CALL OF THE QUANTUM!

An Entangled Mystery

Content guidance: the matter within contains graphic descriptions of medical facilities and treatment, cancer, death, and bodily functions. Topics also include suicide, psychosis, and some mild homophobia.

This book is a work of autobiographical fiction and 44 years have gone by since the time of occurrence of the events depicted. Some characters are based on real persons, some are composites of several individuals, and some are completely fictitious. The key events depicted have a basis in real life while other lesser events are fabricated to extend the story line. All identities, names and places have been altered and their details removed or added for creative purposes.

All Bible verses quoted herein are from the New Revised Standard Version (NRSV), copyright 1952 [2nd edition, 1971] by the division of Christian Education of the National Council of Churches of Christ in the United States of America. Used by permission. All rights reserved.

ISBN:979-8-9879761-2-8

LCCN: 2025902440

Remember the Joy! Publishing
rememberthejoy.com

CALL OF THE QUANTUM!

AN ENTANGLED MYSTERY

A Novel

BOOK II OF THE
QUANTUM MYSTERY SERIES

"DR B! UNIVERSE ON LINE ONE!
THE WIFE ON LINE TWO!"

Roger W. Byhardt, MD &
Lydia Byhardt Bollinger, LCSW

CONTENTS

Cast of Characters

Biedermeier Family

1. Randall Biedermeier (age 38); Chief of Radiation Oncology, Hobbes VA Hospital, Forest View, WI.
2. Zelda Biedermeier (age 31); Randall's wife
3. Kyle Biedermeier (age 8); Randall's son
4. Addie Biedermeier (age 6); Randall's daughter
5. Selma Biedermeier (age 57); Randall's mother
6. Joseph Biedermeier (age 63); Randall's father
7. Peter Biedermeier, Sr. (deceased age 72); Randall's Grandfather
8. Elizabeth Biedermeier (deceased age 26); Randall's Grandmother
9. Adeline Shanefelt (nee Biedermeier, age 54); Randall's paternal Aunt
10. Wondercat; Kyle's cat
11. Milky Way; Addie's cat

Hobbes VA Radiation Oncology staff

1. Grace Lederman (age 35); Radiation Therapy Technologist
2. Molly Sorenson (age 47); Radiation Therapy Technologist
3. Melinda Moore (age 24); Radiation Therapy Technologist trainee
4. Dan Graham, MS (age 30); Radiation Physicist
5. Doris Mims (age 43); Radiation Oncology Secretary
6. MEL (age 11); department 6 MeV Linear Accelerator
7. Judy Janus, RN (age 37); department clinic nurse
8. Elisa Angeles, RN (age 29); department patient care coordinator

Other VA Staff and Employees

1.   Winston Samuels; VA Compliance Officer
2.   Martha Clunes; VA Librarian
3.   Clive Lincoln; Asst. Chief Engineering
4.   Madeline Cornwall, PhD; Chief Speech Pathology
5.   Reggie Clevenger, MS; Chief of Physical Therapy
6.   James Conway, MD; Chief Emergency Services
7.   Clarence Munday, MD, PhD; Chief of Pathology
8.   Clara Sorenson, PhD; Chief of Recreational Services
9.   Lydia Buntwell RD; Chief of Dietetics
10.   Haru Okawa, MD; Chief of Methadone Drug Clinic
11.   Mike Newberry, MD; Chief of Staff
12.   William Sheltie, MD; Chief of Surgery
13.   Robert Munger, MD; Chief of Radiology
14.   Albert Kramer, MD; Chief of Pathology
15.   Sylvia Amory, DDS; Oral Surgeon
16.   Oliver ("Ollie") Oliver, MD; Orthopedics Resident
17.   Ira Roth; Patient Transporter
18.   Joan Zariello, RN; Infectious Disease nurse
19.   Heather Ameche; Chief Transcriptionist
20.   Helen Kiellor; blind transcriptionist
21.   Sandy; 4CS ward secretary
22.   Steve; HR employee, Melinda's "friend"

Dr. Biedermeier's Neighborhood

1.   Fred and Flossie Bush; octogenarian next-door neighbors
2.   Chris and Julie Miller; neighbors
3.   Billy and Charlie Ichner; neighborhood kids

Visiting Scientists

1. Albert Einstein; virtual visit

Other Characters

1. Mary Alice Hoffman, MD, PhD; Randall's Psychiatrist
2. Carol; Mary Alice's Harley riding receptionist
3. Elena Angeles; Elisa Angeles's sister
4. Joseph Shepard, MD; Randall's Psychiatrist friend
5. Chelsea Andretti, MSW, LCSW; Kyle's therapist
6. Juan Angel del Aguilar, MD; Randall's Radiation Oncology mentor
7. James Knox, MD; Randall's Radiation Oncology boss
8. Albert Yard, PhD; Physiologist
9. John Soulder, PhD; Radiation Biologist
10. Dick Mayman; Rat lab technician
11. Ruby Cosgrove; former nun
12. John Bingham, MD, PhD; adult psychiatrist
13. Adele Astravanian, PhD; atomic physicist
14. Simon Escaliente, PhD; psychophysicist
15. Breana Hedley, MDiv; Lutheran pastor
16. Roland Walker; Menomonie Shaman
17. Chase Medley; Chistian Science practitioner
18. Many patients based on reality (with names changed)

CHAPTER 1

—

FORT BIEDERMEIER REDUX

"Speak when you are angry and you will make the best speech you'll ever regret."

—Ambrose Bierce

MORNING CAME BROKEN

Eee eeee eee EEEE!! *Thunk! Mraawawwww*!

"What the heck? Ow! Dang cat. Gotta trim those claws."

At 6:30 AM both the bedside alarm and the cat alarm woke up Randall without mercy. This was fortunate, since he was so deeply asleep neither one alone would have gotten him up. He wiped blood from parallel claw marks on his arm. "Yeah, run away, ya little devil! You're lucky it takes a while for my engine to get going!" He looked around the dark bedroom. There was a glint of winter light filtering in under the window shade.

His wife, Zelda, needed a 200-joule defibrillator shock to bring her out of her usual deep sleep state. Randall suspected she faked not waking up so she wouldn't have to rise or shine. That way, Randall would have to get the two kids up for school. It was 6:30 AM. If he hustled, he might make it to his job at the VA Medical Center in time. It had snowed most of the night and the roads would be a skating rink. He hustled the yowling Wondercat out of the bedroom, called for the kids to wake up, and shut the bedroom door.

First things first. Must pee! shouted Randall inside his head. He shuffled to the bathroom as fast as his wobbly legs could carry him and let loose a stream that lasted long enough for him to regain most of his senses. When finished, he looked in the mirror with bleary eyes. He ran his hand over his semi-gloss pate. No hair had mysteriously grown back overnight. There was no time to polish his scalp. He delayed donning his thick glasses. The morning inspection was kinder without them.

Randall thought to himself as he studied his haggard face. *The face looks familiar, but where did all those lines come from? Oh, I remember. That big one is eight years of Zelda. That medium one is seven years of Kyle and that little one is five years of Addie. These over here must be college, medical school and internship. This blotch must be residency for four years. These crows' feet are war worries and these forehead lines must be miscellaneous categories. Add in the eyebrow scar from when my dog bit me as a kid, and these lovely fresh cat scratches, and I've got a life map face mask.*

Randall stopped counting lines, put on his glasses, and commenced shaving. When he had finished and washed up, he checked to see if the kids were up yet. At the top of the stairs, he could hear them in the kitchen bickering and making breakfast. He wondered if the snowfall had been enough to close school. There had been enough snow the night before for the kids to build a huge snow fort on the front lawn. They had worked for hours to build it and dubbed it Fort Biedermeier.

As Randall was dressing, Zelda emerged from the undead. "Wha… what time is it, Randy?"

"It's still 0F:00, but the kids are dressed and downstairs. You better get down there and see if school is canceled. I know I still have to go in. Cancer doesn't take a holiday! I've got patients out the wazoo today. Everyone wants some radiation for their little cancer."

Zelda harrumphed. "Boy, are you Mr. Sunshine. The whole world is out to get you, eh?"

"Well, yeah," agreed Randall. "I know they are."

Zelda swung pale bare legs out of bed and ran her fingers through her red hair to minimize bedhead. It didn't do much. She shivered and grabbed a green robe. Randall glanced over while she was holding the robe. He admired her shapely body silhouetted by the faint sunlight shining through her thin nightgown. It was so cold that her freckles had goosebumps.

"What are you looking at, pervert?" she inquired with a head tilt.

"Oh, just a nice landscape. You know, hills and valleys. Especially the valley of the Jolly Green Giant, Ho Ho Ho," chuckled Randall. Zelda threw a pillow at him and chased him out of the room.

Randall ran off and went downstairs to his den for his briefcase. The kids had turned on the kitchen TV and learned that all the roads were cleared so school was open. Kyle and Addie were about to have their breakfast cereal, and they were moaning about not having a snow day. They wanted Count Chocula cereal but Zelda made them settle for Raisin Bran. Randall was sipping his first cup of coffee, while Zelda made herself an omelet.

"Hey, Dad," said Kyle. "I turned on the TV to see if we had school today. The news program was talking about this guy in a weird pointy hat that was visiting New York. They had a parade and a bunch of people were on the streets waving. Who is that guy?"

"That would be the Pope Peter of Padua," replied Randall. "He's the head of the Roman Catholics. He lives in a special place called the Vatican in Rome, Italy."

"Are we Roaming Cat Licks?" asked Addie, her mouth full of bran flakes.

Zelda flipped the eggs. "No, we're Lutherans. It's almost like being Catholic. We have a heaping helping of the guilt, but only one scoop of rituals. It doesn't matter, though, because we don't go to church much."

"Yeah, church is boring," declared Kyle. "But I like the Pope's outfit. He kinda looks like Yoda. If we go Catholic, can I wear robes like that?"

"Sure, you'd look good," said Randall. "You could give mass in Klingon."

"Randy!" shushed Zelda. "Stop telling him nonsense. The service is in Latin."

"Same difference. Sounds like Klingon to me," said Randall. "Anyway, Pope Peter is famous for his miraculous recovery from a serious digestive disorder."

"Really?" asked Zelda, smelling a setup. "I never heard that."

Randall buttered his toast. "Well, the media sort of kept it quiet, since it was rather a sensitive matter. Last year a delegation from India visited the Vatican and they had a ceremony in the courtyard. There aren't many Catholics in India, but Peter decided to honor them by allowing a special visitation."

Kyle sighed. "Dad, this story is already boring."

Randall hid his smile. "Worry not, young padawan. Trust the farce." He grabbed the peanut butter jar.

"The Indians flew a trained elephant to Vatican City in a C-130 and then took him to the Vatican in a huge lorry. The pachyderm was all decked out with gilded harnesses and flower garlands. A small boy wearing a large white turban sat atop the elephant and walked the huge animal around the courtyard. The elephant did all sorts of tricks, like standing on his front or hind legs. He sucked water out of a tub with his trunk and blew out a towering spray that cooled the onlookers with a fine mist."

Kyle couldn't help being curious. "Wow, just like in the circus, Dad!"

Pope Peter's elephant

Randall assumed a tall-tale telling pose. "Indeed. The Pope was fascinated by the elephant and asked if he could feed him some peanuts. The Indian boy, sitting atop the elephant, signaled the elephant by prodding him with his stick. It coiled its trunk around the boy and brought him to the ground. The boy directed the elephant to put out its trunk to take a peanut from the Pope. Instead the elephant coiled his trunk around the Pope and stuffed the Pope in his mouth. It swallowed him whole. The Indian boy yelled down the elephant's mouth for the Pope to keep running around inside the beast as fast as he could."

Kyle spewed milk out his nose.

Addie stopped shoveling cereal in her little mouth. "Gee, Daddy, did they get the Pope out?"

"Well, a dozen Bishops with red caps gathered around the elephant. They recited 110 'Hail Marys' and 156 'Our Fathers.' Then, after about

45 minutes, the elephant lowered his rear end, gave a great grunt, and out popped a pooped Pope Peter of Padua, still running. He didn't stop until he'd crossed the courtyard. They hosed him down, changed his robes and he was good to go."

Both kids laughed uproariously.

"Randall! Another one of your stinker stories," yelped Zelda, but then couldn't stop laughing. "I bet the elephant was Hindi and rejected the Pope's Catholic dogma."

"Ha! Daddy told another poop story. Ha Ha Ha! Poopy Poopy Poop!" laughed Kyle, slobbering milk and cereal down his chin.

"Was the Pope hurted?" asked a confused Addie.

"No, he was just pooped out," exclaimed Kyle, now consumed with laughter.

"Well, now that I've created this mess, I'd better head off to work," said Randall. "My damage here has been done." Zelda threw a wet tea towel at him.

Randall deftly ducked. He'd done this dance before. "Oh, before I go, let's check out the front window and see how Fort Biedermeier looks in broad daylight."

FORT KNOCKS

Kyle beat everyone to the front window and let out a loud wail. "Some-one knocked down our snow fort," he screamed. "I can't believe it. It's wrecked!"

Addie, Randall and Zelda quickly joined him at the window.

"I thought I heard some noise in the yard last night as I was falling asleep," slumped Zelda.

Addie stamped her little feet. "I'll bet those nasty Ichner boys did it. They destroyed our snowman last week."

Kyle's face turned red. "Their parents let them roam around late at night. I'm going up there right now and tell on those guys before they go to school." He headed toward the front door, his socks slipping on the wood floor.

"Whoa, boy," warned Randall. "Let's think before we act. We don't know for sure who did it. It could be those other kids from St. Jude's that come through here on the way home from school. The Ichners and the St. Jude's kids are way bigger than you and you would probably get the wrong end of that stick."

"*Hmmmph*. So stupid. It's not fair!!" Kyle grumped and clumped around the room, doing internal calculations. Finally he sighed. "You're right Dad, we need a battle plan."

"You're right," said Zelda. "We may have lost the first battle, but we'll take the second one and win the war. Let's hatch a plan."

HATCHING A PLAN

Randall knew this was not just about a fort, but about family honor. "I might have an evil plan forming in the depths of my gray matter. Tell you what . . ." Randall conducted the kids like a general in the war room. "You guys just finish getting ready for school. I've got a 4:00 meeting at the County Hospital today so I should be home around 5:00. I have an idea how we can rebuild the fort and make Fort Biedermeier II even stronger. If the weather report I heard this morning is correct, I think the culprits are in for a big surprise. Are we all in? We'll all have to pitch in to make this happen."

"High fives all around," cheered Zelda. The kids nodded aggressively. The deal was sealed.

"OK, we'll reconvene here at 1700 hours," said Randall.

"Daddy, what the heck time is that?" asked Addie with frustration.

"It's military time. Five o'clock for you civilians. Everyone, off to your stations!" With a salute, Randall spun on his heel and gathered his briefcase.

They all shrugged into their winter gear and headed out like a *terd* of hurdles.

Randall was able to hustle out of the meeting at the County Hospital by 5:00 and made it home by 5:15. All three members of the battle platoon were waiting for him, already bundled up in their fort building gear. Addie looked tiny in her puffy snow jacket. Her long braids spilled out from under her knit hat.

Randall shrugged on his snow gear over his work clothes and they dashed out into the darkening yard. They started gathering snow in the frozen yard. Kyle wiped his runny nose on his sleeve, his golden brown eyes sparkling. "Hey dad, look! I have a snotsicle!"

"*Ewwwww*!" Addie ran behind her mom and peeked out from behind Zelda's hip.

Kyle ran to his Dad and looked up. "Dad, you have snotsicles in your mustache, too!"

Randall decided not to give the topic the benefit of attention. Randall already had a 12 by 12 by 18 inch wooden box in his workshop. He showed the crew how to pack it with snow to make building blocks. They removed the snow from the walls of the original fort that had been knocked down to make new building blocks. They then stacked these on the parts of the wall that remained. Kyle and Addie used small shovels to load the box and pack the snow. Even working together, they couldn't lift the heavy box. Randall and Zelda removed the new blocks from the box and placed them on the wall. It was an efficient assembly line and they talked while they worked.

Kyle was totally enthused by the project. "Dad, these snow blocks work cool."

"Yeah, this wall is going to be much stronger than the first one," said Addie brightly, equally excited about the project. Her little cheeks glowed pink with the effort and the cold.

"Yep, your Dad is a fart smeller, I mean, smart feller," said Zelda.

"Zel!" exclaimed Randall in mock indignation. "There are children present." Both kids roared with laughter.

"You're right," Zelda remarked. "There are four children playing here."

"Got me there," Randall admitted.

"Some of these dang blocks don't want to come out of the box," Zelda noted as she shook the wooden box up and down with no result. "Keep working, I think I have a solution."

Zelda headed back inside and brought out a cake knife spatula. She ran the spatula between the snow block and the inside of the wooden box. When she turned the box upside down, the snow block fell out easily.

"Voila!!" exclaimed Zelda. "Now we can go faster."

"Ingenious," agreed Randall. "I never would have thought of that."

"Well, I have a PhD in housekeeping and kitchen utensils."

When they ran out of snow from the destroyed parts of the fort, they had to shovel snow into the block box from the snowbank next to the sidewalk. Kyle went to the garage and brought out his sled to haul the loaded box back to the fort. Both kids were working like furies.

"Good thinking, kiddo," said Zelda. "You're working on your PhD, too."

"What the heck is a PhD?" complained Addie. "Would you guys *PUHleeze* stop using big words? I'm just a kid!"

"It means 'Piled High and Deep' like we're doing with the snow," shot back Randall.

"Randy! Don't do that," admonished Zelda. "The kids will never learn things the right way if you keep confusing them. Addie, sweetheart, PhD means . . . er . . . Randy, what does it mean?"

"It means doctor of philosophy. That doesn't make much sense, because the PhD doesn't have to be in philosophy. It dates back to medieval times," explained Randall. "Just because you have a PhD doesn't mean you are a philosopher."

"Daddy, is that like the Phil Ossifer section in the comic page?" asked Addie.

"Umm, that's kind of a different thing. Let's go over philosophy another time, okay?" suggested Randall. "This is getting too deep for me. If we keep talking about this, your mother is going to get angry at me."

"Dad, do you get angry at work?" asked Kyle. "You get angry at home sometimes and you yell at us. Do you yell at people at work?"

THE ANGRY DOOR

Randall paused and took a deep breath. He was somewhat taken aback by Kyle's question. He wanted to make sure to answer him sincerely. "Well, I get mad at work when things aren't working out right. Sometimes I feel like yelling at people. Mostly I get mad about situations that are out of my control. Then, I get angrier because I don't know who's to blame. So, I bury the angry feelings in a secret place inside me. It makes a little hot spot that doesn't go away until I open the angry door in my brain and let it out. I try to wait to open it until no one is around who might get hurt by what I might do or say."

Kyle nodded, as if he understood exactly what his dad meant. He looked intently at Randall as he formulated his next question. "Dad, do I have an angry door?"

Randall knew his answer would be important. He chose his words carefully. "We all have one, son. It takes practice to open it the right way so that when it comes out, it doesn't hurt you or others. It took me a long time to learn how to do it. Even now, sometimes I don't get it right." He put his hand on Kyle's shoulder.

Addie smacked snow into the box with vigor. "Sometimes my angry door opens without warning me."

"Yeah, me too," admitted Zelda. "Sometimes it comes out of my mouth before I can even think about it. I feel bad about that afterwards because I can see when it hurts someone's feelings." Addie nodded her understanding.

Kyle kept packing snow, as if in a daze. His hands made a loud thumping sound, punctuating the conversation. Kyle's voice rose above the pounding. "Or it makes me do something mean and stupid."

Zelda picked up his rhythm, pounding snow into the box. "And once you say or do something you didn't mean to, you can't take it back. It already happened."

Kyle looked at her, as if seeing Zelda as someone beside a parent. "Right! You've hurt someone, and it doesn't make you feel any better. You still feel mad."

"Yes!" Zelda continued. "You can say you're sorry to whomever you've hurt, but they will always remember it unless they can forgive you."

Randall observed the interaction, feeling relieved that Mother and Son were finding common ground they hadn't realized they shared. *All praise snow therapy!*

"Mom, what does 'forgive' really mean?" asked Kyle. Zelda looked to Randall for help. Randall gave Zelda a look that meant she'd have to answer that one on her own.

Zelda shuffled her feet, as if looking for an escape route. Finally, she took a deep breath and tried to explain what it meant to her. "Okay, I'll give it a try. It means that even though you do something or say something that hurts someone, if you say you're really, really sorry they will not stay mad at you. They will agree to still like you or love you even though what you did hurt their feelings. But the downside is even though they may forgive you, they might trust you less."

"Oh," said Kyle and then he went quiet, thinking about what Zelda had said. After a few more shovels of snow, he dropped his shovel on the ground. He ran to Zelda and hugged her. "Mom, I'm really, really sorry that I got mad about the fish sticks and ran away from home. Please forgive me?"

Zelda held him tight. "Kyle, you are my son and I will love you always. I will forgive you, AND there will be a price to pay," said Zelda firmly. Randall winked and gave Zelda a supporting head nod. "There is something you have to promise me," she said. "You have to agree to do this whenever you get angry. Before you do or say anything that will hurt you or someone else, write down on a piece of paper what you're mad about, fold the paper three times and write 'open my angry door' on the outside. Then, bring me or Dad the note."

"But won't that make you guys mad and get me in trouble?" Kyle looked younger than his eight years.

"No. First of all, you're not in charge of our feelings," explained Zelda. "Second of all, we'll make a promise to you. If we get an 'angry door' note from you, we agree to open the note, read it carefully and work through whatever you feel angry about. We want you to feel safe to talk to us about anything that bothers you."

Randall was amazed how well Zelda was handling the question and picked right up on the theme. "Mom's exactly right. We'd rather talk it through than have something bad happen to you."

Kyle was getting used to the idea. "Do I have to keep it nice?"

Zelda seemed to understand. "You can express whatever you feel. We can handle it. That's our job as parents."

"I have an angry door, too," interrupted Addie loudly. "I really hate it when Dad uses all his big words and tries to confuse me. I want it to stop!"

Randall was surprised. "Holy gumballs of goo! You got me. I hadn't realized I was doing that. And I shouldn't complicate things for you. I promise to try to stop doing that."

Addie was getting fired up. "I don't mind learning new words, but the way you're doing it makes me feel stupid," she barked, continuing to vent. "Yoda says there is no try, Daddy, only do. So do it!"

"She's right, Dad," said Kyle, then looked from Randall to Zelda, not sure if his outburst was going to be received safely.

"OK, OK, message received!" Randall raised both hands in a sign of surrender. "How about we just do a word of the day to help build your vocabulary?"

"My vocabulary is fine," insisted Addie. "I'm just a kid, but I know lots of words. And they're all good words." Randall felt like he had just been told to "Go Fish."

"Got it!" Randall felt like he had been bitten by his own dog. "You are a smart kid, and you are learning at your own pace. You want me to respect that. Can we close that angry door?"

Addie nodded, looking satisfied.

Zelda cleared her throat loudly in an effort to redirect the discussion. "Alright, Addie can do the 'angry door' notes, too. There's just one more thing before we get back to building the fort. Then we need to work fast 'cause my feet are starting to freeze. Kyle, I don't want you to use the 'angry door' notes just to get your way. We'll try to be fair, but it's not a blank check."

"What does that mean?" Kyle squiggled his eyebrows.

Randall answered. "Buddy, if you hand us a note that says you're mad because you don't have a new bike, we're not going to just haul off and buy you one. We'll consider it carefully and make a fair decision."

"That's right," said Zelda. "And don't get the idea that you might get a reward for misbehaving by confessing. You know, like when we gave you mac and weenies the night you ran away from home and the cop brought you back. If you do something like that again, don't expect a reward when you come back."

Addie couldn't help jumping in. "Yeah, even *I* know it's stupid to try to walk on the freeway to Grandma's house in the dark just because you don't want fish sticks for dinner!"

Randall stifled that line of thinking. "Addie, cut your brother some slack. Our brains don't make good decisions when we're angry. If he'd let the anger out beforehand, he might not have tried to solve things by running away."

Zelda picked up the thread again. "Dad's right. We gave you the treat instead of punishment because we wanted to welcome you back. You scared the bejesus out of us when you disappeared. We were so happy you got back safely that the mac and weenies were to celebrate that you weren't hurt. We were devastated when you went missing because we love you so much. Please never do anything that drastic just because you are angry. Anything that's bothering you is our concern, too. Just don't keep any angriness buried inside. Always let it out using the angry door and we promise to listen without coming down on you."

"Yeah," said Randall. "Do you understand, Buddy? I know that sounds a little complicated.

Kyle looked relieved. "I think I get it. Let's talk about it more when we're inside. My butt's freezing. Let's finish the fort."

Addie piped up. "You can't get everything you want, you know! But Mom and Dad will make sure you get what you need."

Randall took the cue. "Addie, the angry door is for everyone, for anything. Lucky for you, we parents have got this covered. You get to be a kid."

Addie nodded. "Alright, let's finish. I can't feel my chin."

Fort Finish

The four Biedermeiers set to work again and soon the fort was finished. They decided it was a masterpiece. It had four turrets, a bigger entrance door, and window slits. The roof was high enough that even the adults could sit up straight inside.

While Zelda took the kids inside to warm them up and start dinner, Randall snuck to the garage and took the garden hose off its rack. He took it into the house and went downstairs. There he hooked up the hose to the utility tub faucet. He opened the small basement window, pushed the hose and nozzle outside, and turned on the water about halfway. He snuck back upstairs, went outside, and soaked the entire fort with water.

The outside temperature had dropped to the mid-twenties. The water froze almost as soon as it soaked into the snow. By using the goldilocks method, not too little and not too much, but just right, Randall figured the water would turn the snow fort into an ice castle. When the temperature dropped into the teens overnight, as was forecasted, Fort Biedermeier II would be as good as iron clad. By morning it should be an igloo. Somebody's little toesies were in for a licking from ill-advised kicking.

Randall crept back inside, retrieved the hose, and removed it from the faucet. He hoped he had been stealthy enough not to give his radical plan away to the family. The results were likely to be a great surprise.

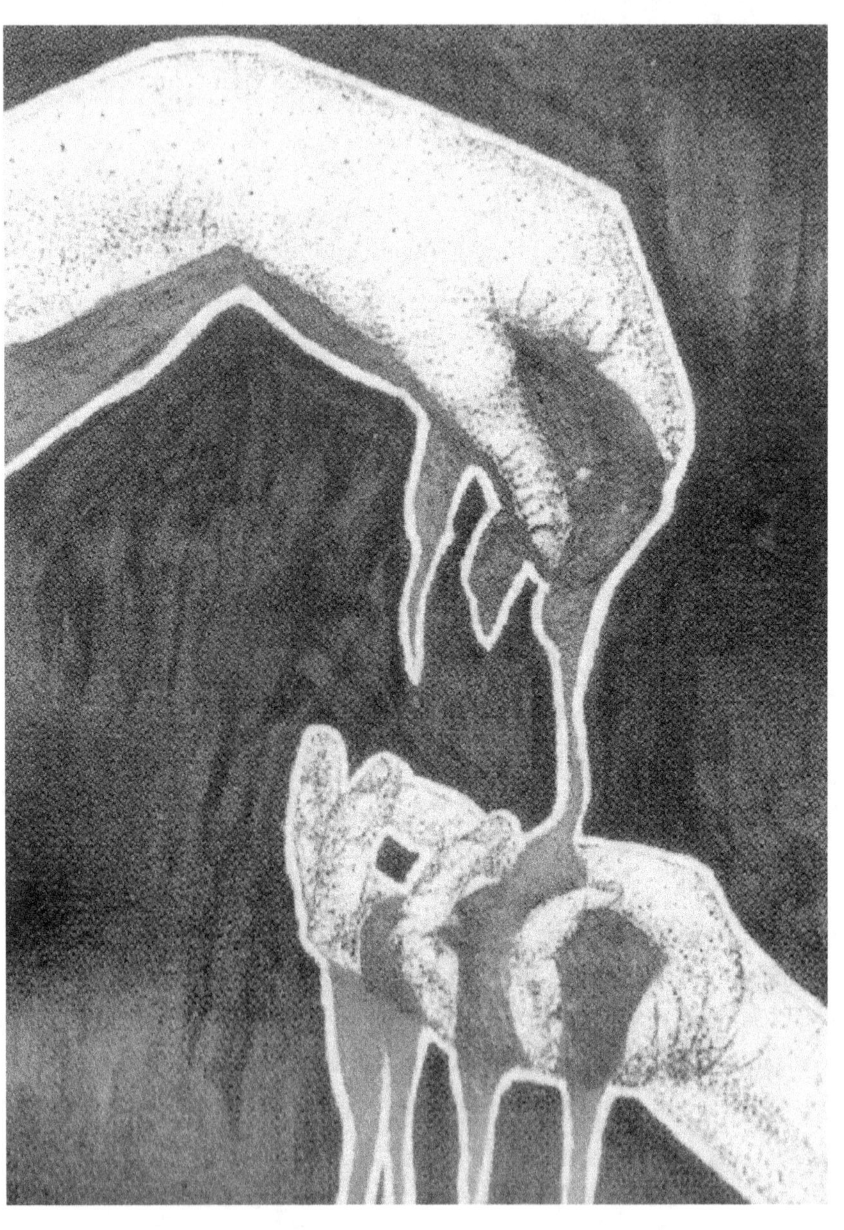

C H A P T E R 2

———

R A D R E M

"… for bravery in no sense is bravado
And prudence is worth more than recklessness."

—Song of Roland

Randall's REM sleep phase usually kicked in about an hour before his 6:30 AM alarm time. The 5:30 AM feature production, obviously fueled by building Fort Biedermeier II, found Randall as an English Crusader in the ramparts of the medieval castle Chateau-Gaillard in 1204. The castle had been built in Normandy along the Seine in 1199 by Richard the Lionheart. Sir Randall was leading a force of British troops fending off a siege by French soldiers during a fierce snowstorm. The siege was commanded by self-declared King Phillip Auguste II, who was resolutely trying to regain possession of Normandy.

Phillip's troops, in great numbers, were scaling the steep castle walls with ladders. From the battlements, the British used the icy conditions to push some of the ladders. The French yelled *"Sacre Bleu"* and *"Mon Dieu"* as they fell to the ground. The English were outnumbered. A burly Frenchman in a filthy fleur-de-lis embroidered tunic scrambled over the wall and charged at Sir Randall, sword drawn. Sir Randall pushed him off the wooden wall walk with a deft flick of his broadsword.

A lanky French soldier quickly took the burly man's place and advanced on Sir Randall, whirling a large broad ax. The soldier's heavy breathing made thick clouds in the arctic air, icicles forming on his beard. Sir Randall stumbled backwards as he parried blows from the ax. He went sprawling into the soft snow, almost sliding off the rampart. He arrested the possible fall by grabbing a support beam, but his attacker came forward with a wide ax swing. Sir Randall was just able to squirm away, and the bloody ax blade became firmly stuck in the icy wooden rampart floor.

POILU

Sir Randall remained tangled in his swash and, at first, could not get his legs free. He tore off his helmet to see better, but things remained blurry no matter how hard he tried to focus. The lanky attacker worked his ax out of the wood floor just as Randall, with a mighty effort, freed up his right leg and used it to deflect another blow. Now Randall had both legs free and, with his left leg set as a fulcrum point, gave a mighty kick that caught the swordsman squarely on the chin and sent him flying off the rampart to his death below. The soldier screamed as he fell and made a gross sound when he landed.

"I got you, you bleeping Frog creep," yelled Sir Randall. "Your *Poilu* ass is grass."

Sir Randall's relief at escaping death by ax was quickly replaced by a mighty rush of pain in his big toe. With that shock of pain, he was whisked out of Chateau-Gaillard. He was fast-forwarded from dream time to real time and found himself back in 1978 in his own bed at 4088 Creekside Place staring at an angry toe.

Randall the Real yelped in pain, grabbed his toe and fumbled for the bedside light. Light on, he quickly assessed that he had unleashed a kick that had landed squarely on the drawer of his bedside stand. The big toe had hit hard enough that the toenail had been sheared from the nailbed. Blood was already collecting under the nail and the nail looked blue. Plus, Randall was freezing cold. The room was frigid.

"Randy, what the hell is going on?" croaked Zelda, rubbing her eyes in confusion as she rose sleepily from the bed. "Did the alarm go off?"

"No, my leg went off in my sleep and I kicked the bedside stand. Call me a medic. I'm badly wounded."

"Were you dreaming again?"

"Yeah. I killed the dang Frog, but he got me bad. I'll never walk again."

Zelda rolled her eyes. "Don't be so dramatic! Let me take a look. You were yelling some weird stuff. What's up with that?"

"Damn. It was so real. I was one of the English Knights Templar defending a castle against a French siege. One of them nearly chopped me up with an ax, but I kicked him off the wall. Turns out he was the bedside stand."

"Where on earth do you dredge up this stuff?" Zelda huffed and rolled out of bed.

"The dream was probably the result of an old movie I saw last week on TV combined with building the snow fort. Who knows where the stuff of dreams comes from? This toe is killing me! I'm getting a hematoma under the nail and the pressure is hurting big time. You are going to have to help me do surgery to drain the blood out."

Zelda recoiled from the toe. "No way, Jose! Just looking at it makes me want to puke!"

Randall waved off her bluster. "Don't panic. It's not that hard to do. I've had the blue toe before. What I can't do right now is run around getting all the stuff I'll need. Would you please go downstairs and get me some ice? Oh, and look in the medicine cabinet on the top shelf. I think I've got some sterile 18-gauge needles in there. I'll need some rubbing alcohol, too. I'll meet you in the bathroom."

Zelda groaned, then set off on her mission, while Randall hobbled to the bathroom. Kyle appeared at the bathroom door rubbing his eyes.

"What's all the noise, Dad? You woke me up." Kyle caught sight of Randall's blue toe. "Did you get attacked? Wow, that looks like it hurts."

"Yep," groaned Randall. "I stubbed my toe a good one kicking a bad guy."

"Is he still here?" asked a still sleep-addled Kyle.

"Nope, I punted him to kingdom come. And he disappeared for good when I woke up." Randall tried hard to sound brave.

Kyle's eyes widened as he caught Randall's drift. "Did you have a night terror, too?"

Randall nodded. "I guess so, Buddy." After a few moments, Zelda came into the bathroom with ice and the other items Randall had asked for. Addie followed, not far behind, in her PJs and bunny slippers, clutching her stuffed unicorn. She looked rather bewildered but said nothing. Zelda had put the ice in a zip lock bag and applied it on Randall's toe.

Randall held the ice bag. "I'll leave the ice on for about five minutes to numb things up before I do the blood-letting."

"Dad, why is your toenail blue?" Addie looked a little green.

"No, stupid, it's purple," corrected Kyle.

"Kyle, don't call your sister stupid! Everyone sees things differently." Zelda started spreading out the supplies.

"Daddy, why is it purple?" asked Addie, still rather muddled.

"I'm trying a new shade of nail polish. What do you think of it?" Randall tried to keep it light.

"OK, kids, your father had an accident and the bedside stand ran into his toe," interrupted Zelda. "When the ice makes his toe numb, he's going to drain the blood from underneath the nail so it doesn't hurt so badly."

"Ooh, can we watch?" yelped Kyle. "I like to watch bleeding."

"Yeah, I've never seen an operation before." Addie peeked around her stuffed unicorn.

"Sure, you guys could learn some new short words." Randall's face pinched in pain.

"Speaking of new words," said Zelda, "when you first woke up you shouted something about a frog and then you yelled a word that sort of sounded like *'Pwaloo.'* What the heck was that about?"

"Hmm. Let me think for a second. I was still half in a dream state." Randall took a deep breath, trying to stave off the pain. Maybe the explanation would take his mind off the pain while the ice did its thing. "Well, I think I was yelling at the French soldier I kicked off the castle wall and called him a frog, a derogatory slang term for French dissolutes. I iced the cake by calling him a dirty *Poilu* which is French slang for 'hairy jerk.' Problem is, that term was first used during WWI and the dream was in 1204. I guess dreams don't require historic accuracy."

Zelda nodded with a perplexed look. "Uh huh, okay, Randy."

House Freeze

Addie shivered. "Daddy, why is it so cold in the house?"

Randall felt the chill too. "I don't know. But you're right—it is cold." Randall turned to Zelda. "Zel, could you check the thermostat and go down to the basement to make sure the furnace hasn't crapped out?" Zelda nodded and headed downstairs to check.

Kyle's teeth chattered. "Dad, what's that old saying about cold and brass monkeys?"

Randall almost laughed, but tried to keep a serious face. "Er, it's as cold as a brass monkey in the freezer."

Kyle shook his head. "That's not it and it doesn't make sense. Everything in the freezer is the same temperature."

Randall nodded and smiled. "You're right. Sometimes old sayings don't make any sense."

Now Kyle suspected Randall was trying to dig out of a hole. "Alright. Tell me a dumb one."

Randall scratched his head. "Well, my grandmother used to say 'You've got to know the difference between a duck.' Whoever she was advising would ask her why. Then she'd say 'One leg is both the same and the higher they fly the much.' See what I mean?"

Kyle shook his head. "No, but your grandmother was probably a nut."

Randall agreed. "Yep. She died before you were born. Now, what were you going to ask me?"

Kyle had almost forgotten his question. "Oh, yeah. The Ichner boys go by our house at about 7:30. Do you think we can watch from the front living room window to see if they try to kick down the snow fort?"

Randall tapped Kyle's forehead. "Good thinking, Buddy. While we're waiting for Mom to get back, go ahead and look out the front window and make sure nothing happened to it overnight." Randall laughed to himself that they might already be in the ER if they had tried booting the fort down.

Kyle ran to the front window of the master bedroom which looked down upon Fort Biedermeier II. Kyle ran back to the bathroom and announced that the fort was A-Okay.

"That's great, buddy." Randall was too distracted to give it much more thought. His toe throbbed with pain. He wanted the toe surgery to be over and done. After an agonizing several minutes, he heard Zelda coming back up the stairs.

Zelda swept into the bathroom with an angry look on her face. "The dang thermostat was turned off! The house temperature is down to 59 degrees and it's 15 degrees outside! How the heck did it get turned off? That's the third time it's happened in the past week. I know I didn't do it. Randy . . . was it you?"

Randall shook his head so hard Zelda thought a marble might come out his ear. "No way! Why would I do that?" He sounded somewhat guilty, even though he was innocent.

Zelda cast an evil eye on Kyle. "Kyle! Was it you?"

Kyle shrank back. "Not me!" He shrugged, helplessly.

Zelda turned to stare at Addie, questioningly.

"What's a thermostat?" asked Addie, looking utterly sweet and naïve.

Randall grunted. "Crap! It's another spook-o-rama. Just what I need."

Kyle lowered his head and whispered to Randall. "Dad, can I tell you something?"

Randall smiled a knowing smile. "Aha, the truth is about to come out. Go ahead and get it off your chest. Did you do it?" Randall still wished a toe truck would come to haul his purple digit to oblivion.

Kyle stammered. "Er, it's not about the thermostat. When I checked out the front window of your bedroom to see if the snow fort was okay, I noticed that the door to the attic was open. You know, the door that's in your closet."

"How in the world would the attic door be open?" asked Randall rhetorically. "It's always closed and latched with a metal pin in the latch. Did you close it or is it still open?"

Kyle backed away. "No, I left it open so you could see. Anyway, I didn't want to go near it. That door kinda freaks me out."

Randall launched himself off the toilet seat, tossing the ice pack aside, and hobbled to the bedroom closet. He found the door to the attic wide open. "Battling bananas on a bunion, of all the . . ."

Things were getting curiouser and curiouser. The attic wasn't heated and now he had an explanation for why it was so cold in the bedroom. He checked the thermometer on the dresser, and it read 50 degrees. No wonder he was freezing when he awoke. He closed the attic door and limped back to the bathroom.

Randall sat back down on the toilet seat. "There will be a further investigation into these matters after I deal with my toe. Zel, pass me the rubbing alcohol."

Randall took a few squares of toilet paper and wet them with the alcohol. He squeezed some on his toe and let it sit there for a minute, while he took the needle out of the plastic packaging and uncapped the holder. He drew out the needle and practiced putting his consciousness outside of his body to minimize the pain.

"OK, gather around kids if you want to see blood," said Randall in an evil tone. "Zel, if you think you might puke, you can look away."

Zelda shuddered. "No, I think I can look. I might need to do the procedure someday."

Randall took the needle and placed it under the edge of the toenail. With a quick push he stuck the needle underneath the nail and pushed it all the way down to the quick. Then he swept it back and forth and withdrew it. Squeezing down on the nail caused a strong ooze of dark blood to emerge from beneath the nail and he soaked it up with a wad of toilet paper. He'd been holding his breath to that point and let it back out with a whooshing sound.

"Oh, gross!" shouted Kyle, with a smirk.

"Icky, icky!" urped Addie, hiding behind her spread fingers.

"Ulp!" squeaked Zelda. "Hasten Chasten, bring the basin. Urp, slop, bring the mop."

Randall kept pressure on the nail for several minutes while the gallery continued to express their disgust and fascination. Then, he asked for the alcohol again and poured some on the toe while he pressed the nail up and down.

Zelda looked aghast. "Oh, goddess, why are you doing that?"

Randall explained. "I'm trying to suck the alcohol underneath the nail to sterilize the nail bed. And holy hamburger hot dish, it burns like a son of a mother. Give me some dry TP, please."

Randall soaked up the alcohol with the paper. He took the antibiotic ointment tube and squeezed the ointment underneath the nail. He wiped off the excess and asked for a large Band-Aid. He wrapped it tightly around the toe, put his foot back on the floor and issued a sigh of relief. He tested whether he could walk on the foot. It was possible, but not without a slight limp.

Randall felt like he'd become the main feature in a circus sideshow. It was time to get on with the day. "Okay, the show is over. Any questions?"

Kyle shook his head. "No, but that was awesome, Dad. Can you do it again?"

Randall frowned at Kyle. "Uh, not for a while. There will be no encore, unless you want me to demonstrate it on you."

Kyle took a big inhale. "No thanks. But I think I want to be a doctor someday. I like blood."

"Not me," squeaked Addie. "Icky, icky, icky."

Zelda weighed in. "Not as bad as I thought, but I wouldn't stand in line to see it. What happens to the nail after this?"

Randall was quite matter of fact about it. "It'll be sore for about a week, and then the nail will start to detach. I'll have to cut the loose parts away with a clipper. Then it will take about six months for the nail to regrow."

Zelda's face was frozen in disgust, her hands on her stomach. She shook her head, as if looking for something else to focus on. "Ok, let's all get dressed and warm while Dad finishes up here. It's still cold as a witch's brass monkey in the house. It'll take a while for the furnace to warm things back up again. You guys need to get ready for school and Dad needs to get set for work. Randy, are you going to be able to walk with that toe?"

"Well, I can't walk without it, so I guess I'll have to bring it along," replied Randall, deadpan.

Zelda laughed. "I'm glad you can still joke about it. I'd be doing a whole bunch of grumping!" She still looked a little green around the gills.

Randall smiled back. "I get that. Well, it was the best of several bad choices. Remind the kids to hurry up because the Ichner kids pass by the house about 7:30 on their way to school and we all need to be at the front window hiding behind the curtains when they walk by. Dollars to donuts they take a swift kick at the fort when they see we've rebuilt it. I can guarantee you we don't want to miss that, because I've prepared a little surprise for them. I won't be the only one with a bruised toe today, if my calculations are correct. And believe you me; I am ready to share my pain with them."

Zelda's eyebrows rose. "What did you do?"

Randall let out an evil laugh that would have made Vincent Price proud. "Let's just say that I've taken steps to improve the structural integrity of the edifice. Wait for it. All will be revealed."

"OK, then," said Zelda. "I will scurry and get myself ready for the show. What about the furnace and the attic door thing? We need to figure out what's going on."

Randall thought for a beat. "Better deal with that tonight. I don't think we have the time this morning. Besides, I need to think it through a bit more. Right now, I can only think of two possibilities. I don't think either of us did it unless one of us is sleepwalking. I don't think Addie did it since she doesn't know what a thermostat is and couldn't reach it if she did know. She couldn't reach the attic door latch either. So that leaves Kyle sleepwalking again, like when he had night terrors a while ago. Could he still have the problem, even though he's been to the child therapist twice? I bet it will take more visits than that to fix the sleepwalking."

Zelda looked surprised. "Jeepers! Sounds like you've already thought it through a bunch. And I agree with your speculations, Sherlock. I don't like them, but I agree with them." Zelda paused for thought for a second "Shit, I'm confused and cold. I'm going to get dressed."

Kick Off Time

Randall glanced at the clock. "Alright, I'll see you downstairs. See if you can get some breakfast in the kids before the front window festivities begin."

Randall put on his clothes and shaved. He skipped the shower because there was no time and didn't want to get the toe bandage wet. He had a bit of a time finding some shoes that wouldn't bind on the bandage but found a pair of old loafers that left the toe enough breathing room to make walking tolerable. He one-stepped down the stairs and walked cautiously into the kitchen for his coffee. It was already 7:25 and he realized he had just enough time to grab a banana and make a PB&J sandwich to eat in the car on the way to work. The kids were finished with their cereal just in time for all four Biedermeiers to hide behind the curtains at the front window in the living room.

Zelda watched Randall limping. "How's the walking going, Hopalong?"

The remark picked up Randall's mood. "Ha ha, Topper. I guess I have a choice between walking fast and walking half fast. I guess I'll opt for the latter."

Looking out the window, Zelda pointed excitedly. "Speaking of walking, look who's coming down the sidewalk!"

Kyle saw two boys walking down the sidewalk and shouted. "It's the lousy Ichner boys."

"Keep your voice down, Kyle," warned Randall. "We don't want to spook them."

Kyle seemed to shrink into himself. "Okay, let's all be super quiet."

Addie pulled on Randall's sleeve. "Look, Daddy! Charlie is walking up to take a closer peek at the snow fort. He's checking around to see if anyone is watching!"

As the family looked on, Billy Ichner joined his brother at the snow fort wall and they started to whisper animatedly back and forth. Charlie got a big smile on his face and motioned his brother to back up a few paces. On the count of three they rushed the wall of the fort as though they were going to punt a football. Each boy reared back and delivered a mighty kick to the wall. Their feet bounced back, and they both fell to the snow, grabbing their feet and howling in pain. The snow fort wall was unmarked. The two boys hobbled away while the Biedermeiers laughed themselves silly. When they finally caught their collective breath, Randall swept his hand toward the window and made a solemn proclamation.

Ice Castle

"I present to you, the Biedermeier Ice Castle. Disney, eat your heart out. The Ichner boys are both suffering from a bad case of ptomaine poisoning."

The kids jumped up and down, cheering. "The Castle hit back, Daddy! It's stronger than those mean boys!!" Addie screeched as she bear-hugged a resistant Kyle.

Kyle waved his imaginary lightsaber with his one free hand. "The force is with us, Dad! We've defeated the dark side!"

Randall puffed with pride. "That's the power of working together. The Force makes us stronger and makes everything we do stronger. Not one of us could have done this alone. Our strength as a family built this, and not even the local bullies can break it apart."

Kyle looked confused. "But Dad, the fort is just made of snow. Why did they hurt their toes kicking it?"

Randall did his best Darth Vader impression. "Kyle. Because I am your father."

"But we're on the bright side, not the dark," yelped Kyle.

"Yes, but that doesn't mean we can't use Vader methods to defeat the evil ones," replied Randall. "Come on, let's go outside and inspect our castle!"

The Biedermeiers all ran to grab their coats, boots, and gloves and headed out into the 15-degree weather. Randall hobbled out behind the galloping troops.

Kyle was the first one to the fort and he lightly kicked the base. His boot just bounced off the fort wall. He called out his surprise. "Dad, our fort is as hard as a rock! It's like magic!"

Zelda poked at the fort with a stick. "This is solid ice! There's not even any scuff marks where the Ichner boys kicked it." She turned to Randall, sotto voce, and said, "Randy, snow doesn't turn to ice just because the temperature drops. Did you do something?"

Randall winked at her, conspiratorially, his shoulders raised in a shrug. He peered up at the sky with a most innocent look on his face. "Well, I may have assisted mother nature to create more cohesive covalent bonds in the hydrogen dioxide."

Zelda shook her head in amusement. "Oh Randy, you've struck again."

Randall and Zelda watched the kids explore the ice castle. Addie crawled in and out of the fort door, and Kyle poked a stick through one of the slit windows. "Pew, pew, pew!! Take that, bullies!" he yelled. Kyle scrambled on top of the fortress, standing proud on the wooden roof. "Look dad, it's strong enough to hold me up!"

Randall limped over to the fort, straightened the little flag on the roof and looked at it proudly. "I believe my work here is done," he announced. "But if I don't buzz out of here right now, I'll be very late for work. And you kids need to get going to school. You can play with the fort later. I can guarantee it will still be standing."

CHAPTER 3

———

BACK IN THE SADDLE

No hour of life is wasted that is spent in the saddle.

—Winston Churchill

HOBBLE MASTER

Randall hobbled back into the house. He hastily gathered up his gear, loaded it into the Scirocco, and started down the driveway. Zelda and the kids stood at the back door and waved goodbye as Randall backed out. Randall stuck his hand out the window and gave them a wave back as he honked the horn. By the time he got to the VA, all the prime parking spots were taken, and he had to use the "back forty" lot. The loafers were no good for traipsing through the poorly cleared lot and up the icy steps. His gimpy foot made the trip very unpleasant. It seemed to take forever to get to the back door into the long hallway leading to the elevators.

Jim Conway encountered Randall in the hallway on his way to the ER. "Hey, Biedermeier, what's with the hitch in your giddyup?"

"Hey, back *atcha*, Jim," replied Randall. "It's just a medieval war injury."

Conway slowed his steps just a smidge. "I'm not even going to further pursue that line of inquiry except to ask if you need me to haul you to the ER for first aid?"

Randall responded with an ironic laugh. "I appreciate the offer. I may take you up on that if my self-repair attempt fails later in the day.

My big toe and its nail had a disagreement. They decided to separate. I fear a divorce is in the future."

"Ouch!" called Conway. "I hate when that happens. Let me know. I gotta go. See ya, don't wanna be ya."

Randall shouted a reply as Conway's speed walked away down the long hallway. "Thanks for the comforting wishes."

Randall shifted into a semi-hop hobble and decided to forgo the stairs. He punched the elevator down button to get to the basement. The door for the brown wallpapered elevator swished open immediately. Randall thought brown was most appropriate for the day he was having. Winston Samuels, the Jamaican born hospital Compliance Officer, exited the elevator as Randall waited to get in.

"*Gud mawnin*, Dr. B," drawled Samuels in his baritone Jamaican patois. "I trust all is well this fine day?"

Randall acted as if he hadn't a care in the world. "Indubitably! I hope you are well. Have you had any further word from your deceased Grandmother?" The elevator door closed as they stood talking in the hall. Randall pushed the down button again.

Samuels feigned sadness. "Regretfully, no. She remains incommunicado. But I am well as always. What serendipity to run into you *heah*! I have just come from your department where I intended to touch base with you."

Randall put a hand to his forehead. "As you note, I am a bit late getting in due to some unforeseen factors. Let's use this propitious proximity for that purpose."

Samuels put on his gleaming nuclear smile. "Ah, you silver tongued devil, ha ha ha! I just wanted to remind you to prepare an agenda for the follow-up compliance meeting we have scheduled for tomorrow at 3:00 PM."

Randall's eyes widened. "Oh, did I know about that?"

"I assume so, since you set the date, ha ha ha!" replied Samuels.

This time, Randall lightly slapped his forehead. "Ah, yes. It all comes back to me now. And we're meeting in the Research Conference room in the old building, correct?"

"Right as rain, that is, if it were summer," parried Samuels. "But not right as snow. Nothing is right about snow. Ha ha ha!"

"Hmm," replied Randall. "I'll have to think of an appropriate phrase for winter. Not to worry, though, I'll have my secretary, Doris, type up an agenda and get it to you by the afternoon."

The elevator dinger dinged and the door opened to reveal green wallpaper. The down arrow lit up. Randall, glad to have the more auspicious elevator color, beat a hasty retreat toward the open door and gestured goodbye to Samuels.

Randall shouted as the door closed. "Say hello to your Grandmother if you hear from her!"

Samuels tried to ask about Randall's apparent injury. "Why are you limp. . . ." But the closing doors cut off Samuels' question. Randall sighed in relief not to have to tell the story of his toe jam yet again.

When Randall got off the elevator, he found a crowd of wheelchairs and gurneys literally blocking the entrance to the department. So he hung a right and went to the backdoor entrance to avoid the traffic jam. On the way by the department entrance, he instinctively looked up at the sign to check if the gum culprit had, again, left a deposit on it. The gum graffiti artist had struck again.

Randall mumbled to no one in particular. "Who in the world has got it in for Radiation Oncology?"

At the back door to the department, he put down his briefcase to open his coat and take out his keys. He kept the keys in his right-hand pants pocket attached to a retractable chain on his belt. This morning, there was exactly nothing in his pocket. In his haste to leave the house for work, he'd forgotten his keys.

He exclaimed loud enough for passersby to turn and look. "Dag nabbit! What's next? The big flood?"

Randall picked up his gear again and started back down the hall for the front entrance. He put his right foot down wrong on the first step, forgetting about the toe. The misstep ignited a jolt of pain. Swearing under his breath, he made his way back to the front door, which was still blockaded by two heavily laden gurneys. Now, deeply annoyed, he pushed one of the gurneys aside a bit too briskly and it caromed into the doorframe.

The patient gave out a yell of pain. A large woman waiting in the hall ran forth to confront Randall. "Who do you think you are, pushing my husband around like that? He's in a lot of pain. He's down here to get his pain relieved, not aggravated."

She came up to Randall and grabbed his coat, giving him the evil eye. Before Randall could respond, Grace and Molly, his two Radiation Therapy Technologists, rushed up to the pair and started to take the gurney away. It was their job to set up patients on the treatment table and deliver the radiation as specified by the doctor.

Despite her advancing age, Molly still moved with the grace of a swan. Grace, on the other hand, wobbled gooselike and grumbled rather ungracefully. She appeared older than she professed, and, often, her particular odor announced her arrival.

Molly addressed the patient's wife. "Mrs. Culpepper, we're taking your husband into the treatment room. Could you please come along and hold your husband's hand while we get him on the table?"

Mrs. Culpepper reluctantly disengaged from Randall to help Grace and Molly. Randall tried to offer his apologies to the retreating woman to no avail. Randall had been saved by the cavalry.

As Grace and Molly departed with the Culpeppers, Randall again muttered to himself. "It was an accident . . . I didn't mean to push the gurney that hard . . . my toe hurts. . . ." Realizing the moment had passed, he quickly beat a path to his office.

Doris greeted Randall as he stumped by her desk in moderate pain. "Good mornin', Dr. B. Why, whatever is wrong with your leg? You're limpin' like a horse with a thrown shoe."

Randall gave no immediate reply and went straight to his desk where he deposited his briefcase, took off his coat and threw it on a chair. He *kaflumped* into his desk chair and took off his right loafer. His sock was soaked in blood at the big toe. Doris walked into his office looking like she was about to give him the business for not saying good morning back and ignoring her question. She was brought up short by the sight of the bloody sock.

"Sorry, Doris, for giving you short shrift, but I had to get off my feet pronto!" Randall held his right foot. When Doris bent over to get a closer look, her wig slipped a few inches forward onto her forehead. She hastily pushed it back in place. The bending over motion also stressed out the zipper on the side of her skirt and it came apart with a zipping noise. She rose up and tried to refasten the broken zipper, but it was no go.

Doris was now flustered and turning red. "Sorry about the equipment failure! I'm like a circus in a windstorm. I guess that's nature's signal that I either need to lose weight or get a larger skirt size. All the sitting and typing is playing havoc with my diet. Plus all the bakery the patients bring in is no help either."

Randall chuckled. "I know what you mean about the donuts. I'm not a 30 inch waist anymore. Someone is going to have to hide the sweetmeats or we'll have to take a willpower booster. By the way, you should get better double stick tape for your head appliance. I tried a topper for a while. It was just such a pain to keep it on straight that I gave up on it. It's sitting atop my plastic skull from med school. It's only good for freaking out kids."

Doris shook her head and the wig moved some more. She readjusted it. "Bald men are acceptable. In fact, I think they're kind of sexy, like they've been ridin' the windswept plains all their god-given life. But not so much for women totally bald from alopecia. As they say, when the hen is plucked, she is not welcome in the yard. Not much of a choice for me, though. And it doesn't help *bein'* a 'traditionally built' woman."

Randall made a *tch tch* sound. "All the more to love. Wait a beat. I think I have some double stick tape in my desk drawer. Either that or we could use chewing gum as a temporary holder."

Doris righted her wig and took a closer look at Randall's toe. "Oh, my. My Spidey senses tell me you have not been havin' a good mornin' neither. Did you stub your toe walkin' in here?"

Randall sighed. "No. I did it at home when I woke up, Walking from the car just re-aggravated it. Looks like I'll need to put a new dressing on it. Do you know where we keep the first aid kit?"

Doris brightened up. "I do. I'll go get it for you. Be back in two flips of a cow's tail!"

On Doris' way out through her office she encountered Mrs. Culpepper who stopped her and asked if the doctor in charge was in. She had an important matter to discuss with him. Doris asked her to wait while she checked with the doctor, but Mrs. Culpepper charged right past Doris into Randall's office. Randall heard the whole encounter and braced himself. Mrs. Culpepper came into Randall's office and stopped in her tracks when she found him sitting there holding his bare bloody foot.

Doris trailed behind, trying to stop her. "The Doctor is not ready to see patients yet!"

Mrs. Culpepper stopped short. "Land sakes," she blurted. "You're the doctor from the hallway! The nurses told me you were the one who started emergency treatment on my husband the other night when he came in paralyzed. I talked to you on the phone before you started treating the cancer in his spine."

"Guilty as charged, on both counts," said Randall. "I'm glad you came into my office, because I wanted to apologize for pushing your husband's gurney so hard. I was hurrying to get in my office and tend to this toe." Randall gestured to his foot, although it was hardly necessary.

"Actually, I wanted to apologize for being so brusque with you," said Mrs. Culpepper. "When we wheeled my husband into the treatment room, I asked him what happened when the gurney hit the doorway. He said his toe got hit and it still hurt. Then, Molly reminded us all that he couldn't feel his toes the day before, so the treatment must be working. He was so happy about it that he started to cry. I just had to come and tell you that it seems like a miracle. Thank you so very much."

Randall seized the moment. "So, I guess we could say that I was just testing to see if he was getting his feeling back."

Doris chortled. "Dr. B, you are incorrigible!"

"I'm what now?" asked Randall with a dense look on his face.

"However do you put up with this man?" joked Mrs. Culpepper. "But seriously, the other night when the ambulance brought my husband down from Iron Mountain to here, I was so worried. He was fine in the morning and then he fell getting up from the kitchen table. He had excruciating back pain and had no strength in his legs. Then they went numb. I couldn't leave right away, because I take care of my mother. I kept waiting for some news and, finally, at 10:00 PM you called and explained that the cancer had collapsed his spine and put pressure on the spinal cord. You explained everything so clearly and said there was a good chance to reverse it because we got to it quickly. I thought you were just trying to make me feel better. Here we are now and he's already better."

Mrs. Culpepper rushed forward and smothered Randall in a big hug and kissed his cheek. Randall was rather nonplussed.

Randall stuttered and cleared his throat. "Ahem, yes, well. I am, uh, pleased as punch that your husband is responding so well. He's a stout fellow."

Mrs. Culpepper stepped back as if to admire her handiwork. "Wait a minute, if you're the night doctor, why are you here now?"

"Well, *um*, I am the day doctor too. I'm also the head of the department. I was on call last week, so whatever comes up after hours, I respond. The therapy techs have to come in, too. We collaborate with doctors from other hospitals and rotate who is on call. We make sure there is always someone available for our patients."

Mrs. Culpepper stood in awe. "I didn't even think of that. Did they call you at home? Did you have to leave your bed and your family to take care of my husband?"

Randall straightened up in his chair. "Yes, Ma'am, that's my duty. And it's my honor to serve your husband as he served our country." Randall hoped the bags under his eyes didn't look too pathetic.

Doris grasped Mrs. Culpepper's elbow and gently led her out of the office.

"I think Grace and Molly need your help again, Mrs. Culpepper," said Doris soothingly. "Let's go on out and check on your husband. Then, I need to help Dr. Biedermeier with dressin' his toe. I think he stubbed it on your husband's gurney. He may need a nurse. I'll call one for him."

Mrs. Culpepper gasped. "Oh, you poor man!" She gathered Randall in a full body hug, pressing his face into her generous bosom. "I am going to send a letter to the hospital boss and tell him you need more help down here!" She released him and waddled down the hall.

Randall could still smell her perfume in the air. Or was it in his nose from the close contact? He gave a sigh of relief to finally be alone with his toe. He asked his toe why it had to be the center of attention today. Once he had the foot elevated for a few minutes, the pulsing pain let up.

Doris returned with a first aid kit. Randall fumbled around with the kit and tried to get in a position to apply a dressing, but failed miserably. "Shoot! I can't do this! Doris, help me out here. I just don't bend this way and my second toe keeps getting in the way."

Doris shook her head. "Dr. B, I'm a wiz at the typewriter and I make a mean plate of grits, but I am not comfortable with doin' a toe dressin' on you. I think it needs more than just a bandage. Let me page Miss Elisa to come down here and look at it. After all, she is a nurse."

Randall felt embarrassed that his patient care coordinator would get to see what a klutz he was. "Geez, Doris. I hate to bother her. She's probably busy with a patient somewhere."

Doris scratched her head. "Would you rather have Grace do it?"

Randall frowned. "Are you kidding?"

Doris looked flustered. "Or maybe Melinda, the new tech student? She's only been here a few weeks, but she seems competent enough. She's gotta get her hands dirty at some point!"

Randall shook his head. "No. Don't ask either one. Alright, go ahead and page Elisa. In the meantime I'll just keep the toe elevated."

"Now that's a good boy," murmured Doris as she went to make the call. She came back a moment later to announce that Elisa was on the way bringing disinfectant and other tools.

Randall grimaced. "Other tools? Did she say what tools?"

Doris couldn't pass up the opportunity. "Hmm. Don't recall exactly.

Somethin' about probes and nippers. Or was it clippers? If'n it were my Granddad, he would fit you with metal shoes! Oh, and by the way, Mr. Samuels called earlier and said he was comin' by soon to see you."

Randall thought that was just what he needed. Another peanut for the peanut gallery. He'd probably show up during his blue toe display. "Yeah, fine. I ran into him by the elevators and he told me what he needed was my agenda for our next meeting. Just send him on in when he gets here. Maybe he can distract me while I'm getting operated on."

"The agenda is on your desk," said Doris. "He told me what he wanted, and you dictated it last week. I finally got time to type it up."

Randall pursed his lips. "Yes, of course I did. Aren't I proactive?"

"That's a word," replied Doris.

Randall held up an index finger. "By the way, after I pushed Mr. Culpepper's gurney aside, I passed Al Kornberg's old office. I noticed Stephanie, Samuels' secretary, sitting at his desk. What's she doing there?"

Doris grimaced. "Muddled mulberries, I meant to mention what we decided would be the best use of her time. Durin' the hours that she's down here, she will sit at that desk, because it's close to the main entrance to the department. She will greet anybody comin' in and sort of triage them to where they need to go. She will take any calls that come in and deal with them. She can direct the calls to where they need to go. A bonafide welcome wagon for the department! It really takes a load off me so I can do my transcription work. When she's not busy with that she'll do compliance forms. She's also doing a desk audit to justify to HR that we need a full-time person in that capacity."

"Will ceases never wonder!" exclaimed Randall. "Maybe there is a Dog after all."

Call a Toe Truck

Doris crossed herself. "Well, indeed there is. Now you just rest here a bit. Stay off that foot 'til it gets tended to."

Randall took a moment to look at the pile of charts and papers on his desk that also needed tending to. He grunted and began to sift through it. In what seemed like seconds later he was startled by an announcement at his office door.

"Elisabet Angeles, RN, reporting for duty. What malfeasance has befallen my leerless feeder for which I may be of assistance?"

Randall turned around to find Elisa standing at full attention and saluting. Over her shoulder, she had slung a tote bag. She looked a bit taller than her actual five foot one height. As usual, her glossy black hair made a perfect frame for her oval face, obsidian eyes and pert nose. But instead of her standard rosebud smile, her red lips were set in a serious straight line.

Randall was at first lost for an apt reply but soon recovered. "At ease, nurse. Come and take a look. I was assaulted by a French *Poilu*. He got me in the great toe. It is but a mere flesh wound, but very painful. Perhaps you brought something to ease the *douleur*."

"Almost correct, my liege. *En mi familia* the word is *dolor*," corrected Elisa.

Randall moaned exuberantly. "*Douleur . . . dolor.* A rose by any other name and all that. It is a hurty pain. Please make it better."

Elisa put her arms akimbo. "I'll do what I can, but don't expect me to kiss it like your mother and make it all better."

Randall laughed. "Heavens, no. Not even my mother would kiss this toe."

Elisa directed Randall to put his foot up on the chair next to his desk. She moved his desk lamp to provide some light on the injured appendage. "Tell me how this happened and what you did afterward." She snapped on her latex gloves in preparation for battle.

Randall recounted the event and aftermath. Elisa shook her head in disgust. "What sort of dressing did you put on the toe after you drained the blood?"

Randall looked up at her with a doleful smile. "My sock."

Elisa looked shocked. "No compression bandage? Did you think to use antibiotic ointment? I hope at least it was a clean sock."

"I only wore the socks for one day. They were mostly clean. And I was late for work," pleaded Randall.

Elisa shook her head and clicked her tongue. "I suppose you're going to tell me you were out sick the day they covered first aid in med school."

"Hmm." Randall shrugged. "I might have been. Yes, that could have been the week I had mono."

"Ah, the kissing disease!" mocked Elisa. She pulled out a cotton-tipped swab from her kit. "That sounds about right. Whatever. Hold still. I'm going to do the job right."

"Wait!" blurted Randall. "Before you start poking around can't we do something to numb the toe?"

Elisa reached in her tote bag. This time she pulled out a styrofoam coffee cup filled with ice. "I have the local anesthetic right here. Stick your toe in the cup."

Randall did as directed. "Yikes! That's cold and it hurts."

Elisa shushed Randall. "Don't be such a baby! The toe will be numb in a few minutes and you won't feel a thing. Now tell me why you were dreaming of French soldiers in a castle. Was it something you had for dinner?"

Randall thought for a second. "Well, I did have a grilled cheese sandwich with French fries and French cut green beans for dinner."

Elisa made a face. "That's your idea of dinner?"

Randall made a face back. "It is when I have to cook. I eat what's there and is quick to make. Besides, I like cheese."

"You eat like my sister Elena," exclaimed Elisa. "Any food, anywhere, any time. I had forgotten how strange her eating habits are until she decided to honor me with a surprise visit this past weekend."

Randall looked surprised. "I didn't know you had a sister."

Elisa nodded. "I kind of left my baby sister out when I told you about my family. She's a free spirit and has been quite peripatetic lately, especially after my little brother died. She just can't settle down in one place. This time she flew in from Los Angeles and I didn't even know she was living there. I thought she was in Boulder, Colorado, but that was several boyfriends ago. I love her to pieces and enjoy her company whenever we're together, but it's always too brief."

Randall nodded. "That's gotta be tough. What inspired her visit?" He barely noticed that his toe was going numb.

Elisa stared away and was silent for a long moment. "That's what's so weird. Whenever she visits she claims she gets a deep vibration that tells her I need her. Then, she just picks up and appears. The funny thing is, something's usually going on in my life that I need help with or support. She's fantastic at seeing the bigger picture and finding creative solutions to whatever crap has befallen me."

"Wow. She sounds like a lucky charm. I wish I had someone like that in my life," observed Randall.

Elisa nodded her agreement. "Yeah. I suppose. But this time it's a little spooky. Usually, I know exactly what is wrong in my life when she pops into it. Now this time, for the first time in a long time, things are pretty alright. I'm a little scared that there's something I'm missing. It's like waiting for the other shoe to drop."

Randall looked sideways. "Well, maybe this time she's just here to share the good times. I wouldn't fret too much about it. You know what? My toe is totally numb. Do your worst."

Elisa smiled and removed the ice from Randall's toe. "*Quédate tranquilo*. Stay calm." She pulled out the cotton-tipped swab, dipped it in antibiotic ointment, and applied it under the nail edge. Finishing up, she wrapped the toe in a compact compression bandage. To Randall's amazement, Elisa pulled a fresh white sock from her cornucopia bag and pulled it onto his foot.

Elisa used her first grade teacher voice. "Today you have non-matching socks. Perhaps you'll start a new fashion trend. Now slip your shoe back on and try walking a few steps."

Randall did as suggested and, after a few tentative steps, was walking with barely a limp and reported that there was very little pain.

Elisa watched the transformation and felt proud of her work. "Looks like my work here is done. Now, if there is nothing else earth shattering, I will take my leave. There are other 'worthys' awaiting my nursing talents."

Randall gave Elisa his best smile. "My thanks to you. And my greetings to your sister. If you two get a chance, come on by. I'd like to meet her. Perhaps she can provide some insight into my vagaries."

"I might just do that," replied Elisa. She waved and took her leave. "*¡Hasta luego!*"

"Pasta lumbago to you!" Randall hoped his attempt at a Spanish accent was at least close. He made a mental note to learn more Spanish.

Elisa laughed at the attempt. "Nice try, but no guacamole. I will grant that you got some avocado."

Sailor woman

Once Elisa had left, Randall busied himself reviewing his mail and memos, then signed off on dosimetry plans for several new patient treatment starts. Next up was a new consultation. While he was reviewing the man's history, he was distracted by an animated dialogue in the hall. He got up and closed the door to Doris's office to block out the noise, but he could still hear a loud male voice. He could make out choice profanity punctuated by what had to be a fist pounding on the wall.

Then everything went silent. The sudden silence made Randall even more curious. He bounded up from his chair, banged his knee on the desk well and gave forth with some choice profanity of his own. When his knee returned from orbit, he went out to the hall. There stood a dazed-looking Doris.

Randall walked over to Doris. "Doris, what was all that shouting and pounding? Are you okay?"

At first Doris didn't seem to see him. She fanned her face with a large yellow VA interoffice mail envelope. "Err, ah . . . yeah. I think so. But that was the strangest woman I've ever laid eyes on since my late Auntie Aggie. If'n you did somethin' Aggie didn't like she'd swear a blue streak and spit a wad of *tobaccy* in your direction."

Randall did a double take. "That was a woman doing all the swearing?"

"It was, indeed," Doris nodded vigorously. "And, for a pipsqueak, she was doin' some pretty hefty fist poundin' on the wall."

"Who is she?" Randall imagined an oversized mouse.

Doris grimaced and shook herself. "Dagnabbit! If I see that woman again, I've got a few choice words for her myself. Couldn't think of them while she was yellin' at me. Now, I've got a passel of 'em. It weren't just the woman by herself. Her husband was with her, but he never said a word."

"Who is he anyway? We have all our morning patients accounted for!" Randall wished he could just get on with seeing patients.

Doris rolled her eyes. "He's your 1:00 consultation. They got here early expectin' he could be seen before his appointment so they could drive back to Green Bay before the traffic gets bad. I told her that you were busy until 1:00 and that they'd have to wait until then. I reminded her that's why we give appointments. Then, she went ballistic. It was like the bull got in with the heifers."

Randall felt his Papa Bear energy kick in. "Did she threaten you?" He wondered if he might have to call his friend from the VA Police.

Doris shook her head. "No. All her venom was directed at the wall. Her husband just stood there while she ranted, like it wasn't even happenin'. Then, she just stopped yellin'. I suggested, gentle-like, that they bide their time by goin' on up to the cafeteria or checkin' out the canteen store. She didn't say another word, grabbed her husband's arm and dragged him to the elevator. They got on just before you came out here."

"That's going in my memoirs notebook," muttered Randall.

Doris raised an eyebrow. "Do you keep one, too?"

Randall's head wobbled a bit. "I do starting now. Maybe, if we're lucky, she'll get tired of waiting and just head back home. I don't think I can cope with any more oddness today. Give me a heads up if they come back. I think I might need to have a few words with Mrs. Sailor-mouth about appropriate deportment in the hospital setting."

Doris put a hand on Randall's arm. "Please don't stew about it and get your knickers in more of a knot. Remember he's just been diagnosed with cancer of somethin' and they're both stressed out. None of us behaves normally when we're that upset."

"You're right." Randall recalled his snow fort discussion with the kids. "I'll do my best to retain my equipoise."

Doris beamed, her mood visibly improving. "Ooh, I love new words. That's going in my notebook. Now get back to work. Your 9:00 consult is waitin' anxiously in the hall. Let's not set off another time bomb."

Randall made a sound like a whip crack. "You're such a slave driver. I'll be in my office."

HR Magic

Randall had just finished dictating the report for the 9:00 consult, when Melinda, the new Radiation Therapy Tech student, came to his open office doorway and gave a tiny knock. Randall glanced up to see her standing there with an ear to ear smile on her face. Her blonde hair was done up in a tidy ponytail and she looked quite fetching. As usual, her tech uniform fit her lithe body without a wrinkle and nicely accented all of her desirable female attributes.

Randall responded to Melinda's presence with a smile that came off as a bit more lascivious than intended. "You look like you've swallowed the Cheshire cat."

Melinda touched her throat. "I almost feel like I did. I just completed my first interview with Dr. Munger, the Chief of Radiology, for one of the two open Radiation Therapy Technologist jobs. I'm pretty sure I aced it."

Randall was pleased. This was good news. "Oh, right. I forgot that it was this morning. So HR approved you to apply for the position, even though you have several months before you finish your RTT training?"

"Yes, they did," she announced proudly. "I have a friend, Steve, up in Human Resources and that may have swung things in my favor." Randall could easily imagine pert Melinda would have many such friends, especially of the male persuasion.

Randall had seen Melinda in the cafeteria sitting with a young man who had a vaguely military look. They were sitting too close together to be just acquaintances. "That friend wouldn't happen to be a young man with a Marine haircut?"

"Dr. B, how did you . . . ?" stuttered Melinda.

"I have my ways," interrupted Randall. "'The Shadow' knows all. But, tell me, what makes you think you aced the interview?"

Melinda winked. "Well, Dr. Munger asked me to explain how the Linac makes X-rays. I started with the Crookes tube, meandered through Roentgen, and wound up at Magnetrons. By that time, he was staring at me with his mouth slightly open and asked how the electrons get bent around the corner. You know, I think he had no clue about Linacs. He was all but taking notes."

Randall had a good laugh. "I'm not surprised." He could picture the rather lecherous Munger pretending to listen to Melinda's Linac tutorial while he estimated Melinda's bra size. "If you followed the basic outline of our talks, I'm sure you nailed it."

Melinda giggled. "I have more news, but I'm not sure I should tell you." She glanced side to side. "I don't want to compromise my source."

"No worries," said Randall, eagerly. "Close the door and sit down. I am a black hole for secrets. Once in, they never get out. Now, tell Uncle Randall everything."

Melinda sat forward in her chair and spoke in a low tone. "My friend, Steve, in HR, has made it known to me that Radiation Oncology has been approved to fill two RTT positions, which you knew already and the part about me being eligible for one of them. But what you probably don't know is that there are three other candidates for the RTT positions who have applied and have been interviewed by HR."

"Do you know anything about them?" asked Randall.

Melinda squinted one eye. "Some. One is an RTT from St. Joseph's in her late 50s. Rumor has it she's a serial screw-up and they're looking to release her for cause. She didn't do well in the preliminary VA HR interview either."

Randall shook his head. "Don't want any of that sandwich."

Melinda continued. "The other two are in their early forties and have been at St. Luke's for about ten years. They are both well qualified but want to leave because they are about to be demoted to Radiology Tech jobs as part of downsizing."

"Good old St. Lucrative's," exclaimed Randall. "Bottom line *uber alles*."

"Right," nodded Melinda. "Word is, HR has eliminated the St. Joe's RTT and wants you to interview the remaining three, which includes me, for the final decision on which two to pick."

Randall's face clouded over. "Oh, joy, can you say 'conflict of interest'?" He felt torn and asked himself what this insider information might cost him in the future.

Randall's face told Melinda all she needed to know. She chuckled a bit. "No pressure. The final call is yours, no questions asked. If I don't get the job here, I'm sure I won't have a problem finding a job elsewhere, because I'm sure you'll give me a great recommendation, right?" She batted her long lashes over her doe eyes.

Randall closed his eyes for a bit to recombobulate. "*Riigght!* That really takes the pressure off. So, do you have any other tidbits to disclose?" He made a mental note not to trust HR with any secrets.

Melinda nodded. "In fact, I do. HR approved Dan Graham as a candidate for the Medical Physics position that Bob Storch just left. I'm sure you remember he's Bob Storch's friend. I think you gave Dan Graham's contact information to HR." Melinda paused to smooth out invisible wrinkles in her white uniform.

Randall grumbled something unintelligible, then found his voice. "So, HR does work eventually. Slow and steady wins the race." It seemed to Randall that there was much more to Melinda than a clean uniform and the contents therein.

"Come on now, Dr. B," scolded Melinda. "The guys in HR work hard. You don't realize how hard it is to find good candidates willing to work at the VA. The salaries are not competitive with the private sector and the facilities are always one or two steps behind."

Randall snorted derisively. "One or two decades, more like! But the job security at the VA is unequaled. Ever try to get rid of a bad VA employee?"

"Of course not, but I've heard the stories," retorted Melinda. "By the way, you get to do the decisional interview on Dr. Graham, too."

"That should be easy enough," groused Randall. "Are you the best drug store in town? Yes, we are. We are the only drug store in town."

"At least he's a qualified candidate," reminded Melinda. "You could be stuck with no candidate. But you'll still have to decide if you want to take a chance on the guy."

Randall sighed. "True enough. Otherwise they will probably contract it out to some physics hack who just comes in here three days a week to spot check the machine and verify a few calculations. That means I'll be stuck doing most of the actual daily physics work."

Melinda made a sympathetic face. "Don't sound so glum. What about going with 'everything will work out?' Or maybe things won't be perfect, but it'll be a whole lot better than what you've had so far."

"True enough," admitted Randall. "Sorry to be so negative. This is really all good news. It means we'll be adding two new RTTs and I'll bet Graham will be just fine. Oh, did they say anything about making one of the RTTs a Chief RTT so we can fill Al Kornberg's vacated Chief Tech position? You remember, our recent heart attack victim."

Melinda tried to remember if HR had said anything about the Chief Tech position. "Nothing that I recall, but Steve did say that Mr. Samuels plans to fill you in on all the details at a Compliance meeting you've got coming up soon. Maybe he'll have something about that."

Randall began to look less downcast. "That makes sense. We're having the Compliance meeting tomorrow and I already have those items on the agenda. It really helps to have a heads up before the meeting to strategize. Do you have any thoughts on who should be the Chief RTT?"

Melinda looked startled. "You're asking me? You know I can't have an opinion about that."

Randall snapped his fingers. "That's true, but you seem to have good instincts. You can tell me the opinion you don't have or any other issues you can see that might be stumbling blocks."

Melinda couldn't help but giggle. "All I will say is that it's hard to teach old dogs new tricks and it's hard for new dogs to accept old tricks."

Randall smiled. "Message received. Anything else?"

Melinda rose from her chair and made motions to leave. "Nothing else, except you were explaining several months ago that the 'powers that be' may add a college degree requirement for Radiation Therapist certification. Is that going to happen soon enough to affect me?"

Randall was glad to be back in familiar territory. "My read is that it will take several more years to make that change. You will probably slide in before that and be grandfathered in. They might ask you to take a supplemental exam to be recertified, but I wouldn't be worried about it. They can't afford to suddenly disqualify all the existing RTTs unless they go to college for four years. But future students will likely need both the training and college."

Melinda looked relieved. "That's good. I was starting to worry about that. I don't have anything else to fall back on and college would be impossible financially. I better get going before Grace comes looking for me."

Randall rose as Melinda reached for the office door. "Thanks, Melinda, for sharing good information. Watch out for the raging bull on the other side of that door."

As Randall predicted, Grace was about to knock on Randall's door as Melinda opened it.

Grace was surprised as the opening door almost hit her in the face. She jockeyed backwards to avoid it, appearing red faced and rumpled. Her mood was the usual brisk and brusque. "Melinda! Where were you when we called for lifting help? Move your fancy behind and come with me. Dr. B, you come too. We need you for a setup check on the table. The patient has a full bladder and he's antsy."

Melinda turned and gave Randall a small wave and a smile. Randall reflected that he needed to tread with care when dealing with Melinda. She functioned at a level way beyond her training. He made a mental note to stay on his toes.

He went to the treatment room, as ordered, and checked Mr. Antsy's setup, then returned to his office. Doris tried to hand the chart for the next consult to him as he went by her desk, but he jigged to the left trying to avoid the handoff. The sudden move tweaked his toe and brought him to an abrupt stop.

"See what you get for tryin' to avoid work?" declared Doris, as she shoved the chart back at Randall. He had no choice but to take the lateral. "This is the last time I'm goin' to warn you; watch your P's and Q's around certain young ladies or be led astray."

"What young ladies?" asked Randall, temporarily bewildered.

Doris put hands on hips. "You know. That dunce cap may cover *your* eyes, but I can still see. You know I have the gift."

Randall's eyes got huge. "I do know! You have the gift. Will I have to watch the rest of the alphabet, too?"

Doris said nothing in response, but glowered at Randall.

Plumbing Accident

Randall limped into his office, chart in hand. He sat down to study the chart, but couldn't concentrate. He felt certain he knew which young lady Doris had been referring to and once more decided to do his due diligence. He put those thoughts aside. There was still the matter of sorting out how he was going to manage the swearing lady when 1:00 rolled around.

He took papers out of his briefcase that belonged in his out box. He spied a yellow sticky note that he'd left in one of the briefcase pockets. The note contained the names of adult psychotherapists that Kyle's Psychiatric Social Worker, Chelsea Andretti, had given him. He'd promised Zelda that he'd make an appointment to see one of them himself. That would need attention soon, so he stuck it on his lamp base.

There were three names on what Randall was calling his shrink list, two men and one woman. Lacking the energy to make such a weighty decision, he returned to the chart review.

Randall quickly read through the patient's recent and past history. The man had a Stage II prostate cancer with too many medical problems to qualify for surgery, so radiation was the default curative treatment. In the doctor trade, when the list reached more than five major illnesses, it was called a positive review of systems. It didn't seem to matter to the surgeons that those factors also made the man a higher risk for radiation. It was nice when you could handpick your cases. Radiation Oncology was at the bottom of the referral food chain. Randall didn't enjoy being a bottom feeder. He sighed, picked up the chart and limped through Doris's office on the way to the exam room.

Randall muttered as he passed Doris's desk. "On my way to see another Stage II prostate with everything."

Doris sometimes served as Randall's moral guidepost. "Dr. B, don't refer to your patients as if they are just tumor-mobiles. They are real people with names who happen to have cancer. You are about to see Mr. Westerfield."

Randall was caught out. "Erk, sorry. I should practice what I preach. You're right. I am off to see Mr. Westerfield of Ozaukee County."

Mr. Westerfield was a slight gray-haired man in his sixties who smelled vaguely of urine but was otherwise well groomed. Despite his multiple ailments he appeared healthier than anticipated. Randall breezed through the interview and had left the prostate exam for last.

Randall rose from his exam stool with the rotating seat and pulled a pair of latex gloves out of the dispenser box. "Okay, Mr. Westerfield. Now I need to have you drop your pants and lean over on the exam table so I can check your prostate."

"Is this going to hurt?" whined Mr. Westerfield.

Randall shook his head and tried to ooze nonchalance. "Oh, not to worry, this won't hurt me a bit, but you might feel a little pinch." He gave a little forced laugh at his attempted joke. The patient did not respond with any sort of amusement. "It does help if you take a deep breath and relax. I'm a professional and I have small fingers. That's why I chose medicine instead of football."

Mr. Westerfield sighed and bent over. Randall found a large prostate with a hard two-centimeter nodule on the right. He swept his finger around the rectum to feel for any other lesions. Finding nothing else, he was about to withdraw his finger when Mr. Westerfield gave a sudden shout urging Randall to be careful because there might be some bowel gas about to come out. Randall stopped, moved to the side, and more slowly withdrew his gloved finger. The sidestep proved to be wise, because much more than flatulence was emitted.

"Clean up in aisle one!" Randall called out to no one in particular. He thought to himself, *most clinics have a nurse to deal with these little unforeseen events.*

Randall grabbed the patient's hips to prevent him from moving. "Mr. Westerfield, don't move a muscle. I have a bit of tidying up to do. Let's just take off your pants. I'll give you some scrub pants to wear home."

After depantsing the man, Randall cleaned off Mr. Westerfield's legs and shoes with wet paper towels. Then he got a towel out of the cabinet, dried him off and led him to a dry part of the floor. There he helped the man put on the scrub pants and asked if he needed to go to the men's room to finish his business. The man indicated that he did.

Randall led the patient down the hall. As they passed Doris's office Randall asked her to get housekeeping to clean up the exam room one. Doris just needed to sniff to figure out the clean up needed. "We'll be back," he announced. "We just have to make a quick visit to the little boy's room."

Mr. Westerfield was embarrassed. "I'm sorry Doc. With the dang irritable bowel, I can never tell when it's coming."

Randall was unperturbed. "*De nada*! My two kids have given me lots of experience in the poopy pants department. All part of the job." Randall waited by the stall for Mr. Westerfield to finish, reflecting on the exotic experiences he'd had in his chosen profession.

Shrink Rap

Randall and Mr. Westerfield walked back from the lavatory. Doris informed Randall that Housekeeping hadn't done the clean up yet, so they moved to exam room two to complete the consultation. After sending Mr. Westerfield off with a return appointment for a new treatment simulation, Randall washed his hands thoroughly, but could not rid himself of the lingering aroma. He wished he could take a shower. Back in his office, the yellow sticky note seemed to stare at him and whisper an invitation to call one of the numbers. If any day qualified him to make the call, this one certainly did. He decided to just do it.

Randall felt he didn't want to spill his psychologic beans to a man, so he somewhat arbitrarily went with the only female on the list, Dr. Mary Alice Hoffman. He liked that name. Mary Alice seemed like the name of someone he'd like to talk to. Like the girl next door, he envisioned she would not be judgmental. She'd listen with sympathy to all his travails and quietly offer suggestions. She would sort of be like an understanding mother who'd just kiss the hurts and make them all better. Besides, her initials spelled MAH.

Randall knew he'd better act fast and call for the appointment before he lost his courage. After all, he'd seen the last morning patient and he'd have plenty of time for lunch after dictating Mr. Westerfield's consult. Then, he could gird his loins for the sailor lady and her husband.

Before he could dither himself to inaction, Randall dialed the number and was told that Dr. Hoffman had just had a cancellation for one of the Saturday morning slots set aside for busy working clients. Randall agreed to the booking, hung up the receiver, and stared at the phone in wonderment. Had he just done that? It had all happened so fast. And it was much easier than he expected.

Randall was good at compartmentalizing some things. He put the thought of the appointment with Mary Alice out of his mind while he ate his brown bag lunch.

Do over

At mid sandwich, Doris walked into his office with the paperwork and a new chart for his next consultation. "Would you like a Morris de Lon along with your BLT?"

Randall looked up. "Umm, sounds like a fine wine. Pour me a chart."

Doris handed him the skimpy records with a flourish. "Here you go, sir. Not much of the chart made it down from Iron Mountain.

Hopefully, it will go down smoothly with a good nose, and not too much tannin." She tried to do a French accent, but it got all muddled in her Southern.

"A consummation devoutly to be wished," pronounced Randall professorially. "And then swished."

Randall completed his BLT and the chart review just as the clock struck 1:00. Since prostate cancer seemed to be the day's blue light special, he was not surprised to learn Mr. de Lon had Stage II prostate cancer. Unfortunately, since most of the records were still at Iron Mountain VA, there was little other patient history to review. Randall would have to get that during the interview. He reminded himself not to mention anything about the swearing/pounding and walked into the now clean exam room.

Mr. de Lon was sitting in the far corner and Mrs. de Lon had pulled up a chair to sit right next to her rather large husband. The man was over six feet tall and had a girth that almost matched. Randall introduced himself, shook hands with the two and took a seat opposite them on his rotating stool.

Randall displayed his 24 carat smile. "So, Mr. de Lon, what brings you here to see me today?"

Mrs. de Lon looked impatient. "I drove him."

"Of course." Randall tried to remain calm. "Mr. de Lon, have your Iron Mountain doctors told you about your prostate cancer diagnosis?" Many times, referrals from Iron Mountain were not informed about why they were sent.

"Yes, he has been told," answered Mrs. de Lon.

"Good," replied Randall, glad that hurdle wouldn't have to be leapt over. "Tell me, what symptoms were you having that brought the cancer to the attention of your doctors?"

"He was having blood in his urine," answered Mrs. de Lon.

Randall turned his stool toward Mr. de Lon. "That's a fairly common first symptom. Were you having any frequent urination or difficulty starting your urine?"

"Yes, he was having that, too," answered Mrs. de Lon.

Randall was getting slightly annoyed. "Mrs. de Lon, if you don't mind, I am asking your husband these questions. Would you please let him reply?"

Mrs. de Lon huffed and crossed her arms. "I would like to let him reply, doctor, but he had a stroke last year and now he can only say a few words. That should be in the records you have, if you'd bothered to read them."

Now, Randall knew what key information he was missing, and knew he'd better not say what he was tempted to say.

Randall took a deep breath. "Tell you what, Mrs. de Lon. I think we both need a do over. I am going to leave the room for three minutes and then I'm going to come back in. We're going to both pretend that we've never met before and we'll start over."

Mrs. de Lon nodded. "Agreed."

Randall left the room, closed the door and waited the specified time. When he re-entered the room, he introduced himself brightly. "Hello, I'm Dr. Biedermeier, but everyone just calls me Dr. B. Feel free to do so as well. Biedermeier is such a mouthful to say."

Mr. de Lon remained seated, but Mrs. de Lon rose from her chair, smiled at Randall and shook his hand warmly. "And you can just call me Mona. No need for formalities."

Randall escorted Mrs. de Lon back to her seat. "That's fine by me, Mona. What about your husband?"

"He prefers just plain Mo. Actually, his friends call him 'little Mo,' but Mo works just fine."

Just plain Mo still hadn't spoken a word, but he nodded enthusiastically.

Randall explained why he had so little case information. "Before I begin the consultation, Mr. and Mrs. de Lon, let me say that most of the records from Iron Mountain failed to reach me. Thus, I know little about your history except for your recent diagnosis of prostate cancer. Are there any other important health issues I need to know about?"

"Yes, doctor," answered Mrs. de Lon, a touch sarcastically. "My husband had a stroke last year and has a hard time speaking, so I do most of the talking for him and take him to all his appointments."

Randall's eyebrows rose in concern. "Oh, I'm sorry to hear that! Can you tell me about the symptoms he was having prior to the prostate cancer diagnosis?"

The rest of the consultation went smoothly. When the three emerged from the exam room laughing at a colorful joke Mrs. de Lon had just told, Doris poked her head out of her office to see what was going on. She seemed shocked to see the trio behaving like old friends coming home from a night at the pub. She just shook her head and muttered. "Dr. B must have sung a siren's song to tame that sailor woman!"

Randall waved to the de Lons as they left. Doris sidled over to Randall, whispering behind her smile. "Mona seems a most appropriate name, *mon cher.*" Randall smiled, enjoying Doris' acute perception and wit, as always.

FRANKEN'S TIME

Randall was ready to pack it up for the day when Melinda and Elisa came to his office. They wanted him to see Mr. Franken, a 38-year-old man with tongue cancer. Mr. Franken was a firefighter at the Verona Fire Department and had been referred from the Madison VA. Elisa handed the chart to Randall. Mr. Franken was two thirds of the way through his planned seven-week radiation treatment.

Randall wasn't sure why he was being double-teamed. "What's up, ladies?"

Elisa was first to speak. "Melinda called me in on Mr. Franken's case earlier today because of some discrepancies. There were some issues regarding the progress of his treatment."

Randall looked puzzled. "Discrepancies? I just saw him in weekly review two days ago and he was doing fine. What's the problem?"

Melinda picked up the rest of the story. "Mr. Franken's wife is here with him and she seemed pretty ticked off. I encountered her in the hallway and she peppered me with questions. She acted pretty hostile. So I paged Elisa to help me because you were way busy. He stays here at the VA Domiciliary during the week and goes home on the weekends. His wife claims that last weekend he was in constant pain and that he'd not been given anything for relief. She wants to know why."

Elisa added her observations. "Yeah, I came down from the Oncology ward and found her sitting in the hallway next to her husband. She said she had driven from Madison to check up on us. She seemed really riled. She went on about us neglecting her husband's pain. I looked to him for corroboration, but he just acted confused and shrugged his shoulders. I put on my best placating face, but nothing seemed to work. The man is pretty young to have tongue cancer, isn't he?"

"Last question first," said Randall. "He's a drinker and a smoker with PTSD and who knows what toxins he's been exposed to fighting fires. He's also a Vietnam vet and was probably exposed to Agent Orange. We see these head and neck cancers much earlier in those who've been exposed."

Melinda shook her head. "That is a cruel payback for serving your country. And I'll bet the PTSD is why he drinks and smokes."

Randall nodded back. "You're probably right. Rather ironic."

"So, what's up with the disconnect between his story and hers?" questioned Elisa.

Randall looked at odds as he paged through the chart to recheck his notes. They confirmed what he recalled. The patient had not complained of discomfort and, on exam, appeared to be responding well. The visible tumor had reduced in size at least 80%. It wasn't uncommon for the wife and the patient to tell two different stories. He'd have to handle this carefully. Randall got up from his chair and asked Elisa to come with him to the exam room.

"What about me?" asked Melinda.

"I don't want them to feel like we're ganging up on them," explained Randall. "Will you please get the next patient set up for review so we don't get bogged down?"

"Dang. I never get to see the good stuff," whined Melinda as she went to do Randall's bidding.

Elisa called after her. "Don't worry, I'll give you a full debriefing."

Randall smiled at Elisa. "Nice save. Let's proceed carefully here, Elisa. I'm not sure what's going on with this guy."

Entering the room, Randall did his usual rapid survey of the landscape. Elisa stood next to Randall with the hint of a smile on her face. The patient sat quietly in the ENT exam chair. As usual, Mr. Franken appeared rather stoic. His wife, on the other hand, was sitting in the guest chair with her legs tightly crossed. The straps of the purse in her lap were being strangled by her twisting hands. She wore an expression of stifled anger. Randall introduced himself and she seemed to stiffen even more.

Mrs. Franken rose from her chair slightly to take Randall's hand. "Good to finally meet you, doctor, I'm Beth Franken. Just what's going on with my husband?"

Randall tried to put some electricity in his smile. "Pleased to meet you as well. I'm glad that you've come in to be with your husband. I'm happy to be able to check him out in your presence. It's always good for the family to understand what's going on."

Mrs. Franken's eyes were narrowed by furrowed brows. "What I 'understand' is that Frank is in constant pain and you've given him nothing for it." She cleared her throat loudly. "Neither one of us has a clue what his progress is. Is he going to make it?"

Randall pushed the "emit reassurance" button in his brain. "Starting with your last question first, yes, he is going to make it. At my most recent exam, I noted that the tumor had shrunken 80% in size, but that he has a moderate radiation reaction in his mouth and throat. He has consistently told us that the pain is not severe and that he prefers no narcotics for it. Instead he's been taking Tylenol."

Mrs. Franken folded her arms across her chest. "Well, then, he's been lying to you, because that's not what I see."

Randall trod carefully. "It seems I am caught in the middle. Mr. Franken, what do you have to say about all this?"

Mr. Franken pulled the corner of his mouth toward his right ear and hesitated. "*Umm*, she's partly right. I've been too chicken to tell you about the pain, because I was afraid you'd stop the treatment and the tumor would come back and kill me. Plus, I'm afraid of narcotics. I've kind of had a problem with them in the past. Plus, the pain has gotten much worse the past several days."

Randall wasn't surprised. Patients often tried to hide the truth. "Okay, let's take another look inside your mouth."

Randall saw a fluffy whitish-yellow coating on Mr. Franken's tongue and soft palette. There were also some red ulcerations. "Ah, Mr. Franken, no wonder you're in pain! It seems you have a common opportunistic fungal infection in your mouth and throat. It looks nasty and painful. I know this might sound alarming, but not to worry. These infections are not unusual at this phase of the treatment. We can treat it with an antifungal."

Mrs. Franken gasped. "That's terrible! You're telling me this is normal? It looks like you're torturing him! How did you even let this happen?"

Randall raised his hands palms up. "I know, it's hard to believe this is progress. The radiation causes a loss of local immunity in the mouth which allows the naturally occurring fungus to grow on the dead tissue. Temporary situation, I assure you. I'll prescribe the antifungal and some low dose narcotics for the pain."

"Is that all you can do?" asked Mrs. Franken dolefully.

"No, there's more." Randall assured her. "When I see a fungal infection of this severity, I like to take a brief treatment break to let the normal tissues recover a bit from the radiation. It helps the affected tissues fight off the infection. This is Thursday and the Techs held your treatment until I could see you. So, I'd like to hold your treatment until Monday next week. That will give us four days of recovery time. I will see you on Monday before treatment is given to be sure the infection is clearing up before we restart. Do you two have any questions?"

Mrs. Franken's anger masked a deeper fear. "Stop treatment? Won't the tumor roar back?"

Randall reached out and touched Mr. Franken's shoulder. "Very unlikely. We use such breaks frequently without an obvious ill effect on tumor control. I suggest he use the time to eat as much as he can tolerate, drink plenty of fluids and get lots of rest. His body has the resources to recover. I know it sounds like one of my mother's old nostrums, but it's accurate. Now, Elisa will take you back out to the waiting area. I'll bring out his prescriptions and some nutritional supplements we have in stock."

Mr. Franken and his wife seemed to be placated for the moment, but both had acquired "deer-in-the-headlights" expressions.

Randall often wished there was more he could do to soothe his patients' fears, or 'magic' the tumor away. *I'm a mere mortal man, doing the best science can offer*, he thought to himself.

He watched Elisa escort the couple gently to the waiting area. He passed them on the way to deliver the prescriptions and supplements to Doris.

Elisa looked rather hopeless. "Dr. B, is there anything more we can do? They're still so afraid!"

Randall shrugged. "All we can do is be compassionate and exude confidence, even if we don't much feel it ourselves. Hopefully, that will instill faith so the patient and family don't give up hope. I believe maintaining hope is just as important as the meds we pass out. Your kindness with them goes a long way to helping them stay hopeful. Your presence matters, Elisa. It's really important for them to know we care."

Elisa looked like she was ready to cry. "It just isn't fair! I can't imagine what it's like to be facing the possibility of death when you're only in your thirties. My God, I'll be 30 next year. It could be me. I'd be so devastated I might just want to end it all."

Randall chuckled softly. "It does feel dramatic! I've already survived three fatal cancers, but I didn't get suicidal. Then I thought Vietnam would get me, but here I am."

Elisa got wide eyed. "Really? Were you in Vietnam?"

Randall shook his head. "Close, but no banana. I served my country in the Baltimore Public Health Hospital for two years. Worst threat was getting mugged walking to the parking lot. No, I had medical student cancer. You know, where you read the chapter about Hodgkin's disease and then you're certain you have it. All imaginary, but just as scary. It's funny. Our will to survive just brings out the fight in most of us. Rarely see suicide in cancer patients. I'm pretty sure that would be you as well. Now, let's get cracking with the next problem and stop being so murky."

Randall touched Elisa's elbow as they scurried off to the rest of the day's patients.

The rest of the afternoon passed in a blur of patients, charts, coffee refills and used coffee donations. The drive home often cleared Randall's thoughts and allowed him to put patients out of his mind. But today, he couldn't get Mr. Franken put away. He couldn't overcome a sense of foreboding.

He wondered what was wrong, then it hit him. *Oh, crap. I'm getting shrunk tomorrow!* Randall knew it was ridiculous and illogical, but he felt deeply afraid that the psychotherapist would deem him crazy, a hopeless case, and a fraud. Just to follow the runaway fear train, he imagined the "crazy" label escalating, leading to him losing his job, then his home, then his family, then being left out on the frozen tundra to die alone.

He shook his head to come back to the here and now.

Dinky
Shrink

CHAPTER 4

DINKY SHRINK

*"I told my wife the truth. I told her I was seeing a psychiatrist. Then
she told me the truth: that she was seeing a psychiatrist, two plumbers,
and a bartender."*

—Rodney Dangerfield

Eee eeee eee EEEE!! Thwack. A pillow flew onto Randall's face.

"What the hell, Randy!?" Zelda threatened him with another pillow. "Why is the alarm going off on a Saturday?"

Randall's heart sank. "Nothing for you to worry about. Go back to
sleep. On my way to shrink visit number one. Gonna go meet my judge
and jury."

"Whatever!" Zelda rolled over and resumed snoring.

MARY ALICE

That Saturday morning was sunny and in the high twenties. It seemed
almost tropical. The traffic on the way to Milwaukee's east side was tolerable and Randall found Dr. Hoffman's office on Prospect Avenue well
ahead of time. There was even street parking available only a block away.
The road was cleared of snow so he didn't have to park on top of pack ice.

The parking spaces were metered and, at 25 cents per 15 minutes,
required six quarters to cover 90 minutes. Randall only had three quarters, so he put those in the meter and hoped he could get change from
Dr. Hoffman's office secretary. As he walked down the sidewalk he noted

that the houses on the block were classic cream city brick two stories, many of which had been converted to offices. Dr. Hoffman's building sported a brass plaque on the wall next to the front door indicating it had been built in 1884 and was an historic site. The building certainly looked vintage enough. Parked at the curb directly in front of the building was a powder blue Harley Davidson Electra-Glide in pristine condition. Randall loved all things wheeled and walked over for a closer look. It had been fully restored and was expertly done. Not his favorite color, though.

Randall walked up the front steps and opened the heavy wooden front door which set off what sounded like sleigh bells announcing his entry. A middle-aged woman wearing leathers looked up at him from behind a raised counter, where she had been typing. "Good morning. You must be Mr. Biedermeier. How many quarters do you need?" asked the woman. "I'm Carol, Dr. Hoffman's receptionist."

Randall was taken aback. "Yeah, that's me. I think three quarters will do the trick." Randall handed her a dollar bill from which to make change. "Boy, I think one of your patients got the best parking space out there. He's riding a beautiful Electra-Glide."

"Well, thanks for noticing!" Carol straightened up in her chair. "That baby is mine. I ride it to work whenever the weather is nice."

Randall was somewhat awed. "Did you buy it that way?"

Carol smiled broadly. "Nope. It was a basket case when I got it. It took about three years to do the resto. Here are your quarters." She dropped four quarters into Randall's outstretched hand. "No charge for the extra quarter."

Randall invoked his best Hebrew accent. "Such a deal! I'll be right back as soon as I feed the meter."

Carol called out to Randall as he headed out the door. "Hurry back, I think Dr. Hoffman has just finished the paperwork on her last patient."

When Randall returned, Dr. Hoffman's office door was open. He looked inside the office and saw a smallish middle-aged woman with graying hair sitting at her desk and puffing on a cigarette. Smoke plumes filled the air. Dr. Hoffman turned and looked at him. She gave him a polite smile and a wave, then turned to take a pull from a heavy ceramic coffee cup. In that brief smile, Randall noted that her teeth were quite stained with nicotine. She motioned that she would be just a minute.

Cartoonia

Randall re-entered the waiting area, again setting off the sleigh bell sound. He was about to sit in an overstuffed armchair when he spotted a rather large book on a book pedestal off in a corner of the waiting room. On closer inspection it proved to be an 800-page collection of New Yorker cartoons. The cartoons were arranged by theme. Randall had always liked New Yorker cartoons and this was a lot easier than looking through the magazine to find them. He couldn't remember ever actually reading any of the articles.

"I love that collection," remarked Carol from behind her counter. "There's a table to your right with a collection of puzzle devices. If you can solve any one of them, you get $50 off your bill."

Randall went over to the table and found an odd array of items. There were nails twisted together, boxes with hidden openings and cords with impossible knots. He decided to go back to the cartoon book, but noticed a shelf with unusual items of ceramic, clay and clever items made from small auto parts.

Carol gestured to the shelf. "That's stuff that Dr. Hoffman's patients have given her over the years. Don't ask me what they are, but they all have some meaning and she never throws anything away that patients give her. See those sketches and paintings on the far wall?"

On the wall indicated were renderings in crayon, pencil, ink and various kinds of paint. The art reminded him of the things you'd find stuck on a refrigerator door in any home with kids. He shook his head in amazement as he perused the postings. The images portrayed were everything from human stick figures to cheery rainbows.

Randall was about to go back to the New Yorker cartoons when he turned and found Dr. Hoffman standing at her open office door waiting for him. The cigarette was gone, but she still held a cup of coffee. The cup looked handmade, with a distorted face sculpted into the side. She was wearing charcoal wool pants and a gray vest over a white collared shirt. The vest was decorated with what looked like hand-stitched question marks and exclamation points. Randall found himself at a loss for words.

Dr. Hoffman motioned Randall to come into her office. "Step into my lair, Mr. Biedermeier. Can I get you a glass of water? Perhaps some hot coffee? One can never wake up too much."

For some reason, Randall continued to feel frozen in place and incapable of speech. He looked into the office and saw it was now, somehow, smoke-free. Then, he became unsure if the invitation had been meant for him, because he didn't recall ever being referred to as "Mr. Biedermeier." Funny, Carol had called him that, too. That was his father's name. The name of a machinist with a tight fist and sharp tongue. Certainly, his father needed to be here more than Randall did. *It's just a case of anxiety.* He reassured himself that he was not psychotic and so had nothing to fear. He thought about dismissing himself right then and there, just walking away. He had his pager . . . he could pretend it went off. But that could just suggest untethered anxiety. Better to look calm and collected than be calm and collected.

"We can start the session out here in the waiting area, if you like," offered Dr. Hoffman, in response to Randall's hesitant, confused state. "There's no one else out here except Carol and she forgets everything she hears, right, Carol?"

Carol continued to type without interruption. "I've already forgotten what you just asked me."

Randall suddenly realized how foolish he must look. What was there to be afraid of? Surely, she wasn't telepathic and couldn't read his private thoughts. Randall knew how to protect himself from probing questions. Dr. Hoffman made another waving motion with her arm and bade him enter the office.

"Now would be a good time to engage motor function, Mr. Biedermeier. The clock is ticking and it's your money. My name is Mary Alice Hoffman." She held out her hand and looked him in the eyes warmly.

"Uh, Randall Biedermeier," responded Randall, taking her hand and shaking it.

Dr. Hoffman had a firm grip despite her diminutive size and maintained a firm hold on Randall's hand as she deftly maneuvered him into her office. She led him over to a comfortable appearing easy chair and pushed him gently into it.

Coffee, Tea or Me?

"I'll get you that coffee. I can see you need it. I'm betting you take it with a dollop of real creamer, not foo-foo juice." Mary Alice grinned knowingly.

"Yes, exactly," blurted Randall, wondering how she would know that. "I'm sorry for acting so flaky. I'm just a bit nervous about this whole thing."

Randall couldn't believe he had just admitted that. That was supposed to remain his secret.

"Not a bit of it," said Dr. Hoffman. "I'm quite used to it. It's a common affliction. First visits are often challenging. But look at me. What harm could I possibly do to a big manly man like you?"

She left momentarily and returned with a heavy ceramic mug, painted clumsily with a mushroom. "Here, take your coffee and relax for a bit while I get my notebook and pen."

Randall wrapped his hands around the rough ceramic, took a sip of the coffee and found it to be surprisingly good.

"Yes, the coffee is surprisingly good isn't it?" commented Dr. Hoffman, again making Randall think she was hard wired to his brain. She took a seat in another easy chair just kitty corner from Randall. "I use a Costa Rican blend which I've grown quite fond of. There's absolutely no reason to drink bad coffee. Life is too short, don't you think?"

Clearly, the woman had mastered the art of observation, Randall thought. It would be best to be cautious around her.

"Yes, it's quite delicious," said Randall. "It's not like that bitter French Roast everyone seems to like. I can't stand that stuff."

Dr. Hoffman held out a small tray with several cookies that smelled fresh from the oven. "Absolutely. Would you like a cookie with your coffee? Carol bakes the best oatmeal raisin cookies."

Randall watched as his hand automatically grabbed the warm delight. "Where do you buy this coffee?"

While Dr. Hoffman explained where to find the coffee shop, Randall took another cookie and was surprised how hungry he was. As he chewed the delicacy and sipped his coffee, he looked around the room, shaking his head. He figured it best to reconnoiter his surroundings while he could. There were floor lamps deployed to create a soft up-glow with no harsh shadows or hidden corners. On the far wall, two tall paned windows with colorful stained-glass inserts flanked a fireplace. On the mantel a vintage Seth Thomas clock marked each second with metallic click-clacks at a pace that seemed way too slow. The view out the windows revealed mature oak trees surrounding a small patio with a lone snow-covered wrought iron table at its center. The snow on the table had accumulated in multiple layers that made it look like a large layer cake with white frosting. Some small fallen tree twigs stuck out of the top of the snow like burnt out candles.

Even though cigarette smoke had recently filled the room, the air smelled clean and exuded an earthiness from several large potted plants. Outside, the street had been noisome with the sound of traffic and people, but this room was as quiet as a sanctuary except for the heartbeat ticking of the clock. Randall imagined that the clock had bradycardia and needed a shot of adrenaline. Dr. Hoffman had remained silent while observing Randall with amusement.

Randall noted that the chair he was sitting in was covered with a blue corduroy fabric and was bolstered by a large matching corduroy pillow. He remembered the joke he often used when breaking the ice with patients. *Have you heard about the new trend in corduroy pillows? They're making headlines everywhere.* That relaxed him and he felt his shoulders finally descend away from his ears.

Dr. Hoffman had been holding a clipboard in her lap, but then she put it down on the wooden coffee table between them.

"Would you like some more coffee?"

"No, I'm good for now," said Randall, feeling a bit more relaxed.

Dr. Hoffman smiled broadly. "Excellent. Then, let's begin. What brings you here today?"

Randall had to restrain himself from saying: "My car, duh." He wondered why he always reverted to high school behavior under pressure. He calmed himself and tried to focus.

Randall was surprised to hear his voice make a clear and true opening statement. "Well, there have been some weird things going on in my life, and I think I could use some help to figure out what's going on."

Dr, Hoffman nodded. "Sounds reasonable, 'Mr.' Biedermeier. That sort of thing is exactly in my wheelhouse. And, look, I know you're a doctor so we can stop the rank charade. You're among friends here. Feel free to call me Mary Alice. When exploring the inner workings of the mind, there's no need to be too formal." The corners of her eyes crinkled as she smiled at him, somewhat disarmingly.

Randall was surprised. "How'd you know I'm a doctor?"

"I do my homework," noted Mary Alice. "I didn't just fall off the potato truck."

Randall's eyes sought the ceiling. "Of course not. I'm sorry about trying to cover that up."

Dr. Hoffman waved it off. "Not to worry. I understand why you did it. The medical professionals that I've seen are always squeamish about letting on that they may be vincible and that coming to my office might somehow disqualify them from retaining their credentials. But, be assured, that is not going to happen. Like Las Vegas, everything that happens here stays here."

Randall's shoulders relaxed in visible relief. "That's good to know!"

Mary Alice gestured to her clipboard. "Oh, and thanks for filling that in correctly on the intake forms ahead of our appointment. That could have been my first clue, if you're counting. I had time to go over them before you arrived. I noticed that you didn't write much in the social history areas, so let's just review some of those details before we start addressing your concerns."

Randall felt somewhat relieved that they wouldn't be delving immediately into the inciting causes for his visit. Filling out the intake paperwork had been a bit strange. He had written up many patient histories, but had found it difficult to put his own information into a few small rectangles on a form. How could anyone write that small, anyway? He began to feel a little more at ease and allowed himself to loosen his tie.

"So, what do your friends call you?" inquired Mary Alice. "For the sake of our new informality, I could refer to you by that name."

Randall responded with a slight stammer. "Depends on the friend.... Well, it's Randall, just Randall." He wasn't quite ready for "Randy" or "Dr. B."

Mary Alice picked up the clipboard and began leafing through the pages. "OK, Randall. Then it will be 'just Randall.' Let's review your information to clarify some points." Taking notes as she asked questions, she reviewed Randall's history. He began to think that the sessions might not be as bad as he'd feared. After all, she seemed to have a good sense of humor. She was old enough to have acquired some wisdom. It could be like sharing his problems with the grandmother he never had.

They breezed through the basic demographic information and medical history—that was old hat to Randall. He confirmed that he was the oldest of four children, had a post-strep heart murmur at age five, and there was a history of high blood pressure in the family. Things got dicier when they got to the social history, where, despite the fact that he had entered N/A, she asked again if he'd had any problems with the law and whether he used alcohol or drugs on a regular basis. He had to make a quick judgment about whether occasional use meant regular in her definitions. He also felt hesitant when she brought up family history of anxiety, depression, schizophrenia or other mental illness. He was also uncertain whether his father's verbal abuse should be mentioned when she inquired about abuse in the family.

As a result, Randall just kept shaking his head. As the questions were asked, he realized that the answers to some of these questions were not simple ones. In his family, some of these topics weren't talked about. Maybe his mother felt sad sometimes about having four kids to raise and a non-communicative husband, but was that depression? His dad yelled at the kids a lot, but was it abuse? And who doesn't have a beer once in a while? This was Wisconsin, after all—beer and cheese country! There was the aunt who committed suicide. He wondered if he should mention any of this. Was it normal?

Not sure what to say, Randall decided on full disclosure. "Well, to be honest, Mary Alice, I didn't know how to fill out some of that. I mean, none of my family were drunks, that I know of, and nobody's been in jail. And as for mental illnesses. . . ." His words trailed off as he remembered all the drinking his Uncle Pete had done.

Mary Alice seemed used to calming the heebie jeebies. "Not to worry, Randall. These are just the standard questions that we ask everyone. They are merely designed to bring out the major issues right up front. Every box of cookies has some crumbles."

The questions moved on to physical symptoms such as headaches, dizziness, numbness and tingling. Then she asked about thoughts of homicide or suicide. It was one thing to check off the "no" box on the form, but it seemed a lot harder to answer the question under face-to-face scrutiny.

The Dam Bursts

Randall didn't want to seem like he was blocking information. He felt pressure to say something credible. Dr. Hoffman sensed Randall was holding back. "Just Randall, you don't need to struggle so hard to say what's on your mind. I'm not going to bite no matter what comes out first."

Randall couldn't hold back what he was thinking. "Well, to be honest, I'm not sure if I should be here at all. You've probably heard that disclaimer before. None of the issues on my plate seem as serious as the stuff you were asking about in my history."

Dr. Hoffman leaned forward. "Is that so? Please expand on that."

Suddenly, Randall's verbal dam burst. "Well, let's see. I don't feel like I want to jump out a four-story hospital window like a patient did when

I was an intern in Denver. Damn near hit me as I was walking from my quarters to the back door of the hospital." Randall shrunk into himself with the memory.

Dr. Hoffman put up a hand. "I wasn't suggesting you're suicidal. It's just part of my history routine. Anything else I should know?"

Randall wanted to be clear he was not around the bend. "I'm definitely not crazy like the patient of mine who saw a huge ship coming through his sixth-floor hospital room window as I walked into the room. Well, that's not right. He did have brain mets. Or like the guy who kept seeing a monkey sitting on the cabinet in my exam room. I certainly don't feel as nutty as when I went without sleep during my 24-hour on-call rotations as an intern."

Randall stopped talking abruptly and looked around the room again. Maybe for an escape hatch. He'd poured out a lot of unsolicited information, despite his self-imposed reservations. Perhaps he sounded a bit manic, but it was said and done. There were no backsies now, but he wasn't sure what direction to go.

Dr. Hoffman broke the ensuing silence. Her tone was reassuring. "Just Randall, from what you've shared so far, it sounds like your life has been full of, shall we say, interesting and perhaps confusing events. These experiences may have engendered some conflicts in your life. It's always good to nip these conflicts in the bud before they have time to fester. You wouldn't want a patient to wait until a lung tumor was impeding their breathing before they sought treatment, right?"

Randall furrowed his brow. "The smaller the lesion, the better the prognosis. Removing or irradiating the tumor when it's still small allows for less damage to normal tissue." Randall felt a lecture coming on, but he restrained himself.

Dr. Hoffman winked and touched her nose. "And the patients with small tumors are no less deserving of attention than the patients with massive growths, right?"

Randall got the point. He realized that Mary Alice had turned the allegory on its head. "Touché. How'd you do that?"

Dr. Hoffman raised her index finger and waggled it. "It's my trade secret. Can't tell you, or I'd have to wipe your memory with my mind-meld laser."

Randall shrank back in his chair for dramatic effect. "Do you have any other arrows in your quiver?"

Dr. Hoffman feigned a sinister face. "Many, so beware."

Randall crossed his legs in mock defense.

Dr. Hoffman dialed back the scary face and lit up with a smile. "Just kidding, of course. You only need to share what feels right to share. Whether you tell me the truth doesn't matter. I'm paid to believe whatever you say. But . . . there's no benefit in trying to outsmart me. So, how about you just jump in and tell me what is bothering you?"

Randall thought about how much easier it was to create a radiation treatment plan for a Stage III lung cancer than to tell a relative stranger the nitty gritty of what was going on in his inner life. That was way out of his comfort zone. *On the other hand,* he thought, *perhaps sharing your baggage with an unbiased person might be easier than disclosing it to a friend or family member.*

Randall relaxed and let out a held breath. "Well, I guess I have nothing to lose. . . ."

Randall launched into purge mode, sharing an overview of the current stresses at work, a few difficult patient interactions, and challenges balancing being a doctor and a father. At first his monologue was logical and connected, but as he went on he became rather tangential and stream-of-consciousness.

Dr. Hoffman sat forward in her chair and motioned for him to pause. "Randall, I'm sorry to interrupt, but I suggest we stop at this point. Let me say that you are doing well."

Randall was somewhat taken aback. "What? I was just getting started. How could I be doing well? I haven't told you about the guy with the face thing, or about the dreams, or my son running away . . ."

Dr. Hoffman paused and took a long sip of her now lukewarm coffee. "Randall, we've already started a long journey that we'll take together. That, to me, is doing well. Trust me. Many of my patients take a long time to even begin to dip their toes in the waters of the mind's inner life. You just dove right in there. However, I see by the old clock on the mantel that we have only five minutes left in this session. It's time to talk about your homework for your next appointment."

Randall was amazed at how slippery time could be. "There's only five minutes left?"

Dr. Hoffman laughed. "Indeed, time flies like nothing and fruit flies like bananas. That's the funny thing—time morphs in the inner world. You've already covered a lot. Now let's decide on our goals for the next week and assign your homework."

Randall's eyes went wide. "Homework? Will there be a test, too?"

Dr. Hoffman smiled as she made an entry in her scheduling book. "And a tickle! Indeed, it will just be an oral exam."

Randall cocked his head to the side like a confused Spaniel.

Dr. Hoffman smirked, knowing she was throwing off his balance. "For the next session we should focus on one topic at a time, rather than take a shotgun approach. I am a firm believer in Einstein's methodology."

Randall sensed another sly shrink joke was coming. "Einstein? What does he have to do with psychiatry?"

Dr. Hoffman didn't answer right away. Randall awaited the punchline, but didn't really get one.

She paused for just a touch more drama. "Well, he was a bit anal compulsive, but that's not why I am referencing him. Einstein's over-arching aim was to find one unifying principle that could explain all natural phenomena in the universe. His theory of relativity came very close to that goal, but it required many others to subsequently verify his equations with observations. Fortunately, we have a much smaller job before us. We just have the unifying theory of Randall to discover."

Randall's face lit up in a smile of surprise. "I'm impressed. You sound like you have more than a passing acquaintance with physics."

Dr. Hoffman mimicked patting herself on the back. "I have an amateur's interest, which is just enough to get me in trouble. Your assignment for next time is a simple one. I just want you to tell me in ten minutes the story of how you came to be a Radiation Oncologist." Her booming voice added a cinematic effect to the last two words.

"That's it?" blurted Randall.

Dr. Hoffman laughed and nodded. "Oh, believe me, it's more than enough, as you will find. Think of it as a meeting presentation. Tell me what story you're going to tell me, then tell me the story, and then tell me the story you told me. Make it clear and understandable. I won't time you to the second but I won't let you run on. After your presentation we will do a Q and A for clarification of any unclear points. Got it?"

Randall took a few beats to digest the assignment. "Uh, yeah, I've got it, I think." The more he thought about it, the less certain he was that such a short timeframe would do the deed. "Ten minutes you say?"

There will be meds

Dr. Hoffman raised her index finger. "Exactly. Perhaps a minute more. Now, let's set your next appointments. I think we should meet twice a week for a few weeks so we can sort through all this and make a decision about whether we're going to need to employ little Mr. Med. or big Mr. Med. Can you come back next Wednesday at 6:00 PM? I have evening sessions every Wednesday for folks who work. I assume you can make it the following Saturday at 10:00 AM as well?"

Randall was not expecting twice weekly sessions. He pulled out his appointment book. "Let's see, I have grand rounds Wednesdays at 5:00, but I could miss it next week. And, yes, I can do the Saturday as well."

Mary Alice marked the dates in her appointment book, wrote them on a card, and handed it to Randall.

Dr. Hoffman's reference to medication finally sunk in and worried Randall. "Can we go back to what you said about medications? I'm not sure I understand what you meant."

Dr. Hoffman made a calming gesture. "I simply meant that we need to decide whether you just have situational anxiety or a neurochemical imbalance involving depression with anxiety. Then, we need to determine if you would benefit from the appropriate medication. Before you ask, anxiety is not necessarily pathological if the situation is stressful enough. Then, it's linked to the situation and we temporarily reduce the anxiety with short acting drugs while we work to decide how to reduce the stressful situations."

Randall thought that could be a good thing. "Does that mean you could give me something today to calm me down a tad?"

Dr. Hoffman nodded. "Yes, we could, if you think you need it."

"I think I'd like to try that, so I can get a better night's sleep and have fewer bad dreams." Randall surprised even himself that he had dropped his guard twice—agreeing to meds and sharing that he had bad dreams. *Am I having brain incontinence?*

Mary Alice wrote a prescription on her pad and handed it to him. "I'd like you to tell me about those dreams next time. I'm giving you a prescription for a low dose Valium in the meantime. I only want you to use it as needed and not more than twice a day, preferably when you're not working."

"What about the second kind of anxiety? Do you think I have that?" Randall felt like a little kid at the pediatrician's.

Dr. Hoffman swept her hand in front of her in a dismissive gesture. "It's way too soon to say on that score. If I think that's what it is after a few sessions, I might want to try you on an tricyclic antidepressant, like Elavil. There's also a new line of drugs being tested called SSRIs that alter brain chemistry in a different way. Both take several weeks to kick in fully. I can explain them in detail next time. Until then, you should understand that if you do have that kind of depression you are not re-sponsible for your brain chemistry. Having depression and anxiety is not your fault. You shouldn't feel stigmatized by having it. But that's water yet to go under the bridge."

Randall took a deep breath and let it out in a rush. "Thanks for telling me that. It's kind of a relief to hear it. I was sort of worried about what that diagnosis could mean for me."

Dr. Hoffman smiled warmly. "You're welcome. Congratulations, from what I see so far, you meet the criteria for 'normal human.' Now, before we finish, I need to tell you that at the end of most initial sessions, the patient usually asks if I can give them any advice about what to do. Were you about to ask me that?"

"The question was sort of in the back of my mind." Randall felt convinced she was psychic. Or had multiple magical eyes, like his first grade teacher.

Dr. Hoffman maintained her soothing manner. "Well, I think the overriding question you have right now is how to explain all the unusual occurrences that have been happening to you. I'm sure some have no obvious or rational explanation. You're probably not sure if it's some problem with your brain or if it's something about the universe we live in. I've been doing this work for a few years now and I can safely say that I have heard some things that would boggle even Einstein's venerated neurological complex." She rose from her seat and started walking to the office door.

Randall stood up in response and followed her. "Hmm, based on what I've seen with my patients, I have no reason to doubt you."

Superstring Theory

At the doorway, Dr. Hoffman reached into a pocket, took out a small card, and handed it to Randall.

Dr. Hoffman ushered Randall out of her office. In the waiting room, Randall stopped to read the card and looked puzzled. "It's a Sherlock Holmes quote by way of Arthur Conan Doyle. It may provide you with some guidance until we meet next. I see my next patient is already pacing laps around the waiting room, so I need to hustle you along. I need to finish my notes on our visit before I can deal with her. She just usually has a round of petty paranoias. I'm not in a rush." She lowered her voice to a whisper. "Don't tell anyone I told you that! By the way, if you're in need of entertainment, try having a conversation with anyone in the waiting room."

Randall was somewhat nonplussed by Dr. Hoffman's remarks and stumbled on a carpet edge. He almost collided with an elderly lady who was, in fact, wearing out the waiting area carpet muttering to some imaginary presence. Randall decided not to interrupt her ongoing monologue. He tilted the card he'd been given to get more light on it and read the quotation: *"If you have competing ideas to explain the same phenomenon, you should pursue the simpler one."*

Randall began his own monologue. "What the heck does that mean?"

The shambolic old lady looked up at him. "Damn crazies always talking to themselves!" She shuffled to the far side of the waiting room.

Carol spoke to Randall from behind her counter. "I see you've gotten your card, Dr. Biedermeier. Don't be alarmed. Every patient gets one after the first visit. They're all different and they're all enigmatic. Ultimately, you'll figure out what it means for you. Have yourself a good weekend. See you next Wednesday. Oh, and Dr. Hoffman suggested that you might understand the card better if you start reading up on superstring theory."

Randall's eyebrows met in the middle, creating a large crease on his forehead. "Huh?" While he tried to come up with something more coherent to say, Carol answered the phone and turned her chair to face away from him. He shrugged his shoulders and walked out, running his fingers over the raised letters on the card. He wondered how and when Dr. Hoffman had given the suggestion to Carol about superstring theory.

BIG
BOY

CHAPTER 5

PAST TENSE

"You better live every day like your last, because one day you're going to be right."

—Ray Charles

JOCKEYING FOR POSITION

It was just after noon when Randall returned from Dr. Hoffman's office. As he entered the back hallway, the Biedermeier cats, Milky Way and Wondercat, circled his ankles and nearly sent him sprawling. Milky Way was a dark-brown and caramel-colored tabby cat, while Wondercat was all black. Milky Way was primarily Addie's cat and Wondercat belonged to Kyle. There was some smell on his shoes that they found fascinating. Zelda was sitting at the kitchenette table engrossed in the newspaper.

Getting no immediate reception from Zelda, Randall called out doing his best imitation of Desi Arnaz. "Honey . . . I'm home!"

Zelda looked up. "So, do you need to buy smaller shoes?"

"Not quite, but my Jockeys feel a bit tight." Randall pitched his voice a half octave higher than usual. "And these dang cats better watch it or I will be demonstrating a feline field goal."

Zelda tried to corral the two felines. "Was the shrink visit everything you expected it to be?"

"And then some!" Randall took off his coat and hung it in the closet. When he came back into the kitchen, Zelda gave him a peck on the cheek.

She sniffed loudly. "Woof, you smell like an ashtray. I have only two questions. One, what have you been smoking? Two, did you bring me any?"

Randall took his usual seat at the kitchen table. "Not me. My Mary Alice likes her coffin nails well done. She partakes between patients. That doesn't set the best example, but who am I to judge? Oh, yeah! An oncologist! Nyuk nyuk!" He wiggled his hand and crossed his eyes.

Zelda nodded. "She probably needs ciggies to wind down after the crazy stooges she sees. No offense."

Randall shook his head. "None taken. I saw some of her other patients in the waiting room. One was several sandwiches shy of a picnic. I'm probably the most sane person she saw all day."

Zelda nodded emphatically. "Of course you are. I'm sure that's what they all say. But not to worry. She'll probably have you shrunk down from XXL to Medium in no time."

Randall groaned. "I hope so, but from what I learned today, it's not going to be a 'one-and-done.' I've got more sessions to go and homework to do. And I have to say, Mary Alice seems to have some special powers."

Zelda dialed up her receivers. "Do tell!"

Randall knew that Zelda had been working up the courage to find a psychotherapist for herself and had been stressing about the decision. She seemed to want only a female counselor. He'd probably have to tap his resources to get her some recommendations. Randall knew she would pump him for details about what to expect. He'd have to be careful to reveal the process but not his personal baggage.

Randall looked about. "Where are the kids? I don't want to start the narrative and get interrupted."

"Don't be so touchy," scolded Zelda. "I needed a time out until you got home so I sent them to play in their rooms. They know not to come down until 1:00 or until I call them. Or if they start a fire. I might have promised to take them clothes shopping so you could have some alone time yourself."

Randall was amazed Zelda would do that for him. "Did I ever tell you what a wonderful wife and parent you are?"

Zelda smiled and shook her head. "No. But now's as good a time as any to start. And repeat regularly."

Randall laughed his fake *ha ha* laugh. "Good one! Got me good."

Zelda looked like a fox in an empty henhouse. "Alrighty then. Give me the Cliff's Notes version of your session with Mary Alice the Great."

Before he started, Randall thought for a moment. He figured he shouldn't be too secretive about what happened, or it might discourage Zelda from going through with her appointment. He reminded himself not to surrender all his inner machinations by having a dam burst like he'd had in Dr. Hoffman's office.

Zelda tapped her foot. "Well, I'm waiting. Cats got your tongue?"

Randall jumped a bit. "Sorry, just getting my thoughts together so I don't miss any important stuff." Randall summarized his session with Dr. Hoffman, deftly glossing over the details of what he had discussed. He otherwise did a fairly complete outline of the session, including the assignment she had given Randall, the unusual Holmes card message, and the string theory suggestion.

PARTIAL DISCLOSURE

Zelda listened intently, at times taking notes. "Is that it? What's your take on the process?"

Randall was temporarily stumped. "Not sure yet without further digestion. I guess what got me the most was the suggestion to study string theory."

Zelda's eyebrows contracted. "Why's that? And what the heck is string theory, anyhow?"

Randall had hoped that the review would be over at this point, but Zelda was trying to open more doors. Time for obfuscating. "Good questions. String theory is related to subatomic physics and quantum theory. You know, the stuff I've been talking about in the group with Joe Shepard."

Zelda nodded. "Oh, the group of eggheads you put together to explain why 'some people' can see the dead and communicate to others without talking. How's that going? You haven't mentioned anything about it lately. Or have all your supposed meetings just been hobnobs with your girlfriend?"

Randall winced. "Oh, ye of little faith. I have no girlfriends except you and Addie. And my group is not a bunch of eggheads. They are all qualified psychologists, physicists and clerics. We've discussed this. We're trying to find evidence that quantum entanglement might explain nonverbal communication at a distance."

Zelda rolled her eyes. "Yeah, yeah. Quantum *schwantum*. Hocus pocus. Out of focus. All I know is that you saw a dead guy at work, a nearly dead guy commanded you to come to his hospital room, and we've had entangled spirits playing with us in whatever house we've lived in. And who can explain it? Does everything need an explanation?"

Randall eye rolled back and stuck out his tongue for greater emphasis. "No, but wouldn't you like one if it exists? And don't forget how Addie messaged us remotely that she was in trouble when she was a baby."

Zelda pointed to her temporal lobe. "Of course, I remember the lawnmower incident. How could I forget? But another option is to just accept that strange shit happens. We just have to learn not to belabor it."

Randall shook his head, surprised that Zelda was arguing against her previous self. "Not good enough for me. If the answer is out there, or in here, I want to find it. It's the scientist in me. What if some melding of neurobiology and quantum theory explains mental telepathy?"

Zelda pursed her lips. "It wouldn't change that it happens without our understanding it."

Randall had not expected this Buddha-like spiritual response from his usually earth-bound wife. It kicked up his frustration a notch, too. "But if we understand how it works, we could exploit it and maybe learn how to use it."

"So, you're on a save the world kick?" countered Zelda. "That's too big a job for little old you."

Randall muttered under his breath in frustration. "What a bitch."

Zelda gave him dagger eyes. "What was that?"

Randall didn't think he'd said that out loud. "I said 'What a switch.' You're usually all in on this spooky stuff. Actually our group has made some progress in our investigations. Next week is our second meeting. We've invited more people to come to broaden the scope of our 'experts.' You're welcome to come . . . if you're at all interested."

There was a long silence before Zelda let out a deep breath. "I suppose it wouldn't hurt to see what you crazies have been doing. I admit I'm just a tad frustrated with trying to explain Kyle's night terrors and spooky ladies in Addie's bedroom . . . among other things like window shades that won't stay down and out of control thermostats."

Randall was relieved. He'd gotten away with the verbal faux pas. "Thank God. I was afraid I'd lost you to the Catholic church."

"There's a few things you could lose me to, but not the Hail Marys," scoffed Zelda. "Now finish your preliminary analysis of Mary Alice's technique. My inquiring mind wants to know."

Randall was starting to see how Dr. Hoffman had fished information out of him. "It seemed she always kept me off guard and used trick plays to gain yardage. She's just started mining but has already uncovered some nuggets."

As Randall narrated, Zelda seemed impressed by the process. "Sounds like she's trying to jumpstart your subconscious to pop out data. It seems like she didn't push too hard for information and refrained from giving advice. I hope my doc is that good."

Randall looked rather weary. "Yeah, I think you've got it. My brain is still spinning."

Zelda looked sympathetic. "Poor boy. You look exhausted."

Randall couldn't tell if she was being sarcastic or sincere. He nodded agreement, just to hedge his bets. Perhaps he could end the inquisition before the hot pokers were employed. "Yeah. I think I need some down time to let it all settle." He shook his head as if to clear it. "I might even do a lay down and take a little nap. It's only noon, but it feels like midnight in my brain."

Zelda touched his cheek in a rare show of spontaneous affection.

"Sounds like a good idea. You look confuddled. I'm taking the kids to Kohl's to buy new winter gear. They've outgrown their coats and their boots are pretty grody. While we're gone it will be quiet. How about you eat something? By then we'll be out of here and you can do a nap."

Randall's head drooped. "Yes, Mother." He got up and gave Zelda a hug, nearly falling asleep in her arms. She shoved him in the general direction of the refrigerator, then set off to prep the kids for departure. He made himself a sandwich, ate, and hobbled upstairs to his bedroom.

Randall was somewhat surprised that Zelda was being so accommodating. Perhaps she fantasized that he had some mental imbalance that was the root cause of whatever marital discord they'd been having and that his visits with Mary Alice would "fix things right up." Or maybe his seeing a psychiatrist smoothed the way for her to get shrunk herself. Whatever, he couldn't process things anymore.

Randall sat on the edge of the bed and took off his shoes. He tossed them in the corner where they landed with two thumps. Shirt and pants were next to land on the floor. He crawled under the covers.

As he lay on the bed drifting away, Randall thought how it always seemed there was an invisible partition between the two sides of the bed that he dare not violate. Not this afternoon. The bed was all his, both sides. He rolled into a fetal position in the exact center of the bed, feeling defiant. *Ooo, risky business, Randy. Living on the edge.* His thoughts circled back to the assignment for the Wednesday session. How had he wound up in Radiation Oncology? As he reviewed the events that led to this destination, he kept circling back to one motivating factor: fear. But before he could suss out the genesis of that fear he was dead to the known world.

Spoiler alert

Randall awoke with a start at 2:30 PM when the shopping trio returned home and began shouting and banging around downstairs. That set the two cats scrambling around like chickens in a rainstorm. Even from the upstairs bedroom, Randall could hear cat claws skittering furiously on the kitchen linoleum in a vain attempt to get a fraction of traction. Kyle pounded up the stairs and burst into Randall's bedroom to display his new snow boots.

Kyle kicked Randall's bedroom door open and found the room dark. He hesitated a bit then whispered loudly. "Dad, are you awake?"

"I am now," croaked Randall. He reached over to the bedside stand and fumbled for the light switch. He tried to look at Kyle, but his eyelids felt glued shut.

Randall heard Zelda shout from downstairs. "Kyle! Don't disturb Dad. He's taking a nap!"

Kyle yelled back. "Don't worry, Mom, Dad's awake! Dad, Dad . . . look at my new boots and snow pants."

Randall groaned. "Sure. As soon as I get my eyes open, Buddy. There. I think I've got one unstuck. Let's take a look at your new waffle stompers."

As Randall inspected Kyle's outfit, Addie appeared at the door to show off her new wares. Randall did his best to show appropriate parental awe.

Zelda rumbled up the stairs and came in as he was doing final inspection. "I told you guys not to disturb your dad."

Randall sat up in bed. "Not to worry. I needed to get up anyway. You know, things to see and people to do. Nice job shopping, Zel. Looks like the sprouts are ready for an arctic expedition."

"And I saved fifty bucks!" Zelda announced proudly.

Randall made an effort to applaud, but couldn't quite coordinate the hand clapping. "Gold stars for you. I've got a boxful in my desk and you get one stuck to your forehead as soon as I can extract myself from bed."

Zelda beamed. "Okay, kids, let's get back downstairs and clean up our shopping mess so Dad can get dressed and join us for some ice cream and coffee."

"But, Mom, I don't drink coffee," corrected Addie.

Kyle stuck out his tongue at his sister. "Dummy, Dad gets the coffee, but we all get ice cream!"

Addie was quick to protest. "Kyle!" she whined. "Mom, make Kyle stop picking on me."

Addie's plea went unheeded, because Kyle made a hasty exit and *kalumped* down the stairs out of ear-shot.

On her way out of the bedroom with Addie, Zelda cautioned Randall about using his own side of the bed, not the whole bed. "Who do you think you are? The King of Sheba?"

Randall was ticked off that Zelda, the rather expressive sleeper, had decided to call him out on the ownership of bed sides. He vowed subtle pay back. With the familial tornado finally cleared out of the bedroom, Randall got up, dressed and washed his face to revive. Then, he went downstairs for treats.

Zelda gestured with her head as she took out the ice cream."Oh, Randy, before you sit down, UPS delivered a large package for you. It's propped up outside the back door."

Randall did a little hop of joy. "Great! That's probably the Kamei spoiler I ordered for the Scirocco. Before we start ice creaming, I'll put the package in the garage."

"Randy, you can take a break from domestic duties this afternoon and install the spoiler thingee," offered Zelda. "You have that kerosene heater in the garage now and it's not too awfully cold today. You always say how working in the garage clears your mind."

Randall was slightly taken aback by the suggestion, since Zelda usually thought his "car capades" were somewhat silly. She liked to tease him about how anal he was with car care. He'd jacked up the Scirocco one weekend and coated the underbody with roofing tar for advanced rust protection, probably adding ten pounds to the car's curb weight. When he emerged from under the car looking like a Vaudevillian in black face, she laughed herself into tears and had not let him forget about it for weeks. It had taken an hour with gasoline and paper towels for her to get his face clean. His clothes had to be tossed.

Randall wasn't sure he'd heard her correctly. "Uh, sure, if you don't mind tending the ranch hands."

"No problem." Zelda sounded sincere, but Randall couldn't be sure.

Randall had to be sure. "So, you're not kidding?"

Zelda laughed. "Oh, ye of little faith. It won't exactly be a sacrifice.

I'm taking Kyle to see the Star Wars movie. Again. Addie agreed to come along, reluctantly. I'm sure you'd do a similar favor for me in the near future if I ask." Her eyebrows raised threateningly. "There's just one thing I don't understand." She put her hands on her hips. "Why would you want to spoil a perfectly good car?"

Randall moaned. "Very droll. Just for that, I might not explain to you what a spoiler does."

Zelda made a stop sign with her hand. "You don't have to. I've actually listened to you when you've rambled on about automotive aerodynamics. A spoiler is a little wing-like device mounted on the rear of the car that provides downforce at high speeds to keep traction on the rear wheels. Plus, as you've noted, it makes the car look cool. I doubt you could ever get the Scirocco going fast enough to employ the downforce, so I am guessing you're going for cool."

Randall was impressed. "Guilty as charged." Randall put his hands out in front of him as if ready for handcuffs. "If you can't make a car go faster, you can, at least, make it look fast. Loud mufflers help, too."

When Zelda announced to the kids that they were going to see the Star Wars movie, Kyle nearly went into a rapture. The two cats picked up his vibe and responded with another round of "zero to crazy in three seconds." Kyle rushed up the stairs to put on his Luke Skywalker gear and was at the back door while Addie dawdled. She complained that she'd rather see a horse movie. Kyle claimed that there were horses in the Star Wars movie. Addie was doubtful but went along reluctantly. The back door banged and they were gone. Finally free of the tumult, Randall sighed in relief. He got on his grubby clothes and went to the garage. He set about unpacking the spoiler, revving up the heater, and prepping the car for the install.

Randall reviewed the installation directions. He needed to apply a template on the tailgate to locate the three spots for the mounting screws. He would then have to work up the courage to actually drill holes into perfectly good sheet metal. That process made the name of the device seem rather appropriate. Double stick 3-M adhesive tape would seal the deal. He put a "Steely Dan" cassette in his boom box and sang along to "New Frontier." He thought it ironic that the song was about having a wing ding. Once he began working, the music faded to background noise. Everything became automatic and he meditated on his "shrink homework."

Un-beckoned, the word 'fear' popped into his mind again. He wondered why. He was used to doing root cause analysis. It would apply here. Exactly what linked fear to his choice of Radiation Oncology? He had a vision of flagstones spaced three feet apart on a winding path through some woods. He stood on the one engraved with the letters "RO" and then stepped backwards. He looked down and saw the next stone had "'Nam" engraved on it. He backed up again and the next paver was marked "WWII." The one behind that said, "Connect the Dots." At first nothing registered. Then, it hit him. They were all connected to war and the prospect of being killed in battle. Had that played a role in his key decision making? And were they really decisions he'd made or just what was on his life menu?

He stared at the smooth paint job on his Scirocco and decided to appreciate the perfection for a few minutes before he drilled the three holes. His father had taught him to measure twice and cut once. He sat back on his rolling mechanic's stool to watch what seemed like a documentary film play in his mind.

He remembered back to 1944, when he was just over two years old. His mother, Selma, told him that he had a father, named Joe. She said Joe was away, across the ocean, a corporal in the Army Air Corps. Selma had shown him pictures of his father. Joe looked tough and formidable in his pristine uniform. Little Randall could tell his mother acted scared when she talked about him. He asked why. She had explained to little Randall that Joe might never come back.

"Doesn't Daddy love us?" Little Randall remembered asking, feeling confused. Selma explained that Joe did love them and wanted to come home, but he had a duty to fight in the war. Selma gently explained that, in war, other soldiers might try to kill Joe. Little Randall could feel his mother's fear and sadness.

Little Randall still couldn't quite understand it all, though, because he didn't have any idea what dying meant. He did understand that if Joe died, he would never come home again, but he still didn't understand about dying. Little Randall tried to imagine having a dad, and then NOT having a dad. All he could be sure of was that he had a mother and he loved her. As long as he had her, things would probably be alright.

A few weeks after their little talk, little Randall found a dead mouse in the basement coal chute. He wrapped it in a paper towel and brought it upstairs to show Selma. He asked if the mouse was broken. She explained that the mouse was dead and would never be alive again. Dead animals and people had to be buried in the ground, she said. That shocked little Randall.

After the two buried the mouse in the garden, little Randall asked when they could dig up the mouse again so he could live. Selma explained that dead things never come back to life. This puzzled little Randall. He couldn't stop thinking about the dead mouse. He wondered about it for weeks. Could being dead ever happen to him? He'd even gone back to the mouse burial site to see if it had somehow emerged from the ground. Of course it never had. He tried to imagine himself lying lifeless in the coal dust in the coal chute, put in a hole in the ground and covered with dirt. It made him shiver.

Recalling the memory, Randall shivered involuntarily in the garage and wiped some imaginary dust off the Scirocco's tailgate. He wasn't cold. The garage had grown quite warm with the heater running at full blast during his ruminations. He got up, turned down the heater, and took off his coat. The buzzing of the heater sounded like bees flying around in the garden and it brought back another childhood memory.

In 1945, after the war in Europe had ended, Joe was discharged from the Army. After crossing the Atlantic on a troopship, he went by train from New York City to Milwaukee. Selma put little Randall in the back seat of their trusty rusty 1937 Dodge and they picked up Joe at the train station. Randall was anxious to finally meet his father. The train was late. When it finally arrived, Selma watched for Joe as other soldiers still in uniform got off the train. After a long wait, she spotted Joe, ran to him and gave him a big hug. Little Randall didn't run. He hung behind and watched the two embrace.

Then Joe and Selma walked arm in arm to little Randall. Joe picked him up and gave him a big bear hug. "There's my big boy. I still remember when you were a baby. While Mom was changing your diaper on the dining room table, your little weeny let go with a geyser and hit my shoes. Looks like you've grown up a bunch since then. You're not going to pee on me if I squeeze you too hard, are you?"

Little Randall pulled away from the hug, embarrassed. "No, sir." This man didn't seem familiar to him.

When Joe put him back down, little Randall thought that his father was at least ten feet tall and he feared Joe might take his mother away from him.

After putting his luggage in the trunk, Joe drove the Dodge back home. Little Randall sulked in the back seat and said nothing even though Joe tried to start up a conversation during the drive home. The three alighted from the car and Selma led Joe into the back yard to show him her Victory garden. It was a hot July day and bees buzzed around the backyard peony bush. Joe had brought home a fancy German Leica camera and the first thing he wanted to do was take pictures of his family. He posed little Randall and Selma in front of the peony for a portrait. As little Randall waited for the photo to be snapped, a bee stung him on the back of his neck. Joe rushed over to help, but little Randall pushed him away, instead turning to Selma.

Little Randall yelled at Joe as he latched himself firmly to Selma's leg. "It's *your* fault I got stinged. Mom told me to always stay away from the peony bush *cuz* that's where the bees are and they might sting me."

Little Randall let go of Selma, marched up to Joe and looked up at him with defiant eyes. "You're not the boss of me! Mom is. *She's* taking care of the bee sting. She knows how!" He plopped down on the lawn and refused to move.

Joe stepped back in shocked surprise, not sure how to react. His first instinct was to show the kid who was boss, but Selma quickly sized up the situation and walked Joe several feet away from the fuming child. Even so, little Randall overheard the conversation.

"He's just a little boy, Joe. He doesn't really remember you at all except for pictures I've shown him. He'll come around when he gets to know you. I'll take care of the sting. I've been the only parent he's known and I'm sure he thinks I'm his alone. You're a threat to him because he thinks you might take me away from him. I know that sounds silly, but welcome to being a parent." Selma soothed Joe with her calm voice.

As that drama replayed in adult Randall's head, it clarified a lot about his relationship with his father. Clearly, he and his father had gotten off to a bad start. He'd remembered picking up his father at the train station and the bee sting before, but not the ensuing dialogue between Selma and Joe. He had no idea what had brought it to the surface now. Was this Mary Alice's magic brewing?

The rattling mufflers of Fred Bush's big Oldsmobile 98 starting up next door brought Randall's mind back to earth. *Damn, I'll never get this spoiler installed if I keep drifting off in the wayback machine. Get your butt in gear!*

After his self-admonishment, Randall got off his stool and reapplied the template to the tailgate. He'd need to mark out the template on the tailgate with a china marker. *Where did that marker run off to?* Somehow, Randall's tools were always wandering off to odd places. He dug through his tool box, but the marker was still hiding.

Randall murmured to himself. "Marker, marker, where art thou marker? Markers mark your place in space and also in time. Photographs are like time markers." It was happening again. His mind had drifted off on another memory eddy current.

In his mind, Randall was back to 1948 and felt like he was watching a black and white newsreel. His adjustment to having Joe back home had taken a while, but things had gradually balanced out. A new brother, Arthur, was born. Everything changed. Now he had to share his turf, including Selma, with a sibling. Also frustrating was sharing a bedroom with a baby who cried all the time and demanded attention. It seemed like he was at war and barely surviving. It took time, but he had gradually adjusted.

When the Korean War had started in the Fifties, young Randall's curiosity about war was rekindled. He asked Joe why there was a war again and why did WWII happen. Joe explained, in simple terms, the causes of WWII. However, Joe wasn't clear on why the Korean War had started except to blame crooked politicians. That helped but young Randall was still confused and wanted to know more.

Joe went to the dining room china cabinet, pulled open a drawer and brought out two photo albums. That particular drawer had been a mystery to young Randall, because Joe had repeatedly told him never to open it. It was "private." Joe put the albums on the dining room table. On the cover they were labeled "War Album 1" and "War Album 2." Joe asked if young Randall was a big enough man for them to look at the pictures together. Randall was more curious than uncertain, so he nodded his assent. They set to looking.

Joe was usually a quiet self-contained man, true to his German roots. He rarely showed much emotion. But as he narrated to young Randall the story behind each picture, he became quite animated. About half-way through the first album they got to a picture of a fellow soldier he'd befriended. They were pictured drinking a bottle of whiskey to-gether and laughing. When young Randall asked if the soldier was still a friend, Joe's cheeks flushed and he teared up. Then Joe revealed the man had died in the conflict. He got up and went to the bathroom. When he returned, he put the albums away and said they'd continue another day.

There were subsequent war album sessions. The two by three inch black and white album photos were sharp but so small you almost needed a magnifying glass to see the detail. The content of some of the photos still stood out sharply in Randall's memory. There were shots taken on the troop ship that took Joe across the Atlantic. They showed the deck crowded with hundreds of men. Others showed long lines of men waiting to use the limited number of toilets. The men sat doing their duty completely exposed. Randall was sure he'd never be able to pee with so many men watching. The pictures followed Joe's progress through England, France and, finally, Berlin, Germany.

In Berlin, Joe was stationed at Tempelhof Airport, which had been turned into an Allied air base. There he was trained to repair the radio systems for B-25 bombers and to be a ground crew engine mechanic. On his way through Germany, his unit had stopped at Dachau prison camp where Joe had taken photos. The pictures documented the horrors of the Jewish holocaust. There were piles of dead bodies, scores of emaciated prisoners, and the ovens in which the dead were burned. After being shown these pictures, young Randall had nightmares for weeks. Once, during a gruesome nightmare, he had fallen out of bed attempting to dodge a charging Nazi bayonet. He vowed to be a "War-No-Morist."

Randall surprised himself by suddenly shouting out loud. "Geez, that's a lot to share with a kid!" He wondered if he would share such intense imagery with his own kids. He recalled Kyle in his Star Wars outfit, and Addie with her unicorn; he couldn't stomach the prospect of filling their innocent hearts with the horror of war.

The other lasting recollection from the war photos was how good Joe had looked in uniform. It kind of didn't fit with Randall's image of Joe from real life experience. Joe looked handsome and commanding in the pictures. But to Randall his dad just looked average and interactions with him often made his father seem woefully inadequate.

Then Randall thought maybe he wasn't giving his father enough credit. After all, he did share his war experience with Randall in his own way. Many veterans never talked about it with their families. He reckoned it must have taken a lot for Joe to risk showing emotion and vulnerability to his young son.

Randall's feet were growing cold. He stomped his legs to get the blood moving, holding them near the heater outlet to warm up. While he warmed his feet, he stared at the sparkling paint on the tailgate where the spoiler was to be mounted. Perhaps if he stared hard enough at the templated area it would speak to him and tell him if it was prepared to be violated by a drill.

Then the car did speak to him. *"Just use the double stick tape. If it doesn't hold, you can always drill holes. But you can't undrill a hole. Turn that heater off before you start a fire. You don't have a fire distinguisher out here, you dummy."*

Randall whacked his forehead. "Why didn't I think of that? That's why I talk to you. You always give good advice."

Randall turned off the heater and, somewhat by accident, found the china marker on the back garage shelf. *Dang car is really smart,* he thought. He gave the car a gentle pat on the fanny and then positioned the template carefully on the tailgate, marking out the outline of the spoiler. He wasn't going to drill the holes, but he marked their location so he could measure out their position to be sure they and the spoiler were symmetrically placed.

Instead of mounting the spoiler, Randall sat down again and tried to think of the next step in his shrink report. It seemed logical to move on to high school. His performance up to junior year was not stellar. He lacked motivation. To him it seemed fore-ordained he'd become a factory worker just like his father, stuck with blindingly dull workdays at low pay. There would be no real purpose to his life. Nothing in school appealed to him until junior year.

Biology struck a chord with teenage Randall and he was fascinated—he even earned his first A ever! This coincided with being assigned a new homeroom teacher, Miss Oole. She saw potential in teenage Randall and encouraged him to believe that he could do the same in his other courses. With her faith, he improved all his grades. She kept pushing him to enroll in college.

Teenage Randall wasn't quite on the ball as the end of his senior year approached. He'd been distracted by a developing social life. Thus, he was late submitting college applications. By the time he completed the forms for the University of Wisconsin-Milwaukee, enrollment there had been full. Marquette University accepted him but the tuition was much higher than UWM. He'd either have to earn big money during the summer or ask his father for help.

Joe had never gotten past eighth grade, growing up during the 30's Depression and having to quit school to work a farm. He had no benchmark for higher education. He didn't see the need for college. So, when teenage Randall announced that he'd gotten into Marquette University, Joe's response had been "Good Luck. I'm not paying the tuition, but you can live at home while you go there as long as you pay your keep." It was actually more than teenage Randall expected and he took the deal.

The sound of Fred Bush's old Olds returning next door brought an end to his shrink prep. Fred's Olds definitely needed a good muffler, but he was so deaf Randall figured he probably didn't notice.

Randall shivered. He reckoned the temperature outside must have fallen. He rechecked the template markup. With no holes to line things up, the install might work better with another set of hands.

Maybe he could recruit Zelda to help, but she was still off at the movies with the kids. It might be an hour yet before they got back. Might as well go inside and warm up with a cup of java. Randall also had a kidney in need of urgent tapping. He went inside, made his bladder gladder and flatter, and started to nuke a cold cup of old coffee. The old clock on the wall indicated it was 4:30. Had he really been out there two and a half hours and only marked up the tailgate with the template? Where had the time gone? Just as the microwave beeped, Randall heard Zelda's car come up the driveway and doors slam shut.

Hot spit and cold saliva, thought Randall. *Alone time is over.*

The thundering herd blasted through the backdoor, invading the kitchen, and taking no prisoners. Right on cue, both cats scrambled underfoot. Kyle could not stop retelling the movie highlights, at high decibels. Addie kept saying, in the background, that there were funny animals in the movie that people rode around on but they weren't horses. Zelda just looked tired and desperately in need of peace and quiet.

"Kids, kids!" shouted Randall. "I'm glad you enjoyed the movie! Now Daddy needs to ask you a favor."

Randall stood there for a few minutes using his best serious stare to get their attention, but gaining no immediate traction. Addie was the first to detect that their attention was required or there would be dire consequences.

Addie hissed to her brother. "Kyle, be quiet and listen to Dad!"

Randall stomped his foot to assure their full attention. "Thank you. Now hear this. Since you've just had a special treat, I want to ask you for one in return. I need your mother's help in the garage for about an hour. If you two could go upstairs and play quietly in your rooms for that hour, you will be rewarded with dinner out at Big Boy's restaurant. But if we hear a peep out of you during that hour, we're staying home and Mom will make lentil soup for dinner." Randall gave Zelda a surreptitious wink. "Keep in mind that if Mom has to cook dinner because you two didn't listen, she will be in a bad mood. None of us wants that, right? Is that a deal?"

"Yes, Dad, we'll do it, won't we?" said Kyle as he poked Addie in the ribs.

"Kyle! Don't poke me," squealed Addie. "Yes, we'll be good."

"Okay, then," said Zelda. "Run on upstairs. The hour starts now." The sound of hoofbeats was followed by the slamming of doors.

Zelda was curious. "So, Randy, what evil do you want me in the garage for?"

Randall shrugged. "Nothing sinister. Grab a jacket 'cause it's a bit cold in the garage. I ran into a bit of a snag and I need another pair of hands. Thanks for parking in the driveway. If you'd opened the garage door it would have let the heat out."

Entering the garage through the back door, they avoided letting heat out. Randall led Zelda over to the tailgate where he showed her the markup he'd made and the spoiler.

Zelda looked incredulous. "This is all you did while we were gone? What's up with you?"

Randall was a bit rattled by the comment. "Well, at first I couldn't decide about drilling holes in the tailgate or just using the tape. Then I decided to let the Scirocco speak to me about what it wanted. While I was waiting for an answer, I kept thinking about the assignment I got from my shrink. The report is due at my next visit. You remember, don't you? I only have ten minutes to explain why I chose Radiation Oncology."

Zelda nodded. "Yeah, Dr. Blabalot. I can see why you're so freaked about it. You tell that story all the time, but in ten minutes?" She had a good laugh. "Good luck with that."

Randall got even more anxious. "Yeah, well, that's why I've been doing all this prep. I want to get it right. So, I engaged the 'way back' function in my brain while I sat here waiting for word from the car. I somehow drifted back to when I was two years old and then wound up in college before the car told me to ditch the holes. I had no idea so much time had passed. I was about to put the spoiler on using the tape when I realized I couldn't line it up properly without help, so I went back inside. And there you were!"

"Hmm, that's very interesting," mused Zelda. "So, what do you need me to do?"

Randall gestured grandly to the tailgate. "As you will note, I've applied the double-stick tape to the backside of the spoiler. With you on the right and me on the left, we'll line up the spoiler with the marks, set it down and hold it in position. Then, I'll grab the little tab of backing tape I've folded over, pull it out from underneath and we press down firmly. If all goes well, the sticky side will hold and we're done."

They did the deed and they did it well. "Voila," said Zelda. "It seems to be stuck on pretty well. Do your final inspection. If it's *el perfecto* I'll get the champagne." Randall perused the installation and pronounced it was all to spec.

College Collage

Zelda stood next to the Scirocco and admired their work. "That wasn't so bad. We do good work! Now, before we go back inside and get side-tracked, I want to hear what you learned from your brain exploration. Let's sit inside the Scirocco and you can spill all."

They got inside the car and Zelda commented how weird it was to sit inside the car and not go anywhere. "Not for me," replied Randall. "When I was a kid, I'd sit inside Dad's Dodge parked in the driveway and pretend I was piloting a B-17 bomber, readying it for takeoff."

Somewhat puzzled, Zelda turned to look at Randall. "I thought you were a car guy. Why airplanes?"

Randall could see why she was confused. "Oh, I was into cars then, too. But, while my dad was overseas, his Popular Mechanics magazines kept coming each month. Each issue had a full color centerfold of fighter planes and bombers. I was fascinated because Mom told me he worked on planes. Of course I didn't know which kind. In my mind, it was all of them. I confiscated the magazines, ripped out the centerfolds and plastered them on my bedroom wall with Scotch tape."

Zelda turned to look at Randall and leered. "So, before Playboy, you got hot and bothered looking at twin props, eh? Figures. Typical randy Randy. Funny what you can learn on the 'way back machine.'"

Randall gave Zelda a light arm punch. "That's a nice segue into what I've learned on my little time travel. My dad may have been the one in the war, but my mother and I were both affected, too. It left me with a pretty deep-seated fear of an ugly death in battle."

Zelda nodded. "Yeah! If you were affected and weren't even there, just think how it must have really messed with your father's head."

Randall punched the steering wheel in frustration. "Hmm, you ain't wrong. That could explain a lot. He lives through the Great Depression and then has to go to war just when things are mellowing out in his life."

Zelda put her left hand on Randall's right arm. "Sure doesn't seem fair, does it? All of that kept him from going to high school. He's probably jealous of you for getting the formal education he never could."

Randall turned to look at Zelda. "I've suspected that too. His post middle school education wasn't formal, but he was self taught and found ways to get by. But it's not the same as having the bona fides. I can think of several times that education envy showed up. For example, once he came up to my room while I was studying organic chemistry. He acted like he knew the subject and asked what chapter I was on. I told him it was 'Catalysts' and he asked what in the world a list of cattle had to do with chemistry. At first, I thought he was making a punny joke, but he wasn't. When I explained what a catalyst was, he just shrugged and walked out of the room."

"That's kind of sad," observed Zelda. "For a guy who never went to high school, he sure is smart in a lot of ways. He was an aircraft mechanic and a machinist. There's hardly anything he can't fix, especially electrical stuff. He taught himself how to repair radios and TVs. He didn't need to feel jealous of you."

Randall went silent and twisted some radio knobs even though the ignition was off. "Emotions and intellect do not always connect. I should know that by now. When everything was said and done, he just didn't have the creds to document his smarts. I had the creds and he didn't."

Zelda nodded. "Yeah, my father always made my mother feel like she was dumb because she didn't run a large lithography company like he did. But she was way smarter than him in other ways and wouldn't let herself get ground down."

Randall shrugged. "Not all folks have the self confidence to do that. It seemed my dad felt trapped long, long hours in a series of boring factory jobs that barely covered the cost of living. I picked up on that vibe and decided I didn't want that life. No 'daily grind' for me. I was going to do something 'worthwhile' and help people, as corndog as that sounds."

Zelda turned to Randall and smiled ironically. "Well, Randy, you got your wish. You are doing something worthwhile, but if you wanted a job with regular hours you kind of blew that part. And let's not ignore the fact that you didn't make any money for ten years after high school and you have a dump-load of student loans to show for it. Otherwise, good show!"

Randall slid down in the driver's seat. "I guess I got both more and less than what I bargained for. If that's even possible."

Zelda looked at her wristwatch. "Hey, we've still got half an hour before our carriage turns into a pumpkin. How about you pretend I'm your free Mary Alice? Continue your story from where you left off, and you'll soon have your assignment done. Just continue your review up to when we got married. I know the rest after that and I'll give you a nice tight summary."

Randall felt like he had just finished a 5K run and sagged in the driver's seat. "Any other observations or tidbits of advice?"

Zelda tried to sound upbeat. "I think the 'worthwhile' part of your career choice outweighs any negatives one can think of. So don't lose heart."

Randall rolled his eyes. "Yeah, I know. But it's hard not to."

Zelda patted Randall's baldspot. "Aww. Not to worry. You're a good boy."

Randall barked like a dog. Zelda couldn't help but laugh. Randall laughed back even harder and felt a load of anxiety fly away. That was followed by a strange mélange of emotions. After some refreshing deep breaths, he decided to take Zelda's advice to heart and sat up straight again to recite the rest of the story.

Randall launched into the Marquette University narrative. After almost flunking out the first quarter, he realized this was not like high school. He upped his game and chose Biology for a major. Living at home limited some expenses, but making ends meet meant side jobs and government loans.

One of the side jobs provided a life lesson. The category was "What we have to do to survive." A home builder hired Randall to get a prospect list by canvassing open houses. He was to be paid by the hour, but the paychecks often bounced. He would have to confront the owner each time and demand cash payment. Randall suspected the owner was full-fledged mafia and never knew if the man was reaching in his desk drawer for cash or a revolver.

Zelda's eyes went wide. "You never told me that! I assume you never got shot."

Randall giggled. "No, but once I needed my pants dry cleaned. That was nothing compared to getting caught embezzling 20 bucks from the insurance agent I did billing for."

Zelda let out a breath. "You stole some money! Mercy me. What did he do?"

Randall laughed again. " I got fired after I paid back the money. Another lesson learned."

Zelda made a clucking sound. "Poor boy! All that juggling to get to all the crap you do now."

Randall shifted in the seat and stretched. "Ah, yes. Those were stellar times. Nothing persists like a bad odor and a penniless student. Somehow I stayed ahead of the bill collectors and got my grades up for the rest of the four years."

Zelda nodded knowingly. "I tried college but went into freefall by mid semester freshman year. It was too damn hard and I had no idea what I wanted. So, I just dropped out. At least you stuck it out."

Randall laughed. "That's for sure—I stuck my neck way out. Between grades and money problems, I felt like I was walking a high wire. With my grades up, my Marquette advisor felt I might have a shot at med school. I thought he was nuts. The tuition was crazy high. I'd thought about it but put it down as a pipe dream. Then he said the magic word: 'scholarship.' We gave it a shot and I was in."

Zelda suddenly felt proud of Randall. She hadn't realized how hard it had been. It certainly hadn't been a slam dunk. "I'm surprised you ever doubted you could do it. It seems like such a natural path for you."

Randall scoffed. "Hardly! I had to let that thought rattle around in my head for a while and battle it out with Dad's low opinion of college. But the more I thought about it, the more it resonated with me. After all, I'd made that vow to myself."

Zelda elbowed him in the ribs and smirked. "You mean besides the vow you made to me?"

Randall laughed. "Whoa Nelly! This was way before I met you, Sweetcheeks. It probably sounds corny saying it out loud, but I wanted to do something 'worthwhile' and to 'help' people in distress." Randall blushed and felt a little foolish. "Probably every medical student says that at the admissions interview, but that's what I really felt."

Zelda grabbed Randall's hand, *tching* like a mama hen. "It's not corny, Randy. In fact, it's one of my favorite things about you. You care about people. And I know that you care about me and the kids. Sometimes your weirdness makes me so mad that I want to skin you alive, but your corny stuff is why I'm still here sitting in this cold garage."

"Holy crap," blurted Randall. "That's news to me. You've never said that before. It makes me feel all eclectic."

"Very punny! That's where we differ," remarked Zelda. "I run on D cells. Now, finish your meanderings, I'm getting cold. But before you get started again, can I ask you something?"

Randall nodded. "Sure, ask away."

Zelda cleared her throat. She didn't want her question to come out wrong. "Well, with you, sometimes I have a hard time telling whether you're making funny or not. Earlier, when you said the car was talking to you, were you being literal? Should I be worried about you?"

Randall grunted. "I love it when you're worried about me. But, no, the Scirocco was not literally talking to me through the car speakers or out the tailpipe. I was just using it as a 'vehicle' for sorting through my internal decision-making process. You've known me long enough to understand that 'normal' for me can be a bit at the outskirts of the bell-shaped curve."

Zelda sighed in relief. "So, it's just your *normal* crazy. We're not dealing with any new phenomena. Then I'm back with you. Please continue the saga."

RANDOM SELECTION

"Well, here's where the military thing creeps in again. Just when I was starting to think the runway was clearing, I received a missive from Uncle Sam's Selective Service." By now, the car windows were steaming up. Randall drew a little envelope in the steam. "It informed me that I'd registered for the draft in high school and that I would be deferred from the draft as long as I was in college or postgraduate studies. This factoid pushed my pucker button. I knew I'd have to study my derriere into non-existence to stay out of olive drab." He drew a swift skull and crossbones.

Zelda shuddered. "Oh geez. This was right before Vietnam. Hard to imagine 'Randy the soldier.' The image is chilling."

Randall shivered, but not from the cold. "I could imagine it quite clearly and almost feel the bullet wounds. Rumors were beginning to heat up about a conflict in Vietnam. I definitely did not want to be drafted and get my butt shot off."

Zelda shifted uneasily in the passenger seat. "I bet you grabbed your gluteus maximi with both hands. I'm guessing you were opposed to acquiring a holy butt."

Randall had to laugh at that image. "I checked on its continued presence a lot during that time. That's why I never have trouble finding it. My scholarship had one hooker. I had to maintain a 3.8 GPA or say bye-bye."

"No pressure! Wait, that was the only hooker involved?" snarked Zelda.

Uncle Sam knocks

Randall held a finger to his lips. "That's enough out of you, vixen! Bad news—the war had already started during med school. Good news— med school deferred me from the draft until graduation. But more bad news—newbie doctors were drafted as officers and deployed in MASH units that were right in the thick of the fighting. Going in as an officer didn't help much because the only weapons were scalpels and Fleet's enemas. My only hope was the war would end before I finished school."

Zelda giggled despite the mood of dread. "I can see it now. Bald man in a brown stained white lab coat. He's holding a full enema bag with long tubes dangling from it. He yells out to the Vietcong. 'Back off or I'll squeeze!'"

Randall laughed. "We doctors do know how to improvise! I think the Hippocratic oath frowns on weaponizing enemas. Sheesh! Anyway, the supraoptimal motivation kept my grades up and tuition got paid. But not without picking up another $30 K in government loans. Med school allowed no time for outside work. Tuition was not the only living expense."

"Oh, and don't forget! interjected Zelda. "You married me in 1968, during your senior year in med school and we had a kid! But that hardly cost anything, right?"

Randall held his head with both hands. "Oh, I didn't forget. I was just coming to that. That takes us to my internship at St. Joseph's hospital in Denver. Good news—I was finally getting paid. Bad news—it was a pittance. Fortunately, the internship gave me one more year of military deferment, but no protection from service after that. I thought I had that solved by opting for Diagnostic Radiology and signing up for the Berry Plan."

Zelda gestured with her index finger. "I remember that all too well. That was the plan that didn't turn out 'Berry' well. After internship, you'd be deferred for three years of Radiology training. Then you'd fulfill your military obligation as a Radiologist at an Army hospital for three years. Bad news—the program was full and they turned you down."

Randall mimed a lame salute. "Right you are. Had they accepted me, I'd have been a free man six years later. My only injury would be a chronic forehead bruise from repeated saluting."

"No doubt, your ego would have suffered some damage as well," Zelda gestured to his belly. "And your tender GI tract."

Randall wrapped his arms around his midsection, cringing at the memory.

Zelda shivered again and looked at the car's clock display. "Randy, we have about ten minutes left. I'm getting even colder. You and I both lived through the story from this point on. I was there with you. Remember?"

Randall did a double take. "Oh, yeah. I guess I was too busy riding on my own parade float."

Zelda laughed. "Yep. You did remind me of a big Goofy balloon."

Randall groaned. "Nyuk, nyuk! Very funny. I'm betting you can recite the rest in about three minutes."

Zelda pretended to hold a magic wand. "Try one minute. Here goes. That miracle midget Radiation Oncologist, Juan del Aguilar, got you out of the Army gig for three years of training with him in Colorado Springs. You did two years of military payback service at the Baltimore Public Health hospital. Then, after one year at Mr. Duke's University we wound up here in Milwaukee. Can we go inside now?"

Randall raised both arms in a gesture of triumph. "That's it! I'll tell it just like that. You're a genius."

Zelda slapped Randall's shoulder. "Now just condense the rest of what you said the same way and you should be golden. My tootsies are numb and I think I am hearing restless natives inside."

The two emerged from the car and as Zelda was walking by the tailgate she stopped to observe it. "You know, the spoiler does look way cool. Way to go, Maynard."

Randall faked a hard punch to Zelda's shoulder. She flinched. "You know what?" observed Randall. "This was fun. We should 'go out' together without the kids more often. You know, like real dates."

Zelda did a non-fake punch right back. Randall grunted in pain, but smiled. "You're right, my randy Randall. It's been a while. I'll see if I can line up that babysitter we had last year. She just lives up the block. We haven't had any recent kid incidents. Perhaps we can go out 'of an evening.'"

CHAPTER 6

BURGER BOBBLES

"Life has got a habit of not standing hitched. You gotta ride it like you find it."

—Woody Guthrie

BRAWNY LAD

Randall and Zelda returned from their sojourn in the garage and found Addie and Kyle sitting at the kitchen table fidgeting. The kids were over-eager to be gone for Big Boy burgers, but were reluctant to break their pledge of silence.

"Who's ready for burgers and fries?" yelled Randall.

Both kids jumped up from their chairs like puffed wheat shot from a cannon. Kyle nearly knocked his chair over. "Me!"

"Me too!" Addie squealed, just a tick behind her brother.

Zelda waved them into action like a school crossing guard. "Then you know what to do. Last one at the back door with coats on is a little rugrat."

The race to the back door was a draw, but Kyle claimed loudly that he'd made it there before his sister.

Zelda waved an arm toward the back door. "Stifle! Just get out there."

The Biedermeiers piled into the orange VW Camper with Zelda at the wheel. She pulled out of the driveway and they putted off to dinner.

Randall had begged off of driving honors, claiming "poophaustion." He'd had a lot of mental strings plucked by Dr. Hoffman. Mental labor sometimes took more energy than physical labor. He figured his adrenaline was nadiring. He stretched out on the back seat to rest during the drive. Randall didn't like driving the Camper. For him, it was too bulky and had only slightly more power than a butterfly fart. Despite that, Zelda drove it with zest, squeezing every last foot-pound of power out of the flat four and she handled it like her old VW Bug.

Randall put his head back on the armrest and closed his eyes. Lying there in the back of the car reminded him of the previous year when they'd gone overnight camping at Wyalusing State Park near Prairie du Chien, Wisconsin. They had arrived at the campgrounds about 4:00 PM, parked, and popped the top on the VW to get the sleeping areas ready. Randall sent the kids off to look for firewood, while he and Zelda readied the food and eating gear. Zelda had pre-made a pot of stew and all they needed to do was heat it up over a fire.

The fire took a while getting hot enough to heat the stew and, by the time it was ready to eat, the sun had set. Zelda got the salt and pepper shakers out of a cabinet in the camper. The top of the pepper shaker was loose but she couldn't see that in the dark. She added salt and pepper and served up four bowls of hot stew. Kyle was really hungry and eagerly took a mouthful of stew but immediately spit it out. Zelda had asked what was wrong with the stew and Kyle responded that it was "too hot." She took a spoonful and spit it out, too, coughing. She clarified that it was "pepper hot" not "heat hot." Randall dipped his spoon into his serving and his spoon brought out the top of the pepper container. Having nothing else to eat, they managed to down the stew using plenty of bread as a buffer. The "Pepper Stew" incident became a part of family lore, with mixed reception.

The van lurched to a stop in the Big Boy parking lot, nearly launching Randall to the floor. He made a woofing sound and grabbed the seat back to forestall Newtonian forces.

Kyle yelled from the front passenger seat. "Dad, are you alright?"

"I'm awake! I was just checking my eyelids for leaks." Randall rubbed his eyes. "I didn't find any, but I did have a momentary dream about 'pepper stew.'"

"Eww!" squeaked Addie. "I remember that. It made my tummy burn all night."

Zelda made a farting sound with her mouth and hand. "Darn tootin'! The fumes were so noxious during the night we had to vent the van windows until morning. That let all the cold air inside."

Randall had to laugh. "But it unconstipated you."

"Yeah, yeah, I remember," groaned Zelda. "You guys reminded me about my pants accident for weeks."

Addie opened the sliding door and ran out into the parking lot, shouting she was going to say hello to Big Boy.

Randall and Zelda got out of the car while Kyle dawdled inside. The two watched Addie hug the Big Boy statue while they waited for Kyle. Randall shook his head. "I don't know why Addie has such a thing about Big Boy."

Zelda did a little girl giggle. "Aww, come on, Randy, he's cute. Don't you just want to wrap your arms around the little guy?"

Randall grunted. "I'd like to wrap something around him. Why would anyone want to hug a four-foot fiberglass statue in 30-degree weather?" He turned up his collar to the wind.

Kyle finally got out of the car and walked over to Addie and Big Boy. He tried pulling her away but she hung on.

As Randall and Zelda watched the play action, their exhaled breath turned to white vapor clouds that almost looked like cartoon dialogue balloons. The night air was crisp. Stars abounded in the cloudless sky. The parking lot looked neatly tailored with its orderly piles of plowed snow. Parked cars looked ethereal covered with a layer of hoary frost. Winter did have its unique qualities.

Kyle finally got Addie disentangled from Big Boy, but not without some minor fisticuffs. Randall and Zelda joined them at the little statue and Randall gave it a closer look.

Big Boy had a grinning round face. He wore a white shirt, black pants and a red and white checkered apron. A forelock of black hair stuck out like a cowlick above the right side of his forehead. Residual snow on his head made him look prematurely gray. Like a waiter bringing an order, his upraised right hand held a plate with an oversized Big Boy Classic burger. There, under the sparkling night sky, it seemed like an offering to the gods. Commercials had embedded the contents of the burger firmly in memory. "Two quarter pound ground beef patties, cheese, lettuce, and special sauce on a sesame seed bun with an extra slice of bun in the center."

Addie jumped up with impatience. "Mom, Dad, hurry up and let's go inside, I'm hungry!" She ran to the restaurant entrance.

Kyle stayed back with his parents momentarily. "Cheesy Chewbacca, Addie is loony tunes."

Zelda shook her head and *tsked*. "Geez, Randy, I wish I could make her move that fast when it's time for school. Should we put a Big Boy statue as a centerpiece on our breakfast table?"

Randall laughed. "You're not wrong. We should be grateful that her first boyfriend is fiberglass."

Zelda guffawed. "Yeah. All we have to fear is night time willies from the sugar overload she gets from Big Boy chocolate milkshakes."

Randall raised his eyebrows. "Good point. We'll have to keep an eye out tonight."

When Randall, Zelda and Kyle got to the entrance, Addie had already gone inside and came running back out. "Mom, Dad, guess what!? They have Big Boy bobblehead dolls inside! And they're for sale. Can I get one? Please, please?" Kyle ran toward Addie.

Randall felt his internal cash register go *ring-ding*. "If they're not too expensive. Great. Now Kyle will probably want one, too."

Sure enough, Kyle and Addie immediately ran inside. When Randall and Zelda entered, both kids were looking into a glass case loaded with bobbleheads marked $4.99 each. Randall just reached for his wallet and paid the smiling clerk for two. He swallowed just thinking how that same money could have taken the whole family out for a movie and popcorn. Not a bad price to keep two kids happy and avoid the inevitable pleading. A little pamphlet on the history of Big Boy restaurants came with the bobble-heads. When they were seated and had placed their order, Addie asked Randall to read the history aloud.

Randall decided just to paraphrase the text. "It looks like there are other Big Boy restaurants around the country and they started in 1958. The restaurants here in Wisconsin are called Marc's Big Boy because they're owned by the Marcus Corporation. They also own most of the movie theaters in town. There are even Big Boys in Florida. Down there they're called Bob's Big Boy. Hmm, some people think that McDonald's stole the burger recipe from Big Boy and changed the name to Big Mac. They thought they could outcompete Big Boy by making them fast and selling them at a drive through."

The conversation was interrupted by the waitress bringing a huge tray of burgers, fries and milkshakes. Little hands grabbed at the goodies with lightning speed.

Zelda huffed and folded her arms across her chest. "People always want their food in the fast lane. Why can't they learn to eat better, not faster?"

Randall agreed. "Soon drive-throughs will not be fast enough. Then what's next?"

"They'll probably bring the food right to your house with a radio-controlled mini helicopter!" smirked Zelda.

"Or bring them by horseback," chimed in Addie, as ketchup from her Brawny Lad leaked down her chin.

"Maybe they can use a Millennium Falcon!" Kyle chipped in through a mouthful of fries. "Then, the burgers would still be really hot when they get to your house."

Secretly the kids hoped they didn't start eating better. Broccoli had nothing on fries! Addie decided to change the topic. She paused, mid-drip. "Dad, what does out-compete mean?"

Randall gestured with a wave of his greasy fork. "If McDonald's does better by using drive-throughs, Big Boy might lose so much business that they will have to close." Randall did his best to keep a serious face.

Addie's face scrunched up. She finished chewing, swallowed, and put down her Brawny Lad. "Then we just have to keep coming here and never buy Big Macs. Dad, promise that you won't let them take Big Boy away." She clutched her bobble head to her chest and started to tear up.

Kyle patted Addie on the shoulder with a ketchupy hand. "Don't worry, Sis. Dad would never let that happen, right, Dad?"

"Absolutely not!" said Randall emphatically. "I have power over the entire universe. Now, stop worrying and chow down. Don't forget to leave room for dessert. Remember, there's fresh strawberry pie and milk shakes with someone's names on them."

Food began to disappear at an accelerated pace. Addie looked across the room and noticed a man at a corner table eating alone. He was clearly enjoying his Classic Burger.

Addie looked around the room. She pointed, flinging ketchup from her finger. "Mom, why does that man have a funny white collar?"

Zelda squinted and looked about. "What man?"

Addie pointed again. "Over there in the corner."

Zelda finally saw the man Addie was indicating. Zelda gently tapped Addie's arm back down. "Oh, he's a priest. A priest is a leader in the Catholic Church. Catholicism is a religion. Like at St. Jude's, the church across the street where all the Catholic kids on our block go to Sunday School."

This got a rise out of Kyle. "Do we have a religion?"

Randall nodded and took the question. "Yes, we're Lutherans, but we don't go to church right now."

"Why not?" asked Addie.

Zelda hesitated. She didn't really want to go further down this road. "Well, that's a long and complicated story. I don't think we should talk about it now, but we will soon, when we have more time and we're alone at home. Right, Randy?"

Randall took the ball and dribbled. He knew it best to agree with Zelda. "Your Mom is not wrong, kids. It's something we've been thinking about, but haven't made any decisions yet. Since you have raised the question, perhaps it's time to talk about it. We did talk about religion after we built the ice castle and the Ichner boys wrecked their feet trying to kick it down. Remember?"

Kyle rolled his eyes. "Dad, that was days ago! I can't remember all the stuff you tell us. I want to know because when I was outside building the snow fort, the Ichner kids walked by. They asked me why I don't go to St. Jude's like they do." Kyle's head drooped. "I just said that I didn't know and they laughed at me. They called me a stupid protester or something like that."

Randall chuckled and tried to decipher the comment. "Hmm, I think they may have said 'stupid Protestant.' That's another religious group and some Catholics don't think much of them."

Kyle felt genuinely confused. "Why does that make them want to beat me up? I thought being religious made people nicer to each other."

"Yeah, you'd think so," smirked Zelda. She tried to hoe and backfill. "Things don't always work the way they're supposed to. That's one of the reasons religious talk gets complicated. Can we drop the subject for now? Say, did I ever tell you I used to be a waitress at the Big Boy at Mayfair?"

Addie's eyes filled with awe. "No, you didn't! When was that? Do you still have the pretty dress?"

Zelda nodded. "You mean the uniform? It was before I met your Dad. I had the job for about two weeks before they fired me. An order of burgers and fries came up for me while I was in the bathroom relieving my bladder. Had to go or I would have wet my pants. So, by the time I brought the order to the table, the food was a little cold. When I came back a few minutes later to ask how the first couple of bites were, the man complained his fries were cold. So, I picked up a fry off his plate and ate it, naturally." She shrugged. "I told him he wasn't wrong. His fries were indeed cold. Then I walked away. Apparently, he complained to my boss and ten minutes later I was standing out in the parking lot waiting for my mom to pick me up."

Kyle's eyes became mostly white. "Mom, that's so rad."

Zelda pumped both fists in the air. "Yesiree, I was a real rebel!"

Addie's mouth was agape with shock at her mother's misbehavior. "Does that mean you were a bad girl once?"

"The baddest," agreed Zelda. "Now, before I forget, I want to tell you guys that next Saturday night Dad and I are going out on a date all on our lonesome. Tomorrow I'm going to call that girl who babysat for us last summer, if I can find her phone number. What was her name again?"

Addie had the answer. "There were two girls that I remember. One was Alexandra. The other was Frances. I remember 'cause it was the same as my book 'Bedtime for Frances.' She read the book to us and said if you spell Frances with an 'i' instead of an 'e' it's a boy's name. Isn't that weird?"

Kyle jumped in. "Are there any other names like that?"

"*Hmm*." Randall searched his cerebral archives. "Gene and Jean come to mind. The correct term for that would be homophonic names. I'm sure there are more." He spelled them both and explained the one starting with "G" was a man's name.

Zelda was tempted to make a comment that *homophonaphobia* was the irrational fear of similar names, but thought better of it. "Very interesting, Randy," said Zelda bitingly. "Maybe we should sign you up for 'Jeopardy.' Can we get back to the point? Your dad and I have had hectic times the last month or so and haven't had much time to have fun together or even talk without interruption. That may have made us a little short tempered."

Kyle nodded enthusiastically.

Zelda ignored him and continued. "So, I think you can both concur that having us be a bit mellower would be good for you as well."

Kyle could see through that. "Aww, you just want an excuse to get all mushy together without us watching."

Randall motioned as if he was pounding railroad spikes with a huge hammer. "Dang! You've seen through our deception. Your Mom and I just want to practice making kissy-face and we don't need you two peeking around a corner giggling."

"Ha-ha," giggled Addie. "We caught you."

Randall did an 'aw shucks' shuffle. "You did! This afternoon Mom helped me put the spoiler on the Scirocco. She did such a good job that we were done super-fast. So we just sat in the car and talked until the hour was up. It put us in a better mood. That's a good thing for everybody."

Addie got the point. "Yeah, Dad. If you were in a bad mood tonight we might not have come here to Big Boy."

"Or gotten bobble-heads," added Kyle.

Zelda pulled her shoulders back. "I can see that you two have gotten a lot smarter just since yesterday. Can you guess what we talked about?"

Addie and Kyle sat up straighter in their pews and looked at each other furtively. Perhaps the ax was about to fall.

"About how good we've been lately?" Kyle batted his long blonde lashes.

Zelda got a *maybe* look on her face. "It was on the list, but the main topic was the homework assignment your dad got from the lady doctor he saw today. He went to see her so he could talk to an expert about all the unusual experiences he's been having lately."

Kyle cocked his head. "Like the night terrors and sleepwalking I've been having?"

Zelda nodded. "Very much like that. The doctor's name is Mary Alice Hoffman. She listened very carefully to Dad, but decided she needed to learn more about his background. Dad has lived a lot more years than you two, so it's more complicated to figure out what's going on without knowing more about him. So, she gave him an assignment to come back and tell her in ten minutes how he came to become the kind of doctor he is now."

Addie frowned. "Wow. Dad's really old. That story must be really long. How can he tell that in ten minutes?"

"Precisely the problem, Rosebud," said Randall. "It is a long story; much longer than you've been a little girl. So, I was trying to put all the pieces together by telling it to Mom. Now I think I might pull it off."

Kyle pondered, looking to the ceiling. "You've told us a bunch of stories about that stuff at bedtime."

Addie's eyebrows shot up. "Yeah, some of them were real funny too, but I bet you're sick of thinking about that old stuff. If you're not too tired, can you tell us one of your cool made up bedtime stories tonight?"

Kyle bounced in his seat. "That would be bad and rad, Dad! Do it, please. We'll even be good for the babysitter next Saturday."

Randall mused a bit. "That's quite a sacrifice to make for a story. But . . . since you're being so generous, I might be able to come up with something."

Addie looked dubious. "Please don't do a story about cars or your patients. Or talk funny or speak every other word."

Randall squinted. "Boy! You're making this hard. Do you want funny or scary?"

"Funny!" squeaked Addie.

"Scary!" blurted Kyle.

Zelda ended the discussion. "OK, it's decided. It will be a funny scary story. Your dad can handle that. Before we finish here and while I still have your attention, I want you to think hard. Can either of you remember Frances' last name or at least which house on the block she lives in?"

"I think it's Smiley," erupted Addie. "I remember because she writes her first name followed by a smiley face."

Kyle rolled his eyes. "Duh, Addie. That's probably her nickname name!!"

Zelda was getting impatient. "Come on, guys. Do either of you have anything useful?"

Kyle loved knowing more than Addie. "I'm pretty sure she lives in the big brown house about four houses up on our side of the street. I think I've seen her riding her bike down that driveway."

"Fantastic, kids! If I can't find the phone number tomorrow, I can take a walk up there and do some checking. Alright, are we all finished eating?" Zelda handed out napkins to clean up fry grease and spilled ketchup. She was tempted to leave Addie's milkshake mustache untouched. "Let's get our coats on and head home. And, yes, Addie, you can give Big Boy a hug on the way out. Don't forget your scarf and gloves."

Addie scrambled to pick up her stuff. "Yes, Mom."

Kyle and Addie put on their coats, grabbed their bobble-heads and made a beeline to the parking lot. Randall paid the check, left a nice tip, and walked out of Marc's Big Boy restaurant hand in hand with Zelda. When they got to the car with Kyle, Zelda called for Addie to stop fraternizing with Big Boy and get in the car.

"What's fraternizing?" asked Kyle from the back seat.

"What she's doing," said Zelda sharply.

"Oh, you mean all kissy huggy," scowled Kyle. "Like you and Dad will be doing on your date."

"Watch your mouth, smart guy!" Randall winked.

Kyle curled his lips up and crossed his eyes, attempting the impossible. "I can't see my mouth unless I look in the mirror."

Zelda was tired of Kyle's lip. "Perhaps I can rearrange your anatomy so you won't need a mirror to see your mouth!"

Kyle made a lip zipping motion as Zelda gave him a mom stare. Addie opened the sliding door and jumped into the car. Zelda backed out of the parking spot with alacrity. As she was pulling out of the lot, Randall looked over at the Big Boy statue. A white unicorn scarf wrapped around Big Boy's neck flapped in the wind.

Before Randall could say anything, Addie piped up. "Don't worry, Dad. Big Boy told me he was cold and asked if he could borrow my scarf." She put a hand on his shoulder. "I can pick it up next Friday when we come back again for dinner. I've got this handled."

Randall smiled despite being manipulated by a five-year-old. "Of course you do." He looked in the rearview mirror at a grinning Addie.

"Home, Jeeves," she commanded.

"What an accomplished negotiator," Randall said to Zelda, sotto voce. "Would you turn on the heater? It's as cold as the jewels on a brass monkey in here."

"You know darn well the heat on this car is *furchtbar*," grumped Zelda.

"*Jah, sehr schrecklich,*" agreed Randall.

DAGOBAH

After returning from Big Boy in the underheated VW van, everyone still felt chilled. Soon Randall got a nice fire going in the fireplace and directed everyone to gather in the living room to warm up while he told a bedtime story. Zelda and the kids formed a semicircle about eight feet in front of the fireplace. Kyle and Addie sat cross-legged on the thick floor carpet with comforters draped over their shoulders. They looked like little Indians gathered around a campfire. Zelda completed the semi-circle sitting in Rex, the wonder chair. The lights were off in the room and light shadows from the fire flickered on the walls. Kyle and Addie sipped on hot chocolates that Randall had made despite Zelda's objection that they'd already had milkshakes at Big Boy and, with the resulting sugar high, sleepy time might never come. Randall told her not to worry since his story was bound to put them all to sleep. The stage was set.

Randall drew himself up deliberately from his chair, cleared his throat and began to pace the floor back and forth in front of the fireplace. Standing between the fire and his listeners, he was backlit and, from the front, all his features were quite dark and shadowy. He looked a bit sinister. Anticipation built in the room, waiting for the story to begin. After several moments of pacing, Randall suddenly raised his right arm to eye level and extended his index finger. He made a sweeping gesture and began the story.

"Tonight!" Randall's voice was so unexpectedly loud that Addie, Kyle and Zelda jumped a bit. "Tonight, I will tell you . . . a rarely heard Star Wars tale. It's called '*Learn the Speak, You Must.*' It is the tale of the very first Jedi Knight." He swept his hands dramatically about the room.

Both Kyle and Addie frowned and looked at each other in puzzlement. Randall continued. "Mark this story well. In it, many lessons are. A tale of the greatest hero from the planet Dagobah it tells. The Dags, short for Dagobahnians, owe their lives and the salvation of their planet to a tall thin boy born to the Decoda family. How this mere lad accomplished the Herculean task has been recorded in a special book, the Decoda Codex."

Kyle raised his hand. "What's a codex?"

Randall was prepared for the question. "Ask your mother. She has a lot of them."

Zelda bopped him on the shoulder.

Randall ignored the kids' confused looks. "Also, it's a special book to record secrets that you don't want just anybody to be able to read. The Decoda family commissioned talented scribes to write down our hero's adventures and, more importantly, the secrets of his special power, *The Speak*. Everything written on the pages used a special blood infused disappearing ink."

Both Addie and Kyle shivered, then looked at each other blankly.

Randall put both hands out in front of him, palms up. "What's the matter?"

Kyle was a Star Wars savant. "I've never heard of the Decoda family in Star Wars. Is it Dakota like in the state of North Dakota?"

Randall shook his head slowly and pointed at Kyle. "Not quite, padawan." He spelled the name for Kyle. "What Jedi Knight, that you know well, might be a descendant of this extraordinary Dag hero?"

Kyle closed his eyes and thought for a moment. "The story's name sounds like Yoda-speak. . . . The hero's name is Yoda Decoda!"

Randall clapped his hands so loudly that the two cats almost levitated. "Right on! The Yoda you know from the movie was indeed a descendant of the Dag Decoda family. Each member of the Decoda family wore an encoded platinum ring on their pinkie finger. If anyone besides a full-fledged Decoda opened the codex without first putting the special Decoda ring in a slot in the back binding of the book, the pages would all appear blank. But if the ring was inserted in the slot, the print would emit a pinkish glow and slowly form visible black lettering on the page."

Zelda failed to suppress a giggling laugh. "Let me summarize what I think you just said. The first Yoda's full name was Yoda Decoda. He and his relatives could read the Decoda Codex entries by inserting the secret Decoda ring in a hidden slot in the binder hinder. And it's not like the coda at the end of a song."

"You ain't wrong!" Randall beamed. Zelda had the summary just right.

Kyle got super excited. "Wow, that is so cool. Can I get a Decoda ring, too?"

Randall nodded his head. "Why not, Buddy? In the Star Wars world, anything is possible."

Addie, not a Star Wars fan and often dubious about her father's veracity, expressed her suspicions. "Daddy, are you spoofing us again?"

Randall's shoulders sagged and he looked disappointed. "Would I ever spoof you guys?"

Addie made a face and protruded her lower lip. Kyle urged Randall on. "Keep going, Dad. Don't mind Addie. Just tell the story."

Randall swept both arms in an arc in front of him to signify the start of the story. "Alright, folks and felines, settle back and listen. Not so long ago, on the planet Dagobah, very, very near to here, the Dags fought to save their planet from takeover by the Siths.

Kyle's face looked fearful. "The Siths?! They're really mean dudes. They fight using scary electric snakes."

Randall nodded. "Those are the ones. The snakes strangle and shock you to death."

Addie was curious despite her doubts. "What is Dagobah like and what did the Siths want with it?"

Randall pointed to Addie so quickly she almost fell over backwards. "Excellent question! Dagobah is a small, ocean planet in the Platoonian Galaxy. It has only one land mass, about the size of Africa, but shaped like a watermelon with fuzzy edges. It is totally surrounded by water. Over the centuries, the Dag population evolved normally, but got stuck at a point where they were just about to invent complex machinery. What we humans would call the industrial age."

Zelda popped a question. "Why did they get stuck?"

"It's rather complicated, but I'll try to simplify it," said Randall. "The people of Dagobah looked much like us humans. Half were tall and long limbed. The other half were short and squat. Both were about as smart as humans, but very short-tempered and always ready to fight. As a result, there were always wars about silly stuff. Eventually, the Shorts wound up living on the right side of the continent and the Longs on the left. Later, they added a wall between the sides and vowed that, to avoid conflict, they'd never interact again. In time the languages of the Shorts and Longs got so different that even if they met accidentally they couldn't understand each other. With the two sides separated they could not make use of the land's resources to make things. So, they just stopped developing."

Addie looked sad. "So, they couldn't make cars and radios and stuff. But were they happy anyhow?"

Randall half nodded. "They thought they were. I guess they really didn't know what they were missing. But then, one day, none of that mattered any more. Sith spaceships landed on Dagobah and the Dags were scared. The Siths were huge reptiles covered with green scales. Even scarier were the large spaceships. Up until then the Dags had only seen birds fly. Even though the Longs and the Shorts couldn't talk with each other, the Siths had devices that allowed all to communicate. The Siths took the Dag leaders of the Longs and the Shorts on board their spacecraft. There the Dags were told how they'd been rescued by the Siths from a dying planet in another galaxy centuries earlier and then relocated to Dagobah to repopulate and evolve."

Zelda slid from a sitting position in front of the fireplace to half reclining. "Is this a short bedtime story or does it have chapters? I'm getting sleepy."

Addie had her own complaint. "Are there going to be horses?"

Kyle was loving the story and urged Randall on. "Don't listen to them but maybe you can talk faster. So what did the Siths want?" He leaned forward as if at the movies.

"Way to get us back on point, Buddy." Randall was glad for the break so he could make up the next part of the story. "The Sith leaders told the Dags that they'd been checking up on them every century or so to see if the Dags were making any progress developing. The Siths had become disgusted with the Dag's constant fighting and stagnation. If the Dags couldn't evolve, Dagobah would be a wasted planet. The Siths were monitoring other failing planets with more deserving populations. The Siths decided the Dags would have to show their worthiness to use what they were given or be relocated. Or perhaps worse."

Addie clutched her stuffed unicorn, Uni, closer to her chest. "Are they gonna kill all the Dags?"

Randall shook his head. "The Siths were angry that the Dags hadn't done better, but they weren't mean, even though they looked scary. They offered the Dags a second chance. Dagobah's lone continent was mostly flat, except for a large mountain at its center that rose 12,000 feet into the bluish green sky. The summit had an irregular peak that formed the silhouette of a horse's head. Hence, the name Mount Horsey."

Addie jumped up. "There is a horse in the story. A really big one!"

Randall nodded. "You have to trust your dad. Now, between the horse's ears the Siths had placed three plaques under a big glass dome, one each of silver, gold, and platinum. Each plaque was etched with a rule that the Siths said were the three steps the Dags would have to follow in order to stay on the planet. However, there was a big BUT."

Kyle began to cackle. "Ha Ha. Dad just said 'big butt!'"

Zelda had almost lapsed to lying down on the floor, but the outburst brought her back. "Kyle! That's not what he said. Do you want to taste test some dish soap?"

Kyle tried to melt into the shadows. "Sorry, Mom. Won't happen again."

Addie giggled behind Uni.

Randall went on. "Mount Horsey had never been scaled to the top by the Dags. There were at least 20 paths up its slopes but they were treacherous. Each attempt to scale it was met with disaster. No climber ever came back to tell the tale. After many failed tries, the Dags gave up attempting it. Since Dag technology had stalled, no special gear was ever developed to assist a climb."

Kyle puffed up his chest. "I bet I could do it. I've got my light saber. And I'm a really good climber. I could climb a construction crane!"

Addie tried to deflate her brother. "Ha! Your light saber's not real. Even if it was, I bet there were monsters on that mountain that would use it for a toothpick."

"How would you know, horsey geek?" shot back Kyle.

Zelda broke up the impending altercation. "Alright, alright kids. Cool your jet streams. Nobody's climbing anything! Let Dad finish his epic."

"Thank you, Mrs. Interlocutor," said Randall. "The big BUT was that the Dags would have to first make it to the top to get the three plaques. The hooker was that the Siths had added some additional obstacles and traps along the paths up the mountain. The Dags would have to overcome these to make it to the top. If and when they could get to the plaques, the Dags would have to follow the three rules for 20 years and demonstrate they could change or they'd be *deplaneted.*"

Kyle was upset. "If the Dags couldn't climb up the mountain before, how could they do it with a bunch of traps? That's not even fair."

Randall nodded. "You're correct. That's what the Dag leaders argued. Finally, the Siths offered a deal. They would alter the layout so that there would be one out of twenty paths that would be safe. The rest of the paths would still have potentially lethal hazards. The Siths refused to reveal what the hazards were. The safe path would only be open for climbing attempts once a year for 20 years. The Dags would have a year to recruit volunteers for the annual ascent attempt. Of course, any Dag was free to try the climb any other time, if they dared. But none did."

Addie shuddered. "I wouldn't volunteer for that. It's no fun to get eaten by some slimy monster."

Kyle's mouth betrayed him again. "How do you know there's slimy monsters? You . . . er. I suppose there could be."

Randall suppressed a laugh at Kyle's quick recovery. "Nobody really knew what was up there. Maybe except the Siths. And they weren't telling."

Zelda sat upright again, suggesting she was actually getting interested. "So, Mr. Grand Storyteller, how did they choose climb candidates?"

"Ah, yes," muttered Randall. "Need to check the archives. Search, search. Here it is. It seems the rules did not limit the number of candidates, but there had to be an equal number from the Shorts and the Longs. They had to go up in pairs, one from each group, spaced apart by five minutes until all the volunteers had gone up. They would stop ascending if one pair returned with the plaques. But that never happened."

Now Randall's audience was moving closer. Kyle asked if there had been any success.

Randall lowered his voice for dramatic effect. "For 19 years, each year's attempt had failed. No climbers came back. Each year the number of volunteers decreased. Most figured it was impossible and it was just a death sentence. In the twentieth and final year no volunteers had come forward and the climb day was just a week away. The Dags were beginning to despair."

Addie looked concerned and clutched Uni even tighter. "Are they all going to die?"

Randall put out a hand in a calming gesture. "Don't lose faith. You never know when an unlikely hero will come forth with a simple solution. Indeed, when least expected, one emerged. Ten year old Yoda Decoda lived with his parents on a farm on the Longs' side of Dagobah. Young Yoda had blonde fuzzy hair and was tall for his age at almost 6 feet. As the twentieth year of the Horsey Mountain challenge was drawing to a close, his parents became sick with a plague. First his mother succumbed and, days later, his father. Fortunately, neighbors helped bury his parents, promised to take over the farm and offered to care for him."

Addie was almost in tears. "Mom, Dad, don't ever get sick and die, okay?"

Zelda moved over to Addie and put an arm around her. "We promise. Please continue, Randy. And no more killing."

Randall promised that there would be no more *deceasements* and continued. "Yoda despaired about his future, while he slowly packed his belongings to move in with the neighbors. He'd always been an unusual child. He never talked much with anyone besides his parents. He lived in his own little world. There were no schools to go to in his remote farming area. Yoda used the *Speak* to talk with most animals, including chickens, birds, dogs and cats. He didn't think it was unusual because his parents had the *Speak* too. He saw so few other people that there were few chances for anyone to tell him otherwise."

Addie raised her hand. "Could he talk with horses, too?"

Randall nodded solemnly. "I assume he could, but the farm didn't have any horses. Horses on Dagobah were the size of our dogs. The chickens were five feet tall and their eggs seven inches around. One egg could be dinner for a family. Nobody messed with chickens. They could easily peck you to death. The summer got so hot on Dagobah that the chickens laid soft-boiled eggs. Most other animals looked sort of like ours on earth except for different sizes and colors. Yoda was pals with a stubborn mule named Deshane who was the size of a Golden Retriever on earth. Yoda often discussed important matters with Deshane since he was smarter than the other animals. Deshane was often quite argumentative, yet he rarely gave bad advice."

Zelda chuckled. "And I suppose the inchworms were a foot long."

Randall ignored the comment. "Yoda felt lost with his parents gone. He felt like giving up. He stopped packing and went outside to talk to Deshane. He told Deshane he didn't want to live with the neighbors. He'd never liked them and they thought he was weird. Yoda brought up the Horsey Mountain challenge and Deshane got excited. After some hee-hawing around, Yoda and Deshane came to a decision. First thing in the morning, they would leave the farm together and journey to the site of the mountain climb. Yoda knew of no rules against having a mule companion in the contest. Without his parents he didn't care if he failed. And who knew? He might just pull it off."

Kyle shot up a hand. "How far was it to the mountain? Did they make it on time?"

"Great question," said Randall. "The mountain was ten miles from where Yoda lived. It wasn't a long way, but half of it was through a swamp. Yoda would not have made it without Deshane's help. They arrived at the challenge site the night before it was set to start. A dozen huge tents were set up for the spectators to spend the night. Thousands of Dags had shown up to witness the contest. Even though there were no contenders that they knew of, this would be a farewell gala before the Siths 'rehomed' them. An event organizer escorted Yoda and Deshane to a smaller tent set up for the volunteers representing the Longs. When Yoda entered, he was shocked. Hundreds of cots were set out on the tent floor, but he was the only Long volunteer there!"

Addie had an idea about that. "Maybe they were all at the dinner tent."

Randall nodded. "That's what Yoda thought at first, but then the escort handed him a green vest to wear for the climb. It had a large number one on it. Yoda asked if the number one meant he would go first. The escort told him that he was correct and that he was also last. The time had expired for new entries, and he would be the only representative of the Longs. Climb time was set for sunrise. The escort handed him a blanket and pillow for the cot and advised him to sleep fast."

It took several moments for that to sink in for Kyle and Addie. Kyle pounded his fist on the carpet. "Didn't they even give him dinner?"

Addie squeaked. "That's not fair! There were no other Longs brave enough to go?!""

Randall sympathized. "You're both right, but sometimes life is not fair. There was no dinner tent. Fortunately, Yoda still had a liverwurst sandwich left from what he'd packed for the trip and shared it with Deshane. The escort tried to make Deshane sleep outside, but Yoda snuck him back inside so they could plan the climb."

Zelda popped a question. "So the Siths didn't give Yoda any idea what perils they'd face on the climb up Mount Horsey? And none of the Dags knew anything?"

Randall hadn't made up that part of the story yet and pretended to have a loogie of phlegm caught in his throat. He hacked and made choking sounds and faked coming up with something. The kids leaned back like they were about to dodge a hairball.

Finally, Randall had the next part of the story sorted. "Harumph! Young Yoda had heard the local farmers talk about it. Most of the talk was rumor and speculation, since it was believed no climber had ever returned to tell their tale. Most common was talk of large cat-like creatures that lurked in the undergrowth along some of the paths. They had hooked teeth and were way larger than most Dag grown men—even the Longs. They'd jump out of hiding and swallow the climber up in several bites, leaving no trace."

Kyle started to make gagging sounds. "Urg! What a way to go. I wonder if they'd recognize me in the cat poop."

Addie looked at Kyle with disdain. "Why did you have to say that? Now I want to puke."

Zelda had her say. "Randy! Could you please skip over the gross stuff? What else was up that mountain?"

Randall put up both hands. "Sorry. I'll just stick to the scary non-gross stuff. Well, let's see. Oh, yeah. The farmers told of pits of poisonous snakes hidden on some paths. Others said the paths could have stinging insects, quicksand, birds that could fly away with you, and even vicious strangling plants. Now, how they knew this, no one could say for sure. Perhaps some had ventured up the paths just out of curiosity, encountered a menace, but escaped back down the path."

"You'd have to be crazy to go up that mountain alone," observed Kyle. "It sounds like a certain death."

"Yeah, I'd never go," agreed Addie. "At least not without Uni."

"But Yoda won't be alone," added Zelda. "He's got Deshane. They can both talk to animals. That might help. And what about the Shorts? Are they sending anyone up?"

"Great question," said Randall. That gave him an idea for the next part of the story. "The Dag escort had told Yoda that he'd go up the starting path with climber number one from the Shorts. It would go for a while and then come to a shallow depression filled with water where it would split into two paths. The escort called it a spork in the path. Yoda and the Short would have to decide which one to take. There would be nineteen more such sporks before he reached the peak, each with a deeper pit. The two needed to make a plan on how to make the best choice at each spork."

Addie looked scared. "I can't think of how I'd do it. Maybe I'd ask Uni for advice. Yoda could do that with Deshane and the Short person. Maybe the pool of water at the spork was full of those little fish that eat people."

Randall smiled. "That's possible. That's exactly what Yoda did. He and Deshane discussed it first. They decided that Deshane would move stealthily just ahead on the starting path as a point lookout followed by Yoda and the Short climber. Each would watch one side of the path carefully as they walked. If one of them sensed a threat ahead, they'd all backtrack and take a different spork."

Zelda raised her hand. "Alright. That might work, but wouldn't it be better if they used some method to help decide which spork to take when they come to it instead of waiting until they run into a trap?"

Randall hadn't thought of that and decided to use it. "Patience, Padowan. You don't get to skip to the end of the chapter. In fact, when morning came, Yoda and Deshane went to the starting point as directed and they met the Short climber. It was a young black-haired girl, also ten years old. She was half the size of Yoda and nicely rounded. Her name was Yodelle, and she was accompanied by her pet dog, Bowsette, the size of an earth cat. Yodelle was wearing a red vest with the number one on it."

Kyle piped up. "Yoda has to do the climb with a girl? What lousy luck."

Addie countered. "Girls are smart too. You watch and see."

"She ain't wrong," asserted Randall. "The escort introduced Yoda to Yodelle and they shook hands. Then, Yodelle introduced Bowsette to Yoda, and the dog replied that she was pleased to meet Yoda. Bowsette sniffed Deshane and greeted him. Deshane sniffed back and told her that she was a very cute dog. She yipped and turned in a circle. At first Yoda thought nothing of the exchange of greetings, then realized they could all use the *Speak* even though he was a Long and Yodelle was a Short. And they could *both* talk to the animals!"

Addie interjected. "Was Yodelle cute too?"

Randall couldn't believe how tangential Addie's comment was when he had just revealed the two ten-year-olds used the *Speak*. Who knew how often that apparent mutation made it into the gene pool. "Indeed she was. Yoda was quite taken with her charms. He asked Yodelle where the other Short climbers were. She just pointed at herself and told Yoda that it would be just the two of them going up the mountain, plus Deshane and Bowsette. Yoda shared his strategy with Yodelle and she thought it a smart one. Bowsette would walk ahead with Deshane so they could assess both sides of the path. The time came and they set off."

Addie began to bounce on her behind. "I can't wait to see whether they make it. They do make it, don't they?"

Randall put up a calming hand. "The chances looked good, but one can never tell without playing the game. The four climbers set off slowly on the starting path to cheers from the gathered spectators. The path brought no hazards as they trod watchfully. Yoda and Yodelle joined Deshane and Bowsette at the first spork and paused. Deshane asked, 'Which one should we take? And what about this pool?' Yodelle replied, 'Let's wait for a sign.' Yoda and Bowsette agreed. So they waited. Yoda said he was hungry because there had been no time for breakfast. He pulled a bag of nutpeas from his pocket and began to munch. He handed some to Yodelle, but one slipped out of his hand and fell into the grass next to the path."

Addie was almost strangling Uni. "How can they eat nutpeas at a time like this?"

Zelda laughed. "Yeah, I'd be so puckered up I don't think I could swallow."

Randall was pleased Zelda was playing along and adding to the high drama. "Just then, a chipmunk jumped down from a nearby tree to claim the errant nutpea. He gobbled it up, wiped his mouth, and looked up at the group. 'Hi guys. My name is Clark. What's up?' Yoda introduced his friends. 'We're climbing to the top to fetch the secret plaques.' Clark made a *chipping* sound and offered his help. Yodelle said, 'That would be so kind of you. We have to pick which of the two paths is safe. Plus there's this pool of water. Is it deep?'"

Kyle was Mr. Anxious again. "Were they surprised that Clark could talk to them? How could they tell if a chipmunk would tell the truth?"

"Yeah," said Addie. "Clark might be a little liar."

Randall shook his head. "Clark might have been a little wheeler-dealer, but he was honest. Clark offered them a deal. 'For one more nutpea I'll tell you which path to take and what the deal is with the pool.

To prove I'm not fooling with you, I'll ride along on your shoulder to the next spork, as long as I can have whatever crumbs you have left. But you smell like flatlanders. I can only ride with a Dag who has cleansed themselves up to their neck in the Sith bath of this spork.' Yoda and the group discussed it and then agreed to the terms. The bath was so shallow that only Yodelle, a Short, could submerge in it up to her neck. She dipped a toe in the water cautiously, and was glad to find it pleasantly warm. No piranhas nipped at her tootsies. Perhaps they could trust the little rodent helper after all."

Addie let out a sigh of relief. "Goodie! Yodelle won't be a fishy snack."

Randall continued. "Yodelle emerged from the Sith bath and shook herself. Yoda took out another nutpea and tossed it to Clark, who gobbled it up and jumped onto Yodelle's cleansed shoulder. Clark announced, 'Take the left spork. The right spork has nasty snakes. I'm too fast for them to catch, but you guys are too slow.' The group set off and made it safely to the next spork."

"I bet they could walk faster now," said Kyle.

Addie shook her head. "I still don't trust Clark. He could jump off of Yodelle's shoulder and just run off. Maybe he made a deal with some creature at the second spork to deliver four victims for a whole bag of nutpeas."

Zelda made a raspberry sound. "Geez. What a trusting optimistic soul! Please get this trek over with, Randy."

"Alright already," grumped Randall. "Enough with the interruptions or I'll never finish. So, at the second spork Clark jumped down and said he couldn't take them any farther, because he wasn't authorized. They'd have to wait for his friend Oppy who was a little slow. Clark thanked them for the snack and was off into the brush in a blink. The four discussed their good fortune while they waited, wondering who they'd get next. After almost ten minutes, a white haired opossum with pink eyes and tail meandered noisily out of the brush. 'Hey, dudes, I'm Oppy, your next guide. Sorry I'm late. I was napping. Looks like Clark gave you good advice and you listened. All the other climbers never do. You ready to roll? All I need is a snack. And one of you needs a bath. You smell like chipmunk.”

The team realized that the tricky Siths had intended the pool not just to be a place to cleanse, but also be a subtle obstacle. If they hadn’t been able to communicate with their helpers they’d never get through.

Zelda laughed. “So there is free lunch in your story. Isn’t poor Yoda tapped out?”

Kyle was worried. “If they don’t have any food left they’re sunk.”

Addie just clutched Uni.

“Not to worry, listeners,” proclaimed Randall. “Our Yoda quartet is nothing if not resourceful. After the usual introductions, Oppy made a deal to guide them for a proper bit of food. Yodelle had a little fanny pack. In it were jerky dog treats she’d brought for Bowsette and a bag of sunflower seeds for her to nibble on the trail. She reached in the pack, took out a large piece of jerky and held it up. ‘Will this work?’ she asked. Oppy began to drool. ‘Indeed, young miss. Just break off pieces and toss them to me as we walk to the next spork. There I will pass you off to your next guide, Robbie. I am not authorized to take you beyond spork three. Oh, and from here on, the big guy just needs to dip his foot in the Sith bath pool.’”

Addie raised a fist in triumph. “Yodelle is just as smart as Yoda. She brought food too.”

Kyle grunted. “Yeah, but I bet she can’t fight like Yoda.”

“Girls are too smart to resort to fighting,” retorted Addie.

“Enough!” intervened Randall. “Meanwhile, at the mountain peak, the Siths had positioned three guard mice around the plaques, Bill, Bob and Morty. They’d been there since early morning. It was noon and they hadn’t eaten lunch yet. The Siths had forced them to look official by wearing thick wool uniforms, helmets and boots. They’d been prom-ised food, but none had appeared. Their job was to check the ID papers of any climbers that got to the top to make sure they were authorized Dags. While they waited, they repeatedly complained to each other about being hot plus suffering through abject hunger, itchy uniforms and boredom.”

"Wait a minute!" burst out Kyle. "Mice to guard the plaques? The Siths must be nuts."

Randall raised his hand. "Ah, but these were Dag mice. They're the size of chihuahuas and have razor sharp teeth. Bloody fast too. Not very bright, though."

Addie reprimanded Kyle. "See, Kyle. The Siths aren't stupid. Remember this is Dagobah."

Kyle grinned and shrugged.

Randall tried to get back on track. "At the third spork, Oppy had just finished his jerky as they arrived safely. He said goodbye and walked away, being a possum of few words. The group looked around for Robbie, realizing they didn't know what they were looking for. While everyone was looking down, a fat red robin landed on Yoda's shoulder. 'Hi. I'm Robbie. Don't bother with the introductions. Oppy already filled me in.' The bird looked at his tiny wrist watch. 'Uh oh. Looks like I'm a few seconds late. I had to scout the path ahead, because they change the hazards every year. Had to go back and recheck one. Glad I did. They changed it again at the last minute. Okay. The deal is bird seed for each spork ahead or no go. That work for you?' Yodelle patted her fanny pack now filled with just sunflower seeds. There was no quibbling—everybody agreed."

"I like sunflower seeds on my salad," remarked Addie.

Kyle could not contain himself. "Is Robbie going to take them all the way to the top?"

"You bet," answered Randall. "At each spork, after Yoda had dipped a toe, Robbie took some seed in his beak, ate it, then flew ahead on the path once more just to be sure nothing had changed. The group made it safely to the peak just as the seeds ran out. They thanked Robbie and he flew away. Just as he was fading out of sight in the sky, he turned around, came back and landed on Yodelle's shoulder. 'Uh. Forget to tell you. Same path choices on the way down, but you have to remember them yourself. Ta ta.' And he was off again."

Addie was aghast. "How could they possibly remember the way back down? There's twenty sporks."

"Yoda and Yodelle looked at each other with wide eyes, but Deshane hee-hawed. 'Don't worry guys. I have a picture perfect memory. I'll get you back down. Let's check out the loot.' With that the mule lit off like a lightning bolt and was first to the glass dome. At the dome were three mice wearing shiny guard uniforms and carrying little swords. They lowered the swords and ordered Deshane to halt and state his business. Deshane hee-hawed and told them he and his friends had climbed the mountain to get the Sith plaques. The mice told Deshane only a Dag could claim them and that he obviously was just a mule. Not to mention he couldn't remove the glass dome without opposing thumbs. Deshane hee-hawed his displeasure but made note that he'd made it to the treasure first."

Kyle was first to comment. "Three mice are guarding the plaques? Their swords must be lightsabers or Deshane is just a scaredy mule."

Randall laughed. "Good point, but Deshane was just being cautious. He was planning to wait for Yoda or Yodelle to remove the dome. When the two, plus Bowsette, caught up with Deshane at the dome, the mice hollered for them to halt and identify themselves. Yoda and Yodelle showed the mice their Dag papers. The mice approved of the papers, but they hollered 'Have you got our cheese? And rice! We've been up here forever, bored and starving. The Sith promised us cheese and rice for guarding this stupid dome. Where's our cheese and rice?'"

Addie's eyes widened. "Oh, no. Yoda and Yodelle are all out of food. They've come so far."

Randall put up a calming hand. "Not to worry. Just then, a huge bald eagle flew towards the mice with three packages hanging by strings from his beak. He did a flyby and air dropped the packages near the mice. The first bag held a fine specimen of roquefort cheese that stank to high heaven. The second had balls of sticky rice. The third held a bag of kernel corn. The mice were overjoyed with their treasure. They had not expected corn. It was really hard to find. They stripped to their underwear and Bob shouted to the group 'Let's head over to Bill's nest to have our cheese, rice and corn. He's got some fresh hootch to wash it down.'"

Zelda began to sing. "What a friend we have in cheeses. Cheese and rice, oh what a friend."

Randall couldn't believe it. Zelda had stolen his punch line. He burst out laughing so hard he was almost in tears, but soldiered on with the story. "Just so. Yoda gave Yodelle the honor of removing the glass dome. She found a note written in fine calligraphy. It read, 'The Dags must take down the wall dividing Dagobah into two halves. Then, in twenty years they must blend back together and achieve each rule of development etched on the three plaques herein. They will start with the silver, then the gold, and last the platinum. If, at the end of the twenty years, that goal is not achieved, the Dag population will be relocated by the Siths to planet X. The Dags will find Planet X to be rather unpleasant.'"

"Ouch!" said Zelda. "That's harsh. What did the plaques say?"

Randall walked in a small circle for a few minutes and then described the plaques. "The silver rule read: 'Do no harm to your neighbor.' The golden rule said: 'Treat your neighbor as you would like to be treated.' The platinum rule read: 'Treat your neighbor as your neighbor would like to be treated.'"

Zelda looked surprised. "I didn't know there was a platinum rule."

Kyle added a comment. "I didn't know there was a gold and silver one."

Randall raised both arms. "Well, you do now. That's the end of the story, but I want you all to think about it carefully. Very soon we'll have another bedtime session and we'll talk about all this further. I want you guys to tell me what the story and those rules mean to you. I pronounce this story over for the night. All further discussion is tabled until next time."

Addie protested. "What does tabled mean?"

Zelda had the answer. "Over until next time. Now you two pop upstairs and get ready for beddy. No complaints."

"But, Mom," protested Kyle. "I've got some questions."

Randall patted Kyle's shoulder. "Great! That means you were listening. Write them down so you don't forget. Then bring them up at the next story time. No more buts and no more butt comments."

Addie looked almost despondent. "Aww, Daddy! Your stories usually have a moral. Can you at least tell us what it is? Then, we'll go to bed now if you promise to answer our questions at the next bedtime story. Do you agree, Kyle?"

Kyle frowned but agreed. "I guess so." His finger started exploring his nostril.

Randall had to think hard and fast. Then it came to him. "Err . . . the moral is this. *There are many baths up Mount Horsey, but the mule at the top is still Deshane. That's the Long and Short of it. Dag nabbit.*"

Zelda groaned loudly. "All the big build up for that!? How about there's no place like the dome?"

Randall was caught out again, but thought of another verse of song. "*Yoda is on the mountain, over to Bill's in our underwear, Yodelle sat in the fountain, and we Sith mice were bored.*"

This time Zelda was caught out and she was hooting with laughter. Meanwhile, the kids looked about wondering what was so funny. When Randall finally caught his breath, he announced the story was officially over and that it was time for bed. He proclaimed that their mother would explain everything upstairs while she put them to bed. The complaints persisted, but ultimately the kids dutifully followed Zelda upstairs while she stared daggers at Randall. He thanked the gods of storytelling for providing not just one moral, but three.

Hard of Hearing

Randall and Zelda prepared for bed, with the kids finally off in slumberland. He washed his face at the sink.

In the bedroom, Zelda stripped to undies and put on her warm fuzzy robe. "Hey, Randy! I've always wondered something."

Randall was rinsing his face when he answered and his response came out in a burble. "What's that?"

Zelda raised her voice to be heard over the splashing sounds. "You have two brothers and one sister. If you do the math, you're all about seven years apart. What's up with that?"

Randall spit the water out of his mouth, cleared his throat, and walked into the bedroom to be better heard. "Rumor has it that there were two causes. First, my Dad was a victim of the seven-year itch and, second, Mom was a bit hard of hearing."

Zelda sounded somewhat baffled. "How the heck did that work?"

Randall laughed. "Yeah, the connection is not obvious. When the seven-year interval would come up and my Dad got the itch, he'd wait until they were alone together in the living room. Dad would be doing a crossword and Mom reading a book. Then Dad would mumble 'Hey, Selma, do you want to go to bed or what?' Then Mom would look up from her book and say 'What?' Well, you can figure it out from there."

Zelda slapped her thigh. "Wow, he must be a straight shooter, just like you. I swear the first time we did it, Kyle went from a glint in your eye to a little piece of fruit pie."

"You could say that," agreed Randall. "So, do you want to go to bed now or what?"

"What?" asked Zelda. "Must you always mumble? You cool your jets for a sec. I'll be right back after I put on the appropriate attire."

Zelda went to the main bathroom and was gone for about five minutes. She came slinking back into the bedroom in a wrap-around black and white kimono robe, her face highlighted by blush and red lipstick. The soft light reflected off her long red hair now let down to her shoulders. The subtle fragrance of "My Sin" perfume filled the air as she slow stepped to the bedside and slowly opened the kimono. [Cue romantic music. . . .]

JUST PULLING YOUR LEG

Later that night, Zelda and Randall were awakened at 2:00 AM by girlish screaming. It was coming from Addie's room. They leapt out of bed and ran to the hallway where they found Kyle. He had been awakened as well and was on his way to check on his sister. The lights went on in Addie's room just before they all entered. Addie was sitting up in bed with the covers pulled up to her chin. Randall rushed to Addie's side and she grabbed him around the neck.

"Daddy!" gasped Addie. "I heard breathing and my eyes popped open. I was a-scared. Then I heard a voice and it said 'you don't belong in this house, you little whippersnapper!' Then something grabbed my leg! Right here, on my ankle! I turned on the light, but no one was there."

Randall surveyed the room and saw nothing awry. Addie started to sob into his shoulder.

Zelda looked suspiciously at her son. "Kyle, you weren't trying to pull a fast one on your sister, were you?"

Kyle put his hands on his chest. "Me?! What the heck? I don't go in her girlie room. It stinks like unicorns in there. I bet it was the Big Boy bobblehead. We should throw them all out."

Zelda rolled her eyes and sat on Addie's side of the bed opposite Randall. Zelda held Addie's hand. "It didn't sound like Kyle's voice, Mommy. It was more like a witchy woman, all high and creaky, like a door in a scary movie. The breathing sounded like gusts of wind with wheezing like when I have an asthma attack." Addie started to shake. "Do we need to hire one of those white-collar men to come to the house and do his exercises? You know, to get rid of a devil woman in the house?"

Zelda stifled a giggle. "No, honey, we can take care of it ourselves. We can make sure there are no bad things in the house."

Addie relaxed a bit. "Good. I don't want to be a snapper whipper. I don't even know what that is. Mommy, can I sleep in your room?"

Zelda nodded and held her close. After Addie finally calmed down, Randall took Kyle back to bed and tucked him in.

"You're not scared, are you, Buddy?" asked Randall.

"I don't think so," said Kyle. "I'm pretty sure it was just a dream. Maybe like the ones I get. I told you Big Boy milkshakes give Addie the jeebs. You can go back to bed, Dad. I'll be okay."

"Did I ever tell you what a good kid you are?" asked Randall.

"I think so, but one more time won't hurt," said Kyle.

Randall gave him a little head rub and kissed him on the forehead. "Good night, little Dude."

"Goodnight, Dad."

Randall went back to Addie's bedroom, where Zelda had crawled under the covers with Addie. The two were all snuggled up. Zelda whispered to Randall that she'd stay with Addie until Addie fell asleep. Randall kissed both girls on the forehead, went back to bed and collapsed into a deep sleep. Randall's last conscious thought was *At least Addie waited until we were finished.*

Einbert Alstein, FD

CHAPTER 7

—

QUANTUM SUMMIT

"Wherever you go, you have to clean up afterwards."

—Fritz the Plumber

BIRTHDAY CAKE

The next Saturday, Addie's birthday was a day away. Zelda was busy making her birthday cake. Addie was "helping," if licking batter off the mixing spoon qualified as assistance. Between licks, Addie was humming a little nonsense tune.

Randall wandered into the kitchen to refill his coffee cup. "Hey, Addie, that's a catchy little tune. Did you learn that in school?"

Addie pointed to her temple. "No, Daddy, I just *'heared'* it in my head."

Randall sidled up and pretended he was going to take a lick of batter from her spoon, but Addie deftly pulled it away. "Mommy said the spoon was just for me!"

Randall laughed. "I was just goofing. Say, how would you like to work out your tune on the guitar with me?"

Addie jumped up and down. "Could we? That would be so fun. Let's make up words, too. 'Kay?"

Randall clapped his hands. "Icing on the cake, Rosebud."

Addie froze. "No! You are not going to sing on top of my cake!"

Randall and Zelda both laughed out loud while Addie looked confused.

Zelda explained. "Icing is another word for frosting, Sweetie. Daddy just meant that adding words to your tune would be extra special."

Addie visibly relaxed. "Oh, I get it, but you guys make me so mad sometimes. I hope that after this birthday I'll know more words so you don't confuse me so much."

Randall tried to wipe the smile off his face. "Don't worry. After you turn six, your vocabulary gets much better. You already know a bunch of big words."

"Daddy, what's the biggest word you know? If I learn that one, the rest should be easy."

Randall looked at Zelda thoughtfully. Zelda shrugged her shoulders. "Let me think," said Randall. Then it came to him. "I think the longest word would be antidisestablishmentarianism. It's got 28 letters. Say it with me."

At first, Addie just gaped at Randall. The first two tries, she got her tongue stuck on her eye teeth so she couldn't see what she was saying. Then Randall repeated the word slowly and after three more tries, Addie had it down. Randall loved the little lisp she put in the middle of the word. "Daddy, what does it mean?"

Randall took a second to deconstruct the word in his mind. "If I remember correctly, it means the belief that the establishment should not be altered or taken apart."

Addie whined. "Aww! What the heck is an establishment?"

Zelda broke in. "It's any group with a bunch of rules put together by people."

Addie squinted. "You guys have rules for me and Kyle. Does that mean you're the establishment in this house?"

Randall raised his arms. "Exactly. Nice job. First prize goes to the little blonde girl. Come on, let's go compose a song. Give me a high five."

Addie nodded and started for the living room. "Okay . . . but we are NOT putting that word in it. It makes my brain hurt!"

Randall grabbed Addie's hand and they went off to write the music and words for their composition. Zelda could hear Randall working out the notes and chords on his acoustic guitar while Addie kept correcting him. Multiple times Zelda heard her yell "Daddy! That's not the way it goes!" Then, Randall would apologize and make changes. After that was resolved they argued back and forth about the verse, but Zelda couldn't make out the details.

Somewhere during the verse composition, Kyle walked into the kitchen. He had smelled cake baking and figured frosting would be next and some mooching was indicated. "Hey, Mom, is that for Addie's birthday party tomorrow?"

Zelda was just about to stir the frosting mixture. "You bet. How'd you like to mix up this goop for me? My arm is tired."

Kyle was eager to help, but had conditions. "Sure, if I can lick the mixing spoon."

Zelda knew that was coming. "Well, I'm not sure my arm is that tired."

Kyle did his "poor kid" moan and put on his most pitiful face. "Come on, Mom. Can I please lick the spoon? Pretty please?"

Zelda pretended to cave under the pressure. "How can I say no to that sad face? Since you asked so nicely, go ahead. But if Addie comes in you have to share."

Kyle eagerly took the spoon. "Fat chance of that. Dad and Addie are too busy howling like cats in the living room. What the heck are they doing, anyhow?"

Zelda shook her head. "Not exactly sure. The message was that they're composing a song from a tune Addie had in her head and putting words to it."

"What the heck for?" asked Kyle.

Zelda shook her head again. "For the heck of it, near as I can tell. But I'm glad Addie is occupied with something else. Some kind of help is worse than no help at all. Don't tell her I said that. As for the song, maybe Dad intends it as a birthday present for Addie."

Kyle shook his head. "Not a present I'd want. I want a Ludwig starter drum kit. Then I could drown out their noise."

Zelda grimaced and passed the buck. "You'll have to ask your dad about that one."

Kyle started his sales pitch. "Billy Ichner told me that Uncle Bob's Music Center has cool used sets for sale . . . and they don't cost that much. Maybe you could drive me over there to look."

Zelda balked at that idea. "Not for me to say, Drumboy. Ask your father."

Kyle banged the spoon on the bowl. "Mom, you know Dad will say no!"

Zelda shook her head. "No, I don't know that. Sometimes you can sweet talk him into stuff . . . if you catch him in a good mood and you show really good behavior. That's for you to figure out. Can't hurt to try." Zelda was wise to Randall's preference for quiet contemplation rather than percussive pursuits.

Kyle went silent for a bit, which made the cacophony coming from the living room seem much louder. "Hmm . . . I think I might have a way. Thanks, Mom. Does the frosting look mixed enough?"

Zelda checked his work. "Just about. One more minute, then get to licking."

Almost as if on cue, the sound of music composition stopped and Addie came bounding into the kitchen. "Mom, Kyle . . . guess what? Dad and I finished my song. It's got words and everything. Come in the living room and we'll perform it for you. Wait a minute! Is that my cake frosting?"

Kyle did some quick thinking. "It sure enough is, birthday girl. It's double chocolate. I was just helping Mom make it. I told Mom you should get first dibs on licking the spoon . . . right after we frost the cake."

Zelda picked up on the tactic. "Yes, Rosebud. We have to wait for the cake layers to cool off before we frost. Let's listen to your song first and the cake should be ready to frost afterwards."

Addie was super excited with that news and felt generous. "I'm ready to sing. Kyle, I licked all the cake batter without you, so you can have half of the frosting to lick."

Kyle was quite gracious. "Thank you, sister of mine."

Zelda didn't trust this temporary detente, so she began to usher both kids to the living room. "Good news, kids, I made extra frosting. You'll both have plenty to lick. May make you sick. But now we have to do music time."

Randall had his music stand set up in the living room with the handwritten sheet music and words ready. Addie had a copy to read from. They prepared to begin while Kyle and Zelda seated themselves in easy chairs.

Randall put the guitar strap around his neck and checked the tuning of his guitar. He motioned Addie to get ready. "This here song was composed by Addie Biederneier with help from her Daddy Randall Biedermeier. It's a folk song we wrote called 'Oaken Annie' and it goes exactly like this . . . this time."

Oaken Annie
Annie came to Oklahoma
With a wagon an' a bed.
Found a farmer who was willin'
Then, one day they up an' wed.
Annie made a real good housewife,
Kept her husband clean an' fed.
But the farmer finally found her
With a cowboy in their bed.

So, he got himself a shotgun
An' he shot ol' Annie dead.
No one would call him a killer,
But jus' gone out'a his head.

———

Zelda and Kyle sat listening with their mouths agape, since the song actually sounded rather good. Almost sort of professional. Creepy and morbid, but still catchy. They both clapped heartily when the tune was finished.

Kyle had the first critical comment. "It would have been better with a rhythm section, like maybe drums. But not bad."

"Thanks, I think?" Randall tried to see the good.

Zelda had the second critique. "Not sure I like the lead character being killed in the end."

Addie stuck out her lower lip. "Yeah, Daddy used my name at first, but I didn't want to be killed in my own birthday folk song, so I made him change it to Annie."

Randall objected to the criticism. "Wait a click. Lots of folk songs are about love and betrayal."

Zelda put an arm around Addie's shoulder. "You're right about that, but it's out of place in a little girl's birthday song. I suggest we make it an instrumental. Besides the drums, which we don't have, maybe we could add ocarina and a tambourine. Who knows what the birthday bobcat will bring."

"The who?" asked Kyle.

"The Who are not on tour right now." Randall couldn't resist.

"What?" asked Kyle.

"What's on third," said Zelda. "Randy, I'm also not sure how I feel about doing a story of adultery for our little girl's folk song."

"Why not, Mom?" asked Addie. "I know what adults do."

"Huh?" Zelda was, unusually, speechless.

Addie explained. "I know what adults do. I've used adultery!"

"Huh?!" That explanation did not register and just alarmed Zelda.

Addie liked to make her point clearer and spoke in a slow, condescending voice. "You know. It's like the cattery at the humane society! Where you can watch how the cats act? I have been watching adults!" Addie could not figure out what had silenced her mother and why her eyes were so big.

Randall and Zelda were a bit relieved by the clarification. The discourse was interrupted when the kitchen phone rang. Zelda jumped up and ran to answer it. She yelled out that it was Joe Shepard calling for Randall. He fast-walked to take the call.

Before handing off the receiver, Zelda covered the speaker end with her hand and whispered to Randall. "Joe says he's calling to see if you can come to some meeting tomorrow with the group you asked him to help set up. What the heck is that about?"

Randall looked surprised. "Oh . . . remember you asked me if I was still going to explore the strange stuff that is happening? And I said I was moving ahead with that? I think Joe may have recruited some experts to look into it with us."

Zelda huffed. "That weird happenings nonsense again? Well, I suppose there's no stopping you. But tomorrow is Addie's birthday. You better not plan anything with him to interfere with your participation in your daughter's big day. You're gonna be there and you will have fun!" Zelda's tone portrayed anything but fun.

Randall put up a stop sign hand. "Heavens no! Don't worry. Tomorrow is Saturday. I'm sure we can work something out that won't interfere. The party kids will be here from 11:00 to 3:00. Give me the phone before Joe falls asleep. We can work this out. Maybe even do a different day."

Zelda looked partly mollified. "Well, alright. But, I warn you. Don't screw things up. We are teaching our kids how adults act. You are part of the adultery!"

Randall scowled at Zelda, hoping Joe hadn't overheard the adultery comment. He took the phone. "Joe! What a nice surprise! I'm glad you called! I was just thinking about you. Weird. This has been happening a lot lately . . ."

"Hey, big guy, what took you so long to pick up the phone? Sounded like you and the wife were having a Congressional debate."

Randall cringed. "Yeah, sorry about that. Zelda is all hyped up about my daughter's birthday tomorrow. She wanted to make sure I don't schedule anything to avoid being here when the gaggle of gigglers arrives. You know, must share the bounty."

Joe hesitated a bit. "Well, uh, yeah. I was able to set up the first meeting of the PCG tomorrow. What time is the birthday party?"

Randall sensed a conflict of schedules might be coming, as he had feared. Could be difficult sailing weather ahead if he couldn't navigate through the squall. "The little girly twerps will be here from 11:00 to 3:00. I suspect there will be stragglers. They might not clear out until 4:00. What did you set up?"

Joe let out a sigh of relief. "Shouldn't be a problem, then. I have a tentative commitment from my friends Ruby Cosgrove and John Bingham for a meet and greet tomorrow night at my house at 7:00. I called Dan Graham, your Physicist, and he's good with it. I just need your presence to complete the startup group. With you, we'll have a group of five. I'm ordering pizza and offering up beer or wine as chasers. Just don't mix them. You game?"

Randall was relieved there would be no conflict with the party and pleased a starter group would finally get together. "Count me in. Thanks for setting it up. I'll need a bunch of pizza and beer after spending five hours in parental hell. By the way, what's PCG stand for? Pizza Charged Gabbers? Politically Correct Geeks? Pretty Clueless Gents?"

Joe made a clucking sound on the phone, his unique version of a laugh. "Did I forget to tell you? It stands for Phantom Cominglement Group. What do you think?"

Randall thought for a bit. "Not bad for a starter. We can always upgrade as we go. But I like it. Better than my names for the group."

Joe mocked sounding mildly annoyed. "Upgrade? Why would we need to do that? Isn't my acronym just the bee's knees?"

Randall had to snigger a bit. "Sorry. It probably is. For now, it's a fine acronym, but we need to allow for possible changes in focus as we go along. After all, no scientific study group startup is worth its salt unless it has a cool acronym. Without it we may be acrimonious."

Joe was partially mollified. "I guess I see your point. Must be ready to roll with the flow. So, I take it we're on for tomorrow night. Do you have an agenda in mind?"

Randall hadn't thought that far ahead, but didn't want to sound unprepared. "Well . . . my idea was to use the first meeting to get acquainted, but I think one of us should review the purpose of the group. You know, develop a mission statement and go over what each can contribute to the mission. I don't want the meeting to be just a BS session."

"You mean, like most of your VA meetings?" Joe interjected.

Randall parried the dig. "Ha ha. Good one. As you point out, that's at the VA, where I try to be consistent with VA culture. I see what we're trying to do as, first, a review of the current state of our understanding of nonverbal communication. Then going forward, we can do proper scientific research into possible connections between that phenomenon and quantum subatomic physics. Don't worry, I'll put a simple agenda together for tomorrow."

Joe thought Randall's explanation sounded like a politician's campaign promise, but agreed. "Sounds controversial already. We'd better keep all this on the down low for now. If it gets around what we're investigating, some folks might mistake us for crackpots."

Randall chuckled. "I'm not sure that would be a mistake. My pot's been cracked for a while. It's how the light gets in. Don't know about you."

Joe guffawed. "Mine must be cracked, too. It's got enough leaks. It's how I water the seeds I plant! Add some manure, and we've got a garden to harvest!"

"That's easy, since we are so full of . . ." Randall started.

Joe interrupted. "Anyhoo! By the way, the whole 'think of you, get a call from you' thing has been happening to me a lot lately, too. Almost like we invoked quantum entanglement just by thinking about it! See you tomorrow. Enjoy the kiddy conclave."

"Yeah, sure." Randall said goodbye, took the receiver back to the kitchen and rejoined the family in the living room.

Zelda wasted no time interrogating Randall about Joe's phone call. "So, what part of tomorrow's party are you going to miss?"

Randall feigned surprise. "Whyever would I miss my Rosebud's big birthday do? Our PCG group will be meeting at Joe's house at 7:00. There will be five of us, including me. Four men and a former nun."

Zelda narrowed one eye. "Former nun? Why is she former? And what is she now? Have you been to Joe's house before? And what does PCG stand for, Pizza Cheese Guys?"

Randall waited a beat. "The answers to your questions, in order, are as follows. Yes, don't know, Yoga instructor, no, and Phantom Cominglement Group. I'll ask why Ruby is defrocked and tell you if she discloses it to us."

Zelda narrowed the other eye. "So, you're just going to leave me to clean up the party mess all by myself? And, you know, this spooky stuff has been happening to me, too. Was there ever a thought about including me in the group?"

Randall tried to read between the lines. Was she just objecting for effect? No, it was never that simple. Randall proceeded cautiously. "Why, heavens no. I'll have at least three hours to help you clean up and spit shine the house. And you won't have to make me dinner."

Zelda narrowed both eyes. "Well, good. That's something. But what if I wanted to do something for adult fun after the girly party? This meeting of yours came up without much notice."

Randall widened his eyes in surprise. "By adult fun do you mean like having a 'date' with me? Like dinner, a movie and bedtime for Frances? Or have you decided you'd like to come with me to the PCG meeting?"

Zelda looked sideways left and right. "I don't know." She paused.

"Part of me would like to go, but the other part of me doesn't think I'd fit in with all you eggheads. I'm just an ignorant cook and bottle washer."

Zelda's comment just hung in the air like a stink cloud. Randall knew he had to tread carefully, since Zelda's tender ego was at stake. Randall rose and put his arm around Zelda's shoulder. "Hey, now. All of us smart people are ignorant about something, but we're not stupid. Ignorant just means someone hasn't learned something yet, but stupid means another someone is incapable of learning that same something. I think you're smart and capable of learning anything you set your mind to."

Zelda looked up at Randall with sad eyes. "You mean that? Or are you just trying to make me feel better?"

Randall gave Zelda an elbow squeeze. "Both. Look, I'm sorry the PCG meeting came up on such short notice. It's something I've been trying to put together for a long time. I, frankly, thought that you'd be too intimidated by the braintrust there that you'd be uncomfortable attending. However, as I think about it further, it makes sense to have a lay person and creative type there to keep us grounded and think outside the scientific box."

Zelda perked up. "Really? How do you mean?"

Randall walked away and paced a bit. "Firstly, you can verify our experiences from your point of view without it being filtered through my scientific lens. Secondly, I want the members to be able to explain their theories in a way that even an eighth grader could understand. Otherwise, the theories won't be easily understood by the general public when and if the time comes."

Zelda frowned. "I think I get that, but are you calling me an eighth grader?"

Randall tried to reword his statement. "Not at all. We, in doctor land, try to follow the KISS rule."

Zelda stuck out her chin. "Now there's consorting involved?"

Randall had to laugh. He was getting in even deeper. "Not at all. It stands for 'Keep It Simple Stupid.' And, no, I'm not calling you stupid. In medicine, we're taught that explanations of complex treatment plans to patients should be at the eighth grade level. It's been shown that the majority of patients, no matter their education level, will understand it then."

Zelda fessed up that she was just goading him a bit. "Sorry. Couldn't help it. I love it when you get all red in the face and start to babble. You probably forgot that you've explained that to me before."

Randall's face did feel a bit warm, but he plowed ahead. "You got me. But let me be clearer about what I mean. Part of the reason for KISS is that us eggheads can get our heads so deeply buried in the sands of discovery that we can't see what's in front of us until a non-egghead points out the obvious."

Zelda was tuned in to Randall's frequency. "Yeah, nobody likes sand in their soft-boiled eggs. So is it kind of like the Bible phrase about how the little child will lead them?"

Randall nodded. "Exactly, but not in the way the original passage meant. I remember it from catechism. The Biblical version means that when the Messiah comes, the wild beasts of the world will be so tame that even a little child could lead them through the wild forest. But it's come to mean that sometimes children can see things more clearly than adults, because their brains have not yet been 'adulterated' by distracting outside input. They see things as they are and are not afraid to speak the truth as they see it."

Zelda frowned a bit, then smiled sweetly. "So, now you're saying I'd be the group's little child sponge absorbing whatever wisdom you PCG guys spout?"

Randall wasn't sure if this was another *gotcha* jest, but decided to play it safe. "Not exactly. In this analogy, you'd only be a child in the sense that you are naïve to the material to be investigated. So you would be our reality monitor."

Zelda's smile broadened. "I was just making your chain tauter, but I like your naïve reality monitor explanation. So, you wouldn't object if I decided I wanted to come to a meeting?"

Randall was quick to respond affirmatively. "No objection from me, if you think you're up for it. Obviously, attending the first meeting won't work out without a babysitter, but I'd be delighted to have you debrief me afterwards. That would give you some additional data and time to decide if you want to come to the next meeting."

Randall and Zelda's discussion was suddenly interrupted by Kyle and Addie, who both came bounding like baby kangaroos into the living room.

"Mom, Mom!" Addie's voice pierced the soundscape. "The cake layers are cooled off. It's time for frosting and Kyle's been sneaking licks from the bowl."

Kyle was quick to his defense. "I just took a taste. Time is ticking. Let's get licking!"

Zelda jumped up. "Dad and I were done talking anyhow, weren't we, Randy? Let's make the cake frosty."

The gang scurried into the kitchen. Soon, there was a whirl of sugar, sticky hands and screeching. When the cake was frosted and mixing spoons licked, Zelda sat the kids down at the table for a glass of milk to wash the sweet taste down. Randall joined them with a fresh cup of coffee.

"That was really good chocolate frosting, Mom," mumbled Kyle in between licking his fingers.

"Yeah, Mom. It was super." Addie's chocolate mustache extended to her ears. "I can't wait to taste the cake tomorrow. I bet I get tons of good presents."

Kyle clanged his empty glass on the table. "You always get the best presents. You're a lucky ducky. Quack quack."

Randall pushed Kyle's glass farther away from him. "Alright. Your birthday was not so long ago, and you got lots of best presents, too. Don't start anything you can't finish."

Zelda followed up. "Better listen to your dad. The birthday nerd is watching. He writes down everything he sees in his little notebook and sends his report to us two weeks before your birthday."

Kyle laughed half heartedly. "Ha! There's no such thing as a birthday nerd. Unless you're talking about Dad. Is there?"

Addie, Zelda and Randall kept serious faces.

"You better listen to Mom," said Addie.

Kyle looked nervous. "Is there?! Come on, you guys! Wait, yesterday you said Birthday Bobcat. I was listening!"

Zelda nodded slowly. "While you're listening, here's some news about tomorrow. After Addie's party we're all going to work on the cleanup, including Dad. After that, Dad has a special meeting at a friend's house at 7:00. He'll be having dinner there. I will not be cooking dinner after hostessing the party, so are there two kids who'd like to suffer through a dinner at Big Boy afterwards?"

Kyle saw a chance to gaslight Addie. "Aw, Mom, do we have to?"

Addie was aghast and kicked Kyle under the table. "Kyle! Are you nuts? You can stay at home and eat stale crackers and dried out cheese for dinner, but I'm going to Big Boy's!"

Kyle laughed. "Just kidding . . . just kidding. Why you always gotta be so serial, birthday goil?"

Randall disapproved of the jibe, but had to give Kyle credit for his cool manipulative skills. And his East Coast pronunciation. *Must have picked it up from his father.*

As bedtime approached, the kids requested that Randall answer some questions they had about the Dagobah Yoda story. Randall limited them to one question. They still weren't sure why the Shorts and the Longs fought so much. Randall thought it an opportune time to discuss the importance of good communication. He explained that it wasn't enough to just have the gift of *The Speak*. One also had to have the gift of *The Listen*. He wasn't sure if they got the lesson, because by the time he got to the listening part they were snoring.

It's My Potty

The Saturday birthday party came and went. When it was finally over, Randall slumped into Rex the Wonder Chair and reviewed the event in his mind. He pictured a blender, but house sized, filled with pink crepe paper, ubiquitous glitter, presents, food, drink and little Barbie dolls. When set on puree, the blender had a soundtrack of giggles and screeches. When done, the contents (two exhausted parents and a flock of sticky Barbie dolls) could be poured into a large sundae dish. Add a topping of hyper siblings and you've got an Addie Birthday Party Sundae.

As far as Addie was concerned, the much anticipated party was a success, mostly. She had consumed two helpings of macaroni and cheese with weenies, then chased it with three pieces of double chocolate cake and half a cow of milk. Randall speculated he might need a forklift to manage all the presents and a leaf blower to clean up all the wrapping paper bits, crepe paper, and glitter.

The only hiccup was that her next door friend, Jenny, tried to out-eat Addie. In due course, Jenny felt a gastric volcano about to erupt, ran upstairs to disgorge the yellow lava with chocolate bits, but mostly missed the toilet. She screamed for help from the top of the stairs. Randall was first on the scene, fearing the worst. Jenny, free of her recycling, was already feeling much better, but the bathroom was a disaster. Randall decided to do the cleanup, since he felt he needed the brownie points.

Zelda came upstairs to see what had happened and gagged. "Urgh! Phew! It smells awful up here. Looks like you've got it well in hand, Randy. You go, boy. I have to get back downstairs and mind the store. Oh, by the way, one of our guests dropped a bomb in the powder room and the toilet is clogged."

"Yeah, sure," replied Randall. "My hand is not the only place I've got it. I might be a while. You look green as a cucumber. Better go before I have to clean up after you. And go find me a plunger." Randall flashed on how he never thought his medical scut work training would be so useful at home.

Zelda smiled weakly. "Randy, you're my hero. I owe you one."

Randall looked up with a leer on his face. "Do I get to choose what 'one' is?"

Zelda grimaced a bit. "Umm . . . probably. We'll see later on. This party has me pretty drained already."

As Zelda walked off, Randall muttered to himself. "'We'll see . . . we'll see,' said the blind man. Promises, promises."

Randall could hear the party goers being sent home, then went down to dislodge what seemed to be an outsized poop for a six-year-old.

He wondered how the little party guest delivered it without an episiotomy. When he was done, he went upstairs and showered to get all the ick off. He put on fresh clothes and figured he'd just have time to make it to Joe's house. He realized he hadn't eaten any lunch. Despite having just wrangled the throw up and a poopy potty, he was salivating for a greasy, cheesy pizza. Manly pizza. With beer. Among adults. Who speak in low tones. Surely he wouldn't have to deal with post-party clean up at Joe's house.

To Randall's surprise, when he got downstairs at 6:30, the kitchen and living room were cleared of all evidence that there had been a party. A note on the fridge informed him that Zelda and the kids were off to Big Boy and that they had all worked hard to do the clean up. The note ended with "Now we're even." Randall shook his head and said out loud to the empty kitchen, "Good news-bad news. Just ain't fair."

Randall walked into the dining room. The table was covered with neatly arranged presents ranging from Breyer horse figures to lacy socks. The haul would keep Addie occupied for at least a week, he thought. He hustled to the hallway, put on his coat and hat, then headed off to the PCG meeting.

Egghead Conclave

At 10:00, when Randall returned home from Joe's house, Zelda was sitting at the kitchen table reading the paper. He greeted her, somewhat lamely, because he was exhausted. He felt like he had just emerged from an "Around the World" whirlpool of scientific theory with nowhere to hang his hat. "Hiya sweetcheeks."

Zelda looked up and smiled. "Hey there, dad stud. How was the meeting?"

Randall gave out a loud sigh. "In a word, intense." Milky Way meandered up to Randall and rubbed cat hair on his pants.

Zelda got up and stood in front of him, peering at his head. Milky Way enlarged her circle to include both sets of human legs. "Ah, yes.

Your head is definitely more egg shaped. Careful you don't crack it open on the pillow tonight. Looks like you need a hug."

Randall's shoulders sagged as he reached out for the hug. "Careful. Don't squeeze me too hard or my brain will come out my ears. I'm totally pooped and full of pizza/beer slurry. Can't guarantee sphincter competence."

Zelda laughed. "That's kinda how eggs come out. Yeah, and you were pooped before you left."

Randall chuckled. "Ha ha. Good one. And puked, let's not forget. I've gotta say, you guys did a yeoman's job of clean up while I was occupied mucking the stall. How did you ever get the sprouts to help? And where are they?"

Zelda grinned widely. "Top secret Mom stuff. The minnows are tucked safely in their little beds searching for eyelid leaks. I wanted to save some time to debrief you on the outcome of the PCG whatsis. I know you're probably tired and it's not the treat you were hoping for, but I did save you a piece of birthday cake and I've made fresh coffee. I hope you're not too stuffed with pizza and beer. And egg yolks."

Randall's face went from crestfallen to resigned in five seconds. "Well, okay. I suppose I'm not in the best shape for hay rolling at this time anyhow. Cake, coffee and talking may be all I can handle. Maybe if you give me a raincheck on a hayroll?"

Zelda looked at Randall coyly. "Let me check my schedule." She pretended to look at her appointment calendar. "I can pencil you in for tomorrow if you fully recover. Or I've got January eighth open."

Randall grinned. "Deal on tomorrow! Auction over. I'll take door number one. Now, let's have the consolation treat. I assume Wondercat is upstairs with Kyle. I'm surprised that Milky Way is down here, not shacked up with Addie."

"Randy, I'm shocked, too. It may be that she might like you. Look at that! She's flopped on the floor for a belly rub from you!"

Randall rubbed and the cat purred. It was a soothing moment. "I bet the cats were freaking all afternoon during the girl twerp invasion."

Zelda laughed. "Never saw hide nor hair of cat tails the whole time. Now, you're like a cat tranquilizer."

Randall chuckled. "Look at me. I'm a catatonic."

Zelda sputtered. "Har har. Now, shut up and eat your cake."

While Randall had cake and coffee, Zelda began the debrief. "Alright, now that I've got you settled, it's time to spill. How did the meeting go?"

"What do you want to know first?" asked Randall.

Zelda waved an arm. "Well, tell me about the people. I'm a people person. I know Dan Graham, your Radiation Physicist. I met him and his wife at the department Christmas party. And you said he's a quantum physics nut. You've talked about Joe Shepard, but I've never met him. And the Nun yoga instructor. I'm curious as hell what she's about. Isn't there an adult shrink in the group, too?"

Randall nodded. "Alright then. I'll start with Joe and work through the list. Actually, I'll start with John Bingham, because I know the least about him. He didn't say much at the meeting. All I can tell you is that he looks like the psychiatrist you always see in cartoons. You know, dark curly hair, Van Dyke beard and mustache, horn rimmed glasses, tweed jacket with elbow patches, black tie and loafers. Answers questions with questions. Very tall and walks with a measured gait."

Zelda nodded, fascinated. "Yeah, John's the shrink from the Ziggy cartoons. Sounds boring. Now do Joe."

Randall took a sip of coffee and cleared his throat. "Well, as far as Joe, if you take a good look at me and squint a bit, it's Joe. Looks almost like me. You know, medium height, skinny, bald and glasses. Brown hair. If you can imagine, he's even more soft spoken than me. But smart like me. Maybe smarter. He's a child psychologist, but he's a grown-up. Curious as a cat."

Zelda looked like her cat curiosity was being stirred. "You must make quite a pair."

Randall enjoyed this. "Actually, we do. We've been friends since medical school. Kinda like when someone has a dog, and they start to look like each other? That's me and Joe."

"Oh, so brothers from another mother?"

Randall touched his nose. "Exactly!"

Zelda snickered. "So, which one of you is the dog?"

Randall went dog. "Arf arf. Depends who you ask!"

Zelda loved playing word ping pong with Randall. "Rats, foiled again. Now, the nun, please."

Randall put up a hand. "Alright, alright. Cool your fuel. That would be Ruby Cosgrove. She's a friend of Joe's wife. That's why she was invited to join the group. She's about 40, with blonde hair, natural, I presume. Also on the thin side with suggestions of curves. Clearly in good shape. Very pleasant, well spoken. Great smile. No makeup."

Zelda's eyes widened. "Wow, Randy, for a married man, you noticed a lot. I liked her better as a nun. I'm going to mentally put a habit on her. Now what's her story?" Zelda couldn't contain her curiosity.

Randall hesitated. "Well, I'm just putting pieces together, but she was raised in a strict Catholic family and groomed for nun-hood from an early age. She took her first vows, became a novice and started going to Marquette University. There she hung out with some male students who kept questioning why she wanted to waste her good looks on celibacy. She wore garb that showed she was a novice. You know, not the full habit yet, but the black formless dress and abbreviated head covering. Later, even though she had made the final commitment, those doubts kept bothering her."

Zelda looked intrigued. "So, later she up and quit? Was there a man involved?"

Randall shrugged. "Not sure. Could be. What she said was that she wanted to work directly with people using an energy connection she had discovered within herself. That led to Yoga studies and she became an instructor to exploit that ability. But the religious training was still there and she has always felt her skill at reading people's energy might have a linkage to both teachings. She's very open to demonstrating what she does and possibly learning more about how it might be related to natural physical laws."

Zelda's eyes got even wider. "Gee. Sounds like someone I'd like to meet. Do you guys have any ideas about what she could contribute?"

"Nothing fully formulated yet. But my idea is to devise a way to quantify if and how her energy connections with others affect a physiological outcome. You know, can we measure the impact of her energy interactions with others?" Randall always got excited talking about his developing obsession. His hands mimed what he imagined to be energy moving through ether. To Zelda, it looked like he was kneading bread badly.

Zelda pursed her lips. "Sounds hard. And very interesting. I believe she probably does have an impact on people, but how can we prove that?"

Randall smacked the table with the flat of his hand. "Exactly. None of this is easy. Since this area of study has always seemed rather hinky, there haven't been a lot of serious investigations. Most scientists are afraid that if they seek funding to explore it, they may do harm to their reputations."

Addie padded softly down the stairs, through the hallway and appeared at the kitchen doorway. Randall and Zelda didn't notice her until she spoke out in her high pitched whiny voice. "I can't sleep. My tummy feels bad. Someone is talking too loud down here and banging on the table. And I can't find Milky Way. Why isn't she sleeping with me?"

Zelda got up, went to Addie and picked her up. "I'm sorry you don't feel good. Maybe Daddy should take a look at your tummy."

Randall came over to the pair and gave both a hug. "Sorry I wasn't here when you went to bed. Did you have a nice party?"

Despite her discomfort, Addie managed a half smile. "Yes, Daddy. And then we eated at Big Boy. Guess what? My scarf was still around Big Boy's neck. But I think I scarfed too much at Big Boy's and now I'm kinda sick."

Randall pushed locks of sweaty blond hair out of Addie's eyes. "Do you have to barf?"

Addie looked sideways as if asking her insides if they wanted to go outside. "No. I don't think so. Maybe if you tuck me back in bed with Milky Way I'll fall asleep again. And please stop banging on the table, okay?"

Randall tapped Addie's nose. "I promise, Rosebud. Hey, Zel, could you grab the catster and bring her upstairs? I'll do a Daddy haul of this little pickle."

"I'm not a pickle, Daddy! I'm a little girl."

Randall booped Addie's nose again. "Alright. Then you're my little girl pickle."

Addie giggled and the group climbed the stairs back to Addie's bedroom. Once tucked and catted, Addie drifted off to dreamland. Randall and Zelda made their way back to the kitchen as quietly as possible, but encountered a sleepy-eyed Kyle standing at his bedroom doorway.

Despite their stealth in returning Addie to bed, Kyle had heard them. "What's up with Addie?"

Zelda waved an arm. "It's nothing much. Just an upset tummy from overeating at the party. Nothing for you to worry about. Let's get you back in bed."

Kyle started whining. "But I'm awake now and I'm hungry. I want some ice cream."

Randall put his foot down. "That would be a definite no. Now listen to your mother and toddle off to bed."

"Aww, come on, Dad. It won't take long. Just a small scoop, please?" pleaded Kyle.

Randall stood his ground and just pointed to Kyle's bed. "Not happening. Get it? Not tonight."

Kyle screwed up his face and tried again. "Please, please, pretty please?"

Zelda stepped forward to reinforce Randall. "What part of 'not' do you not understand?"

Kyle made fists and stiffened his arms at his side. "None of your nots."

Randall had had enough. He pointed and shouted. "Manrope, Granny, Hoop and Gordian! Move it, buster!"

Kyle relented and backed up into his room. "What the heck was that, Dad?"

Zelda was just as puzzled. "Yeah, Randy. You lost me."

Randall gave a sinister laugh. "He wasn't listening to regular 'nots' so I thought I'd try some fancy knots."

Zelda was caught out and guffawed. "Randy! I'm a frayed knot! You are too goofy for words."

Randall shrugged. "Well, he's in bed now, isn't he?"

Just as Zelda and Randall were about to go back downstairs, Kyle called from bed. "Now I have to pee. Can I go?"

Randall was disgusted and shook his head. "You monitor the bathroom tour. I'm going downstairs for something to drink. I'm on my last neuron."

In the kitchen, Randall decided against more coffee to avoid insomnia. He poured himself some cranberry juice and sat down at the kitchen table. Zelda made it downstairs to the kitchen a bit later. She brewed herself some chamomile tea and joined him at the table.

IONS

Randall took two swallows of juice and put the glass on the table. "Now, where were we before the Addie/Kyle intermission?"

Zelda looked thoughtful and squinted, trying to recall. "Hmm, oh, yeah. One of the topics was the difficulty of doing true science proofs of mental connections to the physical world. You know, negative reputation and career effects because of deeply embedded public skepticism."

Randall nodded, impressed Zelda had retained the complex issue. "Right. That was it. And you were suggesting there must be some completed studies by now, despite those risks."

Zelda nodded and shrugged. "I'm just speculating as a lay person here, but it's my impression that most friends and family I talk to are comfortable enough to share stories about strange communication experiences they've had. So, we can't be the first to ever wonder about it. There must be valid studies of telepathy or clairvoyance and stuff like that."

Randall raised his eyebrows. "You're probably right about that. I'll bet a lot of potential investigators got no traction to support that sort of inquiry. Bias exists everywhere. Documentation that our minds can communicate at a distance or affect distant objects would fly in the face of many religious beliefs and much of standard science."

Zelda agreed. "I bet it wouldn't take much ridicule to destroy a scientist's career. Once they'd get labeled as 'goofnut charlatans' that would probably scotch future research grants. Is there any legitimate research you know of?"

Randall grimaced. "It's not exactly my study area, so far, but I have heard of one interesting observation. Cell biologists have noted that the more a culture is observed the faster it grows."

"That's weird." Zelda furrowed her eyebrows. "Is that like talking to your plants when you water them and then they grow better? You know, positive interaction helps plants grow."

Randall squinted. "I suppose it could be. But the biologists aren't sweet-talking the microbes. They're just looking at them through a microscope. Oh, and I also recall something about intercessory prayer."

"What's that?" asked Zelda. "Another Catholic ritual?"

Randall shook his head. "Sounds like it could be, but it's when a large group prays for a person to be healed. They may or may not know the person being prayed for. But the concept is that the more prayer messages God gets about that person, the greater the chance of healing."

Zelda hooted. "Sounds bogus to me. Quantity not quality counts?"

"That was kind of my initial assessment," said Randall. "Later, I found a large national study testing intercessory prayer for advanced breast cancer. The prayed-for group did significantly better than the control group, which wasn't prayed for. The two groups were otherwise matched by type and stage of disease. Oh, and the praying folks did not even know the names of those in the prayed-for group."

Zelda's eyes went wide. "Zowie. Either God was involved in the study or there was some kind of mental influence at a distance."

Randall nodded. "It is an eye opener, but there was a lot of naysaying about the results. Oh, and another study group I read about was founded by the astronaut Edgar Mitchell."

Zelda looked out the window. "Edgar Mitchell? Wasn't he on an Apollo mission, around 1970 or 1971? He walked on the moon, didn't he?"

"Yeah, that's the one," said Randall. "He was the sixth moon walker. When he was journeying back to earth in the space module, he got a pretty long look at the earth from a distance. He later said he experienced an overwhelming sense of connectedness with all the living beings on the planet."

Zelda looked somewhat dubious. "So? I'm pretty sure anyone would feel kind of whacked out seeing the earth approaching again after flying in a tin can to the moon and back. When you go up in a rocket you must have to accept that you could be on a suicide mission. I'd be pretty relieved to be floating back to earth."

Randall nodded his agreement. "True enough! You could say he was a bit stressed out. Anyway, he felt he'd had a transformative experience and decided he would devote the rest of his life to the study of consciousness and connectedness."

Zelda laughed. "I can see it now. They're pulling him out of the ocean and he goes: 'Oh, shit! I made it. I promised God I'd do this big ass consciousness study. Now I'll really have to do it or the Big Man will be forwarding my mail to the hot sweaty area.'"

Randall laughed back. "That's quite an image. Whether or not his ultimate motivation was fear of God, he did go on to form an investigative study group, ultimately named the Institute of Noetic Sciences or IONS just a few years ago in '73."

"Sounds like he became a free radical," joked Zelda.

Randall had to laugh despite himself. *Where had she come up with that?* "Indeed. Very droll. So, you did learn something in high school chemistry."

Zelda shook her copper curls, proud to have made an impression. "It's about all I remember. So, how do you know all this stuff about Mitchell and IONS? One of your journals or something? It's not like there is some grand information database in the sky or in the Amazon. And what does noetic sciences mean?"

Randall was digging the conversation, and glad it was with his wife. "Good questions! Noetic science means the study of intellectual and spiritual capabilities. Remember when our little *fambly* went to the Kennedy Space Center in '75?"

"How could I forget the trip?" said Zelda. "It was April and we drove through snow until we got to Gainesville. The trip was supposed to be just a fun excursion to Dizzy World. Then you insisted that, as long as we were that far and had blazed a trail through a blizzard for two days, we might as well do the Spacey Center."

Randall smiled broadly. "And a good decision it was. Kyle talked more about the rockets than 'It's a Small World.' He's still got the model rocket we bought. Anyway, after the tour, while I was waiting for you to come back from the 'Ladies,' I cruised to the bookshop and loaded up on brochures. I didn't have time to read them all, so I packed them away in my luggage. I found them again the other day looking for something else. One of them was about IONS and Mitchell."

Zelda looked surprised. "Really! That's an odd serendipity. What's it say?"

Randall pulled the dog-eared brochure out of his back pocket. "Glad you asked. I have it right here. Let me read you a quote from Mitchell: 'I realized that the story of ourselves as told by science—our cosmology, our religion—was incomplete and likely flawed. I recognized that the Newtonian idea of separate, independent, discrete things in the universe wasn't a fully accurate description. What was needed was a new story of who we are and what we are capable of becoming.'"

Zelda was confused by Mitchell's odd rhetoric. "Is there more?"

Randall nodded. "If I may read further from the brochure: 'Noetic studies explore how beliefs, thoughts, and intentions affect the physical world.'"

Zelda looked up at the ceiling. "That makes it a bit clearer. What's your translation?"

Randall nodded. "Yeah, I had to read it over several times before I fully grasped the meaning. I think what Mitchell means is that religion and science have been looking for the basic explanation for 'everything' from different perspectives for centuries. That same basis may ultimately be that all things are connected by their very nature. Namely, our subatomic resonance of matter and energy. Religion says man cannot understand that because it was created by a super being. Science has said that man cannot understand it yet, but will be able to with further investigation and no super being is needed."

Zelda shook her head. "Randy! You're talking in code again, but I think I get your drift. Check this out. Here's my simpler Zeldagram. Everything, including animals, plants, rocks, etc., are made of the same stuff, so all are interconnected. If that's true, then intercommunication is a logical probability. If that's true, there's no reason why it can't be proven."

Randall high-fived Zelda. "Couldn't have said it better, my red-headed genius."

Zelda's blush added to her appeal. "Genius? You never called me that before!"

Randall added a shovelful to the pile. "I may not have said it before, but I didn't just marry you for your beauty." He winked at her.

"Now you're gilding the lily," admonished Zelda. "Flattery will not . . . might not . . . get you anywhere. Before you get yourself further out on a limb, let's get back to IONS. If they've been studying this stuff for, what, five years or so, have they gotten any positive results to prove the theory?"

Randall shook his head. "Don't know. All I've got is the brochure. Need to do more research. But I'm betting they have produced some data. Question is where to find it. If it's published, it's not in any journals I read. Probably would be in Psychology type publications. Maybe there's some that cover Parapsychology. I'll have to check with the hospital librarian."

Zelda's eyebrows went up. "Parent Psychology? I know there's Child Psychology, but parent?"

Randall stifled a laugh. "Close but no banana. It's 'para,' like in the word paranormal. As in not quite proven or provable. It studies mental phenomena that are excluded from or inexplicable by orthodox scientific psychology. If you can even consider psychology science. It includes stuff like hypnosis, telepathy, psychokinesis, remote viewing and a host of others that go down a continuum of decreasing likelihood."

Zelda shook her head again, as if in despair. "There you go again; *'bigwordorama.'* I know what some of those are, like hypnosis and telepathy. But does continuum mean the way your *verborrhea* goes on and on?"

Randall smiled somewhat enigmatically. "Oh, come on, my stable genius. You should know continuum. It's like a spectrum. Like white at one end and black at the other with a multitude of gray shades in between. Or like the color spectrum you work with as an artist. Even though there are two finite ends of the black to white spectrum, there are an infinite number of shades in between."

"Right!" Zelda lit up. "And an infinite number of color shades in the visible spectrum of light. Like when you try to pick from the hardware store paint color palette. It takes forever and the shade you pick never looks the same on the wall. And looks different on many walls."

Randall chuckled. "Right! Close enough! As far as the other parapsychology types, telekinesis means your mind is able to influence another physical system without physical interaction, like moving a box or bending a spoon by thinking it. Remember Uri Geller?"

Zelda nodded. "Yep, I remember. He was on the Johnny Carson show three or four years ago. Carson sort of debunked his ability, but Gellar didn't go away. I think people needed to believe he could bend spoons. After that he became even more popular."

Randall felt enthused. "You've nailed the crux of the problem! If people can believe what's patently false, it's just as easy to disbelieve or distrust what's true. So, it will take rigorous science to be convincing. Even then, there are a growing number of science deniers who'd rather quote fake authority than a controlled trial."

Zelda mused. "Hmm.... The whole thing is like a quadruple-edged sword. Okay, so we've got telepathy and telekinesis...."

Randall couldn't help interrupting. "But you can't *tellawoman.* Gotta make it seem like it's her own idea."

Zelda ignored him. "...and the fluid nature of color and light...so, what's remote viewing?"

Randall shook his head. "Not totally clear on that one." He pursed his lips. "But I think it involves seeing images at a distance."

"That would be spooky," murmured Zelda.

Randall nodded his agreement. "So is quantum physics, according to Einstein. Verily, the truth is out there. But back to remote viewing. I vaguely recall this from what little psych I had in med school." He raised his eyebrows. "I think it involves being able to view complex structures from a distance. The government was covertly studying remote viewing as a way to spy on Russian military installations using gifted 'remote viewers.'"

Zelda's jaw dropped a bit. "Did it work?"

Randall retracted the corner of his mouth. "Some say so. But Uncle Sam never formally acknowledged it. Why would he? It would be top-secret and doing a big reveal would be counterproductive."

"True. . . . what about stuff like séances, communication with the dead, and ghosts?" Zelda took a deep breath.

Randall paused for a long moment, considering. "I'm sure they are all in the continuum, too, in varying degrees of likelihood, along with psychic healing. To me, the common denominator is some sort of collective consciousness between everything that is. Maybe that's why we can feel so connected to the land, plants and animals. Also, why, when there is war, hunger, pain and suffering in the world, we feel it deep in our marrow? Or whatever organ we attribute our feelings to."

Zelda wrapped her arms around her belly. "That's so true. My body is like one big radar dish." She shook a bit, as if shaking snow off her shoulders. "You mentioned healing, Randy. You always talk about how you believe being positive and encouraging to your patients helps them heal. If that's true, either you have a special gift or we all do if we are all linked. Which reminds me . . . remember when we read the book *Rolling Thunder* a few years ago? That guy was a Native American healer. I think Cherokee. He was like all into connections with nature."

Randall lit up, remembering the book. "That's right! How could I forget? He always taught that he was connected to nature or 'the spirit of the earth.' He claimed he was capable of telekinesis and telepathy.

Plus, he did some amazing feats of healing while being observed by traditional doctors and scientists. He claimed he could make rain, as well. Hence, the name Rolling Thunder."

Zelda recalled some more details. "I think his 'American' name was Pope, or something like that, and he worked as a railroad brakeman in Nevada. Randy, we're going to have to read that book again."

Randall frowned. "Is that the royal we?"

Zelda started dagger eyes. "Come on. Don't get huffy about it. You've got me interested. Now we're both interested in this stuff. We should both review the book. What else do you remember from it?"

Randall wanted to avoid daggers so he grabbed his chin in thought. The chin grab seemed to reach a memory. "Yeah . . . I remember a story about Mr. Thunder. His teachings attracted a lot of hippie types and a large group of them invited him to give a talk. He was an hour late, but the crowd was mellow and patient. Early or late, they knew his wisdom would be theirs. They all applauded when he arrived holding a chicken. He went to the stage microphone, scratched the chicken's neck and let out a loud, sustained fart. I mean Rolling Thunder, not the chicken. At first, the group didn't know what to make of it. Then, deadpan, he explained 'You have to let it out or it will make you sick. That's the way things go, except when they don't.'"

Zelda laughed herself silly. "That's one attention-getting intro! Rolling Thunder is my kind of guy. I'd love to do that in church. You know, go up to the pulpit to read the gospel for the day and start by letting one rip. The timing would be tough, but I've got good control."

Randall caught the laughing bug. "That's just precious. You've got good tone too. Must be your *om-butt-chure.* Or how 'bout if I would do that to start my paper presentation in front of 500 oncologists at our national meeting?"

Zelda added on. "You could say it's a new form of cancer fighting laughing gas."

That set off another giggle jag. When the two caught their breath again, Randall sighed. "Whooee, how's that for a scientific revolution?

But, seriously folks. I agree we should refresh our recall of Cherokee lore. So, everybody, meet Don and Donna Quixote. We're off to joust at parapsychological windmills. What could go wrong?"

"Where do we go from here, bossman?" asked Zelda.

Randall pointed to the sky. "Into space—into space, my dear."

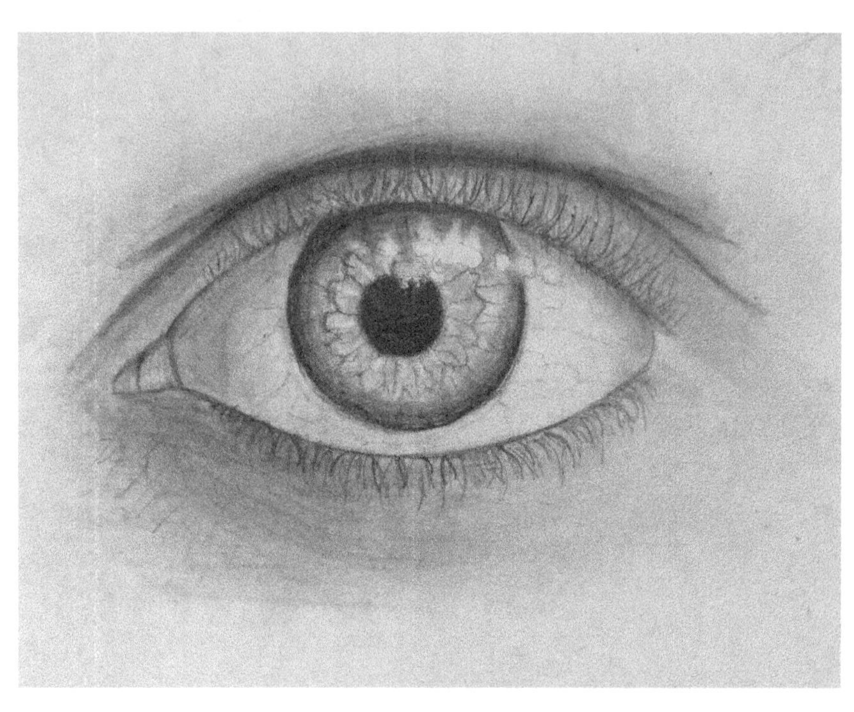

CHAPTER 8

MONDAY, MONDAY

"You don't need something more to get something more."

—Murray Gell-Man

GIBLETS

Sam Gibney waited impatiently in the Radiation Oncology hallway. Sam was too weak to walk and had been brought down on a gurney for his radiation treatment by the volunteer escort, Ira. Afterwards, Melinda rolled him out and parked the gurney in the hall. She paged Ira to return Sam to his ward, where the nurses had decided that Sam was nuttier than George Washington Carver's lunchbox. Ten minutes passed and Ira hadn't yet appeared. Sam felt helpless and frustrated so his 'nuttier' kicked in.

Viewed from the far end of the hallway, all one could see was Sam's bald noggin as if it were perched alone on top of the gurney. It looked like a ripe melon in the supermarket produce section. He raised himself up on his elbows and swiveled his head, looking for Ira. No results. His jowls vibrated as he shouted his dissatisfaction.

Sam was very *foodivated.* "Hey, Melinda, where'd you go? And where's that *dadblasted* Ira. If I don't get back to my room *pronto,* I'm gonna miss my *goldanged* lunch. I'm sick enough already. You want me to starve? Where'd you disappear to, you fluff brain?"

Ira materialized next to Sam's gurney like a genie out of a bottle. Sam was startled and let out a gasp. "*Consarn* it, you cupcake. Near gimmee a heart stroke. I swear, no respect for veterans these days. We put our life on the line, and a little limey libnut like you jumps on me like Mr. Charlie. No respect!" Spittle dribbled off his chin.

Ira extended to his full five feet, seven inches. "Well, as an honorable serviceman, you should also know how to respect us volunteers who give their time and energy to take care of vets like you. Don't you ever call Melinda a bad name again, or I'll leave you in a corner somewhere so you miss dinner too." Ira was rather menacing, but then gave Sam a tissue.

Now somewhat ashamed, Sam took the tissue and wiped his chin. He stuttered a bit and tried to make things right. "Sure, sure. No offense. I didn't mean nuthin' personal by it. You understand? I just need my food."

Ira gave Sam a crooked smile. "Sorry you had to wait. The elevator was slow as a possum in the sunshine. Now I'm here." Ira's words were kind, but his tone said something else. "I just have to leave Melinda a note that I've taken you upstairs. I'm sure you wouldn't mind waiting a few more seconds."

Sam took on a more placating approach. "No problem, Buddy. Do what ya gotta do."

Ira left a sticky note on the treatment console, then wheeled Sam's gurney to the elevator bank. The hall was left unoccupied, except for a lone patient waiting for his treatment. He wore a green striped VA hospital gown and was slumped in a chair sawing logs.

Sam couldn't help himself. He had to give Ira one more jibe. "Hey, man, if you don't mind me asking, what keeps your combover in place? Chewing gum or hair spray? I could never keep mine from blowin' in the wind, so I just shaved it off."

"I'll never tell," said Ira as the doors closed and the elevator headed for the eighth floor.

Doris searched the department for Randall carrying a pink phone memo slip.

"Haven't seen him," said Melinda at the treatment console.

Doris muttered a polite oath. "Where on God's green earth did he go? I just saw him in his office. Disappeared like a little boy at bathtime!"

Grace was standing nearby and grunted a reply. "Try the bathroom. I bet he's 'meditating.' Just shove the note under the stall door. Don't worry, we do it all the time."

Going into the men's lavatory was not the option Doris was expecting. She felt anticipatory embarrassment and grimaced. For a moment she was tempted to send Grace to do the task, but she and the crew were busy with treatments. Doris pumped up her courage, inflated her chest, and murmured to herself. "Tits up, Doris. It's like milking the mean mama cows. Show 'em you got more moxy and don't let anyone get in your way!" She headed to the men's. After all, Dr. Shepard had said it was important.

At the entrance to the restroom, Doris pushed the panel switch that opened the sliding door. She hoped only Randall was inside, but found a veteran patient in green striped PJs standing at the urinal dispensing used coffee. He wasn't phased by the interruption and his stream did not hesitate. Doris excused herself anyhow and spied Randall's familiar salt-stained loafers inside the stall with his pants around them. She was about to shove the pink slip under the door when she noticed the floor at his feet was quite wet. She jingled her necklace, wondering what to do.

Randall saw sensible brown flats from underneath the stall door. "Doris? Is that you? What are you doing in here?"

Doris was rattled. "Yeah. It's me. Sorry to bother you while you're.... Grace said it would be alright to come in the men's. You just had a call from Dr. Shepard. He said it was important and if you called back in two shakes he'd still be available."

Randall was annoyed. He'd told the techs they could check the can for him if it was a patient-related urgent issue, but this did not qualify.

He hated that Doris could see him in such an unflattering, er, posture. "Grace authorized this visit and you listened to her?"

Doris felt herself getting flushed. "When you put it that way, it doesn't sound so good. But, real soon you're gonna be glad I came in. If you look down at the floor, it's very wet and, well, and I think your pants are in the puddle soakin' it up like bread and gravy."

"What!?" Randall looked down and found her assessment to be quite accurate. He hadn't even noticed that his pants had gone swimming. "Oh . . . my . . . God. You're right. Damn, even my wallet is wet. Quick, Doris, get some paper towels and pass them to me under the door. Maybe I can soak some of this up. VA single ply sandpaper won't do the job."

"Sure thing, Dr. B. Quicker than two shakes of a . . ." Doris remembered where she was and blushed. ". . . . Nevermind." She found the paper towel dispenser mounted on the wall by the sink and tore off several sections. After some contortions, Randall got most of the water cleaned off the floor.

Doris regained her composure. "Just wonderin', Dr. B, is it water? Or did somebody . . . have bad aim?"

Randall smelled one of the wet paper towels and concluded it was probably snow melt. "Pretty sure it's just water from someone's boots or shoes. But it could be a cocktail. Now, my problem is soaked pants."

"Ew!" Doris had an idea. "I could give you some more dry paper towels and you could stuff them down your pant legs to absorb the water. Body heat should dry everything . . . eventually. Even the swamp turns pasture sometimes."

Randall scoffed a bit and realized that, short of a change of pants, there was no viable alternative. "Oh, alright, but I may need your help with pants stuffing. Most of the wetness is in the back. You up for that?"

Doris smiled, knowing Randall couldn't see her face. "My stars! Of all the sacrifices I make for you, this will not be the biggest. Pull up your pants, but leave them unzipped so I have room to get the towels down your backside. You want to come out here or have me come in there?"

Randall hesitated a moment. "Er . . . I don't think the stall will accommodate two. I'll pull my pants up and back out. My white coat is hanging on the door hook, so it's dry."

Doris couldn't help but laugh when the door opened and Randall emerged backward. That annoyed Randall. "What's so funny? You've seen me from behind before."

Doris laughed again. "Well, your pants are as clingy as a babe on the teet. I've never seen all the contours so well."

Randall laughed back despite himself. "All right. Just ogle quickly, my butt is getting cold."

Doris pulled Randall's pants away from his back and managed to get several layers of paper towels positioned between wet pant legs and Randall's posterior anatomy. One veteran came in to pee when Doris had her hand and arm down Randall's pant leg to his knee, but he had no comment. Doris freaked out and Randall didn't help her much when he said: "Oh, right there! That's the spot. You really know how to stuff me."

Doris spanked him one and pulled his pants up a little too forcefully. "Watch out, Dr. B. I know where you sit and where you set your coffee. Now get your behind back to your office so we can fine tune this setup. If anybody figures out your pants are soaked, the news will spread and the insufferable ribbin' will commence." Doris tried to look angry, but her barely suppressed giggles gave her away.

Randall donned his dry lab coat, and whispered thanks to the overhydrated pants gods that it covered the offended areas. Job done, Randall and Doris walked back to the department. Rather, Randall sort of walked stiff-legged with all the paper towels in his pants and hoped none of them would emerge from the bottom while he walked. Doris thought he looked rather like a scarecrow.

When Randall got back to his office, Doris asked if she should put the call through to Dr. Shepard.

Randall had almost forgotten about the call. "Sure, go ahead. I hope you can still reach him. I'll just be standing here next to my desk looking at reports. I may have to wait a while to sit down."

Doris placed the call successfully and transferred it to Randall.

Shepard greeted Randall. "Glad you got back to me. I was about to leave for the hospital. How are you doing today, big guy?"

"Pants are a bit wet, but otherwise well," Randall summarized.

Shepard paused briefly. "Interesting greeting. Gotta love the midwest. I'm hoping it was from walking in the slushy snow and not a case of incontinence."

"We *are* on the mainland!" Randall laughed. "Geez, I'm not so old I have to worry about my bladder sphincter yet. It was due to slushy snow, in a manner of speaking. Best to skip the embarrassing explanation. Besides, it sounds like you need to make this call short."

Shepard cleared his throat. "Yeah, I do. I just wanted to see if we could meet at Miss Katie's Diner for lunch soon to discuss the next meeting of the PCG. I've been mulling over the discussion that took place on Saturday night and want to get your take on things so we can plan the next meeting."

Randall had been thinking about the meeting, as well. "That Yoga nun was something else . . . and smart, too."

Joe laughed. "I agree. But that's not among the topics we need to discuss. Better you just dream about her on your own."

Randall felt a bit foolish. "Yeah, yeah . . . just kidding. I've been thinking we ought to debrief together. Great minds and all that."

Shepard couldn't help but interrupt. "I'm not taking off my shorts for you!"

Randall laughed, appreciating the comic relief. "Let's see, this is Monday. Let me check with Doris about my schedule. What day this week is best for you?"

"Wednesday looks good for me," said Shepard.

Randall put down the phone and went to have Doris look at the appointment book. She thought she could probably free him up from 11:30 to 1:30 on Wednesday, unless the unexpected happened. So, Randall confirmed the date with Joe, who made Randall promise to tell the "wet pants" story at their lunch.

Doris, still chuckling, came into Randall's office with the chart for his 10:00 AM consult. "How's the pants dryin' workin'?"

Randall rolled his eyes. "Well, my legs aren't cold anymore, so I think the process is working. No whiffs of ammonia, so I think it was mostly snow melt."

"That's good," said Doris. "The water might have had salt dissolved in it, though. Watch out for white powdery stains on those expensive wool slacks of yours. Wet wool does kind of smell doggy, so don't be alarmed if your legs start barkin.'"

Randall put a hand on Doris's arm and whispered, though no one else was in ear shot. "If you mention a word of this to the girls. . . ."

Doris nodded and made a lip zipping motion. Randall thought the look on her face was slightly devilish.

That's unique

Randall should have been reviewing the medical records for his next consultation. Instead, his thoughts kept returning to the life decisions assignment he'd been given by Dr. Hoffman. It was due in just two days and had proven more difficult than expected. He wrote down a few notes listing landmark life events so he'd have a guide to follow when he presented. The more he tried to make sense of the path he had taken to Radiation Oncology, the more he realized how big a role chance had played. It seemed as though he hadn't really made any decisions at all along the way. It was more like a natural evolution, albeit an improbable one. He decided that was the answer. Just keep it simple and short. When he tried his long explanations, the listener often wound up dozing off.

Melinda strode into his office and broke his concentration. "Dr. B? I've got Mr. Claybourne and his girlfriend in the exam room. All his vitals are normal. Poor man, he's so young to have cancer. He's scared silly."

Randall was glad for the interruption. He took it as a sign that his decision had been approved. He moved the chart over to his right to hide the notes he'd been taking. "Alright, thanks. I was just about done reviewing the records. Let's go in the room together. You can introduce me."

Randall picked up the chart to follow Melinda to the exam room. She hesitated and pointed to the notes he covered up. "Don't you want to take those chart notes with you?"

Somewhat embarrassed, Randall picked up his assignment notes, folded the paper in half and shoved it into his coat pocket. "Oh, it's not chart notes. Just a boring homework assignment." His voice came out pitched a bit higher than usual. "It's tougher than I thought. I'd like to say my dog ate it, but my dog is dead."

"Is it a 'What I did on my summer vacation' kind of thing?" asked Melinda.

Randall nodded. "Sort of."

"If you ever need any help with your homework, I'm available." Melinda grinned slyly. Randall wondered how much she had seen. He chastised himself for doing his personal business at work.

Mr. Claybourne was a 40-year-old man who'd had his right testicle removed as primary treatment for a seminoma. There was a high likelihood of spread to regional lymph nodes not easily removed surgically. Randall was evaluating him for adjuvant radiation to prevent a nodal recurrence. Both Claybourne and his girlfriend were blonde and had ponytails. He was dressed casually in jeans and a snap-up western shirt. He wore well-worn tooled leather cowboy boots and emitted a hint of horse scent. She also wore boots, shiny green pants, a red western shirt and a black leather vest. He was quite handsome in a chiseled kind of way while she was lanky and well-muscled. Randall introduced himself, shook hands with the two and sat down.

Before Randall could start the interview, Mr. Claybourne started talking. "Just so you know, doc, Liz and I ain't married but we might's well be. You can say anything about me in front of her. She's smarter than me, so that's why I brung her. And, please, just call me Luke."

"No problem, Luke," said Randall. "I'm always happy to have wives or even loved ones in on these conclaves. It's best to have two people listen to the explanations of what we do, so there's a better chance of remembering it all. You sure picked a girl who's a flashy dresser."

Luke gave a wry smile and nodded. "Damn straight, Doc. You could even say she's unique. Every day she wears a different outfit."

Luke's remark reminded Randall of a joke Kyle had told him at dinner the previous night and he couldn't resist telling it himself. "Say, that reminds me of a two part riddle. Want to hear it?"

Luke held up pistol fingers. "Shoot!"

Randall rolled his stool to face them both. "How do you catch a unique rabbit?"

"Unique up on it," chimed Liz.

Randall was somewhat amazed Liz knew the answer. "That's right!" Undaunted, he asked the second part. "How do you catch a tame rabbit?"

Liz did not hesitate. "Tame way."

Surprised, Randall rolled his stool backwards. "How in the world do you know that riddle? I just heard it and that's the first time I've used it."

Liz stood up from her chair and walked up to Randall. She turned around with her back to him and asked him to raise her ponytail.

Randall looked unsure. "Last time I touched a girl's ponytail, I was in grade school and I got kicked out of class for it. Luke isn't going to hit me, is he?"

Luke smiled broadly. "Go ahead. I promise I won't hurt you."

Tentatively, Randall lifted the long ponytail and there, tattooed in block letters on the back of Liz's neck, was the word UNIQUE. "Jumping Jehosaphat!" exclaimed Randall. "I am hoisted on my own petard. You are certainly highly qualified to know that riddle. You have to tell me the story behind that tattoo."

Liz explained that she had started tending bar at a western themed saloon several years prior. With the encouragement of her boss, she began wearing colorful combinations of clothing to attract the patrons' attention. New customers would order a drink and often remark that her manner of dress was rather unique. That gave her the idea for the neck tattoo so she could do a big reveal whenever she got the unique remark. It also resulted in big tips.

Randall loved the story. It was one for his repertoire. "You know, the past few days I've been pondering the difference between improbable and impossible. This coincidence definitely qualifies as the former. I dare anyone to calculate the odds that I would tell that riddle to you two the first time I told it?"

"14,313 to 1," responded Liz.

Randall guffawed again. "I think it's time to start my interview before I get in any deeper." The three broke out in laughter.

There was a loud knocking on the exam room door. Randall excused himself and got up to find Grace standing there.

Grace looked puzzled and annoyed. "What's with all the laughing in there? Aren't you supposed to be working? I need you for a setup check."

The remark made Randall want to respond in kind, but he demurred. No point in making a scene in front of the Claybournes. "Not to worry. We're all fine in here. Work is happening. Lead on, Grace. I'll be right behind. Back in a jiffy, folks." Randall decided to take his good mood with him. He wasn't about to let Grace rain on his parade. That would give her too much satisfaction.

Grace spun on her heel and lumbered down the hall with Randall close behind. Randall approved the setup and returned to the exam room. Before he could say anything, Liz had a question. "Did you get a citation from the laughter police?"

Randall laughed. "Yes, I did, but I tore it up. Let her try to collect the fine." He completed the consultation and recommended fairly low dose nodal irradiation. He explained there would be very few side effects and an excellent chance of cure. Doris set up a date for simulation and treatment planning. Luke and Liz left in a sparkle of shiny clothes.

DEATH BY COP

Randall returned to his office to dictate Mr. Claybourne's consult and found Doris about to put a pink telephone note on his desk. "What's up, Doris? Is there something I need to deal with right away?"

Doris had a look of worry on her face. "I think so. It was Mrs. Franken. She just called to tell us her husband died over the weekend. Bless his soul. She wanted to talk to you about it. She sounded as sad as a kitten in a rainstorm."

Randall was surprised. "What? Our Mr. Franken? The Madison fireman I just gave a treatment break?"

"The very one," said Doris.

Randall's heart began to pound and he felt his bowels grumble. Sweat broke out on his forehead. Franken hadn't been doing that badly. It didn't make sense. He hurried to dial the number on the note. The phone was picked up after one ring.

"Hello," said a female voice. "Beth Franken here. Is this Dr. Biedermeier?"

"Yes, ma'am. I'm returning your call." Randall hoped his voice didn't betray his anxiety.

Mrs. Franken sounded quite subdued. "Good . . . thank you for calling back so quickly."

Randall was worried she had called to second guess her husband's treatment. Perhaps there had been a complication he'd missed. Was her lawyer calling next? "Doris just told me your husband has died. Excuse me if I am confused. Did his condition get worse after I gave him the treatment break?"

Mrs. Franken choked back a sob. "Not in the way you mean. When we got back home after you'd given him the break, Frank kept saying that you'd probably given up on curing him. I told him that you'd said nothing of the sort, but he just wouldn't hear anything different. Then, Saturday night, after dinner, he just walked out in the backyard with his Vietnam service revolver and shot himself in the head."

Randall gasped. "Oh, my God!"

Mrs. Franken paused to blow her nose. "I didn't hear the shot because I was in the shower. But my 13-year-old son, Paulie, heard it from his bedroom and ran outside. He found Frank's body."

"That's awful," murmured Randall.

Mrs. Franken took a moment to continue. "Paulie pounded on the bathroom door until I got out of the shower. Very calmly, he described finding Frank dead on the lawn with a large pool of blood under his head. I was so shocked I almost ran outside naked before taking time to put on a robe."

Randall almost had to laugh at the depiction. He chastened himself for having a morbid sense of humor. "I can understand your panic."

Mrs. Franken made a little giggle. Now Randall didn't feel so bad. "Yeah. But I must have looked like such a goof to my son. Then, I noticed Paulie had one of my old perfume vials hanging by a gold chain around his neck. The vial was filled with blood. That almost knocked the wind out of me."

Randall winced. "Blood in the vial?"

"You've got it," said Mrs. Franken. "After Paulie found Frank's body, he ran to my bedroom, and emptied the perfume into the kitchen sink. He fitted it with one of my gold chains and went back outside. He scooped blood from the head wound into the vial, then hung the make-shift necklace around his neck."

Randall forgot his sense of tact. "Whatever for?"

She continued. "He said it was so his father's blood could be close to his heart forever. I was so shocked that I couldn't object. He led me outside to the body and we just stood there looking for a long time. It just . . . just didn't seem real."

Randall suddenly felt responsible for the tragedy. "I–I should have been more positive with him when I gave him the break. I must have given him the impression things were hopeless. I—I. . . ."

Mrs. Franken interrupted. "Nonsense, doctor. I was there when you explained the treatment break and heard everything you said. You weren't at all discouraging. That's why I called you. I was afraid you'd hear my husband had committed suicide and think it was your fault."

Randall couldn't believe that Mrs. Franken had called out of concern for him, despite the recent death of her husband. His throat clutched up and he found it hard to speak. What he came up with sounded lame to him. "Yes, Mrs. Franken. It's my job to present things in a way that the patient remains hopeful."

"Please, doctor," she said calmly. "Don't take the blame for Frank's suicide. It wasn't unexpected. Frank is a Vietnam vet. He had long-standing PTSD and threatened suicide multiple times in the past over at least ten years. He had three previous failed attempts. This time he didn't fail. It's been like waiting for the proverbial other shoe to drop for years. In a way, I'm relieved. I can finally stop worrying about it. I guess that sounds morbid, but. . . ."

Randall had to clear his throat before he could speak. "I guess I understand, but somehow I still feel partly responsible. I knew he had PTSD and had tried suicide in the past. I should have been more . . . something!"

Mrs. Franken let out a long breath. "Well, you shouldn't keep feeling that way, otherwise this call would be for nothing. When I first met you, I wasn't sure what to think. At first, you do come across as pretty serious and intimidating. Yet, after I saw how up front and kind you were with Frank, I could see you actually cared. All weekend I've been thinking that I have to call and make sure you don't blame yourself. I'd hate if you felt badly enough about his death, that it might negatively affect the other patients you're treating."

Randall tried to sound more upbeat. "You've got a deal. I will try not to feel responsible. To seal the deal, let's take a moment of silence for us both to feel bad and sad."

Mrs. Franken agreed and the two were quiet for half a minute before Randall changed directions. "We've taken care of my feelings. Let's shift the focus to you and your son. How are you both taking it all in?"

She sounded resigned and relieved. "I'm doing the best I can and teenagers are just weird. If blood tokens are what Paulie needs to cope, so be it. Who am I to judge?"

"In a way, you've been grieving for a while already. What about the arrangements?" asked Randall. "There must be a lot to deal with."

She responded with a brighter tone. "That's the surprising thing. Frank was well-loved by his fellow firemen and had a wide circle of friends. The fire department has stepped in and taken over everything. They've arranged a big parade to honor him with a big write up in the newspaper. They expect a full house at the memorial service."

Randall responded with self-deprecation. "Wow! That's way more than I'll ever get. Please, send me a copy of the article. Oh, and call me back in a few weeks to let me know how you're doing."

Mrs. Franken laughed at Randall's remark. "I doubt that's true. No need to be so humble. Although, I agree, you might not get a parade. Just kidding. If Frank is looking down from above, I'm sure the sight of all the firemen in dress uniforms will be a beautiful sight to him."

Randall was pleased to hear laughter and kidding. Perhaps the storm clouds were parting. "You are probably right about the parade. That's just not the professional way. We are charged with remaining stoic through good and bad."

"Pish posh," remarked Mrs. Franken. "That is definitely not mandatory. You're proof of that."

Randall wasn't sure what to say next. Some conversations are hard to end without made up excuses. "Well, it seems I am wanted for many tasks. I must ring off. This was horrible news, but your presentation was wonderful. Please take very good care. I'll inform the rest of my staff and we will have a moment of silence for Frank at our morning chart review. You are a remarkable woman. He was a lucky man to have had you for a wife. I'll talk to you soon and look forward to reading about the big do in the paper."

Mrs. Franken had to choke back another sob. "Th . . . thank you for the good wishes, doctor. Go forth and heal without guilt."

"Yes, ma'am. Goodbye and Godspeed." Randall hung up and put his forehead down on his desk. *What an unbelievable turn of events,* he thought. This woman, dealing with the tragic loss of her husband, was reaching out to make sure *he* didn't feel culpable. It was enough to give one faith in humanity. His eyes suddenly felt leaky. He'd controlled himself so well during the call, but now, not so much.

Melinda sashayed into his office with several charts needing calculation checks. She stopped short when she saw him head down on the desk. "Oops, I'm sorry, Dr. B, I should have knocked." He popped his head up and flicked a tear away from his cheek.

"Are those tears or an allergy?" she asked in alarm, ever the observant one.

Randall sniffed and wiped his nose on his sleeve. "I hate to admit it, because big boys don't cry, but, yes, they are tears. It's nothing to be alarmed about, just a momentary jolt. I just had a call from Mrs. Franken. Her husband shot himself in the head over the weekend."

Melinda gasped in shock. "He's dead?"

"Doornail city," confirmed Randall.

Melinda's face got cloudy. She went over and closed Randall's office door. She pulled up a chair. "Please tell me all."

Randall recounted the phone call. Melinda listened wide-eyed. When he finished, she whistled. "Boy, Elisa is going to be really upset when she hears about this. She asked me this morning how he was doing. Then, I checked and he hadn't come in for his treatment. Now I know why."

Randall nodded. "Yeah. Something about his case really got to her." He wondered why he was sharing his emotions with Melinda and not Doris.

Melinda was quick on her feet. "Maybe we should page her to come down here. I'd rather we tell her in person before she hears it from someone else."

Randall nodded and wondered why he hadn't thought of it first. "Good idea. Go ahead and page her. Umm . . . Doris already knows. She took Mrs. Franken's call."

Suicides Aren't Us

While Randall and Melinda waited for Elisa to come down, they sat quietly in his office examining their own thoughts.

Elisa soon padded into Randall's office slightly out of breath. "What's up, boss? You have another conundrum for me to solve?"

Randall marveled at Elisa's choice of words. "Not quite in the way you think."

After Randall delivered the bad news, Elisa looked stunned. "But you said cancer patients rarely commit suicide. What gives?"

Randall crossed his arms. "I never claimed to be omniscient. In med school they taught us never to say never and never to say always. That way you have a better chance of being seen as sage and wise."

Elisa processed that thought and then bounced back with a question. "Did you just make that stuff up about cancer patients not getting suicidal?"

Randall shook his head. "Not at all. It's surprisingly rare, according to the literature. It's the first such case I've ever had, but my sample size is relatively small. When you think about it, it seems odd that it's not more common. You know, the patients are generally older, they've just retired to live the good life, and, kaboom, cancer hits. You'd think they'd just say, oh well, I've had a good run, but now it's time to go. But, instead, they vow they're going to beat it and fight like hellcats."

Melinda gave a half nod. "Yeah, I see your point. I hadn't thought of it that way. I suppose veterans have a lot of extra fight in them. On the other hand, there's teenagers in the prime of their lives, deciding that the peer pressure in high school is just too much so they hang themselves in the shower. Very odd, to say the least."

Randall nodded. "A puzzle. A conundrum. A mystery for the weirdness that is humanness."

"Have you seen suicides in noncancer patients?" asked Elisa.

"Several." Randall thought back. "There was a guy who jumped out of a fourth-floor hospital room window when I was an intern."

Melinda gawked. "Sounds terrible! Tell us more."

Randall leaned forward. "Well . . . I was walking underneath the suicide guy's hospital room window on my way to the ER via the hospital back entrance. I heard yelling from above and I looked up. An older man in hospital PJs was halfway out the open window with a nurse trying to pull him back inside. She was yelling for help and he was yelling for her to let go. He overpowered her and took a swan dive. He face-planted about two feet in front of where I was standing. Sounded like a ripe watermelon when he hit. If I hadn't stepped backwards at the last second, he'd have taken me with him. Two pancakes on a patio."

"Yikes!" exclaimed Elisa. "Could have been a suicide with a side of dead doctor."

Randall nodded. "Nicely put. But, relative to our discussion of suicide in cancer patients, I'm not sure if Mr. Splat qualifies. I don't know what his diagnosis was. My first qualified suicide experience was a lovesick young man trying to make a statement. He made one, alright."

Melinda's saucer eyes encouraged him to spill the details. "I'd like to hear about it, but do we have the time?"

Randall looked right and then left. "As long as no one is beating down the door, let's go for it."

The Oops Suicide

Randall took a deep breath and began. "When I was just a wee lad and a second year resident in Colorado Springs, I was on an ER rotation as part of the training."

Elisa looked surprised. "Your training covered the waterfront, sounds like."

Randall pursed his lips and nodded. "Yep, we had to complete rotations in various specialties. It gave us a chance to taste what other specialties have to deal with. It was a real eye opener. Anyway, about 2:00 AM the EMTs brought in a 20-something guy who had a gunshot wound to the abdomen. I was still half asleep when I got to the ER."

Melinda interrupted. "How'd he get shot? Was he in a gang or did he get mugged?"

Randall waved away the idea. "No, nothing like that. It was self-inflicted kind of by accident. As the EMTs rolled him in, the guy kept shouting: 'I don't want to die, doctor! I don't want to die!' It really freaked me out—it was the first GSW I'd ever seen. There was blood everywhere. Turned out, I was pretty useless. I stood there like a statue, just staring. Unlike me, the surgery resident was very efficient. He started barking orders and things happened real fast. He looked at me and had to shake my shoulder to get my attention. He yelled in my face to get IVs started in both arms and legs. My brilliant response was a resounding 'What?'"

Melinda held her breath. "I would have been frozen in place, Dr. B! I don't much like the sight of blood."

Randall replayed the scene in his mind and paused a beat. "Anyway, when I finished putting in the IVs, the resident sent me running to the Blood Bank to get four units of O neg and bring it to the OR. It was down three flights of stairs and back up four to the OR. I was blowing like a blue bloater when I got to the OR. Anesthesia was ready to gas him as soon as the staff surgeon got there from home. He'd been in bed sleeping. In the meantime, we tried to keep up with the blood loss. The kid kept babbling that he didn't want to die and it was a mistake."

Elisa tried to picture it all. "How was it a mistake?"

Randall shook his head. "Later we pieced the story together from what the EMTs and cops told us. His girlfriend had recently broken things off. He called her after midnight and said that if she didn't take him back he'd kill himself. She laughed and told him he probably didn't even have a gun. He said he did and that it was aimed at his heart. He cocked the hammer so she could hear the click. She figured he could be serious and promised to give him another chance. He was so wound up that when he moved the gun away from his chest he accidentally pulled the trigger when it was pointed at his belly. The girl heard the shot and his cry of pain. She called the cops."

Melinda was shocked. "That's awful. And stupid!"

"Way stupid." Randall shook his head. "The kid had a vise grip on my arm while I was standing next to the OR table. I couldn't get loose even after anesthesia. It was weird." Randall rubbed his arm unconsciously.

Elisa shivered. "What a tragedy!"

Randall grimaced at the memory. "Yeah, it was terrible. While we waited for the surgeon, I kept repeating to the kid that everything would be alright. But when the surgeon got there, put the kid under and made the opening incision, it was clear there was no hope. The abdomen was filled with blood and it poured out of him. Just red everywhere."

Melinda held her stomach, looking a little green around the gills.

Randall continued, almost in a whisper. "The bullet had destroyed the aorta. You know surgeons—they get right to the point. He said 'There's no way to fix this. The damage is too extensive. We don't have a prosthetic graft to patch this. Sam, what are his vitals?'"

Melinda shook her head. "So the kid died? What am I saying, we already know that!"

Randall nodded sadly. "The surgeon told the scrub nurse to record the time of death as 2:15 AM. He pulled his gloves off with a loud snap and told us all to scrub out. He said our work was done."

"What did you do?" asked Elisa.

Randall made a helpless gesture. "I wanted to do CPR, duct tape the aorta, yell at him to wake up, anything! But I just stood there, jaw hanging loose. I couldn't believe it. He'd wanted so much to live. I felt physically sick." Randall's arms wrapped around his belly.

Melinda frowned and nodded. "I guess you could say the kid died from a broken heart." She looked glassy-eyed.

Randall looked into space, lost in the imagery. "When I didn't leave the spot next to the OR table, the staff surgeon came over to my side. He said that it looked like the 20-something guy had a death grip on my arm and asked me if I needed help getting his hand off me. I actually laughed. He asked me if it was my first suicide and I said it wasn't. I told him about the patient who jumped out of a four-story hospital window."

Elisa made a *tsking* sound with her tongue. "Yeah, it would be tough to see someone close to my age die like that. The kid seems to have been a bit unstable, not just an idiot. My sister, Elena, is a little schitzy, but not missing marbles. She lives in Chicago currently. On the other hand, I could see my crazy boyfriend doing something like that. He's so needy and insecure."

Melinda looked surprised, and glad to change the topic. "You have a sister and a boyfriend? I can understand your sister not being around, but I've never seen your boyfriend."

Elisa grimaced. "Carlos doesn't like hospitals and he gets nervous in crowds. He wants to get married, but... I just don't know if he's Mr. Right."

"Tell me about it!" blurted Melinda. "So far, I seem to attract all the Mr. Wrongs. So your sister is in Chicago? Does she work there?"

Elisa shook her head. "Not currently. Mainly, she's there to look after *mi mamá*. I get surprise visits from Elena periodically. She's like the Spanish Inquisition. She says she visits when she gets signals that I need her, but it's usually *her* who's in trouble. Boyfriends, money, busted car . . . you name it."

Randall laughed. "Yeah, some relatives are relatively useless. But we love them anyway."

Elisa nodded her agreement. "Anyway, it sounds like that staff surgeon was pretty supportive, considering the emergency had gotten him out of bed to be there. Some cutters would have just breezed on home and not given two hoots about an upset intern."

Randall sighed. "Yeah, you're right. The surgeon put his arm around my shoulder and suggested I go home and get some sleep. He assured me the ER could limp along without me the rest of the night. It took some time before I could stop seeing the whole thing when I closed my eyes."

Melinda looked a little sick, herself. "I can't believe doctors have to deal with so much death. I always associated medicine with health rather than death. I guess you build a thick skin, and some day it doesn't bother you anymore."

Randall's mind came back to the room, his eyes intent on her. "You guys, the day death doesn't bother me anymore is the day I need to leave medicine. We all need to maintain our sense of humanity or we're not in it for the patients anymore."

Randall and Melinda shared a few moments of reflective silence. Randall started humming the tune to the Eagles song "Victim of Love" and Melinda picked it up and hummed along. They grinned at each other and soon were singing together quietly in a nice harmony.

When they finished, they started to giggle.

From her desk, Doris could only partially hear the singing and outbursts of what she thought was laughter coming from Randall's office. Her mother hen instincts urged her to investigate the questionable activity. She rose and knocked on Randall's office door. The knocking startled the group. Randall jumped up and whispered. "Cheese it. It's the cops come here to arrest us for malingering."

The remark stoked another outburst of laughter which provoked Doris to poke her head in. "Hey, y'all, what was so funny? Y'all sound like a gaggle of gigglin' geese." She fully entered the room.

Randall was ready with a defense. "We were just proving my father got something right."

"We were?" asked Melinda.

Doris disapproved and put hands on hips. "This better be good."

"Well," said Randall. "I'd just finished the call with Mrs. Franken, when Melinda came in with some charts for me and she could tell that I was upset about something. I told her I'd gotten a bit emotional after the call. We talked about the suicide, which was plenty enough to upset me and Melinda. I told her what really got to me was that Mrs. Franken's main concern was for me. She did not want me to feel responsible for her husband's suicide. She was right. I sort of did, but she talked me out of it."

"But why is Elisa here?" asked Doris.

"We thought we ought to break the news to her in person," said Melinda. "So I paged her."

"Okay" Doris softened. "I was upset about the suicide, too. Seems a right proper response for respectable folk. So how do we get to the laughin' part? Were y'all makin' jokes about the dead?" Doris held her cross necklace in both hands.

"Hardly," said Randall. "We got to talking about the rarity of suicides in cancer patients and how ours is a business that has to have a healthy respect for life and death. We make psychological adjustments to cope with death that require not lapsing into the dark side of it."

Doris was still not quite sure if she was hearing a cover-up. "I'm waitin' for the bit about your father."

Randall explained the link. "On the occasion of one of my many screw-ups growing up, I went into a deep funk. My Dad got sick of me moping around the house and began to tease me about it until we both started laughing about the stupid stunt I'd pulled. When we were done laughing, he asked how I felt. I had to admit, I felt better. Then he told me his home-crafted adage: 'There ain't nothing so serious in life that you can't laugh about it.'"

"Well, you might have to wait a few days to laugh at some of them, outta respect and God-fearin'," remarked Doris.

"'Tis true," said Melinda.

Doris was still a bit circumspect about the wisdom of the adage. "Seems to me you three got to laughin' faster than Kentucky Derby horses outta the gate."

"We get too many of these speedbumps to linger on them," responded Randall.

"I don't know," Doris hesitated. "Sometimes I just wonder how you doctors can joke about the morbid. Likely to raise the devil and the dead some day."

Randall gave Doris a sly grin. "It's a special skill."

Despite her misgivings, Doris cracked a smile and Melinda stifled a laugh.

Randall shifted gears. "So, Elisa, what's on your menu this afternoon?"

Elisa winced. "Anything will taste better than this morning's dish! I've got to head back upstairs. I've got a meeting with the Chief of Surgery about participating in our fledgling multidisciplinary tumor board."

Randall smiled broadly. "Better you than me. Dr. Sheltie hates my guts. Maybe you can use your special skills to convince him to stop claiming we cook patients on our rotisserie."

Randall, Molly, Grace and Melinda were gathered at the treatment console trying to resolve a miscalculation of monitor units. Randall scratched his head, trying to figure out what was wrong.

Doris walked up behind the group with news. "You guys look as confused as the little boy who dropped his bubble gum in the chicken coop."

Randall turned and laughed. "I reckon we do. Seems like someone forgot to carry the two, but I can't find it."

"Did you check under the counter?" jibed Doris.

Randall took the suggestion and bent down, pretending to check. "Nope. Nothing. Just a big dust bunny. What's up?"

Doris clapped her hands. "I have news that should make y'all happy. Our lovely Wisconsin winter weather has resulted in five cancellations this afternoon. There's a two-hour gap from 1:00 to 3:00 with nothing to do but drink sweet tea and relax on the porch swing. Oh, and three outpatients on treatment have canceled for the day."

The group let out a collective cheer. That somehow triggered a Randall neuron and he suddenly ciphered out the error. He added another exclamation. "Whoopee! The error was my crappy handwriting. My five looks like a nine. Mea culpa. I'll correct it right now. There. It's done. How about we celebrate by hitting the cafeteria for ice cream? My treat. Who wants to come?"

Doris and Melinda raised their hands eagerly, like children in class vying to be the first to give the teacher the answer.

Molly groaned. "Grace and I would love to join you guys, but there are still patients to treat. See all the green striped pajamas in the hall? I think we can manage without Melinda, right Grace?"

Grace grunted and grimaced. "Sure, why not? She's not much help anyhow. Go ahead and fatten her up. She's too . . . too skinny."

With that, Randall, Doris and Melinda headed out to the hallway and decided to play elevator roulette. Doris pushed the up button. Randall bet on the green wallpaper. Indeed, when an elevator dinged and the door opened, it was green. He took it as a good omen for the rest of the day.

To their surprise, after the elevator door opened, out strode Dan Graham, their new Radiation Physicist.

"Well, fancy meeting you here," said Randall.

Dan's eyebrows went up when he saw the threesome waiting for the elevator in the middle of a workday. "To what do I owe the honor? You guys playing hooky?"

Doris gave Dan her best Cheshire smile. "Not at all. You can blame it on a very angry Mother Nature. The snow storm has given us a two-hour break and we're fixin' to get coffee and a treat."

Dan lit up like a sunrise. "Oh, boy. Can I come, too? I was just upstairs to look out a window and check the storm. It's snowing like there's been a five-year drought. Going home later tonight is going to require extra caffeine and calories."

"Glad to have the company," said Randall. "I hope you have the stomach for today's topic of discussion."

Dan wasn't deterred. "Nothing is going to get between me and ice cream, not even your mind numbing 'discussions.' But we missed getting on the 'up' elevator. Let's take the stairs and burn some pre-engorgement calories."

Melinda set off in a jog, shouting a challenge. "Last one to the cafeteria is a scattered electron!"

Doris rejected the challenge. "Shoot, I don't mind bein' any kind of electron. There's no way I'm haulin' my 'traditionally built' atoms up stairs any faster than necessary. I'm an energy conservationist."

Randall concurred with Doris. "Here, here. I don't have the mustard to keep up either. I'll take measured steps up the stairs at your pace."

Dan started off in pursuit of Melinda and then changed his mind. "Same here. I'll never catch her. There's no rush. When the day shift clears out at 4:30, the unplowed parking lot will be a big logjam. I think I'll stay late and do the monthly PM on the machine. By the time I'm done, the parking lot will be plowed and most of the traffic long gone."

"Good idea," said Randall, hoofing it up the stairs. "PM in the PM."

Doris was confused. "I understand what the second PM means, but what's the first one mean? Hopefully not 'private moment.'"

Dan was surprised Doris didn't recognize the acronym. "You don't know what that stands for? You've typed my PM reports before. That PM means preventive maintenance. Once a month I have to check a slew of measurements on the linear accelerator to make sure that it's making X-rays as it should. Very boring and time consuming. Takes about three hours. Would you like to stay and watch?"

Doris feigned a big yawn. "Oh, I'd like to. But I have to scurry home and watch some wallpaper peel off my bathroom wall. Maybe next time. By the way, just because I type up your gibberish doesn't mean I understand what I'm typin'. I'm not a physicist. It might as well be Yiddish."

Dan had to admit Doris was right. "Sorry. I get that my physics reports are a bit dry. Would it help if I included a few jokes?"

Doris smiled. "Hmm. That might help. But be assured your dictation is not as dry as others in our present company."

Randall barely attended the interchange. His mind was elsewhere. At the first landing of the stairwell, half way up, he spotted what he'd been looking for. "Hey, you guys. Look over here. My candy wrapper marker is still in the corner where I saw it two weeks ago. Housekeeping is as efficient as ever. It hasn't been touched."

Doris was bringing up the rear and already puffing. "Did you leave it there?"

"Not me, McGee," said Randall. "I am just a scientific observer."

Doris stopped on the landing to catch her breath. She started to bend over to pick up the wrapper but Randall called out for her to stop the rash action. "Hey, don't mess with my experiment. I need the data for my report to building management."

Doris withdrew her hand. "Of course. Whatever was I thinkin'?"

At the top of the stairs, they instinctively stood to the right side of the door leading to the first-floor hallway. The door opened inward into the stairwell. There was usually significant foot traffic in the hallway, with people rushing to get through the doorway to the stairwell. It was unwise to stand in the path of the door for long or risk bodily injury. It was a mistake you only made once. Randall reached for the door knob just as two doctors in scrubs came bursting through. The door almost took off his hand. After they passed by, Randall held the door open with one arm and they entered the hallway like three cars merging onto the freeway.

Doris exhaled a sigh of relief. "Good job, Dr. B. For a moment there I thought we were goners."

"Not for the faint of heart," agreed Dan. "Hey, can we take a side trip to the Canteen? There's something I need to get."

The Canteen was halfway down the hall to the Cafeteria. It was a hole in the wall store that sold a variety of snacks, souvenirs and other oddments. However, the biggest attraction was cigarettes. The store was packed with veterans buying cartons of "coffin nails" at half price. Randall thought about the irony. While he was downstairs treating the cancers that smoking caused, the VA was upstairs selling ammunition to the future victims.

Dan asked the three to wait while he went to the back of the store to get a large bag of popcorn. "The popcorn will be my sustenance during PM."

Doris looked at the long checkout line. "It's going to be slow as North Pole molasses to get checked out. Look at the line."

Dan pulled out some folded sheets of paper from his back pocket. "You guys go ahead and save me a seat. I brought homework. I can do it while I'm waiting in the queue. By the way, what's this morbid topic we're gonna discuss? Is it the Packers' chances of making the playoffs this year?"

Randall shrugged. "Not quite as morbid as that, but close. We'll keep a lamp lit for you."

When Doris and Randall got to the Cafeteria, they spotted Melinda waving at them from a table in the corner. Doris waved back and motioned that they were going to get in the serving line and join her after acquiring their respective goodies. Melinda was already working on a chocolate sundae and sipping coffee. Randall liberated a Klondike bar from the freezer and Doris picked out a Fudgesicle. After filling up their large Styrofoam cups with the not-so-bad, but not-so-good, VA coffee, they joined Melinda at the table.

"What took you guys so long?" chided Melinda.

Doris took a seat opposite Melinda. "We were waylaid by a thunderin' herd of Blue Coders. Congratulations. You win. I'm the electron, but I was already scattered."

Melinda was caught off guard and nearly spit out her coffee as she tried to stifle a laugh.

"Looks like you're scatterin' coffee." Doris dabbed at her blouse with a napkin. "Nice of you to share."

Melinda choked and coughed.

Randall sat down. "Going to the Cafeteria for coffee is risky business. I don't think I'm insured for this."

Now Melinda was turning purple. Randall reached out to her. "Shall I call a code?"

Melinda gasped and finally caught her breath. "Woof! And I just washed this uniform."

Jim Conway walked up to the table with a cup of coffee. "Does anybody need CPR over here? Is this an exclusive club, or can anybody join?" Melinda shook her head and looked a bit sheepish.

Randall had to laugh. "Hey there, Jim. No, we are equal opportunity offenders. Have a seat and join in the merriment. Jim, this is my secretary, Doris, and our therapy tech student, Melinda. Everybody, this is Jim Conway. He's the lead physician in the ER. We've gotten some time off for good behavior, thanks to Mother Nature. We're celebrating with ice cream and just sitting around laughing at death."

Jim sat down next to Melinda. "Ah, one of my favorite pastimes. Pray tell. What has occasioned this morbid focus?"

Randall looked around the cafeteria as if searching for a way to summarize. "Well, I just learned that one of our patients under treatment committed suicide over the weekend. Doris took the call and passed it on to me. I talked with the decedent's wife and Melinda encountered me after the call. She noticed I was tad upset so we discussed it and wound up singing and laughing. Doris overheard the end of that exchange and still feels we were a bit callous about treating death so lightly. Is that a reasonable summary, girls?"

Melinda nodded. "Uh huh."

Doris looked a bit huffy. "There you go again, Dr. B. I don't see how you can find humor in someone dyin'."

"Not the light-hearted conversation I was expecting," remarked Dr. Conway. "I feel like I should be wearing my referee striped shirt and whistle."

Doris pointed to Dr. Conway. "We would welcome an outside opinion. If you work in the ER, I'm sure you've witnessed patients die a far piece more than we have. How do you cope with it?"

Dr. Conway backed up in his seat. "I'm no philosopher, but I have picked up a few pearls on the subject over the years. I am willing to give you the three-minute version of my conclusions."

Randall was glad to be off the hook. "Great. I think all three of us will be grateful recipients of your acquired wisdom." Doris and Melinda nodded their heads in agreement.

Dr. Conway swept an arm around the room. "Look around you. Half the people in here are vets and are at an age closer to their ultimate demise. Do they look depressed? Or more depressed than us? No. They have mostly accepted that it's inevitable and that they won't feel any better about it by dwelling on it. It's part of life. We all face it sooner or later."

Melinda furrowed her brow. "I'll take later."

Jim nodded and waved his hand around the table. "So would we all, but we're different from those who become our patients. We've chosen to minister to them in health, to prevent illness, and in illness, to treat it. There are only three possible outcomes. First, we can cure the illness so they get all the time they've been allotted. Second, we can slow the illness so they don't get overtaken by it prematurely. Third, we can ease any suffering from their illness when cure is impossible. In addition, we must attend to both the physical and mental elements of the disease."

Doris placed her hand on her heart. "That's exactly how I look at it. It's what my sainted mother taught me, and you said it beautifully."

Dr. Conway was delighted by the praise. "Thank you, Doris. Now, I am almost glad I sat down. But the story doesn't end there. In the process of our medical ministry, we are obliged to ourselves to remain healthy, both physically and mentally. Dealing with serious disease and death can be a burden on the caregiver. So we have to learn how to protect ourselves from the toll it can take on our health and spirit."

Melinda held up a hand with her index finger extended. "Amen to that! I'm pretty new at this work and that's what I struggle with. Sometimes it's so hard to stay positive. It really saps my energy. What's your secret to not letting it get to you?"

Dr. Conway shrugged. "There's no magic bullet. Do your coworkers cope the same way? Probably not. Some may get so jaded by seeing disease and death that they shut off their compassion for fear of being hurt repeatedly. They may start to see patients as just drains on their battery and treat them as simply distasteful beings."

Doris sighed rather loudly. "Hmm, I can think of some frogs in that pond."

Dr. Conway looked pointedly at Doris. "That style of coping is not the worst. On the next level down are the caregivers who just become indifferent to everything, figuring it's the only way they can retain their humanity."

Randall slumped in his seat as if his air valve was leaking. "So, what's left?"

Dr. Conway nudged Randall with an elbow, who overdid his reaction and pretended to fall to the side. "Come on, you faker. I'm pretty sure you already know the answer to that question, unless I am a terrible judge of character."

Randall sat back upright and forced a smile. "Maybe, but I want to hear you say it."

Dr. Conway gave Randall a dour stare, but continued. "It's really pretty simple, everybody, as I am sure Dr. B has demonstrated many times. You give yourself permission to care about each patient. You purposely make a connection with each one. You strive to be genuine and foster trust. If you do that to the best of your ability, you'll never regret any outcome that some might construe as 'bad.'"

Doris first nodded, then shook her head. "Easy to say. Hard to do. Some of our patients are real . . . difficult. It can be like dealin' with grade schoolers or worse. I'm no kindergarden teacher."

Dr. Conway looked sympathetic and nodded. "I hear you. All you can do is your best. Positive responses are not guaranteed. But, if you've done your job as best you can with the goal of achieving the three possible outcomes I mentioned, that still counts as a success. After all, most patients just want to be heard. To accept that is to accept your own mortality. If you adjust to that concept now through your patients, it permits you to do it for yourself later when you face your fated illness. Hopefully, much later, as our colleague Melinda noted."

Randall grinned slyly. "Geez, you're right. That was almost word for word what I was thinking."

Jim fake-punched Randall in the shoulder. "How do you guys put up with this simpleton?"

"It's a daily struggle," said Doris. They all giggled while Randall stuck his lip out in a pout.

Doris touched her cross necklace. "Seriously, Dr. Conway, that was really . . . profound, if I may use that word. I'm as touched as the beads on a rosary. I'm glad you joined us."

Dan Graham approached the table with his large bag of popcorn. "I see you guys started without me and someone else has my seat."

Randall introduced Dan to Dr. Conway. He explained that Dan was the department's radiation physicist.

"So, what does a radiation physicist do?" asked Dr. Conway.

Dan puffed himself up a bit. "Not much besides keeping the department popcorn supply up to Dr. B's strict standards. Oh, almost forgot. I keep the high energy linear accelerator alive and well so it keeps making X-rays. Otherwise, Dr. B would have nothing to do. I see by your white coat's embroidery that you work in the ER?"

Dr. Conway laughed. "I do. Some people say I'm in charge of the place. Still trying to convince the employees of that."

Dan reached out to shake Dr. Conway's hand. "So you're the head honcho in the ER? Good to know. The way these guys overwork me, I may need your services one day soon. Don't get up. I can't stay. I've just been informed that the X-ray machine I referenced is down for the count. Thus, I will be heading south to see what ails it."

Dr. Conway thought to himself that Dan Graham and Randall Biedermeier were a good fit. "Well, nice to meet you and good luck with your recalcitrant machine."

Randall wondered what other twists the day would bring. "Yeah, Dan. What he said. Try talking nice to the accelerator. Maybe it's just in a bad mood. We'll be back downstairs shortly."

Dan overdid a laugh. "Droll, very droll. A good talking to is probably all it will take." He walked off and fought the foot traffic out of the Cafeteria.

After Dan left, Randall made note of the time. "Hey, Jim, I don't want to keep you here talking if you need to get back to the ER."

Dr. Conway shook his head. "Nah, I'm good for ten more minutes unless they page me. With the storm, the ER has been dead, too. Oops, pardon the pun."

Doris harrumphed. "Well, I'm still waitin' for an explanation about makin' jokes about the dead."

Cadavagins

Randall stifled a laugh. "Fair question. Perhaps the best way to address that is to go back to med school days. What do you think, Jim?"

Dr. Conway seemed to be staring at Melinda's top shirt button as he searched for the applicable memory.

She noticed where he was focusing and snapped her fingers. "I don't think the answer is written where you're looking."

Dr. Conway laughed. "Sorry. It was just a blank stare. But, ironically, the answer is closely linked to what I saw. Anatomy. More specifically, junior year anatomy class. There's a principle that all med students discover there. Some things are so deeply scary that the only way to develop an ongoing relationship with them is to find a humorous side. Those who don't may drop out at that point. I know it may sound callous, but let me explain. Do you agree, Randall?"

Randall began to groan and rub his belly. They all looked at him with concern. "Oh, oh, I think I feel a story coming on." Randall hammed it up.

Doris tried to look disgusted, but a grin belied her effort. "As sure as the sun does rise, Dr. B, you are full of wind and vinegar!"

Randall tried in vain to look innocent and slighted. "Jim, you go ahead while I lick my wounds."

Dr. Conway took the cue. "In anatomy class, we were required to do cadaver dissections over the course of two semesters. The studies covered everything from internal organs to nerves, muscles and eye bones. One cannot imagine the impact of walking into a large room with 25 embalmed dead people lying naked on large tables." Doris and Melinda scrunched their faces.

Randall just nodded his concurrence with the description.

Dr. Conway smirked at their sour looks. "The smell of formaldehyde is enough to make you gag if the visual itself doesn't. The smell gets into your clothes and hair. When you go home, your family wonders why you smell like dead fish."

"The smell was the worst," agreed Randall. "You can't wash it off. You have to keep repeating to yourself: 'I'm going to be a doctor and save lives one day soon. Living people won't smell like this or look this bad. Here, but for the grace of God, will I go. One day, far distant from now.'"

Doris held her cross and shook her head.

Dr. Conway took up the mantle. "Fortunately, you two don't have to go through that like we did. You don't have to be that up close and personal. You just get to imagine it, which is, in some ways, worse."

Melinda looked a little green. "I suppose. Sometimes reality is not as bad as imagination. Although some of the vets we see hint at that eventuality."

Doris' North Carolina voice rang out. "My stars, give that girl a cow and a milkin' stool. She is right! Sometimes reality is worse."

"True enough," agreed Randall. "Let me share a story from my anatomy class. One would think that after all the intense 'ology' courses, my shenanigan spirits would have been schooled out of me. However, let me assuage your concerns. It was not."

Dr. Conway gestured for Randall to take the floor. "As I expected."

Melinda leaned over to Doris. "I'm not sure we want to hear this."

Randall warmed up to his story. "I appreciate your support, Jim. Crucial to learning anatomy is the hands-on experience of dissecting a human cadaver. It's a rite of passage for every medical student. Diagrams in books or slides on a screen just don't capture the true essence of smell, texture, elasticity or hue of a real body. We must become intimately aware of how the body is put together and how it functions in order to create an internal working model. From this we have a baseline to visualize what could be going wrong in a live patient."

"That sounds a bit more erudite than it was," snarked Dr. Conway.

Randall looked offended. "Perhaps. Our anatomy class was divided up into groups of six students per cadaver. We spent a full semester with 'Charles,' a 58-year-old construction worker who'd had a three-pack-a-day smoking habit. Not surprisingly, he had died of metastatic lung cancer. After a time, we got quite used to the sight and smell of his naked cadaver and began conversing with him. He was a great listener."

Doris shook her head in disapproval again. "I do declare. You are pokin' the devil, bless your heart. No respect for the dead!"

"Mine talked back," said Dr. Conway, with a note of superiority.

Randall went on without acknowledging the comment. "I was particularly fascinated with how the small muscles in the forearm channeled through the wrist to move the fingers. I tied a fishing line to each muscle and practiced pulling on the line to make the fingers move and make gestures."

Dr. Conway couldn't hold back a snide question. "Did Charles start giving you the finger?"

"Dr. Conway!" Doris clutched her crucifix. "You're as bad as Dr. B! Best get your coins for the ferryman today!"

Dr. Conway put up a correcting index finger. "As bad, you say? I'd venture a definite worse."

Randall responded with mock anger. "Must you all constantly interrupt? I'm trying to tell a story here. Anyway, late in the semester, my team learned that a group of high school students would be visiting the lab as part of a career day. The anatomy professor suggested that we make the scene a bit more . . . hmmm . . . palatable to the impressionable youth. I found an old lab coat and dressed Charles with it to cover his nuts and bolts. I thought it best, also, to lay a handkerchief over his face."

Now Randall had their attention. There was no more interrogatory. Even Melinda was curious.

Randall paused further, for effect. "Before the career day students arrived, my anatomy team, made up of six med students, prepared the viewing area around the dissection table. We moved the bar stool-like chairs we used during dissection from around the table and stacked them nearby to make space for the 20 high school students we expected. My team gathered around the head of the cadaver table. Our anatomy instructor led the students in and they gathered at the foot of the table looking like they'd rather be elsewhere. Two of the students didn't make it all the way to the table. These two curled up their lips after taking a whiff of formaldehyde and beat a retreat to the bathroom."

Melinda enjoyed the image. "High school students? Greenest of the green!"

"Indeed," said Randall. "And greener by the minute! One brave soul inched closer to the cadaver to get a closer look and said 'Cool, man.' Otherwise, it was deathly quiet. When a few others finally determined the cadaver wasn't going to suddenly pop up his head and say hello, these braver souls leaned in for a closer look."

Dr. Conway chuckled. "I bet they were responding to a dare from another student or two."

Randall pointed at Dr. Conway. "Good call. At that point, our anatomy professor was called out of the room. It was time to activate my devious plan! With a nod to my partners in mischief, I pulled on the fishing line from inside the lab coat. Suddenly, Charles raised his hand, wiggled his fingers, and waved at the career day students. The tallest and most macho looking student screamed like a little girl and fainted dead away into the stacked up dissection stools. The stools tumbled to the ground, sending the rest of the students stampeding out of the room. The noise drew the anatomy professor back into the room to see what the commotion was all about. What he found was the passed out student, a pile of stools, and Charles peacefully at rest attended to by six innocent-looking medical students."

"Oh my stars, Dr B!" Doris called out. "You must have danced with the devil when you were knee high to a grasshopper! I'm just guessin' here, but I'll bet your instructor was none too happy with your dissection team. I'm appalled! What happened next?"

Randall shook his head. "Ha, the rats! They all pointed at me and said 'He did it.' The instructor escorted me to his office despite my innocence plea. He gave me a private lecture about the dignity of the dead and respect for the living. He let me stew in my juices for a few minutes and softened the blow by pointing out that every anatomy class he'd ever had pulled a similar stunt. He explained that making light of death was a human coping mechanism. He cautioned that he would only sanction its use if it was employed in a compassionate manner and added that he could provide further instruction on the technique as needed."

Doris shook a finger at Randall. "I hope you were duly humbled, young man. I'm guessin' you didn't take him up on his offer of further instruction, given your recent behavior. He should have shown you what-for behind the woodshed!"

Randall held up his hand. "Oh, believe me, I was duly humbled. The lesson really sank in when he explained the potential effects that further such behavior might have on the probability of my graduation. He repeated that making light of tragedy and finding the strength to laugh about it releases the emotional impact, but he warned not to take it too far. He described how someone in his class had cut off the penis of a cadaver and thrown it into the sink of the women's restroom. The perpetrator was never caught, but suspicion followed him to graduation. He supposed that the subsequent guilt had been a sufficient lesson."

Doris grunted a grudging acceptance of Randall's explanation. "I'm supposin' you learned your lesson, but remember—I'm watchin' you. Your mother has a subcontract with me. If you don't fear me, fear her."

Randall felt a familiar shame that had been born at his earliest ad*mom*ishments.

C H A P T E R 9

——

F E A R T H E R E A P E R

"If you want a happy ending, that depends, of course, on where you stop your story."

—Orson Welles

DOWN FOR THE COUNT

As Randall droned on about his cadaver escapades, the ice cream in his Klondike bar had softened and was dripping. When he'd bitten into it, a blurb of ice cream had shot out the bottom of the chocolate shell broke, hit the table edge and ricocheted onto his front. Most of it hit his lab coat, but a few splatters had gotten his multicolored tie. Randall wiped at the ice cream on his lab coat with a paper napkin without much success.

"Geez, Dr. B," said Doris. "We can't take you anywhere. Let's get you back downstairs so I can polish you up like pappy's Sunday saddle shoes. Might be a good time to buy me some stock in paper towels."

Melinda sniggered.

"That's what lab coats and ties are for," countered Randall. "This is a multicolored tie. No need to clean it."

"Disgusting!" huffed Melinda. "Let's take the stairs back down. I don't want to stand around and be seen with you while waiting for an elevator."

"Or be trapped in the elevator like cattle with 15 other people lookin' at you," added Doris.

Randall had to protest. "Come on, you guys! It was just an accident. Could happen to anybody. I agree. I'll take the stairs. We need to get back downstairs anyhow to see what's up with our downed Linac."

When Randall, Doris and Melinda got back to the department, Dan had diagnosed the machine fault. The 12-Volt power supply had fritzed out and taken down the magnetron. Thus, the department was closed for business until the next morning, when a drop shipment of the needed parts would arrive from San Diego. Randall went to the waiting area and informed the patients of the bad news. They were rather miffed, since they'd fought through the blizzard to get there, waited hours for treatment and would have to return home untreated. Doris and Melinda called up to the wards to cancel the remaining inpatients. It was 2:00 PM and there were no patients to be seen or treated. What to do? It was a rare coincidence—a machine break down on the day of a massive blizzard. Was it serendipity or dual bad luck?

Call from On High

Doris found a dreaded large yellow VA administrative envelope on her desk. She opened it and found a memo from the Center Director requesting Randall to do an "administrative site visit" at the Detroit VA ASAP. VA headquarters in DC had called the Center Director and suggested Randall to be "volunteered" for the task. They wanted a quality control spot check of the Radiation Oncology Department in Detroit for some "questionable activities" a whistleblower had reported on. "Just routine" noted the memo. Doris presented the memo to Randall.

"What is this?" squawked Randall. He scanned the missive and threw it back on Doris's desk. "What a bunch of nonsense! How can it be 'just routine' and 'ASAP' at the same time!? What bureaucratic quagmire are they dipping me into?"

Doris smiled painfully. "Look at it this way, Dr. B. You get to try out your bright yellow Wellingtons."

Randall was not amused. He grabbed the paperwork again, scowling. "This says I have to fly out there in two days, stay overnight, and conduct chart reviews and staff interviews. They've already booked flights and the hotel. Do they think I just twiddle my thumbs down here? We can't cancel treatments or our other daily functions just like that." He snapped his fingers.

Doris tried to calm him down. "I'm sure we can get someone from the U to cover for you. I'll arrange it. Besides, you could use the break from us. Our department will probably shine brighter than a new copper penny after you see that one."

Randall pursed his lips and made a humming sound. "Could be, but I hate flying. On the other hand, doing the site visit might give me some more leverage to get what we need here. The worst part will be breaking it to the family."

Doris continued to placate. "I'll call Zelda and explain that the call comes from on high and you must obey."

Randall grunted in frustration. "That might help. Maybe you should go home as my replacement."

Doris shook her head. "My job does not go outside the confines of this department. I'm a one chicken coop hen."

Randall nodded. "I hear you. But I have decided to take a stand. I am not going to stand for it. They can go pound sand. The Center Director could have at least asked me first. I'm too angry to write a polite refusal. Can you write something for me?"

Doris nodded and smiled broadly. "I thought you'd never ask."

"Great!" sighed Randall. "What's the worst thing they could do to me that they haven't already done?"

Doris shook her head. "I'm not even gonna answer that one."

STAFF MEETING

Randall asked Doris to assemble everyone for a staff meeting in the Orthovoltage room. It was the only room in the department large enough to assemble seven people. Stephanie, Mr. Samuels' secretary, was helping out that day, so she joined the meeting. Before Randall started the meeting, the group chattered about how lucky they were to have a few hours break from the usual grind and possibly get off early. Randall rose from his seat and the room went quiet. He announced they'd use the free time to have a staff meeting to update everyone on the latest VA machinations. There was some moaning and groaning.

"Aw, c'mon," muttered Grace. "Can't we just get the heck out of here?"

"Well, you could . . ." Randall hesitated. "That is, if you want to forfeit two and half hours of pay. Stephanie just checked with the front office and they are not granting any early release with pay today. Apparently, the snow is being considered a normal storm for January in the frozen tundra."

"Typical," grunted Molly. "No snow day for us slaves."

Randall tried to soothe the savage beasts. "Now, now, don't get your bundies in an undle. There's good news to be had along with the bad."

Stephanie added a comment in her almost comically high-pitched voice. "Don't be such Eeyores. There are good people rooting for you in HR. I'm now authorized to tell you that the department has been approved for a half-time nursing position to help run the clinic."

"Will ceases never wonder," pronounced Dan, with drama.

Randall laughed. "Can I use that comment in the future?"

Dan nodded. "You may, sir. No footnote required."

Randall continued. "As you may suspect, I knew that little tidbit already. Thanks, Stephanie, for the lead-in. There are three candidates for the nursing position. All three are current VA employees who wish to cut back on their hours and want to transfer to a different assignment. Sometimes that's VA code for 'someone wants them out,' so we'll have to do some detective work to make sure they're not bad apples. I want each of you to interview them when they come through. HR will be setting up the visits over the next several weeks. *Verstehen sie?*"

Melinda saluted. "*Ja*, boss,"

Randall saluted back. "A nurse could be a big help down here when we really get busy. That's if we get the right person. If not, the wrong person could really screw things up. So, be thorough in your assessment and report anything hinky to me."

Melinda perked up. "Does that mean I wouldn't have to do patient intake anymore? What a relief! I'll be able to focus on being a tech student again . . . but I did learn a lot doing it." She looked at Randall and smiled demurely.

Randall furrowed his brow. "That's right. And I won't have to do it either. The next item is the Chief Tech position."

Grace raised her eyebrows. "Chief Tech position?"

Randall nodded. "Yes. Another decision HR finally has made with some prodding from Mr. Samuels and Stephanie here. Feel free to give her a round of applause."

There was an occasion-appropriate smattering of applause. Randall continued. "That is to say, they have made sort of a non-decision. They have left the choice up to me. Please, no bribery or altered behavior. That will not influence me. Grace, Molly and Melinda, you will all have a 30-minute interview with me. Before the interview I want you to write a two-page essay on the reasons why you would make the best Chief Tech. Then, you all will take a short test that covers basic Radiation Physics and Radiation Biology. Your ranking will be based on your performance on all three components: interview, essay and test results. Any questions?"

Grace narrowed her eyes suspiciously. "So, the decision is just up to you, *Jefe*? Sure you don't want to add a ballgown or swimsuit competition?"

Randall considered that and winced. "Hmm . . .not necessary. No, it's not entirely my decision. I have asked Dan to sit in on the interviews. He will also review the essay and test results with me. He hasn't known you three as long as I have and may have a different perspective. By the way, the job does have both pluses and minuses. You'll get 20% more pay, but you'll be responsible for fairly representing the interests of the Therapy Techs, both now and when we add a fourth or fifth tech." This information incited some loud exhales and a moment of silence. "Be advised that seniority may be a major factor for how the VA makes employee decisions, but that is not the case for me. I am going for the best fit for the job. If you don't want the added responsibility, decide now and remove your name from the hat."

Grace wasted no time in registering her gripes. "Cripes, it's been a while since Molly and I have studied that radiation stuff, but Melinda has just been getting those lectures from you. That's not fair."

Molly added to the gripe list. "How can Melinda be a candidate? She's still a student. She doesn't have our experience. She might not even want the responsibility yet."

Randall shrugged. "You're both right. But our current lack of viable candidates puts us in this position. Melinda does have the right to refuse the option of being a candidate. To get the job, she still has to outcompete you two."

Melinda squinted and looked away. "Yeah. It's the first I've heard any of this. I'll have to think about it."

The room was quiet for a long moment until Dan added his thoughts. "Sounds fair to me. I'll be happy to help with the interviews and decisions."

"Great!" responded Randall. "There's some other new information that may help with your decisions. You may have heard that, starting this year, the tech licensing board will require evidence of Continuing Education for your annual renewal. You'll need ten CEUs per year. Since we have two work hours left today, I could give Grace and Molly the Radiation Physics talk I gave Melinda, including an update on Radiation Biology. You'll get paid for the two hours, get two CEUs and be better prepared for your Chief Tech interview. Any takers?"

"Oh, alright. You convinced me," said Molly in a low voice.

Grace moaned. "Why not, *Jefe*?" When she noticed Randall's dagger stare, she added, "Dr. B."

Randall relaxed his laser stare and turned away. "That's better."

Randall turned to Dan. "Do you want to sit in and help me, or do you have stuff to do on the Linac?"

"I can't do much until the parts arrive tomorrow," said Dan. "I guess I could *kibitz* during the Physics part. If the Biology part is not too boring, I could sit through that, too."

Randall raised both arms palms up. "What? Me, boring?"

There was a smattering of comments. "Never!" "Are you kidding?" "Not in the least." "As interesting as a door knob."

"Alright, alright, message received and ignored," said Randall. "Unless there's any other new business, comments, criticisms or snide remarks, this impromptu staff meeting is adjourned. Only the CEU participants need to stay. Melinda, you can stay and hear this stuff a second time or complete today's charting."

Melinda stood up abruptly, giving Grace a look of disdain. "I've got the Physics stuff down pretty well. I'll do the charting."

Melinda's answer made Molly and Grace panic a bit. They asked to take a five minute coffee break and reconvene in the Ortho Room. Randall and Dan did the same. Meanwhile, Doris made a graceful exit to finish dictation in her office. She offered to keep an eye on the status of the parking lot and traffic while they conducted the CEU discussion.

Back to Basics

During Randall's physics talk, Dan added useful comments. Molly and Grace surprised themselves with how much they remembered. They were not nearly as well-versed about Radiation Biology, since a lot of the information post-dated their training. A majority of the data regarding the effects of radiation on normal tissue and tumors came from animal experiments, much of it done on rats. For the tumor data, various cultured human tumors would be implanted in rats and, once grown, would be treated with a variety of dosing schedules to determine which scheme was optimal.

Molly was rather grossed out about working with rats. "Good Gawd! How could anyone work with those filthy animals?"

"Oh, you mean the lab techs? They're not so bad," sniggered Randall. "Why, I spent a six-month sabbatical working in Dr. John Soulder's rat lab on the medical school campus. He kept a breed of rats from Reykjavik, Iceland, that had no immune system. The rats had to be kept in a laminar air flow room to keep out bacteria and viruses. Having no immunity, they wouldn't reject implanted tumor cells. To enter the room and handle the rats, I'd have to gown and glove like I was going into surgery."

Molly looked surprised. "Really? You were a rat doctor?"

"You bet I was! At least those patients didn't talk back. My experiment was to implant tumor cells in rat lungs, let the tumors grow and, when they were large enough, I'd irradiate them. I did chest x-rays on the rats to monitor the tumor growth."

Dan smirked. "So, you were a rat radiologist, too?"

"Yeah, just like human X-rays, except the X-ray images were only two by two centimeters. I needed a magnifying lens to read them. The hardest part was keeping the rats alive through the whole process."

Grace recoiled. "Oh, icky!"

"Oh, they're not so bad," said Randall. "They're not like the sewer rats you see in movies. They're all white with pink tails and noses. Cute little whiskers. Big teeth though. You wouldn't believe the size of their testicles."

Grace stared at him with renewed interest.

Dan chuckled. "Yep, I saw them in Dr. Soulder's lab when I helped fix his low voltage X-ray unit. Big-balled little suckers, they are."

Randall looked into the distance, wistful. "Yeah, I had one rat that I kept alive for six weeks. Almost got him through his last radiation treatment. I gave him a bit too much anesthesia and he stopped breathing. I even gave him CPR, but he was a goner."

Grace gasped. "What! Did you breathe into his mouth, too? Maybe it was your halitosis?"

Randall dodged the jab. "Damn! Never occurred to me. Should have used mouth wash that morning."

Dan laughed. "Were you ever bitten by one of your charges?"

"Almost," said Randall. "I was injecting sodium pentothal intraperitoneally for anesthesia into this one rat when he broke free from my grip. He almost bit me, but, before he could reach my thumb, I gave him a flying lesson. He had a crash landing on the wall. No survivors."

Molly stared at him in disbelief. "That's so mean!"

"Yeah, those rats can have a mean streak," replied Randall.

If Molly had been wearing a pearl necklace, she would have clutched it. "Dr. B!"

Randall ignored the comment. "But that sabbatical was not the first time I was a rat wrangler. I had previous experience."

"Let's hear it," encouraged Dan.

Randall was always game to tell a story, but knew those listening were often less enthused. "Are you sure? We've wandered a bit off the mark. I want to warn you that this line of inquiry leads to a rat tale. You sure you want to take the time?"

Molly's gaze went to the ceiling and back down. "Why the heck not? It's 4:15 and my brain is full. We've got 15 minutes left before quitting time. Go for it."

"Yeah, baby, it's cold outside," muttered Dan.

Grace slurped her coffee joylessly. "Whatever."

The Pied Pauper

Randall squared his shoulders and began the rat tale. "The summer after my freshman year in med school, I had to find a job to make a dent in my tuition and living expenses. I applied for a research fellowship in the med school Physiology department working in the lab for a PhD named Albert Yard. He was several yards tall, but not very wide." Randall raised his hand as high as he could reach. "His research project was studying the effect of various drugs on blood pressure and pulse. His animal of choice was the Wistar rat, one of the finest white furred, red-eyed little buggers to inhabit a lab. Me and another med student got the job."

"Did the Wistar rat look like the ones in Soulder's lab?" asked Dan.

Randall was pleased at least one person was listening. "Looked identical, but they had intact immune systems. It was my job, as one of the lowly research fellows, to do the nitty gritty work of getting the data for Yard's experiments. I'd anesthetize the rats with an intraperitoneal injection of sodium pentothal and strap them belly up on a special rat board. The board cost $500. I could have made it myself with plywood and formica for 20 bucks."

"What's intraperito-whatsis?" grumped Grace.

Randall poked his belly. "An injection right into the abdomen. Then, after Mr. Rat went to slumber-land, I would do a cut down on the neck, isolate the carotid artery, clamp it, and insert a tube into it. The tube would be connected to a blood pressure and pulse monitoring device before removing the clamp. After taking baseline measurements, I'd inject different doses of drugs, like epinephrine, and the machine would print and graph the results. Then Dr. Yard would evaluate the data."

Molly furrowed her brows. "Sounds like a difficult surgery, working on something that small."

Randall smiled, loving the comment. "Trains you for working on people-sized stuff. It took a few tries to get it done right. A few rats may have been transmogrified in the process."

Melinda frowned. "Oh, that's terrible!"

"Hold up—where was that lab?" asked Grace.

Randall motioned towards the east. "It was on the sixth floor of the old Marquette Medical School building on 16th Street, just off Wisconsin Avenue. Not much else was going on in the building during the summer. There was no AC and the lab got pretty hot and sticky. Combined with the smell of critter leavings, it got pretty acrid in the lab. So we'd crank the windows open as far as we could to catch any stray breezes." Randall fanned his face with his hand.

Grace was growing somewhat impatient. "Is this another biting story?"

Randall was annoyed with all the interruptions. "Just wait for it. Let's not spoil it for the group. It could be a biting story, but there might be a twisty surprise. Or I can say, yes, and stop here."

"Grace, would you just stifle and let the man finish?" scolded Molly. "You know him by now. It's going to take as long as it takes. We've still got five minutes."

"Shall I take that as a sign to proceed?" Randall asked coyly.

Grace moaned. "Yes, yes. Just get it over with."

Randall rubbed his hands together. "All right. Now, where was I? Ah, yes. I had just had lunch, it was hot, and I was getting sleepy. I got the next rat out of the cage, probably number 21 for the day, and gave the anesthetic. It was a big rat and I suspect I may have under-dosed him. As I was affixing him to the $500 rat board, he suddenly twitched awake, twisted off the board, let out a silent but deadly fart, and the little stinker bit my finger. The two sharp front incisors went clear through my finger tip down to my nail. Out of pure reflex, I screamed in pain, and flipped my hand up and down to dislodge the little pecker-head."

The audience let out a collective gasp.

Randall subconsciously re-enacted the event. "I yelled 'Get it off me!' as I tried to shake the rat free from my finger. In a spray of my own finger blood, the fat rat finally let go and flew in a blood spattering arc right out the open window. It looked like slow motion as the squirming fur ball sailed over the angled glass and on his downward path. I grabbed my spurting finger to staunch the blood and made a beeline to the open window to look below. When I got to the window I saw that Mr. Rat had landed on the sidewalk in front of an older lady with a shopping cart."

Molly gasped. "Zounds! At least it didn't hit her."

Melinda wrung her hands. "Oh, that poor rat!"

Randall held his finger like it had just been bitten. "What about my finger?! My lab partner joined me at the window and noticed my quickly exsanguinating finger. He wrapped it in a paper towel and asked what happened. My inner Dr. Seuss took over. All I could say was: 'Bit . . . fit . . . split! Bled . . . red . . . sped! Fat. Rat. Splat!'"

"That doesn't even make sense," guffawed Dan. "I bet you were in shock."

Randall nodded, still holding his now healed finger. "I must have been! My first reaction was to pretend it hadn't happened. What's one missing rat? Then, I panicked about getting fired and having no summer income or being demoted to cleaning rat cages. By then my lab partner had removed the paper towel and found a small towel to tourniquet my finger. He told me to hold the towel and wait there while he ran downstairs to retrieve the rat."

"Don't rats possibly carry rabies?" asked Molly.

"Funny, that was my next thought," said Randall. "I started to panic again. I could hear my lab partner running down the stairs. Then, the front door of the med school slammed shut and I poked my head out the window to look outside. He was standing between the dead rat and the older lady. I heard him say: 'Don't worry, Ma'am! I'm a doctor. This rat escaped from our lab. He's just sleeping. I'm going to return him and you can be on your way.' He scooped up Fat Flat Fred the Flying Rat and ran back into the building. The shopping cart lady did a double take, shook her head and resumed pushing her shopping cart down the sidewalk.'"

Grace hooted. "That's hilarious! I can see it now. What did your lab buddy do with the rat?"

Randall snorted. "He brought it back up to the lab. We tried to hide it, but Dr. Yard had heard the commotion and came out to check on us. He looked at the rat, then my bloody finger and put two and two together. Without a word, he motioned me into his office."

Dan smirked. "So you were cooked. Like a rat burger!"

"It was worse than I expected," said Randall. "First, Dr. Yard told me that he'd have to cut off the rat's head, put it in a biohazard bag and send it to the state lab to examine the brain for rabies. That would take three weeks and if it was positive I'd have to get rabies shots. Second, he said rat bites in the lab were a common occurrence and the biggest risk was a staph infection in my finger. Rats eat their poop so their mouths are a cesspool."

Molly grimaced. "Eww. That must have been a shock to the system."

"Indeed," agreed Randall. "Dr. Yard sat me down at his desk and went to get the first aid kit. While he was gone, I got up to take a closer look at his shelves. They were festooned with graphic readouts from our blood pressure monitoring work. There were hundreds of readouts. When he came back with the kit, I asked him if the data on the shelves was all his completed work. I was prepared to be impressed. He replied, 'I wish. That's data I still need to collate. I'm a little behind. You guys get data faster than I can process it. Actually, our student lab grants are mostly charity for poor students. Now, let me see that finger.'"

Dan chortled. "So, did you give him the finger?"

"Wisenheimer!" Randall retorted. "The charity thing was a revelation to me. Up until then I thought he was just weird. Well, he *was* weird, but he was also kind enough to help poor med students. And he did a great job cleaning up the bite and bandaging my finger. Barely left a scar."

Randall raised his middle finger and pointed it at Dan. "See, looks almost normal."

This caught everyone off guard. Dan knocked over his empty Styrofoam cup and the room burst out with laughter. "Put that thing back in its holster, cowboy. We know where it's been!" He guffawed at his own joke.

Doris poked her head in through the partially open door. "What did I miss? What was so funny? Y'all sound like feedin' time at the pig trough!"

Dan quickly regained his composure. "Dr. B was just pointing out something to us." The room erupted again and Doris looked lost in space.

Melinda tried to clear things up. "Dr. B was just talking about torturing rats when he worked in the animal lab in med school."

"And that was funny?" Doris shot back. "Rats are livin' creatures, too. I may be a bumpkin from the pumpkin patch, but I was taught that all God's creatures are sacred. It's bad enough they experiment on them, but to torture them, too? Why, I never! There's a handbasket waitin' to take you to hell!"

Dan put out a calming hand. "Whoa, Nellie. Melinda was just exaggerating for comic effect. The rat in question deserved to die and all other experimental rats were 'euthanized' at the end of the experiment anyhow."

Doris turned red and blustered. "As if usin' a euphemistic word for 'kill' makes it any better."

Randall made an "I give up" gesture. "Gee, thanks for your help, guys. That's enough poking the hornet's nest with a stick. May I offer a cogent explanation before Doris has apoplexy?"

Randall summarized the rat-bites-man incident. As he did so, Doris' coloring slowly returned to normal. Yet, she remained adamant that her objection was still valid since all lab rats had an unwarranted death sentence regardless.

Doris blustered a retort. "So, you're makin' this just about you messin' up, not about the rats being doomed?"

Randall still felt obliged to turn down the heat. "That would be one interpretation of the story. Allow me to expand. The rat's failed flight test was an unfortunate consequence of my survival-oriented response to the bite. It's not something one can easily control. And it was the result of my error. Yet, in the end that rat would have been sacrificed anyhow."

Melinda began to see the injustice. "All those rats that ended up deceased in Dr. Yard's lab produced reams of data that was probably never used. What a waste."

Randall nodded his agreement. "I get that. And it changed my views, especially when I was asked to use cats and dogs. I just couldn't do it anymore. I share your overall objection to the use of animals for research. It's a real dilemma. You have to weigh the animal's lives against what we learn from the research that aids healing human illness. I have very mixed feelings about that. I hate the loss of animal life, but I also hate the loss of human life. Although, some people vs. my cat? Tough choice."

Doris sounded a bit more mollified. "I see the problem . . . .You never told me you worked in an animal lab. I see that you did have second thoughts about research on those poor creatures."

Randall sighed. "Well, somewhat in my defense, in the med school lab I was still rather socially naïve and I didn't think too much about it at first, because rats are not endearingly cute critters. They have ugly yellow incisors and, well, ratty tails." He counted off on his fingers. "They poop and pee incessantly, plus their squeal is like fingernails on a blackboard." Randall squinted and curled his fingers into ratty hands. "At the time I was excited about the idea of doing research and that the studies we were doing would make better medicine for human-kind."

"At first?" asked Melinda. "What changed?"

Randall shrugged. "It was what you pointed out, Melinda. When I got a good look at all the redundant, unanalyzed data in Dr. Yard's office and found out we were just doing repetitive busy work, it seemed like a waste of life, even if they were 'just rats.'"

Melinda shivered. "Yuck, but I hate rats! They're disgusting. Ever since I found one in the basement when I was a kid. They're so ugly."

Randall nodded. "Yeah, that was my initial reaction. But then I noticed that the lab next door was using cats for surgery experiments and I love cats. It really upset me that they would use cats to practice on and then euthanize them. I started to visualize my rats with furry tails and perky ears. Their squeals started to sound like meows. It was spooky."

"That ties it," said Dan. "I've been suspecting you were *tetched*, but now I'm sure of it."

"You're not helping, Dan!" Molly snapped. "Kindly let him finish."

Randall tried to remember where he'd left off. "Now you've got me off the rails. Oh, yeah. There was this guy, Dick Mayman, the animal care technician. He liked rats and named each one. I'd go up to the sixth floor to pick up my rat of the day and Dick got it out of its cage. He'd give the rat a last hug and kiss, then put him in my rat carrier. As I walked off, Dick would remind me to be kind to 'Rastus' or 'Doofus' on his last day."

Dan shook his head in wonder. "And I thought *you* were strange." That evoked a round of guffaws.

Randall smiled and joined in the laughter. "I admit sometimes I reach the lower slopes of the bell-shaped curve of normalcy, but Dick was well beyond the edge of the curve."

Dan was on a roll and kept rolling. "You're definitely a data point that's hard to exceed. I heard you once fixed a water leak on the Linac with a twist tie."

"You're mistaking innovation for eccentricity," retorted Randall.

Doris grabbed Dan's arm and tried to rein him in. "Dan, if you keep eggin' him on, I will have to hobble you like my Daddy's mule."

Dan raised his hands in surrender. "Alright, alright."

Randall had planned to stop the story there, but it seemed he was being signaled to continue. Then he recalled a jewel of a story. "Once, when I went up to get Ratus Nextus, Dick gave me a conspiratorial look and asked me if I wanted to 'see something.'"

Melinda's interest had been waning, but this got her attention. "See something?"

Randall's gaze swept the audience. "Yes. Dick took me to a dark corner of the attic. There was a cage that held two immense white rats about four pounds each. Dick had saved them as pets two years earlier and they were well fed. Dick lifted them out of the cage and introduced them to me. Milo and Binkley were named after the characters from the comic strip "Bloom County." Dick handed me Milo. I was so shocked by the sudden transfer of custody that I nearly dropped Milo, afraid of being bitten. I soon found he was a friendly dude that just wanted to be petted."

Grace displayed shock and awe. "He was keeping pet rats on the sly? That's a 9.5 on the Olympic weirdness scale."

Doris added her two cents. "Hold on. Let's consider who's tellin' this rat tale. I bet it gets up to 9.8."

"Indeed," chuckled Dan. "Consider the source."

Randall started to walk towards the door. "Well, considering all the flak this B-17 is taking, it can easily turn around and fly back to England."

Melinda stood and went to block the doorway. "He's quitting the story now over my dead body!"

Randall shrugged and waved an arm. "Well, okay, if you insist! Ahem. Now, where was I?"

"The Four Pound Rat Brothers," prompted Melinda. "I suppose next you'll tell us they sang 'Muskrat Love' in two-part harmony."

Randall cleared his throat, ignoring the comment. "Ah, yes. It seems the animal committee had discovered Dick's little secret on a surprise inspection. They ordered Milo and Binkley to be excommunicated with prejudice. Dick was desperate for someone to assume guardianship. He had chosen me."

Doris was aghast. "You didn't take them, did you?"

Randall did his best to look saintly. "Of course, I did."

Molly did a double take. "Don't you have two cats?"

Randall held up a finger. "At the time we just had one cat, now deceased. She got along with Milo and Binkley just fine. I guess the cat figured it wasn't wise for a five-pound cat to antagonize two four-pound rats. Plus, Milo and Binkley were just sweet guys. They spent most of their time in the *ratatarium*, a nice little habitat that we built for them."

"Do you still have them?" asked Dan.

Randall held up his hands and flapped. "Nah, they lived about nine more months and graduated to rat heaven. The kids were a bit overzealous with rat feeding and rats always eat everything they're given. Dick and I did an autopsy on them. They weighed six pounds each and, near as we could tell, they died of cardiac failure. Not unexpected anyhow. The natural lifespan of a rat is only five to six years."

Doris found herself grieving the rats she had never known. "Bless their big little hearts. Were the kids sad?"

Randall frowned. "Oh, yeah. They were devastated. They insisted I bring back the bodies for burial. They dug little graves in the backyard garden. They made little crosses from popsicle sticks with the rat's names and dates. They cried for days. Probably won't bawl that much when I am released to holiness."

Dan started to say something, then reconsidered. "I'm not touching that last line."

"Darn!" lamented Randall. "I had a riposte prepared for just such a repartee."

Doris ignored their exchange. "My stars! Did you ever actually work with cats in the lab?"

Randall frowned. "No, I did not! The only time it came up was the med school fellowship, before I had kids. Dr. Yard asked me to do our procedure on cats one time and I refused. Passed it on to my lab mate."

"So, rats were okay, but cats were no way?" asked Dan. "You're an old softy at heart."

Randall looked embarrassed to admit it. "I guess. Every time I saw a cat on the lab table being operated on, I would visualize my own cat lying there. It made me want to run into the room and beat the surgeons."

"Sort of revises my view of surgeons," observed Doris.

Randall sort of agreed. "Surgeons do require a somewhat different mindset than other doctors. But you have to respect that they are willing to do what they do. They have to learn to compartmentalize and not become overwhelmed by the magnitude of what you're doing. Whatever the surgeon does happens right now, not sometime in the future, as is the case for us. I'm sorry for the animals that were sacrificed so they could learn how to do procedures safely on humans, but I am glad they didn't use a human as their first test animal."

"Here, here!" cheered Dan. "Better them than me."

Doris still couldn't quite wrap her heart around the concepts. "Your animal pal, Dick, did he handle the cats and dogs too?" asked Doris.

"Yep, he did it all." Randall stated matter-of-factly. "One time I went upstairs for my daily rat ration and he was in the back wrangling a cat. The cat was yowling and hissing its displeasure at being forced out of the cage. I think he sensed doom. Dick donned his special leather jacket and gloves to prepare for the difficult extraction. He asked for my backup help, so I put on protective gear too."

"I guess it would be pretty embarrassing for two grown men to be outwitted by one furry feline," noted Melinda. "I can't wait to see who wins this one."

Randall raised his eyebrow. "Have I told you this story before? As soon as Dick opened the cage door, Whiskers bee-lined out of the cage and through his legs. I tried to head him off at the pass, but wound up on my ass. The animal area was basically an attic with a sloped roof. Whiskers had run to the farthest corner under the roof slope. We had to crawl to get to him. We were sweating bullets in the stifling heat. Every time we got close the cat went zero to crazy and wound up in another hot corner."

Doris admired animal ingenuity. "Cat three, humans zero!"

"But wait!" Randall held up an index finger. "We huddled and came up with a new game plan. Dick flushed the cat out with a broom handle and I trapped it under a metal waste basket. Dick grabbed a square of plywood he kept stashed behind the cage and slid it under the basket. He lifted the covered basket and released the irate furball back into the cage. Dick slammed the cage door shut and told the cat he'd deal with him later."

Melinda let out a breath. "That cat shed at least one of its nine lives, I'm betting."

"Perhaps two," said Randall. "Dick's parting comment to the cat was that the governor had called with a last-minute pardon. The next day I went upstairs and noted that Whiskers was not in his cage. Dick said that, somehow, Whiskers had escaped overnight."

Dan grinned slyly. "That cat was probably named Schrödinger. There was only a 50-50 probability that the cat was in that cage anyhow."

Randall grinned at Dan. "Ah! Very true. He was, in reality, a quantum cat." This drew quizzical looks from the group. "We'll cover that in our next Physics talk."

TEE FOR TWO

"That Dick guy sounds . . . interesting," Grace snarked.

Randall agreed. "He was. I think I learned as much about patient care from him as I did from my so-called professors."

Doris squinted at Randall. "Really? I fail to see how."

Randall readied himself to explain, then paused. "Are you sure we have time for the answer? I suspect the parking lot will be cleared out by now."

Doris glanced at her watch and looked around the room. No one seemed intent on getting up. "It's already 5:00. We all knew this would happen if the boss man got to talkin'. So I'm pretty sure another ten minutes won't bruise our peaches if y'all are willing to stay."

Grace groused a bit. "Maybe if I get paid overtime."

Randall shook his head. "That's outside my purview. Staying on is strictly voluntary. What's it gonna be? I'm guessing it will take ten minutes."

Grace sagged in her chair. "Oh, alright. Why not? We've come this far."

With no other dissenters, Randall went on. "Dick invited me to his house to check out his backyard teepee."

Dan sat forward. "You did say teepee with a 'T', did you not?"

Randall nodded. "I did. Rick had a full sized, by gosh, authentic teepee erected in his backyard. We went in through the tent flap and sat cross-legged on blankets. He had a small wood fire going in the center. The smoke rose and exited through a vent in the peak. The night air was nippy, but it was toasty inside. He pulled out a peace pipe he had carved. It had a stone bowl that he filled with 'special' tobacco. He lit up with a small stick from the fire. After several puffs to get things going, he passed it to me." Randall handed an imaginary pipe to Doris.

Doris recoiled. "Er, how special was this tobacky? I'm purty sure my grandpappy would approve."

Randall swayed side to side, miming the effects of inhaling the special smoke. "Very special. After a while, Dick suggested friendly spirits would bring us visions. Boy, did they ever! We discussed the life spirit inside all living things. He opined that all such spirits are connected, even the Wistar rats and cats in the lab."

Melinda made an observation. "Dick is beginning to sound a little less cuckoo. Did he say anything more about experimenting on animals?"

Randall thought for a second. "Yeah, he did. He told me he took seriously the Native American belief that if you take an animal's life, you are obligated to thank it for its sacrifice. You must assure it that its life is being taken for a greater purpose. That's why he named the rats and gave them thanks when he sent them off to the lab."

Dan seemed impressed. "Sounds like some really good . . . stuff."

"It was," agreed Randall. "The spirits 'talked' to us. Their message was that in whatever form life presents itself to us, it is special. Each life has its own purpose and its own story. It is the responsibility of those called on to look after lives to seek out and protect that story no matter its appearance."

Doris nodded slowly, "The old book and its cover story, eh? Psalm 139. God has a plan for every life. Did the lesson stick with you?"

Randall looked a bit guilty. "It all seemed very profound while the THC was doing its thing, but the intensity faded a bit afterwards. I wondered if the message was just the drug effect talking. You know, maybe the message was a nice fantasy, like Cinderella."

Melinda piped up. "I know what you mean. I've made bad mistakes that make me think I've just learned a great lesson. But, with time, the intensity dwindles and, sure enough, I make the same mistake again. No lesson learned. Did that happen to you?"

Randall nodded. "In a way. The message didn't go away completely. It got reinforced by stuff that happened afterward. Like when I was an intern. I was working late on the medical ward. It was our turn to take patients for admission from the ER. I had already been up working all day and we had admitted six patients to what we called the Rose Room. It was just for patients who were unconscious, but alive. They couldn't give a history, so whatever was wrong with them was a mystery to be solved. I was tired, angry and frustrated."

Melinda piped up. "Why was it called the Rose Room?"

Randall glanced around the room. "That's the very question that came to my mind. I thought to myself 'what a room full of roses I have.' Then, it hit me. 'A rose by any other name....'" He paused. "Who are all these people? They all have a story. They just can't tell their stories any more. I realized it's my job to be sure their stories are respected no matter how they appear to me now. I flashed to lying on blankets in Dick's teepee. I was reminded of why I was there and what my job was."

Doris drew in a deep breath, but said nothing.

Dan commented in his deepest bass voice. "Wow, that's like a well. Very deep."

Randall looked around the room. "A lot of food for thought." He paused, allowing for meaningful silence. "So, before we head out of here, who can tell me how this applies to what we do?"

Doris raised her hand.

Randall pointed at Doris. "The lady in the back."

"Every veteran is sacred?" said Doris with gravitas.

Randall smiled. "Please expand on the concept for those who are hard of thinking."

"What?!" Dan sounded rather offended.

Doris cleared her throat. "Well, even though some of our patients come in lookin' like somethin' the cat dragged in, they are still deservin' of our respect. They have had lives that we know nothin' about and they should not be judged by how they appear to us now. Each one has a story and any judgments should be withheld. Each one is someone's son, brother, or cousin. Could be a father, uncle or grandpappy!"

Dan touched her shoulder. "Well, folks, that's the take home message for the day. Doris, you have my profound respect. You are one deep lady. What you said is a worthy goal, but I suspect it's something that none of us can achieve each day."

"I know I can't," grunted Grace. "Some days I have to force myself to come to work because some of them are so disgusting. And then, for the nice ones, if I get too attached to them, I wind up feeling awful when they pass. So, I try not to get too much into that stuff."

"I get that," sighed Randall. "Doctors deal with that too. And sometimes it's worse, because we're making the decisions that decide life or death and there are no backsies. Some docs just push the 'aloof' button, so we don't have to deal with that feeling. I call that bedside manneritis. It's a dreadful doctoral condition, frequently incurable. It is self-protection with abrogation of the *raison d'être.*"

Melinda squiggled her eyebrows. "Shoot, that sounds like lawyer-speak. Please explain."

"You know . . ." Randall shut an imaginary book. "I'm going to invoke the staff cop-out here. Look it up in your Funk and Wagnalls. Meeting adjourned."

Grace held up a hand. "Wait! What about the Chief Tech thing? Can we have a brief chat about that?"

"I don't see that chat being brief," said Randall. "Let's check the snowpack before we start addressing that."

DECLINATION

Molly attempted to mollify. "I think there's time. Grace and I have been talking and, to make a long story short, we both agree that we don't want the Chief Tech position."

Randall's head spun toward her. "What now?"

"It's simple," huffed Grace. "We don't want the added responsibility. We barely have the energy to do the daily treatments. If we add on all the extra stuff you'd expect from a Chief Tech, we'd be up to our 'you know whats' in alligators. We'd rather be Indians, er, I'm sorry. Native Americans or whatever is PC."

Randall searched his noggin for a response to this rather unexpected admission. "Wow. Now that's a horse with a different collar. Did you discuss this decision with Melinda? Because that means she's the sole candidate for the position if you two drop out."

Melinda pushed back in her chair. She wanted to make sure her response didn't reveal how much she really wanted the job. "What?! Me? No! This is the first I've heard of it. I'm not sure I'm ready to be Chief Tech. I haven't even finished the training yet or gotten my certificate."

Molly expected the response and wrongly judged it as sincere. "We thought of that. We're quite sure you'll finish and pass. You're the brightest student we've ever had. You'll be done in five months. In the meantime, Grace and I could share the Chief Tech designation until you're ready."

Melinda shook her head, smiling inside, but looking scared on the outside. "I can't really wrap my head around this. I'm still just a student!"

Grace had seen right through Melinda from the get go and was having none of it. She waved a hand dismissively. "Oh, get real. You can do it. You may be wet behind the ears, but you're full of . . . moxie. Besides, we don't want to go up against you in an interview, essay or exam. You're fresh off the printing press."

Randall was rolling this little play act around in his head, not sure exactly who was obfuscating. He pointed at Molly and Grace. "Well, whatever. Still, you two will need the CEUs for renewing your certificates. So you're not getting out of more continuing ed."

Molly waved away Randall's concern. "That's no biggie. All we have to do is pass. We don't have to beat out Melinda. I'm sure we can score well enough to get by."

Randall frowned, weighing the new ideas. "I guess I see your points. Melinda will still have to go through and pass the interview process I outlined. I can hold that off until June to give her more time to prepare. That will give the two of you time to change your minds as well. Plus, HR might just spring for a fourth tech position by then. We seem to be among the favored few since we signed on to their little Compliance Program. If so, we'd have another candidate to square off with. What do you think, Melinda?"

Melinda looked up at the ceiling pensively and studied the spaghetti-like jumble of cables running from the wall to the Orthovoltage machine. With a start, she slapped her thigh and nodded her head up and down with vigor. "Sounds like a plan to me. I hope both of you are okay with having a sprout like me being in charge of you two more senior techs."

"No problem," Grace spluttered. "Better you than me."

Molly gestured to herself. "Ditto."

"Great," said Randall. "That saves us a bunch of time and simplifies things. Thanks, Molly and Grace, for being so up front and gracious about this. I was afraid all three of you might be at loggerheads about the issue. Glad we could have this little *tête-à-tête*."

Grace looked like she had a chew of tobacco to spit. "Tay who, now?"

Randall smirked a bit. "Not a Francophile, eh? According to François it means 'face to face' or 'head to head.'"

Grace screwed up her face in defiance. "Smartass. I'm blowin' this pop stand." She sashayed out of the room, waving a limp-wristed goodbye.

Molly rose stiffly from her seat. "Boy, the old joints do get stiff after I sit a spell. Don't pay much mind to Miss Grump. Settling this Chief Tech thing is a load off for both of us. Tomorrow we get to do it all over again. The snow won't keep the patients away for long. Good luck getting home."

Randall wished Molly a safe trip home. Forgetting he wasn't alone in the room, he muttered to himself. "And the battle weary cavaliers retreated to their redoubt for sustenance and the rekindling of spirits."

Melinda's response almost gave Randall a bladder spasm. "You're being very cavalier about the whole thing."

Randall jumped a little bit. "Say what? Dang. Forgot you were sitting there. Do you mean I'm not taking this seriously enough?"

Melinda took umbrage. "Not at all. Just making a play on words. Guess I'm not as good at it as you. Actually, you did a great job handling those two. Maybe we'll get a fourth tech soon and all this angst will be resolved. But, for now, I'm beat. Must go home and hit the books with a baseball bat to force out the essence. One of these times it may work. G'nite Dr. B."

"You too," sighed Randall. "Sleep fast."

CHAPTER 10

———

RUMINATIONS OF THE SOUL

"The suspense is terrible. I hope it will last."

—Oscar Wilde

WHEEL SPINNING

It was nearly 6:30 Monday night by the time Randall made his evening exit from the VA. Somehow the snow-truncated day had still managed to generate enough paperwork to fill the in-basket to overflowing. "Don't need an MD to be a paper plant manager," he muttered as he stepped into the outside hallway and locked the department back door.

Outdoors he found a literal winter wonderland. At least 12 inches of snow had fallen, and it was still coming down in a light dusting. The wind had died down and there was hardly any road noise. It was eerily quiet. The cold front had moved through and the temperature had dropped to the mid-teens. It was brass monkey weather. Most of the parked cars had escaped the lot, but there were snowed-in cars scattered about that weren't going anywhere this night. The plows had cleared the snow around them so that they looked like snow islands with only a faint suggestion of the car beneath.

When Randall got to the spot where he thought he'd parked his car, his Scirocco appeared as just another snow island. He had to remove a patch of snow from the roof to verify it was, indeed, his car. He put down his winter survival backpack and extracted his snow scraper/

241

brush. After ten minutes of work, enough snow had been removed to gain entry and start the engine. Randall thanked the heavens it started on the first try. His lightly gloved hands were already getting numb.

As the car warmed up, Randall pondered his exit strategy. A snow pile at least eight inches deep blocked going straight forward. There was slightly less snow behind. He kicked the snow away from behind the rear wheels to create a tire path. As his loafers filled up with snow, he swore he could hear his mother scolding him for not wearing his galoshes. His punishment was numb feet.

When the exit path was clear enough for an extrication maneuver, Randall put his backpack in the passenger seat and got behind the wheel. Warm air was beginning to waft from the heater vents, so he warmed his hands there for a few moments to get some feeling back. The windshield wipers were frozen in place and useless to clear off the remaining snow. He carried a bottle of denatured alcohol in his backpack for such occasions. He grumbled heartily and hauled himself back out into the cold wind. He poured a splash of the alcohol on the wipers, and they suddenly became unstuck, flipping small chunks of ice in his face. He'd left the wipers on and cursed his moron maneuver.

A fellow employee clearing snow off his car heard Randall's rather loud exclamation and shouted back to ask if he needed help. This ticked him off even more. Someone had witnessed his bonehead botchup. Fortunately, Randall didn't recognize the guy. Randall shouted back. "No problem. I just got a faceful of slush. I'll survive. But thanks for asking."

Randall cursed his "Midwest Nice," counted to ten to regain his composure and returned to the cockpit for takeoff. Momentarily memory-challenged from the facial ice impact, Randall put the car in first gear and gunned the engine. The car lurched forward and abruptly hit the large snow wall. A loud crunching sound indicated a broken front spoiler. Randall yelled some more choice words that his mother would NOT approve of. "You were supposed to be in reverse, idiot! No, I am not going back out there to look at the damage. Nothing I can do about it here. But, shit! I can't wait. I installed the dang thing. I've got to inspect the damage."

Randall banged both hands on the steering wheel and exited stage left. Again. Even in the dark he could see a bracket had broken and the spoiler was hanging loose on the right side, nearly touching the ground. No way he could get home without ripping off the whole thing. His snowbound neighbor was still clearing snow around his vehicle and yelled out again to see if Randall needed help. Now Randall hoped he'd never meet the guy in the hallway some day. He could just hear the greeting.

"Say, aren't you the guy that managed to get a faceful of ice and rip off his spoiler the other day?"

Randall calmly turned and yelled back once again. "No thanks. I got this. Just a broken bracket. I've got a bungee cord in the trunk. Be fixed in a jiffy."

The helpful guy hollered back. "Alright. I'll be here a tad longer clearing snow. Just call out if you need a hand."

Randall waved and shouted back. "Thanks. I will." He cursed his German ancestors for settling in America's Dairyland. Feigning niceness was pissing him off!

The car had to be backed up several feet to get access to the spoiler. Randall eased the throttle in reverse to get the "Goldilocks" amount of rearward propulsion. He was rewarded with a clean exit and now just had to find the "stupid" bungee cord. After rummaging for several minutes through the usual array of frozen trunk detritus, he finally found the bungee. He had to lay down in the snow to find an attachment point on the chassis to hold up the spoiler, but after an 'in the dark' struggle, it was secured.

Randall waved goodbye to the helpful guy, ending his flourish with a hidden bird at the crappy weather. He navigated around snow piles out of the parking lot. He finally relaxed and let out a sigh of relief. There was enough hot air to defrost the windshield. He had forward vision. He had traction. He decided that seeing out the rear window was optional. Now, the question was whether to take the freeway or city streets.

City streets were best to avoid getting stranded on the freeway. Traction was iffy, but Randall made it to Wisconsin Avenue. The road had been partially cleared. The best traction was in the tracks left by other vehicles. Changing lanes was dicey, but he made it to the bridge over the Menomonee Valley. The bridge looked to have less snow, but there was sheet ice under the fresh snow. Almost halfway across the bridge, the Scirocco began to slide sideways. This was because the road surface was canted towards the raised sidewalks for water drainage. No amount of steering correction altered the rightward drift.

Randall backed off on the gas, but the car continued sliding freely with the rear rotating slowly toward the sidewalk and the front toward the center stripe. Braking did nothing to alter course and soon the car had backed itself, with a gentle thud, against the raised sidewalk. Fortunately, only the tires had hit. Randall put the car in first gear and attempted to pull away from the curb, but the front wheels just spun and shrieked. Looking down across the bridge he saw the flashing lights of a squad car parked at the curb at the bridge entrance. A cop emerged from the car and cautiously walked to where Randall was marooned.

The cop motioned Randall to roll down his window.

"Sir, are you okay?" asked the cop.

Randall gave a half-hearted thumbs up. "Yeah, but I'm just stuck here. Road was so slippery my car just had a mind of its own and decided this was the place to be."

The cop was sympathetic. "Not your fault. Bridges always ice up before the roads. I was dispatched here to keep folks off the bridge until we can get it salted. Had multiple accidents on it since the storm hit. My partner was supposed to block the end you entered from, but he's not been able to get here yet. I think I can pull you off the bridge. My squad has a tow line and tire chains. You got a tow hook on the front, I see. You put that on yourself?"

Randall felt proud of his handiwork. "Yeah, I put it on."

The cop was somewhat suspicious about that. "Why'd you do that? Do you race this thing?"

"Er, no, I don't race it, at least on a track," stumbled Randall. "I mean, I don't race it on the road either, ha ha. I just thought the hook would look cool."

The cop nodded. "It does look cool. Nice spoiler on the rear, too.

Nice work on that, but did you know your front spoiler is cracked? Just thought I'd mention it before I hook you up. Don't want you to think I did it with the tow rope."

Randall sighed. "Yep, I already knew. Wrecked it in a snowbank in the VA parking lot. Go ahead and hook me up."

The cop was curious again. "You work at the VA? What do you do there besides hitting snowbanks?"

Randall wasn't sure he wanted to play the doctor card, but decided to anyway. "I'm a doctor. I treat cancer patients using X-rays."

The cop looked surprised. "Well, I'll be dipped. My father is a WWII vet and he's getting radiation treatments there right now. His name is Peter Donahue."

Now Randall was the one surprised. "You don't say. I'm the one treating him. I just saw him today. He's halfway through and doing quite well."

"Doesn't that beat all!" said the cop. "He's told me about you. You look just like he described. You do look like a young Groucho Marx. He says your jokes are almost as bad. You got one for me? It's been a long day. I could use a laugh."

Randall's brain was working on half a charge and the only joke he could come up with was about a traveling salesman. His car hits and kills a rooster on a country road right in front of a farmhouse. He stops, picks up the dead rooster, carries it to the front porch, and knocks on the door. The farmer's wife comes to the door and the salesman apologizes for running over the rooster. He offers to replace it. The wife gives him a strange look and then nods her head. "That's mighty nice of you. Your choice. The hens are out back."

The cop was caught off guard and burst out laughing. "Not bad, doc. That makes my day. My partner will love that one. It was good to meet you. You take good care of my Pop. Remember, I know where you work and I've got your license number."

Randall thought it best to laugh at that. "Good meeting you too. Hopefully you don't get stuck on this bridge too. And hopefully I never see you in my treatment room! You don't want me for a doctor."

The cop chuckled and walked to his squad. He backed it up to the Scirocco without incident. He attached the tow line to the tow hook and easily pulled the Scirocco off the slick bridge. Once off the bridge, the cop reversed the procedure. He got back out of the squad and came up to tell Randall he was good to go.

Randall thanked the cop profusely for helping him off the bridge. "Man, without you being here, I might have sat there for hours and frozen my . . ."

The cop's two-way radio squawked on his shoulder, interrupting Randall.

"Sorry, Doc. Gotta go. I'm gettin' an emergency call on my radio. Don't be racing home now. Your kids are waiting to see their dad."

"How . . . ?" Randall sputtered as he watched the cop head to his car. "Oh well, he'll make a fine detective someday soon."

He pulled away from the curb and after 30 minutes of white knuckle driving he was home. Zelda, Addie and Kyle met him at the door.

"Daddy, Daddy!" shouted Addie. "We were worried that you accidented! It's so late and the snow is so bad!" Her little arms reached up for him.

Randall picked up Addie and gave her a big hug. "Glad to be home. It's been a long and twisty day. I'm fine. No blood was shed, but my car has a minor snow injury and a deflated ego."

Randall put Addie back down with a grunt and gave Kyle a fist bump on the shoulder. "Hey, buddy, how's my big boy?" He added a scalp knuckle rub to his greeting.

"Daaad," yelped Kyle. "Cut that out."

Zelda pushed in for a hug. "Make some room. Saved some dinner for you. We already ate. Get your coat off and get out of those wet shoes. You have perfectly good boots. Do you ever wear them? Get on some dry socks. And give me that filthy lab coat. Geez, what have you got on it this time? It looks like . . ."

Randall pointed at his tie. "It's ice cream! Just ice cream and red china marker and coffee and mustard and a few other things. I'm pretty sure there are no bodily fluids."

Zelda looked at the lab coat in disgust. "Randy, the sleeve edges are literally black. Have you got a frog and a snake in a pocket, too?"

Randall responded like a third grader. "I s'ppose."

This triggered Zelda's "Mom" persona. "I'll bet you have more filthy dirty ones hanging in your office that you conveniently 'forgot' to bring home."

Randall's response stayed in grade school. "I s'ppose."

Zelda had worked herself into a motherly fit. "My 'suppository' is full up. Tomorrow, you bring them all home for a good bleaching. That's the only way to get all the crud out."

"Yes, Mother," squeaked Randall.

Zelda was on a roll. Randall knew she was putting on a show for the kids and was playing along.

"Oh, and by the way, Randy, you're telling the bedtime story to-night. It's titled: 'The adventure of the snow trip home' and I'm listen-ing in. From your looks, I'd say it's going to be quite a story."

Randall deadpanned. "Yes, Mother."

The little drama had been fun, but a wave of fatigue mixed with hunger took over Randall's consciousness. "I'm done for. No more talk until I finish dinner. I'm totally flamed out. But after that, I will tell all. Bring your notebook."

Zelda could see that the horse was dead. There was no use beating it further. "No problem. The kids and I have a game of Monopoly to fin-ish and I am kicking ass. You change and eat what I saved for you. Then we'll gather for your story."

Snow-day Debrief

Randall got out of his wet clothes and started to shiver. He'd gotten rather hypothermic with all the messing about in the snow. He cranked up a hot shower and after 15 minutes of scrubbing and dubbing, he felt good enough to do his Pavarotti impression. His voice sounded almost operatic with the acoustics in the shower stall. He held forth with the only lyrics he knew. He repeated "Ave Maria" over and over in varying registers.

Zelda pounded on the bathroom door and yelled for him to knock off the singing. "Your dinner is reheated and getting cold and old. Stop your caterwauling and get out of there. It won't reheat a second time and still be edible."

Randall yelled back. "Be right down as soon as I dry off!"

Randall put on fresh underwear and wrapped himself in the plush terry cloth robe he had liberated from his stay at the Renaissance Hotel in Chicago. He rushed downstairs and was greeted by a plate of fish sticks, tater tots and Brussels sprouts topped with grated carrots. The ensemble looked as though it had stayed in the bathtub too long. Although the presentation was a bit lacking, he was hungry enough to overcome that minor shortcoming. Besides, a thorough slathering of Ranch dressing could correct most culinary deficiencies.

Randall had almost finished eating when he heard Zelda emit a shout of triumph from the dining room followed by a table slam and groaning from Addie and Kyle. He reckoned Zelda had finished kicking pediatric butt at Monopoly.

Zelda swaggered into the kitchen, both hands raised with index fingers pointed to the ceiling. "I am number one!" She danced around the table.

Addie whined from the dining room. "Mommmm! You cheated."

Zelda did not hold back. "Did not!"

"Did too," rebuffed Kyle.

Zelda shimmied her hips. "Well, maybe a little. Whatever! I'm the Mom and I say I won. Now, it's almost bedtime. You two sprouts have been up too long already. Get upstairs and get your PJs on. As soon as Dad tells me about his day and explains why it took him so long to get home, he will be coming up to tell you a bedtime story about his day. He promised me it would be a good one, so scoot."

"Aw, Mom," grumped Kyle. "I want a second chance to beat you."

Zelda scotched that idea. "Not tonight, Buddy."

Addie registered her indignation. "But you stole the 'get out of jail free' card."

Zelda's voice became steely. "No more lip from you two! You'll get your second chances, but not this night, sirrahs."

The kids clambered up the stairs without further ado and Zelda sat down at the kitchen table across from Randall. "How was dinner? Everything you were hoping for? You could have brought your girlfriends home with you. I made extra."

Randall raised his eyebrows. "Girlfriends? Are you kidding? When was this clandestine affair supposed to have happened? Have you looked outside lately?"

"Well, I called the department this afternoon," said Zelda. "Doris said you guys were shut down for the day due to the snow and a busted machine. When I asked for you, she said you couldn't be interrupted because you were in an important meeting with 'the girls.'"

Randall couldn't tell if Zelda was still playing games. He was annoyed and tired. "I was talking to them about who was going to be Chief Tech! That led to some drama. I softened that up by telling them we might be close to getting a department nurse to help with the clinic."

"I know," laughed Zelda. "Doris told me all that. I'm just yanking your chain. Sorry, I couldn't resist kicking you while you're down. I think it's great that you're finally going to get some help. It's cool how the Chief tech thing worked out. Kind of manna from heaven."

Randall relaxed visibly. "No kidding. You had me going there. I gotta say, it's been a day. I have one nerve left and that one is starting to fray."

Zelda touched his shoulder. "Again, let me say I'm sorry. Let's just take a quick breather right here and laugh about it."

With that, and despite his frustration, Randall burst out laughing, slobbering a half-chewed tater tot onto his plate. It was Zelda's turn to laugh.

"Thank goodness that was your last bite," she splurted. "Randy, here's a napkin." She got up to clear Randall's dishes and asked if he wanted the last piece of a Heineman's cream-filled coffee cake for dessert.

With the food releasing some much-needed energy, Randall was coming back online. "Any coffee left? Can't eat coffee cake without washing it down with a nice cup of java."

Zelda bowed slightly. "Coming up, sir. So, how was the ride home in the snow? I'm guessing it was a Siberian expedition."

Randall whooshed out a loud breath. "It was. Let's save the details for story time, so I don't have to tell it twice. I'd rather hear what's up with you."

Zelda raised her eyebrows. "Well, thanks for asking. After Doris and I chatted about the nurse position, I got to thinking. What would you think about me going to nursing school? I've always wanted to have a career in something more substantial than painting pretty pictures."

Randall was taken aback. This was the first he'd heard about such an aspiration on Zelda's part. His initial response was, wisely, not expressed. His hubby senses flashed red warning signals. This discussion needed to be handled with care. He looked at the ceiling as if contemplating a parallel universe and pursed his lips. "Hmm, interesting," Randall returned his gaze to Zelda, delaying his response. "Tell me more." Buying time was always a good safety net.

Zelda explained her reasoning. "Well, I know I have artistic skills. I realize that it's a gift and I shouldn't waste it. I just keep hearing my Dad's words about how artists don't create anything of real value or that helps people. I see what you do and I'm jealous. You help people every day. It makes me feel worthless and puny."

Randall took Zelda's hand in his and looked in her eyes. "I wish I had your skills! We all have different things we're good at and we should use them. Art contributes a lot to society. It helps us reflect on who and what we are."

Zelda scowled. "Are you saying that I'm not good enough to be a nurse?"

Randall remained steady. "Not at all! You're intelligent and capable. You care deeply about our kids and other people. I'm sure you'd find a way to use your creative skills to be a gifted nurse. The question is whether nursing is something you'd love? Or would it be drudgery? People are always happier doing what they love."

Zelda looked to the side, and down at her hands, considering. "Dang it, Randy! Why do you always have to be so ... wise about stuff?

I guess you're right. If it's just drudge work, I'd probably hate it even if I was good at it. Let's talk about this again after I think about it some more. I'm going to take the kids upstairs for bed prep. You just rest up for a while. I'll get you when we're ready."

Randall nodded. "Good plan."

Bedtime Tale

Randall's gourmet dinner of soggy fish sticks and tater tots churned in his stomach. The meal was going directly to his eyelids and he half-heartedly fought entropy as he slowly slumped forward towards the kitchen table. Gravity won the battle, but he managed to move the empty dinner plate aside before his forehead met the table. The long day had caught up with him. Head on the table, he closed his eyes and saw snowdrifts at the roadside as he glided along in his car like it was on sled runners. In the passenger seat was a pretty blonde he had picked up hitch-hiking. She really seemed to like him, and Randall dreamed he might get lucky.

His sled car swerved toward a ten-foot drift as he stared, distracted, at the bunny hills under the blonde's sweater. When the car yawed right, he tried to correct the veering car by steering toward the skid, but it had no effect. He mashed on the brakes, but nothing happened. His passenger screamed as the car embedded itself, door deep, in the large drift. How pleasant to have a moment's peace, he thought, as his head rested forward on the steering wheel. He longed to rest his head on the blonde's pillows.

A loud knocking on the side window of the car roused him from his torpid state. It was probably a cop tapping the window with a flashlight, he mused. Stupid of him to be caught with another woman in a parked car. The cop would probably think they'd hidden in the snowbank so they could make out. This wasn't good.

Kyle yelled into Randall's ear and rapped on the table with a spoon. "Daaad! Mom says it's time for the bedtime story you promised!"

Randall reached for an imaginary wallet and stuttered. "Yessir, l-license and registration. I have them right here."

Kyle started to yell. "Moommm, Dad's acting squirrely! Make him come upstairs. He's trying to trick me." Kyle pushed hard on Randall's shoulder and he finally came to.

Randall squinted at Kyle through bleary eyes. "Hey, Buddy, what are you doing out in this snow? I mean . . . down in the kitchen? You're supposed to be upstairs going to bed."

"You're supposed to be upstairs telling us a bedtime story!" Kyle's voice seemed to echo in the room.

Zelda came stomping into the kitchen. "What the flaming flyswatters is going on down here, Kyle? What's with all the yelling and pounding? Randy! What's taking you so long? The kids are ready for story time."

Randall moved in slow motion, still stuck in imaginary snow. "Just doing an eyelid light leak check and putting together some thoughts for the story." He hadn't lost his skill, gleaned from being on call as an intern and going from sleep to ready mode in five seconds. "Let me just clean up these dishes and I'll be right up, story in head. Call the Blood Bank for 4 units of O neg. Put in a central line and hang a liter of Ringer's on full open."

Zelda plunked her hands on her hips. "What the heck are you talking about?"

"Oh, nothing," sputtered Randall. "Just an acute episode of deja poo. I'll be sane shortly."

Zelda softened seeing how dazed Randall looked. "Okay, well, we'll be snuggled in our waterbed waiting for you. I'll get them settled in. Don't take too long."

It had become their habit to do bedtime stories with both kids in Randall and Zelda's heated waterbed. The kids liked to lie in it and pretend they were on a ship at sea. When the story was over, they'd be carried off to their own beds, primed for sleep. Kyle was getting just big enough that carrying him to bed was quite a lug. Soon they would need a tug boat.

Randall saluted crisply. "Aye aye!"

When Randall got up to the master bedroom, he found all three under the covers of the king-sized waterbed with Zelda in the middle. "Hey, there's no room for me."

Kyle explained the rationale. "We figured if you crawled in with us, you would fall asleep."

Addie chimed in. "Yeah, then there'd be no story."

Zelda smiled. "Sorry, mister man. You'll have to stay upright and talk. Get started."

Randall began in a wavery voice. "Okay, I'm ready. The story might scare you. Are you guys ready?"

Addie clutched her stuffed unicorn to her chest. "I'm ready and so is Uni."

Kyle tried to sound fearless. "I don't need no stuffed animals to protect me. Give it to us."

Randall took a deep breath and shook his head to wake up. "It was a dark and wintery night. Dr. Braveheart set out on his way home after treating a veritable battalion of sick soldiers. His usual path to his quarters in the forest was so deep in snow he had to take a back road. No one chose to take that path because it led to the troll bridge. He slogged through deep snow for what seemed like hours before he got to the bridge. With any luck, the toll troll would be sleeping in his cave and Dr. B could pass over the bridge unchallenged. It wasn't an encounter he was prepared for. But before we find out what happened to him on that fateful night, let's backtrack a bit and find out how he got there."

Addie shivered. "So this is a scary story?"

"Very scary," said Randall. "Are you sure you're ready?"

"Double ready," barked Kyle. "But before you start, wanna hear the crazy dream about a soldier I had last night?" Randall suspected that Kyle might not be as ready for the scary story as he let on.

Randall's head sagged. "Well, alright, but don't make it too long or it'll be tonight's bedtime story. If I don't tell the troll story tonight I might forget it completely by tomorrow."

Kyle thought that might not be so bad and he sat up in bed. "Cool! In the dream I was a littler kid than I am now. Mom and I drove to a train station. She didn't look like my real mom from now. A big man in a soldier uniform got off the train. Mom gave him a big hug and kissed him. Then, we took him home in the car. It was hot outside. The soldier man had a big camera and wanted to take a picture of us in front of a flower bush. The bush was icky 'cause it had ants crawling all over it and a ton of bees buzzing around it. One of the bees stung me on the neck and then I woke up."

Addie took exception to Kyle's story. "You're just making that up 'cause you're too scared to hear Dad's story."

Kyle stood up in bed trying to balance on the water bed. "I am not scared. Here's proof." Kyle pointed to a spot on his neck, lost his balance and fell back on the bed in a heap. The shock waves sent everybody bouncing up and down. "See, the bee got me right here."

When the bed settled down, Zelda inspected Kyle's neck. She found a red welt just under the hairline. "Dang! It looks exactly like a bee sting, Buddy. Does it hurt?"

Kyle folded his arms over his chest. "Yeah, but I'm tough. It's not so bad. Can you put something on it? It really itches."

Randall was speechless. Kyle's dream story was a near replica of one of Randall's earliest memories. In 1945, when Randall was three years old, his father returned from WWII service in the Army. His mother had driven to the train station with Randall to pick up his father. Randall had almost no memory of his father since he was only two years old when his father was drafted. Kyle's dream was accurate, right down to the bee sting. Randall had no idea how Kyle could know this since he'd never shared it with the kids.

Zelda returned with some ointment and applied it to Kyle's red spot. "Were you around any bees today?"

Kyle shook his head. "No, Mom. I just had it this morning when I woke up. Plus, there are no bees in Winter!"

Zelda shrugged her shoulders. "Well, that was some strange dream, kiddo."

Addie had a stranglehold on Uni. "Mom, Dad. I'm scared. I don't want a bee bite while I'm sleeping."

Kyle had the solution. "Then don't have my dream, dumbhead."

Addie whapped Kyle in the head with Uni. "Kyle called me a dumbhead."

More fighting ensued.

Randall barely registered the sibling melee. He racked his brain trying to figure out where Kyle's dream had come from, but was coming up empty. "I'll say. Strange dream indeed. Not sure how dream bee bites happen. Let's talk more about this later. Let's get back to my bedtime story before it's tomorrow."

Zelda finally subdued the savage beasts. Kyle lay back down and snuggled up to Zelda. "My bee bite feels much better. Thanks, Mom. Go ahead with your icy bridge story, Dad."

As the icy story spun on, Kyle and Addie hunkered closer to Zelda. When it was finished, the audience gave a collective sigh of relief.

"Wow, Daddy," said Addie. "I'm sure glad Dr. Braveheart made it home alive. It was a good thing he made friends with the troll or he would never have made it off that icy bridge."

Zelda patted Randall on top of his head. "Yep, that Dr. Braveheart guy was a fart smeller, I mean, smart feller. He knew how to pay the troll toll."

Kyle was quick to pounce. "Mom just said fart. She has to put a quarter in the swear jar."

Zelda blew it off. "Money well spent. Okay, now, your Dad looks ready to drop over. Time to hop off to your own beds and get tucked in. You're both too big to carry. Hobble off on your own." Kyle and Addie let their feet do the walking and lit out for their respective beds.

Zelda patted Randall's behind. "Nice story, Dad. You should do knitting. You sure know how to spin a yarn."

Randall mustered a weak laugh. "Har, har. Very droll. Next story is on you."

"Deal," winked Zelda. "Go ahead and get ready for bed. I'll finish off the sprouts and join you shortly."

Randall replied with a note of hope in his voice. "To interact?"

Zelda was quick to put a damper on that hope. "Nope, buster, to sleep. 'Charlie' dropped in for a visit today. I am officially on the rag. Besides, you look like you don't have the moxie to raise a ruckus."

"Just my luck," lamented Randall. "Two trolls in one day."

When Zelda rejoined Randall in bed, she was full of curiosity.

"Randy, that was some dream Kyle had. And the bug bite thing was weird. What did you mean when you said we'd talk more about it later?"

Randall had already drifted close to full asleep. "Oh . . . sorry . . . I'm already down to my last sheep. For now, let's just say it's an odd coincidence. Nothing to worry about. But I think our son has some unusual skills. I promise I'll explain it tomorrow. Right now I'm too pooped to pontificate."

Zelda pecked him on the forehead. "Alright. But if you don't, I'll bug you incessantly until you deliver the goods. Say goodnight, Randy."

Randall complied. "Goodnight, Randy."

C H A P T E R 11

———

K ETCHUP BASEBALL

"A whole stack of memories never equals one little hope."

—Charles M. Schulz

S NOW CASUALTY

Morning came fast the next day. It took monumental will for Randall to drag himself out of bed. He'd had dreams of driving down canyons of snow. First, he was stranded in a snowy mountain wilderness with the Donner party. He led them out of harm's way and the wagon train parked in a Big Boy restaurant parking lot full of station wagons. They paraded inside and the lady at the front desk asked if they had reservations.

Randall said, "Yes. It's under Donner, party of 99."

Randall's bladder needed attention at 4:00 AM. He was glad to be awakened, because the Big Boy burgers had apparently not done the job. The Donners were still hungry and were having a cannibal cookout. When his bladder rang, Randall had been saying "no" to a fricasseed foot with jam. Where that had come from, God only knew.

Fortunately, that dream did not reoccur when he went back to bed. Unfortunately, a dream about kidnapping an underage teen took its place and he woke himself up again just before the jury came back with a verdict. He decided getting up early was less taxing than dreaming, but the magnetic pull of the bed was still quite Gaussian.

259

Randall was glad that he hadn't dreamt about his two-year-old self being bitten in the neck by a bee. He didn't want a dream bee bite.

Randall automated through the fog of morning preparations and his cold little Scirocco drove itself down snowy streets to the back forty VA staff parking lot. He stumbled coming through the department's back doorway as his winter survival backpack got trapped by the rapidly closing door. Molly and Grace looked over from where they were sitting at the Linac console, sniggering at Randall's sudden spasticity.

Ever tactful, Grace called out a greeting. "Smooth move, Ex-Lax."

Randall bowed gracefully. "Thanks. I meant to do that just for your entertainment. Glad you enjoyed it." Somehow Randall's backpack strap had become tangled in the door latch. He swore as he freed it up.

Molly had no mercy for the disabled. "Get out on the wrong side of bed this morning?"

Randall let out an exaggerated moan. "Both sides were wrong this morning. And last night was no better. Getting home was like dealing with the VA administration. How was it for you two?"

Molly made a sour face. "About like yours. We're all in a 'mood' this morning."

Randall faked disbelief. "Really? Good to know. Did Dan get the new part installed?"

As if on cue, Dan walked out from the Linac room and said good morning to Randall.

Dan nodded. "That's an affirmative, Boss. We are a go for the show. The girls are going to run the warmup sequence, I'll run the output checks, and, Lord willing and the creek don't rise, treatment may commence."

Randall tried to sound more enthusiastic. "Excellent! First good news I've heard today. By the way, did you know that the C in creek in the expression you just quoted should be capitalized?"

Dan looked puzzled. "My trivia detector is quivering. I hope the explanation won't take too long."

Randall straightened up for a mini-pontification. "The expression dates back to the Indian wars in Florida. It is not about a creek ready to flood, but about the potential for an uprising of the warring Creek Indians."

Dan faked an interested look on his face. "Say, now, that is almost remotely interesting. I'll take note of it—in pencil. At another time. You may go to your office now—please."

Randall waved limply. "On my way."

As Randall headed down the hall, he encountered Doris arriving through the front door. She was limping noticeably.

Randall bowed again. "Good morning, my fair lady. Looks like you have a hitch in your giddyup."

"Yes, a fair bit of one," said Doris. "Slipped on the ice on the way in from the parkin' lot. Well, I didn't really slip. My knee gave out and down I went. Fortunately, I have good paddin' on my stern components and that saved me, but my knee hurts so bad I want to whistle Dixie."

Randall reached out to carry her things. "You want I should take a look at it?"

Doris was glad to be relieved of her carry bag. "I'd be much obliged. I'll get out of my winter gear and meet you in exam room one."

"Great!" Randall proclaimed, then lowered his voice. "I can get into YOUR pants this time."

Doris looked around to see if anyone heard the scandalous remark. "Why, I never!"

"But you did. Can't erase history, sweetcheeks." Randall ticked his internal scoreboard. Now they were even.

In the exam room, Randall tested Doris' knee for range of motion. The findings were consistent with a sprained knee and possibly a medial meniscus tear. She told Randall her doctor back home in North Carolina had warned her, after a previous knee sprain, that if she didn't lose about 50 pounds, she was at risk for further knee problems. If anything, she had gained weight since that exam. Randall offered to get an Orthopedics resident down to check her knee and advise on acute care. Randall wrapped the knee with an Ace bandage and escorted Doris to her desk where there was plenty to take her mind off her knee.

Randall found a similar pile of work on his desk. Although he had cleared it the night before, the paperwork gods had once more scattered manna on his workspace. Boredom would be diverted once more. After a bout of initialing, signing, approving and denying he arrived at the layer pertaining to the day's schedule. There were three new consults to be seen, two of them leftover from the ones canceled the day before. One always paid for time off. It was never free. It was like a layaway plan.

CORPORAL GRUNT

The first consult was one Hardy Haymaker, a Vietnam vet with a history of PTSD, exposure to agent orange and a new diagnosis of inoperable base of tongue cancer. Review of the multiple volumes of old records showed that Mr. Haymaker had made many visits to Psych for counseling and was on some fairly heavy-duty psychoactive medications. Melinda popped into Randall's office and asked if he wanted her to put Mr. Haymaker into a room. He approved of the action and said he would be in as soon as got through reviewing Volume four of the records. Several minutes later, she was back to tell Randall the patient was ready, but they should chat before he went into the room.

Randall glanced up with curiosity. "Is there a problem?"

Melinda shivered. "Several! First of all, he scares the crap out of me. He's one of the strangest dudes I've ever met. He's wearing a white construction helmet that he refuses to take off. There's a name written on the front of the helmet in magic marker and I'm not sure what it means, but he says it's his name."

Randall loved a challenge. "What's it say?"

"'Grunt,'" said Melinda.

Randall shook the cobwebs from his brain. "Excuse me?"

Melinda smirked and shrugged. "That's what's written on the helmet. 'Grunt.'"

Randall shook his head wondering why he attracted all the weirdos. "Hmm, that's what I thought you said. Now that I roll it through my mental printing press, it sort of makes sense. He was in the Army. They like nicknames. What else?"

Melinda frowned. "Well, he's rather disconnected and tangential. He talks nonstop, and hops from one topic to another. You have to interrupt to get a word in edgewise."

Randall nodded. "Makes sense. Tangential thinking is common in PTSD. I'll adapt for that. Is that what scares you?"

Melinda looked at her hands. "Well, no. He's got this big cigar box that's all painted up with scribbles and nonsense. He holds it like there's treasure inside. He says there's something special inside that he wants to show you and only you."

Randall's shoulders hiked up. "Yikes! That is bizarre. I've never even seen the man before. What do you think is in there?"

Melinda glanced over her shoulder. "I know this sounds crazy . . . but what if he has a gun in there and he's, you know, looney tunes. I don't want to get lead poisoning."

Randall took a deep breath. "Hmm. Not what I was thinking, but now that you mention it, I'm getting a little scared." He thought for a long moment and then waved a hand. "Nah, I've dealt with these guys before. Usually more bark than bite."

Melinda didn't look convinced. "Shouldn't we call security down here? A VA cop would be useful."

Randall shook his head. "I think it might just aggravate him. We're going to have to treat this guy. We need to establish trust from the get-go. I think it will be alright if I go in alone and start the consultation. I'll be very careful."

Melinda blurted her objection to the plan. "What? You shouldn't go in there alone."

Randall countered. "So, if it's unsafe, I should risk someone else?"

Melinda took a deep breath. "I'm scared, but I'll go with you. We both stand to his side. If he makes a wrong move, we're both quick. We can get the jump on him."

Randall stood up straight and let out a held breath. "Geez! Let's not manufacture mountains when molehills are ahead. Trust me. It's going to be fine. I'm going in and you can come with me or not."

Melinda rubbed her hands on her skirt. "You're not going in alone. I'm coming."

Randall grabbed the chart from Melinda. "Then so be it."

Randall and Melinda walked with purpose down the hall and Randall pushed the exam room door open slowly. He walked into the room cautiously and found exactly what Melinda had described. Mr. Haymaker was sitting in the exam chair, helmet on and a painted cigar box cradled in his lap. Randall strode up to the patient confidently, put forth his hand and introduced himself. Mr. Haymaker took Randall's hand and gave him an iron grip handshake.

Randall's fingers felt crushed and he couldn't help but grunt in pain. He managed a clenched teeth response. "Just call me Dr. B."

Haymaker's jaw spasmed a bit. When he spoke he sounded like a baked potato was stuck in his throat. "Just call me Corporal Grunt. That's what all my buddies call me."

Randall shook his shaking hand to get the feeling back. "Quite a firm grip you've got there, Corporal. I like your . . . hat."

"Thanks," croaked Haymaker. "I decorated it myself."

Randall pretended to admire the hat. Haymaker took it off and handed it to Randall for a closer look. Randall inspected it like he was a drill sergeant. "Good work, soldier. My aid, Melinda, will be staying in the room with us if that's alright with you." Randall handed the construction helmet back and requested that Haymaker leave it off until inspection was over.

Haymaker gave Melinda a lascivious look. "Don't mind a bit. Like I was telling the boys. You know, I should have bought Polaroid when it was low. How long is this gonna take? My car needs a lube job. You know I can't eat . . ."

Randall interrupted. "I know that, Corporal. It says here in your chart that you can't eat solids. How long have you been on liquids?"

Haymaker's jaw spasmed again and his head twitched to the left. "Liquids. Yeah. I've always liked liquids, especially really liquid liquids. Liquor liquids and liquor lockers. Lacquered liquor lockers . . ."

Randall grabbed the thread. "You're a liquor liker. I see you've been drinking mostly Carnation Instant Breakfast, but you've lost about ten pounds."

Haymaker broke into a rather muffled song. "Away, away, away oh."

Randall thunked his heels together. "Very good, Corporal! I want you to come to attention. It's time for your briefing."

Haymaker saluted. "Yes, sir, Dr. B, sir! What are my orders? Tell me the God's honest. Do I have a chance against the enemy?"

Randall's words came out clear and sharp. "I'll give you honest, Corporal. Before I can give you that intel, you have to answer all my questions straight up, no chaser. I need my troops on board with the program or I muster them out. Understood?"

Haymaker saluted again briskly. "Yessir!"

Randall looked over at Melinda and asked her to take notes. He turned back to Haymaker. "Now, before we start this briefing, we need to reconnoiter and check your gear. What's that in your lap? It doesn't look like regular Marine Corp issue. Open the breech for inspection."

Haymaker nodded and lowered his voice. "Sir, I brought this for you. It's not regular issue, but it's very important. It's 'eyes only.'"

Randall motioned for Haymaker to open the box. "Well, quit wasting our time. Unlatch and reveal."

Haymaker slowly raised the lid, but the contents were still concealed from view momentarily. He reached into the box. For just a moment, Randall envisioned him bringing out a handgun. Instead, he brought out a handful of loose papers. Randall and Melinda both let out a held collective breath.

Randall tried to sound military, but his voice came out sounding like he was going through puberty. "What's that, soldier?"

"This is my novel about Nam, sir," said Haymaker. "All the secrets are in this document. It's taken me years to write, but now I've got it all down. I want you to read it and tell me if it's a good report for HQ. At least it's all true. Here, take it."

Randall took the papers and began to look through them. The pieces of paper were of various sizes, all with scribbled writing on them, mostly in pencil. Each had a date from the mid-sixties written on it. Some were scraps of old menus with writing in the margins or pieces of newspaper. Randall tried to read the writing, but it required some study. One entry read: "6/3/66 Joe got blowed up by a mortar." Another said: "Sunday-Snuffy snuffed by sniper."

"It's a real good story, Dr. B," said Haymaker.

Randall had only read a few entries, but what he'd read revealed a lot of trauma. The man had clearly been through hell. "This is fine work, Corporal. I'll need to read it carefully. You may be up for recognition for these actions. I've got an orderly who can type this up with your permission."

Haymaker seemed to be in a safe world. "Yessir, what are your orders?"

"Melinda," barked Randall. "Take these valuable papers to Private Doris and have her transcribe them. Then have her return them to Corporal Grunt for safekeeping. You're dismissed for now. I'll carry on with this on my own. What follows is strictly 'need to know.'"

"Aye aye, sir," said Melinda crisply. "Are you sure Private Doris can, er, decipher this code?"

Randall smiled and nodded. "She should have no problem. She's been trained to read my code writing. She can handle this. If she needs help, she can confer with me."

Randall completed the consultation with full cooperation of the participant. At the end, he was able to assure Corporal Grunt that he had a significant chance of recovery from his cancer if he went by the book. Grunt confirmed that all orders would be followed to the letter. Randall walked the patient out of the exam room.

On the way out, Haymaker made Randall an offer. "Hey, Doc, want me to make you a hat like mine?"

Randall responded immediately. "You know, I could really use one. . . . so ordered. Make sure to put my rank on the front."

Haymaker saluted again. "Happy to help you out, sir."

Randall took Haymaker to see Doris to arrange further tests and set up a simulation. He went back to the treatment console to explain what he needed.

Melinda brought Randall the chart for his next patient and couldn't help but comment on their experience with Mr. Haymaker. "Holy galoshes! That guy was something else. You *have* done that before. That's the best job of ad libbing I've ever seen. You missed your calling. You should be on stage."

Randall gestured around the department. "Private Melinda, this *is* the stage. Sometimes the script just writes itself. Now, who's next up?"

Melinda looked at the chart. "I've got a prostate on day old white bread or a melanoma on rye. What's your druthers?"

Randall made a face at Melinda's patient menu. "I'd druther you not totally depersonalize our customers. But I do like your ad libs. Just don't do it in earshot of patients."

KINESIOLOGY

Doris rubbed her injured knee and moaned in pain as Randall walked by her desk on his way to start the second consultation. "Knee hurting worse?"

Doris gritted her teeth. "Dang thing hurts like a mother trucker! Must be swellin' up, too, because the ace bandage is tight as a jar of peanut butter at a squirrel convention."

Randall laughed. "My word. A bit of pain sure broadens the scope of your dialogue. Haven't heard those provocative analogies before."

Doris grimaced. "I suppose not. Those expressions are as Southern as Goody's Headache Powder. Speakin' of which, I could use some right now."

Randall was bemused. "And what the heck is Goody's Headache Powder?"

Doris gave Randall a strange look. "Folks 'round here don't get out much do they? It's a mighty potent powder made from Tylenol, aspirin and caffeine. Comes in little packets." Doris held up an imaginary glass and spoon. "Pour a packet full in a glass of water and drink it down. Goes right to what hurts. Tastes disgustin', so you're sure it must be medicine. It's a sure cure for hangovers."

Randall made a sour look. "Hmm, never heard of it. Sounds disgusting."

Doris nodded. "It surely is, but it works. Not available above the Mason-Dixon line. Can't get it up here in the tundra. I've looked. Available only at the 'Good Neighbor Pharmacies' back home."

Randall took a quick look at Doris's knee. "Let's get you back to the exam room so I can loosen up that Ace wrap. It does look more swollen. Listen, I know the Chief Resident in Ortho. Let me give him a call. He may have something more intelligent to recommend."

Doris nodded her agreement. "Sounds like a good idea. You may need to give me a hand gettin' up from this chair."

Randall helped Doris up and led her to the exam room. He had her lay down on the exam table to straighten out her leg. After removing the Ace bandage, he found the knee more swollen and red. It seemed to him there was more damage than he'd thought.

Randall tried not to show too much angst. "Let's keep the leg elevated until I get Dr. Oliver down here. I'll go page him. Just a word of warning. He's a good guy but he doesn't have much of a sense of humor."

"Not much of an exam table manner?" queried Doris.

Randall laughed. At least Doris had not lost her sense of humor. "You could say that! He knows his stuff, better than most of his attendings, but he's fairly blunt. I attribute it partially to the fact that his parents played a lifetime trick on him when they named him Oliver."

"Oliver Oliver?" laughed Doris. "I feel better already."

Randall chuckled. "Yeah, we refer to him as 'O2' At least when he's not within hearing range. If he knows about the nickname, he hasn't said so."

Doris chuckled, then winced. "I can't just lay here doin' nothin' until he comes. There's too much work to do. Walk me back to my desk and elevate my leg there. At least I can type and answer the phone until he can get down here."

Randall held up a finger. "Good point. In the meantime, have you got anything for pain in your purse?"

"You know what?" exclaimed Doris. "I think I have an emergency packet of Goody's in the side pocket."

Randall clapped his hands. "Good! That could do the trick. Otherwise I think we have some ibuprofen in the med cabinet. Let's get you back to your office."

As Randall moved to help Doris up, she hesitated for a bit and looked up at him. "Uh, I saw the look on your face, Dr. B. I'm guessin' you think the knee is not good. Am I right?"

Randall tried to keep things calm. "Let's not jump to conclusions. At least not on that bad knee. You know I'm not an Ortho guy. Don't push the panic button yet." Doris gave an 'I'm not convinced' sigh.

Randall helped Doris back to her office and rigged up a footrest for her. She found her Goody's powder and took it straight up from the packet. Randall paged Dr. Oliver, who called back saying he could come down in about 15 minutes after finishing up a cast. Doris was relieved to hear the news. Randall was ready for the next patient and, just in time, Melinda appeared with the next patient's chart.

Alphabet soup

Melinda held out the metal hospital chart. "Hey, Dr. B. I was just coming to find you. I put your next consult in room two. His name is Oscar Schmidt. Do you have any other paperwork on him? He's on a gurney and he is only semi-conscious. His breathing is funny, too—wheezing and coughing. Seems like he can barely breathe."

Randall reached for the chart. "I don't have anything on him. There was nothing on my desk. But Doris can't get around with her bad knee."

Melinda looked slightly confused. "There's hardly anything inside the hospital chart except this handwritten consultation request and I can barely read it. Looks like code. Best I could make out was something about lung cancer. There's hardly anything else in the chart yet. Not even an order sheet or progress notes. There's a few lab reports."

Randall thumbed through the nearly naked chart. "Hmm. . . . you're right. There's not much here. Wait here. I'll see if Doris has anything more on the guy."

Doris had no other information on Mr. Schmidt. She said the chart had been stuck under his gurney pillow and there were no old chart volumes.

"Just what I need," sighed Randall. "A mystery guest. Give me the chart. Let's see how good my cipher analysis is today."

Randall went back to the consult request and tried to decipher it. It was written in a calligraphy style script, using a broad ink pen tip. The letters were written with a lot of flourishes, but Randall gradually made it out. He read it out loud to Melinda. "Looks like it says: '76 y/o w/m w/ FTT and PPP. CXR w/cav RUL mass. Rt. Br. Obstr. w/ POP. FB r/o. Please XRT sans tissue Dx.'"

Melinda coughed out a laugh. "Well, now I understand it! Not!"

Randall had to laugh as well. "You're right, Melinda. It is in code, but it wasn't produced by the German Enigma machine and we don't need cryptanalysis. The abbreviations are clear to me, at least, if not completely politically correct."

Now Melinda was getting perturbed. "Alright, Dr. B. You've piqued my curiosity. Now, give me the translation."

Randall took a breath. "Piece of cake. Translated from doctor shorthand it says: '76-year-old white male with Failure to Thrive and Piss Poor Protoplasm. Chest X-ray shows a cavitary mass in the right upper lobe. Right bronchial obstruction with post-obstructive pneumonia. Fiberoptic bronchoscopy ruled out. Please treat with radiation therapy without a tissue diagnosis."

Melinda gasped. "Good God! It says all that? So, basically, the man is in such bad shape that they can't even put a scope in to biopsy what looks like a tumor blocking the airway. Is that right? And they want you to treat him with radiation even though they don't know for sure if it's cancer?"

Randall's eyebrows shot up. "That's the gist of it. My star pupil! Go to the head of the class. I never quite understood if that meant sit up front or go to the bathroom, but we'll assume it is the former. So, what do you think? Should we do as asked?"

Melinda pondered. "I don't think so. It could just be an infection. How would radiation help that? What is it you always say about treating without a proven cancer diagnosis?"

Randall looked proud. "You remembered! No meat, no treat."

Melinda nodded. "Yeah. That's it."

Randall backpedaled a bit. "Well, there are some exceptions. This could be one of them. If it's too dangerous to get tissue, we could give four or five treatments. If it is a tumor, it may shrink enough for the airway to open up and clear the pneumonia. Without opening the airway first, they can slam away with antibiotics, but it's unlikely to clear the infection if it's trapped. If the pneumonia improves, they might be able to scope him and get tissue. And find out what kind of bug he's growing to better direct their antibiotic choice."

Melinda squiggled her eyebrows. "Hmm, not an easy choice. So, how do you decide?"

"When in doubt, examine the patient," said Randall sagaciously. "You can see an awful lot by looking. Let's go lay eyes upon Mr. Schmidt."

When Randall and Melinda entered the exam room, they found Mr. Schmidt no longer struggling for breath. He was lying quite still with his eyes closed and his blue lips forming a perfect circle.

Oh Crap, Dead Guy

Randall took one look and knew immediately that Mr. Schmidt no longer needed his help. "Oh, crap, positive 'O' sign."

"Is that more doctor code?" asked Melinda.

Randall moved quickly to the side of the gurney and put his fingers to the patient's wrist, feeling for a pulse. "Look at his mouth. His lips are blue and make a perfect circle. That's the 'O' sign. If his tongue was sticking out to the side it would be a positive 'Q' sign. That's even worse, but both usually indicate death. Plus, he's got no pulse."

Randall listened with his stethoscope for breath sounds, but heard none. He pulled back Mr. Schmidt's eyelids and shone his mini Maglite on the pupils. No pupillary response to light. The pupils were fixed and dilated.

Melinda started to panic. "Dr. B! Should we call a code and start CPR?"

Randall had another idea. "Melinda, check the chart for a DNR slip! It's yellow."

Melinda stared at the newly dead body and didn't respond. Randall grabbed the chart from her and flipped it open. There he found a yellow DNR form taped to the inside of the metal chart cover. DNR did not stand for the Department of Natural Resources. It meant "Do Not Resuscitate."

Randall sighed in relief. "Don't worry, Melinda. We won't be doing CPR today. We just got our 'get out of jail free' card."

Melinda seemed to come to. "So, is he . . . dead?"

Randall uttered some choice four letter words. "Damn straight," he shouted. "Stupid ward! They sent this guy down for a consult when he's got both feet and one arm in the grave. This is the first patient to ever die in the department on my watch. What the heck were they thinking? I have a good mind to go upstairs and ring someone's neck."

Melinda grabbed Randall's arm. "Dr. B! Don't go doing something you'll regret. The nurses were just following orders."

Randall couldn't stop grumping. "Yeah, the orders of an idiot doctor. Whose name is on the consult request? I'll rip him a new one."

Melinda checked the consult request. "It says, C. Newberry, MD."

Randall grabbed the chart. "Let me see that! Holy Mary Mother of a Mongol. That's Carl Newberry, the VA Chief of Staff. He staffs the medical ward for one week every six months to keep his finger on the pulse of the hospital. I should have figured that out when I saw the calligraphy. He's proud of his writing skills and writes all his notes that way. Big flourishes on his signed memos, too. Okay. Deep breaths. Must handle this carefully."

Randall started to dither a bit and Melinda tried to calm him down. "I think it's time to call Elisa for a bail out. We don't have time to deal with this. There's a plethora of patients waiting out in the hall."

"You're right." stammered Randall. "Plethora, huh. That sounds like a lot. Page her right now. Leave the late Mr. Schmidt in the exam room and make sure no one goes in there. Meanwhile, I'll defuse some of the land mines waiting in the hall."

Elisa responded promptly to the page and Melinda filled her in on the situation. Elisa came down to the department just after Randall finished an on-treatment review on a patient in exam room two. She motioned Melinda and Randall into the empty exam room 1 and closed the door.

Elisa explained her proposed solution. "Here's what I suggest the story is. You never had a chance to see the patient. He was brought down and left in the hall. I took him to the exam room for you. I checked his vitals and found him pulseless and not breathing. At first I was going to call a Code, but found the DNR form on the chart. I belayed the idea of calling a Code and went to get you. You confirmed he was deceased and directed me to take him to the ward for a return of the empty."

Randall smiled broadly. "Wow, you think on your feet, Elisa. Sounds like a plan. Probably won't even get back to Newberry. I'd modify the last part of your plan a tad. Let's ask the ward to have that weird transport guy, Ira, come down for the pickup and leave out the dead part. I bet Ira won't even notice the guy has gone back to the factory. Or if he does notice, he'll probably freak out. Don't want to miss that show. By the way, don't forget to get your deposit back."

Melinda gasped. "Dr. B! That's just mean, but I like the idea. That would definitely keep Ira off my back. I bet he'd be afraid to step foot in the department again. He'd probably just leave patients outside by the door."

Randall cautioned. "Let's stick to plan A. Here we are plotting mischief in front of a dead patient. God could be watching. There's probably some commandment against what we're plotting."

Melinda sighed and shrugged. "I figure God gave Elisa the idea, so we're still in the clear. Sounds evil but good—we're just carrying out His orders. I'll make the call to the ward."

Randall covered Mr. Schmidt's head with the sheet and said a little prayer under his breath. He suggested they keep him in the room until pickup lest the body's presence undermine the confidence of the waiting patients. If past experience served, it could take a while for him to be picked up. What Randall hadn't factored into this solution was that he would be asked to sign the death certificate since he was the one to pronounce Mr. Schmidt dead.

THE HARD TRUTH

As Randall walked out of the exam room with Melinda, he felt like he was whistling past the graveyard. He tried to walk nonchalantly down the hall in front of the waiting patients. At Doris's office he found Dr. Oliver chatting with Doris.

Randall waved a hello. "Ah, Dr. Oliver! Thanks for coming down. Doris has sustained a weather-related boo-boo to her knee."

Dr. Oliver frowned at Randall. "Hmm, I'm not familiar with the Radiation Oncologist injury classification system, but I'll be happy to lend some clarity to the situation."

Randall smiled graciously. "I knew I could count on you."

"Is there an exam room I can use?" asked Dr. Oliver.

Randall nodded. "Certainly. Let's go to Exam Room 2. Room 1 is . . . occupied . . . at the moment."

Dr. Oliver put up a hand. "You don't need to come, Randy. I'm sure you have other boo-boos to attend to. I'll get you when I finish. I'm sure Doris can show me the way. Here, Doris, take my arm."

"Well, aren't you a gentleman?" Doris side-eyed Randall. "Dr. B, he's much nicer than you led me to believe."

"Doris," said Oliver smoothly. "Let me give you a word of advice. Only believe half of what that man says. Unfortunately for both of us, I am unable to tell you which half to ignore."

Doris harrumphed. "You and I think alike. He's just like my Uncle Humphrey. Can't believe every other word."

Randall pouted and looked hurt.

Doris picked up a chart from her desk and handed it to Randall. "Here's your next consult, Dr. B. Do have an enjoyable time. I know I did when I first met the man. He needs just your brand of hand holdin'.

His name is Mr. Roebuck. He's in a wheelchair out in the hall. Melinda's waiting there with him."

Randall threw his hands up in the air. "Can't anybody around here walk?" He went to the hall and handed the chart to Melinda without looking at it. She read the patient ID information and laughed. "What's so funny?" asked Randall.

Melinda pointed at the name plate. The patient's first name was Sears.

CATALOGING INJURIES

Since there were only two exam rooms, all Randall could do for the moment was to review the chart in his office and wait for one of the rooms to be cleared. Mr. Roebuck had presented with right-sided weakness and altered speech which was initially thought to be a stroke. It turned out to be a brain metastasis from a small cell lung cancer. Thirty years of smoking two packs per day was the likely culprit for the latter.

Dr. Oliver came into Randall's office. "Hey, Randy—Just finished assessing your secretary's knee. Nice lady. Want to come in with me while I give her the scoop?"

Randall was a little miffed at having a mere resident call him Randy, but suppressed it. "Sure thing." In the exam room, Dr. Oliver sat on the rolling stool and pulled himself up to Doris. His face was so close to hers that she moved her head back as if to protect her personal space.

Dr. Oliver spoke softly. "Young lady, hate to say it, but my odds-on diagnosis would be a torn medial meniscus. From your history, you may have had a minor tear years ago and it just got a bit bigger with your little ice capade. We'd need to do some further imaging studies to confirm it, but it wouldn't likely change how we'd manage it. Given your weight issues, surgery would be a big risk. The surgery would probably fail given the load your knee has to bear. I'd recommend conservative management and weight loss."

Doris was rather self-conscious about her weight and got a bit red-faced. Instead she focused on the complicated words. "Can you explain what a menial *mewhatsis* is?"

Dr. Oliver chuckled. "Sorry. That is a tough pair of words. The medial meniscus is the cartilage cushion between your upper and lower leg bones. Part of it is torn loose and the loosened fragment is caught between the two ends. When that happens, the whole joint gets inflamed and swells up, making things worse."

Doris looked deflated. "Dr. Oliver, I've been battlin' my weight problem for years. I just don't know how I can shed enough pounds to help."

Dr. Oliver nodded in sympathy. "I know weight loss is tough, but it's almost mandatory if we're to avoid surgery or have successful surgery if you need it. For each pound of body weight lost, there is a four-pound reduction in knee joint stress. Losing one pound spares the knee joint from the impact of 4,800 pounds per mile walked. The square area of your knee that has to bear your body weight is small. Normal walking subjects the knee to forces two to three times your body weight. Doris, is all that clear?"

Doris looked at her lap. "I think so, Doctor. Clear as the church bells on Sunday."

Dr. Oliver patted Doris on the shoulder. "Good! I can't really treat you because you're not a vet, but I can suggest some folks to see who can get you started on some pain management, PT and a weight loss plan. I'll rewrap your knee the right way. Sorry, Randall, but not bad for an amateur." He touched Doris' arm. "You'll need to take some of the load off the knee for now. I'll take you over to PT and get you fitted up with a walking cane that you can 'borrow' for a few days. Any questions?"

Doris was unable to formulate a meaningful question and just shook her head.

Dr. Oliver tried to stay upbeat. "That's my girl! Let's grab a wheelchair from the hall and roll you over to PT. Then I have to hustle back upstairs to reduce a dislocated hip. What you've got is nothing compared to that. Randall, there's a babble-head patient of yours out in the hallway. I don't know what's wrong with him, but you better get him into an exam room before he scares your other patients away."

Randall snapped to. "Right, then. I'll take care of him right now. Thanks again for coming down."

Dr. Oliver clapped Randall on the shoulder. "Any time, buddy. You're just lucky I'm not planning to steal Doris away from you. She seems like a keeper." He gestured toward Doris, who made moon eyes and blinked. Then he wheeled Doris to PT.

SEERSUCKER

No one had appeared to pick up the late Mr. Schmidt, so he still occupied an exam room. Thus, Melinda put the wheelchair bound and babbling Mr. Roebuck into the exam room that Doris and Dr. Oliver had just vacated.

Several minutes later, Melinda handed the chart to Randall, shaking her head. "Fruity as an orchard full of ripe apples! One minute he's telling me about the fire in his house and calling 911 to put it out. The next minute he's warning me to watch out for the monkey up on the cabinet."

Randall made a 'what next?' eye roll. "Sounds mildly confused."

Melinda let out a loud breath. "Mild as a jalapeño pepper! I didn't get a chance to go over his chart history yet. What's it say?"

Randall sat back in his desk chair and put his feet up on the open lower drawer, his favorite footrest. The drawer was full of old files, which had accumulated dirt from his shoes. He would joke that he had files with dirt on everyone.

The desk was only slightly less dilapidated than his desk chair. The backrest broke off the chair when he'd leaned back on it one day. The VA replaced it with another used desk chair only slightly better. Randall rebelled and ordered his own chair and had it delivered from an office supply house. VA Building Management had discovered it wasn't VA property on a surprise inspection and put a label on it as private property. That meant they had no responsibility to "maintain" it. In response, he had a brass plaque etched that read "Dr. B Endowed Chair" which he glued to a chair leg.

Melinda settled in the chair next to his desk while Randall reviewed Mr. Roebuck's chart. He read selected parts aloud. "This 67-year-old black male was brought to the ER by the Fire Department Rescue Squad. The patient had called 911 from his home and reported a fire. On arrival, the responders found the doors locked and no outside evidence of fire. They broke down a door and found the patient down on the floor with a bloody gash on his head. They surmised he had fallen and hit his head on the corner of a side table."

Melinda frowned. "That would account for the bandage on his head. Then what?"

Randall continued to read. "There was no sign of fire inside the house. The phone was off the hook. His vitals were stable, but he was out like George Foreman at 'Rumble in The Jungle.'"

Melinda interrupted. "Whoa, there! Rumble in the Jungle? What the deuce was that?"

Randall gawked in disbelief. "Not a boxing fan, eh? Just the heavyweight fight of the century! Muhammed Ali challenged then heavyweight champion of the world, Foreman, for the title. Because of some silly boxing rules, they couldn't hold the fight in the US. So, they fought it out on 10/30/1974 in Kinshasa, Zaire, Africa, at the 20th of May Stadium. There were over 60,000 people there and millions more watched on TV worldwide."

Melinda pretended to care. "Wow. I bet some big US advertisers were ticked."

Randall sat forward. "I'll bet! Foreman was bigger than Ali and claimed he could punch out a cow with his right hook."

"A real cow puncher, eh," mocked Melinda.

Randall twisted his head toward Melinda. "Do I detect a note of sarcasm?"

Melinda nodded briskly. "You do! Good catch. Now finish the story before I sign you up for OAOA."

Randall looked confused. "For owie, owie?"

Melinda laughed. "No, silly, it stands for 'On and On Anon. It's a support group for people who talk obsessively."

Randall gave Melinda a stern look and was tempted to make the tale even longer. "As I was saying. Ali had a secret strategy to beat Foreman. He kept close to Foreman so he couldn't get a full swing at Ali. In the clinch, Ali would whisper in Foreman's ear, egging him to hit harder. Then Ali would back into the ropes which helped absorb the impact from Foreman's angry punches. Throughout the flurries, Ali pretended he was about to topple over. After seven rounds, Foreman was exhausted. Then, in the eighth round, Ali came to life. He attacked with a five-punch combination and a left hook followed by a straight right to the face that put Foreman down at 2:58 for a TKO. When the press interviewed Ali about his strategy, he said it was his 'Rope-a-dope' technique."

Melinda gestured to move it along. "Fascinating, but pointless. Help me out here, Dr. B. Are you having a stroke? What a pile of jock trivia! I never figured you as a boxing aficionado. It's barbaric. Please get back to our case before I reclassify you as a 'dope on a rope.'"

The comment rather deflated Randall. "Er, sorry. I guess I got a bit carried away."

Melinda nodded again. "You think?"

Randall cleared his throat. "Anyway. . . . Back to our patient. The first responders were able to revive Mr. Roebuck with ammonia salts, you know, smelling salts. They didn't need to start CPR. Oh, and Foreman started to get up after the eight count, in case you were wondering."

Melinda shook her head slowly. "I wasn't."

Randall mimed hitting the mat. "But the ref called him down and out anyhow. So, since Mr. Roebuck didn't get right back up, I suppose it was a lame simile."

Melinda was growing even more irritated. "Yeah. Now that you bring it up yet again, what was wrong with a simple 'out like a light'?"

Randall squinted and looked up. "Never liked that one. Seems like an oxymoron. Using the word 'light' is misleading. A light is lit when it's on, so saying out like a light doesn't convey offness. It should be 'out like a switched off light bulb,' but that's a little too long to be a punchy saying."

"But it's way shorter than your boxing simile," carped Melinda. "Should have gone with the light thing. You're wasting time and starting to worry me. Can we let the helium out of the balloon and return to earth?"

Randall's face brightened up. "Good analogy! Round two goes to the lady in the white trunks—I mean lab coat. Er, yes, back to our patient. When Mr. Roebuck came to, he was rambling and not making much sense."

Melinda interrupted. "Just like your boxing story. Now I get your simile."

Randall grimaced. "Very droll. To continue, the responders found papers on the kitchen table indicating that Mr. Roebuck was a patient at our VA and brought him here. After the exam, with a neuro focus, they patched up his head wound and did a CT, suspecting a subdural hematoma or concussion. Instead, he had one big and three smaller round lesions in his brain consistent with brain metastases."

Melinda looked aghast. "You mean a tumor had already spread to his brain? Where did it start?"

Randall shrugged. "They haven't found a primary source yet. Chest X-ray is normal, so that likely rules out lung, but they've got more imaging and bloodwork in the pipeline. The presumptive diagnosis is cancer spread to the brain from an as yet unknown primary. Regardless of the primary, he needs radiation to his brain to reverse the growth of the lesions. It won't cure him but it will prevent further neurologic loss and buy him time."

"Did the tumors cause him to fall down or was the falling down coincidental?" Melinda looked at her two palms as if weighing the options.

"It's hard to be sure," said Randall. "I suspect the big lesion, based on its location in the brain, is responsible for his confusion and loss of coordination. That probably led to the call and the fall. I'd go with the tumor as the cause of all the secondary events."

Melinda nodded. "Seems reasonable, Sherlock."

Randall pretended to be puffing on a pipe. "Hmm, umm, yes. . . . Let's go see the lad."

Randall and Melinda walked past Doris's desk on the way to the exam room. Randall stopped to address Doris, still puffing on his imaginary pipe. He spoke with a bad British accent. "I say, Doris, my good woman, could you please fetch Mr. Roebuck's head CT for review? And, by the by, how doth your errant knee fare?"

"My, my," said Doris. "Who are we today, if I may so inquire?"

Randall bowed with a graceful air. "A medical Sherlock Holmes."

"My knee doth fare mostly well, my kind sir," replied Doris, her British accent twinged with Southern. "With a proper wrap, the swellin' has abated some but still abides. The dolor has ebbed mightily."

Randall waved royally. "Fine, fine. So good to hear of it. Henceforth, I will stick to mine own trade."

"That would be best, sir," said Doris. Melinda waited with tapping toes, knowing that there was no way to speed up this banter.

Randall turned to Melinda. "Ah, such sallies are the glue of good relations, and doth keep us attentive. Shall we away? Sir Roebuck awaiteth, m'lady."

Melinda pinched her lips and sighed as she and Randall glided on to Mr. Roebuck's exam room.

Mr. Roebuck had gotten out of his wheelchair and was squatting under the sink. He looked furtively about the room. Melinda stooped down, took him by the arm, and led him back to the wheelchair. "Hello, Sir. I assure you that the monkey has left the room. I saw him swing into the laundry room. The steam will subdue him until well after dinner."

Mr. Roebuck looked over his shoulder. "That furry mother has big yellow teeth. Don't want him biting me."

Melinda placed a hand on Mr. Roebuck's shoulder. "Sir, this is Dr. Biedermeier. He's the radiation doctor I told you about."

Mr. Roebuck's eyes lit up when he saw Randall. "Why, it's my brother James! I haven't seen you since you died all those years ago. Am I dead too? Or did you come back to see me?" Mr. Roebuck rose from his wheelchair shakily and wrapped Randall in a big embrace. Not quite sure what to do, Randall hugged him back.

"No, Sears," soothed Randall. "You're not dead. I've been given leave to come back and help you. You're a bit sick and I am going to help your doctors make you better."

Mr. Roebuck was delighted. "You became a doctor? That's wonderful. I always knew you wanted to be one . . . How did I get here?"

Randall patted him on the shoulder. "The Fire Department Rescue Squad brought you in when you called them for help. That was a smart thing to do. You were always a smart one, Sears. Say, how about you tell Melinda why Mom named you Sears? You used to tell that story all the time."

Mr. Roebuck turned to address Melinda. "Sure thing! I was Mom's twelfth and last child. When she was about to pop me out, she couldn't decide on a boy name. Didn't know yet if I'd be a boy or a girl. She had a girl name picked out. Still remember it. Sateesha. But she'd done used up all her boy names. In the outdoor crapper one day, she ripped out a page from the Sears catalog to wipe her fanny. Right then it hit her. Name the boy Sears."

Melinda couldn't stifle a giggle. Randall looked away and cleared his throat. "You're a great storyteller, Sears. You told it just like I remember. Now I've got some other questions to ask you and I need to examine you. Melinda will stick around and make sure the monkey stays away."

Mr. Roebuck sat up straight. "Go to it, James! I'm ready. Say, when I was out in the garden yesterday, I found a Howitzer. Neighbor lady came out and complained about it. She's batshit crazy. Need to call the boys to haul that away."

Randall tapped the chart. "Got it. I'll see to it. Melinda, make a note. Get the Howitzer out of the garden. Ladies have been complaining. Now, Sears, let's get you up on the exam table."

When the exam was finished, Randall explained that some radiation treatment would be needed to shrink the spots in his brain. Mr. Roebuck asked if the radiation would keep the monkey away from the Howitzer. Randall assured him that it would be effective in that regard and wheeled him back out to the hall with Melinda trailing close behind with the chart. He asked Doris to have the patient taken back up to the ward.

Doris nodded in response. "By the way, Mr. Roebuck's CT images are settin' on your desk, Dr. B."

"Thanks, Doris," said Randall. "Melinda, let's go take a look at Mr.

Roebuck's head CTs." The two went into Randall's office and studied the images on his viewbox. Randall asked Melinda what she saw.

Melinda pointed to one of the CT sections. "I see some white blobs. There's a big one over here in the back part of the brain and three smaller ones near the front. They have what seem like clear halos around them, especially the big ones. Are they the metastases?"

Randall was pleased that Melinda's assessment was spot on. "You've got it! Those haloes are swelling, or edema, around the tumors. The edema causes a lot of the neurological changes and probably accounts for the Howitzers and monkeys."

"And probably the phantom house fire," surmised Melinda. "Is there a way to reduce the edema?"

Randall nodded. "Good question. Irradiating the brain will shrink the tumors and the edema, but it will take up to a week for improvement. We'll add a course of high dose steroids to get a quicker response until the radiation takes effect. In a day or two on steroids the mental confusion should clear."

"And you'll stop being his white bread brother?" quipped Melinda.

Randall laughed. "Yeah, that too. But you know I'm okay with him as my brother from another mother. He gives great hugs."

Melinda mused a bit. "I can almost see your childhood family photos now ..."

Randall looked up and nodded. "Yeah, Sears was always the tall one! Anyway, the boys upstairs started steroids yesterday after they got the head CT results. By tomorrow, when we start treatment, he will likely be more clear headed. The additional question we have to address is regarding the lack of a tissue diagnosis. You know our golden rule."

Melinda was quick to recall the rule. "Right! No meat, no treat. Should we get them to biopsy one of the brain mets before we start?"

Randall waved off the idea. "That's about as likely to happen as a snowman in July. Under these circumstances, Neurosurgery wouldn't touch him with a 10-foot Pole or two 5-foot Czechoslovakians. Way too much morbidity risk and the likelihood of brain mets is almost standing on top of 100%."

Melinda continued to brainstorm. "What if further imaging can find the primary? Maybe that would be easier to biopsy to get a proven tissue diagnosis."

Randall considered briefly. "Excellent thinking. We can look and we will. But we can't hold off on brain irradiation without risking further neurologic compromise. If the imaging and blood tests, including tumor markers, don't show anything, we still need to treat."

"So, the meat/treat rule has exceptions?" asked Melinda.

Randall's eyebrows shot up. "Yes. Exceptions are rare but this is one of them. There are a few others, but they're not as clear as this one."

Melinda shook her head. "Dang! Just when you think you've got it nailed, you hit your head on the nail!"

Randall pulled his small notebook out and stubby pencil out of his overstuffed lab coat pocket. "Ooh, good one. I gotta write that down. This is a great teaching case. Let's set him up for a simulation tomorrow."

Randall took the film off the viewer and shook it vigorously. The vibration of the shaking film sounded like thunder. It was an excellent way to mask the sound of flatulent gasses escaping.

TB or not TB

Doris knocked on Randall's open office door as he was taking down Mr. Roebuck's films. He rushed to the doorway to keep her from succumbing to toxic fumes. "What's up?"

Doris scrunched up her nose. "There's a nurse here from Infection Control to see you. Do we need to fumigate?"

Randall grimaced. "Oh, geez, is it that bad? Maybe she shouldn't come in here. What does she want?"

Doris looked back towards her office and then whispered. "She wants to talk about a possible exposure."

Before Randall could figure out what that meant, the nurse charged haughtily into his office. She introduced herself as Joan Zarriello, Chief of Infection Control. If she had noticed any unusual fragrance in the office, she didn't make note of it in word or deed. She was a large, squat

Italian woman with scraggly black hair, and a red face. Her nurse's uniform seemed to be under high torsional stress. One hairy arm was strangling a large clipboard.

At first Randall wasn't sure what to do. He reached out a hand and introduced himself, but she seemed not to notice his hand. "What . . . what can I do for you?"

Nurse Zarriello stared at Randall for a beat, then handed him an envelope.

"What's this?" he asked.

Nurse Zarriello's face twitched several times before responding. "It's a notice of your possible exposure to *Mycobacterium tuberculosis*."

Randall was taken aback. "My exposure? How? When?"

Nurse Zariello looked at her clipboard briefly. "A patient that you saw earlier today. One Mr. Oscar Schmidt. He had sputum results positive for a Mycobacterium species, possibly TB. As you know, he is deceased and will be undergoing an autopsy. More samples for culture will be taken at that time. It will take several weeks before we can make the final call on whether we have 'red snappers' or not."

Randall felt himself deflate several PSI. "Geez! Makes sense, though. He had a cavitating lesion on his chest films. What do I do now?"

Nurse Zarriello pronounced the next actions to be taken like a drill sergeant. "You and anybody in your department that had contact with the man will need to have their TB skin test status checked right now." Randall was tempted to stand at attention and salute. "Anyone who tests negative will need a repeat skin test in several months. If they've converted to positive on the retest, they'll need imaging, further testing, and likely several months of antibiotics."

Randall's mental alarms went off. "What if they're positive now?"

"Then a chest X-ray is needed right now," she responded. "If it's negative, we'll repeat it in several months. If it's positive, well, you know the drill."

This was all Randall needed to make his day more brilliant. "I do. Where do we go for the skin test?"

Nurse Zarriello gestured for him to sit, and stay. "You don't go anywhere. I just came to you. Who else do I need to stick? Only folks who had direct contact with the man need it."

Randall reviewed the morning activities. "Well, that would be our student Melinda . . . oh, and the patient transport guy. I think his name is Ira. Weird guy with a comb-over."

"Got him already," barked Zariello. "Go grab your student and go into an exam room. I've got the syringes and paperwork in my clipboard box. Which arm do you want?"

Randall raised his left arm, and half expected to be told to drop and give her 20. He jumped to and scurried off to get Melinda.

Tidying up

Later that afternoon, Randall rolled up his sleeve to see if he was developing a tell-tale red welt at the skin test site. He thought Melinda was probably doing the same if she was also dealing with subclinical panic. He could just picture the mycobacteria setting up shop in one of his pulmonary alveoli. He visualized sending angry, combative immune cells to the injection site and machine-gunning them with 30 caliber antibody rounds.

Randall muddled through the remaining cases for the afternoon, but TB kept going through his mind like an ear worm. He'd checked with Melinda several times to see how she was holding up, but she seemed to be handling it better than he was. He'd finally called his friend, Jason Bugge, who specialized in infectious disease. Jason reassured Randall that there was no risk of spread to others if he wasn't actively infected, but Randall still couldn't settle.

Randall did a good job delivering the TB news to the rest of the department without conveying panic. He'd pretended to be calm as a quiet pond and they had taken it in stride. No doubt, they weren't giving it a second thought.

Doris limped into Randall's office to ask if he was ever going home. Randall sensed that her compassion antennae were on full alert. He assured Doris that everything was copasetic and offered to walk her out to her car to avoid a nasty fall. She graciously accepted. After she was tucked safely away in her Volvo, he walked back to the rear entrance only to find it locked. After a few choice exclamations of dismay, he hiked 100 yards through the snow in his loafers to come in through the ER entrance.

Despite pretending to be invisible as he walked through the ER in wet shoes, one of his old patients hailed him from the waiting area. He recognized Ezekiel Jones right away. He was a drug seeker par excellance and well known for such throughout the hospital.

Mr. Jones yelled out to Randall. "Hey, Dr. B! I needs me a refill on my Percocet. I got a hurting in my 'leader.'"

Randall sighed in exasperation. "In your what?"

Mr. Jones pointed at his right thigh. "Here, in my leader. My 'stint' is plugged."

It took a few seconds for Randall to translate the jargonese. He figured out that the man believed his thigh muscle hurt because his femoral artery stent was blocked. He remembered from his time in North Carolina that 'leader' referred to any large muscle group. At least it did in the South. He figured the whole story was another of Jones's made-up yarns.

Mr. Jones continued to embellish his tale. "I been waitin' here like two hours for Doc Sullivan to see me about it. But now that you is here, maybe you can help me out. I gots to be on an airplane at 9 o'clock tonight to visit my sick mammy in Tampa. My Percocet got stolen outen my pocket at the George Webb hamburger. I needs ten pills to get me through."

Randall resorted to basketball moves to escape. He juked left, then right, past Mr. Jones, and began to sprint down the hall. "Oh, look!" he shouted back. "There's Dr. Sullivan coming to see you now. Gotta go."

Mr. Jones waved furtively in Randall's wake. "But, Doc!"

Having left the department without his key, Randall was fortunate to find the night custodian mopping the floor in the hallway. He cajoled the custodian into unlocking the door. Randall shuffled into his office and groaned when he saw the pile of unfinished paperwork. He told the paperwork to finish itself and then slipped off his wet shoes.

The socks were soaking wet, but he left them on and donned his snow boots, jacket, gloves and hat. He wrapped the loafers in paper towels, and slipped them in an empty desk drawer. Moving quietly, so as not to wake the sleeping charts and paperwork, he snuck out of the office, closed the department door carefully, then tiptoed down the hall. The only sound was the squelching of his wet socks inside the snow boots.

CHAPTER 12

———

SOSDD

"Only those who will risk going too far can possibly find out how far one can go."

—*T. S. Eliot*

RED DOT

When Randall came in the back door, he found Zelda at the kitchen sink washing dishes. He made plenty of noise coming in the back door with his gear, but she did not turn to acknowledge him. A 'hello' got no response. *O Hell, this is not a good sign.* Mentally reviewing what he might have done wrong in the past 24 hours to deserve the silent treatment, he couldn't come up with anything obvious. Whatever it was, she probably had been stewing about it for a while. Randall went into DEFCON 2.

Kyle came tiptoeing down the hall and motioned for Randall to bend over so he could whisper in his ear. "Mom's got a red dot on her forehead. She said you'd know what that means, and she wants everyone in silent mode. She told me that her friend Charlie was here and that I should play in my room. Addie, too. She gave Addie a note for you."

Randall took off his coat and hung it in the hall closet, then walked Kyle into the living room and spoke softly. "Charlie is definitely not a good sign. It's Mom's special lady alone time. None of us have done anything wrong. We all just need to lay low for the evening. Let's go up to Addie's room, look at the note and make sure she understands."

Kyle made his voice even smaller. "Okay, Dad, but who's Charlie?"

Randall searched for the proper words. "Let's just say it's Mom's special friend."

They found Addie sitting at her desk arranging stuffed animals in a way that probably only made sense to her.

Randall walked over to Addie and gave her a kiss on the head. "How are you doing, Rosebud?"

Addie shrugged and spoke softly. "Fine, but Mom is being mean. I didn't do anything bad and she made me come up here to play. I don't care. My animals like me. But I'm hungry. We haven't had dinner yet."

Kyle hung back in the doorway. Randall motioned him to come in and close the door.

Randall placed his hand on Addie's shoulder. "Kyle said Mom gave you a note for me." Addie handed him the note, sealed in an envelope. She stuck out her lower lip, squinting her eyes like she might cry.

The note was short and not very sweet. "SOSDD. Not making dinner tonight. You know why. Take kids out to eat while I'm entertaining Charlie the Red Dragon."

Randall shook his head. *Just another speed bump to add to the day's fun.* "Did either of you read this note?"

The two kids responded in harmony. "No, Dad."

"What's SOSDD mean?" asked Addie.

Randall managed to 'quink thickly.' "It's just a code parents use. It means the same old stuff, different day."

Kyle looked confused. "Is that good or bad news?"

Randall smiled and waved his arm. "No worries, it's good news. The three of us get to go out to Big Boy for dinner tonight. Mom thinks she's getting a flu bug and doesn't want to give it to us. So, she's going to stay home and take care of herself while we have burgers and fries. Who's game?"

"Me!" shouted Addie.

"Me too," echoed Kyle. "Is it a Charlie bug? Like a cold? Is she contagious? Will I get Charlie too?! Or is it like lice? I hate lice."

Addie shuddered and scratched her head. "Ew. Stay away from Mommy!"

Randall sighed. "Don't worry, it's none of those, and you don't need a shot for it." The three headed downstairs to prepare for their outing. Randall announced to the kitchen where Zelda was sitting that they were headed out for dinner. Without turning around, she waved her left hand at them and muttered "Good riddance, peace at last." No one heard it.

On the drive to Big Boy, Randall asked the kids about their day at school. He was regaled with a story of kids getting beat up on the playground during recess, farts during class and a spinster teacher with an errant bra strap. By the time they parked, they all had the giggles.

While getting out of the minivan, a Star Wars figure dropped out of Kyle's pocket and bounced under the car. He started to crawl under the car to retrieve it and Randall yelled for him to stop. "Don't do that. You'll get soaked. Let me move the car so you can get it."

The warning was a tad late. Kyle was already kneeling in the snow and his pants were busy absorbing salty slush. He pushed himself back up soaking his gloves as well.

Randall looked to the heavens for relief. Kyle looked a bit undone. "You're right, Dad. Mom will be really mad at me.'

Randall was sympathetic. "Don't worry, kiddo. Your pants will dry by the time we're home. Trust me. I've been there. Plus, there's spare gloves in the car. I'll get them when I move the car. Here, give me the wet ones."

After the car was moved, Yoda retrieved, and dry gloves acquired, the party of three walked through the snowy parking lot toward the front entrance of Big Boys. Randall tried to change the subject. "Hey, Buddy. Have you had any more bee bite dreams?"

Kyle started skipping while he responded. "No more bee bite dreams, but I did have a dream about Mr. Bush next door. An ambulance came and took him away. Mrs. Bush was all flustered and you calmed her down."

Addie was curious. "What was wrong with him?"

Kyle kicked a frozen chunk of snow and it went skittering under a car. "Goal!"

"Kyle! Answer me!" shouted Addie.

Kyle huffed and puffed. "How do I know? I'm not a doctor like Dad. I'm just a kid."

Addie sounded concerned. "Well, was he okay afterwards?"

Kyle waved it off. "Don't know. I woke up to go pee. When I went back to bed, no more dreams."

Addie was still concerned. "I hope Mr. Bush is alright. I like him. Sometimes he gives me lemon drops. He keeps them in his sweater pocket."

Randall intervened. "Addie, it wasn't real. It was just a dream Kyle had. Don't worry your sweet little head."

Addie turned around and made her square eyes face. "I know that! But sometimes Kyle's dreams come true. Right, Dad?"

Randall grabbed Addie and lifted her up for a hug. "Well, I'm just not sure about that. If it would make you feel better, I'll check on him tomorrow and see if anything is up. Deal?"

Addie smiled and kissed Randall's neck. "Deal. Now put me down and let's go eat. I want two Brawny Lad burgers tonight. I'm so hungry I could eat a cow."

"Don't you mean a cow pie?" chirped Kyle.

Addie curled up her tongue and gave Kyle a juicy raspberry sound. She ran to the front door. Kyle chased after.

After being seated in the restaurant and ordering, Kyle asked Randall about his day. Randall was mildly suspicious. Usually Randall was the one to ask them about their day. *Could Kyle really be interested or was he on a fishing expedition?* Randall complied and gave them a summary of the day's events focusing mostly on the unusual patients he'd seen. The kids laughed at the construction helmet guy, *ooed* at the dead guy, and roared with laughter at the monkey guy.

Then Randall added Doris's knee injury. "You guys remember the nice lady who's my secretary?"

Kyle held out his hands like he was demonstrating a big fish he'd caught. "Yeah, Dad. She has huge . . . sweaters."

Randall wondered whether puberty was closer than he thought, but chuckled. "Ha, yes, I guess she does. Well, she fell on the ice in the parking lot and hurt her knee. We don't know yet how bad it is. She might have to miss work for a few days. I don't know what we're going to do without her. I am really worried."

Randall began to let the day's events show on his face. The kids noticed the mood change.

"Is something else wrong, Dad?" asked Addie.

Randall paused, uncertain whether to share his concerns about Zelda's behavior that day. He decided they needed to understand. "Let's talk about your mother for a bit. I think you two might be a little confused about it. Am I right?"

Addie nodded. "Sometimes she's like the bathtub faucet. One minute you get cold water and the next it's hot water."

Kyle added on. "Yeah, and you never know which you're gonna get!"

Randall had guessed right. "I hear you, guys. You two handled it very well today. When your mother gets like this, it gets me down. It probably is the same for you both. Let me try to explain. It's not something she can always control. It has to do with the changes women's bodies go through every month. The doctor word for it is 'menstrual period.' That's what she means when she says 'Charlie' is visiting. Sometimes it puts her in a bad mood for a few days. It's sort of complicated to explain, but I don't want you two to think it's because of anything you've done wrong. She can't help it and she still loves you. She knows she behaves badly when her period comes, so it's best we just give her space until it's over."

Addie looked a little scared. "When I get growed up will I get a Charlie bug?"

Randall shrugged. "Well, you'll get periods too, but I'm not sure if you'll get as moody as your mom. It affects every woman a bit differently and it can be different from month to month. When you're older I can explain how it works in more detail. That's all you need to understand for now."

Addie made a sour face. "I don't want to know any more right now. I'm too busy just being a little girl."

Kyle frowned a bit and then smiled. "I'm glad I'm not a girl."

Addie smacked Kyle in the arm. "There's nothing wrong with girls!"

Kyle thought about hitting back, but wisely held off. "I didn't say there was anything wrong with girls. I'm just glad I'm not one."

Addie was not going to leave Kyle with the last word. "Well, I'll bet boys have problems when they get older that I don't want either. Right, Dad?"

Randall nodded. "You're both right. The grass is always greener on the other side of the fence."

Kyle looked puzzled. "What fence?"

Randall rolled his eyes. "I'll explain it later. We're getting off topic."

Kyle decided to let sleeping dogs snore. He artfully changed the topic. "You sure that's all that's wrong, Dad? You seem kind of jittery, too."

Randall thought for a second. "You're pretty astute. I guess you're on to me! I've got my second counseling appointment tomorrow and I'm not sure I have my assignment down pat. You know, the one where I have to tell the doc in ten minutes about how I decided to go into medicine."

Kyle looked confused. "Why did you call me an ass toot?"

Randall had to hold his head in his hands in frustration. There was just no way to avoid butts and farts with this kid. He looked up again and decided to play it straight. "It means you're a sharp observer. Now keep your mind above the waist!"

Kyle nodded. "Thanks for explaining, Dad. I didn't know that word. But what's so bad about your assignment? Don't you like having someone to talk to? You haven't done anything bad!"

Randall wasn't really sure what he was so nervous about. Kyle was watching him, and he wanted to be honest with his son. "Well, Kyle, what you say is true. It's just that with a counselor, it's like . . . I mean, she knows stuff about me that I don't share with everyone. And I don't really know what she thinks about it."

Kyle nodded knowingly. "I know what you mean, Dad. It's like Miss Chelsea has X-ray vision or something when I talk with her. Like she knows what I'm thinking."

Randall was surprised that Kyle had the same feeling. "Right! Like she can see through me and can tell if my underwear is clean!"

That got a laugh from Kyle. "Ha! I was nervous about my appointment with Chelsea, but I just slept with my light saber and I was good to go the next day. The visit was a piece of pie. You want to borrow my light saber tonight? Just stick it under your pillow."

Randall gave Kyle a fist bump. "Yeah, buddy. That might just do the trick."

The Big Boy waitress appeared with Big Boy burgers for the boys and Addie's Brawny Lad supplemented with fries and milkshakes. All table talk was put on hold and consumption mode was on fast forward.

After Dinner Surprise

Randall watched in wonder as the kids hoovered up their burgers and fries. Soon after they scavenged all plate contents, their little eyelids began to droop, tummies full and batteries nearing empty. They were tuckered out and ready for bed as Randall drove the family van up the driveway. All three clambered out of the car and in the back door, Randall hushing them to avoid alerting the Red Dragon Lady.

Zelda snuck around the kitchen entry. "Oh, Randall, I'm so glad you're home."

Randall nearly jumped out of his boots at the sound of her voice. But they were tied on too tight. Zelda looked strangely timid and upset, a far cry from her previous 'Charlie' persona. Zelda approached Randall with open arms, gave him a hug, and whispered in his ear. "After we get the kids upstairs for bedtime prep, I have some bizarre news to tell you."

Randall could not imagine what news could have swung Zelda's mood back towards normal so quickly.

Zelda unhugged Randall and turned to Kyle and Addie with her arms spread wide. "Kyle! Addie! My beautiful darlings! Let Mommy give you a hug. Did you miss me? Tell me about your dinner out with Dad."

Kyle looked at Addie with a puzzled face and Addie returned the look. They remained in place like their feet were glued to the floor. They'd been walking on eggshells since they'd come home from school and now . . . ?

Randall could see the kids' confusion and, from behind Zelda's back, smiled broadly and waved them forward. Addie got the cue first and stepped forward to hug Zelda's leg. Kyle shrugged and did the same. The two of them pushed away after a moment. Kyle was the first to speak. "Addie ate two Brawny Lads and half my fries."

Addie took immediate offense. "I did not! Dad helped me finish the second burger and you were so busy watching the girl at the next table that you didn't see Dad sneaking your fries."

"Well, the girl was kind of cute and she's in my class," rebutted Kyle.

Addie saw an opening and took it. "Ha! You're definitely not in her class. Dream on lovey loser."

Kyle was so steamed he couldn't speak. Zelda broke up the potential rhubarb. "Cool it, you two. Addie, apologize to your brother. There's no harm in looking at cute girls and your brother is a handsome young man. I bet the girl was looking at him too."

Kyle spoke up. "Mom's right. She looked at me first."

Addie frowned. "But Kyle made fun of me for eating two burgers. I was just hungry because dinner was so late. That wasn't my fault."

Now Zelda felt a bit guilty. "Sorry, Addie. That was my fault for not getting dinner started on time. I was in a grumpy mood."

Addie spoke before thinking things through. "Yeah, Dad explained that to us at dinner. He said it's a normal lady thing and you'll explain it to me sometime when I'm older."

Zelda's eyes widened. "Your Dad did what?"

Randall was about to defend himself when Kyle intervened. "Don't worry, Mom. It was a good explanation and now we understand better. Nobody is mad at you."

Zelda looked right and then left and just swallowed.

Addie added more padding. "Kyle's right, Mom. Don't have a cow. Kyle, I'm sorry for what I said."

Kyle put his hand on Addie's shoulder. "Me too, Sis. Let's get up the stairs and get ready for bed so Mom and Dad can talk."

Randall's jaw dropped a bit and Zelda muttered her approval. "I'm sorry, too, guys. Sounds like a plan. Get on upstairs. You know what to do. Dad and I will join you soon."

Kyle and Addie dashed to the stairs with just a bit of bickering for good measure.

Kyle began with a hollered challenge. "Race you, Addie! I'll always be faster than you!"

Addie hollered back. "Kyle, that's not fair! You got a head start! And you stepped on my foot!"

Neighbor Bad News

As soon as the kids were in their rooms, Randall asked Zelda what the bizarre news was.

Zelda grabbed Randall's arm. "Randy, let's go to the basement. I don't want to risk the kids overhearing us."

Randall was confused and tired, but curiosity had him by the throat. "Alright. But it's cold down there. Let's grab a blanket and we can huddle under it on the old green couch."

Zelda seemed relieved at the direction. "Good idea, Randy. 'Old Green' has heard her share of stories since we moved here from North Carolina. Remember how we got her down the basement stairs?"

Randall chuckled, remembering the colorful epithets that had accompanied that maneuvering. "Let's just say we can notch that one up to marital fortitude."

After they got snuggled under the blanket, Zelda set to the news. She spoke in hushed tones. "You remember Alexandra, the twelve-year-old who used to babysit for us?"

Randall nodded. "Of course, I haven't forgotten. Her suicide was just a few months back. Why, what happened?"

Zelda drew even closer. "Well, our neighbor Julie came over this afternoon before you came home and wanted to talk about Alexandra. In private. Her kids were home from school so she had to bring them over. I sent Kyle and Addie outside to build a snowman with her kids while Julie and I had coffee in the kitchen."

Randall cocked his head. "What did she have to say about Alexandra?"

Zelda had her own way of telling stories and Randall knew not to try to speed her up. Zelda grimaced before speaking again. "At first, she was concerned that her daughter might catch 'the suicide bug' also. Her daughter is almost the same age as Alexandra. After I pooh poohed the likelihood of that, she started acting squirrely."

Randall had a sudden image of the curly haired neighbor skittering up a tree wagging a bushy little tail behind her. "Squirrely?"

Zelda temporized. "Well, for her, anyway. Normally Julie and her husband, Chris, are pretty steady folks and devout Catholics. Not long after we went to Alexandra's funeral together, she came over without Chris and asked me a bunch of questions about religion. I won't get into the whole conversation, but what it came down to was whether I believed in the soul, what happens after death, and whether I believed in spirits. Of course, you know me, I'm pretty eclectic in my beliefs. I believe in the benevolence of the universe and the ability of that force to communicate with and through us."

Randall knew all this about Zelda's perspective, and was still exploring his own take on the topic. He bit his tongue before making any more commentary and settled on a simple "of course."

Zelda looked around the basement for a visual aid to help with her next revelation. "This afternoon, right after she started acting squirrely, she told me about something weird that happened at her house a few days ago."

Randall's eyes widened. "Something weird?"

Zelda nodded her head slowly with a very serious look on her face. "Judge for yourself. Randy. The other day Julie went into her kids' playroom after dinner and there were toys everywhere. Legos, Star Wars toys, stuffed animals, you name it—just strewn about everywhere. She figured the kids had had a toy fight. Julie is quite a neatnik, so she put away the toys before dinner. After dinner, she gave the kids baths and put them to bed. On her way downstairs, she saw the light on in the playroom and went to turn it off. She nearly dropped her drawers when she saw the toys scattered all over again. The kids had not been out of her sight since she'd put the toys away before dinner."

Randall sat back, inhaling sharply. "Spooky! No wonder she was freaked out. Huh. Maybe she should have left the toys on the floor to see if the mischievous spirit will put them away!"

Zelda felt frustrated that Randall was not taking the story seriously. "Not funny, Randy. This is not a laughing matter. It gets worse. The first day it happened she brushed it off as a fluke."

Randall shrank back on the couch. "The first day?"

"Yep. It happened again the next day. Then the next. She watched where her kids would go after dinner, and it wasn't to the playroom. Each time, the toys that moved were the ones that the kids used to play with when Alexandra babysat them. By this time, the kids knew something unusual was happening and they didn't want to even go into the playroom."

Randall was taken aback. "Seriously? There's some powerful energy happening there."

Zelda nodded vigorously. "And I don't think Julie is making this up, Randy. This flies in the face of everything she believes in. I didn't know what to tell her. I think she felt better just being able to tell me about it and not get turned into a toad or something."

Randall got even more wide-eyed. "Zelda, you are probably the only one in this community she could feel safe telling this to!"

Zelda pursed her lips and nodded. "Yeah, Randy, you're probably right. She runs in a pretty regimented crowd. Oh, boy, what time is it? We better get the kids to bed! I think I hear them arguing more loudly than usual. That's our cue!"

Randall agreed. "No wicked for the rest. There's probably more to come with the Julie saga."

Zelda sat back and smiled. "Wow, Randy! You're precognitive. Julie and Chris are coming over later tonight to talk with us about the very subject."

Randall pressed both hands to his temples. "Apparently not prescient enough to see that coming," he harrumphed.

Julie and Chris

After corralling two overtired kids into their beds, Randall and Zelda were totally drained. Randall had lapsed back onto Kyle's pillow, already in a half dream about dropping a pass from his high school quarterback. He was rescued from the ignominy of his fumbling catch by a loud knocking on the front door. Zelda beat Randall downstairs. She padded in stocking feet onto the cold foyer tiles to peek out the front door window. Julie and Chris Miller bounced up and down in the cold, eager to get inside, away from the frigid wind.

Zelda pulled open the door, wind-borne snow swirling around her feet. "Come in! I'm so glad to see you two." She ushered them into the house, took their coats and sat them on the living room couch. "You guys are shivering like crazy! How about some hot tea?"

Randall finally made it down to the living room and greeted his two neighbors. Julie seemed a bit nervous. Chris looked completely exhausted. Randall didn't know Chris very well, except to exchange baseball stats over the fence or share the odd tool. From those brief encounters Randall had classified Chris as a rather stoic and logical man. His current demeanor did not fit that assessment.

"Chris, can I get you something a little stronger?" asked Randall. "Spirits, perhaps?"

Chris shook his head and gave out a nervous laugh. "Ha. Er, please don't mention spirits just now."

Julie was still a bit tremulous despite being out of the cold. "Zelda, we just had to come see you guys. You've always seemed to be more liberal than the rest of the folks in this neighborhood. We just needed somebody to talk to about what's been happening. From what you've told me about Randy, he has an open mind too . . . for a doctor. Chris has barely slept a wink in days. Tell them about it, Chris."

Chris started to protest, as if he had expected Julie to tell the tale. After a brief pause he shrugged and raised both hands palms up. "Alright. That's what we're here for. I can't deny my own observations. I am a man of reason. I know what's right and what the Bible tells me. But I don't know what is happening to me."

Randall tried to clear the path. "Take your time. There's no rush."

Randall's comment seemed to open Chris's talk valve. "She comes to me in my sleep. It's not like a regular dream. Several times she's awakened me and, I swear, for a moment I see her there in front of me."

Zelda's eyebrows knit together. "'Scuse me? Who appears to you?"

Chris answered with a tight choking voice. "Sorry. I guess I expected you to read my mind. That's how messed up I am. It's Alexandra. You know, the young girl who committed suicide. She comes every night. Appears right in front of me. She touches me. I swear it isn't a dream!"

Randall screwed up his face but said nothing.

Zelda's expression didn't change and she spoke calmly. "What did she want? Did she say anything?"

Chris looked angry. "No, no. . . . It's not like I had a conversation with her! She's dead! I don't want her in my mind or in my home!"

Zelda proceeded more gently. "I know, Chris. This is new and strange. Take a deep breath. You're okay. . . . There you go. Do you trust me?" Chris nodded. "Good, let your mind go back to the dream. What was she doing when she came to you?"

Chris shrugged his shoulders. "I don't know, she was just standing there. She had her hand out. She touched my shoulder and woke me."

"Was she looking at you?" asked Randall.

Chris thought for a second. "Her eyes were open, so yeah, I guess."

Zelda shifted in her seat to move closer to Chris. "Was her mouth moving?"

Chris looked at Zelda as if she were crazy. "What the . . . ? Well, now that you mention it, yes, her mouth was moving. It was like she was trying to talk, but couldn't make any sound. One time she looked like she was screaming."

Randall kept his own counsel. Zelda nodded and smiled. "I know this sounds odd, Chris, but maybe your mind is not willing to listen because the situation is so outside your experience. Maybe she has something she wants to say? Maybe that's why she appears to you. Next time it happens just pretend she's real and maybe you'll hear her voice."

Chris shook his head, hands up, as if pushing someone away. "I'm not gonna do that! This is crazy, I don't believe in this stuff. I just want to get her out of my head! And then there's the crap with the toys in the playroom."

Julie put her hand on Chris's arm. "Honey, you're exhausted. Maybe now that the story is out in the open, the visitations will stop. If it does come back, what's the harm in trying to hear Alexandra? At least give what Zelda said a try."

Chris sighed, staring at his lap. "Randall, maybe I will have a little drink after all."

Randall got up. "I've got just the thing, old man. I'm getting you a hot toddy." He ran off to start the hot water.

Zelda put on some music to "soothe the savage beast" and chatted with the couple until Randall came back.

Chris accepted the hot cup with relief. The first sip hit him with its pungence. "Woo! That's stronger than my mom's tea. What's in it?"

"Oh the usual," Randall said casually. "Chamomile tea, lemon, and honey to calm you down. Oh, and a couple fingers of whiskey, to warm your innards and lubricate your mind."

Chris was done resisting. "Over the lips, past the gums, look out tummy, here she comes!" After a few swallows of toddy, Chris relaxed a bit. "Ah, that hit the spot. Julie, you should try this. I'm not the only one who needs to relax."

Julie reached out for Chris's cup. "I'll take a sip. Hmm, that is good. If it's not too much trouble, Randy, I wouldn't mind one myself."

Randall rose to fill the request. "No problemo, Mademoiselle. Coming right up. I'd have one myself, but the only thing keeping me upright at the moment is a day's worth of coffee and my stiff little spine.

I guarantee one hot toddy won't make things any crazier than they already are." That got a laugh or two and the atmosphere began to settle.

Julie made an observation. "Randy, it seems you may not have had the greatest of days either."

Randall smiled and nodded. "You're right. What doesn't kill you just makes you crazy. Furthermore, I can assure you that I've been drinking hot toddies for years and I'm quite sure that's not what made me crazy!"

Chris looked at his drink and laughed. "So it's safe, then?"

Randall laughed back. "One out of five doctors approve."

Zelda rolled her eyes. "Randy, can't you be serious just once?"

Randall waved his arm expansively. "Well, maybe just once."

Chris chuckled, further breaking the tension in the room.

Randall returned with Julie's hot toddy and settled back on the couch. "Chris, lots of people have encounters with folks who have passed on. I have 'met' several cancer patients after they lost their battle. Sure freaked me out the first few times. I came to realize that there are things in this world I can't explain, but they do happen. You're not crazy. You're human!"

Chris looked like a little boy. "It really happened to you, too?"

Randall put his hand on Chris's shoulder. "Yeah—it's not something people usually talk about over a barbecue. Or anywhere, really. However, in the hospital, facing death daily, we do talk about it. It's more common than you realize."

Chris finally let himself breathe more deeply. "Thanks, Randy. You guys may be right. Maybe Alexandra is trying to tell me something. Not sure why it would be me. What would she even have to say? She killed herself, and that's that."

Julie had a sudden thought. "Hey. What if Alexandra's death wasn't suicide? What if there was foul play or an accident nobody wants to admit to? Or she was abused and felt comfortable enough when she was with our family that she chose us to connect with?"

Chris looked even more startled. "What? You mean there may have been some foul play?!"

Julie continued. "Maybe she saw her father as a threat. You may have seemed like a better father figure or something. Maybe she wants to tell you what really happened!"

Chris shook his head in disbelief. "Oh man, I've been pushing her away. Maybe she is asking for help! I should try to be less scared and more open."

Zelda's eyes popped wide open. "Holy cow, Randy, why didn't we think of that? Julie could be right."

Randall was more circumspect. "Let's not jump to conclusions here. If any of that is true, it puts an even bigger burden on Chris. Maybe Alexandra just wants to say goodbye and you guys aren't the only ones she's tried to contact. Maybe she's already appeared to her parents. If so, that's not something they'd likely tell us about."

Chris and Julie nodded. After a few beats, Chris took a deep breath. "I know her parents pretty well. I don't think there was anything dark going on over there. I'm willing to be her receiver and see where things go. Maybe she's heard our discussion and her 'visits' are over."

Randall was surprised how much more accepting Chris had become. "Sounds like you're less freaked out about these appearances. That's a big step."

Chris looked more settled. "Yeah, I'm tired of losing sleep. If I just go with it and get her message maybe both of us can get some closure. I'm open to that."

Julie stared at him. "You are? You want to hear Alexandra?"

Chris raised his eyebrows. "Surprisingly, yes. It just feels right. She is someone's daughter and deserves to be heard. And I think I can handle it now."

Randall was surprised how quickly the resistance had melted. "I'm glad we could help. You're welcome to come over and debrief us about what happens next. We can figure out together what any messages might mean."

Chris nodded, as if the situation was settled.

Randall thought he wouldn't mind getting to know Chris better.

"Well done, neighbor. We've got a plan. So, what do you do to keep the bill collector away?"

Chris seemed eager to change the topic. "I run a used exotic car dealership in Waukesha. But you might not be interested in all that. What about you? Julie said you're a cancer doctor that uses radiation. Don't know much about that."

Randall shrugged. "Sounds fancy but there's lots of boring physics and smelly patients. But exotic cars, that's in my wheelhouse. Tell me more!"

Once the men launched into car talk, Zelda and Julie repaired to the kitchen to talk about whatever women talk about without men. Usually with visitors in the house after bedtime, Kyle and Addie would have been sneaking downstairs to eavesdrop. Zelda decided to check on them. They were still fast asleep in their beds.

Time passed like nothing and before the group knew it, it was late. Chris walked into the kitchen yawning. "Wow, I am really tired, Julie-san. Time for us freaksters to head home."

Julie looked relieved. "You are so correct, husband of mine. Let's go home and get some sleep."

Zelda gave Julie a girl hug. "Let us know what happens. Come over anytime you want to talk. We could even play board games or have a picnic in the snow. Our future visits don't have to be so heavy!"

The group made some closing small talk, then Randall and Zelda sent the couple off to their home for some version of sleep. Randall looked at his wife with renewed admiration. "Zelda, you're amazing. How did you know how to get milk out of that turnip?"

Zelda put a finger to her nose. "Honestly, I didn't really think about it. I just kinda understood how Chris was scared. I reckoned that Alexandra must have had something to communicate. I tried to imagine what I would do if I were Alexandra—confused, apparently unhearable. Gut instinct, I suppose." Zelda's eyes beamed with otherworldly understanding.

Randall reached out and gave Zelda a squeeze. "You have always had an inner wisdom. But right now you look exhausted, Zel. Let's get our gut instincts to bed."

Zelda just nodded as the wind suddenly went out of her sails. The two weary souls plodded up the stairs and poured themselves into bed.

Beddie-Bye Talk

Despite terminal fatigue, Zelda laid awake staring at the ceiling reviewing the evening's visit with Julie and Chris. The night light cast wavering ghost-like shadows that seemed to move stealthily about the room.

Zelda suddenly shivered and grabbed Randall's arm. "Randy, are you awake?"

Randall grunted and opened his eyes. "I am now. What's up?"

Zelda sat up in bed and pointed to the ceiling. "Do you see what I see?"

Randall cleared a large bolus of phlegm from his throat. "*Herk*! If you mean the ceiling, I can definitely see the ceiling. Is there something else I'm missing?"

Zelda huffed in frustration. "See how the shadows are moving around? Could that be a . . . gh . . . spirit trying to get our attention?"

Randall sat up and put an arm around Zelda's shoulder. All the talk about the deceased Alexandra communicating with Chris had probably worked its way into Zelda's active imagination. "Come on, Zel. You're just overtired and all the ghost talk has got your subconscious working overtime."

Zelda shivered again. "But Randy! What if only I can see her and she's trying to tell me something?"

Randall hugged her tighter. "Good question. Have you gotten any kind of message so far?"

Zelda looked at the ceiling again. "Well, no, not so far."

Randall was still a bit sleep-addled and tried to come up with a cogent response. "Well, then, until you do, let's just assume it's light shadows from the night light. It's kind of been flickering for the last few days. Probably getting ready to fritz out. How about I change the bulb and see what happens? I'm going to turn the lights back on so I don't take an un-scheduled trip on the way. You gonna be okay while I get a new bulb?"

Zelda felt a bit childish, like she had just called out in the night for her father to come to her bedroom and check under the bed for goblins. She gave Randall the go ahead and blinked tentatively in the now brightly lit room. She saw nothing amiss and motioned for Randall to proceed. When he replaced the bulb and turned out the main lights, the ceiling shadows were no longer ghostlike.

Zelda looked sheepishly at Randall. "Randy, you were right. There's nothing sinister going on. I feel so silly, getting worked up about nothing."

Randall patted her shoulder. "Not to worry, my dear. Sometimes nothing can seem like something and vice versa. Lord knows, I've had a few scares like that."

Zelda *harrumphed*. "But you experienced the Chris and Julie visit just like I did and you're not spooked."

Randall shook his head vigorously. "No, no, ma'am. I am just as freaked out as you. Let's just say we're on the same page, but just typing in different fonts. You're in Times New Roman and I'm in ITC Avant Garde. I deal with it by laughing it away until it stops me from laughing."

Zelda nodded her understanding. "I bet it's your doctor's coping skills at work."

"I suppose," said Randall. "Never thought of it that way, but it makes sense."

"I wish I had your coping skills," lamented Zelda.

Randall shook his head. "I'm glad you don't. One of us with those skills is enough. You bring a different skill set to the table. I couldn't have gotten Chris and Julie to open up like you did. What you arranged was like attending church in our home."

Zelda looked puzzled. "How so?"

Randall continued. "You provided a safe place—a sanctuary—for them to open up without fear of ridicule for sounding less than 'normal.' It's like it says in the Bible—I have to paraphrase here. Wherever two or more are gathered to seek answers about the mysteries of the universe, that place becomes a church."

Zelda squinted and smiled. "Not accurate, but close enough. So, I was like Pastor Zelda? That's cool. Never thought of it that way."

Randall squeezed her shoulder. "Well, it's time to start thinking that way. You seem to have a special ability to shine a light so others can see more clearly."

Zelda shook her head. "That's a pile of something. I've never seen a light like that coming from me."

"Of course not," said Randall. "You're the flashlight. You're the source of the light, not what it's shining on. In a dark room, even a small candle can light the way. No need to be a beacon."

"Pish posh," said Zelda. "I'm just a mother and picture maker. And not a very good one of either. When I was growing up I wanted to be something important."

Randall raised his arms. "Are you trying to tell me mothers are not important?"

"Well, my mother didn't do so great with me," opined Zelda.

Randall pooh poohed that idea. "Don't be so hard on yourself. You've given birth and raised two healthy kids. Not problem free, I'll admit, but no kid grows up without a few problems. That's what we're for. We have to keep them moving in the right direction after they go down some garden paths. You've done a great job of allowing them to openly share their fears, hopes and dreams. You help them see they're part of a greater something."

Zelda perked up a bit. "So, you're saying I'm not a total flop?"

Randall shook his head. "Nope. Not 'total' for sure."

Zelda gave Randall a squinty look.

Randall backpedaled. "I am, and we are, both kidding. Not only joking, but also raising kids. Being a mother is very important. And our kids are scientific proof that you are doing a good job. The final outcome may look dicey now, but they are fed, housed, clothed and alive. Something's working right. It will turn out alright in the end and if it's not alright, it's not the end."

Zelda looked about the room, then wrapped both arms around Randall's neck and kissed his cheek. "You can shine a few lights yourself, old man. I don't know about you, but right now I am totally bushwhacked. Let's douse all our lights and count zebras."

That night, Randall was feeling as horny as a brass band, but his overtures to Zelda were being ignored. "What's a guy gotta do?"

Zelda smirked. "Not what you're doing. Pleading is not working."

Randall looked away and pouted. The bedroom was cozy and the sheets fresh, smelling like fabric softener. The kids were asleep and the house was quiet. Zelda was in bed wearing only her diaphanous nighty. This was as optimal as things ever got in the Biedermeier house. Randall had an idea. "Hey! What if I told you an adult bedtime story as a mood changer?"

Zelda scoffed. "One of your shaggy dog stories? Ha! You might as well give me a sleeping pill right now and be done with it."

Randall objected. "No, no. I promise. It will be brief, exciting and to the point."

Zelda turned to her side facing away. "I'll bet you ten bucks you can't keep it under ten minutes. By then I'll be asleep and you'll have to make woo woo to my dead body."

Randall considered that. "Hmm. If that's an option. . . ."

Zelda laughed her dismissal. "Don't even think about it."

"Come on, just give me a chance to prove it," Randall whined.

Zelda turned back to face him, letting the covers fall enough to reveal her cleavage. "Oh, alright. If it will get you off my back."

Randall's mind was one-tracked. "It's not your back I want."

"I know. I know!" exclaimed Zelda. "No need to remind me. Go ahead and tell your story before my sell-by date expires."

Randall rubbed his hands together and began. "Twice upon a time, there was a strikingly beautiful woman named Arabella. She had many admirers, but none of them satisfied her except for Reginald. She was demanding and he was obedient, just the way she liked it."

Zelda interrupted. "You could learn something from Reggie."

Randall nodded. "Indeed. Reggie never asked much of Arabella, but this night was different. She sat at her dressing table, legs crossed, in an ivory negligee. He looked around the room. She had been shopping that afternoon and her new purchases were scattered about. There was a new evening gown on the bed, a fur coat on the lounge chair and red Prada pumps on the floor next to the armoire."

"I like Arabella's taste," remarked Zelda.

"No doubt," replied Randall. "As Reggie studied Arabella's bare legs, he felt a primal urge in his loins and pleaded with her to acknowledge his unfulfilled animal needs. She had been particularly distracted that day and paid him only the merest attention, focusing only on combing her long blonde hair."

Zelda gave a wicked laugh. "Serves the bastard right. Make him suffer, I say."

Randall continued, undeterred. "Finally, Reggie couldn't hold it in anymore and lifted his leg to pee on the red Prada pumps. Arabella was incensed and yelled 'Bad dog, bad dog!'"

Zelda hoisted a pillow and almost knocked Randall over with it. "Bad husband. Bad husband!"

Randall put up both hands in defense. "Ah, but you're still awake! Ten bucks please."

Zelda let out a breath through her teeth. "I'm a bit short right now. Can I offer some services?"

Randall didn't hesitate. "Deal!"

WISCONSIN
RADZ-RUS
America's Dairyland

CHAPTER 13

———

DICTATORS AND TOTS

"Straighten up and fly right/ Cool down, papa, don't you blow your top."

—*Nat King Cole*

END RUN

"Randy, Randy!" Zelda shook Randall out of a dream in which the Packers quarterback, David Whitehurst, had lofted the football to him and Randall was attempting to "run around the edge." A crushing tackle had been imminent.

"Woof," yelped a sleep befuddled Randall. He coughed to clear his throat and tried vainly to open his bleary eyes. "Saved by the wife. I was about to get bone crushed by a Bears linebacker. It was a monster dream."

Zelda laughed at the ridiculous image of her 150-pound husband playing football. "What? That's rich. You were a pro football player in your dream?"

Randall coughed up more throat phlegm and coughed again. He acted highly offended. "Hey, what's so strange about that? I'm a good athlete. I can run like hell when my life is on the line. I was the Packers' running back, Terdell Middleton. I took a screen pass from Whitehurst for an end run, but I slipped on the artificial turf and, well, that's when you woke me up. Nice save."

Zelda laughed even harder. "Ha, that's a good one. So, you were a black man in your dream? You're about as Terdellian as Wonder Bread.

315

It's a good thing I got there before the linebacker or they'd be sweeping up your crumbs right now. Now, get your butt out of bed. You slept through the alarm while I was downstairs with the kids, and you are very late. Today may be the day you start to grow a beard. You have about five minutes to dress and get out of here."

Randall threw back the covers and jumped out of bed almost tripping on his slippers. "Cripes. I couldn't get to sleep last night because I kept thinking about the appointment with Dr. Hoffman this afternoon. It's going to be a Roadrunner mad dash to get there in time. And I didn't get my Acme shipment yet. Plus, I've got a lunch meeting with Joe Shepard at 11:30."

Zelda shook her head. "Tch-*tch*. Sorry to burst your bubble, but the weather man says a nor'wester is hitting us around midday and could drop a bunch of inches of FWS."

Randall slapped his forehead. "Why me, Lord? Why me?"

Zelda giggled. "Because he loves you so much."

Randall blasted through his morning routine in record time and grabbed his gear. He roared down the driveway and up the street hoping for traffic miracles. While waiting at a stoplight he got out his pre-made breakfast of a banana and a PBJ sandwich. He tried eating between gear shifts.

When he was almost to the VA, he reached for his coffee cup but the cup holder was empty. Then he remembered he'd put the cup on the roof of the car while loading his briefcase. He'd done that before. He slapped the steering wheel. *Oh well,* he thought. *I've got enough adrenaline to cover for the absence of caffeine until I get inside and drink from the communal pot.*

Randall was almost caught at a red light waiting for a "slow boat" to turn left, but he cranked the steering wheel hard right, gunned the engine, spun the wheel left again and upshifted so fast that he jammed the banana into the tape cassette slot. He made it through the intersection and started to sing Harry Belafonte's Banana Boat Song. The remaining traffic and stop lights parted before him like the Red Sea.

Randall sang along to the tune but with new lyrics. "Come, mister tape deck man, play me banana! More snow come and me wan' go home . . ." He cruised into the jammed VA parking lot and happened upon a car just vacating a close-in spot. He let out a "Day O!" and pulled into the space, giving a triumphant fist pump. It was 7:58 AM. He congratulated himself for a job well done.

After a brief jog from the parking lot, he made it to his office by 8:02. He walked past Doris to say hello. There he found her all smiles with a large bouquet of flowers on her desk and an open box of Whitman's assorted chocolates.

Randall looked suspiciously at the booty. "Good morning, Doris. Secret admirer?"

Doris smiled somewhat salaciously. "Very good mornin' to you, Dr. B. Admirer, yes. Secret, no. These were given to me by that nice Dr. Oliver. He stopped by this mornin' to recheck my knee and brought treats for the sweet." She put a hand to her chest.

Randall felt an unexpected flush of jealousy. "Oh, he did, did he? Ah, that was . . . very nice of him."

"Yes, it was," agreed Doris, haughtily. "I'm tryin' to remember the last time anyone did this for me. Anyway, the better news is he thinks I just sprained my knee, because it looks so much better now. Isn't that great? He says we can hold off on further imagin' for now. I just have to go easy on it for a few days. I'll still be usin' my cane, though. Careful, or I will use it as a prod for deservin' cattle."

"That's fantastic," said Randall. "I missed my coffee this morning. Ran a bit late. Can I bring you a cup from the canteen?"

Doris nodded demurely. "Yes, you may, Dr. B. I'm glad to see I don't have to prod you. I like the five o'clock shadow. You gon' to grow it further?"

Randall had to think for a second what she was referring to. Then he recalled he hadn't shaved that morning. "Thinking about it. Cream and one sugar?"

Doris shook her head. "Just cream. With all this chocolate, I believe I am already sweet enough."

Randall played along. "Why, yes you are. You're just a step away from diabetes. Say, Doris, can you do me a flavor?"

Doris wasn't quite sure how to take the comment and was wary of the favor she might agree to. "Sure, I think I can spare one."

"How about one of your choclinks?" asked Randall. "I lost part of my banana in my cassette player this morning."

Doris squinted at him suspiciously and was about to ask how he'd gotten his banana in the tape player but, before she could respond, her phone rang. She saw the extension number was the VA front office calling, so she hopped to and answered. "Hello, Radiation Oncology. This is Doris."

Doris shook her head while she listened and took careful notes. When she hung up, she looked rather dour.

Randall noticed the change in mood. "What's up? Who was that and how bad was the news?"

Doris shook her head again and sighed. "Promise you won't be mad, Dr. B?"

Randall tried to look benevolent. "Mad at you? Whatever for?"

Doris looked rather deflated. "I kind of forgot to tell you somethin'."

Randall raised an eyebrow. "You forgot? That's usually my job. You're allowed one or two forgets per year. How bad of a forget is it?"

Doris shrugged her shoulders. "Well, it's not the life threatenin' kind, but it's not the little slip up kind either."

Randall had caught Doris on both ends of a 'forget.' "Okay, I am a just and merciful leader. I will give you a dispensation this one time. Just come out with the truth and no dire consequences shall befall you."

Doris hesitated for a beat. "Well, if you promise I won't be held liable. Two weeks ago the front office called to inform us it was our turn to host an open house. Seems every department has to do one in a regular rotation."

Randall frowned. "Open house? Please define."

Doris's voice got a bit squeaky. "The department shuts down for half a day and invites all hospital staff to come down for a tour narrated by our staff. You know, we give a rundown on all our equipment and our departmental process. That assumes we have a process. Open houses are very popular and well attended. It's mostly because of the food and drink. Sometimes several hundred VA staff show up, but not all at once."

Randall raised both arms in surprise. He tried to picture that many people circulating in his pint-sized department. "Shut down for half a day?! What are they thinking? Have they no idea what we do?"

Doris laughed. "Well, duh. If they did know what we do, we wouldn't need an open house. It's our chance to shine and maybe get some attention from the higher ups for what we need. Gotta show your petals to get a little sunshine."

Randall realized Doris made a good point and smiled. "Hmm. You're right. It sounds like a grand opportunity to make our case for new equipment. I suppose we could reschedule treatments to free up an afternoon. You know, start the first patient at six AM so we're done by noon. That wouldn't be so hard. I think the techs would buy in if they knew there could be a big reward down the line."

Doris smiled back, feeling like she was close to digging herself out of the 'I forgot' hole. "Good thinkin', Dr. B. You are the shiniest marble in the bag. But . . . there is just one other little teensy thing."

Randall looked wary. "Little thing? Pray tell, what may that be?"

Doris shifted in her seat. "As I may have mentioned, the high turn-out at open houses is not so much because hospital staff are interested in what we do."

Randall nodded. "Right. It's the grand buffet."

Doris put an index finger on her nose. "Exactamundo. To meet the high expectations of our prospective attendees, we will need a spread of outstandin' quality and quantity . . . at our expense. Oh, and there's two other minor requirements: entertainment and guided tours."

Randall thrust his head forward like a turkey and tried to stifle a "what next?" It came out as more of a grunt. "So let me get this straight. We have to cater this event, provide guided tours using all of our staff, and figure out some sort of entertainment. What? Like door prizes, raffles, games? A freakin' BEAUTY CONTEST?"

Doris made a half-hearted head nod. "In a word, yes. I hadn't quite worked out the details yet, but those are some good ideas you had there. I may have put the whole thing on the back burner and it got burned."

Randall checked the ceiling briefly, then waved a hand. "Like I said, I will rule this a 'no fault' event. I guess we can make all that happen. Set up a day and time for a staff meeting to plan it. Maybe we can cut costs by bringing in homemade stuff like we do for parties. When does this all have to be done?"

Doris smiled meekly. "Er, that's the little tidbit of news I was not expectin'. Due to reasons that were not explained to me, the date for the open house has been moved up from one month from now to next week."

Randall flailed both arms and sputtered. "What?! Next week?! You've got to be kidding!" He stomped around in a circle like a toddler.

Doris raised a hand and squeaked out a question. "Am I still forgiven?"

Randall blew out a sigh and counted ceiling tiles. Then he reached out and put a hand on Doris's shoulder. "In for a pound. . . . Wasn't your fault they moved it up. Plan remains the same. We'll just do what we usually do: bite the bullet until our gums bleed."

Ear Wax and Fritz

Sometimes being busy at work is a good thing. Dwelling on other worries is difficult while multitasking. Unfortunately, on this Wednesday, Randall had no "multi" to task. Workflow dribbled like water from a leaky faucet, apropos of the day's patients. It was a day of routine follow-ups, mostly prostate cancer patients on long-term monitoring after treatment. Half the follow-ups were late for appointments. When they did come in, the patients were either as terse as haiku verse or blathered on like random number generators. More than once, Randall found himself carried away on his own mental musings during a blather.

With one such offender, Randall had even drifted off to "meditation island." When the patient finished his dissertation, Randall was sitting peacefully, eyes closed and semi-conscious. The patient became confused, got up from his chair and walked over to Randall. As if he was looking for the "on" switch, the patient poked Randall's shoulder and asked if he was okay. Randall started into full alert and got back to business. "Ah, yes!" Randall had said, quicking thinkly. "I find if I close my eyes while you're talking, it allows me to create a cohesive working model of your case. It's a highly scientific method for creating the best treatment plan."

The patient shrugged his shoulders, satisfied. "Okay, you're the doc! Whatever you say." Randall faked his way through the rest of the follow up and beat a hasty retreat to his office. He decided he needed more coffee, stat, perhaps by IV push.

After chugging a mug, Randall thought it best to dictate his unfinished notes before he lost track of which prostate belonged to which patient. When he got to prostate number two, his train of thought tripped a relay switch off to a parallel track while he looked for the correct PSA result. By the time he found it, he'd forgotten where he'd left off and replayed the dictation to find his place. In the process, he accidentally erased about half of what he'd already dictated. That notched his irritation up another level. Suddenly, his ear itched like crazy and it felt like a stalactite had broken off in his ear canal. That dang thing had to come out, so he fished for it with his little finger with no success.

Randall pulled open his pencil drawer to find a paperclip, which he bent open to create a double ended hook. While he did so, he could hear his mother's voice telling him never to put anything smaller than his elbow into his ear. He ignored the warning. Holding the larger hook between thumb and finger, he pushed the smaller hook into his ear canal to pull out the offending chunk of earwax. Unfortunately, when he put pressure on the device, it snapped in half, the smaller hook end of the paper clip lodged in his ear canal. He swore and threw the broken half of the paper clip against the wall and tried, vainly, to grasp the broken part in his ear with his thumb and forefinger. Fearing he'd only push it farther in if he couldn't see it, he did the only sensible thing he could think of. He dialed up Doris on his intercom and calmly summoned her.

Doris limped into Randall's office. "What's up, Dr. B?"

Randall pointed to his ear. "Er, it's more like what's in. Somehow, a piece of paper clip flew into my ear and I can't get it out."

Doris just shook her head. "A likely story. You and little boys! You got a hole and you gotta put somethin' in it. You expect me to remove it?"

Randall smiled and nodded. "You have great hand skills. Anyone who can type 100 words per minute.... There's a headlamp and a hemostat in the exam room. With that equipment you are going to do your first foreign body removal from a body cavity. It goes without saying that this little procedure will remain confidential. And please, don't say a word about elbows in ears."

Doris said nothing and shook her head in disgust. The two walked to the exam room, trying to look nonchalant. Randall talked her through the use of the otoscope and ENT tools. Doris delicately inserted the scope in the involved ear canal and went fishing with an ear wax removal tool. She proved quite deft at small, precise movements and carefully removed the paper clip fragment along with a sizable bolus of wax. Randall sighed with relief as she held out the paper clip fragment for his inspection.

Doris was quite proud of her newfound prowess and walked Randall back to his office. She looked into Randall's still open pencil drawer and noted one of the bins was filled with small piles of dried earwax remarkably similar to what she had just removed from his ear. "Hmm, bless your heart, looks like you've done this before. Even after a few years in the north, there are still some things that startle the Southern right outta me. That's quite a collection. Do you have an ear wax fetish or is there some collector value?"

Randall cleared his throat with embarrassment. "Got me there. The paper clip thing has always worked before. Never had a clip break, though. Must be those cheap VA paper clips. Any way to save a penny."

"And bust an ear drum," added Doris.

Randall raised his hands in defensive mode. "I know, I know. Next time I'll call Earwax Busters before I break another paper clip."

"Not my job, boss," said Doris. "This was a one-time deal. I don't get paid enough to dig for gold. Either use mirrors next time with the proper tools or go up to the ENT clinic. That's an order."

Now Randall really felt foolish. "Yes, Mother. You may be right about that fetish thing. I'll speak with my shrink about it. Thanks for your help. You're really swell. You can go back to your office now. I'm all better."

Doris walked out with a smile and Randall sat back down to finish the dictations. He took several deep breaths and blew them out slowly. He clasped his hands together and rubbed his palms. "Okay, I am calm. I am ready. Let's do this thing."

THE LITTLE DICTATOR

The dictations were going smoothly until Randall reached prostate number five. The patient's active paper chart was as thick as an encyclopedia and came stacked on top of three volumes of old records. Randall had the day's PSA result but couldn't find the previous one for comparison. The active chart was in complete disarray and papers kept falling out of it. It was a juggling act to hold the Dictaphone to his ear and wrangle the overstuffed chart with his left hand.

Sometimes Randall would hold the chart open with his forehead to flip to the next page. When he finally found the page he was looking for, the top clasp holding the chart together broke and the pages went flying across his desk. He swore like a sailor for several seconds and put down the Dictaphone to gather the pages. He muttered more profanities as he tried to put the recalcitrant chart back together. Attracted by the colorful language and random thumping, Doris came in to see what had happened.

Randall was fuming. "What the hell? How can we have high tech machines that can focus radiation within pinpoint accuracy and use x-rays to see into the human body, but the damn chart has tissue paper pages!? Wouldn't it be great if, someday, we have computers smart enough to hold all this god-damned information?" Doris just nodded her assent, staying quiet. The two were finally able to square away the chart, and Randall returned to the dictation.

Doris returned to her desk and muttered to herself. "Poor baby. Tryin' to herd the kittens by himself. What would he do without me?"

Just then Grace came huffing into Doris's office looking for Randall. "Is it safe to go in there?"

Doris looked up and shook her head. "He's been having a thing. That man. I swear. He needs a full-time keeper. I'd wait a few minutes before goin' in. If he were a gestational woman, I'd say he was having his monthly hormonal visitation. Go easy today. He's *man-struating*. What do you need him for?"

Grace rolled her eyes and grunted. "The machine is fritzing and Dan is over at County Hospital for a Physics meeting. We've called him, but with the snow coming down it'll take him at least half an hour to get here and park. There's four more patients to treat and someone has to decide whether the fritzing is bad enough to say we're down for the day."

Doris frowned and her face clouded over. "Oh, my! Is it snowin' already? Not good at all. Tell you what. Let me go in there and dip a toe in the water to see what the temperature is before you deliver the news. Can it wait a few beats?"

Grace had seen Randall when he was in one of his moods. It could be a case of "where angels fear to tread." She remembered one time when she'd ventured into his office after he'd put a sticky note on his door that read "Do not disturb. Enter at your own risk." Randall had escorted her out of his office by the elbow and slammed his office door shut so hard a large framed picture had fallen off the wall. It crashed so hard the glass broke and made a terrible racket. All the waiting patients freaked out. Randall quietly cleaned up the mess and the staff tiptoed around him the rest of the day.

Grace nodded at Doris' suggestion. "I hear you. Better you than me."

Doris waited a few minutes at her desk and, just as she was preparing to go into Randall's office, he came out carrying a stack of completed charts, looking proud.

Randall, plopped the charts down in her out box. "Here you go, Doris. Finished the lot of them. You can send these back to medical records. I thought I'd save your bad knee and bring them myself. They are quite a load."

Doris smiled brightly. "Why thank you ever so much. Are 'we' feelin' better?"

Randall tried to pat himself on the back but couldn't actually reach. "Yes, 'we' are. I am feeling rather proud of myself. It's already 11:00. Patients are done. If I hustle, I might make it in time to my lunch meeting with Joe Shepard. And then I've got a meeting on the east side at 5:00."

Doris pursed her lips, looking a bit confused. "You have a meetin' tonight, too? Don't you have Grand Rounds at County at 5:00?"

Randall shook his head. "Skipping Grand Rounds. My other 5:00 meeting is more important and confidential. I've been preparing a report for it."

Doris thought Randall's mood improvement might make this a good time to deliver Grace's message. "Umm, I don't want to be a wet blanket, Dr. B, but . . ."

Randall's face abruptly turned dark. "But what?"

Doris was alarmed by the sudden mood swing. She proceeded cautiously. "Ah, it seems we may have a slight problem with the Linac."

Randall struggled to maintain his composure. "What kind of slight problem?"

Doris took a second and cleared her throat. "Um, Grace was in here a few minutes ago and happened to mention that the unit was fritzin'."

Randall relaxed somewhat. "Good, just fritzing. That's not the same as down for the count. I'll go check on it. I may be able to handle Fritz. I know some German."

Doris was relieved but tried not to show it. Grace had been listening in the hallway, came into Doris's office, and grabbed Randall's arm to escort him to the treatment room. Randall had no time to object.

When Randall and Grace got to the treatment console, Molly and Melinda explained that the Linac had shut down on its own during a patient treatment and only two thirds of the prescribed dose had been delivered. The patient waited while the techs ran the machine through the restart procedure but had to get back home "to beat the snow."

Randall scratched his head. "Is the unit running okay now?"

"Yes," said Molly. "It came back online without a hitch. We checked for water leaks and low voltage in the power supply, but everything checked out okay. Should we wait for Dan to get here and check the unit?"

Randall looked about the waiting area. "There's four patients waiting for treatment?"

Melinda nodded. "Yep. They said they were willing to wait another 30 minutes if you give the go ahead to resume treatments."

Randall put a hand to his forehead and closed his eyes to think. "Alright. Here's what we'll do. Run an output check. That should take about ten minutes. If that's on the mark, go ahead and treat. If it fritzes again, then we'll hold the untreated patients and Dan will have to check it out when he arrives."

"What about the two-thirds guy?" asked Molly.

Randall squinted. "Dang. Forgot about that. Let's see. You said he's already gone home." Molly and Grace nodded. "Well, I guess we have no choice but to make up for the missed dose tomorrow. I'll write an order for an adjusted dose. Anything else? If not, I guess we're good to go."

"Nothing I can think of," said Molly. "We'll run the output check and if it's kosher we'll restart treating. We'll let you know if Fritz returns."

Randall began to calm down. He'd been afraid that Fritz might interfere with his lunch with Joe Shepard. He swore that MEL, the linear accelerator, had an evil agenda of its own to make trouble whenever it was least convenient. Maybe he had won this round. "That should work, but I have to leave for a lunch meeting in about 45 minutes."

Grace gave Randall a sour look. "You're leaving for a lunch meeting? That's new!"

Randall feared a brush fire was looming. "Don't worry. I'll be here for the first three of the four. There are no other patients waiting and I expect the afternoon ones may not show up with the snow storm and all. Let's treat as I said, but if the Linac craps out again, might as well send these guys home. They can afford to miss one treatment. If the unit is down for the afternoon patients, I'll be back and Dan will probably be here. I've got my pager for other mishaps, sinking ships and fires. Everybody *capisce?*"

"Got it, Dr. B," said Molly. Grace and Melinda nodded their understanding.

LUNCH WITH JOE

At Miss Katie's Diner, Joe and Randall got their usual table near the front window, not that it was a great view. It looked out over the freeway and Menomonee River Valley, both as scenic as peeling wallpaper. The waitress was quick to take their order, knowing the two were always on a tight schedule and the rapidity of service was reflected by the tip. She also knew to start with large mugs of coffee.

Randall took a big sip of his hot java. "Ahh, nothing like Katie's coffee. Puts hair on a man's chest."

Joe laughed. "Just gives me heartburn, which does keep me awake instead of the caffeine. Looks like it hasn't put any more hair on your roof. How's it working for your chest?"

Randall smiled. "Still looking for results. I'll just have to do a dose escalation."

Joe reached for Randall's shirt as though he was going to check for new hair sprouts. It was a nice fakeout. Randall batted his hand away. "Hey, man, watch the fabric!"

"Still having defrocked nun dreams?" asked Joe with a sly leer.

Randall looked slightly embarrassed. "Come on. I'm not that lecherous. But I would like to have been there for the defrocking. The fruit is always sweeter when it's forbidden."

Joe laughed and steered the conversation in a more productive direction. "Okay, now that we've got lasciviousness out of the way, what was your impression of what Ruby said when describing how she practiced Yoga with her clients?"

Randall stroked the top of his head. "Before I answer that, don't you mean licentiousness?"

Joe shook his head. "Nope. That descriptor refers to folks who have a fixation on car license plates and collect old ones, as I believe you do."

Randall laughed. "Got me on that one."

Joe pumped his fist. "Another score for me. Now answer my question."

Randall took another sip of coffee and cleared his throat. "Ruby's comments were a most compelling verification of what we've been theorizing. Plus, they were delivered from a completely different perspective than ours. That tends to make me even more convinced we're on the right track."

Joe nodded. "I agree. I was quite impressed by her account of 'sharing energy' with the Yoga students when she works one on one. I was particularly struck by the way she could detect what part of the student's body was feeling tension or pain. More often than not, the student confirmed her observation even though there was no touching or prior verbal reference to the site."

Randall agreed. "You bet. Sounds spooky, just like quantum theory, which is why it raises my flag. I'd almost like to observe her in action to verify what she says. Maybe she can do a demo for us."

"Just what I was thinking, Randy," said Joe. "Let's get that set up for the next meeting. She's my wife's friend, so I'll see if she can arrange it."

"Excellent!" said Randall. "Now, as far as the others, I didn't hear anything earth shatteringly new. We really didn't have a lot more time to go deep after all the introductions and socializing."

Joe pointed at Randall. "Right. And Ruby kept us occupied inordinately long. I thought your physicist, Dan, has a good handle on the quantum stuff and I think he'll help us a lot. Maybe he can have 10-15 minutes each session to bring us up to speed on the elements of the theory."

Randall nodded his affirmation. "Yeah, there are quite a few elements to review, like superposition, tunneling, entanglement and observational bias. There's some new work that's identified how quantum processes are involved in biologic processes like photosynthesis, enzyme activity, muscle function and the like. It's enough so that there is a small group of biologists and physicists interested in a new field of study they call Quantum Biology. It's so far a very small group but it's global and growing."

Joe's eyebrows went up. "Really? Didn't know that. Any local Quantum Biologists?"

Randall nodded. "Yeah, us. I think we may be the first in this city. Pioneers. That's us."

Joe laughed. The waitress arrived with their lunch and conversation was paused for spirited mastication.

Thoughts...

—

Chapter 14

Give Me A Name,
Any Name

"If he who hesitates is lost, why does he get wasted when he hastens?"

—*Confusingus.*

Dictations

Randall returned from his lunch with Joe Shepard. He walked back to his office through Doris's office just as her phone rang. She held up a finger and Randall stopped walking, reluctantly.

Doris held up the phone receiver to give to Randall. "Here, Dr. B. I've got a call for you from someone named Heather. She says she's the Chief of the Transcription Pool."

Randall grimaced. "Dang, I may have pulled a boo-boo. Put her through to my office line. I'll take it there."

Doris tried to keep a straight face and feigned doubt. "You pulled a boo-boo? Is that even possible?"

Randall looked cut to the quick. "No one likes a smart aleck. Wait 'til I get in my lair and put her through."

Randall's phone rang just as he got to his desk. He punched the extension button, picked up the receiver, and said hello.

"Hello, Dr. Biedermeier?" said the caller.

"Yep, that's me, all day, every day," said Randall. "What can I do you for?"

"Yes, this is Heather Ameche, supervisor in the transcription pool. I'm calling about your dictation from this morning on Mr. LaVonne James."

Randall was expecting the worst. "Uh huh? Was it incomplete?"

Heather suppressed a chuckle. "No, doctor. Perhaps, if anything, it was a bit too complete. I called to ask if the descriptive invective you included in the lab report section was meant to be included in the final dictation."

Randall stuttered audibly for a few seconds. He was thoroughly embarrassed, especially when he heard a chorus of laughing in the background on Heather's end of the call.

Randall tried to compose himself before responding. "Heavens, no. As you may have guessed, I was having a bad day and the patient's chart exploded on my desk. My verbal response to the event seems to have accidentally made it into the dictation when I failed to stop the recording. I wasn't even certain that it might have been recorded. I was trying to decide just how to alert you, but you . . . beat me to the punch."

Heather went with it. "The chart exploded? It must have been an act of sabotage in medical records. We need to investigate."

There was more muffled laughing on Heather's end of the line. Clearly, Heather's line was on speaker phone. Randall figured he was being goofed and decided to just play along. "Yeah. It was a terrible thing. Chart pages everywhere. I have several serious paper cuts."

There was more laughing in the background. Heather finally let Randall off the hook. "Not to worry, Dr. Biedermeier. Actually, I'm not calling to embarrass you. Your dictation was kind of the highlight of our otherwise dull afternoon, wasn't it, girls?"

There was audible cheering in the background. He was grateful there was no visual for them to see how red his face and scalp had gotten. Randall took a few seconds to let the cheering die down. "Glad I could brighten up your day."

There were some more cheers and then Heather changed the subject. "I was going to call you anyway. I noticed on the VA Newsletter that your department is having an open house next week. Would you mind if I brought the transcriptionists down for a tour?"

Randall was glad for the change in venue. "Oh, yeah, the open house. You're all welcome considering the fine work you do and your tolerance of my misdeeds. I don't mind a bit. How many of you are there?"

"There's twelve of us including me," said Heather. "Why?"

Randall thought about reversing the goof. "Just want to make sure we have enough food and drink for your group. We don't want to run out."

Heather was a sharp cookie and deflected Randall's suggestion about her group's eating habits. "Oh, no worries. We are all very svelte like Swedish models, and constantly on a diet. We eat like birds."

Randall went with it. "Great. I'll put bird seed on the menu. If you change your minds, we'll also have home baked goodies, chips, dip and all the soda you can drink. Sorry, no hard stuff unless you BYOB, but then you'll have to hide it in a bag and try to walk straight afterwards. You know, big brother and all. If you don't mind me asking, why all the interest in Radiation Oncology, besides my profligate use of disgusting epithets?"

Heather laughed and faked a chirp. "Well, we're all curious about what goes on in Radiation Oncology, especially with all the non-epithetic new words we've had to learn, like 'Linac' and 'Rads.'"

Randall, thinking tit for tat, replied that he, too, wanted to meet the team that had created so many unique misspellings. That brought some background giggles.

"Oh, and one of the transcriptionists wants to feel your face," said Heather.

"Feel my face?" asked Randall.

There was more background laughing. "Yes, she's blind and always likes to match a voice with a face. She's wondered for quite a while what you look like. She wants to feel the radiation machine, too. She's the one who has been misspelling 'dosimetry' as 'dose symmetry.' She wants an explanation of what that is."

"No problem," said Randall. "I'm a touchy-feely kind of guy. Bring your crew down and I'll give all-y'all the nickel tour. But if you want the good eats, come early before the thundering herds get here. All you have to do to gather a crowd around here is whisper the word 'food.'"

"Oh, and just so you know," said Heather. "We have given you this month's 'Little Dictator' award."

Randall wasn't sure if that was an honor or a joust. "Is that a good thing?"

"It is," responded Heather. "It's based on several factors, including clarity, explanation of difficult words and entertainment value. We love it when you forget to unpress the dictate button and do your ad lib commentaries on life at the VA. May your dictate button be forever sticky. I will be presenting you with a Napoleon bobblehead when we come down for the open house."

Randall let out a loud breath. "Well, I feel duly honored . . . I think. Looking forward to it."

BLOCKBUSTER

When Randall finished the call, Molly came in to tell him that the machine output had been per specs and that they had treated two patients. Dan had arrived and okayed the machine for treatment. It was beginning to look like Randall would make it out of the department on time for his appointment with Mary Alice.

Things were going fine until the last patient. Grace was carrying a 20-pound custom lead block that had been screwed onto its Plexiglas mounting tray. She lifted it to slide into the treatment head of the Linac. The block slipped out of her hands and fell, caroming off the edge of the treatment couch onto the floor, narrowly missing Molly's foot. The Plexiglas shattered when it hit the floor. The block, of course, was fine.

Dan had been standing by and quickly surveyed the scene. No one seemed injured. The block had missed the patient. The treatment couch was dented but intact and functional.

Randall heard the commotion and ran to the treatment room. "Did we have an earthquake?"

Dan was ready with a 'sitrep.' "Nothing that would show up on the Richter scale. No major damage, but I'm afraid we won't be able to finish Mr. Lambeau's treatment today. I'll have to make a new lateral block tonight so we can treat him tomorrow. I'll make a corrected dose entry on the chart. Only one field didn't get treated. You know what they say—anything can happen on Lambeau field. Ha!"

Dan giggled at his own lame Green Bay Packer joke, but Randall was not amused. "Don't quit your day job."

Dan ignored Randall and continued. "Decide what you want to do about the missed treatment field tomorrow. However, you lucky devil, you'll be making out a VA Incident Report before you leave tonight. VA rule. The report has to be on file before the start of the next treatment day."

Randall glanced at his watch. It was 4:15. He figured he could knock out the report in 15 minutes and still make his appointment. Darn good thing he didn't have to run to the County for a staff meeting tonight. He'd probably get there right as it finished. *Staff meeting. What a joke.* That started him fuming again. Randall's rant motor started. *If only The County would stop interfering with my work at the VA with their demands. That damn "Sacony."* Only those in the know understood that was Randall's own derogatory dialect for "The County."

Randall realized he was huffing unnecessarily. He reminded himself not to get distracted and just get the Incident Report done. Randall checked back with the techs. "You guys sure everyone's okay?" Grace and Molly indicated all human flesh was intact and unimpaired by the block fall.

"Dang block twisted my wrist, though," said Grace. "Same one I broke when I fell down the porch stairs last year. I hope it's not sprained or something."

Randall checked Grace's wrist. It was sore on lateral flexion, but there was no swelling. He'd have to include this in the Incident report in case it developed into anything. He recalled the reason for Grace's broken wrist. She had fallen at her house one night after imbibing multiple martinis at Balistreri's bar. She claimed she'd had only "tee martoonies."

Randall gave her management advice. "Ice it as soon as you get home and keep it elevated. Take some Ibuprofen. Put a wrap on it if it swells. I'll check it again in the morning. You want to have it checked in the VA ER?"

Grace growled. "Naah, I'm not a baby. I'll be fine."

Randall suspected that Ibuprofen was not Grace's analgesic of choice. He found and filled out the incident report. He purposely wrote fast, since he suspected no one really looked at the darn forms. If they did, they might be daunted by his rampant poor penmanship and lack motivation to decipher it. Doris had already left for the day, so he placed the report in her inbox for further disposition in the morning. Dan was giving the machine his final blessings as Randall swept out of the department with his survival gear.

"Thanks for busting my machine!" yelled Dan, as he waved farewell to Randall.

Randall waved back. "No problem. Any time. What are friends for?"

Randall let the door slam behind him and didn't hear Dan's reply. He checked his wristwatch. It was 4:32.

Randall jogged as best he could, lugging his survival backpack, and beat a hasty retreat to the Scirocco which was parked in the back forty of the expansive parking lot. His foot caught on a chunk of ice as he took a shortcut through a drift of old snow. He performed some nifty ballet moves to avoid a fall. He stuck the landing and made good headway to the Scirocco. He put down his pack and skillfully performed his Houdini car entry maneuver. The VA back entrance allowed for quicker access to the freeway, but progress was slowed by a VA plow truck dropping salt in preparation for the snow that was forecast for the night. Randall pounded the steering wheel in frustration.

Randall could not get past the plow and distracted himself by fuming about Department staff meetings once more. The avowed purpose of the staff meetings was to iron out the thorny issues of all five of the hospitals staffed by the department, not just the main facility at County Hospital. Some of the outreach sites were as far as 25 miles away. The faculty staff at those sites had to leave their work undone in order to make it to the meeting on time. Sometimes they'd have to drive back to their facilities after a staff meeting to prepare for the next day's work.

After what seemed like an eternity, Randall finally made it to the freeway entrance where he found total gridlock. Before entering, he took some deep breaths to calm himself. He figured there was no sense in obsessing about faculty staff meetings while trying to navigate the traffic nightmare. That was a recipe for an accident. His task was to make it to the east side by 5:00. Better late than lame. He carefully merged into traffic at 4:38.

Eastbound traffic on I-94 slowed further as Randall reached the 35th Street exit. He was in the center lane and thought about pulling off the freeway but was blocked out by right lane traffic. The steering wheel received another pounding as traffic ground to a halt. He decided a feral scream would be in order.

Randall yelled loud enough to attract the attention of the driver stopped next to him. "Rolling roadblocks everywhere!" The random stranger gave Randall the finger assuming, apparently, that Randall was angry at him. Randall gave him a palms-up gesture and shrugged his shoulders. The man mouthed a bad word back at him. Looking ahead, there was what looked like a daisy-chain of red tail lights going off into infinity. Time marched on as Randall sat immobilized in traffic. It was 4:45.

Randall thought to himself. *Geez, do I look as angry as that guy? That's not what I want for myself!* He pictured Mary Alice handing him a hot cup of coffee and some cake. He tried to calm himself by surveying the cars around him and studying the billboards, now lit up as darkness began to take over. *Well,* he thought, starting to rationalize, *maybe I can be five minutes late.*

Randall was startled out of his momentary reverie by a blaring car horn behind him. Looking to the road ahead, Randall found the gridlock had parted like the Red Sea. He popped the clutch, floored it, and was soon lakeside on Prospect Avenue. It was 4:55 and he was a block from Mary Alice's office. All he had to do was park. Randall circled the block twice, frantically looking for an open spot, when a parked car just ahead pulled out of a rock star parking space. Randall did a goose and brake semi-slide parallel parking maneuver and killed the engine as his dashboard clock struck 5:00 PM.

CHAPTER 15

FOURTH DEGREE

"There is no present or future—only the past, happening over and over again—now."

—*Eugene O'Niell*

HARLEY

Before the Scirocco had stopped rocking from the violent braking, Randall flung open the door and erupted from the car. Halfway to Dr. Hoffman's office door, he stopped short and went back to the car to retrieve his backpack. He couldn't risk leaving it in the car in this neighborhood. On the way to the office, he spotted a familiar-looking pristine Harley parked in front of the building. He couldn't help smiling at its beauty. He hopscotched to the front door and entered like he had just come in from a casual stroll.

Carol, the receptionist, looked up and welcomed Randall. "Ah, Dr. Biedenheimer. You're right on time. Dr. Hoffman is running a few minutes late. Just take a seat and she'll be with you in five."

"The name is Biedermeier," corrected Randall. "No worries. Everybody messes it up. Just call me Dr. B."

Carol was not to be outdone. "Sorry, 'B' that as it may."

Randall screwed up his face. "Fifty cents you were setting me up for that."

Carol gave Randall a sly grin. "How'd you guess? Sorry to read a book by its cover, but you look like you've had a rough day."

Randall's cover was blown and he gave out a deep sigh. "Is it that obvious?"

Carol adopted a more sympathetic tone. "Only to those in the know. Hang your coat on the rack in the corner and have a seat. Just do the hook puzzle and you'll be settled down in no time. The doctor will come get you when she's ready."

Randall began to work the puzzle and before he knew it, there was a hand on his shoulder. He was startled by the touch. He was expecting a verbal alert.

Mary Alice ignored Randall's response. "Your number is up. Walk this way."

Randall shouldered his backpack and followed Mary Alice to her office. She walked with a little sashay, which Randall began to mimic. Carol winked as they walked by. Mary Alice directed Randall to sit in the 'comfy' chair and he put his backpack down next to it. Mary Alice went to the adjacent coffee room and came back with a small plate of oatmeal raisin cookies and a fresh cup of coffee.

She handed Randall the cup and put the plate of cookies down on a side table. "Here you go, young man. Have something to eat and drink. I made the coffee extra strong. Looks like you need it as much as I do. Last patient talked my ear off. This time of day the old eyelids get heavy as barbells. Carol tells me you're upset. What's on the top of your head besides bright and shiny?" Randall had to laugh. He'd never heard that one before.

THE FOURTH DEGREE

Randall was confused. "Carol told you that already? Carol and I hardly talked. I didn't see her call you while I was waiting. Is she some kind of telepath?"

Mary Alice wagged an index finger. "How she does it is a trade secret, but that's one reason why she works here. She makes the diagnoses before the patient walks in my office. I almost feel guilty doing the billing." She held her hand up next to her mouth, as if sharing a secret. "Don't tell your insurance company. So, tell me, what gives?"

Randall couldn't answer at first because his mouth was full of cookie. "*Um, er,* how 'bout I finish this cookie, first? I'm hypoglycemic and fading out a bit. It's been a day. Nothing to eat since lunch." Randall wolfed down the cookie he had and reached for another.

Mary Alice put up both hands. "No rush. It's your dime. Take your time. I'll get a warmup on my coffee and re-glue my ear."

Randall stopped chewing and swallowed. "Re-glue your ear?"

Mary Alice laughed. "Earth to patient. Remember I just told you my last patient talked my ear off? Couldn't get a word in edgewise, so I just let her run on fast forward. Had to get it out of her system anyway. Why block traffic?"

Randall almost spit out a cookie chunk stifling a laugh and started to cough.

Mary Alice walked over and pounded Randall's back. "Whoa, boy, take it easy. It's been a while since I did CPR."

"I'm okay now," said Randall, clearing his throat and laughing. "You caught me with my guard down."

Mary Alice chuckled. "Now chew your food carefully, like your mother taught you. While you're chewing, I am wondering why you lugged that big backpack in here? Swallow and think before you answer." She settled gracefully onto her chair.

Randall thought it a strange question. He was becoming aware that Mary Alice seemed able to keep him off balance at will. Was this a trick question or just casual conversation to help him calm down? Randall decided on the latter as he finished chewing and took another swallow of coffee. He could already feel the caffeine starting to percolate through his system and the cookie glucose stimulating his hypoglycemic brain cells.

"That's my survival backpack," explained Randall. "It's filled with all the important stuff I need to carry around. It doesn't all fit in my briefcase anymore and I have a long walk to get to my car in the VA lot, especially in the snow. It weighs about 30 pounds and the weight is better balanced with the backpack."

"Sounds like good aerobic exercise," observed Mary Alice. "But what in the world do you have to carry that would make it so heavy? And why couldn't you just leave it in your car?"

Randall wasn't sure why any of this was relevant, but he tried to explain. "Well, I can show you. Here are my Medical Physics and Radiation Oncology textbooks. About 15 pounds just for those two. Need those to prepare for a case presentation tomorrow. Then, I've got some dosimetry to review, my checkbook, my prescription pad, stethoscope, toothbrush, socks, clean underwear and a spare shirt. Over in this pocket . . ."

Mary Alice interrupted. "I get the picture. But why did you bring it in here? And do you really need a change of clothes?"

Randall still thought the line of inquiry was rather tangential. When was she going to ask him to present his homework assignment? "Well, I couldn't risk leaving it in the car in this neighborhood and having it stolen, could I? As far as the clothes, in the past month I have been pooped on, peed on and gotten a blood bath at work. Each time I had to go home wearing scrubs. You might say my work can get rather 'hands on.' The most recent blizzard almost had me staying overnight at the hospital."

Mary Alice pursed her lips and nodded, but said nothing. It was an annoying therapist trait.

Randall took the silence as his cue to present his report. He picked up the backpack again, reached inside and pulled out some note cards.

Mary Alice looked at Randall sternly. "We're finished going through the backpack."

Randall was confused. "But these are my notes."

"What notes?" she asked.

Randall was getting a bit testy. "The notes for my presentation, you know, the 10-minute 'This Was My Life' summary you asked me to do for today's session?"

Mary Alice smiled and nodded. "Ah, yes. I probably should have clarified that exercise a bit more. It wasn't for you to present to me. It was for you to go through the process of journeying through the choices and factors that led to you doing what you do and being who you are."

Randall slumped. He felt like his breath was being squeezed out of him. He began to whine. "But I've spent hours preparing for this. I've thought about it, wrote about it, discussed it with my wife and even did bedtime stories about it with my kids. It's all right here in these notes."

Mary Alice put up both hands in a defensive gesture. "Whoa. You're not on a podium making a presentation. This is not a scientific paper. Put the notes back in the backpack and put the backpack over by the doorway out of reach. This is the place where you can shed your load."

Randall's defense was to make light of it. "Like in days of old when knights were bold?"

Mary Alice was caught off guard and had to laugh. "Nice attempt at diversion. It's not where we're headed, but I guarantee you'll walk off quite contented."

Randall felt embarrassed, his cheeks warming. So she knew that old rhyme, too.

Mary Alice leaned forward in her chair. "Listen to me. Let's just say that today's first lesson is about just what the old verse says. What we do here is all about lightening loads."

Randall rolled his eyes, turned his head and stared at the wall. He felt a wave of anger coming.

Mary Alice knew that breaking through Randall's norms was the way to open him up to new ideas. She sensed now was the time to deliver her message. "You do not need to recite your personal history to me. It sounds like you've gone through that six ways to Sunday. That backpack may weigh 30 pounds, but the notes probably make up 10 pounds of that weight mentally. Give yourself permission to put all that weight aside. Notice your body—your legs are crossed, you're hunched over. I can tell from your guarded body position that you feel angry. Let's get that anger vented. Your actual 'assignment' was to find the common thread that you found on your journey back through time."

There was a long silence as Randall mulled that through, trying to regain equipoise. He felt like yelling but stifled it. If Carol heard him spout off, she'd probably come in the room and corral Randall in a step-over toehold.

Mary Alice let out a long audible breath, making the exhalation sound like an ocean wave. "Randall, do what I just did and then tell me what you notice in your body."

Randall did as requested. Then he relaxed his arms and uncrossed his legs. "Dang! I feel lighter, but my chest feels tight and my stomach hurts."

Mary Alice straightened her back and she looked pleased. "Good! Breathe into that! We have time. When you're fully relaxed again, tell me what you were so upset about when you got here."

Randall took more deep breaths and gradually the chest tightness and stomach ache faded. "I think I'm ready."

Mary Alice nodded. "Then sock it to me."

Randall opened up like he'd just had a laparotomy incision. In a five minute verbal vomit, he summarized his crazy day and the trip from the VA. He explained how nervous he'd been about presenting his life review. When he finished, he felt like a vintage train engine pulling into the station and releasing a prolonged burst of steam.

Mary Alice tried to calm Randall down. "You have quite a workload and, to boot, things don't always go smoothly. But, just like the backpack, you can leave all that at the door when you come in here. This is your sanctum sanctorum. Relax . . . take some breaths and let the anger go. You must have gone through a lot of snow getting here. Your shoes and pants are full of road salt."

Randall looked down and saw she was right. "Oops. Sorry to drag it in here. I should have wiped my feet better when I came in."

Mary Alice waved off the apology. "Not to worry. I've seen worse." She got up and grabbed a newspaper off a stack beside the fireplace and handed it to him. "Here. Put this on the floor next to your chair. Go ahead and slip off your shoes. Put them on the paper to dry off. Then you can air dry your socks. With all the winter detritus you plowed through, it looks like you're wearing 'Slush Puppies.'"

After Randall released his still cold feet from the wet shoes, he let out a loud sigh. It was rather relaxing. "Woof. That feels better. Actually, these shoes are my 'un-Hush Puppies. My staff got tired of me sneaking up on them and made me buy a pair of squeaky shoes."

Mary Alice laughed. "That's a good one. You haven't lost your sense of humor . . . or your mind. If you were worried about it, I can assure you you're not crazy. Let me refill your coffee while you relax a bit more. Then we can get to today's work. Sound good?"

Randall nodded and let another relaxing breath ease out. "Yeah, I think I'm ready now. I'm not crazy? Boy, you really are a quick study."

Mary Alice's eyes twinkled. "I've got another little task for you. Look inside that overworked brain of yours and see if there's anything besides the backpack that you'd like to unload." While Randall pondered a response, she studied him, head to toe. "Your shoulders seem tight. You seem to still be carrying a heavy burden. This is a great place to loosen your load."

Randall nodded and the lyrics of a rock song played in his mind. "Yeah, like the Eagles say in their song, 'Take It Easy.'"

Mary Alice nodded and looked pleased. "You've got it!" She surprised the heck out of Randall by singing the opening lyrics to the song. Her voice was smooth and lyrical. She gave particular emphasis to the message about loosening his load.

Randall joined in and they both had a good laugh at the end.

Mary Alice complimented Randall's vocal talents. "Nice job! I hope you had only one woman on your mind. Now, settle in and let the chair hold you while I get your refill."

Randall was disinclined to state that he'd been thinking about two women. He felt himself unwind a few notches. He began to think the whole shrink experience might not be so bad after all. Mary Alice returned with a fresh coffee, handed it to him and sat back down in her comfy chair. "So, tell me. How was your trip back in time through memoryland and how did it feel to condense your life into notes on a set of index cards?"

The question gave Randall a moment's pause. He tried to construct a cogent answer. "Well, I worked my tail off. I spent a lot of time just spinning my wheels. Then it got weird. The more I thought about the past, the more long-ago memories came floating up, sort of like bones rising to the surface of the La Brea Tar Pits. One memory would trigger another, and it was like some of the stuff was happening all over again."

Mary Alice leaned forward and rubbed her palms together. "Ooo, tell me more."

GUT INSTINCT

Randall had to think some more before responding. "When the memory would pop up, I'd get the same feeling in my body as when the thing happened. Like when I pushed my little brother into the front hall closet, closed the door on him, and crushed his finger in the door jamb. He started screaming, but I thought he was just scared. My mother came running to the rescue and got him out. When I saw all the blood on his hand, I felt really bad. She rushed him to the hospital and yelled that she would deal with me later. I almost wanted to be spanked with the paddle instead of the dreadful waiting."

Mary Alice stayed calm and present. "That's a strong memory. What do you notice inside your body right now?"

Randall released a tight breath and looked to the side. "Well, my stomach just hit my pelvis. I can't breathe so well. I still feel so awful and guilty! I hate to disappoint my mom! How can I be so stupid?"

Mary Alice nodded her understanding. "Wow, that really hit you in the gut! Some of those memories have a long half-life, if I can borrow a phrase from your parlance. Notice how your verbs went from past tense to present. It may have been long ago, but it still feels alive right now." She gestured to him with an open palm. "Go on."

Randall started to see a connection. "I still get that same sinking feeling in my gut whenever I'm nervous or stressed. It happened a lot before a big test in college or med school. But you don't want to hear about that. It's kind of gross."

Mary Alice dismissed his concern. "Go ahead, everything you tell me is sacred. My office is like Las Vegas. Anything that happens here stays here. And I am not a delicate flower. Nothing you can tell me will be the first time I've heard it."

Randall hesitated and then held forth. "Well, let's just say, I'd spend the hour before a test in the little boy's room reliving past meals and carving my initials in the wood dividers."

Mary Alice chuckled and cleared her throat. "That paints a clear picture. You know, that's a very common reaction to stress. Do you realize that?"

Randall felt a bit sheepish and vulnerable. "So, it isn't just me? I guess I should know that. Doesn't it have something to do with the sympathetic nervous system?"

Mary Alice sat back and nodded her affirmation. "Correct. Sounds like you've recalled some medical school physiology lessons. It's the old fight, flight or freeze response. It's how the nervous system responds to stress. When you feel threatened in some way, your body makes the decision to evacuate your bowels before you can even think about it. When a saber-toothed tiger is about to chase you down, your body decides it can run faster if it lightens the load. Plus, blood gets diverted from your guts to your legs so you can run for your life."

Randall offered his own observation. "I guess that would be the original version of fast food." He laughed at his own clever response. "So, it's like you feel it in your gut first, lighten your load and then your legs light their burners."

Mary Alice suppressed a laugh, but admired Randall's grasp of the concept. "Now you're cooking with gas. Tell me more. I bet you have some strong memories of this feeling."

Randall recalled another early experience with fear and stress. "Right. There was this big kid, Jimmy, who lived up the street from me. Catholic kid. Went to St. Roberts. I went to Atwater across the street. He'd hide in the bushes or behind a tree and ambush me on my way to school. He'd jump out and chase me home." Randall paused, reliving the hazing.

Mary Alice prodded some more. "Why did you run?"

Randall squinted at Mary Alice like she wasn't grasping the obvious. Then he figured maybe girls didn't get bullied in grade school. "I'm not a coward, but he was twice as big as me and threatened to rearrange my anatomy."

Mary Alice could tell she was peeling away more layers of the onion. "I didn't mean to suggest you were a coward. After all, discretion is the better part of valor. Tell me more about what he did and how you felt about it."

Randall shrank into his body, trying to recapture what it was like to be a kid. "Sometimes he would catch me. Then he'd push me down or punch me and run off. I never knew where or when he'd pop up. One time he stole my ball glove. It got so I was afraid to go to school. Sometimes I'd pretend to be sick so I could stay home. It wasn't that hard to pretend—my stomach always hurt."

Mary Alice leaned forward in her chair. "Did you tell your parents?"

Randall shook his head. "Nah, I didn't want to look like a weeny. Dad would have just told me to 'man up.' Ugh, my belly hurts just thinking about it." Randall rubbed his stomach.

Mary Alice pushed a bit harder. "Wow, you had to deal with a lot. Did you ever resolve it?"

Randall stared at random items on the fireplace mantel. It was funny. He'd only recalled the being scared part up until now. He had actually dealt with it. "You bet. One day, I got tired of being scared, so I decided to get smart. I started to take the back way out of the house, cut around the block the opposite way, go through some fields and get to school. Jimmy didn't catch on for a long time. Still, each trip to school I was always checking my back. I guess I chose flight over fight 'cause that guy could have pounded me into the ground."

Mary Alice sensed there was more to the story. "So, did the Jimmy problem finally fade away?"

Randall smiled. "Not exactly. I chose tit for tat. I knew where he lived. One morning I ambushed him by jumping out from behind a huge tree. He was so surprised he stepped back and I punched him right in the nose. He went down with his nose bleeding. Before I ran off, I warned him to stay away from me or pay the price. He never bothered me again." Randall crossed his arms, feeling proud of his younger self.

Mary Alice was rather surprised by this reveal and leaned back in her chair. "Wow. You adopted a hit and run strategy. How interesting. Did that stop the gut response you felt going to school?"

Randall had to think about that for a moment. He closed his eyes and tried to remember. "I'm not sure but I think things were better. I'd still think about it, but didn't have the same reaction."

Mary Alice leaned forward again. "Sounds like finally facing up to the bully took care of the belly yips."

Randall took a sip of coffee. "Hmm. I guess so. I suppose there's a lesson in there somewhere."

Mary Alice nodded but didn't say anything. Her silence made Randall squirm in his seat. He gazed out the window at the solitary tree in the back patio as he paged backwards in his mind for more clues. Ironically, his belly was still talking to him. His ascending colon was doing a tap dance on his hepatic flexure. Something was definitely brewing. *Not great timing,* he thought and swallowed hard.

Randall was definitely feeling a bit queasy. "You know what? It's happening right now. I think my GI tract is giving me signals that it wants attention."

Mary Alice raised her eyebrows. "That's a good sign. It suggests you've relaxed and the tension wants release."

Randall yawned and glanced about. Mary Alice noticed and asked if he wanted a coffee refill. Randall declined. "My chest feels tight. I need to take some deep breaths. I guess that's why I'm yawning. I'm not tired, really. I need to get up and stretch my legs . . . and maybe visit the head."

Mary Alice rose from her chair and went over to the fireplace mantel. "Good idea. I need a stretch too. The head is down the hall on your left. When you get back we can change directions."

When Randall returned, Mary Alice was seated again. She suggested another round of coffee and started to get up for it. Despite Randall's trip to the head, his descending colon was calling for attention again. He didn't want to answer its call within earshot of Mary Alice.

"No, no," said Randall. "I'll get the refills. Be right back, Chief." He quick-stepped into the kitchen and turned on the sink faucet as camouflage.

Blowin' steam

"Just going to wash my hands while I'm here," announced Randall from the kitchen. He effected a controlled release of the gas bolus. He waved his hand in the air to detect any effluvial scent. There was no obvious sulfurous aroma. He refilled the coffee cups, added creamer and left the kitchen, much relieved. On his way out, he noticed a can of citrus air freshener, so gave it a spritz.

As Randall walked back to the office, he stopped to admire some of the artwork on the hallway wall.

"Those pictures were all done by my patients," called out Mary Alice. "Take your time to look at them."

None of these pictures look like they were done by crazy people, thought Randall. There were a few nice landscapes and some watercolor flowers.

Randall returned to the office, handed Mary Alice her coffee and sat.

"Those patients were in worse shape than you."

Randall's eyes widened. "Really? I was expecting bloody knives and nooses. The one with the black sky and full sun seems to indicate some ambivalence."

Mary Alice laughed. "Don't worry, I painted that one." She raised up in her chair and let out a loud burst of flatus. "Oh, and I did that one too." She laughed again.

Randall was shocked speechless. Had she heard him in the coffee room despite his masking efforts? She had obviously made no attempt to hide her emission.

Mary Alice read the surprise on Randall's face. "Come now, Randall. Don't be such a prude. It's a natural bodily function. There's no need to hold back. Would you rather hold it in and be uncomfortable?"

Randall searched for an appropriate response. "So, you're saying it's like the Japanese concept of belching being a compliment to the cook?"

Mary Alice nodded. "In a way. Americans are very conservative about their natural functions. What do you know about the subject?"

Randall wondered how much there was to know. "Enlighten me, Oh Wise One."

Mary Alice put her hands together and held forth. "Well, now. Flatology is an actual area of study promoted by a somewhat anal obsessive gastroenterologist whose name escapes me. He found that the word fart comes from the Old English word 'feortan,' which means 'to break wind.'"

Randall had to laugh. Mary Alice continued. "Most intestinal gasses come from air swallowed during eating and drinking, thus, nitrogen and carbon dioxide make up the large exogenous component. The rest of the mix is produced by the gut bacteria and consists of more carbon dioxide plus methane and hydrogen. The latter two are flammable so that flatus can be ignited, a fact well known to drive-in movie goers."

Randall had to admit this was new information. Maybe he had missed or slept through the flatus lecture in med school.

Control issues

Mary Alice watched Randall as he processed the new data. "I hope you're feeling less … stressed. So, have you contemplated your navel and come up with any other fear/gut focused issues?"

"Yeah, but this one doesn't come much from my own memories," said Randall. "It's from one of those semi-embarrassing family foibles stories my mother would tell at the dinner table during large family gatherings."

Mary Alice nodded knowingly. "Oh, don't you just love those? They make you want to crawl under the table."

"Or worse," agreed Randall. "When I was three or four years old, she said that when I'd get the Number Two signal, sometimes I would just hold it in. To avoid detection, I'd hide behind some furniture, but my grunting would give me away. She'd follow the sound, find me and drag me to the bathroom. She'd plop me on the toilet and 'encourage' me to deliver the goods. If at first, she didn't succeed, she'd read to me from 'Winnie-The-Pooh' until I got engrossed enough in the story and forgot to pucker up. Her tale of my retention problem never failed to elicit a round of family hilarity, at my expense."

Mary Alice cringed in empathy. "Your mother had an ironic choice of reading material! Bowel retention is a syndrome we see in kids who are in family situations of stress. It's like the child senses the need to hold back his emotions or expressions. Possibly because they sense the parents can't hear it or don't want to."

Randall snapped his fingers and pointed at her. "That describes my dad perfectly—he almost always holds back emotions. He is a very stoic man!"

Mary Alice nodded, looking pleased Randall had made a connection. "I bet you sensed that as a kid, feeling it in your body, even if you couldn't say it in your words. Often the body holds back fecal material due to the fear and pain of pooping, pardon my French. Then it hurts the next time, causing more anxiety, and the cycle continues. There is nothing to be ashamed of, but it sounds like your Mom added shame to the pain by making it such a topic of ridicule. I'm so sorry you had to go through that!"

Randall held his belly. "So, I wasn't a bad kid?"

Mary Alice smiled kindly. "There are no bad kids. As far as childhood bowel retention, it's fairly common and can become a serious problem. The bowel muscle can get stretched out to the point that no neurologic signal is generated. It was beyond your control. I hear you say you felt guilty, which is a good social emotion. It means you regret doing something that causes someone else hardship. It's thinking 'I did something wrong.' Which you didn't, really. Right?"

Randall looked more relaxed. "No, I didn't! But I kind of remember I enjoyed the attention I got, but also felt kind of ashamed about how I got it."

Mary Alice nodded. "Kids enjoy attention and will do a lot of off the wall stuff to get it. Shame, on the other hand, is the feeling that 'something is wrong with me.' That's a different kettle of fish. That shame eats away at you. It threatens the very fabric of your connection and sense of safety and attachment in your family."

Randall looked a bit pained. "Seems like I had both. How does that add up?"

Mary Alice shook her head. "Don't ask me. What does it say to you?"

Randall put out his hands palms up and shrugged. "That's not fair. You answered my question with a question."

Mary Alice nodded. "That's what we do. Think hard."

Randall looked out the window again. The tree was still there. Then a thought hit him. "Control! It was all about control. I could control my bowels and, in turn, my mother. And in a strange way there was a pleasurable feeling that went with having a full colon. Sort of like pre-pubescent sex."

Mary Alice looked rather surprised. "That was quite a leap. I really didn't expect you to get to that spot so quickly. I was expecting I'd have to do more prodding. The control aspect is right on the mark and there are some researchers that would make the sex connection."

Randall smirked. "Didn't Freud think sex was the basis for most of what ails us?"

Mary Alice laughed. "He certainly felt it was important and perhaps he overemphasized it. But you have touched on something there. I'd put a somewhat different spin on it. When your father was overseas you had your mother all to yourself. When he came back it threatened that attachment. In your child's mind you conjured up a way to get that back. Maybe a variation of an Oedipus Complex."

Randall looked down at his folded hands. "Dang. You think?"

Mary Alice nodded. "Obviously the complex didn't persist as you got older and more siblings came along. We've gone back pretty far. Let's move forward a little." She got up, took a baseball from the fire-place mantel, and threw it to Randall. He caught it deftly. "Does that ball trigger any other memories?"

Randall rotated the ball and let his fingers wander over the stitches. It had been signed by Eddie Matthews, the former third baseman of the Milwaukee Braves baseball team. He held it to his nose and sniffed it. "This . . . this ball is fantastic. It's got to be a valuable collector's item. How did you get it?"

Mary Alice laughed. "It was a gift from a patient. I'm not much into baseball. I keep it here for when he comes back for follow up. So, don't drool on it. From your reaction, it looks like that baseball has meaning for you. What's the story?"

Randall slowly nodded his head and thought back. "Yeah. My mother and I were dyed-in-the-wool Braves fans. We'd listen on the AM radio to as many games as we could. We lived and died with the team. We'd go in the back yard with our ball mitts and play catch while the radio broadcast the play by play out the pantry window. Mom was a darn good ball hawk."

Mary Alice smiled at the image. "Did your father join in?"

Randall frowned and shook his head. "No way. He couldn't have cared less. I'd ask him to come out and teach me to pitch, but he claimed he didn't know how."

"Why do you think that was?" asked Mary Alice.

Randall retracted a corner of his mouth. "At the time I think I concluded he just didn't care much about me. Looking back on it now, maybe he never had a chance to play ball as a kid. After his mother died when he was 12, he was sent away to live with other families. That meant mostly working on farms with no time for playing games. He could plow a field, but not throw a baseball. That probably embarrassed the crap out of him."

Mary Alice nodded. "So as a child you concluded your father didn't care about you. And you carried that for how long?"

Randall nodded in agreement, feeled rather embarrassed. "The short answer is 'a long time.'"

Mary Alice rose from her seat and stretched. "Stand with me for a moment so we can put a temporary band aid on that hurt." Randall stood. "Today we have learned that children do not yet have an adult perspective and childhood perceptions can last well beyond their shelf life. The good news is that your father is still alive and there is time to correct the misconception. Now, you are a smart adult and only you know how to do that. You can work that out without me."

Randall got a little choked up and knew what he had to do. "Amen!"

Mary Alice and Randall sat back down. Randall was already feeling like a wet towel that had just been wrung out.

Mary Alice looked at her watch. "We've got just enough time for one more area of investigation. Are you up for that?"

Randall squinted and put a hand to his temple. "Don't want to waste my dime. Shoot."

Mary Alice crossed her legs and took a deep breath. "We know your father was in WWII and you had some fears about the possibility of him being killed there. Do you think that may have left you with an underlying fear of conflict in your personal life or being in a war yourself? After all, there were other wars during your subsequent schooling."

"Hmm, I haven't quite thought of it that way," said Randall, reflecting on the question. "How would you jump to that conclusion?"

"Well, staying in college and medical school for eight years kept you out of Vietnam," said Mary Alice. "Were you running away from conflict or towards a career in medicine?"

Randall felt rather insulted at the suggestion that his career choice was motivated by fear rather than passion. "Are you saying it was more self-preservation than pursuit of a career?"

Mary Alice held up a hand. "No, I'm not saying that. I imagine you could consider that both played a role."

Looking away at the big tree out the window, Randall rolled his eyes and licked his lips.

Randall was getting slightly edgy. "Alright, I guess both factors were in play. I'm not sure how they were proportioned."

"Perhaps if you explain in more detail it will become clearer," said Mary Alice, gently.

Randall made another trip through his neural Rolodex. "Maybe about 40% of the choice to go to college was to avoid the draft and the war in Vietnam. Not the only reason I went, but a definite factor. I knew I was deferred from the draft until after college, but I hedged my bets by joining ROTC. I figured if I was drafted I'd go in as an officer and be a less likely target for enemy fire."

"So, it was influencing your decisions to some extent," observed Mary Alice. "Were you having the bowel panic attacks during college other than prior to tests?"

Randall glanced up and to the side. "Yeah. Sometimes, during ROTC drills, I'd imagine myself in the jungle taking enemy fire. Not long after signing up for ROTC, I heard that lieutenants were more likely to be shot than enlisted men. So, I reckoned I needed a better solution. I dropped ROTC, buckled down even more at school, and studied like crazy. That gave me grades good enough for medical school, where I'd be immunized against the draft for another four years."

"Those are all legitimate factors to consider in making a tough decision," concluded Mary Alice. "You can hardly be blamed for considering them."

Randall looked unconvinced. "Yeah, but now you've got me wondering if I went into medicine for the right reason. Was it for the love of medicine or to avoid going to war? Was my desire to help people greater or less than my desire for self-preservation?"

Mary Alice raised her eyebrows. "Hmm. Actually, this is the first time you've mentioned a love of medicine. Only you can answer whether it outweighed fear of war. Clearly both factors were in play, as they should have been. Here's a factoid you need to consider in your evaluation of the balance between the two. Being a dead doctor ain't much fun and can't help anyone. That's just my opinion. What's yours?"

Randall waved his right arm then scratched his nose while trying to find the right words. "To me it's kind of a free will question. I sometimes wonder if I really made any of these choices. It seems doors just opened and closed leaving me with only one viable option. You know, like I wasn't really making a choice at all. Just picking the lesser of two weevils."

"Oh, I get you," said Mary Alice. "You felt like you were being moved around on a chess board by some blasé teenager playing the game in another universe with you as a sacrificial pawn."

Randall aimed an index finger at Mary Alice. "You've hit the broad side of the barn."

Mary Alice clapped her hands together. "That brings us back to the here and now. We have five minutes left. Let's wrap it up and set a time for our next session. Tell you what. I'll let you pick the topic for discussion. Then, I'll decide if there's another assignment."

"What?" exclaimed Randall. "We just started."

Mary Alice laughed. "Yep, it's the way these sessions go. As I like to say, time flies like nothing and fruit flies like bananas."

Randall laughed at the quip. "That's still a good one. I need to write that down. Actually, there are three things that are at the top of my list. First, as a rational scientist, I don't understand the weird things that have been happening to me lately. I touched on them at our first visit. We need to talk about them. Second, you asked me to read about quantum theory. What does that have to do with the price of sliced bread?"

Mary Alice took some notes. "Excellent topics, Randall. I've written them down for next time. What's the third thing?"

Randall smirked. "Oh, haven't you heard? There are three types of people in the world: those who can count and those who can't. Guess which one I am?"

Mary Alice had to laugh again. "I don't have to guess. Anything else before we sign off?"

Randall had an observation. "This session has gotten me thinking that I'm closer to an answer yet farther away. How is that possible?"

"That's easy," said Mary Alice. "It's in Chapter One of all Psych textbooks. The process is always one step forward and two steps backwards. We have to move backwards to go forward. I'm putting you down for this Saturday at 10 AM. Your assignment is further reading about quantum theory, especially quarks. See if you can make any connections to your strange encounters."

Randall nodded and wrote the assignment on a note card.

"AND," she continued. "Allow yourself more awareness of what's going on in your body. You connected with your gut reaction earlier, and then we paired that with some deep breaths. It's repetition of that new pattern—feeling the stress, acknowledging the sensation, then returning to deep breaths—that will begin to retrain your nervous system and unwind this long history of stress in your guts."

"Dang, that sounds much harder than reading about quantum theory. What about meds? Don't you have a pill I can take to calm the jeebies?" asked Randall.

Mary Alice needed to deflect his plea for a quick fix. "Well, we have the fifty-pound pill you can roll uphill every day, Sisyphus. How about electric shock therapy? I've got an eel in the back. I can also offer a week in the sensory deprivation tank. Or the hermitage on the mountain."

Randall got the message. "Alright, alright. I get it. I will pay attention to my body and maybe talk back to it."

Mary Alice smiled and nodded. "I'd like you to try a more mindful approach—just focus on relaxing and deep breathing whenever you can take a break at work, even for five minutes. Talk about your frustrations with your wife. Don't hold so much inside."

Randall was rather overwhelmed. "Easier said than done."

"But more effective than not trying," Mary Alice countered. "Remember, loosey goosey, don't hold it in."

She grinned and sent Randall on his way with his appointment card in hand. Randall thanked her and left quite bemused. He thought to himself, *why do I feel so confused whenever I leave her office?*

Randall walked out of Mary Alice's office as Carol was headed in with a patient chart in one hand and spray can of Glade air freshener in the other. He stopped and gave her a quizzical look.

Carol explained before he could ask. "It's only routine . . . for the cigarette smoke. Don't be so paranoid. Happy quarking."

CHAPTER 16

COLORS AND LIGHTS

"A good head and a good heart are always a formidable combination."

—*Nelson Mandela*

RUBBER MEETS THE ROAD

Randall walked out of Dr. Hoffman's office and out the front door. He paused on the front steps to admire Carol's Harley. It was as clean as a hound's tooth in contrast to the filthy cars parked nearby. Randall couldn't fathom how she kept it funeral clean. He was jealous as hell. He walked slowly down the sidewalk and, lost in thought, almost walked past the Scirocco. He stopped and looked at his car. It had converted itself into a two-tone. It was now shiny gold on the top and matte white on the sides. Actually, he thought it looked kind of cool. The dried salt spray gave the car a rugged character.

He turned and gave the Harley a middle finger salute. To put a finer point on it, he slid into the driver's seat and lit the fuse on the mighty 110 HP 1.6-liter VW 4 cylinder engine. After a few minutes to let engine bits warm up, Randall put the tranny in first gear, turned the steering wheel to a full lock left turn, popped the clutch and floored it. The car responded with a satisfying squeal of front wheel spin as it launched away from the curb and out onto the street.

The trajectory threatened to take the car across the street, but an artfully timed steering correction straightened the path and sent him posthaste down Prospect. It wasn't really a very fast takeoff, but the racket and tire smoke compensated. He hoped Carol was watching out the window. Randall figured Carol didn't really ride the Harley every day; she probably just left it parked there during the day and, at night, kept it in a garage behind the office. She probably got a ride to work from Mary Alice or her husband. The Harley was just an intimidation device; something to mess with the minds of patients. That had to be it, because no one was more anal than him about vehicle care.

Freeway traffic had lightened considerably, so the trip home was twice as fast as the trip downtown had been. As Randall weaved around and past the slow-boats, he considered how he could quickly catch up on the latest thinking on quantum theory and quarks. He was going to have a quark-fest in the near future. He had suspected quarkiness had a connection to his strange visitations and etheric communications. Now, with two references to quantum theory by a board-certified Psychiatric MD/PhD, he had a definite nibble on his fishing line. He would have to reel it in carefully. Stay rational and calm. Don't jump to conclusions that don't stand up to scientific scrutiny.

Soap opera

The dash clock showed 6:25 PM as Randall rolled up the driveway and pushed the garage door remote button. He wondered what surprises awaited him inside. Given the day he'd had, his premonitory senses expected the worst. At the least, no one was rushing out to greet him with bizarre news. So far. He cautiously exited the car and warily approached the back door. He looked in the window and found no waiting greeters. He unlocked and pushed the door open. All was quiet. Wonder of wonders. He did a visual of the kitchen area while unshouldering his backpack. The kitchen and eating area were wife and children-free, but the table was set for four. The smell of food cooking filled the room. Pots were on the stove and the oven was on.

"Great jumping Julia Child!" exclaimed Randall out loud. "They held dinner for me."

In that moment of wonder, Zelda, Kyle and Addie swarmed in from the dining room and yelled, "Surprise!"

Randall dropped his backpack on the floor and grabbed his chest while looking up at the ceiling. "It's the big one, I'm coming to join ya, Elizabeth!" he yelled out, quoting a Redd Foxx line from the TV show "Sanford and Son."

Zelda ran forth with arms outstretched to hug him. "You don't have time to die now, it's time to dine!"

"Oh, alright," said Randall, looking back up to the ceiling. "Elizabeth, I'll call you later."

"Daddy," said Addie, using her 'I'm very annoyed' voice. "Who's Elizabeth?"

Zelda was quick with an answer Randall hadn't thought of. "Sweetie, she is Daddy's long dead Grandmother."

Kyle had to get his two cents in. "Nyah, I bet it's an old girlfriend. Ha ha, Dad's got a girlfriend."

Randall confirmed Zelda's remark. "Actually, kids, it's truly true. My Dad's mother, my Grandmother, your Great Grandmother, was named Elizabeth."

"There were three Elizabeths?" asked a confused Kyle.

Zelda tried to clear things up. "No, you silly billy goat, that's all one person. Three roles."

Kyle shook his head, still confused. "Not rolls, we're having mashed potatoes!"

Randall couldn't believe the density of Kyle's skull. "No, Elizabeth was my grandmother. She was your grandpa's mom. And she's your great grandmother."

Addie crossed her arms and glared at her brother. "Pay attention, Kyle!"

Kyle stuck his tongue out at Addie. Randall knew enough about kid entropy to jump back into his story. "Anyway, Elizabeth died in 1926 when my Dad was only 12 years old."

"Really?" asked Addie. "Why did she die? Was she sick?"

"No," said Randall. "Let me get my coat off and gear tucked away, while you both sit down for dinner and let Mom serve the food. I'll tell you the story after dinner."

The kids scrambled for their seats and Zelda set about putting out roast pork, mashed potatoes, gravy and green bean casserole.

Kyle looked at the spread and announced his pleasure. "Ooo, goody, I love bean shit."

"Kyle, what have I told you about your potty mouth?" scolded Zelda.

Kyle was somewhat abashed. "If I use bad words, I get Ivory soap for dessert. Sorry, sometimes my mouth talks before I know what it's going to say. But don't blame me. It's what Grandma calls it!"

"More contributions to your genome from your father," snarked Zelda. "Try thinking longer before you talk or get your mouth brakes fixed. Better yet, just put a fork in it."

Kyle grinned like a clown. "Ha. Mom said fork."

Zelda knew Kyle's tricks. "Nice try at deflection, Kyle. Watch your language or it's an Ivory soap mouthwash."

Kyle crossed his eyes as if trying to see his mouth.

Addie just looked confused. "What's a genome?"

"It's like diarrhea," answered Zelda. "It's in your genes."

Addie screeched. "Mooommm! You talk in riddles just like Dad."

Zelda motioned Addie to keep quiet. "Well, that's all the explanation you're gonna get." She put the last of the food out on the table just as Randall came in and sat down.

Zelda sat down and directed everyone to take a serving from the dish in front of them and pass it to the right.

Randall took a slice of pork roast and passed the platter to Kyle. "Did I hear someone needs new blue jeans?"

Kyle still hadn't gotten control of his mouth. "Addie needs new jeans because she pooped in hers."

"I did not!" shouted Addie. "Ha ha. Kyle gets soap for dessert."

Randall looked around the table like maybe he'd missed something. "What's all this about?"

Zelda stared at Kyle. "Go ahead, Kyle. Tell your dad what it's about."

Kyle had gone too far and he knew it. He still tried to bail himself out. "Mom thinks I need new brakes."

Randall whistled through his teeth. "What? Now you need new shoes? We just bought you a new pair of Vans. I'm confused. Enlighten me. Can't tell the players without a scorecard."

Zelda kept staring at Kyle with narrowed eyes, giving him her 'better do what I want' stink eye.

Kyle decided to give up before he dug a deeper hole. He let out a deep sigh. "Mom wants me to stop using potty words. I try to put on the brakes before I say bad stuff, but the brakes don't always work. She says I get it from you. She said she'd wash out my mouth with soap if I did it again. Then I did it again."

"Well, son, I've got good news and bad news," said Randall. "The good news is your mother is not going to give you an Ivory soap gargle later. The bad news is I am going to do it immediately upon hearing it once more or hearing of it from others. Is that clear?"

Randall looked around the table and saw no signs of objection from anyone. In fact, Kyle looked rather relieved. Although Randall expected an objection from Zelda, he suspected she didn't really want to have to do it either and was glad for the reinforcement.

Randall amplified his reasoning. "By the way, I admit that sometimes I am prone to opine a few undesirable words as well. I promise that if you catch me guilty of potty mouth you can watch Mom scrub my tongue with hand soap."

That cheered Kyle up considerably and put big smiles on everyone's faces.

Randall surveyed the smiling faces about the table and decided the haggling was over. "Now, chow down or we won't have time for the Grandmother Elizabeth story." He took the first big bite of pork roast and chewed. It was tender and savory. His irritated gut was soon sending him signals of joy.

For the next ten minutes there was silence except for the percussive music of utensils on plates, chewing, swallowing and the occasional eructation. A melody of "Mmm, goods" and "Yum yums" eventually led to a chorus of "I'm stuffed" and "What's for dessert?"

Zelda looked up from her plate and examined the remains of dinner. It looked as though a swarm of locusts had done a hit and run. There was nary a morsel of food left. "Dang! It took four hours to prepare our humble repast and 15 minutes to kill and bury it. Regarding dessert, I've got good news and bad news. What do you want first?"

"The good news," chirped Addie.

Zelda smiled like the Cheshire Cat. "There will be no Ivory soap gargles for dessert."

Randall looked at Kyle and saw the look of relief on his face. "That's good news for a certain someone. Dare I ask what's the bad news?"

Zelda made a frowny face. "We're out of ice cream."

"Aw, sh . . . . . oot," said Kyle with a crinkly smile.

Randall patted Kyle's shoulder. "Nice save, Buddy. Maybe your brakes just need a little more adjustment. Here you go." Randall gave Kyle's ear a moderate twist and Kyle grimaced in mild discomfort. "How do your brakes feel now? Do they need another adjustment?"

Kyle massaged his ear. "Er, no, Dad. I think that did the job."

The Rhubarb

Zelda stood up and stretched out her arms. "Buuuttt, although the ice cream is 86, we do have fresh rhubarb pie courtesy of our neighbors, Julie and Chris. Too bad everyone is stuffed."

Kyle rubbed his stomach vigorously and announced he'd just created a pie slice worth of space in his tummy. Addie did the same. Randall just said he'd had only three cookies to eat all day and could still eat two slices of a cow pie. Zelda looked at Randall with menace and made mouth washing motions. Randall zipped his lips.

When all was quiet, Zelda made her dessert announcement. "So who wants rhubarb pie? How big a slice and with or without Reddi Whip topping?"

Randall slapped the table. "Bring it on! I want a humongous slice and a Reddi Whip mountain."

Kyle echoed Randall's request. "Me too, but I want a Devil's Tower of Reddi Whip, just like in Close Encounters! Give me the whole canister."

Zelda was quick to stifle that suggestion. "No, you'll take what I give you, young man! Last time I let you have it, you filled your mouth from the can. It looked like a scene from 'Animal House'!"

Addie decided not to act like a pig and make her brother look bad. "Mommy, I'll just have a half slice with a little Reddi Whip. If I'm still hungry after that, maybe I'll have another half slice."

Addie's maneuver was not lost on Kyle and he threatened to flip a spoonful of Reddi Whip at her. Zelda's quick reflexes prevented the attempt at mayhem. Before Kyle could carry out his threat, she plucked the spoon from his hand. "Kyle! If I wasn't in such a good mood, I'd send you right to bed. Now stop pestering your sister or I'll take the pie away too. You're not getting any more Reddi Whip, but if this nonsense doesn't stop I'll be ready to whip you. Use your fork and eat your pie!"

Kyle shrank back in his seat, looked right and left, and started scarfing his pie. Addie gave Kyle a triumphant smile.

Randall tried to divert the discussion away from kiddy conflict. "Where in the world did Julie find fresh rhubarb this time of year?"

"It grows prolifically behind her garage," said Zelda. "So, she harvests it every fall, cooks it down and preserves it in Mason jars. She says wild rhubarb grows really well back there because the neighborhood dogs like to pee behind her garage. The dog pee makes great fertilizer."

Kyle spit out his mouthful of pie onto his plate. "Dog pee rhubarb? Oh, yuck!"

"Don't worry," said Randall. "You can't taste it, especially if you use enough sugar."

Addie grimaced and looked like she had been sucking a lemon. Randall and Zelda laughed and almost spit out partially chewed pie. The kids stared at their half-eaten pie. Randall felt sorry for them and explained how plants only use the broken-down chemicals from the soil. He was tempted to point out that farmers often used manure to fertilize the crops we eat, but decided the kids were freaked out enough. Once convinced they were not eating fresh animal waste, they resumed devouring the pie and asked for seconds. Randall and Zelda had trouble stifling giggles.

Randall collected himself and took on a more serious tone. "Why did Julie bless us with this bounty?"

"She wanted to show her gratitude to us for listening to their concerns about Alexandra the other night," said Zelda. "She brought over the pie as a thank you gift this morning and asked if she and Chris could stop over tonight after dinner for a bit of a follow-up. She hoped the pie would grease the skids. I said yes. I hope that's okay?"

Randall rolled his eyes suddenly understanding the reason for the 'special dinner.' He stifled his initial negative reaction and told Zelda an after-dinner visit was perfectly fine. He figured it was a small price to pay for a great dinner and pie.

Zelda was pleased and thought it was a good time to sweeten the pot. "Speaking of follow ups, I made a decision today."

Randall was only partly tuned in. He was thinking of how his evening plans would have to be modified. There was still a morning conference to prepare for.

Zelda had expected a more enthusiastic response. "Randy? Did you hear me?"

Randall jumped a bit in his chair and looked at Zelda. "Yeah, sure. I was waiting for the great disclosure."

Zelda smiled. "I've decided to take Chelsea's suggestion and run with it."

Randall looked puzzled. "You're going to start jogging?"

"Randy, don't be such a pain. I think I should start seeing a counselor. And you're going to help me pick one out."

Randall was surprised and pleased. "Hey, that's great! Glad you will join in on the fun. More than happy to help with that. What are your thoughts?"

Zelda straightened up in her chair and cleared her throat. "Ahem. I'm pretty sure I want a lady shrink. Working with Julie and Chris has kind of given me a taste for therapy. I'm even thinking about becoming one. Well, maybe not a full fledged Psychiatrist. That would take too much school and training. But maybe something a notch or two down from there. And maybe helping Julie and Chris find answers will help us find ours."

Randall grinned widely and nodded. Now he was not sorry about giving up some of his evening.

Kyle had been sitting quietly and listening. His question rather surprised both Randall and Zelda. "What answers, Dad?"

Randall turned his head to look at Kyle. "Well . . .the cure for what ails us. The aspirin for the human condition. You know, take two and call me in the morning."

Addie thought it time to remind her parents she was still present as well. "Great! More riddles. You don't have to explain, as long as you finish the story about Elizabeth."

Randall nodded. "Sorry guys. We didn't mean to put the story off so long, especially since we're getting visitors soon. When I'm done with the story, can you two help Mom and me clear the dirty dishes off the table and take them to the kitchen? Then, go on upstairs and get ready for bed. Deal?"

Addie nodded. "OK, but tuck us in before the neighbors come over."

Kyle started clearing dishes. "Yeah, I'll help, but I don't need no tucking in."

Zelda pursed her lips. "Alrighty then. Only one tuck in. Can I ask that you guys promise to stay in bed when they come over? I don't want any eavesdropping on adult talk from the top of the stairs."

Kyle registered a complaint. "Aww, we never even thought of that."

"Yeah, and bears don't sh . . . out in the woods," said Randall.

Kyle had another mouth brake failure. "Soapy mouth! Dad almost got a soapy mouth!"

"Oh, thanks for reminding me," said Randall. "I almost forgot you're overdue for one."

Zelda held up both hands. "Oh, please, Randy, give the poor kid a break. He's trying to do better. Right now he's full of sugar and can't help himself."

Randall did his best evil laugh. "Aha! Which part of him would you like me to break? How about his little finger?" Randall grabbed Kyle's pinky finger and bent it normally at the knuckle while making a clucking sound with his tongue. "There you go. There's your break."

Kyle laughed in relief.

"Good one, Dad," said Addie. "Kyle, let's clear the table so we can get the story."

With everybody helping, the table was soon cleared and everyone returned to the table for the promised story.

Elizabethan legend

Kyle was turned around backwards in his chair and Addie was standing up in hers. Clearly, the sugar rush had begun. Randall motioned the two to sit back down. When they were settled, he began the story. "My Grandfather, Peter, came to this country by ship, across the Atlantic Ocean, in 1910. He was 22 years old."

"Holy cow, Dad!" blurted Kyle. "That's ancient history!"

Randall wasn't pleased that he was interrupted just seconds into the tale. "Yes, practically the Middle Ages. Please listen with more ears and less mouth. He lived in a country in Europe called Yugoslavia, which was just south of Germany. They spoke several languages there, but he spoke German. His brother, Jacob, had come to America several years earlier and sent a letter to Peter to join him." Randall mimed writing a letter.

Kyle was not about to be restrained from *verbarrhea*. "I bet that was a scary trip.".

"You bet," agreed Randall. "A young man on a big ship leaving home for a new country all by himself. But he knew his brother was there to help him once he arrived. There were big storms on the ocean. Many passengers got seasick and couldn't eat." Randall held his stomach and puffed out his cheeks. "The ship came to port in Chicago and he took a train from there to Milwaukee."

Kyle interrupted again. "What? Chicago isn't on the ocean!"

Randall frowned at Kyle, but decided it was useless to try and stifle him. "No, it isn't. It's on the shore of Lake Michigan, just like Milwaukee. His ship came from New York to Chicago using the Saint Lawrence seaway and then through the Great Lakes. I'll explain it in detail someday. We don't have time now."

"Did he have much money?" asked Addie.

Randall realized the story was going to be a dialogue and would just have to go with it. "Very little. Just enough to get him to Milwaukee. He was very happy to see his brother again. He had a hard time making friends because many people in his new city did not speak German."

Addie scrunched her eyebrows. "But, Dad, English is so easy. Why did he have to speak German?"

Randall smiled and patted her shoulder. "It's easy for you, because you speak it every day. It's hard to learn it as a second language. I learned German in high school, and it was hard! Try saying *'Zwei kleine enten, schwimmen auf dem see. Köpfe in dem wasser,* ärsche *in die höhe.'*"

"*Uhhhhh*, no thanks," said Addie, shaking her head. "That sounds too hard! What does it mean?"

Randall tickled Addie's side. "It's a German poem my dad taught me when I was your age. It translates to 'Two little ducks, swimming in the sea. Heads in the water, tails in the air.'"

Kyle slapped his thigh. "Ha, ha! Dad, that's hilarious! Can I say 'Arsche' and not get soaped?"

Randall glanced at Zelda, now sorry he had picked the duck poem. "Ask your mother! Anyway, Jacob had started a wicker furniture factory and gave Peter a job there. Peter learned English slowly, and was often lonely. Jacob decided Peter needed to meet a good woman, get married and raise a family."

"What did he do?" asked Addie.

Randall continued. "In 1912, Jacob learned from friends that a nice young lady had come to America from a town only 25 miles east of the small town of Erdvik, Yugoslavia, where Peter had lived. Jacob told Peter her name, Elizabeth Meder, but Peter had never met her. She was staying in America with family friends in Cleveland, Ohio. They exchanged letters introducing the two Yugoslav immigrants and finally arranged a meeting."

The kids were on the edge of their seats. Zelda, too, seemed more interested. "I don't think I've ever heard this part of the story before."

As the story tension grew, Randall rose from his seat. "Peter took the train from Milwaukee to Cleveland. Peter and Elizabeth met and spent several days getting acquainted while Elizabeth's friends chaperoned."

Addie shot her hand up. Randall explained what 'chaperone' meant before she could even ask.

Randall stood up straighter for full attention. "Anyway, Peter and Elizabeth seemed to be meant for each other. They discussed their situations and agreed that marriage was a good option. Peter and Elizabeth took the train back to Milwaukee. In 1913 they married and, in 1915, Joseph, my father, was born." Randall held his hands together pretending to hold a baby. "The family lived in a small house behind a bigger house. The small house had been servants' quarters for the bigger house in better days. Now, it was the only dwelling the cash poor couple could afford."

"Sounds like Mother Goose living in a shoe," observed Zelda.

"It gets better," said Randall. "In 1919, my uncle, Peter Jr., was born. Now there were four in the small house. In 1921, Elizabeth had another baby boy named August. Sadly, he died when he was three months old, probably from the flu. In 1924, a baby girl named Adeline was born, my aunt. Her nickname was Addie."

"Just like me!" chirped Addie.

Randall nodded. "Just like you, indeed. And they loved her just as much as we love you. Now there were five in the little house. Peter Sr. still worked at the furniture factory and money was still tight. They still couldn't afford a bigger house. Elizabeth became pregnant again. Then, in 1926, tragedy struck. When it came time to deliver the baby, the umbilical cord got wrapped around the baby's neck and he died.

Even worse, after the baby came out, Elizabeth started to bleed and the doctor couldn't stop the bleeding." Randall stopped there as he started to choke up.

Addie was at the edge of her seat. "Did Elizabeth die?"

Randall just nodded his head. The room was silent for a long moment. Addie had teared up.

Zelda's face reddened. "And then there were four."

The room was silent for another long moment.

Addie broke the silence. "I bet Grampa Peter was real sad. Why couldn't the doctor save Elizabeth? Could that happen today?"

Randall shrugged. "Back in the 1920's, doctors didn't know as much as we do today about women having babies. Even so, it can still happen today, but it's a lot less likely. Now most babies are born in hospitals. Elizabeth had her babies at home."

"Didn't a lot of babies die from the flu during that time?" asked Zelda.

Randall nodded again. "Yeah. If you go to the cemetery where Elizabeth is buried, her two dead babies are there. Hundreds of other children that year died from the flu. They are buried in another section of the cemetery. It's really pretty sad to see."

Kyle found his voice again. "What happened to Grandpa Peter and the three kids after Elizabeth died?"

"That's another story all by itself," replied Randall. "Let's save that for another time."

Addie slowly raised her hand.

Zelda pointed to Addie. "What is it, Rosebud?"

Addie wiped a tear from her cheek. "Did you guys name me after Daddy's aunt? I met her over at Grandma's house last Christmas, right? I really liked her."

Randall nodded and smiled. Addie definitely was a softy. "Yes, honey. I like my Aunt Addie very much. In fact, she helped raise me when I was a little boy. I'll tell you about that sometime. That's one of the reasons I picked her name for you." Addie smiled and put her hands on her heart.

"Did I ever meet Grandpa Peter?" asked Kyle.

Randall thought for a moment. "You did, but you probably don't remember because you were only three years old when he died. Anyway, it's getting late and the dishes aren't doing themselves. You two hustle upstairs. I promise you'll hear more about this in future bedtime story presentations brought to you by your favorite sponsor. Me."

While the kids got ready for bed, Zelda and Randall did the dishes. With dishes dried and put away, they ascended the stairs and got Kyle and Addie tucked away in bed. After calls for drinks of water and closet monster checking, Randall and Zelda reconnoitered in the kitchen to prepare for Julie and Chris.

Zelda sidled up to Randall and gave him a soft hug. "Randy, that was a mighty fine story."

Randall returned the hug and whispered in Zelda's ear. "And that was a right smart dinner. Just what the doctor ordered after the day I had. You know, the usual VA runamuck."

Zelda went right to the heart of things. "How was the shrink session?"

Randall groaned. "Some light, some darkness, with a topping of mild confusion. We're probably getting somewhere, but right now it's hard to guess the final destination."

Zelda gave Randall a hard chest squeeze. "Out with it! I've been thinking about what I would be willing to share with a shrink. Whomever I see would have to get the pot boiling to get much out of me. The process would not be an easy one."

Randall hugged Zelda back even harder. "How about getting the pot smoking?"

Zelda grunted and sucked in a breath. "Slow down there, Bruce. Not before we have company."

Randall thought about giving Zelda a neck hickey. "Maybe they'll bring their own and share."

Zelda scoffed at that idea. "You wish, Randy. Go get busy and make some fresh coffee?"

Randall wasn't ready to get serious just yet. "If we're so concerned about the future, maybe we should hire a psychic."

Zelda picked up on the remark. "And her sidekick. I've always wanted to meet a psychic sidekick. That reminds me, what kind of suit does a guy wear who tries to get information about the future from a fortune teller?"

Randall shook his head. "Duh, no idea. Lay it on me."

"A seersucker!" answered Zelda, bursting out in laughter.

Randall groaned. "Hey, I'm supposed to tell the dad jokes here!

The horseplay was interrupted by the doorbell and pounding on the back door. Zelda rushed to open the door, still laughing.

THE JC SHOW

Zelda flung open the back door and welcomed Julie and Chris. She bade them to follow her into the living room. They both looked much more relaxed than when they'd visited earlier, but Chris seemed to be carrying a lot of lower eyelid baggage.

Zelda guided the way. "Come on in. Sit, get comfortable. We're all safe here. You guys want some coffee and a piece of your rhubarb pie? We snarfed quite a bit of it after dinner, but there is enough left for two. Plus, Reddi Whip."

"Don't mind if I do," said Julie. "How about you, Chris?"

Chris nodded. "Sure, I could use a sugar/caffeine shot. Sleep has been a stranger lately."

Zelda rejoined Randall in the kitchen and soon brought out the promised goodies. Chris was all scrunched up on the couch next to Julie and was still shivering from the outside cold. Randall served the promised Reddi Whip on the warm pie, then sat down. Zelda rushed off and came back with a blanket. She wrapped it around Chris's shoulders, gave him a brief hug and sat down in a chair opposite the couple.

Zelda spoke with a soft and feathery voice as the couple ate pie and sipped hot coffee. "Let yourselves settle in. Feel the warm goodness fill your bodies."

As the pie and coffee disappeared, Julie and Chris became visibly more relaxed. They refused refills and set their empty plates and cups aside.

Zelda took the floor again. "Take some deep breaths. As you breathe out, feel the support of the couch and the earth. Let the experience from last night bubble up to your mind. That's it. Good. Focus on the experience just as it was. You don't have to organize it or make sense of it. Just describe and feel."

Chris leaned back and pulled a pillow to his chest. When he spoke, his voice was hoarse, barely audible. "She was there again last night. I'm not making this up. I could see her, wavering, but definitely there. She was wearing one of those long skirts that go all the way to the floor. Her hair was hanging in front of her eyes, so I couldn't see her whole face. I didn't know what to say. She seemed to be moving her mouth."

Zelda urged Chris on in a soothing voice. "Good, good. Yes. What else?"

Chris frowned and looked to his left. "This is gonna sound crazy. I talked to her, but I didn't say anything out loud. It's like I told her in my mind . . . I asked her to move her hair so I could see her." He swallowed hard. "And she did! She tucked her hair behind her ears, like she did when she played with our kids. She moved her mouth, but her words only came out in my head. She was confused. She didn't know where she was and couldn't find her parents. She wondered why she was in our house, and asked if she was babysitting? Alexandra looked right into my eyes and said she wanted to go home! I didn't know what to do. It felt like my heart was breaking in half."

Zelda gave Chris a hug and patted his head. When she released the hug, Chris looked both drained and relieved to get the story out without getting struck down by a lightning bolt from the heavens.

Zelda stayed calm and collected. "Wow. That is so much to take in. Thank you, Chris, for your bravery. Go on . . ."

"Like I said, I didn't know what I was supposed to say. I just thought of my little girl, and what I would say to her if she were confused. I just told her, kindly, that she had died, and that she was in our house. She could tell me what she needed to say, and then she could find her peace."

Zelda seemed to create a safe space just with her intention. "Wow. Very intuitive of you, Chris. Go on . . ."

Chris looked down at his hands and sighed. "She was quiet for a few minutes, then wanted to know how she died. I told her only what I knew, that she had been found, hanging by her neck. That seemed to open some door to her memory that she hadn't opened before. She disappeared and I slept like a baby. Best night sleep I've had in a while."

Randall encouraged Chris to continue. "That's quite a story. Some would even call it unreal, but I've had to adjust my definition of real these past few months. I've had similar stuff happen to me lately. Was there any further contact?"

Chris nodded. "Then you have a head start on me. I haven't had much time to figure out this weird stuff yet. It's good to hear you've been through it and adjusted. To answer your question, there was one encounter after that. Usually Alexandra would appear to me just in the middle of the night, but she came back again this morning, around six o'clock. This time she was much more serene. Her hair was brushed and out of her face. She had her hands clasped over her chest as she looked me in the eye. Again her mouth moved wordlessly, but she 'asked' me to tell her parents she was sorry."

Chris paused and looked at the floor. Nobody spoke for a long moment while digesting the new information. Chris was afraid everyone would think he was going around the bend and was wondering if he'd shared too much.

Zelda sensed what Chris was feeling and tried to reassure him he was still in the ballpark of normal. "What you lived through is not outside the realm of human experience. As Randy mentioned, he's gone through things just as unusual and I'm pretty sure he's not loony tunes."

Randall laughed. "That's the nicest thing you've ever said about me."

That remark got a laugh out of everybody and it seemed to dissipate the tension in the room.

When the laughter subsided, Zelda took the wheel again. "So, Chris, what do you think you should do next?"

Chris now looked quite calm and collected. "It's pretty clear to me now. I've got to talk to Alexandra's parents. I don't know exactly how

I'll explain it to them or if they'll believe me, but it just seems like the right thing to do."

Zelda smiled and nodded. "If that's what your heart tells you and it seems right, then that's what you should go with."

Randall concurred. "Yeah, crazy as it sounds, any slim hope you can give them is worth it."

Chris smiled and looked around the room. He raised both arms, clapped his hands, and blurted an announcement. "Great Godfrey! I think that's it for sure. I just had a mental flash that assured me that telling her parents is what this whole appearance thing is about. Zelda, Randall . . . I think you cured me. Do you have something stronger than coffee to use for a toast?"

Randall looked at Zelda for an answer and she shrugged her shoulders. Then Randall had a brain wave. "Ah, I have just the thing. My dad gave me some Dr. McGillicuddy's peppermint Schnapps for Christmas. How does that sound?"

"I've heard of it but never tried it," said Chris.

Julie shook her head. "Me neither."

Zelda made a slightly evil smile, knowing that it packed quite a punch. "Stay seated everyone. I'll get it out of our hidey hole and serve some up."

Soon Zelda was back with the bottle and four liqueur glasses on a tray, serving it like a seasoned waitress. She balanced the tray on one hand raised at head level. After distributing the drinks, Chris motioned everyone to stand and he gave forth with his toast. "I beseech all spirits, including those in this glass, to go down easy to their destinations."

After a clink of glasses and a choral "Here Here," the group downed the first dollop of peppermint fire. Julie coughed a bit afterwards, but murmured that it wasn't bad at all. Chris agreed and asked for another to bless the first. Julie went with "Prosit." When that round was history, they decided that all toasts should come in threes.

It was Randall's turn to toast and Zelda poured an even more generous round. Randall raised his glass and smacked his lip to regain some oral control. "Over the lips and past the gums. Look out stomach. Here she comes."

This bigger dollop brought a longer lasting post-swallow silence. Then, Chris made a final pronouncement. "If I drink more, I'll not make the door. Julie, I think it's time we thank the Biedermeiers and take our leave. I think my bed is calling. I foresee a sound night's sleep in my near future. With no visitations."

Randall raised his glass once more. "May it be so."

The Colors

Reunited with their coats, Chris and Julie took their leave after some hugging and hand shaking. Zelda closed the front door, leaned back against it and let out a loud sigh.

Randall laughed. "What's up, Zel? The Schnapps getting to you?"

Zelda hiccuped. "Hardly. It's the other way around. Right now I'm so spooked I may need three more shots of that stuff. Let's go sit in the living room. I need to talk."

"Really? I thought our little meeting went pretty well," observed Randall.

The two settled next to each other on the comfy couch. Zelda took Randall's hand in hers. She turned her head and gave Randall a baleful look. "I agree. The meeting went well. Maybe a bit too well. I need to ask you something. I hope I get the right answer."

Randall wasn't computing. "Ask me what? I give up. Ask away."

Zelda rubbed her hands together. "Randy, did you see anything . . . unusual at the end there when Chris stood up suddenly and clapped his hands?"

Randall thought back for a moment and didn't come up with anything. "All I saw was that Chris went from dour to really animated in like a microsecond. Did I miss something?"

Zelda nodded. "Well, you're correct about the animation part. But I saw something in addition to that I'm not sure I've seen before and it's flat freaking me out."

Randall's curiosity peaked. "Well, now I'm starting to freak too. Come on. Give forth."

Zelda began to pace the room. "Just before Chris stood up, I started to see a faint green and pink aura around Chris. Then, when he stood up, it went to blue, then purple, and then white. It got more intense as I watched. When he clapped, the white just rose away from him, went to the ceiling and faded away. You weren't looking at me, but if you had seen my face, I'm sure you would have found my chin dropped to my chest."

Randall was wide-eyed. "I definitely didn't see any of that. And it was before the Schnapps, so we can't blame that. How did you feel when you saw that?"

Zelda pouted her lips while she recalled the episode. "Well, at first I was downright scared, but, as I watched the colors evolve, I felt like I was enfolded in a blanket of comfort and love."

Randall reflected for a bit. "You know, I sort of felt that at the end as well. I just thought it was because of the Schnapps and that Chris was clearly feeling better about everything. But I did not see any light show. Sorry. Anything else?"

Zelda nodded slowly. "Yeah. There was a voice, but it felt like it wasn't like something you hear with your ears. It felt confined to my head."

Randall had heard voices in his head in the past. It was usually when he had done something against the rules as a kid. Like when he pocketed the money his mother had given him to put in the donations plate at church. At the time he was pretty sure God had seen it and was rebuking him. "What sort of voice? Did it say anything coherent?"

Zelda nodded again. "Yes. I kept hearing the same words: 'She is free. She is loved.' It felt like everything . . . and I mean everything . . . would be okay. I haven't felt that calm and collected in ages."

Randall recalled what he'd felt at the time. "Now that you mention it, I felt like a truce had been declared to a war I was fighting in. One minute I was shooting and ducking behind rocks. The next minute I was ordered to go home and be happy."

Zelda squeezed Randall's hand tighter. "Yeah, kind of like that. Does any of this make sense?"

Randall scratched his head as if dandruff flakes could be read like tea leaves. "Not in a scientific way, but not everything in life makes sense until something happens later that clears up any doubts. Right now, maybe we should just accept it for what it is and let it ripen."

Zelda gave Randall a quizzical look. "I'm not sure what you just said, but I agree with your conclusion. Let's hit the rack. I'm bushed and that Schnapps is taking hold."

Randall looked equally uncertain about what they had decided. "I'm feeling pretty Schnappsed too. Last one upstairs has to put the house to bed."

Zelda was up the stairs before Randall could get out of his chair. He could hear her tucking Addie into bed. He moaned and got up off the couch to put the house to bed. After the house was buttoned up, he staggered up the stairs and joined Zelda under the covers. She was still staring at the ceiling. Randall felt consciousness begin to fade seconds after his head hit the pillow.

Zelda's mind was still spinning. "Randy. Are you awake?"

Randall comprehended just enough of the question to respond. "No!"

Zelda poked her elbow into Randall's ribs. "Yes you are. I've got one more thing on my mind about tonight."

The elbow poke hurt just enough for Randall to raise his alertness a notch. "Ouch! That hurt. Consarn it. Now, I won't be able to get to sleep until you share your 'one more thing.'"

Zelda felt bad about waking Randall, but was too amped up to let it go. "Sorry, big boy, but if I don't get this off my chest, I'll be tossing and turning all night. Here it is. I've had the light thing happen before once or twice. When I was a teen, I saw a light in the corner of my ceiling. I thought it was an angel. My mother said I was just a hormonal teen and it meant nothing. Then, one night, here at home in my studio, I saw it in the window. I may have been smoking too much special tobacco, so I dismissed it."

Randall tried to shorten the tale. He was desperate for sleep. "I agree with both conclusions. Probably estrogen and weed. Any other light moments?"

Zelda didn't want to be dismissed as just having an overactive imagination. "After it happened the second time, I did some research. My Yoga teacher said it's not an unusual experience some people have during deep meditation. I read some other books that agreed with that. I didn't feel scared by the light thing, so it didn't make me think it was anything evil."

Randall waited for more disclosure, but Zelda had no more to say. He decided to go along with Zelda's interpretation if it got him to sleep sooner. "Sounds like the best way to view it. If you don't feel scared now and you feel enveloped in an electric blanket of love, that's what I'd go with. Now, go to sleep, Gracie."

"Alright, George. I love you."

"Ditto."

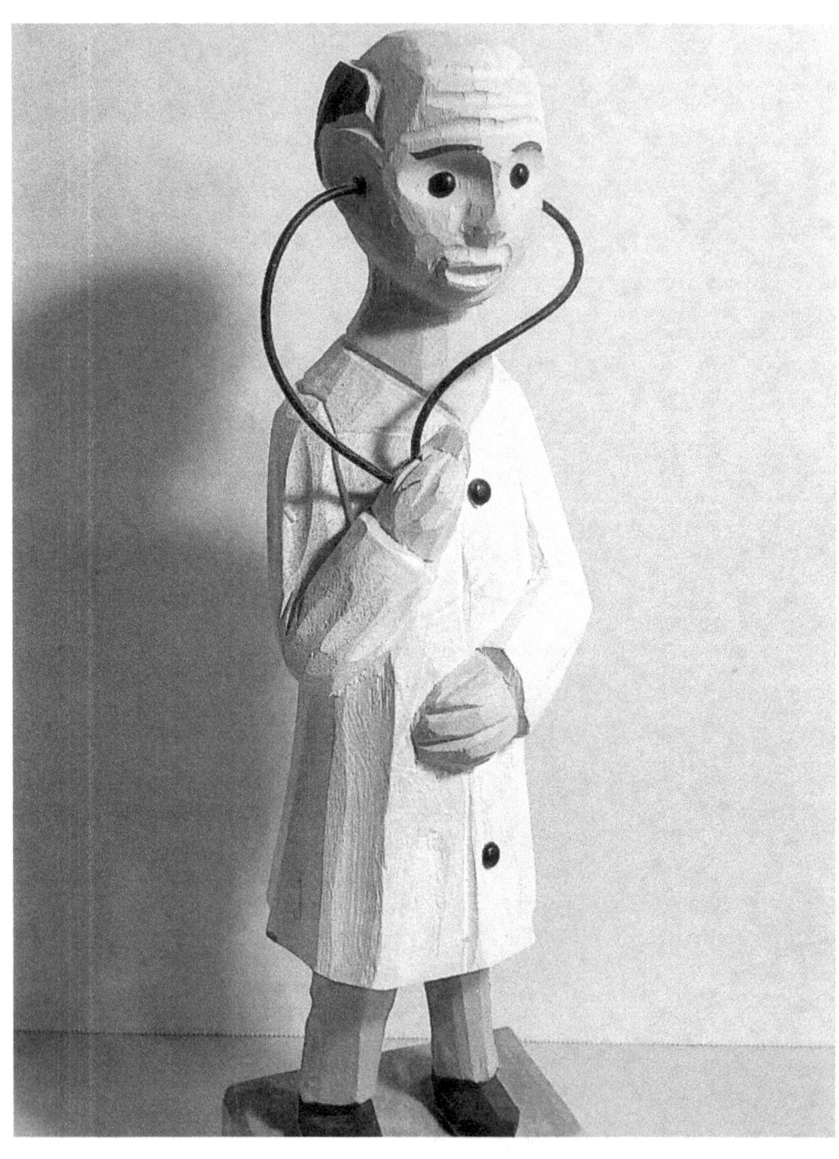

C H A P T E R 17

———

O P E N H O U S E I R A

"Imagination is the only key to the future. Without it none exists—
with it all things are possible."

—*Ida M. Tarbell*

No Foul Ups

Usually, Thursdays at the VA were loaded up with follow-up exams and this Thursday would be no exception. Randall had lost valuable time finding a parking spot, so he had broken into a mini-jog when he was halfway to the building. That set his backpack bobbing up and down on his butt and gave him a butt ache. So he gave up running and accepted his *fateness* of lateness. Nearby the door, a small group of smokers huddled together in shirt sleeves puffing away to get in their last dose of nicotine before starting the workday. They were gathered around a large cigarette disposal station the VA had placed outside the entrances after banning smoking inside the building. It was filled to the brim with butts. The smokers shivered and rubbed their hands together.

We save lives for a living, thought Randall, *but here they are slowly killing themselves.* He shook his head, hoping to push quickly through the smoker crowd. Randall noticed that Ira, the patient transporter, was in the group of smokers standing up close and personal next to Sandy, the young ward secretary from 4CS. It looked like she was trying to get away from Ira who was holding her arm with his left hand.

As Randall walked by the group, Sandy waved and called out to Randall. "Hey, Dr. B. Hold up. Can I talk to you for a second?"

Randall stopped and turned around. He guessed she was looking for an escape from Ira's clutches. "Sure thing. Come on inside with me."

Sandy stubbed out her cigarette and slithered out of Ira's grip on her arm. Ira, looking slightly crestfallen by the maneuver, was shivering in the cold. He was wearing only blue work pants and a thin white shirt. Both shirt pockets bulged. Randall could see the red print of a pack of Marlboros through the thin material of the right shirt pocket. Another red packet was visible through the fabric of the left shirt pocket.

Sandy fast walked and caught up to Randall.

"Hey, Sandy, how's it going?"

Sandy wiped at her arm where Ira had been gripping her. "Great, until I came out for a smoke. Then that little creep, Ira, started hitting on me. If I have to put up with that to get my ciggy fix, I may have to give up smoking."

Randall held his tongue and pulled the back door open for Sandy.

Sandy hugged her arms to her chest and shivered as she entered the building with a whoosh of cold wind at her back. "Holy Eskimos! It's freezing out there, but it's nice and warm in here. I don't know why I put myself through the ice cube treatment just for a few drags of poison."

Randall released his tongue. "Perhaps you should thank the VA powers for making it hard. Keep smoking and you might have to see me professionally one day."

Sandy didn't quite take the bait. "But you're a nice guy. That wouldn't be so bad. The patients on the ward are always raving about you."

That comment went right to Randall's head. He looked at Sandy with a new light and noticed that, from an engineering point of view, Sandy was well constructed. "Don't you mean raving at me? That's a nice compliment, but you won't be happy if you have to see me professionally. My wonderful personality won't offset the downer of having lung cancer. As a favor to me, just quit smoking so we only have to meet socially. Plus, it will help you avoid Ira."

Sandy and Randall stopped walking as they came to the back

entrance of Randall's department. Sandy shrugged. "That strategy would work except for one little inconvenience. I'd still risk encountering him every time he brings patients to and from the ward. Unless I could be forewarned and hide. That's not gonna happen."

Randall shook his head. "Yeah, that's a bummer. I guess the only choice is to grin and bear it. I will contemplate upon the dilemma and perhaps my wily ways can discover a potion that will cure the problem."

Sandy smiled and nodded. "Oh. That would be delightful. I'll pray for success. See you around. I need to get to the ward before the inmates rebel."

Randall waved goodbye to Sandy and opened the department's back entrance. As expected, there was a welcoming committee waiting. His staff were on him before he could get to his office. As he walked they talked. By the time he had doffed his outerwear and settled in his desk chair, he'd learned the machine had been down and now was up, there were two follow-ups waiting that had arrived early and that there would be eight more before noon. Then, Doris came in with a handful of pink phone memos.

Doris began with her usual sing-song greeting. "Good mornin' Dr. B. How are we this fine day?"

Randall pawed on the carpet with his foot like a horse and whinnied. "We are well and raring to go. What have you got for me?"

Doris giggled. "I left the bag of oats in my office. I'll fetch it for you later. Why don't you skedaddle into your office and get settled. Then I'll come in by you and go over these phone messages. None of them are urgent except for one. Dr. Sheltie called about a surgical case he's doin' this afternoon. He said he might need you to place after-loadin' catheters, whatever those are. He said you'd know what he meant."

Open House

Randall groaned. "Great! I detest that blowhard surgeon. He's all 'jump and how high.' Like his lack of planning is my problem. He could have warned me days ago so I could clear my schedule. He'll probably start the case at 1:00 and decide by 4:00 whether he needs me or not. Then, he'll call, I will have to drop whatever I'm doing, go up to the OR and scrub in. Then, I'll stand there another hour before he concludes it's not possible to implant the catheters."

Doris had seen Randall go through the Sheltie ritual before and tried to soothe the savage beast. "Now, now, Dr. B, don't be jumpin' to conclusions. Just sit down and take a breath. You know fat white men can't jump. I've checked my tea leaves and they tell me he's not gonna need you today. So don't you fret none."

Randall decided to trust Doris's tea leaves and relaxed a notch. "Alrighty then, what else is on the stove?"

Doris tapped a pencil on her desk while she formulated his next challenge. "Do you remember that nice young lady from the Transcription Department?"

Randall sensed trouble coming, but hoped he was wrong. "Indeed, I do. The one who made a righteous fool out of me on the phone?"

Doris tapped a *badaboom* rhythm on her desk with her pencil drumstick. "The very one. She called to say that her group is comin' down this afternoon for the open house. She wants so much to meet you and see the department."

Randall jumped up from his desk chair. "The open house is today?"

Doris gestured for Randall to calm down. "Dr. B, take your undies out of a bundle. Surely you remember. We talked about the open house last week and it's right here on your calendar." Doris sounded like a kindergarten teacher. "That's why all the follow-ups are squeezed into the mornin' like eggs in a basket. We've already started to set things up in the Ortho room. In fact, Mrs. Dombrowski brought her husband for follow-up this mornin' and when she called the other day to check on the appointment, I told her about the open house. They came early, as usual, and she brought a slew of homemade sweet rolls to serve. There's at least six dozen laid out in the Ortho room."

"Hot spit and cold saliva . . . I just saw Lady Godiva," enthused Randall. "I missed my breakfast this morning and I'm going in there for a sweet roll before they disappear. If it's the lady I'm thinking of, her bakery is to die for. Isn't she the one who swore like a sailor and pounded the wall the day of her husband's consultation?"

Doris nodded and was pleased the promise of sweet rolls seemed to overcome Randall's displeasure at forgetting about the date for the open house. "The very one. Don't worry. You don't have to run off to snag a sweet roll. I saved out a dozen and hid them under my desk. No one knows."

Randall gave Doris an impromptu hug. "Doris, you're the best!" The hug was hard enough to shift her wig and make her squeak.

Doris smiled shyly and adjusted her wig. "Dr. B! Well, I never!"

Randall smirked at Doris. "Never?"

Doris's cheeks flushed. "Well, not nearly enough, to be precise."

Randall decided it best to change the subject. "Any other pressing news?"

Doris shuffled through her notes. "Almost forgot. You're to call Dr. Knox. He sounded like it was time sensitive, so if'n I were you, I'd call that boss o' yours right away." She ignored Randall's exasperated sigh.

Randall was not happy about having to call his boss. When Knox knocked it was rarely to announce good news. "You sure there's no other storm front blowing in?"

Doris adjusted her wig again. "I think that's it. Wait! Except for one thing. Melinda asked if she could see you briefly before you start the follow-ups. She's also got your first follow up patient."

Randall whistled out a loud breath. "The faster I go the behinder I get. Doris, could I talk you into getting me a cup of java from the department communal coffee pot and a sweet roll from your cache while I check in with Melinda? I desperately need my jolt of sugar and caffeine before I take on the day's vagaries."

Doris put a finger to her temple and looked far left. "Hmm, another new word to look up in my Funk 'n' Wagnalls. Will do. I'll send Melinda in."

Melinda swayed her way into Randall's office, munching on a sweet roll.

"Good morning, Dr. B," said Melinda, through a mouthful of doughy goodness. "You should try one of these. Yummy."

Randall was already salivating. "What flavor?"

Melinda swallowed and smacked her lips. "Strawberry cheese. Absolutely scrumptious. It's my second one. The first was blueberry prune. I can already feel the glucose rushing through my neurons and laying waste to all ill feelings."

Randall nodded. "I need a big dose of that. Doris is bringing me one of those in a minute. Have a seat. What's on your mind besides a sugar rush?"

Melinda sat and was quiet for a beat. She took a deep breath and began. "I need your help with something kind of personal."

Randall couldn't imagine what was on her mind. "Don't worry. What plays here stays here. I have a bad memory."

Melinda decided to go ahead with her issue. "It's about that weirdo Ira. He keeps trying to get chatty with me. Sometimes he sneaks up behind me. I turn around and there he is. How can I get him to bug off without creating a bigger problem? I don't want to be mean, but I don't want to put up with it anymore."

Randall was almost pleased to hear about another instance of Ira caught stalking. "Hmm, funny you should bring that up. You may not be the only one having that problem."

Melinda was somewhat taken aback. "Really? How so?"

"Do you know Sandy, the ward secretary on 4CS?" asked Randall.

Melinda nodded. "I think so. Isn't she a dyed blonde and usually has her hair in a ponytail?"

That was not the descriptor Randall would have chosen, but it was right on. "That's the one. I ran into her coming in the back entrance this morning. She was out with that group of smokers by the back door. Ira was out there smoking too. He was clearly putting unwanted moves on her. When she saw me, she waved and slipped away from him. She and I walked in together pretending we had planned to meet at the door. She said Ira was shadowing her too."

Melinda's eyebrows rose. "Really? So, he's not a monogamous 'perv,' eh?"

Randall smiled and shook his head. "Using my highly honed deductive reasoning, I may have found a way to deter his unwanted advances. It's not 100 percent verified yet, but, with your help, I think we can solidify a plan."

Melinda was curious. "Really? Care to share?"

Randall winked an eye. "Good old Ira may be the missing link in my 'great gum mystery.'"

Melinda was baffled. "The what?"

Randall recounted his discoveries of 'ABC' chewing gum pasted in various spots around the department over the previous weeks.

Melinda gaped at Randall. "'ABC' gum?"

Randall looked at the ground and shuffled his feet a tad. "Sorry, that acronym is from my kindergarten days. Probably before your time. It means 'already been chewed.' You know, it's the dried up gum wads you can find under the seats at movie theaters. Mom would send me to Saturday morning cartoons at the local movie theater. It was filled with screaming grade schoolers. My ticket was on a string around my neck. It was her chance to get rid of me for three hours. My buddies would pick the gum wads off the seat bottoms and dare me to chew them in exchange for a bite of candy bar."

Melinda's face looked like she'd been sucking lemons. "Yuck! I'm glad it was before my time. Don't tell me you actually chewed one."

Randall waved a hand. "Well . . . maybe once or twice when I blew all my candy money on watered down coke. Drank too much once and nearly peed myself on the way home. But that's another story."

Melinda put up both hands. "Please! You can keep that story in your desk drawer. Can we get back to the 'great gum mystery' story?"

Randall was slightly embarrassed that his explanation had wandered off the garden path. "Yeah, sure. Got derailed there. So far it's been a mystery who the gum culprit is, despite my investigations. But with my recent data gathering, I think I have enough evidence to finger Ira. But I'm going to need your help to collar him. Are you game?"

Melinda managed an evil smile. "Where do I sign? What do you need me to do?"

"Not a whole lot, but it will be slightly distasteful," replied Randall. "Fortunately, it shouldn't take too long. When he brings a patient down from the ward for treatment this morning, I want you to cozy up to him and tell how much you'd like him to join us this afternoon for the open house. Say that I want to get a picture of all the people who help treat our patients and I want him included. When he comes down I want your eyes on him no matter where he goes."

Melinda grimaced. "Ew! Well, if I have to. What are you going to do?"

Randall moved a bit closer to Melinda and whispered conspiratorially. He explained what he wanted Melinda to do, and then added, "I haven't worked out the final details yet. What I'll do will depend on how things transpire. I may have to ad lib. I'll signal you with a raised pinky finger when it's your move. Just pull off your assignment and all shall be golden."

Although Melinda was somewhat doubtful whether she could pull it off, she nodded. "Okay, I think I can do that. Perhaps I'll grease myself up like an English Channel swimmer."

Randall cocked his head. "Excuse me?"

Melinda laughed nervously. "You know, the slipperier the better."

Randall exhaled sharply. "Ah, good idea, but you better use *Invisigrease*. Don't want to give away your revulsion."

"Sure thing, I've got some in my purse," giggled Melinda. "Anything else, boss?"

Randall shook his head. "Not for the Ira show. Would you get the chart for my next follow-up and get him in a room?"

While Melinda carried out her task, Randall snuck to the Ortho room to check out the bounty and refill his coffee cup. The room looked like the cornucopia of plenty had burst inside it. Every horizontal surface was replete with mouth-watering and waist-burgeoning foodstuffs.

There were pastries, kuchens, crumbles, kringles, candy, chips, fruit and nuts. There was even a Spanish caramelized custard. It looked "flantastic."

Grace appeared at the doorway and scolded Randall. "Stay out of there, Dr. B. That's all for the open house. No nibbling!"

Grace had appointed herself guardian of the food cache. She stood with hands on ample hips like a Marvel Comics superhero daring Randall even to touch a cookie.

Randall stiffened his back, came to attention and saluted. "Yes, sir! Read you five by five. Cookies off limits to noncoms. Just doing recon. Going to work now. See me leave."

Randall didn't think it possible for Grace to look more disgusted, but she exceeded his expectations. She laid into Randall like a drill sergeant. "Don't get smart with me!"

Randall set off toward the door with a slow shuffle. "Is dumb with you alright?"

Grace pointed to the door and growled. "No backtalk, private! Go. Do. Now!"

Knox NRG

Randall chuckled as he left the room while Grace steamed. When he got to the hallway, he realized Melinda was still prepping his follow-up. He decided to use the brief break to call Knox back. Putting it off any longer would just amp up his anxiety. Any call from Knox, Randall's department chairman, rarely brought good news, only bad news presented as good. He went to Doris's office and asked her to place the call.

The call went through with barely time to fret about it. Knox greeted Randall as though Randall had just won the lottery. "Randy, I have a wonderful opportunity for you."

Randall was immediately suspicious. He tried to sound enthused, but was not feeling it. "Oh, yeah? What's up?"

Knox sounded like a game show host presenting a prize. "How would you like an all-expenses paid trip to Las Vegas?"

Randall figured there had to be a catch. "Las Vegas?"

There was a long silence as Knox attended to something in his office. "Sorry about that. Carmen just handed me a note. Where was I? Right. I need you to fill in for me at the NRG meeting in Vegas on Friday and run the Lung Committee."

The catch was Randall running the lung committee on his own. He'd been to one meeting and witnessed Knox leading the contentious committee. He was certain he wasn't ready. He lacked Knox's leadership aplomb and commanding voice. He needed time to sort out an appropriate response, so he concocted a ruse.

Randall placed his hand partially over the mouthpiece and spoke in a louder than necessary voice. "What is it, Doris? Who wants to see me?" His question echoed in the otherwise empty office. He faked Doris's voice telling him that the Chief of Staff had stopped down to see him on an urgent matter. Randall took his hand off the mouthpiece and told Knox he was sorry, but he'd have to call him right back. Knox seemed to buy the charade and told Randall he'd be working at his desk for ten more minutes and after that had to attend an important meeting. Knox made it clear he expected an answer in ten minutes.

Randall put on his fast forward thinking cap. The National Radiation Oncology Group (NRG) conducted cooperative clinical trials designed to test new cancer treatment techniques. Over 100 large hospitals in the US and Canada belonged to the group. It was funded by a large grant from the National Cancer Institute. The primary focus of NRG was how best to use radiation therapy, but the trials included chemotherapy and surgery as well. Knox had chaired the NRG Lung Committee for five years. It was responsible for a dozen different studies of lung cancer treatment. Randall had attended one previous NRG meeting so Knox could introduce Randall to the process.

Randall's sphincter tightened as he tried hard to imagine his debut as chairman. He didn't think he'd have the moxie to run the NRG lung committee effectively. The members were contentious and ruthless. He'd be eaten alive. Plus, there was only one day to prepare! Randall concluded he'd have to nip this rose of an idea in the bud. He quickly compiled a short list of excuses. There would be no time to prepare.

He had pressing work and family matters that demanded his attention. He wasn't ready for such responsibility. Airline and hotel reservations would be difficult to make on such short notice. He was already late for his daughter's tea party. He was anticipating a serious illness. His dog died. Hark, is that a pandemic on the rise? Now he was in panic mode. His ten minutes were almost up. Despite all of his amazing excuses, Randall feared he would not be able to stare Knox down. When Knox knocked, you answered.

Harbinger of Good Fortune

Melinda strode into Randall's office with his next follow-up's chart and saved Randall from further self-flagellation. "Mr. Harbinger is here with good news. You remember him, don't you? He finished radiation last month for a Stage IIb prostate cancer. He was the first patient that finished treatment on my watch. Pretreatment PSA was 15.2. He had a blood draw yesterday and the PSA was .01. And . . . he brought you a homemade gift."

Randall put both hands on top of his head. "Wow, what a bountiful day! Something just came up. I have a call I need to make. Can you keep the man entertained while I take care of it?"

Melinda nodded. "Sure thing, Boss. He loves to chat. I'll be back in five."

Excuse list in hand, Randall dialed Knox's number as Melinda went off to babysit. Thankfully, Knox was still at his desk.

Knox himself now sounded a bit anxious. "Thanks for getting back to me. I hope your urgent matter went well. While I've still got a few minutes grace, let me give you more details about NRG."

Randall decided to hear Knox out before responding. Better to sift through the fine print first. Before Randall even had a chance to play his hastily formulated fail cards, Knox thumped his trump card on the table.

Knox spoke in his smooth, authoritarian voice. "You needn't worry about writing up the presentation of developing studies. I've been working on it for three months and it's all set. You can use my slides. The trip reservations have already been transferred to you, including a rental car."

Knox's trump cards may not have made an actual table slamming sound when he played them, but they still slammed in Randall's mind. It brought back a childhood memory.

At family gatherings, Randall's mother would send all the menfolk down to the basement so they could smoke cigars, drink beer and play sheepshead. That way they wouldn't disturb the womenfolk who stayed upstairs to coffee klatsch. The kids would also be banished to the basement after making too much commotion. The menfolk didn't seem to notice the extra noise. Periodically, the triumphant shout of a beer-soaked sheepshead player would precede the loud bang of the winning card being slammed on the rickety folding table. The powerful table slam would send half empty beer bottles crashing to the basement floor. The kids loved the *kerplinkity* sound.

"You still there?" asked Knox.

Randall shook his head to clear it. "Yeah, sorry, boss, I'm just soaking all that in. I'm not sure I'm ready to take on that much responsibility."

Knox began stroking and smoothing Randall's ruffled feathers. "Hey, don't underestimate yourself. It will be a piece of pie. I'm sure you're ready. Remember how well your small cell presentation went?"

As Randall started thinking about the opportunity more positively, he realized there might be a benefit to taking Knox's place in Vegas. But, ever the paranoid, he had to make sure there was no hidden agenda. Knox was the proverbial silver-tongued salesman who could sell a rasher to a rabbi. Knox could be *smuuth* as in "beyond smooth" or "too smooth." Randall had been *smuuthed* by Knox before. Perhaps more information would help him decide.

Randall harkened up the courage to test the verity of Knox's story. "So, what happened to keep you from going to NRG?"

Sounding genuinely rueful, Knox responded. "I was just about to tell you. I'm sorry for the short notice, but I'm getting the short end of the stick on this."

Randall doubted that. "How so?"

Knox sounded like he was buying time to fabricate a convincing explanation. "Well, that's a longer story."

Randall looked about for signs of Melinda. Seeing none, he urged Knox on. "I've got a few minutes now. I have a sympathetic ear for administrative woes."

Knox went on to explain that the day before, he'd been "voluntold" to attend an emergency meeting of the hospital finance committee. In four days he was to present a proposal for a 5% cut in the departmental budget. Survival of the department was at stake, so Knox said his choice was obvious. He'd called for "all hands on deck" and had assembled a team of staff to come up with a realistic budget ASAP. He said they would probably wind up working around the clock. Hearing this, Randall was grateful Knox hadn't asked him to be on the budget team. The explanation let all the air out of Randall's feeble bubble of objections. He thanked Knox for the opportunity to improve his CV, consented to go and hung up the phone.

So, Randall's trip to NRG was a *fait accompli*. However, his fate seemed less onerous than what Knox had in store, if there really was a budget crisis. Whichever, Randall reminded himself never to become a department chair. If nothing else, he now had an excellent reason to "86" the request to do the Center Director's requested site visit at Detroit VA. He reminded himself he could do some inquiries about Knox's budget crisis. It was always wise to know for sure if you were being screwed. It might not change the situation, but it's useful information to plan for the future.

Melinda interrupted Randall's musings. "Hey, Boss. Mr. Harbinger told me a hilarious joke. Want to hear it?"

Randall was ready for hilarity. "Sock it to me."

CHAPTER 18

REPRIEVE

"Many men smoke, but Fu Manchu."

—Great Uncle Jacob Biedermeier

Melinda finished the joke. "Then the veteran realized he wasn't paralyzed. He'd put both legs in one pant leg."

The joke was so ridiculous that Melinda had been right. It was hilarious, if not slightly offensive to the elderly. But since a veteran was its origin it was rather self deprecatory, thus not offensive. Randall's laughter somewhat overcame his shame over how handily he'd been manipulated by Knox. No use thinking any more about it. Done was done. "Melinda, I'm ready for Mr. Harbinger. Let's do this."

Grace was still in the hallway guarding the Ortho room as Randall and Melinda entered the exam room. Randall greeted Mr. Harbinger and congratulated him on his good PSA result. It indicated a complete resolution of the man's prostate cancer.

Randall took a seat on his revolving rolling stool. "Melinda tells me you made something for me. Whatever could it be?"

Mr. Harbinger was clutching a small paper bag. "Yes, I did. I made this even before the PSA results were in. If I'd known how low it had gotten, I would have made it out of silver instead of wood . . . if I knew how to do that . . . and had enough cash to buy the silver."

Randall shook his head. "Not to worry. It's the goodness of the heart, not the goodness of the material. Let's see this treasure."

Mr. Harbinger reached into the paper bag and pulled out a small contraption. There was a small rectangular piece of wood as a base, with another small piece ascending vertically from one end. Jutting out of a small hole in the vertical piece was a small iron rod with a piece of wood shaped like a hammer head attached to the rod end. Glued to the base underneath the hammer head was a US quarter. Glued nearby the quarter was a small rectangle of wood painted yellow and drilled with small holes. The hammer device could be pulled upwards and, when released, a spring inside the vertical piece would cause the hammer to hit the quarter. Randall was amazed by the intricate craftsmanship, but had no clue what it was. He didn't want to admit that he was clueless so he just kept studying it, making humming sounds. Mr. Harbinger just smiled and looked proud.

Randall nodded his head and smiled back, still trying to figure out what it was without asking. "Hmm, this is amazing. What fine work you do. It's a perfect example of whatever it is."

Randall looked at Melinda for a hint, but she just did a slow shoulder shrug.

Mr. Harbinger laughed. "Haven't had one person figure it out on first look. So don't feel bad. This is my 'Quarter Pounder with Cheese!'"

Randall slapped his forehead. "Of course, it is! Can't wait for your version of a Big Mac."

Mr. Harbinger beamed with pride. He'd won the first round of 'stump the doctor.' "I'm working on it. Perhaps I'll have it by my next visit. But wait, I've got one more item for you in my little bag."

The grinning patient reached once more into the little bag and pulled out a bottle cap that had been painted brown, with "Dr B" printed on it in shaky writing. Three little matchsticks were glued to the inside rim. "In case you ever want a 'stool sample' from me, here it is. I'll just leave it with you now, on deposit, so to speak."

Melinda put a hand to her heart. "Oh, that's so cute. I want one, too."

Mr. Harbinger produced another "stool sample" from the little bag. This one had Melinda's initials on it. "Here you go, young miss. I came prepared."

Melinda was somewhat overcome. "Oh, you remembered me!"

Mr. Harbinger blushed. "How could I forget you? Your light smiles up a room."

Melinda turned to Randall. "Dr. B, can I take him home?"

Randall shook his head and mock frowned. "You could, but I think his wife might object. As you may recall, she's very protective. I'm surprised she didn't come for the follow-up."

Mr. Harbinger's face clouded over. "She would have, but her doctor found breast cancer after I finished my treatment here and she's recovering from surgery."

Melinda gave the man a polite side hug. "Oh, you poor man. I hope your wife does well. I will cherish my personalized stool sample forever. I'll keep it right on my toilet tank. Now, I better leave you two to finish up the visit. I have to prepare for the next patient. See you next time. Thanks again."

Randall finished up the visit and boogied to the next exam room.

Next was Mr. Dombrowski along with his wife. He had also recovered well from treatment and had a good PSA response. Mrs. Dombrowski was agog with the amount of food the department had assembled and regretted they couldn't stay for the open house. They had a long drive home to Michigan's Upper Peninsula and had to get back on the road. Randall thanked her profusely for the sweet rolls and suggested perhaps they should arrange a follow up on her husband every two weeks.

Mrs. Dombrowski patted Randall on the arm. "We don't want to risk raising your cholesterol, doctor, and being responsible for you having a heart attack. Then who would take care of my husband? Every three months will be just fine."

The rest of the morning burbled along like water down a meandering country stream. It was a rare good day. No recurrences, complications, or complaints. It was a ten out of ten. When Randall finished the last morning appointment, he walked out to the treatment console and asked how things were going. Molly said everything had gone well. No patients were having issues. Grace said they had only two or three patients to treat in the afternoon by virtue of some creative rescheduling. They were prepared for the afternoon onslaught of VA employees coming for the open house. Randall knew that they would get a good crowd. Whenever free food was involved, the locusts would swarm.

Melinda glided up to join the group at the console. "Are you all caught up, Dr. B?"

Randall hadn't seen her coming and jumped a bit. "Yeah, uh, pretty much, I've been dictating the follow-up notes as I saw them, so unless Sheltie calls from the OR for me to come up and implant after-loading catheters, I should be good to go."

After-loading

Melinda's interest was triggered. "I think I know what an implant is, but I'm fuzzy on the details. Can you explain it in a nutshell?"

Grace harrumphed. "*Hmmph,* you want a nutshell from him? Good luck!"

Randall mimed being deeply offended. "I am the personification of brevity. Let me demonstrate."

Grace remained adamant. "Ten bucks he can't keep it under five minutes."

Randall nodded. "Challenge accepted. Don't bother to sit down. It won't take that long. Any time spent on your questions will not be counted."

Molly looked at her watch. "I'll be the timer. Start any time."

Randall smiled and began with a faster than usual cadence. "The case Sheltie has is a recurrence of a rectal cancer. The man's tumor is invading the bladder and pelvic sidewall. The only chance to get it all out is to do what's called a pelvic exenteration."

Despite herself, Grace had to ask a question. "A what now? He exonerates the pelvis? You mean like pardon it for its cancerous sins?"

Randall motioned Molly to stop the timing. "I was about to explain the term, but you interrupted. The term means the surgeon removes all the pelvic organs, including the rectum, bladder and as much of the tumor as possible. He creates a pouch out of a length of small bowel for an artificial bladder and connects both ureters to it. The pouch will drain out a hole in the abdominal wall into a plastic bag. Then, he'll bring out the colon through a colostomy. That will also empty into a bag."

The three techs looked a bit green after Randall's description. "Where do *you* fit in after all that?" asked Molly.

Randall chuckled. "Again, deduct this time for an interruption. If Sheltie can get the tumor out with clean margins, I don't do anything. But if the tumor is invading the pelvic sidewall, he'll take as much tumor as he can and then ask me to implant the afterloading catheters. They're just small caliber plastic tubes that we sew into the tissue that still has tumor. I arrange them in parallel rows about one centimeter apart until the whole area is covered. Then I bring the tube ends through the perineum and pass them through the center of small metal buttons which I'll sew to the skin. I temporarily thread a nonradioactive wire into the catheters and then crimp the center hole of the button around the catheter to hold everything in place."

Melinda grimaced. "I didn't realize a Radiation Oncologist would get so engrossed in somebody's . . . . business. It's like you have to be a surgeon too."

Randall was used to defending his specialty. "Some doctors think Radiation Oncology is all about aiming beams and pushing buttons. That's definitely not the case."

Grace appeared delighted by Melinda's discomfort. "Whatsa matter, Melinda? Thinking of changing fields? What we do doesn't spare us from blood, pus and bodily fluids."

Melinda shrugged off the comment. "So, Dr. B, when does the radiation part happen?"

Randall responded seamlessly. "About three to four days post-op, to make sure there are no postoperative complications, I take out the temporary wire. Then a long thin wire embedded with radioactive Iridium 125 capsules is inserted into the catheters. Each source wire delivers 50 rads per hour at one centimeter, so we can concentrate the dose exactly where it's needed. An external X-ray beam would have to go through too much healthy tissue to reach the tumor area. This technique concentrates the dose right on the tumor.

Melinda held her sides. "Wow, just hearing this makes my gut hurt. That man must be in so much pain when he comes to."

Randall pointed to Molly. "Stop the clock. Another question. Actually, once all the organs are removed, all the relevant nerves are gone. There is no internal pain. The major discomfort is from the incision sites. They sometimes put a mesh hammock inside to suspend the remaining small bowel so it doesn't sit on top of the radiation sources."

The techs seemed actually interested in the topic and had forgotten about the time restriction. "How do you know how much Iridium to use?" asked Molly.

Randall pretended to look puzzled. "We take x-rays of the pelvis with the simulator to determine the position of the temporary wires. Dan maps out their position with respect to metal clips that we put around the tumor margins during surgery. That will decide the location and strength of the radiation sources. Then, Dan orders the sources from the supplier and we replace the temporary wires with the sources."

"Don't you get exposed to radiation during the loading?" asked Melinda.

Randall nodded. "Yes, but we wear several radiation badges to measure our exposure and work as quickly as possible. We use tongs and other instruments to keep as much distance as we can from the sources during insertion. The radiation given off by Iridium is too penetrating to be shielded by lead aprons, so reducing exposure time and proximity is the best we can do. Only one or two people do the loading."

Grace piped up. She had been to this rodeo before. "Tell Melinda how long the sources stay in place."

Randall raised an index finger. "Right! The Iridium stays in place for about three to four days. During this time, to reduce staff exposure, the patient is kept in a hospital room with only empty rooms around him. We leave a lead 'pig' in the room so if a source gets dislodged we have a safe place to put it."

Melinda looked flabbergasted. "Is the lead pig that big cylinder thing on wheels I saw in the physics room? It's huge! Does it take all that to block out the radiation from the Iridium?"

Randall nodded with a very serious look on his face. "Indeed. The walls of the pig are five centimeters thick. The photons Iridium emits from nuclear decay are little bundles of big energy. Can't see them, but they see right through you! When we have an implant patient admitted, we have to train each shift of nurses what to do in case a source wire comes out. Sometimes the patient gets confused and pulls one out. I got a call at home once at two in the morning from a ward nurse. She had walked into the room to check the guy and spotted the Iridium wire on the floor. She freaked, ran out of the room and called me. I drove in and put the wire in the pig."

Grace moaned. "Implants are a giant pain in the posterior. Every time we do one, there's always scared nurses calling us from the ward."

Randall nodded gravely. "You're right. No one sleeps well when there's an implant patient in the hospital. No matter how much training and explaining we do, everyone caring for the patient on the ward is inches away from panic mode."

Melinda let out a big breath. "Phew, let's hope the patient today doesn't need our services, as much as I'd like the experience."

Randall nodded in agreement. "My thoughts exactly. I'd like more time for you to read up on implants before you have to participate in one. If we keep our fingers and legs crossed . . ."

"Everyone will think we have to pee," remarked Grace. "That's where I'm headed—to the head."

"Yes, excellent idea," said Randall. "My teeth are floating."

Gran Tour

The open house got off to a slow start. Randall began to wonder if anyone would show up. All that food and no one to eat it. Not a bad problem to have as problems went. He was sure solutions could be devised.

Randall and Doris decided to station themselves near the department entrance to welcome visitors. They would then conduct five-cent tours ending with the Ortho room so visitors could partake and then wander about with their food and drink. Several view boxes displayed X-ray images of field set ups and layouts of custom blocks.

Randall posted the techs by the treatment console so they could tag team when Randall brought visitors back to the Linac. They would take guests into the treatment room and demo the machine. After handing guests off there, he'd go back to the entrance. Randall would pick up one group, Doris would get the next one. Hopefully, the front entrance would stay tended. Dan was stationed in his office to demonstrate treatment planning and dosimetry or fill in where needed. Elisa volunteered to keep watch on the cache of goodies in the Ortho room and guide visitors to the food stations.

Just as Randall thought the event was going to be a bust, the dam burst. First on the scene was a contingent from Physical Therapy. The PTs appeared en masse in what looked like a football "V" formation. The PT Chief, Reggie Clevenger, led the charge.

Randall intercepted them. "Hey, Reggie! I see you've brought friends to our little shindig."

Reggie nodded. "Yep, I brought a few colleagues. We've always wondered what goes on in here. Seems a bit magical to me. How does it all work?"

Randall laughed congenially. "Oh, you know those hot dog wieners that you see at the ballpark rotating on spits?"

"Yes, I love ballpark hotdogs," said Reggie.

Randall raised a finger. "Well, the radiation machine is nothing like that, despite what the surgeons might tell you."

Reggie gave Randall a knowing look. "I understand. I have met some of those surgeons. I'm guessing you don't use mustard for a treatment dressing."

"For sure." Randall motioned Reggie and his entourage forward. "Come with me down the hall and I'll hand you guys off to our Radiation Therapy Techs. They'll give you the grand tour of the machine that makes the high energy x-rays we use for treatment of deep-seated tumors. Now don't expect to see any x-rays even if they turn it on. But you can see the images they make on x-ray film."

Reggie subconsciously ran his fingers through his shaggy curls. "It won't make me lose my hair, will it?"

Randall chuckled. "Nope. My hair loss is genetic and not radiation related. Plus, I have fathered two children, so no worries about your nether parts. Although my kids were hatched before I started doing this . . ."

Reggie made a show of cupping his hands over his zipper and laughed. "Good to know."

Randall guffawed. "This ancient looking machine is called the Orthovoltage unit. It makes low energy x-rays for treating superficial tumors, like skin cancer. Right now it's turned off . . . I think . . . at least I'm pretty sure. After your tour is over, here is where you'll find refreshments of all types. My patient care coordinator, Elisa, is in charge of the food offerings. She will protect you from over-burdening your styrofoam plates and spilling delectables on yourself."

There was murmuring from the troop of PTs following Reggie. "Ooh. I can't wait for the end."

Reggie knew who the PT was without looking. "Nancy, can't you keep your mind off food for five minutes? This might be interesting."

Nancy responded softly. "Yeah, boss. Interesting."

Reggie tried to make a joke. "Hey Dr. B! Do we get a complimentary X-ray?"

Randall chuckled. "I could do that, but you'd have to sign consent and you wouldn't like the image. I could give you a coupon or we could barter for a back adjustment."

Reggie laughed. "Sure! I'll bend you over backwards! Improves your reach!"

Randall chuckled, motioned Reggie's group ahead and scooted back to his station. By the time Randall could make it back, Doris was already greeting Bill Simmons, Chief of Building Management. He was accompanied by a half dozen of his crew in their familiar green work shirts. Randall came over, welcomed the group, and shook Bill's hand.

As Doris took them down the hall, Haru Okawa suddenly appeared at the entrance and looked around furtively.

Okawa was a slight Asian Otologist who spoke in a very soft thickly accented voice. He gave Randall a slight bow. "Dr. Biedermeier. I am hearing your house is open for looking and there is food for eating?"

Randall bowed back. He took Okawa's small limp hand and barely squeezed it. "So happy you could come down from the eighth floor."

Okawa winced. Randall released Okawa's hand and Okawa carefully put the hand in his pants pocket. "Happy to be here. Have not much to do since nasty Dr. Cornwell take my *crinic*. She not here, I hope." Okawa stole glances over Randall's shoulder.

Randall looked around. "I don't think so, but I haven't seen everybody who might have come in. Do you want to start the tour?"

Okawa sniffed the air like a bloodhound and looked towards the Ortho room. "No, *prease*. Not much time for tour. Start with food first. Please check food room. Making sure Cornwell not there."

Randall stifled a laugh and nodded his approval. He went to the Ortho room and checked with Elisa. She confirmed Dr. Cornwell was not there and he came back out to give Okawa the thumbs up. Okawa shuffled in for the buffet just as ER Chief James Conway and Compliance Officer Winston Samuels appeared at the entrance. Samuels had sent his secretary Stephanie down earlier to help out with the tours.

Randall greeted the two men with open arms. "Ah, my two favorite VA indentured servants."

Samuels raised both arms even higher than Randall and bellowed. "Hah! Is this the place for the big 'Passe Passe?'"

Conway squinted. "The what?"

"You know, mon, the big 'partee' . . . the shindig . . .the gonzo free-for-all," scolded Samuels. "You doctor types are all work and no play. Loosen up and enjoy the day."

Conway gave Samuels a firm slap on the shoulder. "I'm one doc that breaks the mold. If there's food and drink I'm with you all the way."

The three men then began handshaking, high-fiving, low-fiving and side-fiving. Samuels added some hand jive moves and footwork that

Randall and Conway could not match. When they finished, a small audience had gathered and applauded the display of joviality.

With a sweeping gesture, Randall posed a question. "What'll it be, Gentlemen? Coffee, tea or see?"

"How is the food holding out?" asked Conway. "I don't want to get stalled on one of your five-dollar tours while the food vanishes. I missed my lunch and I am starving."

Randall shook his head. "Not sure. It's been five minutes since I looked. The locusts may have descended already. Okawa is in there now and I hear he can really pack it away for a 120 pounder."

"Jah, man," blustered Samuels. "That little man can out-eat me on a good day. I saw him do it at a Chief's meeting that had a lunch buffet. Every time the Chief of Staff asked him a question, his mouth was full, and he couldn't answer."

The three men looked at each other and stampeded into the Ortho room where Okawa was grazing on some chips and seven-layer taco dip. The dip bowl looked quite vanquished. Okawa looked up in surprise and retreated into a corner. "*Herro* Samuels. . . . mmmph."

Conway looked around the room and gasped. "Oh, my goodness. There's a whole batch of pistachio nut torte with cheesecake filling over here. I haven't had that since I left home. It was my mother's go-to dessert. I called it 'green heaven.'"

"Oh, yeah, that's the specialty of my tech, Molly," said Randall. "She makes it for our Christmas party every year with fresh cherries on top. You know, Christmas red and green. It's to die for. You can't eat just one piece. Better sample it before we get more consumers." Conway didn't wait and filled a plate.

Samuels was sniffing a simmering pot of soup with fresh bread on the side. His eyes were wide with amazement. "I must be dreaming— this looks like Jamaican Gungo pea soup. Who made this?"

Samuels had found a pot of traditional down home soup being kept warm over a sterno flame. Randall hadn't realized Dan's concoction was Jamaican. "That's the contribution of Dan Graham, my Radiation Physicist. He's a vegan and this is one of his staples."

"'*Jessum Peace*,' I don't believe this," said Samuels with incredulity. "It smells just like what my Mama made for us. Where is Danny-boy? I 'most want to hug'm."

Dan was off in a corner making love to tortilla chips and guacamole dip. "No man-hugs from you, Samuels. You'll squeeze the guacamole back out of me. Just dig in and enjoy the savory contents. Dr. B won't touch the stuff because it's vegan."

Samuels inhaled the aroma coming off the simmering pot and took a spoonful. He looked like he was in the first stages of ecstasy. "My boy, this is manna from heaven. I not let any man near this pot. I declare, it's '*A Fi Mi*.'"

Elisa had just finished escorting Clive Lincoln, the Chief of Engineering, and some of his staff. She delivered the lean and hungry looking group to the Ortho room for treats. Lincoln and his group waved a greeting at Conway, Samuels and Randall, then bee-lined to the food tables.

Randall walked over to Dan to sample the guacamole. "Dan, it looks like you have acquired an ardent admirer."

Dan looked over to Samuels slurping soup. "Yeah. I like Samuels but he looks lethal. Every time I imagine him hugging me, I picture guacamole exiting each of my orifices and some new ones."

Dan's imagination painted quite a bizarre picture. Randall had to laugh abruptly and spit out partially masticated chips and dip. "Dang! Don't make me laugh while I'm eating."

It was Dan's turn to laugh. "Ha! You just brought my mental image to real life. Now I've got a guacamole shirt."

Grace appeared at the Ortho doorway and motioned to Dan to come out for the next tour group.

Dan grasped at some napkins. "Curses! I'm being cashiered to do the next tour. Help me clean off my shirt before I go out."

Randall helped get most of the aerosolized food off of Dan's shirt. "I did the best I could. Sorry about my food laugh. There's a lab coat hanging on the clothes tree. Put it on. It should cover most of the stains."

Randall went to the hallway with Dan and introduced him to

Martha Clunes, the Chief Librarian, plus a small contingent of assistant and trainee librarians. They all wore cardigans, knee-length dark skirts, and flats. Randall imagined that manner of dress was mandated by the librarian's union. They were cute in a bookish kind of way. Despite their benign appearance they ruled the roost in the library. Randall had nicknamed Martha as Conancy the Librarian. One had to be wary of her swift sword, a deftly wielded pencil.

In the hallway, Dan pointed the way for the Librarians. "Right this way, ladies. Prepare yourself for the show of shows. I am Dan Graham, the Chief Medical Physicist here. Well, at least I must be the Chief, because I am the only Medical Physicist on these premises. It's a job with heavy responsibility and some danger, but have no fear for I am here."

Dan sounded like he was straight from the midway. Randall laughed to himself and turned to the front entrance as Clarence Munday, the Chief of Pathology, appeared with some of his laboratory colleagues. Randall had never really gotten along with Munday, but he put on his professional smile and prepared to lead the tour.

Doris had just finished up with Lydia Buntwell, from Dietetics, and deposited her in the Ortho room. As Randall started the tour for the Pathologists, Clara Sanderson, Chief of Recreational Therapy, appeared at the department entrance and Doris greeted her. Randall wished he'd been a bit slower with Clive Lincoln's group and had gotten Lydia instead of the stuffy Munday. He wondered what forms of recreational therapy she offered, but decided it was best not to explore that further. And he didn't want to risk a slap in the face.

Munday handed Randall a bag of potato chips. "Here you go. I thought I'd bring a little something."

Randall thanked him and told him about the food cache in the Ortho room. "You can just take the chips in there."

Munday nodded. "Alright. What dish did you prepare?"

Randall figured Munday was trying to catch him out about not making any food for his own open house. He also suspected he'd brought the chips so he could go directly to the food without the need for a tour. Randall disappointed the man when he told him he'd made tuna casserole. Randall really didn't care about the chip thing, since he was glad for the excuse not to give Munday a tour.

Munday smiled. "Good to know. I'll avoid it. It's probably radioactive. I'll test it with a geiger counter before I eat it. Just kidding, old boy. Just kidding."

Munday walked to the Ortho room, laughing. Randall mumbled to himself. "I've always hated Munday."

The open house had started slowly, but now there was a substantial crowd of people milling about the department balancing plates of food and drinks. The chatter noise level had risen. VA rules permitted only nonalcoholic beverages, yet the participants were behaving like their soft drinks had been spiked with Jack Daniels. There was even some horsing around, including some minor food throwing. Ira, the patient transporter, poked his head in the front entrance. Melinda had been on the lookout for him and rushed out from her observation point at the treatment console to welcome him in. Ira was so stunned as she approached him that he froze in place.

Melinda approached Ira with a warm welcoming smile. "How nice of you to come, Ira. You've been so good with our patients that I was waiting here to give you a personal tour."

Ira was momentarily rendered mute in surprise. Then he finally found his voice. "What? Me?"

Melinda smiled more broadly. "Why, of course, you."

Melinda took Ira's elbow and led him to the treatment console. There she explained how the equipment worked. When finished she directed him to follow her into the treatment room.

Ira hesitated. "Go in there where the radiation is? That stuff is bad."

Melinda grabbed his arm and shook her head. "There's nothing to be afraid of, you silly boy. The machine is turned off now. There's no radiation to hurt you. At least, I'm pretty sure."

Melinda led the way and Ira shuffled along behind her looking like he was being taken to face a firing squad. Randall watched the scene from the hall with amusement.

Randall watched the entrance to the Linac room for a few minutes, expecting a scream of terror to emerge. When none did, he turned his attention back to the department entrance. Soon after, a small group of young women got off the elevator and made their way toward the department. At first, he couldn't place who they were.

Randall moved forward to greet the group.

An attractive blonde with her long hair pulled into a braid was at the lead and introduced herself. "Hello, Dr. Biedermeier. I'm Heather Ameche, supervisor for the transcription pool, and these are my girls."

Randall's attention was waning slightly after all the new introductions. "How did you know it was me?"

Heather's smile was rather engaging. "I do my homework. Plus, that's what it says on your lab coat."

Randall clicked his heels and let out a lame chuckle. "Yeah, right. Very observant."

Randall momentarily was not quite sure where to go next. Heather helped him refocus."We're here for the tour and food. I hope there's some left."

Randall cleared his throat, smiled, and nodded. "Ahem. Of course you are. I'm pretty sure we have both."

Heather introduced each transcriptionist by name and Randall gave each a gentlemanly hand squeeze. The last one introduced was a woman named Helen Kiellor. Randall put his hand out and Helen moved hers about until she found Randall's hand.

Randall wasn't quite sure what the problem was and was hesitant to ask. Before he could ask, Helen explained. "Sorry, Dr. Biedermeier. I should have told you. I'm legally blind, but my hearing is wonderful. I knew it was you because I recognized your voice. You have one of my favorite voices for a dictator."

Randall recovered quickly and laughed. "I assure you that I am not very strict. I am a rather benign dictator."

Helen flushed a bit red in embarrassment. "Oops, that came out wrong."

Randall took some blame. "Actually it's partly my fault for not *seeing* the whole picture. There's very little about your manner that suggests your sight is impaired. That's a tribute to you. Might I inquire what's so attractive about my dictation?"

Helen's face glowed in response to Randall's compliment. She thought for a moment for an appropriate response. "Well, you speak clearly, concisely and go slowly enough that I don't have to keep rewinding the tape to listen again. You spell words that might be difficult for someone like me who doesn't know the details of what you do. Your voice is just the right pitch for easy listening. But the best is when you forget to turn off the record switch and make your interesting observations about . . . well, VA life."

The group started to giggle and Helen smiled broadly. Randall felt his face heating up.

When the laughter subsided, Heather spoke up. "Helen has two special requests. We're hoping you'll accommodate her."

Randall nodded amicably. "Anything within reason. Ask away."

Helen shuffled her feet. "Request number one is I want permission to feel your face."

Randall hesitated for a beat. "Feel my face?"

Helen had expected a questioning response. "I know that sounds odd at first, but that's how I 'see' what people look like. I've built up an image of you from listening to your voice. I want to 'feel' if my image of you fits the real you."

The request triggered a question from Randall. "Well, here's something I've been wondering. Your crew has never seen me before. What do you say, girls? Does my face fit what you imagined from my voice?"

There was a loud chorus of "no's."

Randall shrugged. "Alrighty then. I guess that's not a good solution." He stepped forward, took Helen's hand in his and brought it up to his face. "Here you go."

Samuels emerged from the Ortho room and looked over towards Randall and the transcriptionists. "Hey, *mon*! What you doin' with those women-folk? Looks like some hanky panky to me. Can anyone join?"

All eyes turned towards the big man. Randall thought including Samuels might be entertaining. "Sure, come on down! Watch and learn. Come closer and see."

Samuels walked up to the group. Randall introduced him and explained what was going on.

Samuels was intrigued. "This *gon* be good."

Helen moved closer and moved her hands over Randall's nose, mouth, cheeks and jaw. She felt his mustache, glasses and ears, finishing up with his sparse hair and bald scalp. She moved to his neck where she felt his prominent Adam's apple. Randall found the examination to be rather pleasant. Helen moved her hands to feel his shoulders and arms and then dropped her arms back to her sides. She seemed to be contemplating her discoveries for a few moments, then announced her conclusion. "Just as I suspected. He feels like Groucho Marx's younger brother!"

Samuels let out a loud guffaw. "Right on, sister!"

The troupe of women gave forth with a round of applause and vibrant giggling.

Helen clapped her hands and smiled. "That wasn't so bad, Dr. Biedermeier, was it?"

Randall raised both arms. "Not a bit of it. Can we go again?"

More laughter ensued.

Randall decided to make more hay while the sun still shined. "For a moment there I was a little worried that you might tickle me to death. And I was both glad and sad when you stopped at my shoulders."

That incited more laughter and some hooting. Samuels boomed a loud cat call.

Heather, rather tongue in cheek, tried to calm things down. "Dr. Biedermeier! I didn't expect the visit to get so raucous. Really!"

Randall took umbrage. "Sorry if I let things get out of hand. But now that we've bonded, from here on, please call me Dr. B, everybody."

As if on cue the group gave a choral response. "Hello, Dr. B!"

Samuels registered an objection. "Hey, don't I get a feely turn?"

Randall pointed and waved an index finger at Samuels. "Sorry, *gyalis mon*. This not be your tour group."

Helen grabbed Randall's arm. "I almost forgot. My second request is to 'feel' your treatment machine. Fearless leader, take me to your machine."

Randall nodded and extended an elbow. Helen took hold and Randall led her and the group to the treatment room.

Samuels shouted after them. "You make a *'maad'* guide dog."

Randall shouted back over his shoulder. "Hey, Samuels. Get back in the Ortho room and guard the food so there's some left when we get back."

Grace came out of the Ortho room and watched the procession go by. "Don't you worry your little head over the food. I just brought in reinforcements from our stash out back. There should be some crumbs left when you return. No pinching behinds."

The gaggle giggled again. Randall had to admit he was enjoying the attention. Life could be much worse. As he led the group into the Linac room, he met Melinda coming out with Ira. She still had a firm grip on his arm. Ira still look totally bemused. The plan was falling right into place. The transcriptionists *'oohed'* and *'aahed'* at the Linac and the description of its workings. Helen felt almost every inch of the unit with both hands. Randall was reminded of the story of the three blind men and the elephant. In this case, Helen was so thorough she would come away with a complete picture of the beast.

By the time Randall delivered the transcriptionists to the food, even more people had flooded into the small department and were in various phases of the tour. He concluded that the overall plan had broken down somewhat like a computer with too little memory for the software to run smoothly. It seemed that most of the late comers weren't really interested in the tour anyhow and had arrived mostly for sugar and caffeine. Thus, he decided he would just mingle.

Randall spotted Melinda and Ira standing next to the treatment console with plates of dessert and drinking from foam coffee cups. He went around gathering up his staff to go stand by the treatment console as well and stay there for a group Polaroid. Soon, he assembled Dan, Grace, Molly, Elisa and Doris to stand alongside Melinda and Ira. Randall recruited Jim Conway to take a group shot. They had to crowd together to get everyone in the frame. Jim had them all yell, "Well, shut the front door" and got the shot. He took another for good measure.

Randall ordered the picture group to stay in position until the Polaroids were fully developed to make sure they had come out alright. While they were waiting, Okawa came out of the Ortho room carrying three oranges. Randall was sure the food hound was blatantly going to steal them.

Juggling for Dollars

Clive Lincoln followed Okawa out of the room and shouted after him. "Hey, Haru, where are you going? I've got fifty bucks says you can't keep three oranges in the air for 30 seconds."

"Not *reaving*," replied Okawa. "Need more room. Food room much crowded. Peoples, please make space. I show this man I not *rying*. I tell truth."

The now very party-like crowd made room around Okawa, apparently thinking this was the planned entertainment. Lincoln stood in the crowd now circling around Okawa with his arms folded defiantly over his chest.

Lincoln taunted Okawa. "Come on, Nip-boy, show me your stuff."

Okawa took exception to the slur. "You not call me Nip-boy."

Lincoln laughed derisively. "Alright, slant eyes, I promise not to call you Nip-boy again. Now get juggling. I've got my timer ready."

Okawa said nothing in response, but glared at Lincoln with narrowed eyes.

Elisa stepped forward and confronted Lincoln. "Mr. Lincoln, there's no need for disparaging name-calling. We are all professionals here."

Lincoln backed away from Elisa and was momentarily at a loss for words. He seemed tempted to keep on ranting, but took a breath and apologized. "Sorry, Dr. Okawa. I didn't mean nuthin' by it. I'm just real competitive. Go ahead and start making some orange juice."

Okawa looked vindicated. He widened his stance, readied the three oranges, and began to juggle. He kept them in the air like a master. The crowd stood in awe and began to applaud. When Lincoln's watch reached 30 seconds, he called out the time, but Okawa kept going until he fumbled one orange at 55 seconds and stopped. He saved the orange from hitting the floor by clutching it to his chest. The applause grew louder, and Okawa took several small bows.

Okawa swaggered over to Lincoln and handed him the oranges. "Now you, Mr. *Rincoln*, must do oranges longer or must give me the money." Okawa's nasal voice echoed in the now quiet hallway.

Randall was dumbfounded by what had just happened. Okawa wasn't a food thief after all. He had made a bet and gone right for the jugular. Adding spice to the atmosphere was the surprise appearance at the front entrance of Dr. Micheal Newberry, the VA Chief of Staff. He had arrived just in time to observe the juggling clinic. Most folks were so focused on the juggling they hadn't seen Newberry come in.

Newberry announced his presence with a clear and penetrating bass. "Well, well, what have we here? Is this a sanctioned competition? Can anyone play? I didn't see this event in the announcement for the open house. And I'm sure there is no illegal gambling riding on this competition."

Randall feared the department was in trouble for being too frolicsome. "Sorry, Chief. I guess I left that off by mistake. We can still give you the tour."

Newberry shook his head and laughed. "Not interested in the tour. After the day I've had, I don't want one of your dry lectures about radiation. I know what you do down here better than anyone. Samuels has been bugging me daily about what you need. What I need is some recreational therapy. I'm sure Ms. Sanderson over there would agree with me. There's a time to pay and there's a time to play. I am not half bad at juggling. I want in on this little event."

Jaws dropped and murmurs erupted. Randall rose to the occasion and said he had some skills in the area and would take up the gauntlet as well. Newberry nodded his approval with a smile. Randall went over to his group gathered by the console and bade them to join him in the competition circle. It was Lincoln's turn next. Lincoln looked nervous and sweat appeared on his brow. Randall was having fun now. He took the timer from Okawa and signaled Lincoln to get ready to start juggling on a three count.

Lincoln started off well and had a good rhythm. At 20 seconds he had a small bobble, but was able to save a drop with a quick hand. Randall called out the time count every five seconds. Lincoln was still going strong at 58 seconds when he missed catching an orange on the way down, but deftly caught it with his shoe top. That set off a heated discussion about rules, but Dr. Newberry made a ruling that his session was complete with a winning time besting Okawa by three seconds. Okawa looked stricken but was comforted by Molly Sanderson who seemed to be quite impressed by the moxie of the little man.

There were no other challengers. Randall suggested that Newberry would go next since his challenge had been posed third and that Randall would follow. Randall also proposed that instead of a monetary exchange, that "door prizes" would be given to the top three juggling times. Only Randall knew that no such door prizes had been planned, but he would improvise. The contestants agreed to the terms and Randall motioned Newberry to step forward to receive the ceremonial oranges. The oranges had survived mostly intact to this point.

Randall stepped back and Newberry readied himself for the count. The crowd murmured approval and support. Chewing and drinking paused temporarily in anticipation. Randall did the countdown and signaled the start. Newberry began to juggle the three oranges smoothly. He threw the oranges higher than his predecessors and the oranges seemed to float in the air as he magically transferred them from hand to hand. It was a thing of beauty. The hallway was dead quiet during the display except for Randall's five-second interval count. Time seemed suspended as the count rose to one minute, then one minute and 20 seconds and finally to two minutes flat when Newberry just stopped without a falter.

After five more seconds of silence, the crowd broke out in loud applause and catcalls. Newberry bowed low once, twice and then raised his arms high in triumph. When the applause subsided, he walked over to Randall and gave him the oranges. Randall looked at the oranges and asked for a minute to consult with his team. He went over and whispered to Grace, asking how much food was left. She whispered back that they were still in good shape. He handed the timer to Dan. Randall whispered something to Melinda, who responded with a brief nod, and he returned to the center of the ring.

Done In

Randall cradled the oranges in both hands and addressed the crowd. "As always, Dr. Newberry is a tough act to follow. But only the faint of heart faint, so here goes nothing. I hope this will be something more than a feint."

Several voices groaned at Randall's wordplay, but the majority shrugged.

Randall put one orange in his lab coat pocket. "Just a second. Let me just warm up with two oranges. It's been a while since I've practiced."

Randall began with the two oranges, throwing them high, then low and finished up by throwing several rounds behind his back or under a cocked leg. This drew a few claps of approval. He stopped and wiped his brow.

Randall pulled the third orange out of his pocket and nodded to Dan. "I'm ready. Give me a three count."

At "go," Randall began juggling the three oranges haltingly, drawing a few audible gasps from the audience when he faltered. He righted himself and got into a nice rhythm. He wasn't as flashy as Newberry, but looked controlled and steady. At the one-minute mark, he had a bobble, but corrected it. Just when things were looking promising, he knuckled an orange and it flew forward onto the floor. It bounced twice and rolled to rest at Melinda's feet.

"One minute and 40 seconds!" yelled Dan.

At Melinda's prodding, Ira stooped over and picked up the fallen orange, whereupon two Marlboro cigarettes and one stick of Big Red chewing gum fell out of his shirt pockets and dropped to the floor. They landed at Melinda's feet.

Randall walked over and took the orange from Ira. "Thanks for the quick pick-up."

Jim Conway still had the Polaroid camera in hand. At Randall's signal, Conway had snapped a shot of Ira picking up the orange. He had taken another shot of the cigarettes and the stick of chewing gum on the floor.

Randall bent over and picked up the cigarettes and gum stick. He handed them to Ira. "Here's the stuff you dropped." Randall reached into his lab coat pocket, pulled out a thick envelope and handed it to Ira. "Here's your special prize for helping me solve a mystery. The note inside explains it all."

Ira looked puzzled but took the envelope. He started to open it but Randall stopped him. "Don't open it here. Wait until you leave. Oh, and if you wish, I can give you a copy of the Polaroid just as a memento of today's events."

Ira couldn't wait to open his prize so he waltzed out of the department to go wherever he went. Randall whistled for the crowd's attention. When he got it, he pronounced that Dr. Newberry was the juggling champion. The mysterious top prize would be first pick of all the goodies in the food room and helpers to assist him with taking the booty back to his office.

Then Dr. Newberry again took the floor and surprised Randall by announcing to those gathered that he had come down not just for the open house, but also to deliver good news. "I am pleased to tell you that your department has just been approved to hire a full-time clinic nurse. I may have done some fancy administrative juggling to prompt HR to approve the position. Mr. Samuels also gave them a nudge on your behalf."

The crowd applauded again. There was a loud cheer from the three techs. They would now be able to do tech work and Melinda would no longer have to prep patients for exam.

The crowd prompted Randall to disclose the results of the juggling contest. He had promised prizes. It was time to ad lib again. The solution came to him in a flash. Without a hitch, he announced that, as the open house host, he was ineligible for a prize. Thus, Clive Lincoln was declared second prize winner. Randall presented Lincoln with the quarter pounder with cheese that Mr. Harbinger had made. Lincoln thought it was the coolest thing ever and beamed with glee. He looked happier than Randall had ever seen him. Randall would harvest that good will in the future to grease the skids for department remodeling.

Third prize went to Okawa who jumped up and down in delight. It was the three oranges, one of them slightly juicy. Okawa was delighted to be recognized. After the prizes were given out, the crowd filtered away. The end time planned for the open house had expired anyway, so Randall shooed out the stragglers and joined his fellow open housers in the clean-up.

Later, Randall and Melinda had several minutes alone together while they finished cleaning up the Ortho room. She had been awaiting Randall's explanation of the interchange with Ira. Finally, she had to ask. "So, Dr. B?"

Randall's mind was elsewhere when he responded. "Yes?"

Melinda suspected Randall was sounding purposely forgetful. "Might I ask what was in the envelope you handed Ira?"

Randall turned away from scraping food debris off dishes. "Of course, you may. Ask away."

Melinda was not amused and made a huffing sound.

Randall laughed and decided to give forth. "Oh, you want an answer, too? Well, put simply, the envelope contained five wads of ABC Big Red gum, plus a cease and desist note worded rather non-delicately.

I doubt we will have any further issues with derelict gum wads or future female harassment."

Melinda beamed. "Fantastic. We got him! Now I can wash his awful cologne smell out of my clothes. You're my new hero. And you juggle pretty well, too."

Randall nodded in appreciation. "Not a problem. All good leaders are juggling adepts."

AMERICA'S DAIRYLAND
QG 5023
AUG WISCONSIN
WIS 79

CHAPTER 19

———

QUANTUM FORCES

"Fight any instinct to be humorless, for humorlessness is the worst of all absurdities."

—*Jean Cocteau*

Randall was wiped out from the open house, but the day wasn't over. He dove into the stack of charts and started on dictations. He was being put to sleep by the drone of his own voice when Knox called to inform him that Randall's former mentor, Juan Angel del Aguilar, MD, had called to discuss some NRG political issues. Aguilar had asked Knox to invite Randall to the meeting. Aguilar wanted to meet Randall for lunch at the NRG meeting hotel to discuss Randall's "future in clinical research." To save time, Knox said his secretary, Anita, would hand deliver the NRG slides so Randall would have adequate time to prepare. Randall figured he'd review the slides on the plane. There was no other time available.

THE CHIEF

Knox was about to hang up when he recalled another Aguilar request. "Oh. Another thing before I ring off, Aguilar wants you to call him in Tampa to discuss the NRG meeting. Anita will call Doris with the number to reach him. Make the call soon. Good luck." Knox hung up.

Randall couldn't think of a reason Aguilar would have any interest in Randall's future. Randall had been a rebellious sort during his residency training and had often drawn Aguilar's ire. Randall would follow orders until they seemed egregious and then work his way to the top of Aguilar's *persona non grata* list. It seemed Aguilar wanted control over issues that Randall thought had little to do with Radiation Oncology and treated the residents as though they were in finishing school.

Randall recalled one occasion in which Aquilar had called Zelda into his office and requested her help in "straightening out" Randall. Aguilar had misjudged Zelda badly. She was already quite disaffected by the whole "doctor business," as she called it. Zelda had listened politely to Aguilar's request and then quietly rose to leave his office. At his office doorway, she paused briefly to give Aguilar graphic "how high, how far" insertion directions.

Zelda's encounter with Aguilar had served to sour Randall's shaky relationship with Aguilar, at least temporarily. Despite this rough patch, Randall had completed the training. He realized now that Aguilar was still a titan of the specialty, even in retirement and it wouldn't be prudent not to cooperate. Knox informed Randall repeatedly how lucky they both were to have been trained in Aguilar's program. Apparently, Aguilar held all graduates of his program in high esteem even if they had rough patches during training. His support was always useful for advancement in the specialty.

Randall was a bit shaky. He wasn't sure why. But he did know he wanted to get the Aguilar call over with. The sooner he got the lay of the land, the better. He walked out to Doris' desk. "Would you please phone Dr. del Aguilar at his Tampa office using the number Anita gave you? Put the call through to me as soon as he comes on the line."

Doris nodded. "That's your old master, right? I mean 'boss.' Can I tell him what the call is about?"

For a moment Randall couldn't think. "Tell him I'm calling about the NRG meeting in Las Vegas."

Doris scrunched her forehead. "In Las Vegas? Don't tell me you have to go there."

Randall made a sour face. "Alright. I won't tell you."

Doris shook her head and made a whooshing sound. "When is this energy meetin' bein' held that you won't tell me you're gon' to?"

Randall pulled back the corners of his mouth like he was in pain. "It's this weekend. And it's not the word 'energy.' It's the letters N-R-G. It's an acronym."

Doris laughed. "What exactly does NRG stand for? More doctor alphabet soup?" Doris paused a moment, remembering a minor issue she hoped Randall hadn't forgotten. "Wait a goldarned minute. I thought you had a VA site visit this weekend in Detroit."

Randall nodded weakly. "Yep. I remember. The NRG meeting is more important. We'll have to 'reschedule' the Detroit thingy."

Doris sensed the rescheduling assignment would be hers. "I assume that's the 'royal we.'"

Randall confirmed her assumption was correct. "I'm sure you can do a better job of that than I ever could." Before Doris could protest, Randall diverted. "To answer your earlier question, NRG stands for National Radiation Group."

Doris was feeling somewhat manipulated, but she reluctantly agreed to set up a new Detroit site visit date. "I *s'pose* I can do that dirty job. I'll call my friend Becky in the front office. I'll make it sound all official-like."

Randall didn't feel too bad about delaying the site visit. It wasn't really in his scope of duties anyway. He would actually be doing the VA a favor that could bear future fruit. "Any other questions before you place the call to del Aguilar?"

Doris nodded. "Just one. What does this NRG group do that's so important you have to have me call in favors from the front office? It may help me convince the powers to release you from Detroit duties."

Randall was glad to clarify. "Good question. It's a national cooperative clinical cancer research group. About 200 cancer hospitals are members and contribute patients to studies that answer important questions about the best way to use radiation for selected cancers. I've been to one meeting before and Knox wants me to sub for him on the committee that does lung cancer studies. It's an important opportunity for me."

Doris was impressed. "So you'll get to hobnob with a herd of cancer big shots, eh? Y'all will be workin' together for the greater good of all mankind and such, right?"

Randall wasn't quite sure how to take the comment, but went with the flow. "Doris, you know how to tag the rooster right on the beak. The NRG group is infused with altruism."

Doris let out a breath. "Dr. B. I'm gon' have to look up that last word in my Merriam-Webster's dictionary." She pulled her dog-eared tome from a shelf and began paging. She found "altruism" and read the definition. "That's a good word. I'll be sure to use it when I call Becky. It will add *gravitas* to my excuse. Lay it on thick like butter on a biscuit."

Randall was getting anxious to get to call over with. "So, are 'we' ready to place the call to del Aguilar?"

Doris nodded and pulled out the note from Anita. She dialed and motioned Randall to wait in his office. Randall returned to his desk and began to review lab reports while he waited for the call.

Randall's attention drifted away from the reports as he reminded himself to gird his loins before talking to Aguilar. Though small in stature, Aguilar's rule had been absolute wherever he was in charge. He had acquired the sobriquet *"el Jefe"* due to his somewhat tyrannical leadership style. After becoming a naturalized US citizen, he had worked hard to master English. He was often embarrassed that his persistent Cuban accent made him sound undereducated.

Aguilar tried to compensate for his accent by using unusual words in casual conversation. He loved confusing listeners with words like "Hobbesian" or an "Ultracrepidarian." Listeners would often feign understanding and weren't aware they'd been insulted until later when they looked up the word in a dictionary. The title *"el Jefe"* was replaced by "The Chief" once he was in charge of a major Radiation Oncology Cancer Center in the US.

After a 30-minute wait, Doris got through to Aguilar and went to Randall's office. "Dr. B, I have Dr. del Aguilar on line two. He talks funny. You can pick it up on line one when you're ready. I wouldn't keep him waitin' though. He sounds *impo'tent.*"

Randall chuckled at the irony of how Doris's accent modified her descriptor. "Thanks. Doris. I've got it. Please close the door on your way out in case I start crying loudly."

Doris made a serious face and nodded. "Dr. B, you be careful now, ya hear? Sounds to me like that man can draw blood over the phone."

Randall muttered under his breath as Doris left. "Yep. He can be a real *futher mucker.*"

Doris was nearly out the door when she turned around. "Pardon my ears! What'd you say?"

Randall had forgotten Doris had super power hearing and called back. "He always makes me feel like another sucker."

Doris snorted. "I see why you don't like him. He was rude to me on the phone and said I reminded him of hominy grits."

Randall waved a hand. "From him, that's a compliment. Don't waste any time fretting about it."

Randall was nervous and he punched the number two extension by mistake. He spent a few seconds talking to nothing and thinking Aguilar had hung up. He could be rather impatient. When Randall realized his error, he hastily punched the one button and blurted rather loudly, "Chief? Are you there?"

Aguilar sounded annoyed. "Yes, Biedermeier, I am. I'm getting rapidly older."

"Sorry, Chief," stuttered Randall. "There was a mix-up on the extension."

Aguilar gave a frosty response. "Not a surprise. I suggest you consider releasing your secretary back to the wild and retaining someone more competent."

Randall chose a placating posture. "I will take your suggestion under advisement. What did you want to chat about?"

Randall had briefly considered saying 'what can you do for me?' but bit his tongue and made a 180. Despite Aguilar's snarky comments about Doris, Aguilar was surprisingly friendly. He engaged in banal chatter with Randall for a few minutes, then abruptly shifted the conversation to the details of the Las Vegas lunch arrangements.

Just as Randall thought the dialogue was about to end, Aguilar segued to clinical research. To Randall's utter surprise, Aguilar praised Randall's accomplishments since leaving his training program. Randall could not imagine what Aguilar was referring to but decided not to ask. He didn't want to appear ignorant of his own "achievements." Aguilar suggested that if Randall played his cards right, he could use the NRG opportunity to make his mark in clinical research. Before he could expand on this carrot, Aguilar had to take a long-distance call he was expecting. He said that they would talk further at the NRG meeting. Then the line went dead without a goodbye. The phone encounter hadn't been as painful as Randall had anticipated, but significant mystery remained.

Roll Call

Randall leaned back in his chair and stared at the ceiling tiles as though they would show del Aguilar's actual intent. The Cuban was still enigmatic.

Doris knocked on his open office door. "What's up, Dr. B? Are there spiders on the ceilin'?"

Randall jerked upright and looked at Doris in surprise. "Yes, and they weave a wondrous web of weirdness. Do you need something?"

Doris nodded. "Indeed those spiders do and yes I do. You have a call from Dr. Shepard. Do you want to take it? He sounds as anxious as a corn kernel in a chicken coop."

Randall looked flustered. "Geez. I'm not sure. I was on the phone with del Aguilar for a while. Are the natives getting restless? How far behind am I?"

Doris shrugged. "Not more than usual. I'd say you've got ten minutes before the mutiny."

Randall raised both arms. "Then fine. Connect me up. But make sure the powder is dry and the bows are strung."

Doris nodded vigorously. "Got it, Chief. He's on your line two. Just push the button."

Randall did as directed. "Hey there, Joe. How's it go? What's on your mind?"

Joe's response did sound anxious. He got right to business. "This weekend's PCG meeting. I'm running into some snags."

Randall slapped his forehead. He'd forgotten all about the PCG meeting with all the confusion about the ill-planned Detroit site visit and the preempting Las Vegas trip. Not sure how to approach the impasse, he obfuscated. He decided that, before disclosing his conflict, he'd find out what problems Joe was having first. "Er, yeah. What sort of problems?"

Joe sighed heavily into the phone. "Well, for one thing, Bingham can't make it this weekend due to some family thing. Also, I'm getting some flak from others about getting some non-professional participants. You know, having someone to bring a lay person's viewpoint and/or a traditional perspective, like Native American."

Randall made a loud humming sound into the mouthpiece. "Too bad about Bingham, but he's already said his piece, so we could probably do without him for one session. The suggestions about a new member have some merit. I may have a few ideas about that."

Joe then dropped the biggest lead balloon into the punch bowl. "Actually, the biggest problem is my wife. She has in-laws coming over to the house this weekend and refuses to reschedule. The only way we could do it this weekend is to find another meeting site, like, maybe, your house?"

It was Randall's turn to drop a bigger lead balloon. "*Umm*. Even if I could talk Zelda into that, I have been *voluntold*, on very short notice, to attend a research meeting in Vegas this weekend. Very politically incorrect to try to opt out of the 'invitation.'"

Joe sighed with relief. "Why didn't you say so to start with? In that case, I don't have a problem. We'll just reschedule for another weekend."

Randall decided to take umbrage. "I was kind of hoping you'd have a reason to cancel so it wouldn't be my fault. I'll bet you were secretly hoping I'd get you off the hook."

They both chuckled at their errant blame-shifting before Joe asked Randall what his ideas were for additional members.

Randall backtracked to refind the thought he'd had. "Oh, yeah. I don't recall if I mentioned this to you before or not, but my wife, Zelda, is what I would call an 'Eclectarian.' She's read everything from the Koran to Edgar Cayce and has tasted many spiritual nectars, while accepting no particular one. I think she could be the 'Jack of all Trades' lay person we're looking for. She has expressed some interest in the group. I suggest she join as an observer. She may be intimidated by all the degrees in our group and may not say much, but you never know."

Joe sounded interested. "It's worth a try. Worst that can happen is we don't mesh. Did you have something else?"

Randall grunted. "Yeah. I've been thinking we change the name of the group to Quantum Entanglement Group or QEG."

Joe sounded confused by the suggestion. "Why would we do that?"

Randall explained his reasoning. "Phantom Cominglement Group was a spur of the moment concoction and sounds like it. As I have been studying up more on quantum processes, quantum entanglement is a real phenomenon, and I think it applies to what we're studying."

Joe made a humming sound into the phone. "Hmm, you may have something there. I like it. We can make the change at the next meeting. I doubt anyone will object."

Tumor Bored

Randall said goodbye to Joe and hung up the phone. Doris had been waiting at his doorway for the call to end and knocked on the open door for attention. "Dr. B? Sorry to bother you again."

Randall was startled by the intrusion and jumped in his seat. "Geez, Doris. I'm going to buy you a Clarabelle horn to wear on your belt so you can warn me when you're coming! What is it now? More patients waiting to storm the Bastille?"

Doris smiled broadly, trying to achieve a more pleasant segue. "Actually, quite the opposite. The two weekly reviews had to leave to catch the Iron Mountain bus back to the UP. The consult that was supposed to come down from the surgery ward was transferred to the eleventh floor, rather unexpectedly. If you catch my meanin.'"

The Hobbes VA had only ten floors. An eleventh floor transfer was code for passage to the great rumpus room in the sky. Randall reacted rather inappropriately. "Great! I could use the extra time to catch up with some business."

Doris was appalled. "Dr. B! That response is as crude and crass as overalls at church. We're talkin' about a human life that has just passed on. Show some respect."

Randall rolled his eyes. "Sorry. But you did say the eleventh floor and not the sub basement. I never even met the man, so I am not vested in his life outcome. Yet I thank heaven that he has risen like a loaf of leavened bread, not the alternative. Also, he showed me respect by rising before I saw him, not after."

Doris paused for a beat. "Hmm. You make a good point. I'm willin' to forgive you, but I'm not so sure about the Lord. Enjoy your 30 minutes of freedom and I'll pray for your forgiveness."

Randall nodded. "Deal! Now, for the next half hour I'm not taking any visitors. Got it?"

"Even if they are Miss Elisa?" countered Doris. "Shall I tell her to try you another time?"

Now Randall had a dilemma. Tell Elisa he was busy so he could ponder the QEG problems or regret not including her in his machinations? Something told him to invite her in. "Of course not. I'm always here for Miss Elisa. Send her in."

Elisa strode smoothly into Randall's office. As usual she was smartly dressed in a flowing floral skirt and colorful matching sheer blouse. Randall rose to greet her and invited her to sit next to his desk where she discreetly crossed her legs.

"So, what's on your mind this fine day?" asked Randall.

Elisa smiled her "I'm proud of myself" smile before announcing her latest accomplishment. "We can check off another box on the Tumor Board task. I have just gotten all the players to sign off on the first meeting."

Randall looked shocked, because he hadn't expected Elisa to pull this off so quickly. "Even General Surgery?"

Elisa slapped her thigh. "Yes! Even that blustery Sheltie, Chief of Surgery. He did spend most of the interview sneaking glimpses of my legs, but mission accomplished."

Randall raised both arms in triumph. "Way to go! Pretty sure my legs wouldn't have cut the mustard. When is the first meeting set for?"

Elisa looked a bit tentative. "Two weeks from this Thursday at 7:30. I know you probably don't like such an early start, but it was the best I could do, allowing for surgery schedules."

Randall waved an arm dismissively. "Not to worry. I expected that would be the case. Besides, the surgeons think they are the only ones who start early and it's their chance to make us plebes get up at the *cracker* of dawn. It's a power thing."

Elisa added more. "Oh, I've got the conference room on 4AS lined up and refreshments arranged. Radiology and Pathology will be there to show films and slides for each case. You'll just have to pick some cases to present. Medical Oncology already has a few selected."

Randall was enthused. The good news was beginning to outweigh the bad. "That's fantastic work! I couldn't have done it without you!"

Elisa blushed. "I'm sure you could have. Just not as fast! I'm sure you have lots of irons in the fire."

Randall nodded his assent. "Boy, tell me about it. And not all of them are VA projects. The good news is one of my inpatient consults 'canceled' at the last minute and I have some extra time to catch up."

Pascua Yaqui

Elisa looked curious. "What sort of nonVA projects do you have, if I may be so bold?

Randall was taken aback. He wasn't sure he wanted to share information about the QEG and wasn't sure how to explain it briefly. Yet an inner voice firmly suggested he try. "Hmm, I'm afraid a good description of my nonVA efforts may take some time. Plus, it's a bit of a weird story. Ask yourself if you're ready for that."

Elisa was undeterred. "Look. You just told me you had extra time now. I've seen weird things before and I'm not easily spooked. My mother always told me that when you have a problem to solve, it's best to share it with others. In the telling, you clarify the problems for yourself."

Randall looked once more to the ceiling tiles for guidance and they assured him Elisa's suggestion was sound. "Alright. I'll take a swing at it." Randall paused to organize his thoughts. "I guess the best place to start is with a brief story of some key events that led up to my project. In short, these events share one feature. Implausibility. They cannot be explained by anything we currently understand in science."

Elisa sat forward in her chair. "Oh, I love this. Do tell!"

Randall began by describing the unusual happenings both at home and at the VA. He said they suggested some form of nonverbal communication between living humans, as well as between living humans and deceased humans. He speculated some sort of telekinesis was moving inanimate objects and some sort of entity was inhabiting his house, creating problems.

Elisa's eyes grew wide. "Give me some examples."

Randall went on to describe how a head and neck cancer patient had, eight hours after his death, appeared to Randall and two of his staff. The experience had left the three of them spooked for weeks afterwards. He described being summoned by a strong mental alert to return to the hospital and receive a final message from a dying patient.

Elisa was on the edge of her seat. "Would you be shocked if I told you that both those sorts of things have happened to me?"

Randall felt a chill. "I would and I wouldn't. I guess what's happened has left me open to a broader world of weirdness. Should I go on? Or have you had enough?"

Elisa nodded. "Please. Keep talking."

Randall went on to tell Elisa of the unusual happenings at the various houses he'd previously lived in with his family. From these encounters he'd concluded the houses had been inhabited by disembodied spirits, in some cases rather malevolent. One of these spirits had moved a cabinet in front of the door to his baby daughter's bedroom. This prevented him from getting to her to remove a blanket that had mysteriously wrapped itself around her neck and was choking her. Somehow the child's distress had signaled Randall's wife, Zelda, to return in haste from a shopping trip. Even his young son had picked up on the warning. He noted he had a friend with a similar experience. He went on to describe the various exorcisms they had done which had rid them of these visitations.

Elisa interrupted. "I am familiar with those sorts of inhabitations as well."

Randall was taken aback again. "Pray tell, please explain how you have had such experiences at your young age."

"Please, Dr. B," said Elisa somewhat scoldingly. "I am 30 years old. I am not a spring chicken any more. More of a summer swan. I am afraid I would have to tell you more of my background for you to understand."

Randall nodded. "That we can do. First, let me just say that there are more stories like these that have led me and a small group of others to explore these phenomena. Being scientists, we have agreed to use experimental but eclectic investigational approaches. These range from standard science, like psychology, psychiatry, neurobiology and physics, to various religious or spiritual disciplines."

"That sounds quite ambitious," said Elisa. "Many philosophers and spiritual experts have been pursuing those ends for decades. What makes you think your group will get a breakthrough? Is there something new to your approach?"

Randall shrugged. "Perhaps. We are including and looking closely at subatomic physics for a clue. We think there might be a window using some elements of quantum theory. We've named ourselves the Quantum Entanglement Group or QEG. But more about that later. Right now, I want to hear about your background."

Elisa shifted forward in her seat, formulating her thoughts for a coherent delivery. "Okay, Dr. B, I'll try to keep it short. The bottom line is that I come from a lineage of folks who have a special gift. Some family history may help."

Randall nodded, quite curious. "Ah, yes, family history. In the beginning and in the end everything is in the genes. And I don't mean Levi's."

Elisa chuckled. "Very droll. As I may have mentioned before, my family originated in Puerto Rico. That's only half right. My mother, Juanita, was Puerto Rican. She claimed to be a fortune teller and she could sometimes get visions."

Randall was hooked on the story already. "That's a hoot! What about your grandparents? Did they have any 'gifts'?"

"There were some rumors that they had some special abilities, but I'm not sure about that," replied Elisa. "My grandfather ran a small tavern in Ponce with his brother Ronaldo until 1944."

"What changed then?" asked Randall.

Elisa leaned further forward. "World War II. Ronaldo decided to move to the US and start a cantina near the Mexican border. Soon after, my mother moved to the US and wound up helping Ronaldo."

Randall's face lit up. "I think I see where this is going. I'm betting your father was one of those cantina drinkers and met your mother at ye olde watering hole."

"You are correct," said Elisa. "In 1944, my mother was 20 and a certain fresh-faced lieutenant was 23. His name was Juan Angeles and he was very handsome. He noticed a barmaid named Juanita and she noticed him. Soon they were sitting at a private table every night sharing stories."

Randall couldn't resist adding a twist. "And soon they were sharing more than stories."

Elisa smiled and nodded. "Indeed. Turned out, Juan was from a small town in Sonora province called Magdalena de Kino. He was not Mexican. Rather he was a Pascua Yacqui Indian, a Native Mexican Indian tribe descended from the Aztecs. His family had a Shamanic background."

"I'm sure that's fodder for many tales," noted Randall. "So, both your mother and father had gifts for unusual perception. One would assume there are stories that you have about their abilities. And I would deduce perhaps you have inherited some of those gifts."

"Indeed, Mr. Holmes," announced Elisa. "You have surmised or perhaps foreseen the truth as we know it. I have tales that would startle the average listener. But I believe you are not average. I have a few more questions about your group and whether the membership is closed."

There were sounds of repeated loud throat clearing coming from Doris's office, followed by a firm knock on Randall's open office door. "Dr. B, I don't mean to interrupt, but there are some restless natives beginnin' a ritual dance outside in the waitin' hallway as I speak. Do you wish to address their grievances now or after the pendin' assault?"

"Dang!" uttered Randall. "Time to address the elephant in the hallway. I am most intrigued by what you have told me, Elisa. Let's continue this soon. I want to hear more details. I think I have just the spot for you in the QEG group, if you are so inclined."

Elisa held her hand to her heart. "Me? Really? I was just meditating yesterday on how I would love to deepen my connection with my spiritual roots, but I didn't know how. And now you offer this. Great!" Elisa glanced at her watch, and grabbed her clipboard. "I'll depart stage left to avoid the slings and arrows. I'll be in touch." She skipped out of the room.

Randall sat in wonder, pondering what machinations of the universe had been conspiring to bring Elisa to the department. *Did her inherited gifts explain her ability to read people, disarming their hard edges and stingers? Was this another quantum energy connection?*

Randall pondered further. The QEG meeting wasn't happening for at least a week or two, depending on what Joe Shepard could set up. Randall was anxious to hear Elisa's stories, but it probably would have to wait until he returned from the Vegas trip. The delay would give him time to bring Zelda up to speed and prepare her for the meeting. Randall hated waiting, but there was nothing for it but to hold fire.

Come On Down

It had been midafternoon by the time the open house was over. After all the phone calls and Elisa's visit, Randall had to hustle to catch up with the remaining work. He thanked the gods that Dr. Sheltie had not called down for after-loading catheter placement. He'd almost forgotten about the prospect of that further interfering with the day's work.

Randall tried to finish his mountain of paperwork, but had trouble concentrating. He kept flashing back to what abilities Elisa's parents might possess. He wondered how much of it might have gotten handed down to Elisa or, indeed, her sister. He imagined successful rain dances, conjuring of spirits, and miraculous healing ceremonies. Maybe even resurrections!

Randall's mental disconnect persisted throughout the rest of the day. During one follow-up, he fell silent while taking the patient's recent history. Thoughts of the NRG meeting repeatedly distracted him. The patient waited for Randall to continue, but when he didn't, the patient finally got up and shook Randall's shoulder to see if he was alright. Randall jerked to attention and responded that he was fine, just considering the man's symptoms. He struggled to stay focused on his work for the rest of the day. However, the effort drained him to the point that when he finished with the scheduled patients, he decided to head home early even with the large pile of unfinished paperwork on his desk. His brain was full.

At home, Randall went right up to bed, laid down and fell immediately into a deep dreamless sleep. When he didn't respond to a call for dinner, Zelda came upstairs and found him totally zonked. She sat down on the bed next to him and gently shook his shoulder until one eye fluttered open.

"Hey there, big boy," she said softly. "Where have you been?"

Randall opened a second eye and looked rapidly right and left. "Where am I?"

"Dead asleep in your little bed," replied Zelda. "Where did you think you were?"

Randall cleared his dry throat several times before speaking again. "Harumph . . . harumph. . . . I think I was in Mexico in an Indian sweat lodge."

Zelda raised an eyebrow. "Indians in Mexico? That's rich!"

Randall pulled himself partially upright on his elbows and coughed. "It's not so weird if you know anything about Mexican history. Descendants of the Aztecs living mostly in the northern parts of Mexico lived there for centuries. They were persecuted by the Mexican government and ethnically cleansed. A few tribes still remain in Sonora and southern Arizona."

Zelda looked befuddled. "Wherever did that piece of trivia come from to land in your dream world?"

Randall coughed again. "That's a longer story."

"How about I get you a fresh cup of joe to help you wake up for dinner," offered Zelda. "Then, you take some time to tell me. Dinner will keep for a while. The tuna casserole is still in the oven."

"Oo boy!" croaked Randall. "Tuna slop! That will hit the spot."

Zelda rose from the bed. "Thanks for using the correct 'S' word. Be right back."

When Zelda returned with his coffee, he reckoned he'd be better telling her about Vegas sooner than later.

Randall propped himself up with another pillow under his head, grabbed the hot cup and took a sip of coffee. "Ah! That spots the hit! Before I unravel the Indian story, I've got good news and bad. Which do you want first?"

Zelda squinted at Randall. "I'll bite. Start with good news."

Randall smiled. "I don't have to do the Detroit VA site visit this weekend."

Zelda smiled back, thinking that the bad news couldn't be worse than the Detroit trip. "Alright! What's the bad news?"

Randall pulled back a corner of his mouth and half closed one eye. "Instead, I have to fly to Las Vegas for the weekend for an NRG meeting. Del Aguilar orders."

Zelda raised both arms. "What? He's not in charge of you anymore. What do you mean 'have to'?"

Randall put down his coffee cup and made a calming gesture with both hands. "Now, now, don't get upset. I was going to have to go somewhere this weekend anyhow and this was the better choice. It was the lesser of two weevils and could benefit us in the long run."

Zelda was only partially appeased. "Is that the royal 'us?'"

Randall explained the call with del Aguilar and Zelda gradually understood. She became less miffed. Her opinion of del Aguilar hadn't improved since he'd called her into his office to help "control" Randall during residency.

Zelda sighed in disgust. "Alright. I get it. I still don't trust that Cuban midget. I guess the Vegas trip is the best of two bad choices. Enough about that. Tell me more about the Mexican Indian thing."

Randall recounted the conversation he'd had with Elisa and his interest in learning more about her Shamanic background. Zelda was equally fascinated. The subject of Zelda's possible involvement in the QEG meetings arose again. Randall was glad for the segue and told her about the phone call he'd had that day with Joe Shepard in which they had decided to add one or two lay people to the group of experts.

"That's a fantastic idea, Randy," chirped Zelda. "Professors and Pastors aren't the only ones with valid opinions about this weird stuff. So, you're saying you'd want me in the group too? And why?"

Randall nodded vigorously. "That's easy. You may not realize it, but you've already done a lot of research into multiple religions and traditions. You've done explorations of spiritual energy and experiences with non-physical entities. You've read Khalil Gibran, Edgar Cayce, Course in Miracles, the Koran and the Bible. It hasn't been formal course work, but that makes it even better. You've been free to choose what fits best for you, not to accept some proposed doctrine or go to Hell without a return ticket. From your visits to the spiritual buffet, you have constructed a working theory of the unifying ingredients of many beliefs and built one unique to yourself."

Zelda rose from the bed and gave Randy a wet kiss on the cheek. "Dang! I never thought of it that way. You may have something there. If that's really the way you feel, you can count me in for your group. I'd love the chance to show up those stuffed shirts. Of course, I don't mean you, but . . . well . . . you know. Just one little problem."

Randall frowned. "Problem?"

Zelda pointed an accusatory finger at his nose. "Yeah, big boy. Did you forget we've got two little urchins? If we both go to the meeting we'd have to get a sitter or bring them along."

"Hmm, good point," mused Randall. "Then, we'll just have the QEG meeting here at Casa Biedermeier."

Zelda's face performed cartwheels of emotion. "Umm . . . here? Wow, I get to rub shoulders with the bigwigs! Show them the value of the creative mind. Umm . . . All those important people here, in our kid infested, disorganized artist den of a house? I'll have to clean the windows . . . and polish the wood floor. And. . . ."

Randall saw where this train was going. "Zel, it's alright. Slow down. We have time to think about it. And it can be somewhere else. Maybe even Joe's house."

Zelda flipped her indignant switch. "What, our house isn't good enough for them? No, sir, we are having it here, and proudly share our bounty! When the heck is it, anyway? Certainly not this weekend, cuz you get to go play in Vegas." Zelda crossed her arms and huffed.

A heavy blanket of despair settled on Randall's shoulders, urging him to go back to sleep. "Yes, dear." He snapped himself back to the moment. "We will figure it out, darling. I'm hungry for some of your famous tuna casserole. Ah! The elixir of life."

Appeased for the moment, Zelda led Randall down to the kitchen and served up the delectable tuna casserole. Randall 'ooohed' and 'aahed' the meal throughout dinner, easing back into her good graces for the rest of the evening. They poured themselves into bed for the night, grateful there was just one more day in the work week.

CHAPTER 20

———

JUST STALLING

"We think too much and feel too little"

—Charles Chaplin

FLORENCE NIGHTINGALE

Randall woke up surprisingly refreshed the next morning. He was delighted to find that Zelda was also in good spirits. He surmised this meant that she was still feeling positive about the QEG meeting. He had no time to get involved in another discussion about it this morning. That could happen after work. He had an early meeting at the hospital to interview the new nurse promised by Mr. Samuels.

The traffic gods blessed him. He arrived in time to park and visit the executive bathroom for comfort. He sent heavenward prayers of gratitude that the Center Director's wingtip shoes did not peek out from under the stall door.

When Randall got to the department he stopped at Doris's desk. "Good morning young lady. You're looking well."

Doris frowned. "I guess looks can be deceivin'. Be warned. They's a GI flu bug goin' 'round. I spent the night worshippin' at the porcelain throne. But amazingly, I'm feelin' right better this mornin'. So good, I couldn't justify stayin' home. Oh, and Elisa won't be in today. She done got it too. She had to go to the ER for feedin' and waterin.'"

447

Randall shook his head in sympathy. "Creeping grunge! That's the worst. Hope both of you get a ride on the road to recovery. What's the morning look like?"

Doris pointed to Randall's office. "Your nurse candidate, Judy Janus, is already waitin' in your office. She's a might early. She seems nice. Try not to scare her off. After that, it's business as usual."

Randall smiled. Doris was well enough to jibe him. "Sure thing. I'm feeling fairly benign this morning."

Randall walked into his office. The slender young woman sitting next to his desk rose and offered her hand in greeting. Her coffee with cream colored skin was further highlighted by her white nurse's uniform. Tight cornrows framed a face that was rather cherubic. Rising from the chair, she stood a full two inches taller than Randall. She reached down slightly to shake his hand.

The woman greeted Randall with a melodic voice. "Hello, Dr. Biedermeier, I'm Judy Janus, your new clinic nurse. Please call me Judy. I believe Dr. Newberry told you about me. So nice to meet you. Your secretary asked me to wait here in your office."

"Ah, nice to meet you as well, Judy," replied Randall. He took her hand and squeezed it politely. "I was expecting you, but you beat me here. Please, everyone calls me Dr. B. If you're pressed for time, you can just call me DB. Saves one syllable. Hiring you was unusually fast work for the VA."

Judy laughed brightly. "Yes, apparently someone upstairs likes you, Dr. B. Or your wheels have been squeaking loudly."

Randall laughed back. "Hopefully, both. Have a seat again and tell me about yourself. Are you a new hire or an in-house transfer?" Randall alit in his 'endowed' desk chair.

Judy began her story. "I'm an in-house transfer from the ER. I'm really looking forward to working with you and learning more about your department. You've got a really good reputation in the hospital. I don't know how you do it, considering the challenging nature of a government hospital!"

Randall suspected he might be getting buttered up, but he was enjoying it anyhow. "I'm not sure either, but I have a feeling we're about to get better at it. What's your VA story?"

Judy was surprised by the unexpected praise. She blushed and smoothed her skirt before responding. "Well, I completed my nurse's training at this VA. I started in the Internal Medicine ward on 4CS. I spent half my time on the ward and the other half helping to staff the outpatient clinic. I liked the job alright, and did it pretty well. I guess no bit of competence goes unpunished, so the nursing service transferred me to the ER."

Randall took a deep breath. "Well, I'll have to make a note to cut back on my competence. Wouldn't want to end up there! Go on. . . ."

Judy chuckled. "I've been there for about four years. It was challenging at first and I enjoyed it. But lately . . . well . . . it's just become too demanding. I have come to realize that I don't like to make quick decisions under pressure. I get more satisfaction out of spending some time with patients so that I can develop a relationship. In the ER it's just 'one and done.'"

Randall nodded. "I get that. That's one of the reasons I like Radiation Oncology. You see the patient over a longer period and really get to know them. The patients under treatment come daily, Monday through Friday, and we see them in review at least weekly. After treatment, they come for follow-up at regular intervals depending on response and outcome."

Judy was pleased with Randall's description. "That sounds ideal for me. Also, over the last few years, I've developed an interest in Oncology and I want to learn more about it. I'm hoping you can help direct me to some foundational reading to catch up on the basics. Do you have an idea about how you want to use me to help run the clinic?"

This was already more than Randall was expecting. He was getting a good feeling about Judy's transfer to his department. "I can give you the broad brushstrokes. After that, I'm hoping you can take the ball and run with it. I'm too busy to plan it all in detail. I'll leave that to you. The biggest problem we might have is to get buy-in from our staff to any changes you try to make. Even if it's for their own good, they abhor change in their routine even if it's a bad routine. You will have the job of selling whatever you come up with."

"I understand," said Judy. "It's nothing I haven't encountered before. I'm pretty good at the 'soft sell'."

Randall gave Judy a thumbs up of approval. "Excellent! That's my philosophy too. No part of the VA likes rapid change. You have to sneak up on it. To get to the nuts and bolts, I'd like you to basically run the clinic. For that, you'll have to coordinate with the three Radiation Therapy Techs, Grace, Molly and Melinda. They set up the daily treatment schedule and keep track of when the patients need on-treatment reviews. Also, you will have to work with Doris regarding the new consults and follow-up patient scheduling. You've already met Doris. I'll take you around and introduce you to the other staff when we're done here."

"Will I have an office to work out of?" asked Judy. "I like to be efficient and thorough."

Randall wasn't prepared for that query. He thought fast. "I was thinking, *just seconds ago*, you could use the office just to the left of the main entrance as you come in. It was previously used by our Chief Tech, Al Kornberg, until he retired. Now, it's just used a few days a week by Stephanie, Mr. Samuels' secretary. She helps Doris with some coding we're piloting for charge retrieval. That office would be an ideal spot to meet and greet the patients as they come in. I'll leave it to you to figure out how to share the space with Stephanie."

Judy had been taking notes on a legal pad. She finished writing with a flourish. "Oh, yes, I saw that office when I came down here. That's all the questions I have. Do you have anything else you want me to do?"

Randall smiled and slowly nodded. "Actually, lots else. You will be responsible for developing the routines to take patients into exam rooms and setting up charts for me. You will do an initial interview, get vital signs, weigh the patient, and notify me when the patient is ready. There will also be other nursing duties, including, but not limited to, skin care for patients with radiation skin reactions, assistance with procedures, injections, etc. And let's not forget scut work that could include clean-ups of . . . hmm . . . bodily fluids."

Judy had expected worse and laughed in relief. "Sounds familiar! I guess no department escapes that tidbit. I do have one related question. How much authority do I have in working with the other staff?"

Again, Randall had to pause to process the question. He tapped his pencil on the desk and Judy waited patiently for his answer. "How you get all that I described to work is up to you, but I expect to be kept in the loop so I don't get caught out. I'm fairly certain that when changes start to happen, I will have a parade of folks coming into my office with comments and criticisms. If I don't know the plan, I won't know how to respond."

Judy sat forward in her chair. "I understand. That's more guidance than I ever got in the ER. They set me loose and I had to figure things out on my own. They'd only 'talk' to me when I didn't guess the rules correctly."

Randall pressed his lips together and gave Judy a knowing nod. "Tell you what. To ease the transition, I'll have you shadow me for a week to get a feel for the operation. Then, you'll have some time to de-velop a plan and present it to me. You and I will go over it. After some massaging, we'll finalize it, and I'll have you present it at the weekly staff meeting. There, we'll take all the comments and write them down, promise to modify as needed, and implement."

Judy raised an index finger and pointed to Randall. "Got it! No buy-in from staff without a sense of involvement." She made a few more notes on her paper.

Randall added a slightly sarcastic addendum. "Plus, you never know, the staff might actually suggest something better than we think up."

"Yes, there is that," agreed Judy, smiling broadly. "I think I get the picture. You know, I have the afternoon off and don't officially start here until Monday. We could start the shadowing this afternoon."

Randall gave three pencil drum beats on his desk. "That's fine with me. Just one more question before we finish."

The train of conversation was derailed momentarily when Doris knocked on the open door and waited for a response.

Randall held up a finger and turned to Doris. "What is it, Doris?"

Doris looked a bit strained. "Sorry to interrupt, Dr. B, but I've got bad news that's good news and good news that's bad news or good news."

Randall and Judy looked puzzled trying to parse out Doris's riddle.

Randall motioned Doris into the room. "Come on in and spill the news, Doris. We have no secrets from our new clinic nurse. I presume you two have already met?"

"Yes, we have," said Doris. "I don't know how we got so lucky to have such a pretty petunia in this onion patch. We had a nice chat while we waited for you to reappear. I might have already known about the new clinic nurse part. Mercy me, my poor little brain can't remember how I know that."

Randall had to chuckle. "I know. With you it's always something about a diminutive avian. So, what's popping?"

Doris giggled. "Little birdies are my magic helpers. Anyhoo, that little old bus that brings our follow-up patients down here from way up north at the Iron Mountain VA broke down near Green Bay. Even if they get it fixed today, the bus won't make it in time for appointments and then they're stuck 400 miles from home. Basically, a bunch of your follow-ups and consults for the mornin' and early afternoon are canceled, but fear not. There are still some locals that will be comin'."

Randall was confused. "Let me get this straight. Is that the bad news that's also good news?"

Doris nodded then shook her head. "It's also good, because Dr. Newberry called to inform us that we're gettin' an unannounced 'Congressional' today. So the time you won't be spendin' with those canceled patients will be spent meetin' with Dr. Newberry and our State Representative."

Now Randall and Judy were really confused. "What's a 'Congressional'?" asked Judy.

Randall shrugged his shoulders.

Doris invoked her sixth grade teacher's voice. "Apparently, some of our veteran patients have written Representative Sensenheimer, from our District 5, about some veteran issues at this VA, includin' some about our department. So, the congressman and his entourage are conductin' an on-site visit to look into things. Oh, and the best part, he's bringin' along a reporter and photographer from the Milwaukee Journal. The VA drops everythin' for these visits, so when they say 'jump' we say, 'how high?'"

Randall stood up from his chair. "*The* Representative Sensenheimer? The one that's always in the news squawking about veteran's rights?"

"The very one," said Doris. "He's a friend of Senator Hobbes' family. You know, the dead Senator this place is named after? I've heard he's influential in gettin' fundin' for this VA. Somethin' about the House Committee on Veterans Affairs. He's a mighty rooster to this flock."

"Faith and begorrah!" muttered Randall. "Be strong, my heart." Randall flopped back into his chair, feeling suddenly weak in the knees.

Doris put a hand on Randall's shoulder. "Don't worry, Dr. B. Judy and I will be here to support you. Right, Judy?"

Judy was quick to agree. "With faith and friends, one can overcome anything. I'm with you all the way. You know, I'm surprised Congress cares about what affairs veterans are having."

Doris got the joke first and burst out laughing. "My goodness. The lady has a sense of humor. I hope we're keepin' her."

Randall caught the reference a few beats later and had a good laugh. He let out a breath. "We are, indeed. But be warned. I take a dim view of those who try to best me in the terrible joke department."

The laughter had Randall feeling better about the coming challenge. "Alrighty then! The gauntlet has been thrown down and the lemons served. Let's make lemonade. Doris, get the Ortho room set up for visitors. See if anyone brought in bakery and get some coffee perking. Get some goodies down from the Canteen if necessary. Something to eat always calms the savage beast."

Doris made a curtsy and headed out to get things prepared. Randall looked back to Judy. "Now, for that last question I was about to ask."

Judy spread out both arms palms up. "I'm ready. Ask away."

Randall cocked his head and pursed his lips. "Assume that I am paranoid and that I never take anything at face value. I could call upstairs and ask a lot of questions of your previous supervisors. Or I could just ask you what are the worst things they would tell me about you."

Judy glanced around the room, considering her options. She decided to be totally honest and not obfuscate by saying something like "they would say I work too hard." She sighed and spoke quietly. "I think they would tell you that sometimes I got too close to my patients."

Randall wasn't sure how to take that. "How would that be a bad thing?"

Again, Judy carefully considered her response. The interview had been going well and she didn't want to scotch her chances. She decided on full disclosure up front. "As in I would spend too much time with some patients and not be as efficient as I could be. And . . . and there was an issue with what they called proselytizing. I called it praying with dying patients and providing comfort. They said VA rules don't allow espousing religious beliefs with patients."

Randall had not previously heard proselytizing was a VA issue, but figured the hospital had to be non-denominational. "I see. My next question might be too personal to answer. You can choose whether to answer it. If you decline, I won't press you further. What led you to use prayer with the patients?"

Judy knew she had best continue on the full disclosure path. Randall would find out anyhow if he went through her HR records. "You should know that the transfer of departments was not just my decision. You see, I was diagnosed with acute lymphoblastic leukemia two years ago and spent six months on sick leave while I underwent chemotherapy."

That fact came to Randall out of far left field. "Wow, that's awful. You must have been really sick."

Judy's face started to cloud over and tears were brewing. "I was. The chemo was terrible. I lost 40 pounds, but I got through it with the help of Jesus. I gained back 20 pounds, so I don't look quite as bad as when I finished." She patted her short hair.

Randall noted that Judy's close cropped hair wasn't just a hair style. "I'd say you look just fine now. If you hadn't told me, I wouldn't have guessed."

Judy placed her hand on the silver cross necklace that hung near her heart. "I had a complete response and I've been disease free for almost two years now. My mother is a devout Christian, but it never caught on with me until I got sick. I'm certain it was with God's help that I'm sitting here talking to you now. The VA let me go back to full time work a year and a half ago, but I found I just can't tolerate the pace of work in the ER."

Randall looked up at his picture of a 1935 Duesenberg hanging behind where Judy sat. "Tell me more about your leukemia treatment. I'm guessing it was pretty rough. That is, if you're comfortable talking about it."

The brewing tears finally spilled over but Judy didn't cry. "After my third round of chemo, my white blood cell counts tanked and I got pneumonia. I was in the ICU for three days on a respirator. My mother would visit and pray for me. I was so scared. At night, when I was lying there alone, I started to pray to Jesus to save me. It might have been a dream, but one night I opened my eyes to the touch of a hand on my forehead. There he was, at my bedside, in his robes and blessing me. I felt clear-headed and free of any drug-induced stupor. From then on, I knew I would be alright. And I was. I still am. But I'm different."

"Wow!" said Randall. "That's quite the experience."

Judy nodded faintly and she wiped her eyes with a tissue. "I know it sounds crazy when I say it out loud. But since my recovery, I've tried to bring that same hope and comfort to my patients. The VA rules just didn't have any tolerance for it."

Randall felt a bit like crying himself. "Have you told any of this to your nursing supervisors or staff?"

Judy made a stop gesture with her hand. "Not a chance. They already were shunning me when I came back to work. They just looked at me like I was the 'about to be dead' nurse. Nobody wanted to be friends with the 'walking dead.' I didn't want to add 'crazy' on top of that. Then, one day they caught me praying with a patient and, well, you know the rest."

"Umm," mused Randall. "So, you and the VA mutually decided a change would be best for all concerned?"

Judy nodded. "Well, actually . . . I had prayed to Jesus the night before to help me get out of the ER job. The nursing supervisor pulled me out of the ER and told me I was moving. That's about it."

Randall wasn't sure why Judy had trusted him with a story so personal. "So, why did you feel safe telling me what you've been holding so close? After all, you barely know me."

Judy squinted and looked away for a second. "I honestly don't know. I may not know you from personal contact, but I know you from what others say. I guess I figured that it would be okay and that we could start with a clean slate; you know, tabula rasa."

Randall put a hand gently on Judy's arm. "That's good enough for me. The VA may frown on mixing religion with patient care, but I believe that spirituality and human connection have a huge effect on patients' hope and ability to heal. That need is particularly strong in cancer patients. It seems to have been the case with your leukemia. Just telling my patients your story is more inspiration than I can provide. And it sounds like your prayer helped bring you here, too. As I said earlier, as long as my goals are met, and I see no publicly overt proselytizing, I'm good. Are you up for that challenge?"

Judy breathed a sigh of relief. "I think so. And I can adjust to each patient's spiritual belief system, whether it's God or the Universe, Jesus or even a Unicorn!" She laughed. "I'd better be up for the challenge if we're going to survive the 'Congressional.'"

Randall smiled at the veracity of her joke, and felt relieved and ready for the next challenge. "Good. I'm glad you said 'we.' Let's take the busman's tour and go meet the troops. I'll grab some charts and show you how the charting system works. The Radiation Oncology record is kept separately from the hospital record because we have so many other forms to document what we do. Some copies of our work are added to the hospital chart. We also keep all the X-rays we take for treatment setup separate from what Radiology stores. That should occupy us until the firing squad calls for us to stand before the wall."

Judy smiled and wiped her eyes. "So, we have to store all those records down here?"

"We do," said Randall. "That's what all the filing is in your new office space. That's what makes it ideal for setting up patients as they arrive. You'll have to order the hospital charts from medical records for all new patients and follow-ups. Come on, let's start the tour. We'll end up with your future office."

Congressional

Randall took Judy around and introduced her to the rest of the staff with Doris tagging along. Everyone was surprised at the turn of events and they were very welcoming. Judy seemed to make a good first impression. They ended the tour at Judy's new office, as promised.

Judy looked around. "I didn't notice it before, but there's a window in the wall facing the hallway. You can see right in to my desk. That should help to spot patients when they come in."

Randall waved his hand towards the wall window. "Yeah, it was meant to be an opening through which the department receptionist could meet incoming patients, but we never got a receptionist. Before I got here, my retired Chief Tech used the desk and had the VA put a window in."

"Whatever for?" asked Judy.

Randall rolled his eyes. "He told me he didn't want patients popping into his office. The window allowed him to wave them along."

Judy was stupefied. "He couldn't even do that simple job function? What kept him so busy he couldn't meet and greet patients?"

Randall shrugged. "You catch on quickly. Apparently you've learned about the VA culture. He was basically lazy. Mostly he sat at his desk smoking his stinky pipe and getting tobacco on the floor. Then the VA banned smoking in the building and he was at a loss for what to do. He never helped treat patients or interact with them or the techs in any way. He did order supplies. He was fairly good at spending down our micro-budget."

Judy had to laugh. "So, prototypical VA employee, huh? Didn't do much, but worked hard at it."

Randall chuckled. "Yes, aptly put. I'm afraid there's still some of them around. Present company excluded, of course."

They shared a mutual nod of understanding.

Randall kept the tour moving. "Okay—here's an example of one of our Radiation Oncology charts. It's divided up into sections as shown on this table of...."

Randall was interrupted by a knock on the office's hallway window. He turned to see the Chief of Staff, Dr. Newberry, standing in the office doorway with a small group clustered behind him. He hadn't expected the visit to come so soon, since he was told his small department would be inspected near the end of the visit. Dr. Newberry was wearing his power suit with a bold red tie. That meant serious business.

"Uh, oh," Randall uttered to Judy, under his breath. "Don't look now, but the barbarians have arrived. Follow my lead and smile a lot."

Randall put down the demo chart and took Judy's arm. He led her forward to greet the Chief of Staff.

Randall reached out to shake Newberry's hand. "Ah, Dr. Newberry, our local juggling champion! This is Judy Janus, the clinic nurse you so kindly expedited for us. This is her first day here. I believe she will do a great job. I was just giving her an orientation."

Newberry took Judy's hand and gave it a gentlemanly squeeze. "Good to put a face to a name. Welcome aboard, Judy."

Judy beamed an angel's smile. "Sirs, I thank you both, very much, for the opportunity. Who are these other fine folks you have with you?"

Randall was impressed with Judy's seemingly effortless segue.

Newberry held out an arm towards his entourage. "This group makes up the Congressional Tour that I called about earlier. First, I'd like to introduce the Honorable John Sensenheimer, our state's Congressional Representative from the fifth district. As you know, this VA is in his district."

Randall and Judy shook Sensenheimer's hand. He was a tall, stocky man in his fifties with thinning hair and the look of a former athlete going to seed. He had a good head start on jowl formation. His grip was a bit limp and he had little to say in greeting, but he did break a slight smile when taking Judy's hand.

Sensenheimer gave Newberry an odd look. "What's this about juggling champion, Newberry?"

Randall intercepted the question. "That's the honorary title we've given Dr. Newberry for his ability to juggle resources."

Sensenheimer just grunted. Newberry gave Randall a quick look that said "nice save."

Newberry continued his introductions. "These two ladies are Representative Sensenheimer's top aides; Mary Kelly and Sylvia de Camp. Did I get that right?"

Mary Kelly bowed slightly. "Yes, doctor."

Newberry continued the introductions. "Mary Kelly and Sylvia are here to take notes and be an extra pair of eyes." This time, head nods replaced handshakes. "Lastly, these two gentlemen are from the Milwaukee Journal. Forgive me, but I've lost sight of your names. Please introduce yourselves." Newberry waved a dismissing hand.

A bald man with thick glasses responded first. "Sure, doc. I'm Alex Barthelmy. I do feature articles for the Journal and this is my photographer, Joc Pietersen. The camera equipment hanging from his neck gives it away. Ha ha." No one laughed. Alex handed out his business card.

Joc freed up a hand from his camera gear to wave a greeting to Randall and Judy. "Yeah, all Alex has to carry is a notepad and pencil."

Alex reached out a hand to both Randall and Judy. "Yeah, Joc is always jealous 'cause I don't have to lug a ton of gear."

Randall was anxious to learn the reason for this special visit. "If you don't mind me asking, what exactly have you come here to see?" All eyes turned to Randall as if he'd asked a forbidden question. He felt his mouth go a bit dry. "I mean, in order to best help you, and not waste your time, 'cause I know you're all busy people. . . ."

Representative Sensenheimer was used to guarded reactions to his visits and responded in a pastoral tone. "Don't worry, Dr. Biedermeier. You're not in trouble. I get that reaction a lot on these visits. I'm here in response to some constituent letters I've received, all quite positive regarding this department. However, some were rather negative about some other VA services. I want to learn more details about what you do here, how you do it, and how we may help you to do it better. In addition, what we learn here may help us improve other departments."

Randall had not expected this and needed to revise his strategy.

Judy filled in the silence gap, hardly missing a beat. "Well, sirs. I've just completed my first tour of the department. It's all new to me, but from what I've seen so far this department is well buttoned up. I didn't know much about Radiation Oncology before, but I believe working here is going to be a wonderful adventure for me. I'm sure Dr. Biedermeier could give you the same tour."

Judy's words of praise gave Randall time to rearrange his mental synapses. He dove right in. "I certainly could!"

Judy took the reins again. "Dr. Biedermeier has set up a room for us to gather after the tour and chat about what we've seen. During that time I'm sure he can discuss his vision for the future of the department. His secretary, Doris, has requisitioned some refreshments as well."

Sensenheimer cracked his first smile since arriving. "Is there coffee?"

Randall stood straighter and raised an index finger. "Yes, there is. And pastry!"

Senseheimer's smile broadened and Joc Pietersen let out an "Oh, boy!" Randall lifted his gaze to the heavens with a silent prayer of gratitude to the guardian angel who brought Judy to the department.

Judy began to herd the group along for the tour. "Alright, everybody. Follow me and listen while Dr. B narrates."

Newberry moved the group along from the rear. "'Lead on, McDuff.'"

The open house had given Randall the opportunity to refine his patter for the department tour. As the tour progressed, he painted a clear picture of the treatment and follow-up process. He answered questions with alacrity as they went along. Judy suggested photo ops at key locations. The department staff were well prepared to answer questions

about their duties. Barthelmy and Sensenheimer's two scribes took pro-
digious notes as they went. Newberry piped in with appropriate sub-
stantiating comments at key moments. Finally, the participants pleaded
for a coffee break and Randall brought them to the Ortho room.

Doris was already there, waiting for the group. Laid out before
them, along with fresh fruit, were three different varieties of Racine
Danish Kringles: apple, strawberry and cream cheese. Their alluring fragrance could be detected out in the hallway. Doris was posted next to
the kringles, guarding them from poachers or escape.

Sensenheimer walked into the Ortho room and threw up both
hands. "Oh, happy days! Kringles! My favorite pastry in the world.
How did you know?"

Randall motioned towards Doris. "Meet the department's secret
weapon, sir. This is my secretary, Doris Mims. She selected the pastry.
She is all knowing and all seeing. No one knows how it's done, but we
just accept her powers."

Sensenheimer nodded in agreement. "Indeed, a good aide makes all
the difference. Mary and Sylvia are my surge protectors. Can't survive
without them. Too many balls to keep in the air at one time."

Newberry chimed in on that. "You got that right. In my case, it's
Sharon O'Bannon, my Assistant COS. Without her behind the scenes
work, I'd get nothing done. In fact, it was her poking around that en-
gineered the pair up of Miss Janus with Radiation Oncology. I predict
good things."

Doris became the cruise director. "Well, thank all y'all kind gentlemen for speakin' so highly of us comfort keepers. I say that's enough
sweet talk for now. It's time for some sweet munchin'. Y'all dig in and
start piggin'."

Sensenheimer gave Doris an initial harsh look that quickly melted
away to a guffaw of laughter that the group soon joined in on. With no
further delay, they began to graze on pastry. Kringles and coffee quickly
disappeared. The caffeine and glucose filled the room with a buzz of
conversation and laughter until Sensenheimer signaled the group to
freshen their coffee one last time and take their seats.

When everyone was settled, Sensenheimer began speaking. "Let me explain in more detail why we are here. My office has received a number of letters from veteran constituents lauding the care they received in this department. How many was it?"

"Nine, sir," chirped Mary Kelly.

Sensenheimer nodded. "Right, nine. Thanks, Mary Kelly. And, in almost every one of the letters, mention was made about a notable lack of resources provided to the department. The inadequacies included lack of space, outdated equipment, and under-staffing to care for a large patient load. There was some suggestion in the letters that a certain Dr. Biedermeier may have coached these veterans to write to their state representative, but I'll rule that as hearsay evidence."

Randall nodded his head trying to look innocent. There was momentary silence as this disclosure sank in.

Newberry broke the silence. "I think I can explain, sir."

Sensenheimer flicked his hand, dismissing the idea. "No need. I know the drill. The VA allots you a budget pie based on an outdated paradigm and you have only so many slices to go around. You spackle and fill where you can to keep things going, but there's never enough pie for all the mouths you have to feed."

Newberry nodded his assent. "That's about right, sir. Great analogy."

Sensenheimer chuckled. "It should be. I got it from you."

Newberry flushed a bit when he remembered he'd used the pie analogy when pleading for money to support the cardiac cath lab.

Sensenheimer continued before he could respond. "Based on what I've seen today, I'd say that you all have been doing the best you can, but you can't do better without some outside help."

The two aides busied themselves taking copious notes.

Sensenheimer zeroed in on Randall. "So, tell me, Dr. Biedermeier, in a nutshell, what would it take to bring you up to speed? Are there published standards for space, staffing and equipment based on workload?"

Randall took a deep breath. He had a sales pitch that had been brewing for years! "There are. The American College of Radiology has put out consensus-based criteria in their national journal. The basic numbers they use to set the requirements are new patients seen per year, patients under treatment per day, number of treatments per year and follow-ups per year."

Newberry knew the data, but asked Randall to tell Sensenheimer. "What are your numbers?"

Randall had the numbers etched on his retina. "We see 450 new patients per year, do 10,000 patient treatments per year, average 40-45 patients under treatment per day, and see about 1,000 follow-ups yearly."

Randall paused a beat to let the data sink in.

The Congressman raised his eyebrows. "Really? I had no idea the workload was that high. What resources do the ACR criteria say you should have to handle that number of cases?"

Randall rattled off the numbers like a Tommy gun. "They say we should have 5,000 square feet of space. We have 1,500. We are like the old lady in the shoe. We should have two high energy treatment units. We have one. We should have a fluoroscopic treatment simulation unit, but the cupboard is bare."

Sensenheimer raised his finger. "What is a simulator? What does it simulate?"

Randall pointed to Dan Graham, who was picking Kringle crumbs off a platter. "This is Dan Graham, our Radiation Physicist. He's more qualified than I am to answer questions about simulators. He was busy with some calculations when your group arrived. He came in during our Kringle feeding frenzy."

Dan swallowed, grabbed a napkin and wiped some Kringle crumbs off his tie. "Hmmmph. Well, hello, everybody. Nice to meet you all. A radiation simulator is used to prepare the treatment setup before we use the Linac. We use fluoroscopic images to visualize the area we are going to treat. It's a dry run of the process and then we don't need to use the treatment unit to set up the patient. It saves resources and time. Plus it improves treatment accuracy."

Randall nodded. "That's right! It would definitely make us more efficient."

Dan thought of another urgent need. "Oh, and we would like to be able to have better equipment for implanting and monitoring radioactive sources. Remote after-loading devices and dosimetry monitoring systems would be high on that list." Dan paused, composing his list. "Right now, we have to send patients who need that over to County Hospital and pay them on a per case basis. We'd save the cost of the new equipment in one year if we didn't have to send those patients away."

Sensenheimer looked like he was trying to comprehend it all. "Is that everything you need?"

Randall couldn't stop himself chuckling. "Not even close! We should have six Radiation Therapy Technologists. We have three. We should have two Radiation Physicists and one Dosimetrist. We have one and none. We should have two secretaries, one receptionist and two nurses. We have one, none and one. Oh, and I almost forgot, we should have three Radiation Oncologists and we have me."

The resulting silence was deafening. Sensenheimer shook his head and looked around the room. Everyone else studied the floor.

Randall decided to give himself a plug. "But I'm pretty good."

The room erupted in laughter.

"We'll hold off on that judgment," responded Newberry.

Sensenheimer just smiled. "Sounds like you have been working with about half of what you need. Which means you've been working double time, unless you have a stunt double?"

Randall blushed. "It's all me and my team, but we're certainly ready for help."

Newberry took the lead. "Look, I know all those numbers. Randall has been drilling them into me for a while, but the congressman is correct. The budget just does not cut it. And I want that off the record. I do not want to see that in tomorrow's paper, understood?"

"You got it, Chief," said Alex. "We understand the position you're in. We're going to write this up to reflect the good that happens here and the better times ahead. I am sure, given the Congressman's past record, he will find a way to direct some resources on this department's behalf."

"Indeed, my son," confirmed Sensenheimer. "It's what I intended. Don't think you've intimidated me in that direction. But your point is duly noted. I take veteran's care seriously and I think we have a chance here to make this a center of excellence."

Randall decided to butter the bread. "That would certainly show, sir, how we have thrived under your leadership. How can we help with that?"

Sensenheimer puffed up. "Write up a report detailing what you just told us, including what corrective steps are needed. Put together an equipment and salary budget with recommendations for vendors. Work with Dr. Newberry on expansion plans and a budget for construction. That will be a bit longer in planning, but we need something to act on. Can you do that?"

Randall saluted. "Yes, sir. I can deploy memos I have already written to provide that. I'll do an executive summary to simplify it with a detailed attachment for the particulars. May I ask how you are planning to help?"

"Sure, you can ask," replied Sensenheimer. "But I must retain some mystery. The magician doesn't give away his tricks. Let's just say I have ways to make it happen. Most of them are legal." He chuckled at his own joke. "Now, enough of this boring stuff. I have ten minutes left. I have a question I want to ask Dr. Biedermeier. Guys, this is off the record stuff, so I hope you don't mind if I ask the reporters to leave?"

Alex stood up. "No problem. We've got places to go and things to investigate. Don't worry, you'll like what we write."

"I'd better," warned Sensenheimer. When the reporter and photographer had left, Doris asked if everybody else should leave, too. Sensenheimer suggested they might want to stay.

Randall was mystified. "I've had my say, what else do you want to know?"

Sensenheimer looked right and then left. Then he looked Randall right in the eye. "You may find this odd, but indulge me. I'm known for my spellbinding stories, jokes and riddles. I like to collect good new ones. I have a sense that you've seen plenty and are a good storyteller. If I'm right, Doris, Judy and Dan will want to stay. Mary and Sylvia have to stay and take notes."

Randall shrugged. "What is it you'd like to hear? I've got some good riddles that I learned from my kids, like why was the number six afraid of the number seven?"

Sensenheimer shook his head. "No, nothing like that. Think back to some of the most unusual cases you've seen. Pick the weirdest one you can think of and tell it to me so I can repeat it to my colleagues. It should have a humorous element and the terminology should be simple enough even I can tell it."

Doris sighed. "Don't expect any short stories from Dr. B! He's as long-winded as my grandpappy after the chili cook off!"

Randall raised both arms. "Doris, give me a break. I can keep it brief."

Dan guffawed. "Yeah, and ducks don't like water!"

Randall sighed. "Geez, I'm gettin' it from both sides! Oh, boy . . . there's so much to choose from. Give me a minute to go through my mental Rolodex."

Randall got up to refresh his coffee, had an 'aha' moment, and walked back. He remained standing to tell the tale.

Before he could start, Sensenheimer had to ask. "I give up. Why was six afraid of seven?"

"*Pshaw*, that's an easy one," laughed Randall. "Because seven, eight, nine."

Sensenheimer nearly spit out his coffee. "I'm going to use that at tonight's school board meeting!"

Randall laughed. "I'm pretty sure the teachers all know that riddle."

Sensenbrenner slapped his thigh. "Makes sense. It's been a long time for me since grade school. How 'bout your shaggy dog story?"

NO ONE NOSE

Randall put his thumb and forefinger together and twisted them like he was winding up his storytelling motor. "My spring is wound tight. Here you go. Feel free to take notes. Come springtime, a Norwegian bachelor farmer, 'Big' Al Dente, living quite alone in his cabin in the Upper Peninsula, set off to Manistique to shop for supplies. His most recent grocery shopping foray had been the previous spring and he was running low on baked beans. The paper money he'd saved up from odd jobs was kept rolled up in an empty soup can. He pulled the wrinkled bills out of the can, counted them and figured he had just enough."

Doris could not contain herself. "My stars, sounds like a typical Yooper recluse! Like my afore-mentioned grandpappy in the Carolina mountains. I bet Big Al takes a bath every Spring with the chickens whether he needs it or not. Probably chain smokes Marlboros."

Mary was confused. "What's a Yooper?"

Doris was pleased to clarify. "Well, UP is shorthand for Michigan's Upper Peninsula and someone from the UP is a Yooper."

Mary made a face, then smiled. "Oh. Now I get it. But who'd want to live up there? It's cold, isolated and gets buried in snow every winter . . . ah, a recluse. Nevermind."

Randall smiled. "I'm glad you all are following along. Doris may be a Southern lass, but she's learned some Northern lore. She's exactly right about Big Al. Anyways, once he found his lost tin of chewing tobacco, he set off for the 40 mile drive to town in his 'pickem' up truck. His tangled hair hung to his shoulders, his mustache hid his mouth, and his beard straggled below his first shirt button. The cherry on top of the sundae was a tattered, sweat-stained fedora."

Judy laughed. "Sounds like hygiene and grooming were not in his skill set."

Randall gave Judy a thumbs up. "Exactamundo. Big Al walked into the General Store in Manistique and grabbed a shopping cart. There weren't many customers and with all the hair and the drooping fedora, no one really noticed Big Al's face. That is, until he stepped up to the checkout counter and started to unload his cart. The cashier looked up to see a man with a hole where his nose should be. She screamed and fainted to the floor."

"Oh, my golly," exclaimed Judy. "What happened to his nose?"

Randall was warming to his story. "Patience, my dear. You don't want to skip to the last chapter. You gotta read the whole book! Hearing the commotion, the store manager came out to see if they were being robbed. His first sight was his cashier lying on the floor and he ran to check her. She was just coming to. She pointed to Big Al and managed to choke out the words: 'He has no nose!' The manager looked up, made an audible gasp, and confirmed the absence of a nasal appendage."

Sensenheimer was on the edge of his seat. "Didn't Big Al know he had no nose?"

Randall shrugged his shoulders. "Apparently not. The manager took Big Al aside and asked what had happened to his nose. Somewhat irrationally, he was worried that the nose had somehow been amputated by an accident in the store. You know, a store liability. Al admitted his nose had been a bit sore for a few months. He had wanted to check it, but had no mirror in his cabin."

Dan was flabbergasted. "No mirror? Was something wrong with his hands that he couldn't feel there was no nose there when he blew his nose? Maybe he blew his nose too hard. That's why you should always check your tissue after you blow chunks out your nose. Did you treat this guy before I started here?"

Randall wove their awe into the magic. "I share your wonderment at his 'obliviosity,' if I may coin a word. And, yes, he was down here the year before you arrived. I'm sure Doris remembers him."

Doris nodded her agreement. "I got the picture durin' your intro. The memory is etched in my noggin, like initials carved on a tree."

Sylvia had been quiet, but found her voice. "So, how did Big Al wind up down here?"

Randall turned to Sylvia to answer. "Excellent question. It was a circuitous journey, to be sure. The store manager took Big Al to the men's room so he could look in a mirror. At first, Big Al was befuddled and groped the area previously occupied by his proboscis. Then he decompensated and became combative. He ran out of the men's room, out into the store, where he started knocking down displays of fruit and throwing canned goods."

The image of a noseless man rampaging through a grocery store was both tragic and comical. Sensenheimer couldn't stop himself from bursting out in laughter. "Oof! I shouldn't be laughing, but . . ."

The comment triggered a chorus of laughter from the group. When it died down, Judy was the first to speak. "I guess even tragedy can be funny. I'm sure we're all sorry for the man underneath the oddity of the situation. How did they calm him down?"

Randall cleared his throat and continued. "Some customers subdued him and the local constabulary was summoned. They arrived and seemed to take the whole thing in stride. Considering the presence of other such recluses in the area, it's likely they had seen the unusual before. They took Big Al off to the Iron Mountain, Michigan, VA for disposition."

Sylvia had another question. "I should know this, but how far is Iron Mountain from Milwaukee?"

Doris had the answer. "It's 214 miles or three hours and 22 minutes by car. Oh, and it's roughly 4 hours by VA bus. That's how long Dr. B's Iron Mountain follow-ups have to travel."

Sensenheimer looked shocked. "Dang! I did not know that. Newberry, we need to talk about that soon. So, Biedermeier, what happened after our recluse showed up at Iron Mountain VA?"

Randall answered. "The doctors there confirmed the nasal deficiency. They suspected skin cancer had eaten away his nose. Biopsy confirmed it was a basal cell skin cancer and he was sent here to Hobbes VA for further treatment."

The group wasn't sure the story was over. There had been several very funny parts, but Randall had not indicated he was done.

Sylvia seemed the most confused. "So is that it or is there more story?"

Randall nodded. "Yes. There's more to the story. I'm just pausing to make sure I'm keeping the facts straight."

"Or maybe making up new 'facts,'" suggested Dan.

Randall looked annoyed. "If you're bored, we can stop here."

Doris punched Dan in the upper arm. "Bless your heart and shut your mouth! Let the man finish, or we'll be followin' the cows home!"

Dan grabbed his arm and hollered. "Ouch! That hurt. Will the abuse never end?"

Randall cleared his throat and continued. "Big Al was seen by all the specialties and it was concluded that the skin cancer had eroded away the nose and was still active at the margins. So, our tumor board decided that the margins would be removed surgically, followed by radiation for any microscopic leftovers."

"Wait a minute," said Sensenheimer. "My mother used to tell us kids a story about an old woman who had a blanket full of holes and she fixed it by cutting out all the holes. The treatment plan for Big Al sounds a lot like that."

Randall smiled and nodded. "Sort of. We were left with a bigger hole after surgery, but, after radiation, the area remained tumor free. We were able to save both eyes and a good portion of his upper lip. Then we sent him to the prosthodontist for a new nose."

"Wait a minute," said Sensenheimer. "Isn't that a dentist?"

"It is," replied Randall. "At the VA, they specialize in making more than dentures. They make prosthetic eyes, noses and ears. After taking a plaster cast of the face, they made an acrylic nose and upper lip section that included a mustache. The nose was attached to a pair of glasses and magnets implanted in the cheeks helped hold the whole thing in place. Two sets were made for Big Al, one for winter with pale skin and one for summer with tanned skin."

Mary Kelly blurted out in unedited adolescent wonder. "He's a real-life Mr. Potato Head!"

Sylvia looked aghast. "Mary Kelly, we do not call patients potatoes! Clearly he is more like an all-season Ken doll."

Randall chuckled. "Unbelievable, right? When I first saw Big Al with his new nose, I was flabbergasted that it looked so good. You had to look twice to tell it was fake. He was a new man."

"The haircut and shave helped a lot," said Doris. "Not to mention the bath. He was one ripe fellah. I swear that man lost three pounds of dirt! Dr. B, Don't forget to tell him what you said, in all your patient sensitivity."

Randall blushed slightly. "Oh yeah. I was so surprised, I couldn't help joking. 'You pick that nose?' Big Al was ready for that, because he said, 'yep, it fits my picking finger.' I nearly nosed my coffee imagining the prosthetic boogers."

Sensenheimer joined in the laughter at the absurdity. "Wow, that's quite a story!" He seemed to suspect the story was over.

"But, wait, there's more," warned Randall. "Or I can save it for next time."

Mary pleaded to her boss. "We can stay for a few more minutes, can't we?"

"If you insist," said Sensenheimer.

"The story is almost over," said Randall. "When everything was all fitted up, we sent Big Al back home on the Iron Mountain bus with all his new accessories. Several weeks later, I got a call from the Iron Mountain doc who'd sent Big Al down to Milwaukee initially. It seemed Big Al still needed to buy groceries, since he'd never finished the first time."

"I bet they didn't recognize him anymore," said Sylvia.

"Indeed," agreed Randall. "All was going well until Big Al rolled his cart to the checkout line. There were several carts ahead of him so he lit up a Marlboro while he waited. The line moved a bit quicker than he'd expected, so he took big puffs to finish the smoke before he got to the checker. Not noticing that the butt was growing dangerously short, the final drag lit his mustache on fire and an even larger and fouler cloud of smoke was sent airborne."

"Oh, my heavens," said Judy. "Did he burn himself?"

"Not exactly," said Randall. "Apparently, Big Al failed to notice that it was his mustache burning until the checkout clerk looked up and saw the flames. She yelled out: 'Sir, your mustache is on fire!' Big Al looked down, threw down the cigarette butt, ripped off his fake nose assembly and tossed it on the floor. He stomped on it to put out the blaze which had spread to the acrylic nose. Stripped bare of his new nose, the clerk shouted: 'It's you again!' and passed out on the floor once more."

"Criminy!" shouted Sensenheimer. "What goes around comes around. That is a keeper!"

Everyone squealed into bouts of laughter.

"Hooeee!" said Sensenheimer after catching his breath. "Now all I have to do is some serious editing to get that puppy down to tellable size and I'll be golden."

"Told you," said Doris. "No unexpurgated stories when Dr. B tells them. They're all dinghummers!"

"Well, thanks, for adding that to my repertoire, Dr. B. And Doris, thanks for that new word," said Sensenheimer. "You've earned a follow-up visit from me in which we'll review progress toward our mutual goals and, hopefully, I will be regaled with another repeatable story. I'm sure you have more in your back pocket."

"I may have one or two left," Randall made a show of checking his pockets. "This job may not pay very well, but it provides a wealth of story material. Perhaps next time I'll tell you the tale of the turban tumor. I think you owe me a good story as well."

"Believe me," said Newberry. "The Congressman has a few. Some are even fit for a mixed audience. But, I have to warn all of you, sometimes Dr. B's stories just leave people mixed up."

"Good one, Chief!" Randall pointed and winked.

After all the handshaking, goodbyes and 'see you agains,' the entourage departed. The remaining Radiation Oncology staff looked at each other with relief. They had survived the Congressional. Perhaps two more steps forward had been taken. Time would tell.

Shaboom shaboom

Randall was quite relieved when the Congressional entourage finally departed at noon. They had spent two and a half hours in his micro department. That suggested significant interest in his plight.

Randall's machinations were interrupted by an urgent bladder message. He'd been chugging coffee all morning without a break. He dashed off to the used coffee depot and when he returned, he found Elisa sitting at his desk with two brown bags.

Randall was surprised to see Elisa at work after Doris's description of her battle with the grunge. "Wow! You're up and about. Doris said you were pretty sick yesterday."

Elisa nodded. "You could say that. I had the 24 hour flu in 12 hours. Really knocked me out. But the rehydration at the ER perked me back up again. The ER doctor said some of my labs were a bit off. He wants to repeat them in a few days. Nothing too worrisome."

Elisa held up the bags like prizes. "Oh, master of Congressionals, your lunch is served. A mother hen told me you hadn't packed a lunch today. So, I took the liberty of delivering your favorite: tuna salad sandwich, chips and a pickle from the Bagarette on International Avenue."

Randall raised both arms. "The day just keeps getting better! Did you bring one for yourself?"

Elisa nodded. "Yes, but mine is a Reuben. I love sauerkraut. Shall we lunch together? I thought I could wait to tell you about my parent's Shamanic exploits but I can't. The stories are burning a hole in my brain, they so want to be told."

Randall snorted at Elisa's analogy and signaled her to begin.

Elisa looked at the wall clock. "I think we have some time. I checked with Doris and you don't have anything until 2:00. She blocked out extra time in case the Congressional ran late."

Randall whacked his desk with an open hand. "Wow! That's even better news. Do you want to eat lunch here in my office or go up to the cafeteria?"

"Too much noise up there," said Elisa. "I prefer the peace and quiet here and the view out your window picture of a bright, bright sunshiny day."

Randall grabbed his bag lunch and began to open it. "Then, here it is! Let's eat first then you can start the stories flowing."

They both unwrapped their sandwiches and began to munch and crunch. Randall managed to talk between bites of sandwich. "Usually, I eat my PBJ sandwiches while reviewing dictations or test results. This is a welcome change from that."

Elisa spoke with her mouth partially full of chewed chips. "Yeah. *Mmph.* For me too. I'm usually on the run somewhere . . ." She paused to swallow. ". . . and scattering food bits around the hospital. I swear you could probably find me by following the trail of crumbly bits."

Randall laughed and opened his desk drawer. "Look. I could probably feed birds from the food scraps I've dropped in my drawer. If Doris saw this mess, she'd probably unload some down home aphorism on me like 'Dr. B! Your desk drawer looks like the floor of my Meemaw's chicken coop. Bless your heart." Randall's voice cracked as he tried to mimic Doris's high pitched voice.

That little flub tickled Elisa and she had to cover her mouth to stifle spitting out a bite of sandwich. With a struggle she finished chewing and swallowed. "Don't make me laugh while my mouth is full."

Randall crossed his heart and raised two fingers. "Scout's honor." Elisa had to laugh again.

With the special lunch quickly polished off, both were wiping their mouths with napkins and cleaning up the debris when Doris waltzed in with fresh coffee for both of them.

Elisa was impressed. "Well, Doris, aren't you the most gracious hostess?"

Doris didn't miss a beat. "Why, of course I am. I have more talents than my Do-Si-Do and my ability to type 100 words per minute."

Elisa wasn't done. "Your timing is also impeccable. However did you accomplish that?"

Doris waved a dismissive hand. "Oh, that's easy. I've got Dr. B's office bugged like a flea on a frog."

Randall gave Doris a look. "Doris?"

Doris waved again. "Oh, don't worry your little self. I don't need no bugs. I just use my special powers, as you well know."

Randall squinted and nodded. "Good to know. Now, Doris, if there's nothing else?"

Doris nodded. "No worries. I'll be at my desk."

Randall turned to Elisa with a weak smile. "Lovely lady. Full of surprises. So, what's this you're all fired up to tell me about your folks? And what's it got to do with you?"

Elisa had a big smile on her face and cleared her throat to begin. Randall settled back in his desk chair to listen. "My mother, Juanita de Leon, started out as a fortune teller in Ponce, Puerto Rico. Her father, Juan, and his brother, Ronaldo, ran a small cantina there in a poor neighborhood. From the age of ten, Juanita helped at the cantina washing and cleaning up. Sometimes she would fill in behind the bar and enjoyed talking to the customers. By the time she was 16, customers would seek her out to tell her their problems and she would give good advice."

Randall tried to remain serious, but couldn't hold back a comment. "Don't tell me! You're a direct descendant of Ponce de Leon and you're really 120 years old."

Elisa gave Randall an irritated frown, then laughed despite herself. "Almost right. I'll be 220 next August. Do I need Doris to come in here and referee or can I continue?"

Randall pushed away the idea with both hands. "No, no! Anything but that. Sorry. Poor impulse control."

Elisa put a finger to her lips, then continued. "Juanita became so in demand that Juan decided to set aside a quiet corner table for her so customers could speak with her privately. He began charging customers two pesos to have sessions with the 'special' girl and gain insights into their future fortunes. Mostly she 'saw the future' by 'reading' her clients with artful questioning. Sometimes, maybe one in ten times, she would get someone with whom she seemed to have a genuine connection. With these people she claimed to have visions about them either at the meeting or later in dreams. At first, she didn't make much of the visions. Later, after getting follow-up information indicating that what she'd seen had come to pass, she realized there might be something more to it."

Randall sat forward in his seat. "Wow! How'd she react when that happened?"

Elisa waved at an imaginary fruit fly. "At first she was afraid she might be *loca*. She discussed it with her mother, my *Abuela* Rosa, who had suspected Juanita had the gift of 'special sight.' Rosa explained it was a 'gift' that many of the de Leon women had possessed through the generations. Juanita wasn't as sure about it being a gift."

Randall rubbed his chin. "Hmm. I can see how she'd feel that way. It's not what 'normal' folks call 'normal.' What did she do about it?"

Elisa leaned over in her chair and picked some bits of potato chips off the floor. She pitched them in Randall's waste basket. "Ah! A three pointer. I never miss . . . anyway, despite Rosa's portrayal of the special sight as a blessing, Juanita didn't like all the attention she got in Ponce. After some of her visions proved true and word got around, people looked at her differently. They acted as though she was the village Shaman and giving them advice was her duty. They didn't want to pay for it. They'd come to her on the street and ask about prospective marriage partners or the sex of an unborn baby. Everybody wanted free advice. Juanita wanted no part of it and decided to emigrate to the US."

Randall's mouth felt fuzzy. He realized that was because his mouth had been open so long it had dried out. He licked his lips. "Fascinating! When did she emigrate?"

Elisa thought for a second. "Must have been around 1944. Yeah. That's right. She was born in 1924 and I remember she said she was 20 when she moved. Why do you ask?"

Randall adjusted his glasses. "Well, I would think by 1944 most Puerto Ricans would have stopped believing in Shamans and moved into a more modern world-think."

Elisa shook her head. "Oh, no. It might have been 1944 in some parts of the world, but for Puerto Ricans the world of tribal behavior and medicine men was still very real. Those customs go back hundreds of years and are hard to break. For example, even though the Catholics seeded Christianity into Latin American countries for centuries before the modern age and claimed conversion of the old ways, that's not quite the true story."

Randall looked puzzled. "Oh? How's that?"

Elisa looked right and left as if she was about to tell Randall a dark secret. "The old ways got integrated into Catholicism and vice versa. For example, there might be a celebration of Easter that just happened to coincide with a Puerto Rican fertility rite. The priests didn't mind that the natives gave it a flavor of their own as long as it coincided with an actual Catholic holy day."

Randall winked. "Sort of like a macrophage engulfment."

Elisa narrowed her eyes. "Excuse me? Analogy *obscuras*."

Randall waved an arm. "Sorry. That was a little unclear. How about 'we are what we eat?' How did your mother survive in a new country?"

Elisa started to feel tired and thirsty. "Do you think there's any coffee left in your communal pot? I could use a boost."

Randall nodded. "It's hot, but probably not fresh. Will that do you?"

Elisa smiled. "Doesn't matter. Need . . . caffeine. . . ."

Randall got up and retrieved the last two cups of sludgy coffee. It had been simmering for hours and was probably potent enough to give Lazarus a kick start. He returned and handed one cup to Elisa. "Be careful. It's hot and potent."

Elisa blew steam off the hot liquid, raised the cup in a salute, and continued. "Back to my mother's big adventure in America. Juanita first stayed with a shirttail relative in Brownsville, Texas. Her welcome wore thin after a few months of not really fitting with ranch life. She was not suited for wrangling. Around that time, she learned that her uncle Ronaldo had also immigrated to the US not long after she'd left. He'd opened a cantina in Douglas, Arizona, near the Mexican border. She contacted Renaldo. After some negotiation, it was agreed she would move there and help him at the cantina, like before, but sans fortune telling. He had an extra room above the bar she could stay in."

Randall shook his head. "My goodness. It's a long way from Texas to Arizona."

Elisa agreed. "But Greyhound buses eventually get anywhere you want to go, except overseas."

Randall was curious. "Why did Ronaldo set up a cantina in Arizona, of all places?"

Elisa bit her lower lip. "To use a multisyllabic word, it was multifactorial. Since the late 1930s, the US Army Air Force had set up multiple training airports in southern Arizona. They desperately needed more planes and pilots for the war effort. Arizona was flat, dry, and could be used year round. Douglas was the site of an army airbase for an Advanced Flying School for twin engine bombers, mostly B-25's."

"Douglas, Arizona?" asked Randall. "Not sure I've heard of it."

Elisa nodded slightly. "Most folks haven't. It's a small border-crossing town across from Agua Prieto, Mexico. Ronaldo figured he'd have a captive clientele with all the troops rotating through Douglas airbase and the bar could also attract customers from Mexico. He knew enough English to get by with the GIs. Plus the old cantina he bought was cheap. It needed lots of work, but he fixed it up. And he was right. Soon, business was booming and he needed more help."

Randall pursed his lips as he processed the information. "So Juanita fit right in. Did she refrain from fortune telling?"

"For the most part," said Elisa. "She was still a good listener, but gave only noncommittal advice. When she went on break she sat at her special table. The soldiers would be attracted to her and sidled over to chat her up. Ronaldo saw an opportunity to make some money and put a tip jar on the table. It was often filled by closing time. Mostly the chatters were just lonesome young men, scared and away from home for the first time. And she was quite lovely."

Randall made the connection. "Don't tell me. Let me guess. And one of those lonely guys became your father."

Elisa concurred. "Indeed, as I mentioned last time, that's where Juanita met Jose Angeles, a 23-year-old US Army Air Force second lieutenant."

Randall connected more dots. "Oh right! I remember. Jose is from that town in Sonora, Mexico! Margarita something? I remember you said he was a descendant of the Pesky Yacqui Indians."

Elisa guffawed. "Close but no banana. The town's name is Magdalena de Kino! Named after Mary Magdalene in the Bible. And it's 'Pascua' Yacqui. Pascua means 'Easter.'"

Randall blushed, accepting the correction. "Yeah, if I recall my history, isn't their story much like our Native American Indians? You know, been around for centuries until the oafish outsiders invaded, in this case the Spanish, and drove them to near extinction?"

"Exactly," affirmed Elisa. "In the early days, some of the Yacqui practiced peyote rituals, but not the Pascua. They did have Shamans or native sorcerers/healers who claimed to be able to alter the weather and foresee the future, among other skills. Jose's father had been a Shaman until the Mexican government forced the Pascua out of Mexico. The Angeles family then moved to an enclave of Pascua in Phoenix in 1922 when Jose was only three years old."

"That must have been rough on the family," observed Randall. "Was Jose's father able to continue as a Shaman in the Phoenix enclave?"

Elisa nodded but retained a severe look. "Yes, but it wasn't easy for them. The Pascua remained a very tight knit group and *Abuelo* continued with his Shamanic role. It turned out that Jose had even stronger visionary abilities than his father. However, his dream to fly airplanes was very strong. He gave up on the native ways and went to college to take aeronautical engineering. He was a brilliant student, but left school during his junior year, 1944, to join the Army Air Force. After initial flight school training at Davis-Monthan field in Tucson, he was assigned to Douglas Field for bomber school."

Randall put two and two together. "And that's where Juan met Juanita and soon their gifts were combined to make you. I'm pretty sure that combination of DNA has made something special. I have a feeling I know only part of the story."

Elisa maintained a look that gave nothing away. "The book cover does not tell the whole story. Before I do the reveal, first, a bit of history about the Yacqui."

Randall suspected what was to come and egged her on. "I'm all ears."

Elisa paused to collect her thoughts. "One can't talk about Yacqui Shamanism without discussing their relationship with plants and the spirit world. This is not just true for the Yacqui, but tribal cultures across the world, including Asia, Europe, Australia, Africa and Latin America. Each of these cultures attempt to achieve a connection between the daily 'real' world and the spiritual world. Often that entails using healing and psychoactive plants to help connect to the spiritual world and correct imbalances. Sometimes it's just the unique abilities of the medicine men or women Shamanic practitioners."

This rang a bell for Randall. "Yeah, like Carlos Casteneda wrote about using Peyote for seeking an alternate reality. I think he also suggested the drugs were just a way to train the brain to see outside of our limited perception."

Elisa nodded. "Yeah. It's still debatable whether Casteneda is just a charlatan, but I believe there's a universal truth in much of what he says.

Anyway, the plants, in and of themselves, are considered sacred by many tribal cultures and that within the plants, provided to us by nature, are supernatural powers. Shamans, using these psychoactive plants, enter into trances, from which they have the power to heal disease, combat evil spirits, control the weather and predict the future. In those states of mind, they can understand both the real and spirit worlds. They determine if the two worlds are out of balance and try to create a balance between the two."

Randall blinked as he tried to make sense of what Elisa was explaining. "Okay. That's a lot to digest, but I think it makes sense to me. But what about the Pascua? You said they don't use drugs for their visions. That implies to me that drugs aren't always needed to see the spirit world. There must be some 'gifted' ones that already have a brain function that can send and receive 'spirit' messages. By inference, that could be an inherited trait. And, if it is, how does it work? That's the stuff the QEG is investigating."

Elisa was delighted Randall was "getting it." "To use a radiation related comparison, you and I are on the same wavelength. I've witnessed the things that my parents have done over the years, ranging from predicting the birth sex of newborns to causing rainfall after weeks of drought. I saw my father heal chronic arthritis and put cancer in remission. My mother stopped a serious infection after antibiotics failed and doctors gave up. Never once did they use psychoactive drugs. Want to find water in the desert? My father will bring his divining rod."

Randall was dumbfounded. "This is what I want you to share with the QEG. These kinds of stories. If you're willing. So, has the 'gift' been passed on to you? If so, in what way?"

Elisa frowned and studied her lap. "Here's where it gets confusing. I think I have inherited some abilities, but not exactly like my parents. I get vivid dreams that repeat themselves and sometime later they get acted out for real. Nothing major or earth shaking, but definitely spooky. Lately, I've been having recurring dreams about some evil force that's out to harm me. Like a bad disease is lurking. I feel hands on my body and I try to kick them away. I wind up with my bedclothes in a bundle when I wake up."

"That is scary," said Randall. "I get those too. Once I dreamed that a pirate was trying to run me through. In my dream, I kicked at him so hard I hit the bedside stand with my big toe and tore off my toenail. In the dream, I got the bugger good. In real life I got my toe just as bad."

Elisa laughed. "I never connect. I'm a bad kicker. The other thing that I've noticed is that with some patients it's like I can read their thoughts and it directs me how to help them. Like the paranoid schizophrenic guy you had me talk to to get him to consent to treatment. Once I entered his vision of the world, it was easy to see how to guide him. And it's not just patients. Like the first time I met you, it was like I'd known you for a lifetime. You're the first person outside of my family I've told any of this stuff to."

Randall winced. "Wow. That's deep. I sort of had the same feeling when I first met you. I think you're right. Some people have an inherent ability to connect." He held his hands like a pair of radar dishes. "They have good receivers and transmitters. Basically, the QEG operating theory is that it's a neurobiological skill we all have. We are part of quantum entanglement, a basic subatomic function that connects us with all and everything." He noticed Elisa's eyebrows squinching. "Yes. I know. That's even deeper still. But with time I'm sure you can understand it as we do."

Elisa wasn't so sure and grimaced. "Maybe."

Randall went on. "Be warned. It is still just a theory. The QEG goal is to understand it better and prove it."

Elisa nodded her assent. "Makes sense to me. Nothing to lose in trying. Why do you think some people have the connectivity and not others?"

Randall shook his head. "Not sure. The group has some theories about that, but nothing solid yet. Could be a mutation that favors success of an individual and, as a result, the group they run in, so it's selected for by Mr. Darwin. He's a natural selector. We might all be born with it, but lose it with all the white noise of the world as we get older. Maybe never growing up is the answer, like Peter Pan. Interesting quandary."

Elisa had a connected thought. "Oh! I should mention that my weird sister has some odd ability that I can't easily quantify. Elena still lives in Chicago to help out my Mom, but rarely keeps in touch with me. Except . . . occasionally she'll show up on my doorstep, unannounced. She'll just explain that she got a message that I needed her. I'll swear to her that I sent no such message and I don't need help, but she insists on staying with me anyhow. Then, a day or so later some crisis will hit. My refrigerator dies, my dog gets hit by a car, or I nearly slice off my finger. She helps me through the mini-crisis and then disappears for months. How does she do this?"

"Good question," replied Randall. "Seems like she foresees only minor bad stuff. Maybe she doesn't respond to the big stuff. Too much effort."

Elisa laughed. "Good call. You've pegged her. But here's what worries me. She just showed up again two days ago and is sleeping on the living room floor on an air mattress."

Randall had to laugh himself. "Geez. Now I'm worried too."

"Holy smokes!" exclaimed Elisa. "Look at the time! I've got to move my derriere. I've a meeting five minutes ago. I may have a gift, but not the kind that makes one punctual. Let me know when you're holding the QEG meeting and I'll be there. I'll prepare some of my best Shamanic stories."

Randall gave Elisa a thumbs up and escorted her out of the office. As they passed by Doris, she offered an opinion. "I was just about to come in there and pry you two apart. From what I was hearin', things were getting' as tight as my grandpappy's britches after Thanksgivin' dinner."

Randall ignored the comment and returned to his desk. He wondered if Elisa's message of dread was real or imaginary. For reasons unclear to him he had a nagging worry about her. That worry was displaced when Doris reminded him not to forget to take the presentation slides with him when he left for home.

OuttaTime

Randall flogged the Scirocco through the maze of back roads that led out of the VA grounds to the freeway. He had made the drive so often it had become nearly reflexive. In his mind, he ticked off all the tasks that needed doing before leaving for Vegas. There was packing, sorting through the slides and notes Knox had given him, and dealing with what was sure to be the typical "pre-Randall's going away for a meeting" family chaos. The kids would be hyped to the gills and Zelda would be, well, "unpredictable." Lord only knew where she'd be on the nuts-o-meter. He would have to ad lib his responses. He hoped he would have the energy to dodge and weave enough to avoid a TKO.

Randall let the Scirocco coast quietly up the driveway and killed the engine. He decided to reconnoiter stealthily before making his presence known. He quietly exited the car and tiptoed to the back door to take a peek. Halfway there, his plan was scotched as the yard light came on and the back door was flung open by two yelping kids who ran out to greet him. Kyle grabbed Randall's briefcase and announced he'd carry it inside. Addie grabbed Randall's leg and squeezed hard.

"Daddy, daddy," screeched Addie. "We've been waiting and waiting for you to come home. Mom says you're taking a trip tomorrow and we should be extra nice to you. How are we doing so far?"

Kyle was struggling with the weight of Randall's briefcase and let it drop to the driveway. "Wow, this thing weighs a ton," he exclaimed. "I'll have to use both arms. What's in it?"

Randall laughed. "A bag of cement mix, Buddy. I thought you could lift one of those. Nah, just kidding. It's heavy duty science papers."

Kyle gave Randall the stink eye, knowing Randall was referring to a Kyle misadventure several years earlier. Kyle had dumped half a bag of cement mix in a neighbor's car seat as payback for not getting invited to dinner with his playpal. At the time, Kyle had professed his innocence. Randall had gone along with the lie, then had snuck in with a casual phrase. "Wow, it must be really hard to lift such a heavy bag that high!"

Kyle had taken the bait and replied, "No, Dad, it was easy! I just put my legs like this . . ." at which point Randall just pointed at him and the gig was up. Now Kyle was craftier about his coverups.

Kyle used both arms and manhandled the briefcase to the doorway. "I'm not a baby anymore, Dad! Where are you going tomorrow, anyway?"

Randall jumped up and landed with spread feet and arms raised. "I am flying to Las Vegas, Nevada, gambling capital of the US of A."

The two kids responded in spontaneous loud harmony. "Can we come too?"

"I want to play the slot machines," said Addie.

Kyle made his hands into claws. "I want to ride a tiger!"

Randall was just as quick and loud to reply. "Not a chance! How in the heck do you know about the slots?"

By this time Zelda was at the door and stepped outside. "I told her about them. Yeah, why can't we all go?"

Randall lowered his head into his hands and just groaned. "Lord. Give me strength."

Then Zelda laughed. "Just kidding. No need to fret. We're just giving you the business. I told the kids all about the trip and Las Vegas. They know it's too late to get plane tickets and that it's just a business trip that the department paid for. Definitely not a private little Daddy boondoggle."

Randall detected an edge of sarcasm and wondered just how okay Zelda really was with the concept. "Yeah. Your Mom's right about that. Maybe someday soon we can all go to Vegas and have good family fun, including a little excursion in the desert. But right now let's get inside. It's cold out here and I'm hungry."

Inside were the familiar smells of pork roast in the slow cooker. Randall's mouth began to water. He still wasn't sure where he stood with Zelda. The superficial signs were good, but was there an undertow beneath the calm surface? They all settled around the table after the food was served. The pork roast was so tender it could be cut with a fork. There was fresh bread, gravy, baked potatoes, string beans and a side of sauerkraut. The food stars were aligned.

Zelda announced they should all hold hands around the table while she said grace and prayed for Randall to have safe travels. "Dear Mr. or Mrs. Great Spirit, wherever you are, please bless this food which I have so painstakingly cooked for my family . . . , especially my hard working husband. Let them be sustained and nourished by it. May it give Randall the power to resist the temptations in Las Vegas. May he be able to look away from the lure of beautiful women dancing wearing only feathers. May he not be led astray to the gambling tables and squander our limited resources. May he spend all his time on boring academic and career pursuits. May he come back with all his parts attached and nothing extra. Amen."

The kids understood little of the prayer, but responded with an echoing "Amen."

Randall looked around the table feeling like he should defend himself. "Err, thanks, I think, for the blessing. Just to be clear, this meeting is not for fun. I was 'voluntold' to go at the request of my former mentor to take my boss's place. It will be mostly work. There will be little time for cavorting. The meeting could actually help me get started in clinical research and maybe lead to a promotion. That, in turn, could increase my income and make vacation travel to fun places for the entire family more likely."

Zelda was unfazed. "We understand all that completely. We just want you back safely."

Addie stood up on her chair. "Before we eat, I have something to say."

Randall put down his fork. "Yes, honey, I'll try to be good and come home safely."

Addie waved a hand and pulled four quarters out of her pocket. "Yeah. That too." She held out the four quarters and gave them to Randall. "Take these and put them in your back pocket. When you get to Vegas, take a few minutes and put them in a slot machine. They're special quarters and I know they will win. I want every penny back that they earn. Do you promise?"

Randall nodded slowly.

Addie reached out her little finger. "Now we have to pinky swear."

Randall reached out his little finger and wrapped it around hers. He frowned. "What makes you think these quarters will win?"

Addie looked surprised that Randall would even ask such a dumb question. "My Unicorn, Uni, told me. What he says always comes true."

Randall nodded. "Of course. How could I forget?"

With that, Addie sat back down and made another pronouncement. "Nice meat. Let's eat."

Randall was taken aback by Addie's behavior. She seemed 20 years older than her stated age. Somehow he knew the quarters would return a nice payoff. As he ate the delicious meal, he concluded that he had been given a vote of confidence but it was conditional. He decided that, of all the tasks he had to do before he left the next day, the most important one was to use the occasion of this dinner to have a good time with his family. There wasn't really that much to pack and he could review slides on the plane. After dinner he suggested they play Monopoly until whenever. Everyone was cool with that.

As the game progressed, Addie was breaking everybody's bank with rent from her monopoly on hotels. She was lording it over her opponents, who were, by now, just going through the motions. "Nyah, nyah. I'm winning big time. You guys are losers."

Zelda was almost bankrupt and had lost interest. She asked Randall about the upcoming QEG meeting to pass the time. "Hey, Randy. Just checking here. You still want me to attend that squeegee meeting of yours or was that just PR?"

Randall nodded. "Of course I still want you to attend. By the way, the group's name is QEG. Here's why I want you there. When you look back at all the reading you've done over the years, you have a much broader perspective than half the superbrains in the group. My guess is that it will be your chance to shine. Since it'll be your first meeting, consider it a chance just to put your toe in the water. Just take it all in or, if you feel comfortable, take a dive. Can't demote you any from where you are now and might give you a kick start."

Zelda raised her juice glass and nodded. "Yeah! What you said. Hey, look at the time. Shouldn't we all be hitting the hay? Tomorrow is an early day."

"Cripes! You're right," blurted Randall. "Addie, I pronounce you the Monopolist champion. Now let's all get to our beds and lay down our heads."

In a sing-song duet Kyle and Addie begged for a bedtime story. Zelda stifled that by pointing at the clock and then the stairs. "Mommy has to help Daddy pack his stuff and then she has to pack him in bed."

Randall looked up at Zelda hopefully. She just smiled and shook her head. "Dream on, cadet."

AFTER HOURS
L. Voell

CHAPTER 21

———

LOST VAGUS

"From there to here, from here to there, funny things are everywhere."

—*Theodor Seuss Geisel*

The next morning, Randall had his alarm set for a predawn wake up. His flight to Las Vegas departed at 6:20 AM. When the alarm went off, he was briefly disoriented, because Saturday morning was usually not an early wake up day. At first he panicked, thinking he'd forgotten to prepare for his Thursday morning tumor conference. A moment later his brain booted up all the way and he realized that wasn't it. He was panicking about getting to the airport. Not a relief. "Oh, crap!" yelled Randall loud enough to wake Zelda.

Zelda sat up and punched him in the arm. "Just because you have to get up, why do I? Can't you do it quietly? Jerk!" She rolled over and pulled the covers over her head.

Randall apologized and popped out of bed, heading for the bathroom. He went into speed mode. Dressed and ready to head out in record time, he dashed back to Zelda's side of the bed. He pulled the bed covers off of her head, planted a kiss on her forehead and pulled them back over her head again. Zelda grunted and he zoomed downstairs, stopping in the kitchen only long enough to nuke some coffee to go. It was already 5:30 and the airport was at least a half hour drive. More with bad traffic. With check in and security, it could take even longer. He decided to pretend the trip was an autocross.

As Randall hauled his briefcase and carry-on down the concourse toward the gate, he patted his back pocket to be sure Addie's four quarters were still there. He patted his pocket yet again to be sure the quarters were still there and they were. Their presence was surprisingly reassuring. He decided the four quarters were his good luck charm.

Randall still had strange misgivings about the trip. It went beyond the worries about the committee and Aguilar. He felt like a malicious entity was pulling his strings and shadowing him.

The feeling recalled a "Twilight Zone" TV episode in which the protagonist becomes convinced that someone is following him. With quick head turns to the left and behind him he tries to get a glimpse of his pursuer. No matter how quickly he turns his head, he is never fast enough to see anyone behind him. He is certain a demon is stalking him to take him to hell. He becomes so obsessed with the idea that the backward look becomes an uncontrollable tic. Finally, he looks behind his shoulder while crossing a busy street and is hit by a car. He lies broken and dying on the pavement. He looks up to the sidewalk where he dimly sees an old man standing at the curb propped up on a cane. The old man smiles broadly and waves goodbye. The screen fades to black.

Randall was startled from day-dreamland by the announcement from the overhead PA that his flight was ready to board. He shivered involuntarily, grabbed his briefcase and queued up at the gate.

Flight of Fancy

Randall was assigned to a port side window seat overlooking the wing. The view outside was blocked by the wing and was not optimal for in-flight sightseeing. No matter, he had to get Knox's slide printouts down pat for the presentation at NRG. Lord knew he wasn't the bright light that Knox was, so he reckoned he should use his time wisely. If the Lord knew that, maybe He knew some other answers. Randall thought perhaps he could call God from the hotel phone. The operator would probably know the number. He thought it odd that he knew Satan's number, 666, but God's number was unlisted.

Randall had acquired a deep loathing of the number 666 for a different reason. A somewhat notorious patient of his had died under suspicious circumstances on June 6, 1966. Randall had been blamed for her death and it had taken weeks for the toxicology report from an autopsy to show she'd taken a lethal dose of cyanide. It wasn't clear how, since there was nothing evident in her stomach. After far too much time, he was exonerated when they figured out she had chosen a port of entry for the drug in a more southern orifice. Since then, Randall considered anything with those three numbers as a bad omen for him. If he saw a car with three sixes in the plate number, he would drive away from the car as soon as possible.

Randall shook his head to clear the negative thoughts and rubbed his right-hand back pocket. All was good. The pilot announced they had reached a cruising altitude of 35,000 feet and were slicing through the air at 530 mph. That cleared Randall's brain. He looked out the window and could see miles of geometrically demarcated farmland. He reckoned that either cows were not visible from that altitude or they were in the barn having lunch. He wondered if they used forks or mostly ate finger food.

Randall refocused his mind, took the slides from his briefcase and started to review them. Each slide was printed out but he could also make them out by holding them up to the window. He had to give Knox credit. The talk was well written. Happily, he knew most of the data, so it flowed well. The plane was halfway to Las Vegas when he got to the eighteenth of twenty slides. Slide 18 outlined a newly proposed lung cancer study that the NRG Lung Committee had discussed at the previous meeting. At the time it had been referred to as the hyperfractionation study. No official study number had been assigned. Now the study was designated NRG-79-666. This was an internal shorthand used by NRG. The first two digits represented 1979, the year the study was to open. The next three digits were a code. The first number of the code meant it was the 6th study approved in 1979 and the last two numbers meant it was approved on June 6th of the year.

The dreaded number had appeared again! Randall gasped out loud. "What the heck?"

A young woman in the aisle seat next to Randall looked up from her paperback. "Excuse me, are you OK?"

Randall looked up and saw the woman was rather attractive. Randall hadn't realized he'd spoken out loud. He tried to make light of his remark. "Sorry. Mind and mouth connection suboptimal. Can you believe what they charge for the stuff in the airline catalog?"

The woman nodded and smiled. "Yeah. It's outrageous, but I guess they figure they've got a captive audience that compensates for boredom by buying stuff they don't need. My mouth does that sometimes, too. I'd love to chat, but I've got to get back to my novel and find out if Agatha has killed off Inspector Poirot."

Randall nodded. "No problem, I understand the passion of Agatha Christie fans. I have work to do myself. Happy reading."

Randall turned back to his slide review. He chided himself for being so silly about a stupid number. There was no deep mystery here. Coincidences can be strange. He needed to get the review done. *Just stop fretting and finish the slides, doofus!*

Randall took a deep breath and casually looked left, out the window, to recalibrate himself to his environment. He noted clouds were beginning to form. Before he turned back to his review, the plane's wing began to bend languidly upwards like a bird flapping its wing in slow motion. The upward excursion reached about 60 degrees above horizontal before returning to normal position. Randall held his breath, now worried the plane would start falling out of the sky any second.

Randall looked around the cabin and saw no alarm among his fellow passengers. There was no change in the plane's ride or attitude. Perhaps his imagination had briefly gone into overdrive. He looked back out the window to recheck the wing and was alarmed to observe the graceful, flapping motion of the wing repeated several more times. The panel lines of the wing curved and stretched as though elastic. Still, the flight remained perfectly smooth. Randall looked to the right to check the starboard wing. It was in standard position and stable. This did not compute.

Randall stared at the seatback in front of him and spotted the plane information placard. He pulled it out, hoping it would contain some information about the flapping wing phenomenon. Perhaps it was a new feature. The card identified the aircraft as an 84 passenger McDonnell Douglas DC-9. Exits were front, back and sides. Date of production was 2/4/75. There was nothing about an auxiliary flapping function. He looked for the part of the placard that would read something like, "*Welcome to the new and improved McDonnell Douglas DC-9. To enhance your experience and improve our fuel efficiency, we have added the patented 'bird in flight' feature to our wings. Do not be alarmed by the bending motion of the wings or the sudden sinking feeling. You may also notice an increase in repeated sixes. Please note there are extra air sickness bags in the seat pocket in front of you.*"

Finding no such disclaimer, and afraid to look anywhere but straight ahead, he mentally reviewed possible explanations for what he had seen. He went through a differential diagnosis listing the worst things first. Was something going haywire in his noggin? Maybe it was a delayed symptom of getting beaned by a softball playing baseball with the kids. Or he could be developing a brain tumor. How about early stages of a bipolar disorder and his brain had chosen this plane ride to go 'round the bend? He reminded himself to start with the simplest explanation first. More likely, it was just stress and an overactive imagination. If that were the case, it should be safe to look left again, but he decided to think it through a bit more.

His rumination was interrupted when the stewardess approached and asked his rather comely seatmate if she wanted anything to drink before the inflight meal. She ordered a Scotch. A drink sounded like a great solution. Randall definitely wanted a drink. A drink was just what he needed. He ordered a gin and tonic. No matter what turned out to be outside the plane window, a drink would help.

Thus emboldened, while he awaited his drink, he took another look out the window. There were no clouds now. The sky was clear, and the sun was still behind them to the East. The wing was in its place and stayed there.

Randall muttered aloud. "Good, no flapjacks. I hate flapjacks, but I love *blintzes*."

His seatmate looked up from her novel. "What? They never have pancakes on the in-flight menu."

Randall realized he'd done it again. "Sorry, brainless mouth strikes again. I was just replaying an argument I had with my wife this morning. Pay me no mind."

The woman was sympathetic. "Don't worry, strange replays of my life happen when I fly alone. That's why I read. It keeps my mind from meandering down some strange garden paths."

Randall's gin and tonic arrived. He took two healthy sips and chanced another look to the left. The port wing was doing its normal wing thing. He needed to get his mind off of the wing, so, as long as they were drinking and awaiting a meal, he decided he would chat with the nice young lady to his right. He tried a favorite opening line. "My favorite bulb is 60 watt, what's yours?"

The woman turned her head and gave him a squinty look. "Excuse me?"

Randall tried to maintain an innocent look. "Sorry. I am kind of a nervous flier and thought it might calm my nerves to participate in a little 'light' conversation before lunch."

The woman was no dummy. She nodded in amusement. "Oh. Well, I actually prefer 100 watt. It provides better illumination. I do a lot of reading."

Randall was a little embarrassed he'd started the conversation. He didn't want the woman to think he was hitting on her. "Obviously, the reading keeps your mind very sharp. You caught on right away to my rather obscure reference. I hope you don't mind being taken away from your book."

The woman laughed. "Not at all. Inspector Poirot has reappeared safe and sound. I can resume reading after lunch without fear that it will depict his funeral."

The two seatmates had an enlightening chat during lunch. Randall stole several glances out the plane window and everything with the miscreant wing continued to be hunky dory. To his relief, there was no further wing flapping. The healing effects of gin were kicking in. The flight attendant removed their empty trays and he used the rest of the flight to complete the slide review.

Randall then checked the NRG program schedule. It showed that most of the Saturday agenda was set up for budget reports and business meetings that he had no role in. He had the day free until 4:00 to 6:00 PM when the Lung Committee met and he'd have to give his presentation. Following this was a dinner and reception. Randall had no intention of attending. He felt he was incapable of hobnobbing with the elite oncologists of the world, despite del Aguilar's recommendations to mingle and make himself known. Just as Randall concluded this, the pilot announced their imminent landing at the Las Vegas McCarran International Airport, where the temperature was a balmy 96 degrees.

The landing was uneventful. As the passengers deplaned, his seatmate thanked him for the enjoyable conversation. She bid him goodbye as she headed for baggage claim. She started to walk away, then stopped and turned towards Randall. "I'll keep a lamp lit for you."

Before Randall had time to process the suggestive comment, she had disappeared into the concourse crowd. He lamented his slow uptake, but concluded it was all for the best.

The Marquis

Randall's next stop was Amos car rental. The agent had one customer at the counter who finished up as he approached. Randall handed the agent the reservation papers Knox had given him and waited as he looked it over.

The agent took his time, squinting and making humming sounds, before he spoke. "Yes, we're all set here. Sir, if you would just look over these forms, we can get you going. And I have good news. You have been selected for a courtesy upgrade to a full-size car."

Randall was concerned about the desert heat. "Does it have air conditioning?"

The agent laughed as if that was a silly question. "Of course, Sir.

After all, this is Nevada. It's warmish here. It's a fully optioned Mercury Grand Marquis."

Feeling slightly slighted, Randall shot back. "Does it have the 'de Sade' option?"

"Excuse me, sir?" said the agent.

Randall chuckled, figuring he'd won the sparring match. "Never mind, it's not important. Which boxes do I initial for the insurance? I want to be sure I've got the maximum coverage." Randall always double checked.

The agent turned the packet of papers around and pointed to a spot on the triplicate form. "Just initial these two spots and sign at the bottom. I'll need to make an imprint of your credit card and I need a form of ID."

Randall opened his wallet. "Here's my Master Card. I have a distinctive scar on my knee. I got it playing baseball with my little brother. Would you like to see it?"

The agent managed a weak smile. "Very droll, sir. Your state driver's license will do. I need to make a photocopy for the records."

Randall complied, and the agent gave him directions to downtown Vegas. He pointed him towards the exit where the rental lot shuttle was parked. When Randall stepped outside, the hot desert air hit him like an oven blast.

It was a short trip to the rental lot, but the air conditioning in the shuttle couldn't compete with the heat. When it deposited him at the lot office, he was already sweating profusely. He exchanged paperwork for car keys and went back out into the heat to find parking space 36F. The Mercury looked like a dark red police cruiser. Randall burned his hand on the sun-soaked door handle and screeched a little when his delicate behind hit the hot black leather. He started the engine, fired up the AC, and set the fan on high. Only a blast of hot air came out the vents.

Following signs that directed him out of the airport, he turned right onto Las Vegas Boulevard and headed north toward Sahara Avenue. From McCarran, the boulevard runs south to north along the 4.2-mile strip, which is actually south of the Las Vegas city limits in the unincorporated towns of Paradise and Winchester. Many people "go to Vegas," but only stay on the strip and then fly back out of the airport. They don't realize they were never actually "in Vegas."

The Vegas strip presents the newcomer with dramatic architecture. There's a bewilderment of multistory towers, marquees, flashing lights, and burbling fountains. Tourists wander everywhere—walking, talking, and gawking. The wind swirls little pieces of paper debris across the road. There are posters on every wall, lamppost and phone booth window, advertising "other kinds" of strip services. It's exactly what one expects to see, but is, nevertheless, surprising in a garish and American sort of way.

Vegas Sahara

With all the sights to see along the strip, it was hard to focus on driving, let alone finding the intersection of Las Vegas Boulevard and E. Sahara Avenue. It turned out Randall didn't need to spot a street sign to find the Sahara Hotel and Casino. After he passed the Fontainebleau Hotel, the Sahara appeared on his right, looking like a movie set for an Arabian Nights tale. Randall wasn't sure where to park, so he pulled over to the curb to check the hotel information Knox had given him. He hadn't thought to look at the stuff before. The hotel brochure was lavishly done. It described the Sahara Hotel and Casino as "a jewel of the desert and a 20-acre oasis of modern luxury and comfort. The entrance pylon and marquee are drawn from exotic cultures fringing the African Sahara Desert." It was all of that and a whole lot more.

With no apparent entrance to a parking structure, Randall pulled into the porte-cochere and was greeted by a parking attendant in a uniform and white gloves. The valet informed him that the hotel offered valet parking for only $20 a day. Randall figured he wasn't paying for it anyhow, so he may as well go first class. He got out of the car and opened the trunk. A bellhop, dressed like a Genie just released from his lamp, unloaded his luggage. The valet gave him a claim ticket, took the car keys and shuttled the Mercury off to the parking structure with a chirp of the tires.

Randall wondered if he'd ever see the car again. He figured he should have no worries, it was only a rental with insurance coverage out the wazoo. The bellhop escorted him into the expansive lobby of the Sahara and to the front desk for check-in. Randall could see the gambling area through an ostentatious archway. The casino was replete with one-armed-bandits, gaming tables and gamblers of every stripe, many armed with drinks. He felt very much out of his element, in his wrinkled khakis and sensible, salt-stained brown hush puppies.

Randall looked about on his way to the registration desk, gawking at the ceiling and columns, entranced by the lights and illusion of opulence. Customers wandered around dressed in everything from tuxedos to overalls. The cacophony of conversations was almost deafening. He got in line for check-in.

When it was his turn, he was summoned to the front desk by a slick looking reservations clerk. "Hello, my name is Craig. Welcome to the Sahara Hotel and Casino. Checking in?"

At first, Randall had trouble finding his voice. "Uh, yeah. Here's my credit card. The reservation should be under my name. The correct spelling is on the card."

Craig searched and shuffled for a bit, then frowned and regretfully indicated he had nothing under that name. "Alright, sir, I'm not finding you on my list. Just one moment while I check it again."

Randall got a sinking feeling in his stomach. Arriving at a hotel for check-in and not having a room was one of his fears. Could it be happening? "Maybe it's still in the name of my boss. I'm here in his place. Try looking under Knox, James Knox."

The clerk ran his finger down the list again. "Ah, yes, sir. Here it is under the name Knox, as you said. Indeed, there's a note indicating that you are to use his reservation. Very good, sir."

Relieved, Randall waited while the clerk completed the check-in process. When done, Craig smiled broadly and handed him the keys. "Here you are, sir. You're very lucky to have secured accommodations in one of the exclusive villas on the hotel grounds. The main tower rooms are also excellent, but the villas are superb."

Craig's tone made it sound like the main tower rooms were only fit for the unwashed. Craig directed the bellhop to take Randall and his luggage to Villa 6B.

Randall followed the bellhop, dressed as a genie look-a-like, out a side entrance and down a circuitous stone pathway. After about 50 yards they came to a cluster of small apartment-like units intermingled with desert gardens and palm trees. Each villa resembled an Arabian tent but built with faux adobe walls. It was sort of Lawrence of Arabia goes Navajo.

The bellhop unlocked and opened the door to villa 6B. After ushering Randall inside and depositing his luggage, the bellhop gave him a brief tour of the amenities. There was a sitting room with a fireplace, a small kitchen and two bedrooms. The bathroom included a shower and a whirlpool bath. His job done, the bellhop casually held out a hand and asked if there was anything more he could do. Randall was not well traveled but he reckoned this was bellhop code for tip time.

Randall reached for his wallet and pulled out a five dollar bill. Before he handed it over, he thought of something. "Actually, yes, can you tell me the location of the NRG meeting that is being held here tomorrow? I forgot to ask at the front desk."

The bellhop pulled some papers from his pocket and after a brief search found the right sheet. "I think this is it. Looks like the NRG meeting will be held in the Ali Baba Conference Room in the North Tower starting at 8 AM. You go back to the lobby and take the east elevators to the 40th floor. The doors will only open on that floor with a special code."

Randall waited for the answer, and finally spoke up. "A code. Really. And what is the code?"

The bellhop held out his hand again. Randall ignored it and waved the bill. The bellhop rolled his eyes and spoke. "Simple. Just punch 3666 into the elevator keypad when you get to 40, wave your hand at the door, and say 'Open, Sez Me!'" The bellhop deftly whipped out his hand with a flourish, grabbed the fiver out of Randall's hand, and smiled a broad smile, displaying unnaturally bright white teeth.

Randall was slightly miffed, but impressed. "You're quite the showman. Are you in one of the night club acts?"

The red-vested bellhop did a pirouette and flashed another smile. "No, but I'd like to be. I practice my routine whenever I can."

Randall kept a straight face and tried a gambit. "You know, I could be a talent agent working for the hotel. What else have you got in your act besides a bit of sleight of hand and fancy footwork? Do you think you could make me laugh? Are you funny?"

The bellhop looked at Randall dubiously, but took the bait. "Where are you from?"

Randall raised an arm and circled it in the air. "Wisconsin."

The bellhop put an index finger to his temple and lightly tapped. "Then you must know about the lumberjack camps they used to have in the north woods of Wisconsin during the depression, right?"

Randall nodded his head in affirmation.

The bellhop leaned forward and stared at Randall. "I'll bet you don't know this story. In 1935, a midget, carrying a big ax, shows up at the Big Pines logging camp near Minocqua. The foreman asks him what the heck he wants. The midget says he's looking for a lumberjack job. The foreman laughs in disbelief. The midget walks up to the foreman, looks him straight in the belt buckle, and offers to demonstrate his skills with the ax. The foreman points to a 4-inch diameter pine behind the midget. The midget directs the foreman to back up a few steps. Without turning to face the tree, the midget swings the ax backwards in an arc over the top of his head. Swoosh, the pine goes down in one stroke." The bellhop mimicked the ax swing with a dramatic wave of his arm.

Randall acted unimpressed but goaded him on. "Okay, then what?"

The bellhop continued. "Well, the foreman looks shocked as hell and asks the midget where he learned to swing an ax like that. The midget says: 'I used to be the foreman of a crew that clear-cut the Sahara Forest in Africa. We could clear 10 acres a week.' The foreman says: 'The Sahara is a desert, not a forest.' The midget says: 'Yeah, well, *now it is*.'"

Randall could not hold back a low groan. "Ah, a Sahara routine for the Sahara Hotel. You know, it's so bad it's good. Mind if I use it?"

The bellhop grinned broadly. "Not as long as you credit me as the source."

Randall smiled and reached for his wallet again. "Don't worry, I wouldn't have the nerve to claim that joke as my own."

The bellhop sensed another tip might be coming and smiled broadly. Randall checked his wallet for a smaller bill, but hesitated when he found only a lonely ten and a few twenties. He hesitated to pull a bill out. Was the lame logging joke worth it? He pretended to look at the bellhop's name tag to buy some time to decide.

The bellhop saw Randall glance at his nametag. He looked down and realized the full name was partially hidden by a shirt fold. "The name's Mickey, sir, like in Mouse, Mantle, Rooney, or Finn. You decide whichever fits the best, but I prefer Mouse. Mick works, too." He gave a Boy Scout salute.

Randall feigned disappointment and folded his wallet up again. "Darn it, Mick, I'm sorry to hear that, because I was thinking of calling you Aladdin."

Mick made a quick ad lib. "I'll have my name tag changed by tomorrow!"

Randall had to give Mick credit for being entertaining and quick witted. He unfolded his wallet again and pulled out the tenner. It suddenly vanished from his hand as if by magic. Randall thought that was quite a slick stunt and no longer felt bad about giving up more money. Mick had earned it. Plus he had a great story to tell. Mick bowed slightly, wished him good luck for the morrow and departed.

Mick had set the AC to high when they'd come in. The room had already cooled off considerably. It beat the oppressive heat outside. The locals claimed the heat wasn't so bad because it was dry heat, but to Randall it was just hot heat. He changed into some lighter clothes. He planned to hit the casino before dinner and take Addie's quarters to visit a user-friendly slot machine.

Randall opened the front door of the villa to check the outside temperature. The sun was now low on the horizon and the desert was beginning to cool off. He turned off the AC and stepped outside to leave, but hesitated before closing the door behind him. The hesitation was due to a phobia he had developed from recurring nightmares about locking himself out of hotel rooms. He had never actually locked himself out of a hotel room, but the fear of doing so always made him double check his pockets before the door closed. After the flapping wing vision, now was no time to take chances.

In the hotel nightmare, he'd find himself in a hallway wearing just a dress shirt, underpants and socks. His wallet and room key would be in his pants which, of course, were in the locked room. He would sneak downstairs to the lobby to get a spare key, hoping no one would see him. It was alright for the desk clerk to see him half-dressed, but not anyone else. Desk clerks were trained to remain professional while interacting with underdressed patrons. He'd use the stairs to get to the lobby to avoid sharing the elevator with some lecherous old lady. Just before making it back to his room with the spare key, he'd wake up sweating. Using low cost self-analysis he surmised that the dream was about the fear of losing control. He didn't need a shrink to figure that one out.

No worries about getting trapped pants-less in an elevator outside his cozy villa. Nevertheless, he made sure the room key was, indeed, in his pants pocket, and that his pants were, indeed, on. He closed the door and headed down the path to the casino. Once there, he was startled by the frenzy of activity. There were so many people and so much ambient energy. Randall heard a man's voice yelling to his left. At first, Randall thought the man was calling his name, but, when he turned to look, it was just a drunk patron protesting his ejection from the casino. Randall wanted to go back to contemplating fountains again but reminded himself that all he needed to do was find a slot machine, insert Addie's quarters, and leave. No need to panic. It was only 1:00 PM. He still had plenty of time before the Lung Committee meeting to test out Addie's quarters.

Randall looked straight ahead with eyes focused and found his way to the slots. Down one row, a beery old lady had a choke hold on the lever of a slot machine that looked like it dated to the 1960s. She was cursing it for not paying off after more than an hour of play. She threatened mayhem if it took her last quarter. She force-fed the coin in the slot and yanked the arm down. The machine's wheels spun, but there was no payoff. The harridan whacked the one-armed bandit with her purse, insulted its parentage, and stomped away muttering a cascade of disparaging invectives. Randall decided her misfortune would be his good fortune.

Randall figured the slot the old crone had been using was due for a payout and it had probably developed an intense dislike for the lady of profane. Randall would be nice to it and treat it with respect. Before committing his first quarter, he inspected the machine. A placard framed in brass sat on its top declaring the slot to be the "Money Honey" model by Bally Manufacturing. Randall introduced himself to the unit, complemented its unique charm, and gave it a reassuring pat on the side. He pulled out the first of Addie's quarters and placed it gently through the money slot. The quarter thunked reassuringly into the bowels of the "Money Honey." The lever arm had a nice feel to it when he pulled it and released it. Blurred images spun in the three windows. When the spinning stopped, there was an orange in each window. Gears ground and levers clicked followed by the sound of coins cascading into the payoff tray.

Randall decided that perhaps this gambling thing wasn't so bad after all. He counted his take. There were 25 quarters or $6.25. Not a bad return for just one quarter invested. Randall put the booty in his left front pants pocket. There were still three more of Addie's quarters to go in his right rear pants pocket. The next quarter brought three horses and a payoff of 30 quarters. The third delivered three cherries and 35 quarters. Randall was up another $16.25. There were too many quarters for his pockets to hold without his pants heading south. He'd have to deal with that before playing the fourth quarter.

A cocktail waitress appeared at his side with a complimentary drink and a basket. She offered her hand in greeting. "Pardon the interruption, sir, but management sent me over to help you. My name is Grace."

Randall had not expected this at all. This Grace was definitely unlike the Grace he knew, in every way. He took her shapely hand in his and noticed the rest of her was as shapely as the hand. He was hesitant to give his real name. "It's nice to meet you, too. Uh, my name is Carlos."

"You don't look like a Carlos," said Grace.

Randall gave Grace a knowing nod. "It's from my mother's side of the family. I get that a lot."

Grace put a scented hand on his arm. "Well, Carlos, why don't you take the quarters out of your pockets and put them in this basket. Then, you should definitely continue. This machine is lucky for you. You seem to be on a roll!"

Randall shook his head. "Oh, no. I can't use these quarters. My daughter, Addie, gave me four quarters to use on the slots and bring any winnings back to her. Then I was planning to quit."

Grace knew she had Randall nearly in her grasp. She just needed to tighten her grip. She leaned forward and put a hand atop Randall's shoulder, giving him a compelling view of her twin sisters. She whispered in his ear. "I have an idea, Carlos. You put the quarter in the slot and I'll pull the lever. I have a special touch."

Randall gave Grace a nervous smile. "Er, sure. No problemo. What could go wrong?"

Randall rubbed the last new Bicentennial quarter for good luck. He poised the quarter in the slot. Before releasing it he declared: "Bombs away!"

Grace made a show of pulling on the slot machine lever with her whole body, then gave a little yelp as she grabbed her elbow.

Randall looked at her with concern. "What's wrong, Grace?"

Grace shook her arm. "Oh, it's nothing. I'm just getting over a case of tennis elbow."

Just then the slot machine made dinging and whooping sounds. Grace looked up at the machine and pointed. "Oh, my God, look at the little windows! It's about to spew quarters."

The slot machine had stopped at three sixes. Bells kept going off. It was another jackpot, only way bigger. Quarters gushed into the tray and spilled onto the floor. Randall was amazed at this positive turn of events. Grace *was* a good luck charm, indeed.

Suddenly the tune of a church hymn came to mind. Randall began singing it but with new lyrics. "Amazing, Grace, how sweet the sound, you wrenched your arm for me. I once just lost, but now I've found the winner I can be." He was slightly out of tune, but made up for it with a sweeping flourish and a bow. It was straight out of Mick's handbook of bellhopping.

Grace shimmied her hips as he sang. When Randall finished his ad libbed hymn she jumped up and down and clapped. "Oh, Carlos. You're better than our lounge singer!"

Randall blushed beet red and was ready to keep playing the slot. *Then he had a spooky thought.* The winning number was a triple six. He was dazed and confused. How could a bad omen bring good luck? What was he missing?

Grace stooped and began to pick up the quarters that had fallen on the floor. Randall just stared. Her stooping was definitely conquering Randall. She stood back up holding a handful of quarters and put them in another basket. "See, Carlos, you *are* on a roll. You should keep playing. Between the two of us, we could beat the house."

Randall was enthused but cautious. "I would like to play some more, but, like I told you, I can't use *these* quarters."

Grace frowned but wasn't deterred. "Oh, right. I almost forgot. Not to worry. We can just go over to the cashier and get paper money in exchange for these quarters. That will make it easier to carry back home . . . for your daughter. Then, you can exchange some of your money for quarters and keep playing. I'm sure you'll do just as well on your own with me by your side."

Randall felt rather stupid for not figuring that out on his own. "Yeah, sure, that's a great idea."

Grace accompanied Randall to the cashier and directed the conversion of Addie's quarters to paper money. The winnings totaled $49.00, even. Randall should have been feeling great about converting one dollar to forty-nine, but he was puzzled by the reappearance of 666. He decided to further test if 666 was a good or bad sign by playing his own quarters. He put the paper money from Addie's quarters into a separate compartment of his wallet. He gave the cashier a twenty dollar bill in exchange for a trayful of eighty quarters. He imagined the payoff could be huge.

Grace took Randall's elbow and led him back to 'their' slot machine. "This should be fun. Let me get you a drink. What would you like?"

Randall didn't think a drink was such a good idea, but demurred. "What the heck! How about a gin gimlet?"

Grace went off for the drink. She looked just as good going away as walking up. "I'll be right back. Don't start without me."

Grace returned with a rather large drink glass and Randall took a hefty gulp before starting with his own quarters. She pressed up against him as he sent quarters down the coin slot and she pulled the lever. Despite his algorithmic processing, all 80 quarters went in the machine and none came back out. It was like the joke about the guy who wanted to win a pun contest. He submitted ten puns hoping that at least one would win, but no pun in ten did. He chuckled at his own joke, then started to feel panicky and thought about the airplane wing. After the last quarter disappeared into the slot abyss, all he wanted was to get out of the casino and *pronto*.

Grace didn't want her fish to escape, but her allure had suddenly disappeared for Randall. He turned and ran out of the casino like a scalded cat. Grace watched him go with a frown on her face and hands on hips. "Dang, we were so close to the blackjack table!"

C H A P T E R 22

———

LOKI

"Wherever you go, there you are."

—Joseph Biedermeier

DARK DESERT HIGHWAY

Randall didn't stop running until he was standing outside under the *porte-cochere* of the Sahara somewhat out of breath.

The parking attendant gave Randall a strange look that said "why was this guy running?" After a long pause the attendant had to ask politely. "Can I help you, sir?"

Randall had been oblivious to the attendant's presence until the question. He glanced over at the man and said the first thing that came to mind. "Er, no. I'm good. Just came out for a breath of hot air. Way too cold in there." He took a deep breath and almost scalded his lungs. After inhaling, he gasped loudly. The afternoon heat was stunning.

"You sure you're alright, sir?" asked the attendant.

This was way more attention than Randall wanted. "Yeah, sure. Quite alright. That was just what I needed. Dropped a bunch of quarters in there. You know what I mean?"

The attendant nodded knowingly. "Got you. Anything you need. I mean anything. You just ask old Tony. I'll fix you up."

Randall smiled and nodded, trying to look cosmopolitan. "Good to know, Tony. But I've gotta go now. Gotta meet a man about a horse."

509

Tony the attendant winked and gave Randall a thumbs up. Randall responded in kind and checked his watch. It was already 2:30 PM. He needed to get ready for the Lung Committee meeting. He rushed back to his villa and fumbled with the front door key before getting it into the lock correctly. He kicked the door open and shot inside, the door slamming shut behind him. He was hot and sweaty, so he shed his clothes.

In his underwear, Randall paced around the bedroom trying to sort things out. He was feeling a tad bleary from the gin and tonics Grace had given him. Questions roiled in his head. How had Addie's quarters given a windfall, but the 666 left him with nothing from his own money? And what had happened to the wing on the plane? The feelings of dread and bad omen led his mind down a rabbit hole.

After more mind meandering, Randall tried to kick himself into gear. The Lung Committee meeting was approaching fast. He needed to clear his head to get ready to "knock 'em dead." The AC was set to full arctic and, in just his underwear, he started to shiver uncontrollably. Instead of dressing, he crawled into bed with the slide printouts to do a final review. Yet, with the bedclothes up to his chin, he could only just lay there staring at the ceiling.

After a while, a *largoid* spider crawled into view and began investigating a ceiling crack. Randall was fixated on the spider's explorations. He recalled that the Hopi believe some spiders can be a manifestation of Loki the Trickster. If you ask Loki a question in his spider form, he is obligated to bring you an answer. Randall explained his dilemma to the arachnid and begged for help. There followed no obvious feedback from Spidey land.

Frustrated he couldn't come up with an answer that fit the situation, Randall leaned over and pulled out the top drawer of the bedside stand. There he found what he was looking for. Bless those Gideons, whoever they were. They had made it to Vegas. He let the Bible fall open to a page and put his finger down randomly. It landed on the Bible verse Isaiah 40:3. Reading it aloud, he decided its message would serve as his guidance.

It read: *"A voice is calling, 'Clear the way for the Lord in the wilderness; Make smooth in the desert a highway for our God.'"*

Randall's moving finger had written and having writ he knew what he must do. He would take a predawn Power Walk in the Mojave. After his Lung Committee presentation he would come back to his little villa, order room service for dinner and hit the hay so he could rise at 3:30 AM. With a local map provided by the front desk, he determined the most direct route west out of town and into the desert. The desert would be dessert.

This new plan finally settled Randall down again. He decided he already knew the presentation well enough. No need to prep further. One just has to be confident. He spent the remaining time methodically dressing in his finest set of power clothes. He shaved once more, combed his remaining hair and put on dabs of Old Spice. He still had 15 minutes to get to the meeting.

Randall made it to the North Tower with time to spare. He was not surprised when he punched the 3666 code into the elevator keypad and the door opened for the Ali Baba room without the need to say "Open *sez* me!" The hallway led to a huge chandeliered conference room with some folks already seated and the rest milling around and chatting. As soon as Randall entered the space, del Aquilar trotted forward in little duck steps to greet Randall.

The Chief looked somewhat frazzled. "Where have you been? I've been trying to reach you to touch base about some changes to your talk. Knox has contacted me with some new data to add to it when he couldn't reach you. The front desk said there was no one here by the name of Biedermeier."

Randall frowned in surprise. "Really? I've been in my villa most of the afternoon . . . er . . . getting the talk ready. Oh, wait a minute. My room was first registered under the name Knox. Maybe that's what caused the mix up."

On hearing this, del Aguilar turned livid and exclaimed. "*Mierda!* Las Vegans are such *cabrones*! Come with me to the AV room and I'll show you the new slides to add and explain them. We have five minutes before I introduce you."

Five more slides were added and del Aguilar went over them with

Randall. He offered to clarify any uncertainties from the audience if needed. "You were a good *estudent* for me. I'm sure you can handle this little hiccup."

Randall nodded numbly. "*De nada*, Chief. You taught me well. I roll with the punches."

The Chief looked at Randall with a crooked smile. "But I did not punch you."

Randall laughed. "It's just a pugilistic American colloquialism."

Del Aquilar gave Randall a light fist bump to the upper arm. "Ah! *Entiendo*! Go sit in the front and come up after I introduce you."

The introduction made Randall sound like a newly minted savior of those afflicted with lung cancer and his best Radiation Oncology trainee. Randall wondered if del Aguilar had him mixed up with the Mormon who'd trained with Randall. Randall had three steps to ascend to get to the podium and felt like he was trying to walk in high heels. His legs stiffened when he got to the top and he had to take baby steps to avoid tripping on wires taped to the floor. His mouth was dry and his throat was as tight as a fat lady's shoes.

Randall was planning to start out with the usual 'thank yous' for inviting him, but when he tried to utter the "th" of thank you, all that came out was a fricative rush of air. He coughed and cleared his throat right into the microphone, causing a loud annoying feedback. Someone came up to him with a glass of water which he accepted gratefully. After a few gulps he was able to clear the runway. Following some off-microphone coughs and hacks, Randall was in full voice and managed to get enough airspeed to take flight. After that, he breezed handily through the presentation, including the new material, with minimal help from the Chief.

Afterwards, there was an engaging give and take with the audience. The response to the new study results was very positive. There was even a motion to make Randall a nominee for membership on the committee. Little did Randall know, but no one wanted to be on the committee since the outcome of most lung studies was mostly dismal. Still a small improvement in dismal can be bigger than a small improvement in successful. And much bigger than a huge improvement in nothing.

After some friendly interchanges with attendees after the talk, Randall found himself almost alone in the large room. Even del Aquilar had left to get to the dinner with a request to see Randall there. That wasn't happening. Despite the successful presentation, Randall had other plans and he nearly jogged out of the room to the elevator. The walk back to his villa was much more pleasant than earlier. The sun had just set and the air was cool.

Eyes Unfocused

The night sky was a dark canopy limned with a diaspora of stars. A frail gibbous moon hovered on the horizon. Halfway back to the hotel, Randall came upon a man-made fountain with a gentle waterfall in the center. It was backlit with colored lights that created a kaleidoscope effect in the thin veil of flowing water. He was fascinated by the shifting shapes of color it created. Randall decided to sit for a few minutes and relax. His thoughts drifted back to the Castaneda book he'd been reading.

Castaneda was fascinated by Shamanism and the concept of alternate perceptions of reality. Looking into the wavering colors, Randall was reminded of Castaneda's different way of seeing. The shifting colors were like the way one gets mesmerized staring into a campfire. That thought reminded Randall of what he loved to do as a child. He'd lie on his back on the living room couch with his head upside down over the edge of the seat cushion. He would imagine that upside down was right side up. He'd giggle as he watched his parents walking on the floor that was now his ceiling.

Other memories came back that Randall hadn't recalled for a long time. When he was six or seven years old, he'd often fret about dying and what it would be like. He'd go for walks along Shorewood sidewalks canopied by huge elm trees. He'd tell the trees about his fears and the trees would tell him not to worry. He recalled a recurring dream in which he could walk ten feet off the ground and move at will in any direction. He was certain then that someday he would be able to walk in the air while awake. That was an alternate reality he'd love to live in.

Sitting in the dark, looking with slitted eyes at the Sahara's rainbow waterfall, he saw dancing faces and flitting birds. Right here was the perception versus reality conundrum of his youth once again. One of Castaneda's tasks was to learn how to use his subconscious brain to merge new and unfamiliar data into his already established mental construct of reality. Randall thought perhaps that's what he had been doing as a little boy upside down on the living room couch.

One task Castaneda was given was called "power walking," which was to walk through the desert at night in total darkness without running into any trees, cacti or other obstacles. His only guidance would come from looking up with "unfocused eyes" at the horizon. There would be no need to see the ground. He just had to keep his mind open to the signals around him in a kind of darkness peripheral vision. Despite his doubts, Castaneda accomplished the task. Randall saw no reason he couldn't do it as well. And perhaps he would try it here.

Randall had also read that Tibetan monks, trained as messengers, used the technique of "eyes unfocused" to travel at night in order to avoid detection. The monks believed that the technique uses peripheral vision to detect the few photons of light available in the dark. This faint amount of light is not enough to form a conscious image in the brain but is subliminally processed in the subconscious. After some practice, the process easily becomes a kind of walking meditation and sensitizes the subconscious to process the information well enough to navigate in limited light.

Randall muttered to himself. "Well, maybe not so easy. We'll see. Might just be an efficient way to gather cactus spines."

Walk This Way

There was little foot traffic on the Sahara's villa pathway to disturb Randall's waterfall meditation. A giggling young couple had walked by, but otherwise he'd been pretty much alone. Randall needed to have this brief down time to collect himself and make further sense of the day's events.

"Hey, Doc, how are you doing? Can I get you something?" said a voice behind him.

It took Randall a second to come out of his meditative fog. He turned and Mick the bellhop was standing there looking concerned.

Randall stammered. "Oh, er, hey there, Mick . . . Alladin. Sorry, my head was elsewhere. No, I don't need anything. Just thinking about a few things. Thanks for rousing me."

Mick bowed slightly. "You know, I sort of like the name Aladdin. I'm going to test it out tonight." He turned on his heel and padded away.

As Randall rose to leave the contemplation bench, Mick suddenly reappeared and startled Randall again. "By the way, I've got a riddle for you. What's the difference between a bellboy, bellman, bellhop and porter? Don't answer now. Wait 'til I see you again. And don't worry, you will see me again."

Before Randall could respond, Mickey/Aladdin disappeared into the dark. Randall took the cue and went back to his villa for a room service dinner and some sheet time.

Having a plan, even a slightly crazy one, seemed to calm Randall down and he dropped right off to a dreamless sleep. The alarm chimed while it was still pitch dark outside, but he shot out of bed and got dressed. With java brewing in the Mr. Coffee, he shaved and showered. Breakfast was a five dollar Milky Way candy bar sourced from the mini-bar. It went down surprisingly well with the coffee. Randall dressed in some lightweight casual clothes and donned his running shoes. He jogged from his villa to the front entrance where he found Tony, the valet, sitting at his station half asleep. Tony questioned Randall's sanity, but reluctantly shuffled off to fetch the Grand Marquis.

Tony came back with the car, got out, and handed Randall the keys. Randall took the keys and asked Tony what he was doing on station at four in the morning. Tony raised both arms and smiled. "What else? Lost a bet. After all, this is Vegas."

Randall and Tony had a good laugh together. Soon Randall was on the road and headed west out of the city on Nevada State Highway 159. He planned to stop when there was no sign of habitation in any direction. He didn't want to see power lines, buildings, or human debris.

As Randall hustled the Marquis toward the desert, the word *debris* made him chuckle as it usually did. It reminded him of a story his college friend, Frankie, had once told him during a shared lunch on campus. Although Catholic, Frankie had grown up in a predominantly Jewish Philadelphia neighborhood. By osmosis, Frankie had absorbed a lot of Hebrew tradition. In eighth grade, his English teacher wrote the word *debris* on the blackboard and motioned for Frankie to stand up. Frankie's job would be to pronounce the word correctly and define it. At first, Frankie drew a mental blank, but then he recalled a recent party hosted by his Jewish neighbor to honor the birth of his son. That gave him the clue to continue. No Hail Mary pass would be needed. Frankie confidently averred that debris was pronounced 'dee-*bris*' and that it was the name of a surgical procedure to reverse a circumcision. The class hooted and jeered. Debris, thus, became Frankie's nickname.

Randall then recalled his own oratory faux pax committed during a 6th grade geography lesson. His teacher had pointed to Iraq on a map of the Middle East and asked the class who could pronounce the name. Randall raised his hand eagerly and when the teacher chose him, he said with great confidence that Iraq was pronounced "Ear-a-cue." Randall decided that his embarrassment was worse than Frankie's, because he had voluntarily betrayed his own ignorance, whereas Frankie had been forced to display his.

The drive west soon reached the outskirts of the city. Randall noticed the buildings and houses were spread farther apart. *Getting closer to pure desert.*

In his mind, Randall kept rehashing the classroom embarrassment that he and Frankie had experienced. He wondered why that memory had persisted all these years. *We were both just ignorant. Better to be ignorant than stupid. Ignorant can still learn. Stupid means you're too dumb to learn, i.e., hopeless.*

Randall drove on in the darkness contemplating whether he was being ignorant or stupid reliving the incident. He heard Doris's voice in his head. *No use plowing that field again. Just focus on the goal. Find the Power Walk starting point before sunrise.*

Fifteen minutes out from the city limits, highway 159 was devoid of car traffic. The speed limit rose to 75 mph so Randall goosed the pedal on the right. It wasn't long before the trip odometer rang up 35 miles. His mental radar indicated he had reached the appropriate coordinates. He pulled off the road and got out of the car to reconnoiter. There was no sign of human habitation in any direction. This was it.

How Dry It Is

Randall pulled to a stop well off the road and killed the engine. He climbed out of the air conditioned car and locked it. The presunrise desert air was not as hot as midday, but still warmer than inside the car. He had the sense that as soon as the sun rose, things would get crispy rather fast.

Randall looked around again to check for signs of humanity, but found none. The silhouette of the Spring Mountains loomed on the western horizon. He reckoned the highest peak should be Mount Charleston, which rose to 9,000 feet above the Pahrump Valley. If the sky remained cloudless, the entire range should be visible in detail at daybreak.

Although it was still dark, to the east there was the faint glow of impending sunrise. He tried to look at his Timex but, in the dim light, just couldn't see the dial. Randall estimated he might have 30 minutes of darkness before the rising sun began to illuminate the surroundings. Before setting off, he checked the perimeter to see if he could make out anything on the ground. All he could discern were some vague shapes that might be sagebrush, rocks or clusters of cacti. *No worries, I'll probably recognize them when I run into them.*

Randall trained his crossed eyes on the western horizon and set off, his shoes crunching along on the desert floor. He was bound for answers. Gideon had promised there would be answers out here. From the early going, his walk went well. He navigated the desert darkness with few problems. He would avoid looking at his watch until the sun rose. He soon lost a sense for how long he had been walking.

Gradually, it was possible to see more definition in the distant mountain range. He stopped walking and looked down at the landscape around him. In a slightly brighter light, he could now see details. The brown desert surface was a mix of hard packed sand and variegated small stones. Scattered about, helter-skelter, were some good-sized boulders among clusters of creosote bushes, sagebrush, yucca, and small cacti. His assessment of his nocturnal navigation skills might need to be down-graded slightly, since the sparse vegetation left a lot of unfettered space. There was a low chance of unwittingly running into anything. Nevertheless, when he had occasion to recount the story, he decided he would still claim full credit for his prowess.

About 30 yards to the south was a large boulder that looked like it would be a good perch from which to view the forthcoming sunrise. Up close, the boulder proved to be just the right size for the task. It was about two feet in height and had a shallow divot on top that was a nice fit for his posterior. His trusty Timex indicated 5:16 AM. Randall settled into his rock spot and, with elbows on knees, watched the sun's ascent.

Waiting for the full sunrise, he reviewed his mental encyclopedia of rocks, acquired as a Boy Scout. The three basic types of rock were sedimentary, metamorphic and igneous. He recalled the Great Mojave Basin was made up of mostly sedimentary rock in the form of sandstone. Metamorphic rock was found less frequently and was formed when heat and pressure from shifting tectonic plates restructured the existing sedimentary rock over millennia. The reformed metamorphic rock could display a myriad of contrasting and intertwined layers. The layers of rock types and colors could sometimes turn ancient rock into modern art.

The sun usually does not give one a sense of its movement during the day, but with the unobstructed eastern horizon as a reference, one could actually detect its movement. It was like watching a time lapse film of a flower blossoming. The sight was a textbook demonstration of earthly astrophysics. Randall was a speck on the surface of a rotating sphere of massive dimension. He watched mesmerized as the full sun came into view and lit the Mojave in red-toned rays.

Tin Can Alley

A sudden noise from the south startled Randall. It sounded like a tin can being kicked and skittering along the ground. He looked in the direction of the sound but saw nothing to explain what he'd heard. There was only a small clump of cacti and a creosote bush. He got down off the boulder and walked south to search the area. Perhaps he had misinterpreted from whence the sound had come. Puzzled, he listened intently for several minutes. As he started to walk back to the boulder, the kicked can sound repeated, this time from the east. He turned and walked east, but again found nothing. Perhaps a small animal was playing with a can. He found no animal tracks or scat. And no can.

Randall was a bit spooked. He briefly entertained the thought that a person might be hiding behind boulders and playing tricks on him. Perhaps he had become the target of some sadistic prankster. Or maybe it was the trickster spider he had conversed with on the ceiling of his villa bedroom. It could have shape-changed and was now having fun with him.

The more possibilities Randall imagined, the more nervous he got. He tried to calm himself down and approach the situation rationally. Clambering to the top of the boulder for a better view of his surroundings, he scanned the area. He neither heard nor saw anything unusual. That calmed him down, but he decided that he'd done what he'd come for. It was time to leave. Make like an amoeba and split.

Randall jumped off the boulder. Before he could take the first step, the "kick the tin can" sound happened again, this time even louder. His anxiety spiked again and registered "scared as H-E double toothpicks" on his personal scare-o-meter. The sound had come from the north, off to his left. He felt like the sound was daring him to look left. He was tired of being fooled with. He shot a look left and saw nothing. Anger crawled up his spine and stiffened it. He clenched his fists at his side.

Randall loosed a cascade of oaths at full volume designed to repel any human intruders. He sprinted to the north about 30 yards and stopped beside another large boulder he thought must be the point of origin. He circled the boulder looking every which way, but there was nothing suspicious to be found.

Randall stomped his feet defiantly on the baked desert floor. "Is anyone there? If someone's out there, show yourself!"

All Randall heard in response was the echo of his own voice. With the fresh charge of endorphins, he was now too angry to be scared. "If anyone is there, show yourself now, or else . . . !"

In the silence that followed, he could hear bees buzzing around nearby flowering cacti. The buzzing grew in volume until it filled his head. He clapped his hands over his ears.

As the buzzing sound reached a crescendo, a booming voice blossomed inside his brain and commanded him to look down at the ground. The voice seemed to come from both within and without simultaneously. He goggled his head around desperate to identify a source for the voice. Nothing but desert in every direction.

The inside out voice boomed again. "Look down!"

It was a directive not to be ignored and Randall obeyed. There was a dark gray and white rock lying at his feet. He picked it up for a closer look and it fit nicely in his hand. Despite his fear, the rock-hound in him was intrigued and classified the rock as metamorphic, unlike any of the other rocks he had seen in the desert. White bands were embedded in the contrasting dark gray and distinctly formed two white capital letters "I" and "Y."

Randall muttered to himself. "What the heck does 'IY' mean? Ignominious Yakima? Indecent yogis? Irritable yowl syndrome?!"

Randall's brain tied in knots and he shouted out loud. "I've trekked to Vegas, gone on a retreat into the desert only to listen to tin cans rattling and find this hunk of metamorphic rock? None of it makes any sense! If you, whoever or whatever you are, have gone this far, at least tell me what it all means!"

Instead of a response from the booming inside out voice, a calm inner voice did the talking. "'In Yourself,' young one, all answers lie within yourself. No longer look out there. Look inside yourself."

It was almost like his mother's essence was inside his head pointing out the obvious. His chest grew warm. He felt wholly himself, and yet somehow completely changed. One might even say he had metamorphosed, like the rock in his hand.

Randall again looked to his left and still saw nothing sinister, only the beautiful sweep of the mountains. His search for answers had led him to isolation. Isolation had led him to himself. He was the only intelligent resource in the desert vastness, except for . . . the mysterious inner voice? God? Spirit? He didn't even know what to call it. Whether he acted as a conduit or a repository was his mystery to solve. Either way, he had found the simple wonder of being him. He wasn't quite sure who or what he was talking to, but announced out loud. "I should have known I had it in me all along."

Randall shook his head and smiled. He pocketed his "IY" Rosetta stone and surveyed the desert one last time. Content, he walked back to where the Grand Marquis sat waiting beside the road. He would ride the wings of Mercury back to Aladdin and Ali Baba.

As Randall drove back to Vegas, and so called civilization once more, he turned on the car radio. Maybe an evangelical station would be broadcasting the explanation for his desert encounter. The radio was already tuned to a Vegas rock station. The DJ announced the next song. It was Steely Dan's *Any Major Dude Will Tell You.* Despite Donald Fagan's nasal singing voice, Randall understood the lyrics loud and clear. To paraphrase, it said you can run, but you can't hide from what's inside.

C H A P T E R 23

———

FOUR QUARTERS

"You get what you pay for and you pay for what you get, sometimes twice."

—Selma Biedermeier

RETURNING HERO

Randall's return trip from Las Vegas was surprisingly uneventful. The long flight gave Randall enough quiet time to plan for the reception he might get from Zelda at the home front. Despite Zelda's fairly benign send off, it had some rough edges. His call home before departure from Vegas had been met with a slightly frosty response. He decided just to be prepared for anything. He was so caught up in his planning that he didn't notice the plane was landing until the wheels hit the runway.

Randall lugged his gear through the obstacle course of deplaning fellow lemmings, then down the concourse. He chuckled at the sign that greeted travelers who had just passed security. "Recombobulation zone." He sighed as he recombobulated his brain in preparation for arriving home.

When he reached the parking structure, he couldn't recall where he'd parked. He stopped and swiveled his head around looking for a clue. None emerged. The only choice was to walk up and down the aisles until he spotted the Scirocco. It didn't help that his car was tiny and every other vehicle was a pickup truck. He looked up at the ceiling. "This would be a great time to throw in a tin can sound!"

After searching long enough for a cake to rise, he realized he was on the wrong level. Sure enough, at the next level, the Scirocco was sitting just feet away in the row closest to the elevator. Randall thought he could hear the car giving him a derisive laugh out the radiator. It continued to mock him by being reluctant to start. After spouting choice epithets and pounding the steering wheel, he got the engine to fire up. He took off with a tire squeal and spiraled quickly down the exit ramp only to find a line up at the payment booth. With that dispatched, he assaulted the freeway, but still didn't roll up to his house until 5:30. That was way late for dinner. He feared there could be hell to pay.

To Randall's surprise, when he walked in the door, Zelda greeted him warmly and said dinner would be on the table soon. *Was this a set up for a big fall?* He took a deep breath to stifle his alert system.

Zelda could be as unpredictable as the local weather. There was a saying among Milwaukeeans: "If you don't like the weather, just wait five minutes."

Kyle and Addie ran to Randall and gave him big hugs. Randall lifted Addie up, gave her his Daddy super-squeeze, and she whispered in his ear. "Mommy was really worried about you while you were gone. She said she had a feeling like something bad was going to happen to you. It's a secret though, cuz I'm not allowed to tell you she's glad you're back. But something else is bothering her."

"Thanks, Sweet Pea," said Randall more loudly than needed. "You give really good hugs."

Kyle ran up and pulled on Randall's coat sleeve. "How was the trip, Dad? Did you bring us anything?"

Randall set down the squirming Addie, stomped his feet, and extended both arms. Yep, I did. Me!" He imagined a big red bow on his shiny scalp.

Both kids looked less than pleased. Zelda laughed and stated the obvious. "Earth to Randall. I think they mean goodies from Las Vegas."

Randall feigned revelation. "Oh, right! They want surprise goodies! Hmm, I might just have something for you two. If I could only remember."

Addie looked worried. "Daddy, what about my quarters? Did you lose them? Did you spend them?"

Randall raised his hand with a flourish. "Of course not! Well, not exactly. Your Bicentennial quarters went into the slot machine. They didn't come out again but a bunch of other ones did. I got so many I couldn't carry them all, so the casino converted the quarters to paper money. I've got them here somewhere. Now, where did I put all that money?"

Randall shuffled around in his pockets dramatically and then gestured with his arm. "Oh, yeah! The envelope is in my briefcase." He pulled out loose paper and folders quite clumsily until finally finding an envelope stuffed with bills. He slapped it on the kitchen counter. "Here you go. Look what happened. Your quarters had babies."

Addie squealed and grabbed the envelope, pulling out two twenties, one five and four singles. She labored to count it. "Jumping jingle berries! It's $49! I'm rich! Thank you, thank you, Daddy."

Kyle looked somewhat crestfallen. "Is there anything for me?"

Randall waited a beat to draw out the suspense. "But you didn't give me any quarters for the slots. Let me try to remember. . . . It was so busy at the meeting. I didn't have much time to shop. Oh, wait. Ah, yes. I did pick up something at the hotel gift shop you might like. Now where did I put it? I hope I didn't leave it in my hotel room."

Kyle began to hop up and down. Randall reached into the briefcase once more, and after some unnecessary shuffling around, produced a small box. He handed it to Kyle, who tore off the gift wrap revealing a box labeled with the Star Wars logo.

"Leaping lizards!" yelped Kyle. "A Boba Fett Star Wars figure. I don't have that one!"

Randall smiled a broad smile. "Yep. I knew that. Well, now you do, Mr. Skywalker." Kyle flopped on the floor and set to wrestling the figure out of the box.

Zelda looked a bit disappointed, but she didn't say anything. Randall raised his right index finger and slapped his forehead with his left hand. "Almost forgot! Come with me, my lady."

Randall led Zelda to the living room and sat her down in Rex the

Wonder Chair. He bowed and retrieved a small object from his pocket. The kids scrambled into the room, almost bowling him over. Randall opened up a fancy black flip box, revealing a silver ring set with turquoise. "Size seven if I do recall. Blue-green goes well with your red hair. Underneath the cotton are matching earrings. Handcrafted by Navajo silversmiths working in teepees while smoking natural grasses."

Zelda was floored speechless. She 'oohed' and 'aahed' at the booty. She tried on the ring and it fit perfectly. The earrings fit her pierced ears just fine and looked great. She gave Randall a sloppy kiss.

Randall had one more surprise. "Pull out the bottom layer of cotton from the box."

Zelda pulled out the cotton and found a small folded piece of paper upon which was written: "This certificate is good for one round trip by personal automobile from Milwaukee, Wisconsin, to Louisville, Kentucky, for some horsing around. Side trip possible to Claiborne Farm, the 3,000-acre, 57-year-old farm that is home to the 1973 Kentucky Derby winner, Secretariat. Or, perhaps to the Calumet Farms, home of several other Derby winners."

"Oh, my heavens," burst Zelda. "I didn't think you knew any of that. How did you get all that information?"

Randall looked proud. "I have my ways." He gestured to the encyclopedia set that took up the entire wall of the living room.

"Randy, that might be the cleverest thing you've ever done for me," gushed Zelda.

Randall went into his "Aw shucks" mode. "We all deserve a Spring break and we can do something you and Addie would enjoy. March will be Spring in the South, but here it will still be frozen tundra. So, the perfect time to go."

Kyle stared at the encyclopedias as if for the first time. "You learned all that stuff just from reading those big books?"

Randall reached up and patted the encyclopedia bindings. "Yep! And you could learn whatever you want, too. Just pull down a book and open it up. Information at your fingertips."

Kyle gagged a bit. "No way! Too much work!! I want to tell a machine to find the information for me. Invent that, Dad! Make me a magic box with a button I can push to learn whatever I want."

Randall's eyebrows soared. "Actually, I was just in the Chief's office, and he had a computer installed that was small enough to fit on his desk! Can you believe it? Cleared out a whole room of equipment that did the same thing. It can store lots of information."

Kyle got excited. "Can you ask it questions and get answers?"

Randall shook his head. "Not exactly. It can do calculations for you. Who knows? Maybe someday."

Kyle got a far away look. "Yeah, maybe when I grow up they'll make one. Dad, that would be clever! I want one small enough for me to carry around. And then it can plug into the wall and talk through the wires to the sky where it can get all the information in the world!"

Addie joined in the fantasy. "Yeah! And we can use magic cameras to talk to Grandma and Grandpa!"

Randall and Zelda laughed and slapped their thighs. "That *would* be amazing. Your dad's clever, guys, but he's not a wizard. That's impossible!"

Kyle's face twisted into a sly, slightly evil smirk. "Hey, Mom, what was the un-cleverest thing Dad ever did for you?"

Zelda squinted her eyes. "Hmm, let me think. There're so many to choose from. I've got it. Randy always leaves the toilet seat up. I'd go to the bathroom at night to pee, half asleep, and think the seat was down because that's where I had left it. I'd sit down on the john and my butt would go right in the water. Then I was wide awake and had to dry my fanny. I'd go back to bed and whack your Dad with a pillow."

Randall looked shameful as the kids laughed riotously and pointed at him.

Zelda continued, enjoying the laugh fest. "So, your Dad got tired of the pillow whacking. He installed a pressure activated switch on the toilet seat so that when the seat was up a small desk lamp on the toilet tank would turn on to show the seat was up. If the light was off, that meant the seat was down and it was safe to sit."

Addie looked at her Dad with admiration. "Wow, that's really cool. Dad, you're smart!"

Zelda shook her head slowly. "I thought so, too. We both thought that was worth a patent until one night, when the light was off, I got a wet butt again. Turns out the light bulb was burned out and he got pillow whacked again."

Randall held up his hands in defense. "You have to admit, it was a good idea, but, in hindsight, it had that one flaw. No pun intended."

This caught Zelda by surprise and she laughed, despite herself. The kids joined in even though they didn't quite know why. Randall gave a small bow.

Randall was suddenly the most popular Dad in the house again. Kyle ran upstairs to get the rest of his Star Wars figures and set them up on the dinner table around his place setting. Addie counted her paper money again. Zelda checked out her earrings in the mirror. When the three were done admiring their swag, Zelda announced that dinner was ready and they all ran to the kitchen and dug in. For the next twenty minutes the only sounds were of utensils scraping plates, chewing and dinner time happy banter. Randall was pleased that he seemed to have appeased the Las Vegas gods. Yet Addie had warned that something else was on Zelda's hit list. Randall couldn't wait to find out.

Sahara Redux

After Zelda cleared away the dinner dishes, Randall volunteered to wash them while Zelda readied Addie and Kyle for bed. Both kids were still hyped up and pleaded for a bedtime story. "Come on guys, you know I can't tell stories like your dad. Ask him to tell you a short one though, because I need to talk to him about some important stuff before we crash. Maybe a ten minute story, alright?"

Addie looked disappointed, "But, Mom, I want him to tell me about how he won my quarters and Kyle probably wants to hear how he found Boba Fett. You know Dad can't tell that story in just ten minutes."

Kyle stood up and bounced a bit. "Yeah, Mom. Addie's right. Plus, he needs to tell you how he found your jewelry stuff. And maybe other important things that happened."

Zelda knew she couldn't win this round and gave in. "Oh, alright! I'll double it to twenty minutes. How's that?"

"Deal!" said Addie.

"Ditto!" said Kyle. "Can we call for Dad to come upstairs?"

Zelda gave a resigned head nod. "Sure. You have permission to yell from the top of the stairs and break the sound barrier."

Both kids went to the stairs and hollered for their dad to come up right away. They didn't break the sound barrier, but a small chunk of plaster fell off the ceiling. Randall came running up the stairs to see what the commotion was about. "Who's hurt? Do we need to go to the ER?"

Zelda put a damper on the need for an ambulance run. "No injuries, Chief. The kids just need an emergency bedtime story."

Kyle ran up to Randall and pulled on his sleeve. "Dad. Tell us about your trip to Las Vegas. What were the casinos like? I bet they were cool."

Addie pulled on Randall's other arm to get his attention. "Yeah, and I need to hear how you outsmarted the slot machine."

Kyle could see Randall trying to retreat. "Don't worry, Dad. We know you're tired from the trip. You don't have to tell us about the whole trip. Just the stuff we asked about. Oh, and Mom's present. Mom said we had permission for a twenty minute story. Then she has something important to talk with you about. You know, probably adult stuff."

Randall was relieved his speaking engagement would be short. He was, indeed, wasted. But what the heck was this private session with Zelda all about? He remembered Addie had mentioned it when he'd first come home. "No problem, kids. I'm sure I can cover those topics in twenty minutes. Go ahead and get settled in and we'll begin." Randall thought to himself. *If I can stretch it out longer, maybe I can sort out what Zelda's going to be on about.*

Kyle jumped into his bed and got under the covers. Addie joined him there. Wondercat and Milky Way seemed to like story time, too, and wandered into Kyle's bedroom. Each cat burrowed in the downy covers next to their respective cat-designated kid. After the cats stopped turning in circles, Zelda settled in at the foot of the bed. Randall was set to begin the tale. It would be easy because he didn't have to make it up.

Zelda gave out a warning before Randall started. "Randy. Remember. Keep it to twenty minutes. I need to talk to you before we go to bed."

Randall felt his stomach knot up. No sentence starting with "we need to talk" was ever a good omen. "No problem. I'll just cover the stuff you want to hear, not the boring meeting events."

Zelda scoffed. "Ha! I've got a whacking pillow ready for you if you go over 20 minutes."

Randall involuntarily jumped back as if hit by a pillow. Then and there he revised his plans for the story and spoke slowly in his spooky voice. "I'd better get started, then. Actually, as I think back on it now … some strange and spooky stuff happened besides the boring meeting."

The kids pulled the covers up to their chins. Zelda looked curious.

"What happened?" squeaked Addie.

Randall motioned as if he was flying. "On the airplane, I was sitting in the window seat. When we got to 35,000 feet, I looked out and the wing started flapping up and down like a bird's wing. It scared the stuffing out of me. I looked away and asked the stewardess for a drink to steady my nerves. I didn't look again until I had downed half of the drink. When I finally dared to look back again, the wing was flapless and remained that way until we landed."

Kyle and Addie shivered and looked at each other with dread.

Zelda interrupted. "Randy! Please don't scare the kids by making stuff up."

Randall put up both hands in a defensive gesture. "I promise. I'm not making this up. Anyway, the flight landed okay and I rented a car, drove to the Sahara hotel and checked in. Beautiful place with a big casino on the first floor. Every kind of gambling you could think of, but it scared me and I didn't want to go inside the casino. Hundreds of people and you know how I hate crowds. Gambling has always seemed a bit evil to me. My room was actually a little villa outside the main building. It was really nice with everything anyone could want."

"What's a villa?" asked Addie.

Randall thought for a moment. "It's kind of like a fancy cabin. This one was designed to look like something Arabian."

"Did it have a TV?" asked Kyle. "Did you watch some neat movies?"

Zelda let out a breath. "He probably watched some triple X flicks."

Kyle looked interested. "What are those?"

Zelda was sorry she'd brought it up. "Never you mind, little dude. Not now. When you're older."

Randall let that one roll by. "Yeah, there was a TV, but, you know, I never turned it on. I was still kinda freaked out by the flight and the *casinophobia*, so I stayed in my cabin and read the Bible."

Zelda's eyes popped open so far, Randall thought he might have to look for her eyeballs under the bed. "You read the Bible? You're in Las Vegas and you read scripture? You hate church."

Randall again took a defensive posture. "Well, that's what the Gideons put the Bibles there for. For comfort in times of need. And it felt like a time of need."

Kyle started laughing. "Daadd, you're pulling our legs, aren't you?"

Randall nodded and then shook his head. "Maybe. Maybe not. The storyteller can tell the story any way he wants to. It's for the listener to decide what's the truth."

Addie pushed up on her elbows. "I believe you, Daddy."

Randall smiled. "Thank you, Sweet Pea. During the day it was so hot outside, I decided to wait until dusk to go outdoors."

"How hot was it?" asked Zelda.

Randall pointed to Zelda to acknowledge the assist. "It was so hot the chickens were laying hard-boiled eggs."

Both kids laughed like baboons. Zelda joined in.

When everyone settled, Randall went on. "And the cows were giving evaporated milk."

That started another round of heeing and hawing. Randall put his hand under his chin and pondered. "Hmm, now where was I? Oh, yeah. There was a beautiful walking path between the villas. The path had flowers, plants and little water fountains. I walked the path a bit and sat on a bench next to a fountain. I looked up at the darkening sky and marveled at all the stars I could see. Many more stars than you can see here in Milwaukee. While I was sitting there, a bellhop named Mickey walked by and started a conversation. He was dressed in an outfit that made him look like a character out of an Arabian Knights story. I nick-named the bellhop Alladin. Like Ali Baba maybe. You remember that story, don't you?"

"Yeah, I remember," said Kyle. "We got the book for Christmas one year and you read us all the stories. And then I got a rubber sword for my birthday. It's in my closet next to the light saber and my rubber tortilla."

Randall nodded. "Yep, you are well armed to fend off the Boogie Man. Anyway, it turned out the bellhop was also a standup comedian when he wasn't hopping bells. He told me lots of funny jokes and sto-ries. That got me in a better mood."

"Can you tell us one of his jokes?" asked Addie.

Randall told them the story of the lumberjack from the Sahara for-est. Zelda got it and groaned a woeful groan. The kids were slack-faced. She then tried to explain the story to the kids without much success.

"That joke is awful," said Kyle. "He shouldn't quit his bellhop job. Why do they call them that anyway?"

Randall thought for a moment. "Good question. I'm guessing it's be-cause bellhops wait in the hotel lobby for when people check in with lug-gage. When the desk clerk rings the bell on his counter, the bell hop has to hop forward and take the luggage to the room. So, it's like ring bell and hop to. Dang! Mickey promised he'd see me again and explain the differ-ence between bellhop, bellman, and bellboy, but I never saw him again."

"Move it along, please," said Zelda.

Randall came back into focus. "Right. After Mickey left, I decided to brave the casino and try the slot machines with Addie's four quarters. I was kind of shaky, but I walked in and looked around until I found a slot machine I liked."

Randall recounted the bonanza of winnings he got with Addie's quarters and the total flame out with $20 worth of his own quarters. He concluded Addie's quarters were probably lucky because of the unicorn spell Addie had put on them. Addie agreed solemnly and looked immensely proud of herself.

"Then what did you do?" asked Kyle. "Did you try more gambling?"

Randall dismissed the question with a wave. "No, I was actually feeling so claustrophobic by then that I went back to the villa and decided to hit bed early. I wanted to get up before sunrise and drive out into the desert to where I could see no sign of mankind and watch the sun come up."

Zelda looked startled. "You got up before dawn? I warned you about making stuff up."

Randall gave Zelda a look that said "Oh, ye of little faith" followed by a head shake. "I know. But I did. Found a spot about 30 miles out of town and parked. Walked in the dark until I found a rock to sit on."

Randall gave his micro audience a short version of the sunrise, the kicked can sound and the God-like voice. All three audience members were convinced he was making up another story. He paused for drama, then pulled the "IY" rock out of his pants pocket for show and tell. His rapt audience just gaped for a long beat.

Zelda took the rock from Randall and studied it. "Wow. This is really unusual. No wonder you were *flabbervasted*."

Kyle grabbed for the rock. "Let me see it." He and Addie studied the rock and handed it back to Randall.

Zelda looked at the bedroom clock. "Would you believe it? You have five minutes left. Is there more to the story?"

Randall shook his head. "That's it for the interesting parts. The rest of the weekend was meetings and more meetings and the flight home. Any questions?"

Kyle sat up in bed again. "Hey, wait. You didn't tell about Boba Fett and Mom's present. You did Addie but not us."

Addie saw her opening. "I bet your part wasn't as interesting as mine."

Kyle tried to punch Addie in the arm, but she dodged it. "I bet my part was more interesting. So there!"

Zelda broke up the potential brawl. "Kids, kids. That's enough! Settle as of now. Randy. Fill us in on Boba Fett and Navajo jewelry and, by God, make it equal to slot machines."

Randall had to laugh at Boba Fett, Navajo, and slot machines being used in the same sentence. "Hee hee. That's rich. Okay. Here goes."

Randall nicely fit the missing story parts into four minutes and was proud of himself for making them sound of equal importance to winning $49 with four quarters. Everyone looked happy.

Zelda jumped in. "Randy, the story was great and you have avoided a pillow stomping. It's past time for the kiddos to be stuffed under their covers. Addie, get to your room and I'll tuck you in. Dad will do Kyle. Then your Dad and I are going to have a Q and A session of our own."

Randall was done worrying about the third degree. "Fine with me. What did you kids think about tonight's story"

Kyle scratched his head. "I think you make up great stories, Dad. I was kind of scared while you were telling it, but I'm not anymore. Cans don't move by themselves and God doesn't talk from the sky. The Boba Fett part was great."

Addie nodded in agreement with Kyle. "Yeah, I was a little scared by the plane and desert parts, too. But I believe it's probably true just like the quarters story."

Randall was curious why Addie thought the stories were true. "Why'd you decide that?"

Addie let out a sound like "duh." "Because you'd never give me 49 dollars for no reason. What do you think, Mom?"

Zelda snorted. "I'll let your Dad know later on what I believe. It's time for lights out, kids!"

Zelda and Randall made their way down the stairs to the kitchen. It was almost 9:00 PM and Randall was starting to feel groggy.

The Phone Call

Zelda motioned Randall to sit down at the kitchen table. She looked quite serious. Randall *uh ohed* inside. "Have a seat, buster. I have a few questions."

Randall sat as directed but his head sagged to the table. "If this is going to be a long inquisition, I think I need a coffee tune up."

Zelda sat down and pointed to the microwave. "Go ahead and nuke away. There's enough cold brew left for a small cup."

Randall went through his mental Rolodex for clues to what might be up. Nothing came to mind. He tried to make his face reflect innocence. He returned to the table with his heated cup of coffee and sat down. "Do I need a lawyer?"

Zelda laughed and looked him in the eye. "Do you know a young lady named Elisa Angeles?"

Randall jerked back his head in surprise. "Err. . . .Yes, I do. She's a nurse who recently started working in the department as a patient care coordinator."

"Why haven't you mentioned her to me?" asked Zelda.

Randall was flummoxed. "It never occurred to me to bring her up. Why do you ask? How did you hear about her?"

Zelda was turning a deeper shade of red. "She called the house on Saturday afternoon asking for you! She apparently didn't know you were in Vegas. If you, indeed, work together, wouldn't she know you were out of town? And how would she know our home number? And do you want to know why she called?"

Randall rummaged his mental attic for appropriate responses. "The entire department knows our number in case of emergencies. I've been concerned there might be something healthwise going on with her. What did she want?"

Zelda looked almost ready for tears. "Elisa was crying and said she needed to talk to you. She just found out she's pregnant and her doctor is concerned about something wrong in her pelvis. She said she needs your help. Then I hung up on her."

Now Randall was upset. "You what? Why'd you do that?"

Zelda was about to spout tears. "Tell me you're not the father, Randy."

Randall nearly jumped out of his chair. "What!? Are you kidding me? Why would you ever think that?"

Zelda shrunk down in her chair. "Is she cute? She sounded cute on the phone."

Randall got up and put his arms around Zelda's shoulders. He laughed, then kissed Zelda's forehead. "Yes. Elisa is very cute, but she has a boyfriend and they've been talking about marriage. Am I attracted to her? Of course. Any red-blooded man would be. But she's too short for me. Besides, I'm in love with you."

Zelda wiped her eyes with a hankie and sniffed. "Oh, really?"

"No. O'Reilly!" joked Randall. "You're the only one for me. Think about it. If she and I were that close, she would have known I'd be in Vegas this weekend. She'd also know it would be stupid to call the house and risk getting you on the phone. And she'd be even dumber to tell you she was pregnant."

Zelda hiccuped several times. "I suppose. But maybe she was calling to rat you out to me if you'd blown her off after she told you she was PG."

Randall nodded. "Possible. But unlikely. If she wanted me to help her pay for an abortion, let's say, it would be more likely she'd blackmail me for the money threatening to tell you if I don't come through for her."

Zelda nodded slowly and sat quiet for a beat. Then she started to cry again. "Oh, Randy. Now I feel so stupid for hanging up on her. I could have at least waited to get more information. We should call her back right now, but I never got a call back number. I hope she didn't do something rash."

Randall thought for a moment, and sighed deeply. "I think she said her sister had come to visit. So she's not alone. It's pretty late to call now. I don't think she'd do anything radical."

Zelda started. "Radical?"

Randall grimaced. "You know what I mean. Pull an Alexandra."

Zelda jerked. "Oh. Right. That makes it even more important to call. There must be some way to get a hold of her. I won't be able to sleep until we find out more."

Randall looked pensive for a long moment, shook his head in misery, but then jumped up. "Of course! Doris puts out a monthly call sheet for emergencies. You know—if I get called in for an emergency treatment, I have the home numbers for all the staff needed to begin a treatment. I'm pretty sure all the staff are on it. Elisa should be too."

Zelda looked up hopefully. "Where would you have it?"

Randall thought for a second. "I think it's in a folder in my briefcase." He retrieved his briefcase from his den and found the list. "Bonanza! Here it is. Elisa Angeles. 414-781-9990."

Zelda reached for the wall-mounted phone in the kitchen. "Randy, let me make the call back. After all, I made the big booboo. I should at least apologize. Then, I can pass it over to you."

Randall agreed and read off the number again. The phone rang four times before it was picked up.

Zelda jumped to respond. "Hello? Is this Elisa?"

There was a pause on the other side of the line. "No. This is Elena. Elisa is resting. Who's calling?" The voice sounded small and tired.

Zelda did some quick thinking. "This is Zelda Biedermeier. I'm returning Elisa's call from earlier. We . . . ah . . . got disconnected and I didn't have the number to call her back. Are you Elisa's sister? My husband told me about you. Randall just got back from Las Vegas and I got this number from him."

Elena didn't respond immediately and Zelda gripped the phone like it might escape.

Finally, Elena spoke. "Yeah, well. Elisa said you hung up on her. But maybe it was just a, as you say, disconnect. She wanted to talk to your husband. If he's available to talk now, I'll see if I can get her to the phone."

Zelda nodded, then, again, realized that Elena couldn't see her. "Um, yes, he's right here." Zelda pointed at Randall and then at the phone.

Randall waved his acknowledgement. "You first, my lady. Do your apology, then transfer it to me."

There was a long delay and then Elisa got to the phone. "Hello? Who is this?"

Zelda adopted her "friendly neighborly voice" which came out a bit more singsongy than she expected. "This is Zelda Biedermeier. My husband is back home now and anxious to talk to you. I am so sorry about before. I took your meaning the wrong way and jumped to unwarranted conclusions. I apologize profusely. After you finish talking with Randy, I mean my husband, if I can help in any way. . . . Well, here he is."

Zelda handed the phone to Randall before Elisa had a chance to respond. "Hey, Elisa. It's Dr. B. What can I say, but hello? What's up?"

Zelda motioned Randall to hold the phone so she could hear the conversation.

This time Elisa had better control of her emotions. "I'm really sorry to bother you at home, but I was beside myself with worry." Her breath caught in her throat and she paused.

Randall feigned ignorance. "What about? How can I help?"

Elisa started strong. "Remember how I was talking about something that may be going on with me? Well, I didn't want to go into detail about it then, but I'd missed two periods. I sort of ignored it because my periods are usually pretty irregular, especially when I'm under stress. And, believe me, I've had plenty of late. Then the last few weeks I've also been having nausea in the morning. Sometimes with the *urpsies*. So I saw my doctor on Friday and my pregnancy test was positive."

Randall let out a sigh. "I'm sorry to ask this, but do we have a suspect for the father?"

Elisa struggled to hold back a sob. "Yes, I do. My idiot boyfriend who's already flown the coop several weeks ago. And good riddance. I want nothing more to do with him. He's a self-centered two-timing son of a mother. And he's the only semen donor possible!"

Zelda smiled broadly.

Randall winced involuntarily. "One mystery solved. How do you feel about the baby?"

"Just fine," blurted Elisa. "But there's another complication. And it's a big one." She began to sniffle.

Zelda's expression became drawn. Randall urged Elisa to take deep breaths before continuing.

Elisa collected herself, then went on with the story. "On the pelvic exam my doctor thought I was already three months along and he felt something suspicious in my pelvis. That got me an ultrasound, which confirmed the three month pregnancy. But there was a mass on the right side of the pelvis, and he said it needs further investigation. He's thinking it's an enlarged lymph node, but he's not sure without further imaging. That possibility made him check all my lymph nodes again and he found enlarged nodes in my neck and under my arm. I'm set up for a biopsy of the neck node on Monday."

This was the end of Elisa's calm and collected voice. The sound of soft sobbing echoed through the phone line. Zelda began to cry in sympathy. Randall looked at the ceiling. No answers there, just ceiling tiles.

Zelda grabbed the receiver from Randall's hand and the next few minutes were filled with unintelligible girl talk. To Randall it sounded like a pilot talking on the radio to flight control. There was nothing for it but to let it wane on its own.

Zelda asked Elisa to hold for a second and put her hand on the receiver. "Randy, she's still pretty upset. Do you want to talk to her?"

Randall pursed his lips. "Nah. Not just yet. Keep the girl-talk going until she settles a bit more. Make an excuse for me."

Zelda took her hand off the mouthpiece. "Randy wants to talk to you, but he had to run to the bathroom. It could be a while. In the meantime, tell me about the baby. Is it a boy or a girl?"

Elisa sobbed softly and then spoke. "That's another unknown. The baby was turned funny and they couldn't make it out. But they saw a heartbeat and thought the baby was healthy. The doctor said the ultrasound wasn't the best quality. That's why they're still unsure about whether they're seeing an enlarged pelvic node or an artifact."

Zelda had hoped to raise her spirits with the inquiry, but now felt bad she might have compounded things. "So there are still a few unknowns, but they could all be nothing down the line. Best case, you have a healthy baby and nothing else. Boy or girl makes no difference. Let's picture that and not be sucked down an imaginary sinkhole."

Elisa was quiet for a beat. "You're probably right. I tend to focus on the worst case. That might just make the outcome a self-fulfilling prophecy."

Zelda nodded in assent then, again, realized Elisa could not see her. "Er, yeah, you bet. Better to hope for the best and prepare for the worst."

Zelda surprised herself and went on to invite Elisa and Elena to the house for dinner Monday night so they could all discuss choices and options. The convincer was an offer of chicken enchiladas, salad, and homemade guacamole. Randall felt like a fifth wheel when Zelda finally gave up the phone to him.

Randall wasn't quite sure what to say. "Well, sounds like you and Zelda had a fine little chat. What was it you wanted from me?"

Elisa sounded perfectly calm and professional again. "Zelda was very helpful. She knew just how to get my emotions out of the sky. I'll need your medical expertise once we get the biopsy results back. There will probably be some tough decisions to make that are way beyond my skill set."

So it's "we" now, Randall thought to himself. *How do I get caught up in this stuff?*

"You still there, Dr. B?" asked Elisa.

"Yeah, sure. Right here with you." Randall tried to clear his head. "Who's doing the biopsy and at what hospital?"

"It's Dr. Blankenship at County Hospital," she responded.

"Well, good," said Randall. "They usually do a frozen section for preliminary pathology results. I can call over there and get a verbal report. I know most of the Pathologists. I should be able to call and get the results by dinner time tomorrow. Then, if it's negative, we can celebrate the potential arrival of a newly minted Angeles."

Elisa hesitated before responding. "Hmm. I hadn't really thought of it that way . . . yet. But why not practice some positive thinking? See you tomorrow. Say goodbye to Zelda for me. And thanks again. We'll bring some wine for you and grape juice for me."

CHAPTER 24

LIGHT SHOW

"Outside of a dog, a book is a man's best friend. Inside of a dog, it's too dark to read."

—Groucho Marx

With the Sunday phone call to Elisa finally ended, Randall leaned back in his chair. He announced loudly that the large bolus of coffee, not to mention the disturbing news from Elisa, had him on full alert again.

Zelda echoed the remark. "I'm so hyped up now I could work a third shift. How in the heck are we going to get to sleep? Plus, I'll have to do some major shopping tomorrow if we're having guests over for enchiladas and all the fixings."

Randall nodded his agreement. "Yeah. It's like when I was a kid and got overhyped playing with my cousins at family picnics. I became an Energizer Bunny. Mom would have to peel me off the wall. She'd say I was overtired. That never made sense to me. I thought that if you were over being tired you were asleep. But now I get it."

Zelda got up from her chair and began hopping around hunched up like a monkey. She started scratching her armpits and hooting. "Yeah, 'Mister Doctor Man,' what are we gonna do now to get under tired?"

Randall got up and joined Zelda, mimicking her movements. They bounced, hollered and hooted until they were both out of breath. They staggered back to their chairs and sat back down, puffing loudly.

Randall got his breath back first and smacked the table with his open palm. "Boy! Have we got a wicked case of the jeebs."

Zelda slapped the table even harder and the sound echoed off the kitchen walls. "Your mating ritual sucks, monkey boy."

Randall's response was preceded by a loud and juicy raspberry sound using lots of tongue. "If mine sucks, yours Hoovers! But give me a hug and I'll upgrade your score."

They both laughed uproariously, rose from their chairs, and wrapped their arms around each other.

Randall finally pulled back from the hug. "Boy, if the kids could have seen us cavort like chimps, we'd never live it down." He heard giggling at the dining room door and looked in that direction. Kyle and Addie were both standing there trying to stifle laughs. "How long have you two been standing there?"

Kyle scratched his armpits. "Long enough to see your monkey dances. All the yelling and loud noises woke us up. We were scared and came down to see if you guys were fighting."

Zelda felt like she'd been caught with her undies around her ankles. "Oops! Sorry, kids. I guess we were a little loud."

"You think?" observed Addie. "Did something happen after we went to bed?"

Randall tried to explain. "Actually, yes. We talked on the phone to a friend from work. She's having some problems that made us both worried. So, we were just blowing off some nervous energy to get tired enough to go to bed."

Kyle looked dubious. "Did it work?"

Zelda nodded. "I think so. I'm starting to feel like a rag doll." She waved floppy arms to illustrate her point.

Addie laughed. "That's funny, Mom. How do you do that?"

Zelda demonstrated again. "It's easy. You just pretend there's no bones in your arms."

Addie tried, but couldn't quite make it look like her arms were made of rubber. Kyle tried and was even worse at it.

Randall decided it was time to roll up the magic carpet. "Alright, chipmunks. We can practice floppy arms tomorrow. Let's get you guys back under sheets and blankets so Mom and I can have some quiet time. Otherwise we'll be real testy tomorrow. I'm sure you all don't want that."

Addie wasn't quite ready to go quietly into the good night. "Who is the friend from work? What bad thing happened to her?"

Zelda knelt down and hugged Addie. "Oh, you dear heart. You are always concerned about the welfare of others. That's great. Elisa's story is too complicated to go into right now. But, good news. Elisa and her sister are coming over for dinner tomorrow. You'll have a chance to meet and talk to them. How's that?"

Addie nodded and smiled. "Okay. I bet she's nice."

Kyle was feeling left out. "How do you know that? She could be a witchy woman."

Addie stuck out her lower lip. "Because she works with Dad. He only works with nice people. Right, Dad?"

Randall nodded. "A consummation devoutly to be wished. But, yes, she's very nice. You'll see. Now, let's shuffle on off to slumberland."

It didn't take long to reinsert the kids into their bed slots with both Randall and Zelda doing the insertions. When done, they reconnoitered in the living room, sitting side by side on the couch. Randall took Zelda's hand and patted it softly. "Nice work tonight. Not a cakewalk, any of it."

Zelda let out a loud breath. "Thanks. You too. But, seriously, monkey boy, how are we going to get settled enough for bed without resorting to liquor?"

The Green Light

Randall contemplated briefly. "Hmm. I've got it. How about we just start a fire in the fireplace and lie on the rug in front of it? You know, just to relax the old body parts. We can pretend we're camping out and looking at the stars . . . and telling ghost stories."

Zelda clapped her hands together. "Great idea. There's already fresh wood in there. I'll get some old newspapers and we'll be cooking in a few minutes. While you build the fire, I'll mix up some hot toddies."

Randall agreed. "That's a bit of kit! And some blankets to crawl under."

Zelda stopped what she was doing and questioned Randall's turn of phrase. "A bit of kit? What the heck does that mean?"

Randall laughed. "Sorry. I just heard that last week from one of my patients who is a World War II vet, but in the British army. It means something like 'that's perfect for the task at hand,' as he explained it. Sometimes in more mundane usage, when referring to the shape of a woman's derriere, it's modified to 'a piece of kit,' if you get the drift."

Zelda *tsked* and chuckled. "Oh, that's perfectly clear to me. Is that a lewd suggestion of what might happen in front of the fire?"

Randall looked deeply wronged. "Heavens to Betsy, no. You have cut me to the quick. I was using the most benign version."

"Yeah, sure," taunted Zelda. "There will be no ass grabbing tonight. Just talking. Got that, ape man?"

Randall bowed in deference. "You bet. No hinder pinching on the menu. Yes, Ma'am."

Zelda chuckled despite herself. "Ha! You look so needy. I have something weird to talk about with you. Perhaps, if that goes well, we can reconsider my ruling."

Now Randall was curious what "weird" meant and he decided to keep quiet. Soon, the fire was going strong and they were huddled under the blanket with their feet getting toasty and the hot toddy warming their innards. Randall moved his leg until it was touching Zelda's. She moved hers away. "Too soon, Bucky. Ready for the first question?"

Randall acted like his stuffed teddy bear had been taken away. "Oh, alright. If you insist."

Zelda's question wasn't even close to what Randall had expected. "What were you doing about 5:30 on Saturday afternoon?"

"What?" Randall thought for a second. "I was making my presentation at the NRG meeting. Wait a minute. They're two hours behind us. It would have been 3:30 there. What has that got to do with anything?"

Zelda held up her hand. "Wait for it. Just answer the question."

Randall remembered the time well. "As memory serves, I was freaking out about lots of stuff, lying in bed in my undies. I was staring up at cracks in the ceiling, when this huge-ass spider started crawling right above me. My addled brain immediately thought it was Loki the Trickster of Navajo legends come to trick me."

Zelda gave out a gasp. "You mean like when a Shaman inhabits his animal spirit?"

Randall shuddered. "Exactly!" He began to think the alcohol was fast tracking to his brain's spooky center. "Please explain why this is of interest to you."

"Well, Chucky...." Zelda had an odd rasp to her voice. "At that very time, I was sitting in front of a fire in front of this very same fireplace."

Randall raised his head. "In the middle of the afternoon? Whatever for?"

"It was cloudy and dark. Snow was falling and the house was chilled. For some reason I couldn't get warm and kept shivering. The kids, too. They asked for the fire. We were sitting here with the cats enjoying the warmth when.... Randy, you remember when Chris and Julie were over here and we had hot toddies together?"

Randall blanked out on the reference. "Chris and Julio, who?"

Zelda sounded disgusted with Randall's recall. "You know. Chris and Julia!" Zelda emphasized the 'ia' of Julia. "Remember? Alexandra was 'visiting' Chris in his dreams?"

"Oh! Yeah. That Chris and Julia," blurted Randall. "So, go on."

Zelda sat upright to continue. "Then you should also recall that I saw a green light show on the ceiling above him as he started to recall what had happened to him with Alexandra."

Randall nodded. "I surely do remember that. Did Alexandra appear to you and the kids?"

Zelda shook her head. "Nope, but I saw the green light show on the ceiling above us again. It was dancing all about. I asked the kids if they saw anything unusual on the ceiling. Addie thought I was nuts and said she didn't see anything but flickering light from the fire. Kyle said he thought he saw small bugs crawling down the wall. We all got scared and went to the kitchen for some hot chocolate. Both cats stayed right where they were and just stared at the ceiling."

"Holy flaming enchiladas!" exclaimed Randall. "You hadn't been smoking any magic cigarettes had you?"

"No siree, Bob!" swore Zelda. "I was stone cold sober. I'd like your interpretation of the events, mister smart guy."

Randall sat up and shook his head several times. "I'd like very much to do that, but for the moment I am at a loss for anything rational."

"How about something irrational?" asked Zelda.

Randall chuckled. "Well, now you're cooking with gas."

As if on cue, both cats meandered into the room and jumped on top of the blanket, neatly landing on Randall and Zelda's respective bladders. That led to unscheduled bathroom breaks and when they rejoined under the blanket, Zelda seemed to have gotten friendlier. She rolled over on her side and put a leg over Randall's outstretched legs.

Zelda patted Randall's bald spot. "Don't get excited, little man. This is just to protect our bladders from bouncing felines."

Randall harrumphed. "Why would the mere closeness of your skinny butt get my little man excited?"

Zelda countered with a zipper pull. "How's that grab you?"

Randall nodded. "Getting warmer."

Zelda pulled the zipper back up. "Before things get too warm, I want your unadulterated opinion on the green light issue before I give you the green light."

With that promise hanging in the air, Randall thought furiously. "Well, my thought is that we were connected in that moment by a basic neural connection mediated by quantum entanglement. I think that, under stress, we can more ably use it to connect with those close to us. I think the kids have it, too. Kyle, maybe more so."

Zelda sounded frustrated. "There you go again with that mumbo jumbo about quantum *enfranglement*. You keep bringing it up, but I don't really get it yet. I don't know whether it's a good thing or something to be spooked out about."

Randall nodded while the cats sauntered into the room again looking for targets. "I get that. I'm just beginning to understand it. Even the experts admit it's unclear and beyond our usual way of understanding the natural world. In fact, that's what our QEG group is struggling with. We all believe there are various capabilities of the human brain that we are just beginning to understand, but proof is very difficult."

Zelda was only mildly mollified. "Okay. I get that. But I don't yet know enough about it to know what I don't know. If you know what I mean."

Randall reached out and stroked Zelda's red hair. "Surprisingly, I get you completely. Tell you what. As you know, I want you to join us for the next QEG meeting. It still has to be set up, but should be the next weekend or two. And I'm hoping Elisa will agree to come. We can confirm that when she and her sister come for dinner tomorrow."

Zelda collapsed back. "But I feel completely unprepared for that meeting of yours with what little I know about the topic."

Randall gave Zelda a reassuring pat on the arm. "I am aiming to fix that. I've been thinking about using the dinner as an opportunity to give you and Elisa my Quantum Elixir shortbread summary version. It should be enough to bring you both up to speed. It's too long to get into tonight, especially with how wasted we both are. Let's get a good night's sleep and aim for clarity on the morrow."

Zelda raised a hand. "Sounds like you're quoting Shakespeare, Dr. English major, but I'm drifting right along with you. Sounds like a plan."

Both cats began to howl in a duet that could not be stopped.

Zelda jumped up. "I think Milky Way and Wondercat are demonstrating for their version of hot chocolate. Let's service them now and then service each other."

Randall's eyebrows shot up and he hustled to the kitchen.

Mr. Lucky

As Randall was preparing Milky Way's treat, Zelda came up behind Randall and wrapped both arms around his waist. She kissed his neck while she undid his belt buckle and rubbed her pelvis up against his backside. She murmured into his ear. "Hey, Mr. Lucky, you ready for beddy or what?"

Randall felt his knees go weak with a combination of accumulated fatigue and shock. He'd expected the living room couch for the night but was now being offered the honeymoon suite. He felt like a man who'd been crawling through the desert being offered a drink of cool water by a genie. *Was it real?*

Randall tested the waters. "Err, I'm dead tired from the trip. And I've got a 7:30 tumor board in the morning. If I don't get right to sleep, I'll never make it. Can I have a rain check? Do you have a layaway plan?"

Zelda moved her hand down the front of his pants. "Sorry, Big Boy. This is a time limited offer. You've primed the pump and it's ready to start pumping. Lay right away or lay awake. That's the best offer I've got."

Randall's eyes went wide. "Umm, works for me. Suddenly, I'm wide awake. You know, I can sleep during tumor board. They never listen to what I say anyhow. Last one up the stairs has to be on top."

Randall won the race and sat on his side of the bed. Zelda went into the bathroom and didn't come out for 10 minutes. When she did, she crawled under the covers. "I've changed my mind, Randy. I'm way too tired. Can I give you that rain check?"

Randall groaned. "Come on. I don't want to do it in the rain. Give a guy a break!"

Zelda laughed despite herself. "Randy! You know what I mean."

Randall nodded reluctantly and got into bed with Zelda. He removed his glasses and placed them on the bedside stand. He laid back on his pillow. "Woof. What a day. I could hibernate for a week. Someone needs to invent a time suspension cocoon so a guy could get the right amount of sleep."

Zelda let out a breath. "Amen! And gals, too. Randy, get down to your workshop right now and build some time cocoons. Just think. We could go to bed at 2:00 AM, set the cocoon for eight hours and wake up four hours later at 6:00 AM with eight hours of sleep."

Randall rolled over on his side towards Zelda. "Love to. Then we'd have extra time for other stuff. But I have to plan out the schematics first. My brain's blueprint section is doing it right now."

Zelda teased again. "Oh, goody. Has anything come up yet?"

Randall snuggled up closer. "Only 'little Randy.' Want to check it out?"

Zelda turned and poked Randall in the chest. "Good luck with that. You can't ride a dead horse. Nice try, though. Now turn out the lights."

Randall groaned loudly, turned back over, and switched off the lamp. "Say goodnight, Gracie."

Zelda chuckled. "Goodnight, Gracie."

Randall was drifting rapidly off to dreamland when, out of the engulfing mists, he heard Zelda's voice. "Randy, psst. Are you asleep?'"

Randall wasn't sure if he was dreaming but he answered the question. "Yes. I'm asleep."

Zelda took that as a sign that he was awake. "Good. We need to talk about something."

Randall thought it was one of those bad dreams where the wife asks the husband that fateful question. Husbands with any experience know the question never leads to anything good. "I didn't do anything. I don't even know the lady. I was never there." His voice drifted away as he descended back into somnolence.

Zelda was perplexed and shoved Randall's shoulder. "What lady? Where?"

Randall came awake. "Yeah. What lady? Dang. I was sleeping."

Zelda laughed. "Sorry. My mistake. Go back to sleep."

Randall turned over on his side again and huffed. After several moments he spoke. "Okay. Now I'm awake enough to worry about what was so important you had to wake me up. I won't be able to sleep until you get it off your chest."

Zelda felt bad. "Don't worry. It wasn't that important. We can discuss it another time."

"Not happening!" said Randall gruffly. "Spill it now."

Zelda sat up in bed. "Well, if you insist. You've been seeing Mary Alice for several months now and you haven't shared anything about how it's going. Is there any reason you're keeping me in the dark?"

Now Randall was really getting ticked off. "Now if that isn't a case of the pot calling the kettle black. Likewise. You've told me squat about your progress with your shrinky dink."

"Well, can't you tell by my improved behavior?" retorted Zelda.

Randall snapped the bedside lamp on again and looked daggers at Zelda. "You apparently haven't noticed my new calm demeanor either."

Zelda responded rather meekly. "Touché! I don't mean to pry into your private baggage, but I guess I just want your opinion about how it's working for you. Like, is it helping you with coping and handling stress?"

Randall was quiet for a bit, hoping to tone down the tension and let some of the high pressure bleed off. "Honestly, I think it's helped a lot just to have someone not involved in our situation to talk to and get feedback from. She gives me a lot of reinforcement and perspective. At first, we met twice weekly. I'll admit it was pretty nerve-wracking and intense. I guess I was a mess! She saw past my BS and pushed me to dig deeper. You probably noticed I was pretty frazzled for a while."

Zelda nodded, recalling. "I did notice you were on edge, but, frankly, it didn't seem that unusual. I figured there was a new VA policy you had to enforce or something like that."

Randall shrugged. "Fair enough! When we dug down far enough and started rewiring some stuff, I felt a lot more clear-headed. After a few weeks, we reduced it to once a week, and she's just decided we can meet every two weeks. Now, when we meet, it's more like we're just two friends getting together for coffee and a chat. We share the weekly news of what's going on in my life and there's not as much obvious 'therapy' happening. I guess I got used to shifting gears on the fly rather than running myself into the ground and needing an overhaul."

Zelda laughed and nodded. "Yeah, you would be a car in this scenario! That's exactly what's happening with my lady shrink and me, but I'm more of a horse. At first I was all bite and kick, and she figured out how to calm me down until I felt safe. We're still on weekly sessions, so we're not quite as advanced as you and Mary Alice, but I feel like I can cope with things better. I get to choose my own pace, rather than some mysterious rider whipping me. Like now, for example. If we'd have had this talk before the shrinks, I'd be off and running by now and you'd be Billy Goat Gruff."

Randall reflected for a moment. "I suppose you're right about that. So, I guess I'd give the process a B plus or even an A minus. But I don't think we need to share all the inner workings of how we got there, do you?"

Zelda put up an outstretched hand. "Heavens no. That's why they're private sessions. And I wasn't trying to find out if you have secret Mommy issues or perverse thoughts."

Randall laughed. "Ha! You know me well enough to know that I do have perverse thoughts about you. I do love my Mommy, but I'm not out to make you a replacement for her. No one will ever make pies like she does."

Zelda faked a huff. "I can so make good pies, but that doesn't mean I'm going to spend all my time baking."

"Easy there, Trigger!" Randall stroked Zelda's forehead. "So, what grade would you give your brain adjuster?"

Zelda was a bit less generous than Randall. "Perhaps a B minus. But that could just be me. I kinda wanted a magic wand or a bottle of horsepills to do the work for me. I'm probably a more intractable case than you."

Randall laughed again. "Your words. Since you brought up the issue, we might as well debrief on Chelsea Andretti and Kyle."

Zelda smiled and pulled the covers down to her waist, improving Randall's view somewhat. "You read my mind. I'm very pleased. I got a call from his teacher today. She wanted to report that his deportment was much improved, and he was more attentive in class, even raising his hand to answer questions. I think she was fishing for information, but I attributed the improvement to good parenting and didn't mention outside professional help."

Randall beamed. "Hey! That's great. He hasn't been as pouty around the house. And he doesn't pick on Addie as much as before. The two seem to play together better. It's been a pain taking him there every week, but I'm glad we've been able to take turns doing it."

Zelda sighed. "Yeah. It's been easier since she just meets with Kyle alone now. I can draw or read while I'm waiting for him to come back out. It's a nice hour break in my day."

Randall agreed. "I bring some VA paperwork along and I usually get it done while I watch the strange people she gets in the waiting room."

Zelda nodded. "Good. I appreciate that she brings me in at the end so we can review what they worked out, and Kyle can practice telling me what he wants. What sounded impossible months ago is actually working out. The only question I'm left with is, what is the end game? How long before we're pronounced 'done?' It is not like baking, where you leave the cake in the oven for 45 minutes. Or when the little button thing pops out on the turkey."

"Hmm," mused Randall. "Hadn't thought that one through yet. I suggest we make that our objective for this week. Let's ask our respective shrinks that question and see what they say. I hope we don't hear something like 'You want to know when you'll be fixed? Ha ha. In your case I can't say for sure. It may take years.'"

Zelda guffawed. "In your case maybe, but not mine. I'm not broken. I'm just organized like a Picasso."

Randall threw his pillow at Zelda and vice versa. The noise of their "discussion" had woken Addie and she spoke up from the bedroom doorway. "Mommy, Daddy? Why are you fighting?"

They broke up laughing and Zelda motioned Addie to come in for a hug. "How long have you been at the door, Rosebud?"

Addie squeaked out a reply. "I've been listening for a while. Will I need to get shrunken like you guys? That scares me. I'm already pretty small."

Randall got out of bed and hoisted up Addie and her little unicorn. "Don't you worry about that. You are quite small enough and you will get bigger. I promise. Now let's get you back to bed."

Zelda piped up. "Addie, don't worry. We don't actually mean shrinking. That's just a silly word for people sorting out their thoughts and feelings."

Addie looked relieved and relaxed on Randall's shoulder. "Daddy, you are so confusing. Maybe you need to go to talking school."

Randall sighed and walked to the other side of the bed. "Cute. Now let's give your Mommy a kiss and go back to bed."

That done, Randall took Addie back to her room and tucked her in like a bug in a rug. He sat with her for a bit and soon she was sawing lumber. He checked Kyle on his way back to bed. He was down for the count. When he returned to his bedroom, Zelda was waiting for him, sans nightgown.

Randall gawked. "What have we here?"

Zelda gave him a pert smile. "I've already unwrapped your surprise gift."

C HAPTER 25

———

F RUITS OF O UR L ABOR

"You only live once, but if you do it right, once is enough."

—Mae West

W HIRLING D ERVISH

When Randall sauntered past Doris's desk the following Monday morning, he had a Cheshire cat grin out to his ears.

Doris took immediate notice. "Hey, Boss. Had a good weekend, did 'we'?"

Randall tried to take the wide out of the grin, but failed. "One might could say 'we' did, but I can't speak for you."

Doris knew the look but implied otherwise. "Were 'we' lucky at the slot machines?"

Randall managed to tone down to a smirk. "Ah, yes, a bit of it. And with a few other ventures. But funny, I didn't see you there. What do 'we' have on today's menu? Any new news 'we' should know about?"

Doris shrugged. "Sorry to use the royal 'we', but usin' it makes me feel like I was there too and had just as much fun. Most of my fun is vicarious. As for the menu, I'm afraid it's just the usual scrum, plus one little oddment. Oh, and Elisa called in sick today. Hope it's nothin' serious."

Randall tried to respond to Elisa's absence without letting on that he knew anything about the cause. "That's too bad. I'm sure it's just something that's going around."

557

Doris pulled back the corner of her mouth. "I hope she doesn't bring it around here. That's the last thing I need."

Randall spoke before he thought. "Oh, it's nothing contagious . . . er, probably."

Doris changed the subject. "Pray tell, what did the Missus think of you agreein' to go to Bluegrass Country?"

Randall's ridiculous smile reappeared. "She was tickled pink. And I thank you for bringing me up to speed on horsey trivia. When I mentioned Claiborne Farms and a few other equestrian tidbits she thought were outside my wheelhouse, she was totally taken aback. I threw in some references to Churchill Downs and Lexington, Kentucky, and she melted in my arms . . . metaphorically, that is."

Doris nodded and grinned. "My guess is that it was less metaphorical and more metaphysical. At least that's what my special female senses detect. And judgin' from the bounce in your step."

Randall shrank back in mock alarm. "Why, Doris, let us not go down a lustful pathway."

The two spent a long moment looking at the ceiling and giggling. Randall came forward with a diversionary question. "Say, Doris, how is it you know so much about thoroughbred horse racing? I only lived in Durham for a year, but I don't recall any pari-mutuel race tracks in North Carolina."

Doris got up and walked to her file cabinet. She pulled out the bottom drawer and rummaged around a bit. Near the bottom she found what she was looking for. She pulled out an old five by seven black and white photograph and studied it for a moment. "Ah. That's the one I was lookin' for."

Doris handed the photo to Randall. "That's me when I was 13 years old. I'm standin' with my Daddy, bless his soul, in front of the chestnut thoroughbred, Whirlaway, after he won the Preakness on May 31, 1941. I mean, Whirlaway won the race, not my Daddy."

Randall nodded as he looked at the picture. "I kinda figured it was the winning horse because of the big bouquet of flowers around his neck. But, look at you! You were quite a thoroughbred yourself back then."

Doris struck a girlish pose with her hand behind her ear. "Why, thank you, kind sir. Yes, that was in my pre *avoir du pois* years. You might say I've bulked up a tad since then. My Daddy loved the big races. He drove up to the Pimlico race track in Baltimore every year to watch the Preakness. 1941 was the first time he took me with him. He didn't want to miss it that year, because he had a connection to Whirlaway. He'd already won the Kentucky Derby and had a chance to win the Triple Crown. The horse, I mean."

Randall was impressed. "Of course, the horse. How in the world did you get to pose for this picture? The jockey is still sitting on the horse."

Doris pointed to the ridiculously small jockey atop the majestic horse. "The jockey is Eddie Arcaro. He was pretty famous in those days. My Daddy knew the trainer, Ben Jones, and he set up the photo op. My Daddy knew Mr. Jones before he went to train Whirlaway at Calumet Farms in Lexington, Kentucky. It was named after the Calumet Baking Soda Company. The millionaire who owned the company started the farm and paid big bucks for Mr. Jones to raise Whirlaway. Mr. Jones is the guy holdin' the reins."

Randall knew the jockey's name well. "Oh, yeah. I remember Arcaro. He was pretty darn good, as I recall. I saw newsreels about him when I was a kid. My mother sent me off to Saturday morning cartoons at the Shorewood Theater. They showed the newsreels in between cartoons." Randall looked at the ceiling, searching for the rest of the memory. "I don't remember the cartoons, but I do remember seeing Arcaro riding and winning a bunch of races. Didn't Whirlaway win the Triple Crown that year?"

Doris nodded proudly. "Yes, indeedy. My Daddy was so pleased, bless his heart. He got to see Whirlaway win the Derby on May 3rd that year, at Churchill Downs, but couldn't make it to the Belmont Stakes in New York. My Daddy had a heart attack in early June and was still recuperatin'. He never got well enough to go to more races, bless his soul."

Randall put his hand on Doris's shoulder. "That's a shame. I mean both the heart attack and not being able to see Whirlaway win the third race."

Doris clutched the small cross that hung from a gold chain around her neck. "Yeah, I think it broke his heart even more. But I'll never forget that Preakness. It was a memory that will stick with me 'til my last breath."

"Why's that?" asked Randall.

Doris laughed sardonically. "Oh, the way that stupid horse won. Whirlaway literally just walked out of the gate at the start of the race and looked like he wanted to get off the track and just get some breakfast. Then, somehow, Arcaro coaxed him to get going again. But, by that time, the fool horse was 20 lengths behind the pack. At half track he shifted into high gear, like, all of a sudden, he remembered he had to catch the other horses. After that he ran like his tail was on fire, caught the other horses and finished five lengths ahead. Everyone was stunned. Mr. Jones just laughed about it later and commented that the horse just had a moody personality."

Randall didn't know that part of the story or didn't remember it. "Unbelievable! It's a real life 'never give up' story."

Doris laughed again and slapped her thigh. "Turns out Mr. Jones was right. Even though Whirlaway won the Triple Crown that year, over his racin' career he lost half his races—badly. Some days you feel like racin' and some you don't. How about you? Up for a race today, Dr. B?"

Randall slumped at the prospect. "I am so sleep deprived right now . . . and jet lagged from the Vegas trip . . . that I will be happy just to remain part of the human race for the next 12 hours. I can't wait until I can go home and hit my nice soft bed. It's beckoning to me now."

Doris shook her head. "You poor dear. Bless your heart. Then you're not gonna like today's menu."

Randall's imagination raced. "Why? Are there 10 consults and 42 follow-ups?"

Doris took some papers off of her schedule book and turned to the correct page. "No, just the usual number. But here comes the oddment I mentioned earlier. There are two VA attorneys that wish to see you for a briefin' on the Chester case. The 9:00 consult canceled, so I booked them in that spot. They're comin' down here to talk. I put the patient's radiation therapy chart on your desk for review."

"Goody gum drops," griped Randall. "Great day starter."

Doris could tell Randall wanted to find some sand to bury his head under. "Pish posh. Don't despair. They said that you shouldn't be upset about the case. They've already done a thorough case review and they don't think we have a significant liability risk."

Randall wasn't convinced. He hated encounters with malpractice lawyers, although nothing bad had ever befallen him as a result. He still had to grumble. "Yeah, and the Pope doesn't wear a funny hat. Well, such things are unavoidable in this litigious world. Better to get it out of the way, I suppose."

Doris almost had to laugh at Randall's rapid descent into despair. "That's the resigned but positive attitude we've been lookin' for. Now, I suggest you review Mr. Chester's records while you wait for the lawyers so you can keep all the details straight. We don't want to seem uninformed about our case, now do we?"

Randall painted a smile back on his face and stood up straight. "'We' definitely do not. I'm off to chart-land right now. Rather, after I warm up my coffee. Need that caffeine to kick in."

On his way to the departmental coffee resource, Randall was stopped in the hallway by Grace for several calculation checks. He did the math and handed the charts back.

"Anything else cooking?" Randall asked.

Grace thought for a moment. "Well, Mr. Arthur starts at 9:30 and Dan doesn't have his blocks made yet. Maybe you can light a fire under him."

Randall thought fire lighting might improve his mood. "Alright. I'll do a drive by. Is Melinda in today? She hasn't been hovering around me."

Grace made a *tsking* sound. "She is and she isn't. Had to go up to personnel for some paperwork processing about being hired here as a tech. Personally, I think she's too green, but when has my opinion ever mattered?"

Randall *tsked* right back. "All suggestions in the suggestion box are taken into consideration and duly processed anonymously."

"Of course they are," said Grace, dryly. "But you'd probably recognize my handwriting!"

Randall knew better than to get drawn into Grace's lame arguments, but couldn't resist a riposte. "Not if you type it!"

Grace sneered. "I don't DO typing. Fine, you're not getting any of my suggestions." She snorted as punctuation and buried the topic. "By the way, I heard you had a hot time in Vegas this past weekend and got lucky. Anything you want to share?"

Randall wondered how Grace could know anything about his trip, because he had discussed it with no one at the VA except Doris. She would not have had time to talk with Grace about it—unless some little someone was eavesdropping. So, he decided to play it up for effect.

Randall looked expansive. "Oh, you betcha. Killed at the slots. Needed several buckets to haul away the booty. And I found treasure in the desert. Had the attention of a bevy of beauties, too. And I met a real genie! All kinds of luck."

Grace just stared dumbly as he walked away to check on Dan in the block making room.

NRG Recruitment

Randall strode quietly into the block room. He loved silently approaching from behind and scaring the bejeebers out of staff. Before Randall could say anything, Dan greeted him without turning around. "Hey, boss. Heard you were a major player in McVegas. Don't worry about me. What happens in Vegas. . . . Oh, and you can tell Miss Grouchy that Mr. Arthur's blocks will be ready in five minutes. She's always got her *bundies* in an *undle* over something."

Before Randall could ask how Dan had detected his silent entry, he noticed a mirror strategically placed on the shelf above the block work area. He decided not to mention it directly, but he was impressed with Dan's resourcefulness. "You are a great observer of the obvious."

Dan turned and smiled. "Why, yes, I am. So, really. How was the casino experience?"

Randall shrugged and tried to make light of his Vegas experience and focus on the research aspects. "Look, I only gambled with four bicentennial quarters that my daughter gave me to put in the slots. Each one paid off and I won $49.00, which I had to give back to her along with the four quarters. Then, I lost $20 of my own and left. The rest was mostly all business. You know, lung cancer protocol stuff for the NRG. By the way, they need a Physics consultant. You interested?"

Dan had to laugh. "Nice segue. My truth detector is trending positive. As far as interested others are concerned, I'll tell them you told me that you broke the bank. Any time you leave Vegas with more than you came with is considered success. Tell me more about NRG."

Randall explained what Dan's involvement in NRG would be. "Well, it would be helping to make sure that the radiation physics in new state of the art clinical trials is up to par. That would include being certain all sites are using uniform techniques and setting a standard of excellence. It's an opportunity to be at the forefront of treatment innovation."

Dan took all that in but did not appear impressed. "Nice advertising pitch, but it sounds like a lot of work for free. As I recall, we don't get paid by NRG for the effort put in."

Randall was a bit disappointed that Dan had seen through the car salesman approach. "Did I mention that our department gets paid for patients we put on the study?"

Dan frowned. "When was the last time that money has trickled down to us worker bees?"

Randall had to admit that hadn't happened yet. "True that. But did I mention that when you help write a study, your name appears on the author's list of numerous resultant NRG landmark papers. Those publications can all be added to your CV and lead to promotions and pay raises."

Dan suddenly looked like a lightbulb had lit above his head. "Now you're talking a language I can get behind. As long as there is a reward down the line, I can be magnanimous about my contributions. Plus, my sacrifices will make my grandchildren proud, even though they won't understand why."

Randall could sense success. "Did I forget to mention that the meetings are always held in quite favorable locations and that all travel expenses are paid for by an NIH grant?"

Dan decided he could sacrifice the time away from home. "I know my family will miss me, but absence makes the heart grow fonder. As long as we're doing critical cancer research. Are there any other downsides?"

Randall spoke quietly, as if conveying a secret. "Well, there's a bit of wrangling and writing involved. You have to convince other Medical Physicists to do things your way and collaborate with them in writing the Physics sections of 60-page protocols. The work could become a bit tedious. But just think of the greater good you'd be doing."

Dan had an idea. "How about if I go to the next meeting and observe before committing?"

Randall nodded. "I think that's a reasonable solution. Test drive before you buy. The next full meeting is in July in Philadelphia. Philly is the location of NRG headquarters. The full group meets every six months. The meeting I attended was just for the Lung Committee to do vetting on new proposals that we wouldn't have time for at the regular meeting. Too many axes to grind."

Dan raised an index finger. "I assume the winter meetings are usually somewhere warm?"

Randall smiled. "Do tight shoes give you bunions?"

Dan laughed and stretched out his arms indicating he had connected all the dots. "I'm liking this. I spoke with Knox last week. He said if I want to get promoted to Assistant Professor, I have to start beefing up my CV. This could do it, wouldn't you say?"

Randall touched his finger to the side of his nose, Santa style. "You have correctly identified my primary motive for continuing this academic pursuit. Knox gave me the same 'encouragement.' I figure that if I have to build my CV, I'll be better off joining a collective effort than trying it on my own. I'd never be able to design a study that could recruit enough patients to be meaningful just using accrual from our small group of hospitals. With NRG we can accrue hundreds of patients, because the group draws from over 200 cooperating hospitals. That's why protocol design is so critical. The design has to be doable by all 200 hospitals and they don't all have the same capabilities."

Dan nodded and smiled again. "Like Paul said on the road to Damascus, and I'm paraphrasing here, I'm beginning to see the light."

Randall was pleased. He thought Dan would make a great traveling companion. "I thought you'd like the concept. I'll pass the word along and get you an invite."

Grace steamed into the block room and stood at the doorway, hands on hips.

Dan looked up and started pushing the cart with Mr. Arthur's completed blocks. "Your block order is ready, Miss, sunny side up. Where would you like them served?"

Grace gave out a grunt and a comment. "You don't really want to know. Just follow me."

Dan waited until Grace's back was turned. Then, he turned his head back towards Randall. "She wants us to 'walk this way.'"

Randall caught the reference to a Monty Python routine. He and Dan walked behind Grace with Nazi steps and pronounced hip shimmies.

Boxing Cigars

Randall had only twenty minutes to review Chester's chart before the VA attorneys showed up. Heading back to his office from the block room, he mused that the NRG meeting had some hidden benefits despite all his prior misgivings. Things might turn out better than he initially expected. When he got to his office, Doris was placing memos and mail on his desk.

Randall was still feeling set upon and growled softly. "Great, more work."

Doris gave Randall a sideways look. "Dr. B, don't be so negative. It's nothin' important. All it needs is your initials. Do the chart review first before the suits get here."

Randall was still floating down the river of self pity. "So, I don't have to read the stuff you just dumped on me?"

Doris stiffened. "Make paper airplanes out of it if you want. You're the boss. I'm just doin' my job."

Randall realized his grumbling had gone too far. He wasn't sure why he'd gone from positive to negative just moving through two rooms. Perhaps his mood had just gotten "entangled" being too close to Grace. "Sorry, Doris. It must be the sleep deprivation. No need to take it out on you. Please forgive me. I must say, I really enjoyed your Preakness story. Like I said, I didn't suspect North Carolina folk to be into horse racing."

Doris relaxed a bit. "Well, you're right about that. My Daddy knew all the history and told the stories often. There used to be a lot of horse racin' in the Carolinas in the 1800s and early 1900s, but then the gamblin' part messed it all up. The state passed laws makin' bettin' illegal and most all the track activity died. The biggest track was Pinehurst Track down near the southern border. It's still there, but now it's just a historic site. The Amphidrome was built there in 1917, or so, and they held all kinds of events there during state fairs. There are horse barns, paddocks, harness shops and a clubhouse. No racin' now. Neat place to visit, though."

Randall nodded. "Yeah, now North Carolina is most noted for car racing. I guess the car really did replace the horse. Say, can you show me the old picture again? There's something I want to check."

Doris got the Preakness picture out the file drawer again and returned with it. Randall examined the photo more closely and pointed at her father's image. "Yeah, I thought so. He's got a big stogie in his mouth. And I love the big fedora he's wearing. That is so 1941. You realize I was born in 1942? I remember my Dad always wore a fedora just like that and had a love affair with cigars."

Doris put a hand to her heart. "Land sakes! My Daddy, bless his soul, sometimes wore that hat to bed at night. I think he just forgot it was on his head. Before his heart attack, he would rarely be without a cigar at the corner of his mouth. My mother always complained that he'd rather kiss the dang cigar than her ruby lips. After the heart attack, it was a different story. She hunted down his cigar supply and excommunicated every last one like they were the devil incarnate." She crossed herself instinctively.

Randall laughed. "Sounds like how my Mom felt about it. She restricted all cigar puffing to the basement."

Doris continued her cigar tale. "My Daddy got real mad at mother after tossin' out his cigars, because she threw away the boxes, too. He loved those old cigar boxes. They had full color lithograph labels on the covers of royalty, sports stars and sometimes famous racehorses. Those he treasured. His favorite was the box with the thoroughbred Alcazar on it showing him standing in front of his paddock with his winning times on a gold medallion. I think they were from the Kentucky Derby."

Randall stood looking at Doris, amazed. "You're not going to believe this, but my Dad had that same cigar box. I remember it clearly. One day, when I was about four or five, I found it on a shelf in his workshop. He used it to store electrical parts. I thought the horse looked spectacular, but I figured I could improve its regal looks with my little paintbrush. Days later, when my Dad found my artistic endeavor, he sought me out and demonstrated his appreciation with the repeated application of his belt to my little behind. The belt made quite an impression on me. I still remember Alcazar's best winning time was 2 minutes 20 ½ seconds. I wondered how you could measure a half second. I don't know which race track it was set on. Maybe the Derby."

Doris clutched her cross again. "I'm not sure either. But the Derby is 1 ¼ miles. I'm bad at math. How fast would that be?"

Randall took the challenge. "Let me see. If the horse goes 1.25 miles in 140 seconds, that means he'd go 1 mile in 112 seconds, give or take."

Doris looked confused. "Oh, there you go again, doin' all that math in your head. How do you do it?"

Randall knew he should be reviewing the Chester chart, but he was on a roll, and this was much more fun. "It's the art of estimation, with some physics thrown in. And a little magic, for spice. So, we continue, noting that 112 seconds is almost 2 minutes. It's a circular track, so we add a little Pi, apple for the horses, of course. Then we consider the average horsepower of the engine, in this case, one. There's also drag, which would take into account the stickiness of the earth, the moisture in the air, and horsehair friction."

Doris had to laugh at Randall's conflated explanation. "Dr. B, I do declare! You sure you haven't left somethin' out?"

Randall put a finger to his temple and squinted. "You're right. There are other factors, but they are unknowns. Has the horse just eaten? Was it oats or Purina horse chow? What was the jockey's weight and coefficient of friction? Adding a fudge factor for those variables, I'd estimate that in 60 minutes the horse would go about 30 miles. That means he'd be running 30 to 33 mph. You're the horse expert. Is that possible?"

Doris shook her head. "Ask a simple question and I get a comedy standup routine. I think horses can run as fast as 40 mph, but not for 30 miles. Even Secretariat would be pooped going 30 mph."

Randall nodded. "I guess that explains why jockeys are a bit smallish. Got to hand it to those 120 pound dudes driving a ton of horse."

Doris tried to redirect Randall. "Speaking of tons. You have a ton of reviewin' to do before the legal eagles descend and not much time to do it in. No need to panic but maybe get a little anxious?"

Randall snapped back into focus. "Very observant. Now I've got five minutes. Better make them count."

Lawyer Land

Randall found that he didn't even need the five minutes to refresh his memory about how he'd planned and delivered Mr. Chester's treatment. He was more than ready when the VA attorneys showed up, just a few minutes late. The man and woman were very cordial and rather benign. The review lasted just over 30 minutes, the time it would take a good horse to run 15 miles. They concluded that Randall's treatment plan and delivery appeared up to current standards. They also noted that two Radiation Oncologists from other states would review and comment on the case as expert witnesses. Randall could expect their written reports in several months and would have a chance to comment on them.

Randall bade the two attorneys goodbye and retreated to his office again. It was easy, he thought, for them to be blasé about the lawsuit. They didn't have any skin in the game. Whenever someone told Randall not to worry about something, he took it as a red flag that perhaps there was, indeed, something to worry about. Otherwise, why would they issue a warning not to worry?

Randall remembered the conversation with Zelda from the day before. They had decided to keep looking at the sunny side of life, always on the sunny side. Now would be the time to start practicing that philosophy. No need to dwell on a future problem when there were problems on his plate right now. Heck, he'd first have to live long enough for it to become an issue. After all, no tomorrows are guaranteed. He could get hit by a meteorite or attacked by a killer bee before the legal thing reappeared. Putting worries about the future aside, he trooped into Doris' office for his next assignment.

Doris looked up from her typing. "How did it go with Dewey, Cheatum and Howe? By the look on your face, you must have vanquished their evil spells."

Randall forced himself to smile even bigger, but just succeeded in looking like a clown. "Today it was just Dewey and Howe. They were both positive and uplifting despite my embedded negative and downtrodden. After I thought it through, I decided I should assume their positive outlook presages a successful outcome."

Doris nodded. "That's a good attitude to take, but I'm bettin' you still dread the long wait for the outcome to be announced."

Randall's smile faded. "You're bang on. But the wait time will pass whether I worry or not, so why burden myself with worry until it's necessary?"

Doris clapped her hands. "That's my boy!"

Randall was reinvigorated. "All I need is a jolt from the coffee urn and I'll be good for a 30 mile run."

By the time Randall had topped off his serum caffeine level, the next follow-up was waiting in an exam room. By some good measure of luck, the remaining cases for the morning were without drama or major pathology. He thought perhaps the positive attitude thing might be working. But there was a whole afternoon to go and something could be lurking wickedly just around the next corner. And there he was armed only with a stethoscope and a reflex hammer.

Randall walked reflexively through Doris's office on his way to sit at his desk and finish off dictating the morning's progress notes. The appointments had been scheduled back to back so that he only had time for hand scribbled notes. He needed to decipher them before he forgot what his abbreviations meant.

Doris walked into his office with some completed dictation. She noticed that Randall seemed to be sagging in his chair. "Hey, Dr. B, here's some more stuff to review and sign. You look like you're in a voodoo trance."

Randall rose from his chair, stood up straight and saluted. "Name, rank and serial number. That's all you'll get out of me. Heard nothing, saw nothing and said nothing." He began walking in circles around his office like a mime imitating a robot.

Doris couldn't help but chuckle at Randall's antics. "Dr. B, sometimes you are such a clown. I'm goin' to buy you some big, floppy shoes. And when are you goin' to wash that lab coat? It's filthy. Just think of the terrible impression you're givin' others. How do you expect your patients to trust you? Would you go to yourself if you were the patient?"

Randall stopped miming. "Why do I bother to go home when I can get nagged right here at work? You'd make someone an excellent wife. I'll have you know my patients love me . . . mostly. Except for the ones who don't. Besides, a dirty lab coat shows that I have been working, not lazing about just to keep it clean."

Doris feigned outrage. "Oh, yeah!? Well, what about the ripped pocket and the coffee stains?"

Randall looked down, surprised. "The ripped pocket is new. I caught it on a doorknob."

Doris disputed that claim. "Not hardly. The pocket has been like that for at least a month. The coffee stains suggest you're a closet alcoholic that needs coffee to stay awake and you have the shakes so bad you can't keep the coffee in the cup."

Randall held up a fist. "Why I oughta. . . ."

Judy walked in to see if Randall needed anything before she went for lunch. She had overheard a lot of the exchange between the two. "For Pete's sake. You guys sound like an old married couple. Give it a rest. Here's a clean lab coat. Take off the one you're wearing and I'll take it home, wash it, and repair it."

Randall and Doris looked at each other and broke out laughing. Judy looked confused.

Doris tried to clarify. "Did you think this was serious? Oh, my Lordy. We didn't think anyone was listenin'. We've been doing our Honeymooners routine since Duke University days. We both loved the old show and when we need cheerin' up he plays Ralph Kramden and I play Alice. We do a typical argument, ad lib, until Ralphie boy here gets so steamed he offers to send me on a trip to the moon. Then, whatever was botherin' us just melts right away."

Judy burst out laughing. "Well, you fooled me. Next time, warn me ahead of time so I can play Trixie Norton, the next-door neighbor. Then, we'll see who goes to the moon."

Dan entered stage left. "Hey, Ralphie boy. You stink just like the sewer, but I didn't see ya when I was workin' down there."

Randall didn't miss a beat. "Norton! You are not going to steal my lunch again or I've got a special trip to send you on."

It was so spot on that the quartet of people laughed uproariously.

Grace hollered from down the hall. "What's with all the hollering and laughing in there?! What did I miss?"

Dan yelled back. "Nothing, mother!" That rekindled the rebirth of mirth.

When things settled again, Randall felt much better. There was nothing so cathartic as a good laugh. He thanked the stars for the strange chemistry that catalyzed comic relief in the group. Judy turned to leave with his decrepit lab coat, but Randall called after her. "Slow down! I've got some follow-up notes in the top pocket. I need them to dictate from."

Judy pulled the somewhat crumpled papers out of the pocket and unfolded them to make sure that's what they were. "You call these hieroglyphics notes?"

Randall grimaced and defended himself. "Does the physician abuse in this department ever end? Give them over. The notes are written in Biedermeier shorthand code; you know, for the sake of patient confidentiality."

Judy handed over the goods and stifled a chuckle as she walked away. Doris just stood looking at Randall, shaking her head and giving him a mild *"tsk tsk."* He just smiled and returned to his desk.

Randall wondered why he and Doris got along so well despite their bickering. Obviously, their interaction was not encumbered by intimacy issues or shared parenthood, but they had a closeness that somewhat defied logic. Randall speculated that perhaps Doris fantasized that she was twenty years younger and she was married to him. The "marriage" was an unusual one in which they were only together at work. When Doris got home it was all imaginary. At work, Randall certainly trusted Doris and relied on her opinions. Whatever was going on and for whatever reason, the two of them had become, for want of a better word, *entangled*. They had been through a lot of trials together and had a deep mutual respect.

Randall thought it rather remarkable that a homebody in her fifties, who'd never left North Carolina, except once, to go to Baltimore with her Daddy for a horse race, would have the moxie to pick up and leave her home in the rearview mirror. Plus, she'd left home just to keep a job working with him! Go figure. He knew he'd never been a chick magnet. The Midwest's cold and snow hardly offered a better climate. Why had she done it? He wasn't sure. He hoped it wasn't because he'd led her on somehow and she expected something more. Whatever the case, the reason was just beyond his ken. Whatever had incited the bizarre decision, Randall was glad Doris had come with him. He wasn't sure he could have tolerated the VA without her as a buffer. Whether it was quantum induced or otherwise, he was glad they'd become entangled.

No Meat, No Treat

Randall checked the time. He was shocked that it was already almost 5:00 PM. He'd almost forgotten to call over to County Hospital Pathology to get the report on Elisa's neck node biopsy. He hoped someone would actually pick up the call this late. He checked his directory and found five different extensions. The first one he tried rang ten times before he hung up.

Randall tried the second extension. This time someone picked up and answered. "I heard you the first ten times. I hope this is important. I'm trying to get out of here."

Randall recognized the gruff voice. Jim Kramer was a great Pathologist, but had some rough edges. "Hey, Jim. You're in a better mood than usual."

Kramer was not at all perturbed. "Shit, Biedermeier! If I'd known it was you, I would have dialed it up a few notches. Why are you disturbing me so late in the day?"

Randall cleared his throat. "Well, I was hoping you could do me a biggie."

Kramer growled. "As I recall, I've already done you one that you haven't paid me back for. Why should I comply?"

Randall thought fast. "I have nothing to offer at this time except a boatload of good karma that you can bank in St. Peter's desk drawer. Lord knows, you need all you can get."

Kramer bellowed a loud laugh. "Ha, ha! Biedermeier. You got me there! Whaddya need?"

Randall tried to sound more serious. "One of my nurses had a neck node biopsy today done by Sam Blankenship. She asked me if I could get the results rather than wait for Sam to get back to her. He's out of town for two days at a surgery meeting. I know Sam. He probably won't mind. If it's a cancer diagnosis he'd probably ask for our opinion anyway. Plus he hates to give bad news. My nurse and her sister are meeting with me later today. Can you help?"

Randall heard a big sigh and then a long silence.

"Well, you know as well as I do that patient confidentiality rules are a bit misty about such a transfer of patient data. The admin boys would probably frown on me disclosing the diagnosis to you, but . . . the way you explain it, I guess we're covered. What's the young lady's name?"

Randall gave Kramer Elisa's details. Kramer groaned. "Of course! It would be my mystery case of the day. Would you believe I was just working on those slides? I read the frozen sections right after the biopsy, but they were inconclusive. Just looked at the fixed sections. I have a preliminary diagnosis, but I'm waiting on some special stains to make a final call."

"What do you think so far?" asked Randall.

Kramer gave out a loud huff. "Geez, Randall, I'm afraid it walked and talked like Hodgkin's lymphoma. Let me see if the special stain slides are done yet and, if they are, I will give you a final diagnosis. Can you hold for a few?"

Randall was stunned. He distractedly agreed to wait on the line. While he waited, he struggled with how he could possibly break the news to Elisa that she had the Big C. His right knee bounced up and down while he listened on the line to the random noises Kramer made while fishing around for the slides and coming back to his microscope desk.

Kramer made a bunch of rustling noises and picked up the receiver again, but it slipped out of his hand and he dropped it. The loud bang when it hit the floor made Randall wince. Kramer's loud apology seemed even louder than the drop bang. "Sorry about the butter fingers! Got the slides. Let's take a look. Give me a sec to study them."

Randall half expected to hear elevator music during the pause, but all he could hear was the sound of Kramer grunting and clicking his tongue. The wait seemed interminable. At last, Kramer rendered his conclusions. "Okay. Looking around I see lots of characteristic

Reed-Sternberg cells. There's a background of reactive lymphocytes and a few plasmocytes. I'd say it's definitely Hodgkin's and most likely lymphocyte predominant. As you know, that's pretty uncommon, but has a good prognosis."

Randall was partially relieved. If it had to be Hodgkin's, at least it was a favorable subtype. "You've only looked at the slides briefly. Do you think the cell type could change on further review?"

Randall could hear Kramer drumming a pencil on his desk before he answered.

"Hmm. Not likely. I did a quick look at the other stained sections and I'm not seeing any nodularity or mixed cells. I'd say I'm pretty solid on the diagnosis, but let me study it a bit more to be sure. Give me your home phone number and I'll call you a bit later with the final. Will that work?" Kramer sounded as if he was describing a plumbing project.

Randall found it rather jarring to be on the receiving end of Kramer's depersonalized manner and nodded as though he was in the same room with him. A few seconds later, Randall realized Kramer could not hear his head nod. He blurted out a verbal "yes" and recited his home phone number.

Kramer jotted the number down and had a question. "Does she have any systemic symptoms or other nodes?"

Randall thought for a moment. "I don't think she's had any night sweats or weight loss, but here's the kicker. She's about three months pregnant and, besides that benign growth in her pelvis, the imaging suggests a possible nodal mass in the pelvis on the right. That's still an unknown and may need further study."

Kramer made low moaning sounds. "Well, Biedermeier. Now you know why I chose pathology. I just make the diagnosis and report the results to dolts like you. Then, you're the one who has to deliver the bad news. Seriously, though. I'm sorry this had to happen to your nurse. I'm sure she's totally undeserving of this fate. I wish you all the best. Keep me posted. I may be a mean bastard, but at least I'm not a heartless lawyer."

Randall thanked Kramer for his help and hung up. He was not quite prepared to be the bearer of this chunky news.

On the way home that night, Randall realized that even the huge dose of caffeine he'd consumed that day was not keeping him awake. The news about Elisa was making him feel like he'd rather just curl up in bed for a long winter's nap.

On the drive home, perhaps fueled by all the horse race talk with Doris, his brain was replaying scattered lyrics from a Spike Jones album. The song was a sendoff of a horse race. In it, the band plays a heavily doctored version of the William Tell Overture spiced up with pots, pans, and bicycle horns for instruments. One of the band members, Doodle Weaver, announces the fake race mimicking a famous horse race announcer of the day, Clem McCarthy. Real horse names from the time were borrowed but changed to silly versions of their real names, like Dogbiscuit for Seabiscuit and Stoogehand for Stagehand. Other fake horse names were added for comic effect.

At first, the lyrics eluded Randall, but, through some mental trickery, the melody triggered the memory to come back. He started to belt out the words: "And they're off. Heading into the first turn, it's Cabbage by a head. AAANNNDDD, last out of the gate, wait, look . . . it's Beetlebaaaaaum. Around the turn they go. It's Girdle in the stretch. Image is fading away. And the winner is . . . da da da dum ta dum . . . Beetlebaaaaaum!!" In the recording, the Beetlebaum announcement is followed by a big musical crescendo with cymbal crashes and brake drums hitting the floor.

Randall tried but couldn't quite duplicate the percussion section. The rest of the way home, He kept repeating the tune and lyric fragments. Finally, he grew tired and just kept muttering: "It's Girdle in the stretch. HA HA. GIRDLE IN THE STRETCH!" and singing out "Beetlebaaaaaum" at the end in his best basso profundo.

The silly Spike Jones routine was probably all that kept Randall from falling asleep on the drive home. His father, Joe, had acquired the Spike Jones record, a 78 rpm '40s relic, just after coming back from active duty in the Army Air Force in 1945. Joe had played the record repeatedly when Randall was a child growing up and the songs had been etched into his brain, though some of the etching was fading a bit. Now, it was possibly saving his life by keeping him awake.

When Randall arrived home, he drove carefully up the narrow driveway and parked, not bothering to mess with the garage door. He staggered out of the Scirocco, through the back door and dumped his briefcase and gear in the hallway. The smell of cooking enchiladas was redolent in the air. Zelda and the kids came out to greet him.

"Hail, the conquering hero," pronounced Zelda. "He has returned from the arena after besting all the challenges put before him by King Kong VA." She followed up with a big hug and the kids followed suit. "How was your day?"

Randall obfuscated. "Illegitimus non carborundum. By the way, when are Elisa and Elena expected to arrive?"

Addie screeched. "Daddy! You're doing it again. What do all those big words mean?"

Randall was startled by the outburst. "Sorry Bedbug, I didn't mean to confuse you. Translated from the Latin, it means 'Don't let those who were born illegitimately grind you down.'"

Addie screeched again. "I still don't get it! And I am not a bedbug. Ew!"

Randall raised his arms in surrender, picked Addie up and kissed her cheek. "Sorry again. Don't worry, my little pea pod. You were born very legitimately."

Now Kyle was worried. "Was I legitimate too? Was I? And what does it mean?"

Randall put a finger to the side of his nose and looked puzzled. Zelda punched his arm and Randall finally responded. "Of course you were. But it was so long ago I had to think. Quite simply, it means we were wed way before the babe hit the bed."

Before the kids could ask more questions, Randall raised his forefinger again. "And, once more, when are the sisters coming?"

Zelda nodded. "Right. They said around 7:00. We've got about an hour before they arrive. I'm planning on feeding the kids first so we can dine without little pitchers nearby. They have permission to watch TV while we eat. Besides the food I promised, there will be Riesling, the elixir for tongue lubrication."

Randall moaned. "Oooo . . . need Riesling, stat."

Zelda went to fetch Randall the wine. He was glad Zelda hadn't asked about Elisa's diagnosis. He didn't want to explain it twice, once to Zelda, then again to Elisa and Elena. Besides, he wasn't ready to explain anything quite yet until he did some boning up on Hodgkin's and got the final call from Kramer.

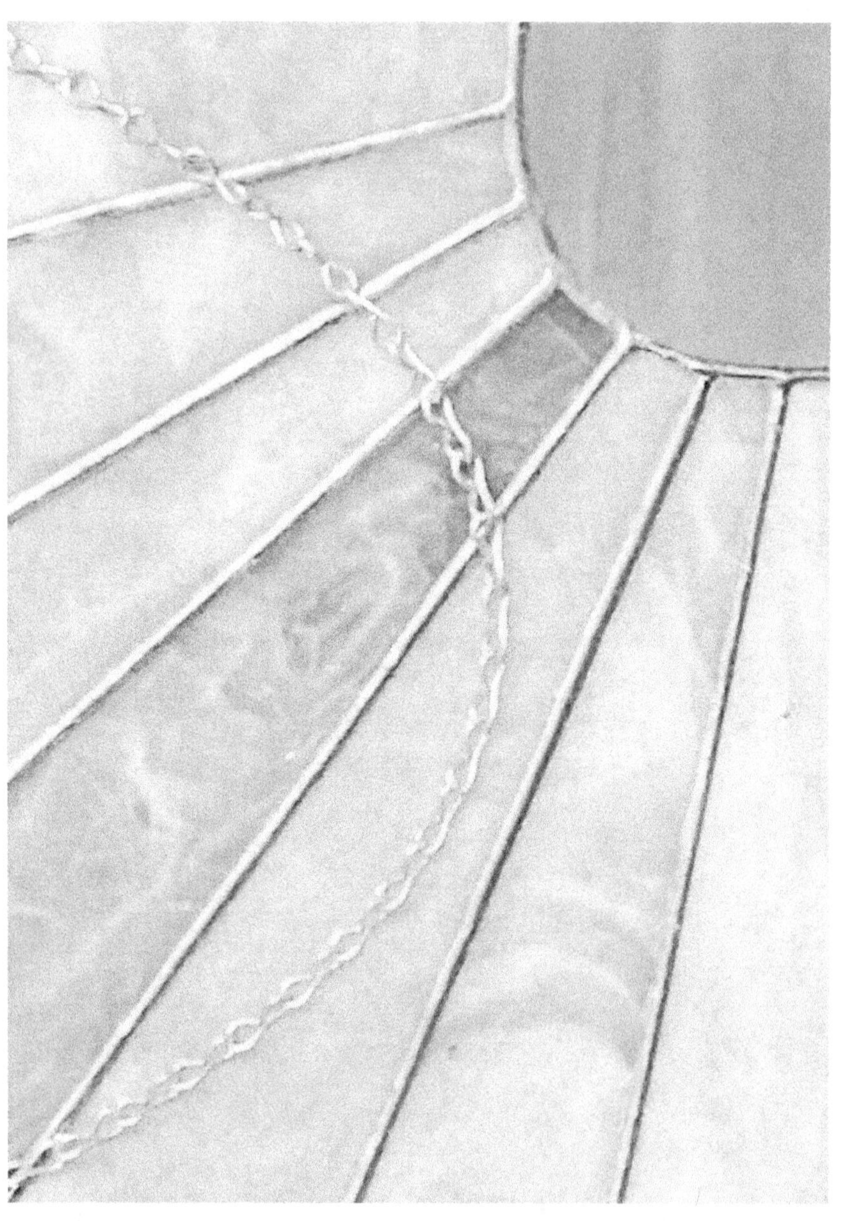

CHAPTER 26

ROCKY CHOICES

"Start by doing what's necessary; then do what is possible; and suddenly you are doing the impossible."

—Francis of Assisi

DINNER WITH THE SISTERS

While Zelda fed the kids, Randall went to his study to reread his textbooks on Hodgkin's disease. He didn't see the disease very often, since it was relatively rare in the veteran population. He wanted to be as up to date as possible. As he read, he sipped from a rather large glass of Riesling. It might have been a delusion, but the wine seemed to improve the flow of information from the printed page. He decided to study this way more often.

Randall's oncology texts confirmed what he already knew about Hodgkin's disease. The lymphocyte predominant histologic subtype was favorable, but the outcome also depended on the stage. If the disease was confined to the neck nodes it would be stage I, which had a high cure rate with chemotherapy and/or radiation therapy. If the disease involved nodes below the diaphragm it would jump to stage III with the same treatment options but a worse outcome. Elisa's suspicious pelvic nodes would determine which way the pendulum would swing.

The next conundrum was how the pregnancy affected everything. In all likelihood, treatment would involve chemotherapy, especially if it was stage III. If it was stage I, radiation alone could work as recent studies had shown nodal irradiation above the diaphragm, so-called "mantle field treatment," could still provide a good chance of cure. The problem with chemotherapy was the danger to the unborn fetus. In all likelihood, chemotherapy at this early stage of pregnancy would result in a miscarriage. The risk of this happening with radiation was much less.

If chemotherapy was necessary, a difficult decision would be needed. It was a devil's choice: sacrifice the baby to save the mother or risk the mother's life by delaying the chemotherapy until the fetus is viable. With delay, the disease could advance to a less treatable stage. There was good evidence to suggest that most women of child-bearing age could still become pregnant after recovery from chemotherapy and the disease. Only the patient could make that decision after being presented with the options and the odds.

Randall slammed the text shut and pushed back from the desk. He despaired of having to explain this objectively and mentor a good decision. "This is what I signed up for!" he said to the room. "Man up and do the best you can."

Zelda had been standing at his office door for a while, but Randall had been so deep in thought that he hadn't noticed her. "And that's just what you're going to do, husband of mine, if I may express an opinion. Just so you know, the kids are safely stationed in front of the boob tube and we have about ten minutes to make final preparations for our guests."

With that announcement, the doorbell rang. "Make that zero minutes," corrected Zelda. "Get your shoes back on and put on your happy face. I'll get the door."

Elisa and Elena had come to the front door, which was rarely used. Zelda tried to open it, but it was stuck fast, probably frozen in place. She yelled out for Randall to help and it took both of them to tug the door open. Two rather forlorn and cold young women stood at the doorstep and were ushered in by Zelda with a flourish and a friendly welcome. Randall was blocked out until they cleared the foyer into the front hallway. He reached out, gave Elisa a big hug, and introduced her to Zelda who also gave her a big hug.

Both women, especially Elisa, had red-rimmed eyes and looked quite tired.

Elena just stood to the side during the display of warmth until Randall turned to her. "And you must be sister Elena." Randall gave her a gentlemanly hand shake and bowed slightly.

Zelda couldn't help but take the opportunity to launch a zinger. "Good guess, Randy! You had so many choices."

The remark seemed to break the ice and everybody chuckled as Randall bowed his mea culpa bow with a hand outstretched.

Elena reached out her hand for his. She resembled her sister, but was taller and had darker hair. "It's so good to meet you, doctor. Elisa speaks highly of you." Randall noticed her clothing was a bit muted and rumpled, in contrast to Elisa's well-pressed skirt with matching blouse and colorful scarf.

"All the good stuff is true," quipped Randall. "I can't account for the other stuff. Welcome to our home! Give me your coats and Zelda will take you into the living room. Sit in front of the fireplace and warm up a bit. We've got a nice fire going. When I return I can bring you something to drink. May I offer some nice Riesling wine?"

Elena took Elisa by the elbow and spoke. "Thank you. That would be nice. But before we sit down, I have to ask, because we are both so anxious. Have you received word of Elisa's diagnosis yet?"

Randall stood there tongue-tied for a moment just holding their coats. "I . . . don't have the final results quite yet, but my pathology colleague should be calling me any time now with that answer. So, I suggest you just take a breather in the living room and I'll bring your drinks."

Elisa wrung her hands a bit, but she let Elena guide her. They followed Zelda into the living room and sat. Elisa slumped in a chair and set her purse on the floor. When Randall returned with their wine in stemmed glasses, they seemed less tense.

Drinks in hand, Zelda proposed a toast to good health and opened the interrogation. "So, Randy tells me that you both have a Shamanic ancestry. Tell me about it."

Elisa and Elena frowned and looked at each other with question marks etched on their foreheads. Given what they thought they had come for, the question seemed odd. Elena was the quieter of the two and looked to Elisa for a clue.

Elisa paused for a moment collecting her thoughts. "Well, yes. I suppose you could say that. My father, Jose, was a descendant of the Pasqua Yacqui in northern Mexico. He was born in 1919. The Pasqua go back to the ancient Aztecs. His father was a Shaman and practiced many of their ritual ceremonies, including rainmaking, fertility rites, healing and fortune telling."

Randall gave Zelda a look intended to tone down the interrogation, but she either didn't get it or ignored it.

Zelda ignored Randall's look and leaned forward. "Did your father have the gift of seeing the future?"

They were all distracted by Wondercat sneaking into the room and sniffing at the new visitors.

Elisa smiled at the black cat. "Hmm, looks like you have a familiar?"

Zelda blushed at the implication. "Not me. She loves the kids, but doesn't hang out with the adults."

As Wondercat sniffed Elena's shoe, Elena found her voice. "Zelda, you asked whether my father was a fortune teller. He always seemed to know what mischief I was into and I never figured out how he knew. But I think every parent has that skill. His abilities swung more towards those of a shaman, like those Elisa mentioned." She took a sip of wine. "Now my mother, Juanita, is another story. She was born in 1924 in Ponce, Puerto Rico. Even as a child she could predict things and when she grew up she called herself a fortune teller. From what Elisa and I saw, she was right more often than wrong."

Zelda sat forward with interest. "Intriguing! Can you give us an example?"

Randall tried to redirect the questioning. "Now, Zel, I think the sisters have more on their minds right now than storytelling."

Zelda waved him off. "Oh, Randy! Don't be such a killjoy. I bet the girls have thought enough about their troubles. A little diversion won't hurt."

"You're probably right," agreed Randall. "But only one story and then we should talk about more pressing issues, okay?" Everybody agreed to the compromise.

The two sisters collaborated for a moment, deciding which example to use. Elisa told the tale. A young boy in their neighborhood in Tucson disappeared on his way home from school. He was missing for three days despite searches by the police. The boy's parents knew of Juanita's abilities and asked for her help. She came to the house and went through the boy's belongings. That night she had a vision that he was trapped in a local canyon. The authorities were doubtful, but had run out of options, so they agreed to check out the canyon. Sure enough, a rescue party found the boy in that very canyon with a broken leg but alive.

Zelda was duly impressed. "That's so cool. I assume there are other examples?"

Elena nodded. "There are many and she had regular clients, but they mostly asked about love and marriage prospects. Dad did mostly private healings and some rainmaking for farmers."

Randall knew this train could career out of control. "Zel, why are you so interested in this?"

Zelda raised two fingers. "Two reasons. Firstly, if you recall, you invited both Elisa and me to your UEG meeting and I want to find out what talents she might bring to the table."

Zelda paused to *shoo* Wondercat away from digging around in Elisa's purse. "Secondish, I want to find out if she or Elena may have inherited some abilities from their parents that they can tap into to help with the big questions we have to wrestle with tonight, those being the pregnancy and the possible cancer diagnosis. There! Now I've said it and it's out in the open. No more need for pussyfooting." Zelda stomped her foot, and Wondercat skittered from the purse (on her pussy feet).

The sisters looked rather shocked and wide-eyed by Zelda's rather blunt statement. And the cat's punctuation.

Randall let out a whoosh of air. "Nice segue, wife o'mine. By the way, the acronym is QEG, but your moniker may be more accurate considering how little we know. Now that we've let the cat out of the bag, so to speak, I suggest the following. . . ."

Zelda groaned, yet Randall carried on.

"We still have to wait for my pathology colleague to call with the biopsy results. Let's use our little cocktail time to talk about the cookie in the oven. Does that work, ladies?"

Elisa let out a loud breath. "*Whoo*! I'm already feeling Mr. Riesling doing his magic. But I'm still nervous as a chicken in a fox house. I should ask for a refill."

Elena interrupted. "Wait a minute, sister! We both forgot. You're pregnant and one glass is enough for you. Zelda, do you have any orange juice?"

Zelda slapped her forehead. "How dumb of me to have overlooked that tiny fact. Randy! You're the doctor here. Why didn't you stop me from giving wine to Elisa?"

It was Randall's turn to head slap. "Would you buy terminal fatigue or just total professional lapse?"

The girls had to laugh at Randall's reaction. Elisa came to his rescue. "I may be nervous, but I'm not stupid. I know the risks of alcohol during pregnancy. But I decided that the baby was nervous too. So . . . I decided 'what the heck?' Tipsy would be okay, but flopsy not so much. Notice I said I 'should' ask for a refill? That didn't mean I was going to."

Zelda thought that was hilarious. "Elisa . . . you are a kindred spirit. I think we're going to be good friends."

Baby Talk

After glasses were replenished, Elisa's with orange juice, Zelda decided to kick off discussion about the pregnancy dilemma. "From what Randy has told me, Elisa, you just found out you have a little uterine invader and are already three months along. The first question I have is simple. Do you want this baby?"

Elisa coughed and cleared her throat. She took a large hit of OJ. "The simple answer is yes. I would never have an abortion. It's against my moral principles. Besides, it would be difficult and cruel to do at three months gestation." She began to tear up a bit and dabbed at her eyes with a tissue.

Randall waited for Elisa to regain her composure. "You told me that the father is a nonstarter. Is that still the case?"

Elisa scrunched up her face. "I don't have the words to describe how ill-suited the sperm donor is to be either a husband or a parent. He's moved to a planet far far away. And good riddance. I'm fully prepared to have the child and raise it by myself, if necessary."

Elena took Elisa's hand. "You won't have to do it by yourself. I've got your back and your front."

The comment evoked an outburst of laughter, but it was lubricated by more female tears. Even Randall got a bit choked up.

Randall collected himself and made a pronouncement. "So, we are hereby resolved to welcome Elisa's little cookie, whether it be a Lorna Doone or a Gingerbread Man. We vow that her cookie will not crumble!"

Zelda punched Randall in the arm. "Randy! You are such a goof. But I have to admit you are correct. Let us toast to hallowed cookies! No matter what the morrow brings us, the biscuit, as the Brits would say, is in the breadbox."

The group chuckled and clinked glasses. The toast was interrupted by Addie's call from upstairs. "Mom, Dad! Kyle won't let me watch my program!"

Randall rolled his eyes and rose from his chair. "Duty calls. Please excuse me."

Kyle called downstairs. "What she wants to watch is lame!"

Randall shook his head and yelled a response. "I'm coming up there. Cool your jets. Sort it out before I get there. Or else!"

As Randall stomped up the stairs, Zelda tried to lighten the moment. "Kids are so curious. They probably just want to know what's going on down here. I should probably start getting our dinner on the table. You girls finish up your drinks while I get things ready. I'll call you when it's time to sit down. Feel free to talk amongst yourselves and reconsider whether you really want kids. They do grow up to pester the heck out of you. Ha ha. Just kidding!"

Dinner Time

Randall returned from upstairs and walked into the living room. Elisa and Elena were huddled together holding hands.

"All quiet on the western front. We finally found a program the two could agree on. Where's Zelda?"

Elena looked up. "Zelda's getting dinner ready. We should go see if we can help."

Randall pointed to the kitchen. "You ladies go on ahead. I'm allergic to pots and pans. Besides, I'm all pooped out from kid crisis intervention. Call me when dinner's ready. I'm going back upstairs . . . to check on the armistice."

Upstairs, Randall attempted to call Dr. Kramer's office again to see if he'd made the final diagnosis, but the extensions just kept ringing. He hung up, banged the wall with his palm, and whisper-yelled. "Dang! Left hanging again! I need that answer before dinner starts or things will get really awkward."

Randall realized he would have to come up with a plausible excuse for not having the results if Kramer didn't call. The question of Elisa having the baby was sort of settled, but that could all change depending on the node biopsy results. Best to keep a happy face for now and not raise anxiety levels any higher. He was already pretty sure what the diagnosis would be and he hoped he was prepared to break the news in the best possible way, if there was a best way.

Sounds of laughter wafted from the kitchen as Randall descended the stairs. Zelda had a gift for breaking through barriers and she seemed well on the way to loosening up the sisters, judging from the girlish giggling he was hearing. There was more nonsense than food preparation going on when he made his appearance in the kitchen.

Randall spoke loudly enough to be heard over the racket. The three ladies were startled by his stealthy entrance. "I just settled down wrangling kids upstairs. Do I have to do it again down here?"

Zelda was startled and nearly jumped out of her shoes. "Randy! Do you *alwish* have to *schneak* up on people?"

Randall smiled at the slurred speech and made a grand gesture. "Why, *yesh* I do. That's my job. How else am I going to catch malefactors?"

Zelda and Elena had a little giggle fit. When they regained control, Elena offered an explanation of their behavior. "I think Zelda and I . . . have had a bit too much, urp, winey. We probably ought to . . . eat something. I'm already *sabilating* for those enchiladas. I mean . . . my mouth is *droobli*ng."

Elisa was more terse. "Boy, you two are cheap drunks. Let me guide the two of you to the dining table. Randy, help them get seated and I'll start serving. Everything is ready."

Soon, they were all seated around the table with the steaming food laid out. Elisa raised a hand for attention. "Before we start inhaling food, Dr. B, has your doctor friend called yet? I didn't hear any ringy dingy."

Randall had to think fast and answer without fibbing. "We did communicate earlier this evening. It seems we'll need to wait a bit longer for slides to be finished. He ran some special stains and was waiting for them to do a final reading. They should be ready soon. We should have plenty of time to eat before we hear from him. Shall we dig in?"

Zelda raised a forefinger. "Before we *schtart* eating . . . does anyone who can still talk *schtraight* wanna say grace?"

Randall was suddenly tongue tied. Elisa surprised everyone by volunteering. "Let's all close our eyes and hold hands. Good. Universal Spirit, we thank you for this fine meal of which we are about to partake. We thank our gracious hosts for sharing this meal and this time in our lives with us. I am eternally grateful for the blessing of a new life, a life which I vow to help raise and guide along with my beloved sister. There are questions we anxiously await answers to. I pray that the answers are benign ones. But if they are not, give me the wisdom and strength to face any challenges they bring. Amen."

The room was silent long after the answering amen. Zelda felt Elena and Randall's hands squeeze hers. She opened her eyes and looked across the table at Elisa. Everyone else still had closed eyes. Zelda was shocked to see a brilliant red aura surrounding Elisa. It pulsated with intensity, at times sending off fragile plumes of color, almost like solar flares. When everyone else opened their eyes again, the red aura disappeared. Zelda blinked her eyes in disbelief.

Randall focused on the food. "Great God. Great food. Let's eat. Take what's in front of you and pass to your left."

Everybody did as directed except Zelda, who just sat there trying to sort out what she had just seen. She remembered from her Yoga classes that auras were thought to be the electromagnetic field radiating off our bodies. She remembered Randall saying that, according to quantum theory, we are all composed of energy, so the body emitting radiation made sense. What she couldn't remember was what a red aura meant. Was it good, bad or indifferent? Then, in another memory flash, she remembered the green aura she'd seen around their neighbor, Chris, while discussing his visions of the deceased babysitter, Alexandra. A shiver went up her spine. Meanwhile, everyone else at the table had begun to wolf down their enchiladas, salad and guacamole.

Randall looked over at his wife. "Hey, Zel! Wake up and pass the guacamole. Why aren't you eating? Did you lose your appetite?"

Zelda started a bit. "No, I'm plenty hungry. I was just thinking about Elisa's beautiful blessing. Plus, I forget to put out the hot sauce. I'll be right back."

In the kitchen, Zelda found the hot sauce, then went to the cabinet where she kept her Yoga notes. After some shuffling she found the section on auras. It described how a photographic plate could be used to image auras as a glowing discharge of energy around the body. It was called Kirlian photography. Some people could see auras and some could not. Auras for a particular person were usually constant and consistent with their personality, but could change depending on what was happening in their life.

Zelda's reading was distracted by more laughing coming from the dining room. Then Randall called out. "Zel! Did you fall in the fridge? We are Jonesing for hot sauce."

Zelda tried to buy time. "Be there real soon. The old hot sauce was spoiled. Have to find a new jar." She read on and found the information on colors. It said that red was connected to major life changes, like marriage, job changes, moving, etc. It also represents the root chakra, which is to ground us and be our foundation. It's the place where people feel safe and secure.

Randall had waited long enough. He got up and went to the kitchen where he found Zelda pouring over her notes. "What's up, wife o'mine?"

Zelda looked up furtively. "Hold your horses, buster. I'm on a mission."

Randall raised both arms. "What mission?"

"A red and green one," said Zelda. She got closer to his ear and whispered. She quickly explained the aura she had just seen and what it meant.

Randall was wide-eyed. "That's another one for the books. What's it say about green?"

Zelda paged some more. "Here it is. Green. That's the heart chakra. It's about self-nurturing energy and being more open and generous with others. Basically, if you love yourself you can spread the love. You can also use the energy to overcome a challenging situation."

Randall chuckled softly. "So, that's like the Kermit the frog chakra? It's not easy being green."

"Very droll, lunkhead," responded Zelda. "Not quite sure how it fits with Chris's situation, but, yeah, I can see a connection."

Randall nodded. "Not quite sure what a chakra is though. Say, we better get back to dinner before the troops get suspicious. Please explain chakra later, *dudette*."

Zelda put her Yoga papers back in the cabinet. "Yeah! Here's the hot sauce. I'll bring in another round of enchiladas. Serve some more fluids, my *studlet*."

When Randall and Zelda made it back to the dinner table, Elisa asked what had taken them so long. Randall replied that he had been taking advantage of the cook. That set off a round of laughter and he turned beet red. Then, talk returned to the sisters' parents.

Through a mouthful of enchilada, Zelda asked how Juan and Juanita had met.

Elisa shook her head. "I could tell you, but you may not believe the story."

Zelda had switched to orange juice and the food was absorbing some alcohol. "Try me. I'm not easily fooled."

Elisa began the tale. "Okay. Elena, you help me if I leave anything out. When Juanita was a teen, she immigrated to the US and wound up living with her Uncle in Douglas, Arizona. He owned a cantina and she helped out there. When they discovered her fortune telling abilities, she was given a special table to 'entertain' customers for a fee. One day, Juan Angeles, an Airforce pilot in training, came into the bar and spotted Juanita at her table. It seems he immediately saw something in her, or I should say, around her and vice versa."

Zelda rose to the edge of her seat. "What was that, pray tell?"

Elena jumped in. "Should we tell her or make her guess?"

Elisa smiled and looked enigmatic. "I say give her three guesses."

Zelda could not hold back the answer that came into her head like a flash. "They both had brilliant auras! Hers was red and his was green!"

Both sisters gasped and clasped a hand to their mouths. "If that means something like a halo, you're exactly right. How ever did you guess that?"

In the next five minutes Zelda explained about seeing Elisa's red aura and her previous experience with Chris, the neighbor. The sisters listened with rapt attention. Randall was as quiet as a mouse with laryngitis.

When Zelda was finished, Elisa was first to respond. "So, it seems you have the gift as well. Can you see the future, too, like my mother?"

Zelda shook her head. "Unfortunately, no. And I'm not sure I would want to. This aura thing is something new to me. It's just started happening. Maybe it will become something bigger. I think my son, Kyle, has something like it. He has dreams that seem to come true, but nothing with auras yet. Randy has had some weird contact with the spirit world and nonverbal communication. That's why he's working with his group on the quantum entanglement thingy. That's the think tank he wants us to be part of."

Randall broached another question. "How about you, Elena? Any connections with the Twilight Zone?"

Elena looked to the side and pursed her lips. "Only a weird connection to Elisa. Like whenever she has a crisis I get the sense that I have to go help her. When I show up at her doorstep she claims that nothing is amiss, but shortly after I arrive chaos ensues. That's why I show up unannounced. If I called first she'd worry longer. She won't admit it, but I can usually help her weather whatever little storm has rolled in."

Elisa pouted a bit. "I do so appreciate your help. It's just that your ability can't seem to distinguish between a bad hair day and a car accident."

Elena nodded. "Well, we have had a few false alarms."

Randall looked at his wristwatch. As if on cue, the kitchen telephone rang. Everybody jumped perceptibly. Zelda raced to the kitchen to pick up the phone and directed Randall to his study to take the call.

The Call

Randall picked up the phone receiver. "This better be you, Kramer. What took you so long?"

"Loosen your BVDs, Biedermeier. I had the dreaded call from the wife at home that starts without a hello and begins with 'Where are you? Did you forget? Your boss, his wife and I are waiting for you to come home for dinner and it's getting very cold!' And she meant both the dinner and her shoulder."

Randall could relate. "Oh, boy. Sorry about that. Been there. Done that. Paid the price. It was dear."

Zelda *harrumphed* on the extension.

Kramer gave out a big sigh. "I'm more worried about my failing memory. Probably was your case that sabotaged my attention. After I struggled my way through the dinner, I came back to the department to finalize the report. I feel even worse about the news I'm about to tell you."

Randall's gut clenched. "Oh. Give me the bad news."

Kramer cleared his throat. "Nothing's really changed from what I told you earlier. It's still a lymphocyte predominant Hodgkin's lymphoma. So far, with just the neck node, it would be stage I, but, if that pelvic mass is involved, it could be stage III. You know the treatment options better than me, but, with the pregnancy, it becomes a sticky wicket."

Randall couldn't come up with actual words. "Uh huh."

Kramer couldn't make out Randall's response. "What's that, Biedermeier? Did you get all that?"

Randall shook his head to connect brain with mouth again. "Yeah. I got it right between the eyes. My nurse and her sister are still over here for dinner. We're just finishing up. They know the call is from you. Fortunately, they're in a relatively better mood than when they arrived. I hope that will help tone down the bad news."

Kramer coughed. "Hard to believe a good mood will make any difference. Better you than me. Best of luck."

Randall coughed back. "I'll need it. Thanks for all your help on this. You went above and beyond. Sorry it got you in the doghouse."

Kramer laughed. "No doghouse for me. I get the living room couch. At least I won't have to listen to her cacophonous snoring tonight."

Randall saw his opening. "Nor she yours!"

Kramer guffawed and hung up noisily. Randall stretched and prepared to deliver the news.

When Randall returned to the dining room all eyes were on him. He sat back down and requested they all hold hands again. He didn't have to say anything for everyone to figure the news was bad.

Randall skipped any preamble and went straight to the presentation of facts. After disclosing the diagnosis, he basically repeated the summary he had read earlier in his oncology text. Elisa and Elena took the news stoically, then asked a few clarifying questions. Zelda rose during the discussion and put both hands on Elisa's shoulders. Elisa placed her hands on top of Zelda's hands. A few tears welled from Elisa's eyes and Zelda's face became carmine. Elena's face turned white. For a long moment no one spoke.

Elena broke the silence with a question. "Well, where do we go from here?"

Randall cleared his suddenly thick throat. "Good question. From everyone's serious faces, I sense resolve and courage. This is a complicated situation, but not a hopeless one. It seems pretty clear that the little cookie is a keeper, so all plans henceforth will be based on that assumption. Agreed?"

All heads nodded. Randall went on. "The obvious next step is to figure out whether the pelvic mass is involvement by the lymphoma or something unrelated. We may be able to sort that out with a lymphangiogram. That's done by injecting X-ray contrast into lymphatic channels in the groin to visualize the pelvic nodes. If that shows a large lymph node, it's likely involved. If they're normal sized, it's probably not involved. We'd have to get clearance from Radiology to use diagnostic radiation on a pregnant woman. Considering the radiation dose is low, the fetus fairly well developed, and the need for a diagnosis is high, they may approve it. I checked with ACR guidelines and it says that such imaging should not be withheld if the situation demands it."

Elena raised her hand. "The American College of Radiology actually considers this? That's pretty forward thinking. What about a biopsy of the mass?"

Randall shook his head. "Needle biopsies are tricky with lymph nodes, especially in that location. With the pregnancy, a laparotomy to get at the node would be dicey. I'd say we start with the lymphangiogram and a surgical consult for an opinion on how to sample the pelvic mass, if necessary."

Zelda quivered with compassion. "If the pelvic mass is negative, what's the treatment?"

Randall smiled. "That would be our best case scenario. The lymphoma would be stage I and we could irradiate the nodes above the diaphragm without much risk to the fetus. The dose to control Hodgkin's is about two thirds of that needed for other cancers. The cure rate is excellent and it would give the fetus time to mature enough for delivery."

Elisa was looking less traumatized. "What about chemotherapy? Would that work instead of radiation?"

Randall nodded. "It would, but it couldn't be used until the fetus is mature enough to deliver. That will take at least another three months. In that time, the disease could advance to a less treatable stage. So, if we are firm on keeping the baby, there would be no chemo for at least three months. And you would have to understand that you'd be risking your survival to save the baby. That could mean the baby survives without a mother."

Elisa and Elena looked at each other, downcast.

Randall pushed on with the difficult question. "Is Elena prepared to step in if that path is taken?"

Elena pondered for a beat, then stood up at attention. "She is! But that would only happen if the stupid pelvic thing is Hodgkin's. With the Great Spirit's help it will be a non-issue."

Elisa looked with gratitude at the people around her. She had big decisions in front of her, with no one clear answer. The silence extended for a few moments.

Zelda broke the quiet. "Are you okay? Elisa, what's going on in your mind right now?"

Elisa took a deep breath in and let it out slowly. "Surprisingly, it's actually in my heart. While my mind is full of worries and 'what ifs,' my heart feels sure that my soul will be alright. All this is part of my spiritual journey, and I chose it before I got to Earth in this incarnation. I feel the connection of my body to the Earth and those around me. The lessons that are coming to me now are part of my growth. If you saw that my aura is red, that's probably because that's exactly how I'm feeling."

Zelda applauded. "Here here, I say. That's the moxie I was looking for!"

Elisa gathered her strength and stood up with Elena. "Thanks, Zelda. Bottom line, I think we all agree on the path forward. Dr. B,

Zelda, Elena . . . I don't think I could have faced this by myself. Without your support I would have been a blithering mess right now. Somehow, I expected we might have these immediate connections. I don't know for sure how I knew that, but from what I've learned tonight, I think I have a clue. Can we do a group hug?"

"You bet," cried Randall. "I am very much in need of one at this moment."

The four gathered with arms wrapped around each other, humming and swaying. Wondercat wound herself in between them to soak in the love.

When they finally broke up the hug, they looked for tissues to wipe eyes or blow noses. Zelda followed up a loud nose snort with a proposal. "How about some hot cocoa for the road?"

Randall raised his hand like a grade schooler and jumped up and down. "Oo, oo, I want one!"

Elisa and Elena followed suit and copied Randall. Zelda laughed at their antics. "Alright, you kids. Sit down at the kitchen table and behave while I concoct my special brew."

While they waited for their hot cocoa, Randall made a suggestion. "Hey, Elisa, you should consider taking next week off and just concentrate on getting to your tests and making it to your appointments."

Elisa shook her head. "Thanks, but I'd rather stay working between that stuff. It'll help keep my mind occupied. I just ask that you and the VA stay flexible."

Randall nodded. "I get that. I'll make it happen."

Kyle and Addie had slunk down the stairs without drawing the attention of the adults. They appeared at the kitchen door in their PJs.

Randall looked up in surprise. "What are you two doing downstairs?"

Addie squeaked out a response. "Kyle and I want hot cocoa too. And we want to meet your work ladies."

Kyle added his two cents. "Yeah, can I have a scoop of ice cream in my cocoa? Say, your work ladies are real pretty. I bet Mom is jealous."

Elena and Elisa laughed at the remark. Elena put a hand to her chest. "Why thank you, young man. You're not bad yourself." She reached out her hand to Kyle. Kyle took it and kissed it instead of shaking it, drawing more *oohs* and *aahs*.

Zelda was aghast. "Why you little pervert! Wherever did that come from? I am not the jealous type. These work ladies are my new friends."

Kyle took the comment in stride. "I saw it on TV. Nice men always do that with pretty ladies." He turned to Elisa. "May I kiss your hand too?"

Elisa blushed and complied as though she were a shy teenager. "Oh, sir. You are most kind."

It was Kyle's turn to become flush faced. But he recovered quickly. "Now, how about that cocoa and ice cream? Both of us have been good and we didn't bother you during dinner."

Addie piped up. "And we didn't eavesdrop on you talking about the baby."

Elisa gave Addie a stern look. "Are you sure?"

Addie shuffled her feet. "Yeah, mostly."

That got everyone laughing again and now Addie turned red.

Before the ice cream was served, Elisa rose from her chair. She announced that it was time for her and Elena to leave. "You have really sweet kids. We suggest you make them even sweeter by filling them up with all the ice cream they can hold. We'll leave you now and avoid the sugar rush that's coming soon. Good night and thanks for everything."

Zelda directed them to the back door and held the door open for them. Randall was right behind her as the sisters stepped outside. "You two drive safely," yelled Zelda.

"See you tomorrow," shouted Randall. "We'll get everything squared away."

Randall and Zelda stood at the open back door and watched as the sisters got into their car and pulled away. When the car's red tail lights were out of sight, the two were already shivering and rushed back inside.

Zelda was first to talk. "Poor girl. I feel so bad for her. Randy! You better do your best work helping those two. Let me know if there's anything I can do."

Randall hugged Zelda in the hallway. "Thanks for putting the dinner together. That was a big help towards showing our support and that she isn't alone in this. Perhaps you can stay in touch with her. Besides her sister, you could be the new girlfriend she needs right now. Who else understands her condition and circumstances as well as you?"

Zelda kissed Randall on the cheek. "She's lucky to have you too. She gave me her phone number and said she'd welcome my call. I plan on doing just that. I'm sorry I acted jealous of her earlier. I shouldn't have worried about you. I should have been worried about Kyle."

Randall burst out laughing. "Yeah. I never expected him to come on like that. That boy is going to turn into a Casanova one day soon."

Kyle yelled from the kitchen. "Quit the mushy stuff and get us our ice cream!"

Zelda chuckled. "Well, maybe not so soon."

I scream, you scream

Things got a little wild during the phagocytosis of the ice cream when Addie accidentally launched a spoonful into Kyle's lap. That, of course, led to retaliation and escalation before peacekeeping forces could be deployed. Somehow Randall and Zelda got involved before entropy reclaimed control. After Kyle and Addie wolfed down all the ice cream, with some help from Randall and Zelda, they were launched back upstairs and bound for bed.

After finally getting the kids settled with a short fabricated bedtime story, Randall and Zelda returned to the kitchen for cleanup.

Randall cleared the dirty dishes from the table and brought them to the counter next to the sink. Zelda womanned the sink and somewhat mechanically washed and rinsed the seemingly endless stream of dishware.

Zelda tossed the dishrag at Randall. "Randy, will this ever end? I can't believe we used so many dishes."

Randall brought her the empty enchilada cooking pan. It was a mess of fused cheese on pyrex. "Settle down. This is the last of it."

Zelda exhaled loudly. "Woof, that's a relief! You get to drying this stuff so we can sit down and decompress."

When the task was finally done they collapsed on the living room couch. Zelda closed her eyes and Randall followed suit.

After studying the inside of her eyelids for a long moment, Zelda decided to discuss the red aura mystery with Randall. "Randy, why do you think I could see Elisa's aura during grace at the table, but not later?"

Randall wasn't prepared for the question and made a long humming sound. "Hmmm. Not sure. Maybe it's something you can only 'see' when you focus your mind in a certain way."

Zelda nodded. "Yeah, that makes sense. That might explain why some people can do it and others can't. It may take both a natural ability and some training to refine it. It seems I may have it. That could be both a blessing and a curse."

Randall wasn't sure where this was headed. "How so?"

Zelda hesitated for a bit. "Well, if I don't have total control over when it happens, that means I could get uninvited messages about folks. Then, am I obliged to reveal to them what I've seen?"

Randall thought about the possibilities. "I wouldn't think you're obliged to do anything unless you think it might have a significant bearing on the person involved. And you're clearly not alone. Elisa, and maybe Elena, seem to have it as well. You were going to explain more about chakras?"

Zelda cleared her throat. "Yeah, well . . . I'll do my best to remember what I learned in Yoga. Basically, they are the main energy points in the body and the ancients thought there were seven of them located at various points along the spine and the head. The locations correspond to nerve bundles and major organs. I think it dates back as far as, like, 1000 BC or maybe 1500 BC. Anyway, it was a long time ago. The theory goes that the energy points need to be 'open' or disease may follow if they are 'blocked.' Each has a number and color linked to it."

Randall looked dubious. "Sounds a bit like Astrology. I bet the descriptions of each chakra are vague enough to be interpreted to fit any situation."

Zelda nodded. "You could say that. Now red is linked to the root chakra in the tailbone area. Its meaning is physical identity, stability and grounding. Remember, a chakra is thought to be a vortex of spinning energy inside the body. The heart chakra and aura are both green. They are both pretty strong. They say the heart aura can be projected as far as five feet away."

Randall was confused. "Wait a minute. Didn't you say that a red aura is the root aura? You just said the root chakra is red. Are they the same?"

Zelda shook her head. "Red is the color for both the root chakra and the root aura. They are both located in the tailbone area, but the chakra is the internal and the aura is the external manifestation of the body's energy. If that makes sense."

Randall nodded slowly, making connections. "This sounds like . . ."

Zelda interrupted. "You might even say it fits with your refinement using quantum energy theory. The ancients didn't know anything about atoms and subatomic behavior, but it was still there in 1500 BC."

Randall slapped his thigh. "Now that's the most brilliant observation you've ever made! That really links the puzzle pieces together! You and Elisa are going to be a major hit at the QEG meeting. I need to call Joe Shepard first thing tomorrow and find out when we can schedule our meeting."

Zelda was excited. "Randy! I am so ready for that. I'll call Elisa tomorrow and rev her up about the meeting. It will be a good new focus for her. Lord knows, she needs something to distract her from the awful news she just got."

Randall got excited, too. "You know, when you think of it that way, the person with the aura is a broadcaster and those who can see the aura are the receivers, no, the perceivers. You are the energy perceiver."

Zelda felt proud. "Yeah, we see through the window clearly."

Randall jumped up. "Talk about both sides of the spiritual coin— the Yogi just referred to the Bible! Isn't that Corinthians?"

Zelda held her hands together in front of her heart. "Whatever. I just know that in the duality of contrast might we see our divine wholeness."

Randall felt a rush of energy. "You are the Yin of spirit and I am the Yang of science."

Zelda jumped up and put out her hand. "Nice to meet you, Dr. Yang."

Randall bowed, took her hand and shook it gently. "The pleasure is mine, Dr. Yin."

C H A P T E R 27

———

T H E L O O K I N G G L A S S

For now we see through a glass, darkly; but then face to face: now I know in part; but then shall I know even as also I am known.

—1 Corinthians 13:12

BABY ANNOUNCEMENT

The Tuesday morning after the dinner with the Angeles sisters came so quickly, Randall could not remember sleeping. On the drive to the VA he was distracted by three issues that kept spinning around in his sleep deprived brain. When he got to the parking lot he tried to settle himself before getting out of the car. If he was going to be any good at work he'd have to put thoughts of pregnancy, Hodgkin's disease and QEG meetings on his mental back burner. He took a last sip of now cold coffee from his travel mug and exited the car stage right.

During the walk to the building, Randall switched his brain focus to Quality Assurance, or QA, in hospital speak. In his department, Tuesdays at 7:30 were reserved for Chart Rounds, never mind that the charts were rectangular. QA was a somewhat boring, but necessary, practice designed to appease the hospital certification gods. It was the official moniker for just minding your Ps and Qs. It wasn't as though hospitals had invented QA. As far as Randall was concerned, minding one's Ps and Qs had been pioneered by his mother.

Randall had looked up the origin of the "Ps and Qs" aphorism once before. It basically meant "watch what you're doing." Some etymologists believed the phrase dated to the mid 1800s and regarded the possible confusion between the lowercase letters p and q in school penmanship and printing typesetting. Others pointed to a poem by Charles Churchill, published in 1763, that ends with "And to instruct him how to use, His As and Bs, and Ps and Qs." Even older references traced it back to old Scotland, where barkeeps kept track of pints (Ps) and quarts (Qs) in logbooks. Whatever the case, in some form or another, QA had been around for a while.

In Radiation Oncology, the QA process required checking and double checking that every aspect of the treatment plan was being followed and properly recorded. It wasn't enough just to verbally instruct the department staff to double check everything. There had to be a formal written Policy and Procedure document on file outlining what all the steps were. Even the checklist had a checklist to verify that the verification was being done verifiably. It was massive redundancy, but the process had proven its worth in picking up errors and miscues that might have gone undetected and ballooned into larger problems. It had taken months to drill the value of the process into the staff, but eventually they had bought in.

To make the QA process more palatable, Randall had worked out a rotation schedule for one of the staff to bring donuts or bagels to the weekly meeting. Also, the VA canteen had a standing order to provide a coffee urn weekly. However, from the transparency of the swill, one might say it was delivered weakly. It was amazing how carbohydrates could motivate. The meeting was also one of the few times the entire department could all assemble together. Thus, Chart Rounds often became a time for news, announcements, comments, criticisms and gossip.

When Randall entered the Ortho room, the staff had already begun to assemble and most hovered near the food and drink. Grace came in just behind him and eyed the week's caloric offerings. "My stars! Racine kringles! I love those. Apple and cream cheese! My favorite! Hey, Dr. B! Here's your favorite, pecan." Grace gave out a rather malignant chuckle.

Randall made a choking sound. "Ugh. I hate pecan and you know it. Don't eat all the apple and cream cheese. Those are my favorites."

Grace made a show of loading a large helping of apple and cream cheese kringle onto her paper plate, which folded in half from the weight. The whole serving plopped upside down on the floor.

Dan Graham burst out laughing and rushed over to scoop up the mess with a triple thick plate. "Five second rule invoked! I pronounce the kringle to be free of all contamination. Here you go, Dr. B."

Randall wrinkled his nose, but still selected a piece from Dan's offering and placed the slightly disheveled kringle on his plate. "Thanks, I think. Not to worry. My stomach is so hyperacidic right now, it's unlikely any self respecting bacteria will survive."

Grace had turned a deep purple by then and Randall could swear she had a brown aura. Randall made up a triple paper plate, loaded it with two slices of kringle and handed it to Grace. "Here you go. No harm, no foul."

At first, Grace couldn't decide what to say and then uttered a weak "thank you."

Randall acknowledged Grace with a "You're welcome" and then made shooing motions. "Now, everybody pick your poison and get seated. We've got 41 charts to go over and I can't turn the clock back, although I am working on an invention to pause time."

Dan looked up in interest. "Does it involve quantum finagling?"

Randall's facial expression became enigmatic. "Could be."

Doris seated herself, but hadn't taken a kringle. "I don't believe in the five second rule. You can keep the kringle. Besides, I don't need the calories. I'm on a diet."

Judy pulled out a chair to sit. "Oh? When did you start?"

Doris smiled and took a sip of her coffee. "Just now. No time like the present. Even though the road to H-E-double hockey sticks is paved with good intentions."

The group was about ready to start when Elisa entered the room. She offered a cheerful good morning to the group. "Buenos Dias, everyone. I hope you all like the kringle. It was my turn to bring the sugar and lard ration for the week."

Randall was somewhat shocked to see Elisa at the early morning gathering, but did his best to hide his surprise.

Dan was first to respond. "Love your choice of kringle. Heard you were under the weather. You look pretty good to me. Did you have a 24 hour bug?"

Elisa laughed. "Something like that. Turns out it's a nine month bug. Saw my doctor last week and he said I have a bun in the oven. My GI symptoms are not uncommon with that condition."

Dan rose from his chair and gave Elisa a hug. "Congratulations! I love pregnant women with kringles. Well, not pregnant with kringles. You know what I mean."

Elisa laughed and was given similar greetings by the rest of those assembled. Randall was the last. He was somewhat stunned that Elisa had come right out with the news, but said nothing about it. Everybody knew she wasn't married, but made no bones about that. They had just risen up and supported her. He got rather choked up at Elisa's courage and the compassion of his crew.

Randall raised his coffee cup. "Let's give a toast to Elisa and her bun. Er . . . does anybody have a good one?"

At first, those assembled just looked at each other and shook their heads. After an uncomfortable silence, finally Doris stood up and raised her cup. When the rest of the group followed suit, Doris gave her toast. "May the blessin' of new life grow gently in your heart. And when your time comes, may everythin' come out okay."

Smiles lit up the faces of the toasters and they clinked their cups.

Always the critic, Grace had to ask. "Is that the best you could do?"

Doris looked defiant. "Well, it's better than what you came up with, which was zip. Like a herd of heifers with no bull."

Grace had to admit that was true and the laughs escalated.

Molly put an arm on Elisa's shoulder. "Honey, is there anything you need? Most of us have been in your shoes before. Baby clothes, toys, bassinet or old diapers? Anything you need, just ask."

Elisa looked somewhat overcome. "You guys are great, but right now I just need my schedule to be flexible. I've got more doctor visits and tests to get done over the next several weeks, so I'll be in and out a bit. I've already shared the news with Dr. B and he said that would be okay. My sister is up from Chicago to help out so I should be alright. So, I suggest you stop fawning over me and get this Chart Rounds started before I have to pee or Dr. B blows a head gasket."

Randall did a double take. "Me? Blow a gasket? Why, I am the personification of calm and clammy. But, yeah. Let's get this row on the shoad. I've got the first chart right here. It's Charlie Applebaum. He's a 73-year-old vet with stage III lung cancer, two weeks into treatment. Dan, could you put his sim films and beam films up on the view box?"

Dan rose, still chewing the last of his kringle. "Got it, boss."

Reverse Handoff

As Chart Rounds labored on, Randall made frequent eye contact with Elisa. From this communication alone he was able to discern that she had decided to be upfront about her predicament. He sent the mental message that he approved of her announcement. That assured her support from the entire department staff and spared awkward disclosures later on. It made sense not to bring up Hodgkin's just yet, since much of that was unsettled.

Doris seemed to pick up on the eye messaging and did some of her own. As usual, her sixth sense had detected there was more going on with Elisa than met the eye. She was hard at work trying to sort it out. She developed her plan. She would wheedle the information out of Randall after Chart Rounds.

Despite the earlier delay in getting Chart Rounds started, Randall pushed through all 41 charts and they finished at 9:00 AM. The techs hauled a cart with all the charts back to the console. He and Doris walked together towards his office.

Doris was about to begin her inquisition. "*Whooee!* That was some horse race to get through all those charts. You were whippin' us like a Kentucky Derby jockey."

"Yep," said Randall. "And Beetlebaum won the race."

Doris stopped walking. "Excuse me? You make as much sense as a pig on ice skates."

Randall was sorry he'd brought it up. Now he'd have to explain.

"Sorry. It's an obscure reference to a Spike Jones album my dad used to play when I was a kid."

Doris slapped her forehead. "I knew I remembered that name from somewhere. My dad used to play that old 78 too. Beetlebaum is the slowest horse but he wins."

Randall laughed and nodded. "That's the one! I don't believe it. You and I must be more mature than I thought."

"Well, we are older, but only one of us qualifies as 'mature.'" Doris went to her desk and sat down. There was a large pile of charts in front of her.

Randall stopped and stared at the pile. "Oh, my word. Are those for today?"

Doris nodded. "They are, indeed. Before we start on these, I have to ask you a question."

Randall nodded his assent, but was not expecting what came next.

Doris raised an index finger. "You and Elisa seem as tight as a pair of prom shoes. I may be gettin' a bit motherly, but might I inquire about the daddy? I recall she no longer has a boyfriend."

Randall frowned. "Oh, that. Yeah, I'm surprised but glad no one asked during Chart Rounds. Be assured, the father is not standing in this office. The only male in this office is way too mature to be a suspect in that crime. The departed boyfriend is not only the leading suspect but the perp. He's also way out of the picture, so she's trying to cope with the concept of being a single mother."

Doris nodded slowly. "Are you sure that's all that's afoot?"

Randall shook his head. "I'm not at liberty to discuss that at this time. I've made some promises and I'm also too mature to break them. And too forgetful to remember any lies. However, be assured that all the bases are being covered and a relief pitcher has been summoned from the bullpen."

Doris's demeanor shifted to a look of concern. "Oh, the poor child! I can only imagine."

Randall put a hand on Doris's shoulder. "Well, don't let your imagination run away with you. When the time is right, all will be revealed.

I know you are mature enough to be patient and to be supportive when the time comes."

Doris wiped away a tear, got up from her desk, and grabbed a large chart off the top of the pile. She handed the chart to Randall, but didn't release it right away. "I do detect preliminary signs of maturity in you, Dr. B. Sometimes you do make me proud. Now muster that same maturity and go see Mr. Lyle Underbridge. He's waiting for follow-up in exam one. He's a bit late, though not like Elisa, I dare say. He was delayed up in oral surgery. We can go over the rest of these charts when you're done with him."

Randall was taken aback. "Oral surgery? What's he need them for?"

Randall had treated the patient two years earlier for an inoperable, locally advanced, base of tongue cancer. At the most recent follow-up he had been tumor free. The patient had already had full mouth teeth extraction prior to radiation for advanced periodontal disease, so he couldn't have a tooth problem. Randall hurriedly checked through the chart but found no notes from Oral Surgery yet.

Randall turned to Doris. "Any idea why they saw Mr. Underbridge?"

"Not the foggiest," said Doris. "But he does have a funny bandage around his jaw. If the patient can't tell you, I've got the extension number for Dr. Bishop in Oral Surgery."

Randall's stomach hit bottom like an elevator free falling and suddenly stopping at basement level. He had an idea what the problem was and didn't like it one bit. "Thanks. I'll just go in and see the man. He's usually a pretty reliable historian."

Randall walked out of Doris's office and down the hall towards the exam room. He encountered his nurse, Judy, as he was about to enter the room.

"Dr. B, I just put your next patient in the room and was coming to get you."

Randall was glad that Judy could give him a heads up before he had to go into the exam room. "Hey, Judy, so, you've already talked to Mr. Underbridge?"

Judy nodded. "Yeah, briefly. He's anxious for you to come in. He says everything was fine until three days ago when he was eating a sandwich. He bit down and got a horrible pain in his right jaw at the angle of the mandible. The jaw swelled up at the site of pain after 24 hours and he hasn't been able to take solid food since."

It was the worst case scenario that Randall had imagined, a fractured mandible. "Why didn't he come in right away?"

Judy gave Randall a puzzled look. "Don't you remember? He lives way up in the UP. At first, he thought it was just a muscle spasm and would go away. When it didn't, he got concerned, but figured he'd wait another day to come down for this appointment." She shuffled through the chart. "Looks like it got so painful on the bus ride down to Milwaukee that he stopped in the ER to get some pain meds. After he got a shot of Demerol, the ER doc sent him to Oral Surgery for an exam and Panorex."

Randall's stomach now approached the sub basement. "Err, what did Oral Surgery have to say?"

Judy shrugged her shoulders. "Not sure. They haven't put a note in the chart yet, but the patient keeps saying a word that sounds like 'osteocrosis' and that it caused a fracture of his jawbone. He says they think the radiation caused it. Could that be true?"

Randall tried to push his gastric "up" elevator button, but his stomach was still stuck in the sub basement level. "Yeah, unfortunately, . . . it could be very true. I think the word he was trying to say was 'osteoradionecrosis.' We abbreviate it as ORN because it's easier to say. Any idea what that means?"

Judy was relatively new to the department and didn't have, as yet, a good grasp of the terminology. "Hmm. Let's see. If I break the term down into three parts, it would be 'osteo' means bone, 'radio' means radio, and 'necrosis' means breakdown or decay. So, perhaps if he listens to the radio with the volume turned up too high, the strong auditory vibrations from the ear canal destroy the adjacent jaw bone?"

Randall couldn't help but laugh out loud. The analysis rather cheered him up and he felt the elevator move back to the first floor. "Nice try at etymology, but, in this case, the 'radio' part of the word means radiation. As in, an overly high dose of radiation to the mandible damages the metabolism of the bone and it starts to break down and weaken resulting in a fracture when it's overstressed."

Judy put an index finger to her jawbone. "Oh, that doesn't sound good. You mean the treatment we gave could have caused his jaw fracture? Did you, I mean, we mess something up in his treatment?"

Randall shook his head. "Not exactly. You see, he had a very locally advanced tumor and we had to treat him with radiation alone. With no assist from chemotherapy. So we had to use a relatively high dose to have even a remote chance of controlling it."

Judy looked puzzled. "Why didn't he get chemotherapy along with the radiation? Or surgery?"

Randall was pleasantly surprised that Judy seemed to be catching on quickly, asking all the right questions. "Mr. Underbridge refused chemotherapy after hearing the possible side effects. Surgery could have been done, but would have required removing most of his tongue and half of his mandible. It would have left him unable to eat normally. Any radiation after surgery would be fraught with complications. Surgery after the radiation would be almost as debilitating and healing would be impaired."

Judy shook her head. "Not a lot of good options. It makes sense to try radiation and reserve surgery for salvage if the cancer recurred after radiation. Only take a chance with surgery if absolutely needed."

Randall smiled and nodded. "Excellent analysis, Judy. Let's review his treatment plan before we go into the room. I want to see where the highest dose areas were. I suspect it was at the fracture site."

Judy had seen radiation treatment plans before, but didn't really understand them. Randall needed room to unfold the trifolded pages of the computerized treatment plan, which were stapled in the back section of the radiation treatment chart. He went over to the countertop next to the treatment console and flattened out the pages to give Judy an overview. "Okay. This first page shows a body section through the angle of the mandible. You can see that we used three beam directions to concentrate the total dose of radiation around the tumor volume. See how I've traced it out in red?"

Judy looked confused. "I see the red outline around the tumor volume, but I'm not sure I understand where the three beams are coming from."

Randall had grown so used to looking at the plans, he had almost forgotten how confusing all the different lines of radiation dose were. "Sorry. I should have given you more basics. These green lines represent the different beam directions. Two beams come in at oblique angles aimed at the center point of the tumor volume. One is a 40 degree anterior oblique and the second is a 120 degree posterior oblique. These two beams contribute 80% of the dose. The third beam is a left lateral aimed at the same center point, or isocenter, and it delivers the remaining 20% of dose."

Judy nodded. "Okay. I see that now. So, three beams meet at the tumor. That way the tumor gets 100% of the dose, but the healthy tissue around doesn't get a full dose. This spreads out the radiation in three areas. Right? But what are these sort of concentric wavy lines around the tumor volume?"

Randall thought Judy was really following the logic of the plan quite well. "Excellent next question! The computer has summed the doses together for the three beams and represented them as individual lines of the same total dose. We call them isodose lines. For example, this isodose line surrounds the entire tumor volume and gets 100% of the daily dose of 180 rads. The next line outside of it gets 90% or 162 rads per treatment. The total daily dose falls off progressively as we move away from the tumor volume."

Judy smiled broadly as the concept became clear. "Oh! It's just like a topographic map where the lines show areas of the same elevation! Or like a weather map showing areas of the same temperature! And if we move inside the 100% isodose line, which is all in the tumor volume, it looks like the isodose goes up to 120% at the highest point. I bet that part of the tumor gets really cooked."

Randall nodded and murmured. "Indeed it does. That's bad for the tumor, but also bad for any mandible in that area. Obviously, if tumor and mandible occupy the same space that's unavoidable."

Judy frowned. "Boy. It's like a deal with the devil. If you don't give that dose, the tumor comes back. If you do, the mandible gets damaged."

Randall threw his pencil down on the counter. "You got that right. Plus, there's still no guarantee the tumor might not come back anyhow."

Judy let out a helpless laugh. "More fine print in the devil's contract."

Randall picked up his pencil to use as a pointer. "Well, let's look at the highest doses to the mandible and how large an area they cover. Let me find the right page. Alright, here's several images that show the mandibular dose well. Let's see. Looks like some areas of the mandible, about where the back molars would be, got between 7,000 and 7,300 rads. That dose given over seven weeks would put the risk of ORN at around 20-25%. In other words, it's likely we were the cause."

Judy frowned. "If you knew the risk was that high, why not give a lower dose?"

Randall raised an index finger and waved it. "Why, indeed? If we were to lower the mandible dose, it would result in an inadequate tumor dose. Why put the patient through seven weeks of treatment with a low chance of success? A recurrence would be nearly 100% fatal."

Judy's frown dissipated. "So, better to deal with a radiation complication than a tumor recurrence? A 25% risk of necrosis sounds better than a 100% risk of death."

"Bullseye!" said Randall.

Judy looked pleased with herself. "But we still have to deliver bad news to the patient. I hope you explained the risks well enough that he understands and accepts what happened."

Randall nodded with vigor. "That is our greatest fear. No matter how well you explain things up front and how clear the consent form is that they sign, you never know how they'll remember everything. Especially when you consider how mentally foggy most patients are when they're first diagnosed with cancer. Many are so anxious to get treatment started, they would probably sign anything. Then, later, their recall is quite selective. You want to come into the exam room with me to see how well my explanations took hold?"

"I would," said Judy. "One quick question before we go."

"Shoot."

"You said his teeth were extracted before the radiation. Was that just before the treatment started or years before?"

Randall paused to recall the details. "Good point. As I recall, Mr. Underbridge still had half of his teeth left when the tongue lesion was biopsied. The remaining teeth had advanced periodontal disease. That means they were at high risk of requiring extraction after the radiation. Radiation causes dry mouth and interferes with blood supply to the teeth. To pull the teeth after radiation would risk non-healing of the extraction site and result in mandible necrosis, so we usually recommend pulling any bad teeth prior to radiation. The extraction sites need to heal for 4-6 weeks before we can start radiation."

Judy whistled. "Wow. I'll bet sometimes it's a race between the extraction sites healing and the tumor growing bigger."

Randall did drum beats on the treatment plan with his pencil. "You got that right. In some cases, the tumor can double in just three weeks, so, when push comes to shove, we'll take our chances with healing and start treatment because the growing tumor is a greater risk."

Judy shook her head again. "Dang. It sounds like a constant balancing act. I don't know how you do it and stay standing at the end of the day."

Randall made a sweeping down gesture with his arm. "Sometimes gravity wins and we fall down."

Judy made a sweeping up gesture with her arm. "But then you get right up again and keep running, right?"

Randall moved his head sideways and rolled his eyes a bit. "Mostly. Some days it's a bit slow getting back up again."

Judy put a hand on Randall's arm. "Well, let's see how well you did with Mr. Underbridge. Take me in so he can testify."

Randall and Judy put on their bright and cheerful faces as a shield against evil and entered the exam room. Mr. Underbridge was already seated in the ENT exam chair but popped out of the chair when they came in. Despite his obvious discomfort he attempted a smile. Randall reached out to shake his patient's hand with his right and added a left handed warm grip to the man's forearm for icing on the cake.

Mr. Underbridge returned the handshake in kind. His voice was mumbly and shaky. "Doc, I'm so glad to see you. The last few days have been a nightmare. I've wanted to talk to you so many times since last week, but I didn't want to bother you. I know how busy you are."

Randall waved off the man's concern. "It's never a bother to hear from a good patient. I wouldn't have minded at all. Tell me everything. Leave nothing out."

Mr. Underbridge had somewhat slurred speech due to limited mobility of the mandible. Randall had to listen carefully to catch all the words.

The patient started with how he'd made a sandwich with some leftover pork tenderloin that was rather chewy. "As soon as I took the first bite, I felt an awful pain in my jaw. Right away, I remembered what you explained to me before treatment. If you hadn't gone over it with me before we started treatment, I would have been scared as hell. So I wasn't totally afraid when it happened. I figured it didn't have to be the cancer coming back."

Judy nodded and smiled during the story. "It sounds like you were very brave and did all the right things. Too bad you live so far away. That must have made it hard."

Mr. Underbridge wiped at his eye. "Yeah. Wasn't easy, but I got here. When I got to the docs up in Oral Surgery they took x-rays that showed a fracture in my jaw. It was right where you said the radiation could make a fracture. But they had good news. They said there was no sign of the cancer on their exam or on the x-rays. The oral surgeon, she's a cute little lady, said she can fix it. They've got me scheduled for surgery in a few days."

Randall clapped his hands and Judy joined in. "Here, here. You must have met Dr. Julie Amory up there. She's very good, but she looks like she just graduated from high school. Cute as a button. She can work on my mouth anytime."

Mr. Underbridge's thought train was momentarily derailed. "Anyway, I've been worried that you'd hear what happened to me before I could explain it and you might take the blame for the fracture. But I want you to be clear on this. I knew it could happen. And, as long as the cancer doesn't come back, I'm golden with this."

Randall was quite taken aback. He had an explanatory speech all planned and was now at a loss for words.

Judy took up the slack. "Dr. B is a good explainer, isn't he?"

Mr. Underbridge turned his head slightly and paused. "A bit long-winded and repetitious sometimes, but you're not gonna forget what he says."

Randall nodded vaguely. "Thanks, you two . . . I think."

Randall got back to business. A thorough head and neck exam showed no gross sign of local recurrence, but he'd add a CT scan to be more certain. Promising he'd follow Mr. Underbridge during his surgical stay, Randall had Judy transport Mr. Underbridge up to 7CS in his wheelchair. Randall paged Dr. Amory.

She responded almost immediately in a birdlike voice. "This is Amory."

Randall answered back. "Boy, that was quick."

Dr. Amory laughed. "Yeah. I figured you were probably stressing about Mr. Underbridge. I know what that angst feels like."

Randall laughed back. "You just made my A list. I just finished reviewing the radiation treatment plan and up front we figured there was at least a one in five chance for mandibular ORN. On exam I didn't see any sign of pathology except for the fracture. I'm getting a CT to be more certain. I'm curious how you all are going to repair the fracture."

Dr. Amory giggled softly. "Of course you are. Easy peasy. Just a bit of super glue."

Randall was taken in. "You're kidding!"

"Of course I am," said Amory with a sly laugh. "We'll go in and debride any necrotic bone and take biopsies of any suspicious areas that look like they might be harboring residual tumor. We'll cut back to viable bleeding bone and graft in new bone from the posterior iliac crest."

Randall hadn't heard of doing bone graft repairs on the mandible. "Really! Does that work in a heavily irradiated mandible?"

Dr. Amory made a raspberry sound with her lips. "Have ye no faith in your own dosimetry? If the entire mandible gets the maximum dose, no repair will work except mandibulectomy. But with the dose concentrated to a small area, the way you treat now, it works pretty well."

Randall had a key question. "How many cases of ORN have you repaired that way?"

Dr. Amory paused to recall the total count. "We've treated about eight to nine such radiation necrosis cases at County Hospital with this repair approach and it's worked, I'd say, 80% of the time. I'm in the process of writing them up for a paper. The failures were cases that had been referred to County from outside hospitals that don't use your more advanced techniques. Given that you treat more head and neck cancer at the VA than County, you should be pleased to have only one case of mandibular ORN."

Randall was taken aback. "Well, go figure. Some days you can't lose for winning."

Dr. Amory laughed. "There you go. Your existence is justified for another day. Gotta go. I got mouths to open and teeth to pull."

Randall laughed back. "Happy yanking."

Judy returned from 7CS as Randall hung up the phone. "Mr. Underbridge is admitted and tucked in for the day. You've got quite a fan."

Randall had to laugh again. "This is turning into quite the fan day. There must be some evil lurking around some corner."

Judy gave Randall a knowing look. "Yeah, well, we were all worried how you'd react to Mr. Underbridge's case after dealing with the lawyers on the Chester case."

Randall felt a bit like he'd had his dark underbelly exposed. "To be forthright, I was wobbling a bit between the two events, but Mr. Underbridge was the tonic I needed. I think I am going to be just fine, now. At least, I'm determined to be so."

Judy gave Randall a crooked smile. "Attitude is everything. And the only thing we can control."

Randall looked sidewise. Judy had found the kernel. By the time he looked back, she was treading down the hall away from him to grab the next follow-up chart, her sneaker soles squeaking quietly on the waxed green tile floor.

Randall felt a commercial coming on and sang it out loud. "Plop, plop, fizz, fizz. Oh, what a relief it is."

Then a quiet female laugh came from Doris's office. Randall decided to count his blessings and coffee up. There was still a long day ahead.

Lymphogram

Later, Randall was still regrouping when Elisa dragged into his office looking a bit wrung out.

"Hey, Elisa, what's up? You look like a chewed up cat toy."

Elisa laughed harshly. "Best quasi-compliment I've had all day. I was doing alright with stress management until my doctor called to say I have a lymphogram scheduled for tomorrow morning. Just as a joke I told my doctor I wasn't a *lymphomaniac* and didn't need one. He didn't laugh. I just stopped by to let you know I won't be in until at least 10:00 AM tomorrow."

Randall put down the chart he was reviewing. "That's no problem. I'll bet you're wondering what that procedure is all about. It's definitely not like a candy gram."

Elisa stuck out her tongue. "I never even made that connection. But, yeah. What do they do? My doctor said you could explain it better than him. I think my lame joke put him off."

Randall shook his head in disgust. "What a lazy bum! That's a backdoor compliment if I ever heard one. But he's right. I probably can."

"So what's involved? Does it hurt?" asked Elisa, grimacing.

Randall grimaced right back. "Well, let's just say people aren't exactly lining up to get one. Here's the deal. We need to visualize the pelvic lymph nodes clearly. As a nurse, you probably know most of this already, so my summary will be just a refresher. The lymphatic system is a separate set of vessels from the blood-carrying arteries and veins. The lymphatics carry clear tissue fluid that has escaped from blood vessels into soft tissue spaces and return it to the blood circulation. Lymph nodes are clustered along the lymphatic vessels and act as filters for any foreign material, like bacteria, cancer cells or toxins, that may have gotten into the tissue fluid."

Elisa nodded her understanding. "Right. And if a cancer cell gets filtered out by the node, it can grow there and enlarge the node. It stops cancer from spreading there for a while, but eventually can escape to the next node and beyond. I get that. But how do the radiologists make the nodes visible?"

Randall made a pencil sketch of the legs and pelvis with the lymphatics and nodes drawn in. "First, they pick a spot near the groin and inject a small amount of blue dye below the skin. As the adjacent lymphatics take up the dye, they can be visualized through the skin. As larger channels show up, they freeze the skin above a large lymphatic, make an incision and place a small tube in the lymphatic. Then they inject a radio opaque dye in the tube and it goes north to the pelvic nodes which denotes them on X-ray. They wait 24 hours for more dye uptake and image them again. Any node above a certain size threshold is considered pathologic. The X-ray would show if it is enlarged due to either tumor involvement or infection."

Elisa crossed her legs, imagining the process. "Yuck! Needles in my groin! I hate needles anywhere, but down there? I may need some kind of relaxer premedication."

Randall chuckled. "Now that you mention it, I wouldn't be too fond of needles in that neighborhood myself. Maybe a few stiff drinks before I go in."

Elisa just sat quietly for a long moment processing the information. Then she let out a deep sigh. "If they see large nodes, then that means my stage is higher, so I'll need chemo sooner than later." She sighed again. "Well, I've got to do what I've got to do. No two ways about it. Can I ask a favor?"

Randall smiled warmly. "You don't need permission. Shoot."

Elisa looked to the side and studied Randall's large picture of a red

1935 Duesenberg SJ. "I really like Zelda. She's so open and spiritual. I feel like we've known each other for years. Would you mind if I came over to your house one night this week so I can talk 'girl talk' with her?"

Randall looked a bit puzzled. "Girl talk? You mean without me butting in?"

Elisa put up a hand. "Yes and no. I'd want to do it after my lymphogram results come back so I can talk with both of you about the decisions for treatment once we know the stage. What I want to do is a *'mujer-a-mujer'* with Zelda around the whole pregnancy and childbirth thing. That's pretty foreign territory for me and she's gone through it twice. I'd be alot more comfortable if I got it straight from the mare's mouth."

Randall chuckled. "I get it. Sounds like a great idea. Maybe bring Elena along for that rundown as well since she's going to be playing the Dad role. And I think we can all do some collective decision making about treatment choices. I know this may sound a little crazy, but how about we include the kids in the discussion? I don't believe in protecting them from life's crises and sometimes, as they say, 'out of the mouths of babes . . . '"

Elisa paused. "I don't want to make Zelda cook for us again. . . ."

Randall cleared his throat. "That's easy! Marc's Big Boy. You take us there and the kids will love you forever. We should have the results by Thursday. Let's plan for then, pending approval by the Big Boss."

Elisa smiled broadly. "I assume you mean Zelda."

Randall chuckled. "Nobody else has that job description. I'll confirm with you tomorrow and bug radiology to give me prompt results."

Elisa smiled slightly. "Thanks. I'm pretty overwhelmed." She rose to leave, but turned and came back. "Oh, and I almost forgot. If you want both Zelda and me to come to your 'squeegee' meeting, I need a primer on that again. You already explained about quantum theory, but I could use a rebriefing. Perhaps we could do that on Thursday also."

Randall laughed. "Correction. It's a QEG meeting. I hope some of what I said previously has stuck. No problem. My kids have heard me expound about it so often, they could probably explain it. Just kidding. Zelda needs a refresher too. So we'll add that. I have a special 15 minute Quantum Elixir presentation."

With the plans decided upon, Elisa headed off to see a patient who
needed her expertise and Randall resumed his chart review. Six follow
ups, three consults and two minidisasters later, it was time for Randall
to head home.

On the drive home he pondered the best way to break the news to
Zelda about the Elisa dinner without generating another minidisaster.
He couldn't come up with a scheme he liked so he decided on immediate full disclosure. To Randall's surprise, Zelda was very receptive. In
fact, she was quite touched that Elisa thought so highly of her. Another
plus was that she didn't have to cook dinner.

Big Boy Balm

By the time Thursday rolled around, Randall had heard from Joe Shepard that the QEG meeting would take place at Joe's house on Saturday
next at 2:00 following a buffet lunch. Zelda arranged for Mrs. Bush to
watch the kids that afternoon. Zelda was all in on the meeting.

Kyle and Addie were super hyped about going to Big Boy for dinner. They couldn't wait for Elisa and Elena to arrive.

Randall decided to mess with the kids. "Kids. Are you sure you
want to eat at Big Boy tonight? You know their food gets you all sugar
rushed and you can't fall asleep at bedtime. It's a school day tomorrow."

Addie was first to protest. "Are you nuts? You know I love that
place. I promised my Big Boy bobblehead I'd take him there with me."

Kyle chimed in. "You know I love the Brawny Lad burger. And I lost
my bobblehead. I want to get a new one. I have my own money."

Randall slumped dramatically. "Well, I get that, but we're going out
with Elisa and Elena. You remember them from the other night, right?
It might be kind of boring for you two, since we're going to be doing a
lot of adult talk. Grown up stuff. We could have Mrs. Bush on alert next
door until we come back. Mom could make you guys sandwiches and
chips to eat here while we're out."

Addie stuck out her lower lip and frowned. "Daad! That's just crazy.
We like adult talk. That's when we learn the good stuff."

Kyle jumped up. "Yeah! We learned a lot when you guys were talking at the dinner table. We were listening from the. . . ." Kyle stopped talking abruptly when Addie kicked him in the ankle.

Addie filled in the blank. "Kyle means you guys were talking real loud and we could hear you from upstairs."

Randall looked surprised. "Oh, is that right? How much did you hear?"

Both Kyle and Addie closed their mouths like clamshells. They tried to look innocent.

"Answer your father!" ordered Zelda.

Kyle decided on full disclosure. "Well, when you guys were in the living room, we heard you all talking about Elisa having a baby."

Addie followed her brother's lead. "Yeah, and you were talking about cancer at the dinner table. It sounded like Elisa might have it. Isn't that the stuff you treat, Dad?"

Randall nodded. "Glad you remember. Anything else? Full disclosure or no Big Boy for you two."

Addie squinted. "Oh, and you were talking about your *physicky* project. I don't get any of that."

Zelda gave Randall a malevolent look. "Randy! Stop threatening the kids. They did nothing wrong. We're all going out together and no Brawny Lads or chocolate shakes will be missed. This is just your dad's silly way of warning you we'll be discussing serious matters tonight with the two ladies. In the past we've protected you from that kind of talk, but now we think that you're ready. You guys need to understand that life isn't always easy and that it helps to share the hard times."

Addie spoke up. "Like when Alexandra suicided?"

"And when I ran away from home and needed to talk to Chelsea?" asked Kyle.

Zelda embraced both kids. "Exactly, my little dumplings."

Kyle protested. "I'm not a dumpling! Ha, Mom, you said 'dump.'"

Zelda glared at Kyle. "Work a little harder to control that potty mouth, Buster, or you might go from dumpling to dumpster!"

Kyle was surprised he'd even made the remark. He had been working hard to pump the brakes before blurting. "Sorry, Mom. My tongue brain wasn't working."

Zelda was surprised at the apology. Usually Kyle dissembled for a while before admitting guilt. "Don't worry about it. I know you're trying to do better. Just try a bit harder."

Kyle stood up straighter. "I promise Addie and I will be as serious as adults if we have dinner with the sisters. I really lo . . . like Elisa. Er, well, Elena is nice too. Is Elisa in a lot of trouble?"

Randall had to suppress a laugh at Kyle's rapid turnaround and expression of fealty towards the sisters. "I'm glad we have your full attention. I want you guys to be part of this. You're both very smart and sensitive to other people. You two have a special gift to read people and I bet you can help us make some decisions tonight. You guys up for that?"

Addie looked very concerned. "Daddy, does Elisa have something really bad? Could she die?" A little tear rolled down her cheek.

Randall turned his head to the side to conceal his emotions. "Zel, can you give them a briefing on what we're facing?"

Zelda raised both shoulders. "Me? You're the expert on this stuff."

Randall put a hand on Zelda's arm. "Not all of it. You tell them in your words."

After Zelda explained about the cancer, the baby and the upcoming QEG meeting, both kids stared at each other for a long moment.

Addie was first to speak. "I get it. I may be just a kid but I know stuff. I'll need to bring Uni along to Big Boy. Then, I can tell you what he thinks."

Kyle looked very serious. "And I'll bring along my Yoda figure. He always helps me make big decisions. He helps me see stuff too."

Randall clapped his hands. "Great! Sounds like all loins are girded and digits crossed."

Zelda gave Randall a mock stink eye. "Should I bring my ouija board, too?"

Randall shook his head. "Nah. Too bulky for a restaurant. Maybe save it for later. I think we're all on the same page. Let's get ready to go. They'll be here soon."

Not long after departure preparations had begun, car lights shone in the driveway. "Red alert," shouted Randall. "Everyone, on me at the backdoor." Car doors slammed shut in the driveway.

Both Kyle and Addie were first to the back door. They ushered Elisa and Elena in and gave them both big hugs.

Zelda was the next big hugger. "No need to take your coats off, ladies. We're going to head straight for the restaurant."

Elena had begun to take off her coat, but stopped. "Do we need to hurry? Do you have reservations?"

Randall laughed. "I gather you've never been to Big Boy. They don't take reservations, but we've been there so often that they have a table with our name carved on it. Kyle did it."

Kyle looked gobsmacked. "I did not! I just drew it on the placemat with crayon. I just pressed too hard and it went through the paper mat."

Zelda poked her husband in the arm. "Randy! Will you stop baiting the kids?"

"But it's so much fun," complained Randall.

Zelda couldn't help but laugh. "I swear. We're a non-nuclear family. One wife and three kids. Everybody can fit in the van so we can all drive together."

Soon the six were seated at a large round table at Big Boy with food ordered. Addie took out her Uni the Unicorn stuffed animal and placed it next to her plate. That prompted Kyle to put his Yoda Star Wars figure next to his plate.

Randall explained to Elisa and Elena why they'd brought Kyle and Addie along. "I hope you don't mind sharing our discussion with them."

Elisa smiled broadly at Randall. "Not at all. That's what family is all about." She turned to look directly at Kyle. "Especially if one of them is a handsome young boy."

Kyle made a silly grin and blushed.

Elena looked directly at Addie and put a hand on her shoulder. "And one of them is a lovely little girl."

It was Addie's turn to blush.

Randall looked over at Addie. "Tell the ladies why you brought Uni along."

Addie picked up Uni and introduced him to Elisa and Elena. "I brought Uni so he can give us good advice."

Zelda patted Addie's head. "Good thinking, Rosebud." She turned to Kyle. "And I suppose Yoda is here for the same thing?"

Kyle nodded. "Yep. Rosebutt isn't the only smart kid at the table."

"Mom! Kyle called me a bad name!" yelped Addie.

Kyle put his hand to his mouth and muttered. "Oops!"

Randall stifled the impending dispute. "Addie, you will look even smarter if you just ignore Kyle."

Addie turned and stuck out her tongue at Kyle. Kyle just smiled and asked when the waitress was coming with the food.

Elisa decided to use a diversionary tactic. "So, Addie, tell me about Uni. You said he gives you advice?"

Addie grabbed Uni and hugged him to her chest. "Yep. And he tells me stuff too."

Elena was curious. "Really. What kind of stuff?"

Addie looked uncertain. "I'm not sure I should tell. It's just between him and me. But it's big stuff."

Kyle was not to be outdone. "Yoda tells me real stuff. Not fake stuff like Uni."

Zelda gave Kyle her mother's stare. "Elena was talking to Addie. You'll get your turn."

Kyle let out a loud breath. "Aw, alright."

"Go ahead and tell us just one thing Uni has told you," prompted Elisa.

Addie got excited and stood up on her chair. "Uni told me you have a little baby boy in your tummy."

Elisa put a hand to her heart and Elena gasped. Kyle tried to punch Addie's arm. "That's what Yoda told me. I found out first!"

Zelda caught Randall's eye and gasped in amazement. "How do you kids know that? Nobody knows that yet."

Elisa cleared her throat loudly and all eyes turned to her. "Actually …

they're correct. I was waiting for the right time to tell you all. The repeat ultrasound got a better look at the baby's little private parts. It is a boy!"

Randall raised both arms in the air. "Holy Smuckers grape jelly! What sort of freaks am I raising? Brilliant, scary freaks!"

The adults were silent for a minute then started to laugh. At first, Addie and Kyle looked at each other wondering what was so surprising about their news, then they joined in. In the midst of the laughter, their waitress came over to the table and announced the food orders would be out in a few minutes. She asked if anyone wanted a drink refill. Everyone raised a hand. The waitress asked if she could bring them anything else.

Kyle raised his hand. "Have you got any more Big Boy bobbleheads? I didn't see any out front."

The waitress shook her head. "I'm sorry, Sweetie. They're all sold out. But we might get some more soon. Keep on coming back to check."

Both kids got upside down smiles and went quiet.

Elisa was the first to speak after the waitress left. "I wouldn't call Kyle and Addie freaks. I would call them special and, perhaps, gifted. Whatever the case, I'm glad you brought them along. They've already been a big help."

Both kids glowed with new found self-importance.

Randall decided to make use of the long wait for food. He informed Elisa and Elena that the QEG meeting was set for the following Saturday and hoped they could attend. They agreed to try their best.

Randall noticed their relaxed shoulders. "You two look decidedly more upbeat than the last time we were together. Are you taking happy pills?"

Elena laughed in response, but her eyes were moist. "If you've got happy pills we'll take some, but we got happy news. Elisa's lymphogram didn't find any enlarged pelvic lymph nodes! They even repeated the ultrasound to confirm. None of the blood tests were abnormal. Her doctor thinks the Hodgkin's is only stage I and can be treated with either radiation or chemotherapy."

Zelda beamed. "Wow! That is very good news!" She began to sing out loud. "Oh, Happy Day!" She shimmied her shoulders and snapped her fingers.

The kids shrank in their seats. They always got embarrassed whenever Zelda sang in public.

Kyle whispered from under a napkin. "Mom. . . . Stop it! You are so weird! The waitress is looking at us! And so is Elisa!" His face was mortally red.

Elisa clouded over a bit, ignoring Kyle's desperate state for more pressing matters. "The dilemma is that for chemo I'd have to wait until the baby is old enough to deliver safely. And for radiation there's a risk too."

Zelda shrank a bit. "Oh dear, honey, that's hard. Why?"

Randall elaborated on that. "The doctor's right. The radiation is directed at the neck and chest with the pelvis shielded from the direct beam. However, a small dose of radiation gets to the pelvis because the radiation bounces around inside the body. It's a higher dose than you got from the lymphogram, but it's not so high that it will cause significant damage to fetal tissue that's already formed. However, it can damage newly forming tissue and cause genetic mutation. The effects of these mutations may not show up until later in life. So, a bunch of unknowns there, but I'd judge it could be done if you felt uneasy about waiting."

Elena rolled that around for a beat. "So, if I do radiation now, there's no way to avoid some risk to the fetus?"

Randall shook his head. "Nope. The only way to avoid that risk would be to remove the baby now and it would be too immature to survive."

Addie looked ready to cry. "You mean the baby would have to die if it got borned now?"

Randall nodded and the group went silent as they took in the news. There was some sniffling. Randall tried to improve the mood. "Well, we're here to help decide just what to do. Who can tell me what the alternative treatment choice is?"

Kyle raised his hand. "Can we wait until the baby gets born before using radiation or that other stuff?"

Zelda looked proud. "Excellent question, young man. Let's ask who knows that one."

Elisa raised her hand. "My doctor said that full term is nine to ten months and 95% of babies born at eight months survive. At seven months, survival drops to about 80%. So, ideally, I'd have to wait four to six months for the baby to be born safely. The Hodgkin's could advance to a higher stage in that time. That might lower my chance of survival and increase the amount of treatment I would need. Waiting could also put the baby at more risk. It's a three pronged dilemma."

A cloud of doom loomed over the table. Randall attempted to clear the skies. "Let me just remind everyone that this dilemma is a much more favorable one than if the lymphogram had shown involvement in the pelvis. It gives us more time to play with. Let's give thanks for that."

The waitress arrived with platefuls of food carefully balanced on her arms. "Sorry it took so long. We're really busy tonight and we're short one cook."

"No problem," said Randall. "We've had plenty to talk about. Do you need a taller cook? I could help out."

"Good one, Sir. I can tell you're a Dad," placated the waitress. "Don't let my comment affect your tip."

When everyone was served, Zelda suggested they all hold hands, close their eyes, and say grace. There was a collective sigh after the "Amen." There wasn't much talk after that. Mastication trumped communication. The kids had been slightly disappointed because the Big Boy bobbleheads were sold out, but the arrival of their food was a balm.

DECISIONS, DECISIONS

Perhaps all the Big Boy calories taken in facilitated decisional clarity for the attendees. It seemed a conclusion was near. Randall pushed back from the table and emitted an involuntary eructation. It was a sort of page marker. Kyle took it as a challenge and tried to match his father's volume, duration, tonality and embouchure, but didn't quite pull it off. Addie gave it a try with some swallowed air, but only managed a girly hiccup.

Elisa blurted out an involuntary laugh. "In Japan they make those sounds to flatter the cook. Should I go back to the kitchen and get him?"

Randall turned a bit red. "Excuse me! That was not a premeditated comment of culinary quality. But these two? Probably not the case. What do you say, Kyle and Addie?"

The two replied in unison. "Thank you!"

"Close enough," said Zelda. "Is there anything more we need to discuss before we head home?"

Elisa held up her hand. "I have nothing more to discuss, but I do have an announcement. I've made my decision. Who wants to hear it?"

No one had expected a final decision so soon. The Biedermeiers looked around at each other for a beat and then raised their hands. Elena quickly followed suit.

Randall waved an arm toward Elisa. "You have the floor, young lady."

Elisa sat forward in her chair. "I've decided that I want to give my baby boy and myself the best chance to survive. To do that I have chosen not to expose him to any more danger from either treatment choice. Obviously, that means I will wait until eight months so that he has the best chance of survival. Then, I will take treatment. We'll follow the cancer closely during that time. If there's progression, I'll have to rethink it. But I now have faith and an unexplainable certainty that it will all come out well. Any questions?"

Zelda raised a hand. "So you're not going to take any treatment right now? What are the chances that the Hodgkin's could progress rapidly?"

Elisa turned to Randall for the answer. Randall paused, still processing the information. "Ah, well . . . the histologic subtype is the least aggressive, so I would say that favors your choice. Besides, we can easily follow the size of your neck nodes by physical exam and repeat the pelvic ultrasound to see if the pelvic nodes remain stable. If the neck nodes get bigger too fast, without the pelvic nodes changing, we could always plug in neck and chest radiation with minimal risk to the baby boy."

He stroked his chin in thought. "Worst case would be the pelvic nodes begin to enlarge, which would lead us to use chemo. With the subtype you have, control with chemo is pretty good even if we have to delay until eight months to start it."

Elena had a question. "Are you sure you don't want just to start radiation right now to give yourself the best shot at survival?"

Elisa shook her head. "No. I've meditated on what my purpose in this life is. The spirits are telling me it's to give life to this gift I've received. They say I will be protected so that my baby can survive and that I can raise him. This meeting with you and your children has shown me how precious these little lives are. You've helped me so much, kids. And your Uni and your Yoda." The kids glowed with the affirmations.

Randall retook the floor. "Any more questions?"

Zelda had one. "I thought you wanted to hear the gory details about pregnancy and delivery."

Elisa smiled. "Oh, Zelda. There's time enough for that. We have months ahead of us. We'll get together again. So, are we ready to vote?" Heads nodded round the table. "All in favor of my decision, raise your hand."

Everyone raised a hand. There were no dissenters. The Biedermeier table erupted with spontaneous applause that drew the attention of the nearby Big Boy diners. Kyle squirreled under his napkin again.

The commotion got the attention of their waitress who came over with the check. "You all look like a bunch of happy folks. Having a celebration?"

Elisa tried to grab the check but Randall was faster. Elisa looked up at the waitress. "These kind folks have just made me part of their family. Do you serve champagne here so we can make a toast? I wouldn't drink any, of course."

The waitress shook her head, but smiled slyly. "No, but how about I bring you a Bigger Boy super sized hot fudge sundae to share? On the house. If you've got room to spare."

Randall shook his head. "Thanks, but not for me. I'm stuffed. Probably everybody else is too. Right, guys?"

Kyle almost sprung from his chair. "Not me! I've got plenty of room. I always have dessert space in my right leg."

Addie was quick to follow. "I gave part of my burger to Uni. I've got plenty of room left."

Zelda laughed. "Go ahead and bring it on. Some of us other adults will help the kids out if they need assistance finishing it off."

Randall shrugged. "Okay then. Bring it on. I'll sacrifice and stand by in reserve."

CHAPTER 28

LOOK AGAIN

When you change the way you look at things, the things you look at change.

—Max Planck

BIG BUOYED

The Biedermeiers and the Angeles sisters were greeted by cold gusts of wind as they exited the Big Boy restaurant. They scrambled through the frigid parking lot as fast as they could with full stomachs. As they piled into the yellow VW van, there were choral complaints about the bitter cold temperature. For some reason, yet to be disclosed by scientific research, the digestive gasses that had been accumulating during dinner decided it was prime time to make their collective exit.

Kyle took credit for the first flutter of air, but no one owned up for the subsequent ones. There was, however, quite a bit of girlish giggling and window cracking.

Randall laughed from the driver's seat. "Dang! I can't take you guys anywhere! Careful of the open windows, you could float away. Don't you worry, though. You're among friends. Oh, and if you're shivering cold, I can guarantee the heater will be cranking out actual warmth by the time we get to our driveway."

Elisa denied being a contributor to the soundscape, but didn't sound convincing. "That's reassuring, Dr. B. I may be a *corpsicle* by then."

That got the group laughing again. Zelda suggested they should start telling jokes to take their minds off the cold and windy conditions. The kids started it off with some grade schooler riddles.

Kyle yelled out his riddle far louder than the space required. "Where did the little King keep his little armies?"

Before anyone could answer, Addie followed with hers. "What do you call a cross between an elephant and a rhinoceros?!"

None of the adults could get them right. Kyle and Addie refused to give the answers. Kyle was left cackling since the kids had stumped the adults.

Elisa tried to save face for the adults. "Okay! So we don't know any of your kid riddles. Here's one for you, smart boy. How in the world did your Yoda figure know my little unborn baby was a boy?"

Kyle stammered a little. "I sat on my special stool in my room, held Yoda in two hands, and closed my eyes. This was after I heard you guys talking downstairs. I asked if you'd be alright. He didn't tell me anything right away, but. . . ."

Kyle was interrupted by Zelda screeching. "Randy! Red light! Red light!"

Randall skidded the van to a stop just before the intersection. "I saw it! Sort of. Kyle's story distracted me and I turned to hear him better. Sorry, guys."

Kyle continued. "That was fun. Can we do it again?"

Zelda responded sternly. "Not a chance, Buster. Now keep talking. Finish before the next light. And talk louder."

Kyle dialed up the volume. "No problem, Mom. I sat on my stool some more. Kind of longish. Maybe I nodded off. Then Yoda told me to get a pencil and paper to write down what he said next. When I opened my eyes again my writing was on the paper and it said a baby boy was coming. The words were sort of *poemy*. Nothing like what I'd write. I don't remember it exactly. The paper's at home."

"Randy, red light ahead!" yelled Zelda.

"I see it! I'm stopping already," retorted Randall.

Elena was stupefied. "Are you sure that's what happened? I hope you know where the paper is. I definitely want to see that."

"Me, too," said Elisa.

"Ditto," said Zelda.

"Ditto, ditto," said Randall. "We'll be home in about ten minutes. I can feel some heat coming out of the vent. You guys feel anything back there?"

A chorus of "no's" echoed from the rear of the car.

"Good," said Randall.

Addie spoke up. "Mom, can we have ice cream when we get home?"

Zelda let out a loud gasp. "Are you kidding me? You just got done stuffing yourself with a burger, fries, a milkshake, a hot fudge sundae and now you want a second cold dessert? Amazing! Speaking of amazing, would you kindly inform us how Uni told you about the baby?"

Addie laughed. "I was just kidding you about the ice cream. I was trying to make everybody laugh some more to warm up. But it didn't work."

Ironically, that set everybody laughing. When it settled down again, Elisa requested that Addie do the reveal.

"You guys will think I'm silly," protested Addie.

"No problem," prodded Kyle. "We already think you're a silly bird."

Addie made a threatening fist and Kyle moved farther away. "Alright space boy, here it is. I got on my bed and sat against the headboard. I took all my stuffed animals and put them in a rainbow in front of me with Uni in the center. I started the meeting and told them about Elisa. I asked them if everything would be okay."

"And?" asked Zelda.

"It was a hard question and Uni was quiet for a long time," continued Addie. "Then, my 'Tiny Chatty Brother' doll said 'I love you.' That's the doll Mom used to have when she was a little girl. You know, where you pull the string in the back and it talks? It says 'Let's play school' and 'I hurt myself,' too. That's when I knew."

"Holy string pulling Mattel dolls from the 60s!" exclaimed Zelda. "I loved that stupid doll. The spring must have been stuck and let go on its own. That's hardly. . . ."

Randall interrupted. "I agree. But it's dang spooky. Another 'mouths of babes' moment. I don't get messages from stuffed critters or action figures, but my dreams have been giving me the. . . ."

"Randy!" Zelda interrupted with a loud outburst. "Just ahead on the left! Car running stop sign!"

The car ahead hit the brakes and managed to stop right in front of the van. Reacting without thinking, Randall slewed the van right and then left. He missed the car and wound up neatly on the other side of the car still in his lane. His passengers had been swayed left and then right in their seats and let out little squeaks and screams. Everybody was buckled up and unhurt.

Randall let out a loud breath. "Hoowie! Just missed her! The Great Spirit is truly watching over us. Have faith, you sinners. I shall not lead you astray."

Zelda grabbed Randall's arm. "Randy! I don't know how you did that but you kept our body parts from going astray."

Randall suddenly got a massive adrenaline rush from the near disaster. He started to shake and sweat. "I don't know either. It was just automatic. Now, I just need to keep from soiling my tighty whiteys."

Elisa tightened her seatbelt a notch and uttered a mild expletive. "*Mierda!* That was close. Dr. B, when Zelda yelled I looked over at the car and saw the lady driver putting on lipstick while looking in the rear view mirror. Can you believe that?"

"Perhaps she wanted to look nice in her casket," suggested Elena.

Elena got a lot of nervous laughs with her comment and the anxiety level dropped a notch. Randall pulled over to the curb and stopped the car. He turned around in his seat. "Is everybody alright back there? No whiplash or bumps?"

There were no discouraging words. Elisa called out her thanks to Randall for his driving skills. "Dr. B, I don't think I could have done a maneuver like that. I'm sure we're all grateful that we'll live long enough to read Kyle's message from Yoda."

"Plus, I'm wide awake now and ready to absorb your *physicky* lecture," added Elena.

Zelda made a loud gagging sound. "Yes, I'm sure we'll all be highly enlightened. Drive on, McDuff."

Yoda's Note

With no further mishaps, Randall pulled the yellow van into the Creekside driveway safely. He put a pretend microphone to his mouth and made an announcement. "Ladies and gentleboy, we have arrived safely at our destination. Please return your seat backs to the locked and upright position and prepare to decar. You will all note that, as promised, your conveyance heater is now dispensing a modicum of heat. Please watch your step and no tripping other passengers."

Instead of laughter, there was a lot of complaining about cold feet as the group clambered out of the van. They stamped their feet on the driveway to get feeling back while they waited for Randall to unlock and open the back door.

Zelda huffed. "Fat lot of good that stupid heater did. Let's put more wood on the fire and gather in the living room to warm up. I'll get us fresh coffee. That will help with the warming and should keep us awake enough to get through Randy's talk. You kids need to get to bed before that happens. It's a school day tomorrow."

"Aw, Mom, do we have to?" whined Kyle. "I've still got to find my Yoda note and we want to hear Dad's talk."

Randall was surprised. "That's a ripe one. If you're interested in my science talk, it would be a first. What do you say, Addie?"

"Well, I think Elisa and Elena are pretty fun," Addie replied. "And I don't want to stop being with them. So, if all I have to do is listen to you talk, I'm used to that and it will help me fall asleep."

Randall's eyebrows headed for his hairline. "Resounding endorsement. Looks like Addie has gone for honesty as the best policy. Kyle, do you agree with what Addie just said?"

"Actually, yeah," said Kyle, looking rather sheepish. "I'll just go up to my room and look for that note."

Zelda donned her evil smile. "Great idea."

When Kyle returned, he found the group gathered near the fireplace sipping hot coffee, except Addie. She had hot cocoa.

Kyle skipped into the living room and spotted Addie sipping hot cocoa. "Hey! How come she gets. . . ."

Zelda interrupted. "Your cup is right there on the side table. Quit griping. Did you find the note?"

Kyle nodded. "Yeah, Mom. Sorry. I didn't see the cup. Thanks. Do you want me to read the note?"

Elisa patted Kyle on the shoulder and he beamed. "Yes, I would love to hear it in your own manly voice. Take a swallow of hot cocoa first to warm up your throat."

Kyle did as suggested, put the cup down, and stood an inch taller. "Okay. Here goes. 'Born, there will be, a baby boy. A font, he will be, of endless joy.'"

Randall wrinkled his nose. "You really wrote that?"

Kyle shook his head. "I wrote it down, but I didn't write it. It's what Yoda said. Besides, I don't know what the word font means. Is it a real word?"

Zelda came to Kyle's defense. "Yes, it's a real word. In that usage, I think it means 'a source' or a 'fountain.' I believe you couldn't have written that on your own. I have no idea how you did that unless your brain is an open channel receiver." Kyle cocked his head like a confused dog.

Elisa was dumbstruck by the message and began to tear up again. She went over to Kyle and gave him a hug. "I don't care where the message came from. You are the one who delivered it to me and I am so grateful."

Kyle didn't quite know how to handle the affection and went into "aw shucks" mode. "Aw. I didn't really do that much, but I'm glad it helped you."

Elisa kissed his cheek. "It did, Kyle. It really did." Elisa stood and turned to Zelda. "Now, Zelda, have you had any messages you haven't told us about?"

Zelda thought for a moment. "Nothing really definite, but I've been around these two kids long enough to tell you they're right more often than not. If it's not Gospel it's the next best thing. Randy, you should tell the sisters about what happened on your trip to Las Vegas."

Randall rubbed his extensive forehead. "Geez, I'm not sure we have time for that."

"Come on, now," urged Zelda. "You told the kids the essence of it as a bedtime story when you got back. It didn't take that long."

"Yeah, Dad," said Addie. "That was a good story. I want to hear it again."

Randall tried stalling. "But you kids are headed for bed."

Kyle activated puppy eyes. "Not if Mom says we can stay up, right, Mom? Besides, isn't Mom the boss of bedtime?"

Randall laughed. "Well, you've got me there. Then, ask your Mom." They didn't have to ask. She was already nodding and smiling.

Randall gestured to the rest of the room. "What about the two sisters? Do our special guests have the time for that?"

Elisa and Elena nodded their assent and Elisa raised her hand for attention. "I have to say. I've had more affirmation of a favorable future tonight than I ever could have expected. I am so grateful to all of you for that. I feel like I've received a joyous gift this night. It reminds me so much of how our native traditions would have helped me. I have to believe it has come from them through you. Elena and I very much want to hear your Las Vegas story."

"Well, then, I would be honored to tell it," gushed Randall.

Zelda shook her head. "Just keep it short and economical, Talking Bear."

"Yes, Laughing Hyena," retorted Randall.

To Randall's surprise, Zelda had no witty comeback.

Randall started the story with the plane trip and the flapping wings, related the feelings of evil at the casino and finished with the lone desert walk. The climax, of course, was the loud voice in his head and the discovery of the IY rock. He finished with his interpretation of the possible meaning of the IY message, noting that one has to take the true meaning as a matter of faith, not fact. He told them that the best test of its truth is what your heart tells you.

Elisa nodded, her eyes moist. "This is what my guides are telling me. They say what you are saying. 'Only you know what's in your heart, so only you can know your truth.'"

Randall smiled wider than his whole face. "Exactly!" He hugged Elisa, and the group sat in silence for a long while.

Addie contemplated, her face puzzling over a concept. "Daddy? Does that mean that the IY rock told you that if you're looking for the truth you have to look inside of yourself?"

Kyle's face lit up suddenly. "Yeah, you can run around outside in the snow all day and never find it. And never make it to Grandma's."

Zelda chuckled at Kyle's insight. The adults just nodded, with nothing more cogent to add to the story.

The Seven Directions

The IY tale had taken only ten minutes. That surprised everyone. There was scattered sniffling and watery eyes. Elisa stood up, sensing what was needed next. "Do you all know the Prayer of the seven directions? It basically expresses gratitude for all the good things in life."

Zelda jumped up. "I do! Let's do it. Wait a sec. I have to get some of my gear."

While Zelda was off to her art studio, Randall decided it was time for some comic relief. "This could take a while. Zelda's art studio is rather . . . chaotic. Say, did you guys hear that the Olympics is adding a new running event strictly for guys with very little hair? You know, like me."

Elisa sensed a Randall groaner was coming but bit anyway. "No, but I'm sure you're going to tell us about it."

Randall continued. "Yeah, they figure that men with hair have more wind resistance and that slows them down. So, to be fair to the hairy guys, the hairless guys will run a separate 100 meter sprint. That means I might qualify."

Elena had to laugh. "You in the Olympics? That's a stretch."

Randall frowned. "Hey! You may not know it, but I am quite the runner. I do about 10-15 miles a week."

Elisa looked doubtful. "Kids? Is that right? Does your Dad run that much?"

Kyle nodded. "Yep. I think he's nuts. But he runs all the way up to the freeway and back."

Now, Elena was getting curious. "So, what are they calling this new event?"

Randall smiled. "It's going to be the 100 meter Balderdash."

Elisa groaned loudly. "I knew it! I got sucked in again. That is so lame that it's almost funny."

That comment set off a round of groaning and chuckling. Zelda returned with her gear in the midst of the laughter. "What the heck is so funny? Did I miss something?"

Elisa slapped her thigh. "No. You missed exactly nothing. At least nothing worth repeating."

Zelda grimaced. "Oh, I get it. I bet Randy tried his Balderdash story on you. It's as lame as a one-legged duck. Am I right?"

That set off the laughing again. Randall had achieved his goal with a story that needed a crutch. Zelda couldn't help but join in. When Elisa finally stopped giggling she asked Zelda about the gear she had dumped on the coffee table. "Hey, Zelda. Why did you bring down a candle, feathers, stones, dry leaves and this powdery stuff? And what's this stick?"

Zelda began to assemble the supplies. "That's easy. While we're doing the seven directions prayer, I'll light the candle, burn some sage, and waft it with the feathers. The stick is *Palo Santo*, from South America. The stones are crystals that help focus our energy to the seven directions."

Kyle and Addie jumped up. "We know the seven directions thingy too," shouted Addie. "We can help."

Wondercat and Milky Way sauntered silently into the room on little cat feet as if attracted by the ambient energy. They settled down to watch the proceedings. Zelda lit the candle and started wafting the sage smoke.

Soon everybody was standing and following Elisa's movements and absorbing her recitation. She began by facing East and gave a brief instruction. "I will say words about the meaning of each direction and then say a prayer. When I finish, please repeat it after me."

Elisa stood seemingly taller than her nominal height and faced East. "This is the direction of the sunrise." She spoke slowly, with gravitas. "It brings hope and promise. Hope plus action makes miracles. We pray to be open to those gifts." Elisa exhaled slowly, while the group repeated the prayer and Zelda wafted candle smoke with her feather.

With a quarter turn to the right, Elisa faced South. She breathed deeply again, establishing a rhythm. "This is the direction of growth and fertility. We pray for these things this day." The group missed a few words, but repeated the prayer as Zelda wafted.

With a quarter turn to the right, Elisa faced West. "This is the direction of the setting sun where our dreams and new beginnings lie. Pray that they are fulfilled." More in sync now, her breath and words were echoed by all except the cats. Again, Zelda wafted.

With a quarter turn to the right, Elisa faced North. "This is the direction of strength and purpose to help us face our challenges. Pray that we embrace them this day." Before the group could respond, both cats approached the wafting area and howled. The group took a collective deep breath.

Zelda stopped wafting and tried to calm the group. "Don't worry. The cats have just approved this blessing ritual. Elisa, you may continue."

With a final quarter turn to the right, Elisa faced East once more but instructed everyone to look up. "This is the direction of Father Sky, the One power that made us part of the universe. Pray this day that we not forget He watches over us."

Before anyone could speak, Addie spoke up. "I can't remember all that. Can I just say Amen?"

The group laughed again and Addie looked a bit embarrassed. Elisa patted her head. "Of course you can. Everybody please just say Amen." The group complied. Addie looked relieved. Zelda wafted.

Elisa instructed everyone to look down. "This is the direction to reach down and touch our Mother, the earth. Let's all touch the floor and pray that everything we do will be to honor Mother Earth. You can just say Amen." There was a hearty *Amen*. Zelda added some *Palo Santo* to the wafting.

Finally, Elisa told the group to put their hands on their hearts. "This is the direction of the spirit that lies *within you*. Pray this day that your spirits continue to grow and thrive. Say one at a time that you invite the seven directions to enrich your hearts." Each person recited their version of the prayer in turn. Then the room was quiet. Zelda wafted with an extra dab of sage and *Palo Santo* and a subtle humming.

The cats got up and body rubbed Elisa's ankles. She looked down in awe. "I guess that makes it the prayer of eight directions. It's an added bonus. You guys did great. I'm so impressed. You have given me so much to absorb tonight. I truly thank you all."

Zelda approached and put her hand on Elisa's belly. "Let's add one more direction. The direction of the unborn baby. Let us pray that you continue to surround it with positive energy."

There was a collective *Amen* that outdid all the previous *Amens*. Elisa blushed and smiled. "I promise to do my best." She paused as if listening inward. "And so does he!"

Zelda turned and used her announcer's voice. "Now, it's Randall's turn to tell us about his version of great spirits. But let's all take a potty break before he begins."

As everyone but Randall headed for a toilet, he shouted out. "You all come on back when you're done. I don't want to be talking just to my own self."

Then, as Randall received neural feedback from his own bladder, he realized his only option was the basement drain. He ran downstairs. Soon, the group reassembled, ready for quantum talk.

Quantum Elixir

Randall motioned everybody to take a seat around the dining room table. He knew his talk could bring on heavy eyelids and he didn't want his audience too comfy. Plus, seated around the table he could make eye contact and use sketches to make his points. He was a strong believer in diagrams with circles and arrows. He had put out notepads, pencils, and scissors for the group.

"Is everybody comfortable? Bladders empty?" queried Randall. The adults nodded.

"Why can't we sit on the couch?" whimpered Addie.

Randall put up both hands. "You volunteered for this duty. So I want full compliance."

"What's *fulcum* lions?" asked Kyle.

Zelda explained. "That means it's Dad's way or the highway, which, in your case, means bedtime. Got it?"

Both kids nodded. Kyle looked at Addie. "We don't want to go to bed before Elisa and Elena leave, right Sis?"

Addie nodded again. "No. I promise I'll pay attention."

Kyle jumped up. "Even if there's lions."

Randall smiled. "Good! Then I will begin the tale. I'm also hoping it will help me make sense out of what happened to me in the desert. Just to be clear, everything I said that happened out there was for real."

Zelda looked mildly surprised and stammered. "For really real?"

Randall swished a hand in the air. "For really."

Zelda looked newly surprised, as if she had previously thought Randall had been telling her a fairy tale the first time. Or had just been embellishing a bit. "I remember you talking about Quantum Theory before, like when you first started going to see Mary Alice. Didn't she ask you to study up on it?"

Randall nodded. "She did. I read about it in my Physics text and talked with Dan Graham. Dan's got a real interest in Quantum Theory. I brought up the topic with you a couple of times after that, but I don't blame you if it kind of went South. Even the experts don't really understand it and usually disagree about what it means especially when it comes to how it may affect human biology."

Elisa pointed at the notepads. "Are we supposed to take notes?"

Randall laughed. "It's not quite that serious. You don't need to take detailed lecture notes. It might help to write down some unfamiliar terms. Make some sketches. They will help you visualize what I'm describing."

Zelda gave a medium eyeroll. "Awwright, professor. Lay it on us."

Randall ignored the eyeroll. "The first thing I want you to write down is 'electron.' Zel, you took chemistry in high school, didn't you?"

Zelda folded her arms and puffed out a short breath. "Yeah, I did, but I didn't exactly ace it. I'm the artsy-fartsy one, remember? The electron is a little orbitty thing. It's kind of like the moon around the earth. How am I doing so far?"

Randall nodded. "Not bad. Go ahead, everybody, and draw the earth and moon. Yeah, like that. Now, we'll call the moon the electron and the earth the nucleus. Together they make a decent model of a hydrogen atom. The earth/nucleus is made up of two subatomic particles, a proton and a neutron, with a net positive electrical charge."

Zelda drew a big plus sign in the middle of the planet. The others mimicked her drawing.

Addie's puzzled face squished like an accordion. Randall had predicted this would be a difficult concept and pulled two magnets out of his pocket. "These magnets might help. See how one magnet attracts the other?"

Kyle had seen magnets before. "Even I know this one. They push each other apart, too, if you turn one around."

Randall nodded, then pointed to the smaller circle "The moon/electron has a negative charge and is way tinier than the nucleus."

Zelda made a negative sign in the orbiting moon.

Randall pointed at her picture. "Exactly! The opposing charges keep the electron from leaving its orbit and flying off into space. But the cool thing is that while the electron orbits the nucleus, it also spins around its own axis." Randall circled his finger in the air.

Elisa was pleased with her drawing. "Axis, eh? Haven't heard that word for a bit, but it's coming back to me now. If another hydrogen atom came walking by, they could start dating and share electrons. Then, for a while, they could become H2. Instead of an engagement ring they could get a covalent bond."

Randall was impressed by Elisa's quick grasp of the analogy and her cartoon of two hydrogen atoms holding electron hands. "Very nice drawing. I think the kids can understand this stuff with your sketch."

Kyle got excited. "Yeah, I get it. Mr. and Mrs. Hydrogen. Their kids are a gas."

Addie joined in. "Yeah, I like Mom's Earth and Moon drawing. But not Kyle's gas."

Zelda allowed herself a proud moment. She was always a bit touchy about not finishing college. "Thanks. I guess my art is good for something. Now, what's the big deal about electrons? What do they have to do with your wanton theory?"

Randall gave Zelda the slant eye look. "Nice try. It's Quantum theory."

Zelda lightly punched Randall's arm. "I know. I'm just yanking your chimes."

Randall chuckled and waved off the statement. "Whatever. Draw two electrons side by side. That's it. In order to better understand what electrons do, scientists recruited midget dwarfs to get into a Hydrogen atom and take a closer look. When they came back from their expedition, the midgets reported that electrons either spin up or spin down."

Elena joined in on this one. She drew an 'up' arrow next to her first electron and a 'down' arrow by the second. She then added elaborate fletching to the arrows, giving them a Robin Hood vibe. "Like Yin and Yang."

"Yeah, like man and woman," said Randall. "Here's the cool part. If the two electrons share space in close proximity to each other for a while, one of the pair will always spin up and the other will always spin down."

"Like they share good vibes?" asked Kyle.

"Sure, like that," agreed Randall. "Now, here's another cool part. Take these scissors and cut out the two paired electrons."

Zelda carefully cut out the spin up and spin down electrons so they were on two separate pieces of paper.

Randall took one of the pieces. "You hold the spin up electron and

I'll hold the spin down electron. Now, what do you suppose happens if you turn yours upside down so it spins down?"

Zelda pondered for a moment. Wondercat came wandering into the dining room, meowing for a treat. Zelda shooed her away. "Umm. It won't let me reverse its spin?"

Randall put his thumb and forefinger almost together. "Close. My electron instantaneously reverses to upward spin. No delay at all."

Zelda looked amazed. "That's really weird. How in the world does it do that?"

Elisa and Elena looked puzzled as well. Addie almost got up out of her chair. "Yeah, Dad. How does that work? Are you just making this up to *confuscate* me?"

Randall shrugged. "Sorry to disappoint you, but nobody knows for sure how this happens. I warned you it's strange science, not just me. Now, the even better quantum quandary here is this—suppose my down electron is on Mars when you flip your electron down. What's your guess?"

Elisa raised her hand again. "Oh, oh! Don't tell me. Your little down electron still flips its lid?"

Randall pumped his fist. "You've got it! Somehow the two electrons are still linked and behave as a pair, even at a distance and still instantaneous. Here's your first quantum mystery word pair. It's called 'quantum entanglement.' Write it down. Einstein knew about this phenomenon in the 1930s and could not explain it with his theories. At the time he didn't quite believe it. But it's been well studied since then and verified as real."

Zelda couldn't help but reference a goofy TV show featuring Lancelot Link, the Secret Chimp. The kids loved how it had chimps instead of human actors. "What's it all mean, Lance?" Zelda curled her arms and scratched her side, monkey style.

Randall got distracted as Wondercat put both paws on his leg and gently dug in sharp claws to send a tactile message that cat treats had been ordered and had not yet been delivered. This was followed up with a meow and a yowl. Randall got up from his chair and went to retrieve the treats, as ordered.

"Why is it always me that has to get your treats?" grumbled Randall.

"You are '*catangled*,'" joked Zelda. "You two share one vibrating neuron each."

Randall scattered a few treats on the floor to make Wondercat work a bit harder and stay quiet longer. "Very droll. There, that should hold her for a while. Now, where were we?"

Elena was first to respond. "The relevance of quantum 'whatevers' to the macro world we live in."

Randall cleared his throat and went on. "We still don't have a good explanation for the relevance of quantum entanglement at the macro level. That's the level of experience we live in. Some physicists have resolved this conundrum by concluding that quantum actions only affect events at the atomic level. Basically, they're saying that large objects, like two chairs side by side, don't change positions when one is moved, because it's not a quantum function."

Zelda patted her forehead. "Now that's a convenient and feel good solution."

Randall agreed with a head nod. "Indeed. One might even say it's a cop out, because the true explanation probably does not fit into a nice little box. Quantum entanglement is only one weird part of quantum functions. There's also the wave-particle duality of electrons and electron superposition, among others. These are beyond today's starter version."

Everybody's eyes glazed over a bit, especially the kids. Randall figured he might have filled up everybody's pitcher already. Then Zelda surprised him. "Randy. I hate to admit this, but I think I get it. I'm not sure I could repeat it all, but now I wish I hadn't quit college. I could have taken Physics."

Elisa squinted a bit and sort of agreed. "I'm getting the drift, but the Physics I had in college didn't go this far."

"How are the rest of you doing so far?" asked Randall.

Elena didn't have her sister's nursing background and was a little behind the mark. The kids said they were "sort of" getting it. That was a lie. They just didn't want to go to bed. Randall knew the truth but wanted them included anyhow. Tonight was not a night for discipline.

"So, ladies and kids, have window shades gone up from what I've explained so far?"

Zelda's face lit up with a flash of insight. "I'm beginning to see where you're going with this. The electron does all these weird quantum things. The stuff that happens in the body depends on chemical reactions that mostly happen with electrons. That would mean biology probably uses quantum behavior, too."

Elisa suddenly saw the connection as well. "Yes, maybe it could explain a deeper level of communication between humans."

Elena blinked. "Sure, like between Elisa and me. I always know when she needs me."

Addie's eyes lit up. "And how Yoda tells Kyle stuff. And when Uni talks to me!"

Kyle stared at her. "Yeah, what she said."

Randall was very pleased. "Right on the mark, everyone. You are grade A students. As you have intuited, there is a field of study looking at how quantum interactions might work in the function of living beings. It's called Quantum Biology and has been a field of study for several years already. Researchers have found all sorts of ways that quantum interactions affect important biologic functions, ranging from photosynthesis to the action of enzymes."

Elisa's Biology class was coming back to her. "Well, it makes sense that it would work at a chemical level inside a single organism."

Addie's wiggled her eyebrows. "What's an *N-zime*? Is it before an *O-zime* and a *P-zime*?"

Kyle giggled. "Or a *Poo-zime*?"

Randall was pleased that at least the adults were getting the drift of his quantum explanation. It was heady stuff. He'd expected Kyle's descent into potty land to come much sooner. He ignored the remark and congratulated Elisa on her insight. "Exactly, Elisa! And it's not just at a hidden subatomic level. We can see it in action in biological systems."

Zelda looked dubious. "Oh yeah, Dr. Wisenheimer. How about some examples we can understand?"

Randall put his hand to his heart and feigned being slighted. "Do you distrust my pronouncements?" He paused for effect. "Here are just a few. Muscular activity is an important one. Even bird navigation depends on quantum entangled chemical reactions. A chemical in the bird's retina responds to the magnetic field of the earth! Then there's digestive enzymes. A quantum entangled electron on an enzyme acts as a tiny biologic on/off switch. Very little is known about what brain functions might depend on quantum activity, but I suspect a lot of it does. Neural activity could use a switching mechanism like that."

"Oh, my goddess!" burst Zelda. "We've all heard scientists say that we only use 10% of our brains. I've never believed that. Maybe the rest of the brain is operating on the quantum network! Why would we have such big brains and then not use them?"

Elisa had a sudden revelation. "Yeah! Man didn't evolve by being mentally lazy. Even if what they say is true, we'd still have 90% of the brain *in* our noggins. That 90% must be doing something even if we don't consciously know what it is. We may not be aware of it, but our subconscious is always in there doing its thing. What it does can probably cross over to our conscious brain like when we get dream messages while we're sleeping."

Elena finished Elisa's thought process. Sister to sister brain waves must have been connecting. "Why not when we're awake, too? We'd just have to be tuned to the right frequency."

Zelda paused, deep in thought. She turned to look Randall straight in the eye. "What if we have quantum transmitters in our brains that can communicate with quantum receivers in other brains that have become entangled with ours? Randy, that is so cool, and it could explain how your dead patient said goodbye."

Randall raised both arms in celebration of Zelda's flash of insight. "Not to mention Uncle Phil calling me to come up to his hospital room while I was walking to my car in the parking lot. Or Addie yelling for help from her crib when she was entangled, pardon the pun, in the bunting of her blanket. Or, say, you knowing Gary Ballasco broke his leg skiing with me before I got home with him and took him to the ER. It's a long list of strange communications when you think about it."

Zelda's brain ticked through her inner rolodex of experiences. "Or how you came to me in a ball of green light when I was scared. Or the light with Chris. Or how Kyle and Addie knew the gender of the baby!"

Kyle and Addie stared at each other as if seeing something that previously had been hidden.

Elena picked up on the theme. "Yeah, like how many times have you just been about to call someone when they call you? Or the way you can sense someone behind you? How does that work?"

Randall had another thought. "What if we get these entangled messages all the time, but only 'hear' them when we can distinguish them from all the noise of our daily life?"

Elisa pondered. "We don't spend that much time truly listening these days."

Zelda nodded. "You're right about that."

Milky Way mewled loudly, padded up to Randall and again poked him in the leg with extended claws. Her message was that the palliative treats Randall had provided earlier were not filling her empty stomach. The cat's pathetic plea for sustenance and the claw poke didn't register with Randall. He was lost in space somewhere.

Zelda was annoyed by the *cateruption*. "Randy! Earth to Randy. I thought you were going to feed the feline. Is anybody home in there?"

Randall snapped to attention. "What? Er . . . sorry. I was having a daydream. Yeah, the cat. I only gave the cat some treats to shut her up. She can wait a bit longer without a health risk."

Zelda snorted. "It's not the cat's health I'm concerned about. Where the heck has your brain wandered off to?"

Randall straightened up in his chair and stretched his arms. "Sorry. I just had this strange flashback to when I was a kid. When I was maybe 7 or 8, I would get these 'brain messages' from somewhere while I was walking alone outside." His voice drifted off again as he remembered. "I didn't know where the messages came from. It was just talk in my head. But I soon found that listening to that voice was a good choice. I told my friend's mother about it once and she looked at me like I was a strange little boy and walked away. So I learned to just keep it to myself.

When I got older, I either stopped hearing the message voice in my head or it stopped talking to me."

Kyle's mouth opened. "Dad. That kinda sounds like when Yoda talks to me. Do you think it's the same thing?"

Randall shrugged. "I don't know, Buddy. It could be."

"Funny you two should say that," offered Elisa. "I kind of remember something similar happening to me when I was growing up. But I usually didn't listen to the voice because I thought my mother had implanted the thought into my brain. That might explain why I always seemed to get into trouble. My guess would be that, as we get older, we're bombarded with so much other input that the voice gets lost in the white noise."

Randall nodded. "Makes sense. In order to get tuned back in to those messages from wherever, we may have to make a voluntary effort to separate the wheat from the chaff. Like meditating, praying, or just keeping an open mind to not just outright dismiss things that don't have neat logical explanations."

Kyle scooched his chair closer to his dad. "Sometimes the voices just scare me."

Zelda was still trying to connect stray dots. "It might explain our neighbor's experience with the dead babysitter. Kind of makes me feel better about death. I've always felt like my grandma is still talking to me, even though she passed when I was a teenager."

Milky Way had stopped pleading for food and rubbed up against Zelda's legs. Both kids nodded.

Zelda looked at the kids and nodded back. After a pause, she turned to Randall. "Hmm. I'm just remembering one of my yoga teachers. She could tune into someone's energy and get what she called 'divine downloads' that showed her what was going on for them. You think this has anything to do with your Vegas voice episode?"

Randall scrunched up his face. "It could be related. Good thought. You know, it's getting late. Before I go further with the quantum stuff, maybe I had better stop here so you all can digest what we've gone through so far."

Whether Kyle was just fishing for more Elisa time or truly interested in Randall's talk will never be known. "No, Dad. This is good stuff. Keep going. I think Addie gets it too."

Addie frowned and looked at Kyle. "I do?"

Kyle lightly kicked Addie's leg under the table and she got the message.

She opened her eyes super wide. "Yeah, Dad. I understand, mostly. You can always remind us with bedtime stories."

Zelda made a dubious face and checked the clock. It was approaching 10:00 PM. "It's already past your usual bedtime. Are you guys sure about that or just fibbing to stay up longer?"

Kyle put on the most sincere face he could muster. "Honest, Mom. This is real cool stuff. If we don't get the whole thing, Dad can tell us again."

Zelda pursed her lips. "It's against my better judgment, but there can never be too much education. Randy, continue palavering. You ladies up for more?"

Elisa nodded. "Not a problem. Like Kyle said, this is cool stuff."

Randall looked a bit unsure, but continued. "Alright then. A closely related topic is something called String Theory. It's oddly named, but it says that if you keep slicing and dicing subatomic particles like the electron, you finally get down to a basic level where the electron is made up of tiny ribbons of energy, or strings, that vibrate in different ways to give each its unique function."

Kyle loved food analogies. "Like a wiggling bowl of spaghetti?"

Randall nodded. "Sure. Why not? Now, here's an even spookier part."

Elena piped up. "That's hard to believe. It's already spooky enough."

Randall held up a hand. "You got that right. Here's the even weirder part. For all the calculations in String Theory to work out correctly, the physicists had to posit that there are as many as ten parallel dimensions, or universes, probably folded within the vibrating ribbons of energy. If that's true, it seems possible that our brains might be able to receive signals from those universes via quantumly entangled neural-sensors in our brains."

Zelda held on to the table, as if trying to put on the brakes and slow down the train. "Holy crap! If one of the universes is parallel and a bit out of time sync with ours, could our brains receive traces of future events in our lives?" She held her hands close together, imagining parallels. "You know, not little things like 'I'm going to get the flu,' but big things, like 'in two days I'm going to have a massive heart attack.'"

The corner of Randall's mouth pulled back. "Cripes, I never thought of that. But, if it applies, it could explain the stuff that happened on the Vegas trip."

Zelda's face was a question mark. "In what way? I didn't want to bring this up, because I thought I was just being my usual paranoid self, but for the past several weeks I've been having a general sense of dread. I couldn't put my finger on what the dread was about."

Randall drew his head back in surprise. "Really? Me, too. It sort of started when I got the call from Knox trying to sell me on the trip to Vegas. I usually have a low-level sense of *ominosity* as my baseline, but his invitation sent my needle past 100%. I had no idea why."

Elisa was next to make connections. "Here, here! That's a good descriptor for what my past week has been like."

Zelda nodded vigorously. "Same here. Randy, when you told me you were going to Vegas, the little electrons in my brain started spinning. At first, I thought it was because you got to go on a boondoggle and I was being left behind to mind the store. But, after you left, I kept imagining your plane crashing. Later, I saw you gambling away all our money or getting lost in the desert and turning into dried fruit. I was so glad when you made it home safely. There's just one problem."

Randall scrunched up his face so tightly he looked like he'd just sucked an entire lemon. "Problem? What do you mean?"

Milky Way's meal messaging resumed. She jumped into Randall's lap and massaged his thighs with sharp claws. It caught Randall by surprise and he reflexively swatted the cat off resulting in several needlepoint skin piercings. "Damn cat. Just what I need. Inaccurate acupuncture."

Zelda straightened up in her chair and started to laugh. "Oh, poor baby. Now that was something to worry about. I think you'll survive.

Want to go in the other room and drop your pants so Mommy can kiss your owies and make them better?"

Randall stood right up and pretended to unbuckle his belt. "Best offer I've had all day. Let's just go upstairs."

That set off a round of laughing and giggling.

Zelda quickly dispelled Randall's notion. "Dreamer. Not in front of company. All you're getting is Bactine spray. Plus, you're not going to be excused until this debrief is over."

"I'm so close already. I could de-brief right now," said Randall.

"Go right ahead, if you dare. It would be a show not worth seeing," retorted Zelda.

Elisa and Elena began to applaud and encouraged Randall to go ahead. Addie and Kyle just looked confused.

Randall blushed and sat back down. "Can't blame a guy for trying."

"You're right. You are very trying," said Zelda.

Randall cleared his throat and straightened an imaginary tie. "Now, Zel, what's this big problem of yours?"

Zelda's face went serious again. "I thought the bad feeling would go away after you came back home, but I've still got it, big time."

"Yeah, me too," grunted Randall. "Do you suppose there's still something out there to worry about?"

Kyle piped up. "Should I ask Yoda? Addie could ask Uni."

Zelda shook her head. "Thanks for offering, kiddos. But this one is for adults. Your Dad is the quantum expert. Randy, what do Einstein's tea leaves tell you? Tell me how you think the electrons could be involved."

Randall assumed a somewhat ethereal meditative pose with his hand to his chin. "Let's review the 'facts.' I did see the port wing of the 727 flap up and down. It either really happened or I imagined it. I did hear the tin can noise in the desert with no human or animal or wind to move a can and I never found the can. Again, real or imagined, but this time with hearing, not sight. I did hear a loud booming voice in my head telling me to look down and then found the rock with the 'IY' on it. Then, it told me what the 'IY' meant. Hearing and sight. Still have the rock. I wasn't on drugs. I had no alcohol. The question then is how to explain it, assuming I am sane and rational."

Elisa and Elena looked back and forth from Randall to Zelda as if they were watching a tennis match. The kids sat forward in their seats in suspense.

Zelda mused for a moment. "Well, if you're crazy, then I am, too. Speaking just for myself, I may be weird but I'm not crazy. If you're crazy, then Grace and Molly are, too, because they saw Mr. Swindell along with you."

Randall looked relieved. "Whew. Good point. I'm feeling better already."

Elisa interjected a thought. "Is that your patient who rose from the dead? Wow. The water is getting pretty deep for us mere humans, right, *mi hermana*?"

Elena nodded her head. "Yep. I followed this for a while but now I'm lost at the bakery."

Zelda prodded Randall to continue. "So, Mr. Junior Einstein, put your quantum brain to work and tell me how your quantum stuff could explain things."

Randall heaved a big sigh. "I'll try. Einstein's theory demonstrates that all matter and energy are interchangeable. That applies to living beings, like us. If, as quantum theory postulates, all matter is made up of sub-subatomic vibrating strings of energy folded into multiple dimensions, it seems logical that matter can communicate with energy using a process like quantum entanglement."

Zelda was reserving judgment. "Okay, I follow that so far."

Randall went on. "Plus, the signals may cross dimensions or universes. I think our brains are capable of processing that form of data. However the data received is so outside of our normal plane of cognition that it gets dismissed as fantasy. You know, as not real."

Kyle looked pensive. "Like what I see at night when I'm dreaming? It's real to me but it's really not."

Zelda was surprised that Kyle made that connection. "So, dreams could be a window to another world?"

Randall looked up at the ceiling, searching for answers. "Possibly? I kind of think so. Like I said before, I think kids are more in tune with the data because they are blank slates. Their frequencies are wide open for reception. They haven't yet developed a standard model of what 'real' means."

Zelda bounced in her seat, energized by the possibilities. "Yeah, they're all tabula rasa, a blank slate. Like in sleep, able to relate to alternate realities and timelines. Maybe even dimensions where they don't have a body!"

Kyle squinted at his mom. "Have you been in my no-body dreams?"

Elisa raised her hand. "I hope this isn't too macabre, but . . . so, like when we die, we could pass from matter and energy to all energy?"

Zelda followed her thread. "Yeah . . . if that energy can still vibrate like the ribbons in our human electron signaling, maybe we could perceive them for a while before their signal gets too weak. Geez. Like spirits and visitations?"

Elena continued the thread. "Or from all energy to matter, like a developing baby! Or the connection between family members. Maybe it could explain telepathy and telekinesis."

Randall nodded in agreement, but put up a cautioning hand. "Slow down, folks. If we go down this road too fast we might miss something. But it's way cool we're coming to similar conclusions. Let me add one more thing I've thought of. When I was first contemplating this, I went so far as to think that perhaps what we call 'love' is the quantum entanglement of our electrons through genetics or just close association over time. Which means falling out of love may be possible if the reaction can go in reverse."

Elisa saw the line of thinking. "Maybe it's quantum *dis*entanglement. Like your electron strings start vibrating at different wavelengths. I wonder if my little oven bun can communicate with me already. Every time I think about him, I swear he tells me he's alright."

Zelda got a faraway look.

Randall didn't want to lose the momentum of their intellectual leap-frogging. "It seems the universe puts families together with that mysterious entanglement, linking our energies through time and space."

Zelda returned to the here and now. "That would certainly explain why we all were able to receive Addie's distress signal in Colorado when she got the blanket bunting around her neck. But I don't get how the file cabinet moved."

Randall again put up a cautionary hand. "Hey, we're not going to solve all the puzzles tonight."

Elena jumped in. "I'm sure if we put our minds to it, we could all come up with more inexplicable events that we've forgotten. Maybe, when these strange things happen, and we can't explain them, we dismiss them. If the events create tension with our concept of reality, our reality-based brains can't cope. So, it's easier to do a memory delete."

The group was quiet for a long moment, letting Elena's suggestion sink in. Then Zelda raised a finger and asked another question. "Randy, are there any other mysterious electron behaviors that we should know about?"

Randall nodded. "There are. I believe they only add more fuel to the little reality fire we've started. Besides being able to behave both as matter and energy, which the Physics folks call 'electron duality,' electrons can also pass through physical barriers. Weirdest of all, an electron does not exist at a specific spot. You can calculate where it's likely to be, but the act of observing it in one spot changes its characteristics. Without explaining this in further detail, let's just say it indicates the electron is capable of far more that our concept of a finite world would predict."

The group looked exhausted and almost full up with the new way of conceiving reality. Elisa summarized. "To me, what that means is that if the electron's behavior is that 'unreal,' none of the speculations we've been making are beyond the pale."

"Wow, that's very pithy," commented Randall. Kyle's head popped up, wondering if his father had just used a bad word.

Zelda gave Kyle a preemptive stare. "Kyle, do not say what you're thinking. Randy, careful with such words. Your son is on the lookout for word choice errors."

Randall realized he had tempted Kyle to go off course. "Sorry. I wasn't thinking. Brain is fried. It is getting late. Let me wind things up.

If we accept that the uneasy feelings we've been having have a basis in quantum theory, meaning they could be real, what are we to make of our premonitions of dread? Do we take them seriously and let worry befog our future plans? That's no way to live."

Elisa looked at the ceiling. "I agree. I say we take it as a sign to be cautious and prepared in everything we do. You know, do due diligence but don't let worry get in the way of living our lives."

Randall couldn't help himself. "I love doo doo diligence."

Kyle's patience was rewarded and he cackled. "Ha! Dad said 'doo doo!'"

Addie rolled her eyes and looked disgusted.

Zelda diligently avoided stepping in the doo doo and just ignored the two 'boy-men.' "If we stay wary but positive, we've done all we can do. Otherwise, how do we know when to stop worrying? We shouldn't let it paralyze us."

Randall heartily agreed and went on to suggest that perhaps they were too prone to focusing on the negative and the speculative.

Elisa raised an empty water glass. "Yeah, right on. I'll drink to that. We are in control of our thoughts most of the time." She smiled and glanced at Randall and Kyle who grinned back weakly. "We control how to spin things."

Randall raised an empty coffee cup. "Amen! When you take a hard look at things, we all have pretty good lives. We've had our trials, but they pushed us to learn and grow. If we stay entangled, we'll always spin in sync."

Zelda smiled gently and reached over to tap his wedding band. "Yes, we are entangled."

Randall felt all warm inside. "Life gives us situations that are hard to handle at the time, but they become the lessons that guide us on our journey. You know the saying: 'The universe never gives us anything that we don't have the ability to handle.'"

Zelda nodded, her hands on her heart. "You sound like Conan the Barbarian. 'Vat don't kill us, makes us *stroooonger*.' I prefer 'Just when the caterpillar thinks the world is ending, it becomes the butterfly.'"

Randall broke into a wide grin, almost ear to ear. "Hey, this is great.

Dueling aphorisms. You win. In other words, we should be grateful for all we have. Ladies and kids, I think this session is done. Any questions, comments or criticisms?"

Elisa rolled her eyes before speaking. "I have lots of questions, but I think I'll save them for a later time after I have mused on this some more. I've absorbed enough to say that I feel much better about my situation. I will listen to what my heart tells me and let things unfold in their own time."

Elena added a thought. "Our mother had a saying that applies here. *'No puedes abrir una flor con forza. Hay que esperar a que se desarrolle.'*"

Zelda applied her limited Spanish. "Something about a flower and waiting?"

"Ah yes, I remember that one," said Elisa. "'You can't pry open a flower. You have to wait for it to unfold.' And Dad often said that you have to listen to that still, quiet voice inside. In my case, there are two voices inside, my baby's and my heart. That's your lesson, Kyle and Addie. Keep listening to Uni and Yoda. They tell you the truth that's in your heart."

Both kids placed their hands on their hearts, as if finally feeling understood. The energy field filled with love.

Milky Way jumped up on the table, meowing loudly. It was *catlish* for "Can I finally get some dinner!?"

RICA'S DAIRYL

IY

WISCONSIN

CHAPTER 29

———

QEG

"We are slowed down sound and light waves, a walking bundle of frequencies tuned into the frequency of the cosmos, we are souls dressed up in sacred biochemical garments, and our bodies are the instruments through which our souls play their music."

—attributed to Albert Einstein

Friday came and went in the usual blur of busy-ness, school and family. Saturday morning seemed to drag in anticipation of the 2:00 QEG meeting. Kyle and Addie made one last plea to join their parents at the meeting, but Mrs. Bush from next door lured them across the driveway with fresh baked cookies and a promise of Monopoly.

Kyle ran into her house, planning to lick every cookie before Addie could get one.

Addie plotted her victory strategy to claim Boardwalk and Park Place early on.

Zelda grabbed Randall's hand on the way to the car. Randall felt surprised by this show of vulnerability.

"You are the sly one, little fox," he reassured her. "Let your wisdom shine!"

SHEPARD'S HOUSE

The members of the QEG group seemed to arrive at Joe Shepard's house at the same time as if choreographed.

Randall and Zelda walked to the front door just as Elisa and Elena arrived. Zelda greeted the pair. "Hey, you two. Or should I say you three? You ready for this little escapade?"

"As ready as we'll ever be. Are you sure the group will be alright with us being here?" asked Elisa.

Randall waved an arm. "No worries. I cleared it with Dr. Shepard by phone. He said 'the more the merrier.' You two certainly qualify as the merry more."

The front door opened before Randall could ring the bell. It was Joe Shepard there to escort them in. "Are these the lovely young ladies you told me about?"

Randall smiled broadly and nodded. "They are, indeed." He stepped to the side and extended a hand towards Elisa and Elena. "Joe Shepard, these are the sisters, Elisa and Elena Angeles." The two gave small curtsies and Joe shook their hands in turn. "You remember my wife, Zelda."

Joe gave Zelda a polite hug and ushered the group inside. "Please come in. The rest of the group has already arrived. I've made name tags. Please put one on so people know who you are, then go on over to the buffet and grab some lunch. Feel free to mingle. We'll start the meeting in about 30 minutes."

Randall and his three cohorts walked into the living room as a tight group, somewhat surprised to see about a dozen people scattered about with plates of food and drinks. A few were chatting together, but there wasn't much mingling.

Elisa looked about and stopped walking. She leaned over to Randall and whispered. "Geez, Dr. B, I thought you said this was going to be a small group!"

Zelda was surprised, too, and quietly echoed Elisa. "Yeah, Randy, this almost looks like a funeral reception. Nobody is mingling and they look like the corpse is laid out in the next room."

Randall backed up a step. "Er, yeah. I hear you. At our first meeting . . . let's see . . . we had about five or six members. But Joe did say he had some other possible members in mind. The extras could be them.

Let me check in with Joe and see what's up. In the meantime, go ahead and visit the buffet. Looks like good grub. Joe went all out."

Zelda put a hand to her mouth and muttered. "Or his wife did."

Randall made his way over to the dining room where Joe was refilling his plate with sandwich fixings, cole slaw, sauerkraut, and German potato salad. "You didn't need to do all this, Joe. It's quite the spread."

Joe continued making what looked to Randall like a Dagwood Bumstead sandwich. "Hey, no worries. I asked the wife to put together some lunch fixings. Let's just say she's no hand in the kitchen and not motivated to do extra work. She waved her magic credit card and made a caterer appear with the goods. Of course, she got a discount. You can pay up your half later. So eat up all you can before the bill comes. It will reduce the pain."

Randall winced. "Ouch! Suddenly I'm ravenous. Just one question. How did our group double in size? Do we have rabbit genes?"

Joe chuckled. "The math is easy. You brought three more. Dan Graham brought a subatomic physics friend, Adele Astravanian. John Bingham—you remember him, he's the psychiatrist—brought a colleague of his, Simon Escaliente, who's a psychophysicist. My wife invited the assistant pastor from our church, Breana Hedley, who's a smidge on the eclectic side. I invited Roland Walker, the father of one of my kid patients. The man happens to be Shamanic elder in a northern Wisconsin Menominee tribe. He's quite the trip. He's kind of the Menominee version of Rolling Thunder. You know . . . the self-proclaimed Shoshone Shaman in Nevada who claimed he'd done a bunch of miracles. Finally, I called the local Christian Science council and they sent over one of their people, Chase Medley, to fill us in on their views."

"Wow! You have been busy," remarked Randall. "I spotted Ruby Cosgrove, the former nun yoga instructor, chatting up the Walker guy. She was here for the first meeting."

Joe nodded. "Oh, right. I forgot she's here too. Not sure how I forgot. She's rather, er . . . unique."

"Shame on you for not being perfect," teased Randall. "This group may not be our final one, but it sure covers the waterfront. How are we going to deal with all these new members? Any thoughts?"

Joe waved off Randall's concern. "Half the group knows each other already. So, I suggest once we're settled in the living room, we go around in rotation and have each person introduce themselves. You know, brief bio, area of speciality and why they are interested in our little quest. With twelve folks at five minutes each that will cover the first hour. What do you think should come next? We've got two more hours after that."

Randall thought for a long moment. "Coffee break for sure after hour one. Maybe ten minutes for some face-to-face social time. Then, I'd better give them a 10-15 minute summary of our quantum entanglement theory of nonverbal communication. Probably allow another 15-20 minutes for discussion after that. More if we need it. Then, I suggest I pose a moral-ethical dilemma to them and see how their solutions compare."

Joe frowned and briefly covered his eyes with his right hand. "Oh boy, when I hear you say it all out loud, this task sounds rather Herculean. Well, we gotta start somewhere. If we stay flexible for impromptu changes, that should be a reasonable framework. I'm not sure I want all these people in our core group. I'd like the freedom to inform them up front that final membership in the group is dependent on the approval of the two of us. If we do not believe one of them is a good fit, they may not be invited back."

"Hmm, I like that," said Randall. "Right now, I'm going to plunder your buffet and get my licks in. You be the time keeper and ring a bell or something when it's time to gather."

"You got it," said Joe.

Randall walked back to the living room, his plate piled high with food, dessert on top. Randall's three ladies were seated together on the couch having a strained conversation with two young women seated across from them. The two young women appeared to be in their late thirties and rather attractive. Their name badges read "Ruby Cosgrove" and "Adele Astravanian." Ruby was lithe and tall with shoulder-length blonde hair. Adele was almost the opposite. She had dark hair cut in a pageboy, was medium height and well rounded. Randall settled on the armrest of the couch. "How's my little entourage doing? Great food, eh? Looks like you've made friends already."

Zelda looked a smidgen uncomfortable in the surroundings, but managed a sociable introduction of Ruby and Adele. "Ladies, this is my husband, Dr. Randall Biedermeier." Zelda seemed to choke a little bit on the 'doctor' part. "He's a Radiation Oncologist. He and Dr. Shepard organized this little weeny roast. Randy, this is Ruby Cosgrove. She used to be a nun, but chose something a bit less cloistered. Now she's a yoga instructor. Isn't that cool?"

Randall nodded. "Yes. Hello again, Ruby. How are you? We met at the first QEG meeting. But your friend here is new to me."

Randall offered his hand. Adele took it and allowed a gentle squeeze before withdrawing. "I'm Adele Astravanian. I've just now met Ruby, but I'm an old college friend of your Medical Physicist, Dan Graham. I'm into subatomic and particle physics. Dan and I have been exchanging thoughts about quantum theory for some time. He asked me to come and add my two cents to your conclave."

Randall hadn't yet had a chance to touch any of his food. He was taken by the intelligence displayed by Adele's Russian-tinted words, not to mention the fullness poorly hidden under her well-tailored top. His plate hand slipped a bit due to lack of concentration, but he corrected before everything slipped off his plate. Adele shifted backwards reflexively and Randall apologized for his clumsiness. "Whoops! That was close. Well, glad to have you join our group. I'm sure your expertise will serve us well."

Zelda gave Randall the side eye and stifled a chuckle at his awkwardness in the presence of female vibrations.

Adele rose from her easy chair to avoid being a food target. "I'm looking forward to it. Listen, I need to use the powder room. Please take my seat so you can better wrangle that cache of food on your plate. We may not have much time before the discussion starts."

Randall obliged. "Very thoughtful of you. I don't think Joe or I were expecting quite this many people. The seating is a little sparse. Talk more later."

Randall began to eat and looked around the room. There were indeed some unfamiliar faces. The first new man he spotted was definitely not a Christian Scientist practitioner. He was clearly Native American and very tall. He wore his hair in braids that fell below his shoulders. He was dressed in blue jeans, a white cowboy shirt buttoned to the neck, and a bolo tie. He was shod with snakeskin cowboy boots.

Zelda looked to where Randall was staring. "Randy, is it my imagination or do you think that looks like Tonto over there?"

Randall put a finger to his lips. "Zel! Keep that to yourself. I may be mistaken, but I think most Native Americans would take that as an ethnic slur. Plus, he looks big enough to pound me into the ground, so don't aggravate him."

Zelda made an evil grin. "How, Chief!"

Randall poked Zelda in the ribs. "Very carefully. Now stifle, Edith!"

Elisa laughed quietly. "Hey, how about that dude in the wire rim glasses over there by the mantle chatting up the lady that looks like Aunt Bea from The Andy Griffin show? Did Dr. Shepard shed any light on those two?"

Randall nodded. "He didn't point them out specifically, but my guess is that the guy is the one sent by the Christian Science Church, given the black suit and tie. Joe said his name was Chase something. It reminded me of the character Harvey Korman played in 'Blazing Saddles,' Hedley Lamar. Now I've got it! Chase Medley. The other guy Joe mentioned had a Hispanic name and our glasses guy is definitely not one."

Zelda had a sudden flash of recognition. "Wait. I think I recognize Aunt Bea. Remember when we tried that Tosa Lutheran church?"

Randall nodded. "You're right. Wasn't she the assistant pastor? But 40 less pounds ago?"

Zelda pointed at Randall. "And her name was something like the Medley guy."

Randall laughed out loud. "That's it. Her last name is Hedley! What a riot. Hedley and Medley! When Joe said her first name I thought 'banana' with an R as a mnemonic."

"Was it Breana?" asked Zelda.

Randall high fived Zelda. "That's it! You nailed it."

Elisa and Elena had been watching the exchange and laughed at the dynamic.

Elena caught her breath and sighed loudly. "You guys are like that old comedy duo, Abbott and Costello. It's just a riot how you fill in each other's blanks. Is that what marriage does?"

Zelda nodded. "Yep. It's marital entanglement. It's mostly good, but it makes it harder to keep secrets from your spouse."

Randall raised a finger. "You're right Elena. But, just to be clear, I'm Abbott and she's Costello."

Zelda raised a fist. "What's that you say? You've got that turned around."

When Randall saw the look on Zelda's face, he changed course. "Wait a minute. Isn't Abbott the short one?"

Zelda shook her head with menace.

Randall raised a calming hand. "You're right. I'm the funny short guy and you're the tall straight man, er, lady."

Zelda nodded and smiled. "Now, you've got it straight. Wait! Are you saying I'm not funny?"

Elisa decided to break up the dispute. "Guys! Guys! You're both funny, as in humorous. And you're both straight, right? Can we just get back to people watching?"

Randall and Zelda laughed. Zelda was first to speak. "Oh, we weren't really arguing. It's a little spontaneous play acting routine we do when we're nervous while waiting."

Elisa seemed a bit annoyed. "Well you could have fooled us. Let's get back to business."

Randall nodded. "Good idea. See, Zel? We are getting better at our Honeymooners bit."

Zelda nodded agreement. "Yep, old Randy one. There's just one more player to ID. See the guy going back to the buffet for thirds? He definitely looks like he's from the 'hood. Note the white floral button-up shirt hanging over his low riding pants. There's some tear drop tattoos on his face. Not a likely look for a guy with a PhD in Psychophysics. But

I'm not really sure what Psychophysics means. Never heard of it before. It might be a somewhat fringe group of, you know, semi-professionals."

Elisa made a humming sound. "Hmmmm. . . . Did Dr. Shepard mention his name?

Randall nodded. "He did. I remember Simon like in Paul. Last name . . . I remember the word is like the Spanish for hot."

Elena spoke up. "*Caliente?*"

Randall frowned. "Almost. Now I have it. It was like it started with an S."

Elisa got it. "Was it Escaliente?"

"Bingo!" said Randall. "What's it mean?"

Elena translated. "To heat up. Looks like Juan is stoking the coals. He just went back for more *comida*. I suppose we'll find out soon whether he's a psycho physicist or just a hot dude."

Elisa stared at Elena. "Not now, *hermana*. We are here as professionals!"

INTRODUCTIONS

With the identity of the guests partially analyzed, Randall's little group finished the rest of their brunch and headed back to the large coffee urn for refills. The rest of the group was doing the same and finding their seats in the living room with fresh drinks in hand. Joe Shepard went to stand by the fireplace and clinked an empty glass with a knife for attention.

Joe waited a beat, then spoke in a loud clear voice, totally unlike his usual quiet manner. "In the immortal words of Milton Berle, ladies and germs, please settle down and choose a place to sit. Let's quiet the chatter so we can get started with this battle of unique perspectives. Most of you know me already, but, just to be thorough, I'm Joe Shepard and this is my house."

A male voice from the back of the room spoke out loudly before Joe could continue. "I know all that. I'm still not clear what QEG is and why I'm here."

Joe looked up. The speaker was Simon Escaliente, the Psycho Physicist friend of Joe's psychiatrist friend, John Bingham. Joe pointed at the man. "Patience. I was just about to explain that."

Simon yelled out again. "Then get on with it."

Joe became noticeably irritated. "I'm trying! Please. Let's all stay calm. For those who don't know, I'm a child psychologist. Beyond that, I've always been interested in the unusual ways humans can communicate. That's an interest I share with my friend and colleague, Randall Biedermeier."

Joe pointed to Randall. He rose and came forward. He was still eating a large piece of chocolate cake and brought the plate and plastic fork with him. His mouth was full, so he just waved to the group. Joe continued. "Together, we started this so-called Quantum Entanglement Group. That's a lot of syllables, so henceforth we'll just refer to it as the QEG. Randall, for the benefit of the newbies, please say a few words about our purpose."

Randall looked up in surprise with his mouth full of chocolate cake. He wasn't expecting to be spotted out so soon and was slow to swallow the sticky cake. Joe saw the hesitation. "Come on, Randall. You usually can't stop talking, so a few words shouldn't be a hardship for you."

The assembled group roared in laughter, easing the tension several notches.

Zelda took the opportunity to add to Randall's embarrassment. She stood up and spoke out loudly. "Dr. Shepard, you really do know my husband."

Randall blushed and couldn't help but start to laugh himself. However, he had a mouthful of cake and started to choke. Zelda rose and ran to Randall with a napkin. He managed to spit out the bolus of chewed cake with a cough. Zelda collected the cake in the napkin and took it to the kitchen, along with the rest of the plate.

The room went silent. Joe was concerned. "Randall, are you alright?"

Randall smiled then looked slowly left and right. He cleared his throat loudly and made a little cough. "For my next act, I will reassemble the cake. But before that, I would be grateful if someone could fetch me a fresh cup of coffee."

Randall's response roused a round of applause. A cup of coffee magically appeared. Randall downed the whole cup in a few swallows. Joe sidled up to Randall and asked if he was ready to proceed.

Randall cleared his throat like a bellowing cow. "Why, yes. I'm good to go."

There was some tittering from the group. Randall cleared his throat once more and proceeded with his requested introduction. "Well, if you all insist, I guess I can manage a brief introduction, now that my airway is restored, thanks to my wife, Zelda. As Joe mentioned, this is the second meeting of the QEG. As the name suggests, we are exploring that quantum entanglement as a possible explanation for what we are calling non-verbal human communication. Simply stated, that would include telepathy, visions, healing, and contact with the dead. How's that for brief? Any questions, raise your hand."

Roland Walker raised his hand. "Are all of your introductions this dramatic?"

Randall laughed politely. "Why, no. Some are way more dramatic."

Roland laughed in response. "Lord help us. Next time, please do give us some forewarning. My real question is this. What's your background and why are you interested in nonverbal communication?"

Randall nodded to Roland. "Good questions. As my wife, Zelda, mentioned, I'm a Radiation Oncologist. I treat cancer patients using radiation. In my practice I've witnessed several of the phenomena I mentioned, including an appearance of a deceased patient, transmitted messages from patients, and even a mental distress signal from a distance."

Ruby Cosgrove raised a hand and spoke. "I assume you will describe these to us in some detail?"

Randall nodded and looked towards Joe Shepard. "I will certainly do so, as will Joe. He has similar experiences to mine. When we learned this, we decided that the topic deserved deeper investigation from a more serious and varied point of view, not just from us. We wanted to include others with different, shall we say, spiritual viewpoints and include what I'm going to call 'regular lay people.'"

Zelda decided to stand and deliver. "Folks, by lay people, he means people like me. I'm just a wife, his, and a mother. But, as my five-year-old daughter would say, I know stuff too."

Randall looked mildly embarrassed. "Yes, dear. I was just about to get to you. Thanks for the cake rescue." The group laughed and Zelda turned a bit red. "What I was going to say is that before we start any discussion on tonight's topic, I'm going to go around the room and ask each of you to stand in turn. I'd like each of you to give us a brief bio and explain what you think your area of expertise might bring to the group."

Roland Walker was still standing and Randall pointed to him. "Sir, since you're already standing, let's start with you."

Roland made a slight head movement in response, but his face remained blank. "Your wife is correct about your speaking. My Menominee tribe would name you Long Talker. I am Roland Walker. I am a Shaman. I do many rituals that reach into the spirit world, but mostly healing. I, too, have seen many things your medicine could not explain. I will share these later." Roland sat back down.

Joe stood up. "Mr. Walker, you are clearly a Short Talker. Let me fill in some blanks. He is the father of one of my patients, a young man dealing with unusual dreams. After getting to know Roland, I invited him to attend our meeting because I wanted a Native American point of view. Thankfully, he agreed. Randall, please continue."

Joe sat back down after surrendering the floor to Randall.

"I'll continue by introducing three attendees I invited, all new to the group. First is my wife, Zelda. Zel, I don't think you need to raise your hand. Everyone knows who you are now. My second invitee is a very special nurse from my department, Elisa Angeles." Elisa raised her hand. "Third is Elena, Elisa's sister." Elena raised her hand.

There was some buzzing from the group. Randall continued. "I think we can all agree that these three ladies increase the average beauty of the group significantly. Their P value is at least .05. Zel, would you please go next? Please stand and tell us more about yourself."

Zelda pointed at herself and mouthed a silent *me*? Randall nodded. Zelda stood uncertainly and cleared her throat. "*Errhaug*! I'm accustomed to speaking, but not to a large group of super educated people.

As I've said, I'm Randall's wife. I'm also a mother and an artist, not necessarily in that order. I'm just one of those common folk Randall mentioned." Zelda looked over at Randall and shrugged questioningly.

Randall got the message. "Keep going. Tell them about the diverse reading you've done."

Zelda perked up. "Oh, yeah. That stuff. My mom dragged me to a bunch of different churches, but none of them stuck for her. She wound up in Christian Science, but that seemed lame to me, so I started reading other things, like the Quran, some Bible and even Edgar Cayce. I picked up a lot from Khalil Gibran and then *A Course in Miracles.* I never settled on any one of them, but I selected some from each one. Oh, and I read a lot of Carlos Castaneda and Rolling Thunder. I'm like the 31 flavors of religion."

Joe Shepard chuckled. "A regular patchwork quilt, I'd say. Or, Zelda, the Technicolor Dreamboat." That got a big laugh. "What was your reaction when Randall told you about seeing a dead patient or when your baby daughter's distress call reached you from miles away? How did those experiences fit into what you'd read?"

Zelda put her hand to her chin in thought. "Oh, that's right. I guess Randall told you the whole story before. I suppose it was that everything I'd learned seemed to say that it was possible and not unusual, since unusual stuff had been observed for centuries in so many ways. But those observations couldn't explain what caused the events to happen, so the observers just assumed it was a divine or mysterious greater power. And the greater power was just pictured differently by each writer. You know, like the blind men and the elephant."

Joe had a followup question. "This may be a bit premature, but when Randall explained his quantum entanglement ideas to you, what did you think?"

Zelda put both hands in front of her like she was grabbing a basket. "Well, I figured I didn't have to look for an explanation that's way out there in the sky. If what we're made of is a power we all have, then it's already in all of us. Randy can explain it better, but that's what I think now."

Zelda's comments got scowls from Chase Medley and Breanna Hedley and smiles from Ruby Cosgrove and Roland Walker, who rarely smiled. Randall and Elisa looked proud. Zelda looked ready to be done.

Randall read her body language and motioned her to return to her seat. "Thanks, Zelda. I'm sure we'll hear more from you later on. Next, let's hear from Elisa Angeles. Please rise and tell the group what you're about."

Elisa felt a surge of energy and rose. She looked around the room, making brief eye contact with each group member before she spoke. "Looking back several weeks, this is the last thing I would have thought I'd be doing. But it's amazing how quickly life can rise up and bite you in the fanny." There were some chuckles and knowing nods from the group. "As evidence of that, here I am. Dr. Biedermeier hired me as a nurse patient care coordinator for his complicated cancer patients. I love the job and I really get a chance to help people."

Elisa took a long pause to collect her thoughts. Simon Escaliente broke the silence. "Miss Angeles, are you willing to tell us what part of life bit your backside?"

There were scattered laughs after the question and Elisa smiled. She decided to put it all out there. "Simply put, I suddenly found myself single, pregnant and a cancer patient. I haven't quite decided how to manage all that. It's complicated."

The group seemed to take a collective breath. Escaliente looked embarrassed. "I'm so sorry for asking such a personal question."

Elisa shook her head. "*No pasa nada.* It felt good to get that off my chest. My current dilemma is not why Dr. Biedermeier invited me here, but that is the reason I came. He asked me to come because of my family heritage. My mother was a Puerto Rican fortune teller and my father was a Native Mexican Pasqua Shaman. Like Mr. Walker, my father performed many healing rituals and other traditional ceremonies. My sister, Elena, and I witnessed many of them." She gestured to her sister with pride. "Growing up, we thought what we experienced in my family was normal, but later we realized that, to many others, they would seem like miracles. My mother's predictions were correct more often than not. Again, when young, we thought all mothers could do what ours did, but we were wrong. Isn't that right, Elena?"

Elena stood up, nodding her head. "Elisa is correct. And I believe that the two of us inherited some of our parents' abilities. We're not identical twins, but I always know when Elisa is in trouble and Elisa senses when troubles are coming for her and others around her. Dr. Biedermeier thinks his quantum ideas help explain these things. I did not come to be a member, but as a guest to listen and learn from those who know more than me." Elena folded her hands together, lowered her head and sat back down.

There was polite applause. Randall took the floor again. "That was very brave of the two of you. Elisa, perhaps the group can help you with your dilemma later in the discussion. Are there any questions at this time?"

Ruby Cosgrove raised a hand. "Elisa, Sweetie, how far along are you? Do you have a sense of how things will turn out with your cancer?"

Elisa was quick to respond. "I'm three months along. And, yes, I do have a general sense of my disease outcome, but I'm not quite ready to believe in it."

Randall closed the discussion. "Okay, folks. I think that's enough for Elisa and Elena right now. Ruby, since you asked that last question, please take the floor and tell us about yourself." Elisa sat back down.

Ruby stood to speak. She didn't look much like just a nun with no habit. The impression she made was more like that of a fitness instructor. She had long blonde hair done up in a ponytail with a large yellow ribbon, long lithe limbs, tight fitting yoga pants, and a somewhat revealing silk blouse. Randall noticed a small tattoo on the back of Ruby's neck.

Ruby started out with a tribute to Elisa and Elena. "I think you'll all agree that we're very glad to welcome both Elisa and Elena to our group. They seem to be very bright and I'm sure they will have much to contribute. Let's put our hands together in welcome."

There was a vigorous response to the suggestion and both Angeles sisters turned rather red.

Ruby took a long deep breath. "Now, half of you already know me, so I'll keep it brief. It's true I was a nun in a previous life and had my little self married to Mr. Jesus. But we didn't see eye to eye about some holy trinity stuff and we got divorced. Let's just say I could never get into the habit." She paused for the collective groan and chuckle.

Randall couldn't let that go. "Er, Ruby, only the MCs are permitted to be funny. Watch yourself." That evoked more chuckles.

Ruby looked at Randall with a smirk and continued. "Anyway . . . I started looking for something that involved the spirit world without so many rules. That's when I found Mrs. Yoga and we got married. I guess that makes me a *Lesbotarian*. I'm not bragging when I say I can feel other people's energy, especially when it's all messed up. The messed up ones come to me for a front end alignment. I guess that makes me a soul mechanic. That's all for now, folks."

Ruby sat back down with the grace of someone quite comfortable in her body. There was some female tittering in the group. The men just stared. Randall got up again and congratulated Ruby for her straightforward and terse delivery. "Okay, then. That will be hard to follow. Before we go all physics, let's hear from the psychiatry contingent. John Bingham, will you please come on down? Ha, ha. I always wanted to be Bob Barker on 'The Price is Right.' Actually, you can just stand where you are."

Bingham rose awkwardly. He was a tall, gawky man. He wore a tight-fitting black suit, white shirt, and black bow tie. His Prince Albert beard was going white way before his sparse, close-cropped hair. Bingham adjusted his wire rim glasses with a long slender hand. His facial expression said "I'd rather not be here."

Bingham surveyed the room before clearing his throat and speaking. "Ahem! Yes, thank you, Randall. I am, er . . . pleased to be here, once again. I found the first meeting to be quite edifying if not a bit stupefying. I must admit, physics is not quite my cup of tea. I prefer the science and art of psychiatry—the brain and the mind. Some of the QEG theories the two of you posited at the first meeting rather have the ring of PC. For those of you in the dark, my PC does not mean 'politically correct.' Rather, it means 'poppycock.' No offense. I am a man of science and demand repeatable proofs of verity. When I see some, I may change my point of view. Now, is there anything more you need from me? Do I need to further clarify?"

Randall's initial impression was confirmed—Bingham was wound rather tightly. "Umm, no, Dr. Bingham. I think you've made your position quite clear. Just one thing. Could you please introduce your new invitee?"

Bingham waved an arm toward Escaliente who was standing in a corner that provided a good view of Ruby Cosgrove's decolletage. "Of course. May I present to you Dr. Simon Escaliente. He has a PhD in Psychophysics. My clinic has employed him as a consultant, working with patients who need his special methods of psychometrics. I'll let him sum that up for you." Bingham sat back down, perched on the edge of his seat.

The audience shared quizzical looks around the room. Randall nodded. "That would be great. I, for one, am not quite familiar with that line of investigation. Dr. Escaliente, if you will."

Escaliente stepped forward and moved to the center of the room. His baggy low-rider pants and loose shirt contrasted greatly to Bingham's habitus. He put out an arm and rotated slowly on the balls of his feet. "*Hola, amigos y colegas.* Thanks to the leaders of this *elite* assemblage for inviting me. I am not sure I am worthy after what I have heard and seen so far. I am from humble beginnings in the *barrios* of Los Angeles. Since I was a little *muchacho*, I always want to see how things work. I take apart things and put them back together. Then I want to find out how people work. I owe it to my large family for supporting me through my education. I am so fortunate to finish with a PhD."

Dan Graham raised a hand. "Excuse me, doctor, but can you explain that? I am a radiation physicist, but I've never heard of psychophysics as a branch of physics."

Escaliente nodded. "Of course, sir. That is because it is not a branch of physics, but it is a branch of psychology. I deal with the relationship between physical stimuli and the sensations or perceptions they produce."

Dan Graham frowned. "All I know for sure is that I'm not sure what you just said. But I do know now that it has little to do with my sort of physics."

That got a laugh from the crowd. What Randall got out of the exchange was that Dr. Escaliente was not the poor *muchacho* from the *barrio* that was initially suggested by his exaggerated Spanish accent. He encouraged more clarity. "Perhaps you can rephrase your explanation for Dr. Graham."

Escaliente smiled somewhat triumphantly. "Certainly. I use various testing techniques to determine how individuals process information derived from visual and other sensory systems. For example, each of us has a different threshold for their response to sound intensity. One person may not notice music playing in the background, but another might be totally distracted by it. You can imagine how these differences could drive behavior." Randall noted that Dr. Escaliente's accent had smoothed out dramatically as he delved into his area of passion.

Dan Graham followed up. "So, do you have techniques that could modify these stimulated sensory behaviors? Say, like eating disorders, light sensitivity, and so forth?"

Escaliente nodded. "Indeed. Those are but a few examples."

Zelda popped a question. "What about extrasensory perception? I mean stuff that some of us can detect without obvious stimulation of our known sensory systems?"

Escaliente smiled broadly and spread his arms. "An insightful query. That is exactly what I am exploring in my research. It is why Dr. Bingham invited me, although he takes quite a dim view of my 'hobby,' as he calls it."

There was some loud murmuring from the group. Randall decided to move on to another new member. "That is very interesting, Doctor. We look forward to hearing more from you later on. Right now, I must move this along. Let's see. Since we're sort of on a physics path, let's hear some more from Dan Graham and his invitee. Dan?"

Dan stood up and smiled. He was an affable looking man in his mid-thirties with light brown hair and bright blue intelligent eyes. He wore blue jeans and a green turtle neck sweater over a white collared shirt. "Thanks, Dr. B. By the way, we call him Dr. B at work. It's way easier than four syllables. I like him well enough except for his habit of sneaking up when I'm deep in thought and scaring the bejeebers out of me. The last time he did that, he grilled me about quantum theory. It's not quite a main area of study for radiation physics, but I've always been fascinated by it and keep up with the literature when I can."

Roland Walker interrupted without a hand raise. "Dr. Graham . . . when are we going to hear what the quantum theory of Dr. B is all about and how it relates to what these shrinks are all about? It sounds like it could be something simple all wrapped up in fancy white man words."

Dan pointed a finger at Walker. "Very keen observation. Dr. B and I have discussed it at length. We use all the accepted physics terms when we do, but they're not easy to understand. He told me the other day that he intends to do a mini-tutorial to explain it later in this meeting, right, Dr. B?" Randall nodded to the crowd. "He calls it his 'Fifteen Minute Quantum Elixir talk' and he has vetted it using his grade school kids. He said they got the idea . . . mostly."

There were a few chuckles from the group. Walker squinted a bit as if doubtful, but sat back down.

Dan nodded. "I understand you all being a bit dubious. I haven't heard the talk yet and I'm wondering if he can get the concept across in 15 minutes, because many physicists, including a certain Dr. Einstein, haven't been able to wrap their heads around it. Albert himself called it 'spooky science.'"

The group members nodded and chuckled. Walker spoke up again. "Ha! And you white folks call our rituals spooky."

Dan nodded and laughed. "You got me there. But here's an observation of mine. What we don't understand, we fear. Like good wine, new and unfamiliar concepts need some time to age in one's brain. I don't expect you to be any more comfortable with quantum ideas than I am with what goes on in a sweat lodge."

Walker nodded his agreement. "Umm. This white man speak truth." That got a laugh from everyone.

After the laughter died down, Dan continued. "I'm glad you think so. I'm sure we are both here for the truth. For you and for everybody here, don't feel bad if you don't get the concepts right away. We'll have made progress if we just get a peek in the window. What quantum theory says is counter to everything you or I have ever been taught in classical physics about the world around us. This will not be a sprint, but a cross-country meet. If we all work together, we can trim that down to a relay race. Any questions?"

The room was quiet for a stretch until Zelda raised her hand. "So, to put it in mommy terms, we'll have to put on our thinking caps."

"Exactly," said Dan. "Now, I'd like to introduce my invitee, Adele Astravanian. Adele, please stand and be recognized."

Adele rose gracefully and smoothed her skirt. She looked poised and confident.

While she stood for everyone to size up, Dan gave a brief biography. "Adele and I both got our degrees at UW and were often study mates. Don't read anything into that. We're both married, but not to each other. Just friends, folks, just friends. Anyway, she focused on particle theory and subatomic physics, while I studied radiation. But the two are so closely bound that you can't really learn one without the other. Much like paired electrons, am I right?"

Dan waited for laughter, but was met with blank stares and an awkward silence. "Ok. . . . too soon, I guess. So without further ado, I present Adele Astravanian."

Adele made a sweeping gesture with her arm so as to encompass the entire group. "Hello, everybody. Before you ask, as you say in this country, I will tell you I am not from around here. When I was ten, my parents move to the US from Leningrad, Russia. My father is also physicist. He was persecuted under Communist rule and forced to leave his country. We almost get caught, but now I am here. Dan is correct. Quantum theory very hard, but like Rice Krispies to my family. Very simple and tasty. As we talk more, I am hopeful to help you understand. I thank for being here."

Adele sat back down. Dan had remained standing in support of Adele and motioned Randall to retake the floor.

Randall took the cue and responded again, channeling his best Bob Barker. "Thanks to you and Adele for agreeing to help with our investigations. Now, let me see. We're getting close on our time limit. If there are no questions for Adele, I must move the intros along. There are two more to go. I believe Joe Shepard has invited both of them, so I'll turn it over to him. Joe?"

Joe got up and joined Randall. "Randall, please stay up here with me and help me wind this up. I guess we'll do ladies first. My wife is responsible for inviting our next new member, Breana Hedley, MDiv, who is the Assistant Pastor and Director of Christian Studies at St. Michael's Lutheran Church in 'Tosa. I will admit that I am not an avid church-goer, but my wife is. Breana teaches a course at the church about the origins of Christianity and has some interesting views on the topic. In the interest of time, I'll leave it there and turn the talking stick over to her."

Breana Hedley rose and made her matronly way to the fireplace. "Hello, everybody. I feel rather out of place without my vestments, but since Dr. Biedermeier isn't wearing his white lab coat, I conclude I can probably remain unfrocked without loss of import. I wasn't sure what to expect from this assemblage. However, I suspect we may all be dealing with the same mystery draped in different clothing and named with different pronouns. As with science, in spiritual matters, truth is studied about and written by men and women. Unfortunately, spiritual studies cannot use the scientific method of experiments and proven results. Our conclusions are always subject to opinion and interpretation. By definition, therefore, it can be subject to flaws. My hope is that this group will seek truth and not some fictionalized version. That's all from me for now. Amen."

When Pastor Hedley turned to Joe after her statement, he found himself at a loss for words, just staring at her. He felt like he'd been hypnotized. Something about her presence made him feel like he was a kid again back in Sunday School. He'd always felt out of place there. After an awkward pause, he stuttered out a response.

"Yeah, right. Amen. Are there any questions for Pastor Hedley?" Joe surveyed the group for a question, but there were only blank stares. The group looked like he felt. Finally he snapped himself out of the weird trance and decided to ask a question to at least seem more professional. "Could you explain what MDiv means?"

Pastor Hedley looked somewhat bemused at the group's response to her little presentation. It had gone exactly as she'd planned. "Certainly, Dr. Shepard." She overemphasized the word "doctor." "It means Master of Divinity. It's the degree one gets after graduation from a four-year divinity school, like Wisconsin Lutheran Seminary, my alma mater."

Joe nodded his understanding. "Thank you, Miss . . . Breana. You've most certainly given us much to consider." He gestured for her to have a seat.

Joe looked around the room trying to identify the last new invitee. He was pretty sure he'd spotted the right man. "Now, our final new member is an invitee of mine. I must admit that I do not know the man personally. I felt we needed someone from a . . . er . . . less traditional spiritual vantage point for comparison and contrast. Therefore, I called the local headquarters of the Christian Science church, explained our purpose, and asked if they could send a representative. They have kindly done so. May I present to you—Dr. Chase Medley."

Chase Medley rose from the couch he was occupying at the front and, with a stately walk, ambled to the fore. He straightened his black suit coat and adjusted his narrow tie before speaking in a gentle Virginia drawl. "Ah, yes. I thank you all for havin' me. Let me explain my correct title. I am not a doctor. Our church has no ordination process. We are all lay leaders. Before I arrived I had little idea what this meetin' would be all about. I merely followed the request of my administrator."

Bingham spoke up loudly from where he was seated in an easy chair near the back of the room. "Hmm. I must say, Medley. Now that you've heard the introductions, have you changed your mind about being a participant in this rather professional group?"

There was some murmuring from the group in response to Bingham's remark, but no one spoke. Medley was used to ridicule and took the barb in stride. "Since you bring it up so forwardly, I must respond in kind. In a sense, you are correct. After hearing the testimony of this group, I am at odds to see how I can contribute much of value. In contrast to the beliefs of our righteous last speaker, Christian Science practitioners believe that only God and the mind have ultimate reality and that sickness is an illusion that can be overcome by faith and prayer. What you seem to be calling nonverbal communication may simply be prayer and the intervention of God. But I will wait and see what path your jargon takes. Any more comments or criticisms?"

Breana Hedley interrupted. "Is it true that you use the Bible for worship but do not believe that Jesus was the savior?"

"That's mostly true, but we do believe that Jesus was holy," clarified Medley. "We feel similarly about Mohammed."

Randall sensed a holy war brewing. Pastor Hedley continued her questioning. "Why do you use the word 'Science' in the name of your religion if you don't believe in medicine?"

Medley was starting to get upset and tried to hide it. "We don't prohibit practitioners going to doctors or dentists, but we do believe prayer is more effective."

Zelda could take no more of Medley's explanations and popped up from the couch. "Why use the term 'Christian' if you don't believe Jesus Christ died for our sins? My grandmother was a follower of Christian Science. She fell and broke her hip and never got medical care. It healed badly and she was in pain until she died. That's hardly Christian!"

Medley backpedaled a bit. "Now, now! I wasn't around when Mary Baker Eddy created the name in 1879. And nothing stopped your grandmother from seeking an orthopedist."

Randall could see it was time to extinguish the burning bush. "Alrighty, folks. Thanks for that lively exchange. By the old clock on the wall I can see that this portion of our meeting must come to a close. Let's take a fifteen minute break. I believe there are some new desserts out on the boarding table and fresh coffee. When we reconvene I will regale you with the grade schoolers' edition of Quantum Elixir. See you then."

Chase Medley shuffled away muttering to himself. The group, grateful for an end to the little dustup, beat a hasty path to the treats. Thankfully, the sugar rush soon soothed the average savage.

Plane Ahead

As Randall and Joe had expected, it took longer than 15 minutes for the group to reassemble in the living room and remain quiet. Apparently, the earlier introductions had ruffled some feathers and there were some 'dynamic interpersonal exchanges of thought' during the break. Off in the kitchen, Randall and Joe had a mini-meeting to decide on next steps.

Joe seemed frustrated. "Randy, this is a tough crowd. I'm tempted to pare us back down to six members. I'm not going to name names, but some of these religious types seem like real nut jobs."

Randall was sympathetic. "You don't need to name names. I can guess a couple of them, but they do add the contrast we can use to our exploratory advantage. I'd leave it for now. Before we summarize our quantum theory, I wonder whether we shouldn't give two more real world examples first."

"Such as?" asked Joe.

Randall looked around to make sure he wasn't being overheard and spoke quietly. "I suggest you tell your treehouse story and I tell my Las Vegas trip story, but I focus on the sunrise in the desert and the Big Voice part. We take no more than five minutes each. I want them to get another taste of these oddball communications before we belabor the group with tough physics."

Joe mused a second and nodded. "Good idea. I'll go with that. Build them up more before making them work. You've already mentioned your baby rescue story, but they've not heard the details yet. We could keep that one in our back pocket if they press for more."

Randall smiled. "I was just kind of thinking how we could use that."

Joe smiled like an evil professor. "Great minds! Or QE?"

Randall laughed. "Yeah. That should get their ears pricked to really concentrate on QE 101. Ready to go back?"

Joe hesitated briefly. "Err, you mentioned posing some kind of dilemma to them for the last hour. What did you have in mind, if I may be so bold?"

Randall put his hand to his forehead like the Great Carnac without the envelope. "At the time I wasn't quite decided, but after seeing their reaction to Elisa's story, I want to play that out further. What do you think? Have you thought of anything better?"

Joe scratched his nose and raised an eyebrow. "Great galloping ghosts. That's what I was hoping you'd say. The only other thing I was thinking is that we've only scratched the surface in our selection of members to represent religious sects. We've left out big chunks, like Judaism, Buddhism and a host of others. But it's not our job to relive the Diet of Worms."

Randall's gut gurgled in response to the reference. "I know that was a meeting of the religious bigwigs in Germany in the 1520s, but it still gives my bowels the heebies when I think of it. The Jesuits at Marquette loved to talk about it. You're right, we need balance. That's why I brought Zelda. She's read enough to know the essence of most of the biggies. I think we have enough clergy here to act as a counterpoint. Maybe we can use Zelda to fend off any doctrinal clashes."

Joe looked convinced. "Gotcha. Sounds like a plan. Let's give a ten-minute warning and resume the *munera*."

"*Munera*? Do we need more on top of the worms?" asked Randall.

Joe shook his head, chuckling. "It's Italian. Really from ancient Rome. It means like a gladiator contest in the colosseum."

Randall looked a bit green. "Sounds like Greek to me. You have no soul, do you?"

Joe looked triumphant and took Randall by the arm, directing him back to the living room where they jointly gave the ten-minute alert.

Story Time

The group seemed to have formed cliques while on break, since the seating arrangements had subtly rearranged. Randall laughed to himself as he recognized old high school group behavior. They were arranged by either ethnic group, belief system, family or friendship. He reasoned that was just the way of things. So be it. Both Randall and Joe stayed standing up front for this session.

Joe began. "Welcome back, everyone. I hope you enjoyed the tasty pastries. Our mental exercises require a lot of unsanctioned fuel. The next hour will be divided into illustrative stories and Dr. B's Quantum Elixir talk. I know you wanted his talk first, but we thought some examples would better whet your appetite and enhance your desire for understanding."

There was some subdued moaning in response to this information. Randall countered that. "Don't worry. The boring hard stuff will come soon enough. Before we get to that, Dr. Shepherd has a tale to tell you. He promised it would only take five minutes. Joe?"

Joe began his treehouse story. He told of how he had fallen out of a tree house as a child and broken some ribs, knocking the breath out of himself. His parents were not nearby, yet he automatically yelled out to them for help but could not make a sound. He went unconscious briefly and awoke to find both parents tending to him. After he found his voice again, he asked how they had found him and they said they had heard him calling for help. He decided not to tell them he hadn't been able to say a word out loud. The group exchanged glances and someone said something about the Twilight Zone.

Joe smiled and looked around the room. "Dr. B, how about you tell your two stories now?"

Randall smiled back at Joe as though they were evil conspirators. "If you liked that story, I've got one that will shiver your timbers."

Zelda erupted with a comment. "That's it, Randy. Give them your testimony."

Randall raised a clenched fist and began. He recounted the essence of the lawnmower incident in Colorado Springs where he received an emergency mental message from his 10-month old daughter, Addie, while he was outside mowing the grass. The message was so clear that he was convinced to stop mowing, run inside and check on her. He found the door to the room blocked. When he was able to push it aside, he found the obstacle was a file cabinet that had somehow moved. Addie was in her bassinet choking from a blanket bunting that had wrapped itself around her neck. Five minutes after he rescued her, Zelda and their son, Kyle, who had just headed out to go shopping, returned home, wondering what had happened to Addie. They had also gotten the red alert!

Roland Walker turned to Zelda. "Is that true? Can you validate that?"

Zelda smiled and nodded. "I sure can. We were driving and suddenly Kyle started yelling for me to turn around and go home, because Addie was in trouble. He was only three years old! I sensed it too, and sped back home. I found Randy on the living room couch holding Addie. She had just stopped crying and was in the sucking air mode."

"Spooky!" muttered Adele. Others nodded in agreement.

Randall continued. "If I hadn't found her when I did, our little girl might have. . . . she was turning blue when I got to her." He allowed a tear to well up for effect.

Walker had another question. "What about the file cabinet? How do you figure it got moved?"

Randall shook his head. "No idea."

"Were there other unusual things happening in the house before that?" asked Walker.

Randall was somewhat surprised by the question. "Umm, yes there were. Lights on that should be off, thermostat turned up, voices in the dark . . . things like that."

Walker put a hand to his heart. "Was there ever a death in the house?"

Now Randall was getting spooked. "Yeah, the previous owner died of cancer. Nobody in the neighborhood knew much about him. He was a loner, but was meticulous about keeping up the house."

Walker muttered something that sounded like it was in his native language, then spoke English. "Sounds like the *anamakiu*, Menominee evil underworld spirit. Usually mischievous but not that harmful. Causes what you white men call a 'haunting.' Owner who died does not want to leave and wants to drive away new owner. What'd you do after?"

Randall shivered. He had not expected this perspective. "An impromptu exorcism," replied Randall before thinking how that might sound in the current setting. "Er, using a Bible."

That got a nonverbal response from Breana Hedley consisting of a poorly stifled laugh. There were looks exchanged around the room. Randall got even more uneasy and looked around the room for rescue.

His gaze landed on Zelda, who shrugged, but Elisa, sitting nearby, raised her hand. "Dr. B, what you describe is not that unusual among my ancestors. The Pascua Yacqui healing witches, or *morea,* are recognized for their great amount of *seataka,* or mental strength. These haunting spirits or *pascolas* are thought to be malignant or children of the devil. The *morea* are the only ones with strong enough *seataka* to expel them. I witnessed my father, who is considered a very strong *morea,* do it many times."

This time Breana Hedley's laugh was not contained. "What a bunch of rubbish! And I can't believe a pedigreed physician like you believes any of it. Of all the...."

Chase Medley joined in the clerical critical commentary. "Looks like you were served an icy glass of *pascola,* Dr. B. Sounds like a fizzy soda to help move your bowels."

There was no laughter outside that of Hedley and Medley. Randall felt the bile rising in his throat. "Very Christ-like, you two. And open minded."

The room was silent enough to hear a mouse fart until Joe Shepard came to the rescue. "Sooo, it seems we have run into a bit of controversy. Randall and I would like to confer on content going forward. We'd like a five minute break to decide that. Take the opportunity to honor your bladders before we resume. Chop chop. Everyone move along."

The group did as they were bade, but not without an undertone of hushed chatter that almost sounded like the soundtrack from a beehive.

Randall and Joe huddled in the kitchen. "Joe, I'd like to suggest something, but I want to run it by you first."

Joe raised his eyebrows. "Alright. Start running."

Randall first looked about the kitchen to be sure there was no one to overhear them. He reviewed Elisa's dilemma about her pregnancy and the Hodgkin's diagnosis to make sure Joe understood it. "I would like Elisa to share her situation with the group, if she is willing to be exposed that much. It could bring out some good discussion that will help us compare and contrast. Plus, it could help her make a decision about what course of action she's most comfortable with."

Joe was a bit unsure at first. But, as he considered the suggestion further, he smiled and nodded his assent. "You know, I think that might work. Let's get her in here and see if she's willing."

Randall found Elisa surveying the food table for strays. He put a hand on her shoulder and asked her to follow him into the kitchen. He and Joe briefly outlined their proposal. To their surprise, Elisa didn't hesitate to agree.

The group was more subdued and seemed ready to resume when the three returned to the living room. Joe Shepard surveyed those seated. "Hmm, it seems we are two members short. Looks like the Hedley medley has left the stage. No worries. I think we've gotten the gist of what they represent."

"Yeah, and gist in time," came a disembodied voice from the back of the room. That evoked a round of chuckles, as folks looked for the ventriloquist.

Joe pointed to Randall standing beside him. "Roll 'em, Lester. Tell us about the Vegan desert."

Randall raised both arms like a game show host. "Thanks, Joe. I'll do my best to keep it succinct. This all started when I was *voluntold* by my boss to attend a lung cancer research meeting in Las Vegas. It wasn't on my list of favorite things, but when has that ever mattered?" That comment evoked a round of chuckles.

Randall did an impressive job of keeping the story short enough to resemble a campfire story, where you try to finish before the s'mores are burned to ash. All eyes were wide when he finished by pulling the IY rock out of his pocket and displaying it. There was much *oohing* and *aahing*. He asked for volunteers to offer their opinions as to the lesson of the tale.

Elisa raised her hand. "This may be cheating, because I've heard Dr.

B's story before, but the meaning rings true to what we've already heard tonight. That is, if we are seeking truth we can find it already right here inside of us." She put her hand to her heart. "Even if you look 'out there' for the answers, the 'out there' will tell us to look inside. The 'out there' and the 'in here' are one in the same when you consider the nature of the way our world is made up of the same tiny subatomic particles of energy." She paused to look at the astounded faces in the room. She mistook their awe for lack of understanding. "In other words, all and everything is connected by its very nature. I may not be using the terms correctly, but Dr. B is about to explain it to us."

Randall raised both arms as if in triumph. "Elisa, I couldn't have said it much better."

The crowd agreed with nods and hums. "That made it much more understandable!" came a voice from the back.

Randall put his hands together as if in prayer. "That makes a great segue for me to move on. Before I do, are there any questions?"

Simon Escaliente rose. "I wonder. Do you think there is any local Nevada Native American lore that correlates with your experience?"

Randall frowned. "I'm not an expert on the topic, but I would guess there may be. Mr. Walker, any thoughts?"

When Walker stood, he seemed stronger and taller than his physical body alone. "There is more here than you can see with your eyes and your logic. I have been a long time follower of the teachings of Rolling Thunder, a Shoshone Shaman from the deserts of Nevada. His white man's name was John Pope and he worked for the railroad. Anthropologist Doug Boyd wrote about his Shamanic practices. Rolling Thunder believed in a desert spirit and invoked it in ceremonies. His rituals were for healing, making rain, death ceremonies and much else."

The crowd was silent, taking in the presence of this man who now seemed bigger than life, and more mysterious than the science they knew. Walker took another meaningful breath, drawing them all in. "I tell my wife I want to be like him. She says to keep trying, because so far, I am just Roland Blunder."

The group gave a hearty laugh at this self-deprecating remark.

Randall walked over and touched Walker's shoulder. "Thanks, Roland. I am sure your wife is only half right. Any more questions?"

John Bingham, the psychiatrist, spoke up. "Where do you think the voice and other sounds came from? Did they sound like they came from outside yourself or from inside?"

Randall thought. "Hard to tell. Almost like both at once. I know what you're thinking. Some kind of hallucination or seizure. Namely, an organic disorder unique to me. I considered that, but given there was no postictal state or reoccurrence of the event, it seems less likely. That's why we included someone of your background. I'd like to explore that with you in more detail."

"Sound thinking," said Bingham. "From what I've seen, you seem unusual, but not pathologic. But I reserve a final conclusion."

Randall nodded, surprised that Bingham had stuck around and was curious. "Fair enough. Now, if there are no more questions, let's move on to the Quantum Elixir talk."

Dan Graham stood up. "Before you start, I have a request. Next time you go to Vegas, can I give you some quarters for the slots? Oh, and if you get stuck on any quantum details, Adele and I are here to help."

Randall laughed. "Heck, you can give me dollars. And conversely, if I mess anything up, feel free to correct me."

"Quarters will do and I've prepared my spitballs," shot back Dan.

Randall wasted no time running through the Quantum Elixir talk, aided and abetted by Dan and Adele. He covered most of the main points. He used tennis balls to represent the spinning electrons. Electrons could become paired through quantum entanglement. Such pairings occur in biology, including in the brain, and could be the on-off switches that control transmission and receipt of non-verbal signaling. Such signaling may occur between some as yet unidentified part of our subconscious brains. We all have the ability, but it manifests more strongly in some. The group raised many questions and he made valiant attempts to make things clear. In the end, Randall was mostly convinced that the main points were mostly understood.

Randall let out a loud breath when he finished his quantum summary.

"We can't go any deeper right now, folks. Consider this just a primer we can build upon. We have one more session left for today. Before I give you another body break, are there any spinning electron questions?"

Ruby Cosgrove rose and stretched gracefully, drawing some admiring male glances. "It seems to me that what Elisa and Roland described about their Native American Shamans, what was it, having *seataka*, or mental strength, sets them apart. It rather dovetails with your concept of all of us having different levels of ability to communicate nonverbally through our subconscious connectivity."

Joe added in. "Yeah! I was just thinking the same thing. We all have it, but to different degrees."

Ruby continued. "This may sound like I'm honking my own horn, but I think that's an ability I've always had. Since I was a child. That's one reason I became a nun. I could always read people. And it's what I do now with my Yoga clients. I read their energy which connects directly to their physical and mental state. In another life my *seataka* could have made me a Shaman. If I told some of the things I've done and seen it wouldn't sound so different."

Randall looked like he was having a mini-epiphany. "That's . . . that's really interesting. I want to know more about how you read people's energy. But we'll have to explore that further when we have more time. Thanks for sharing that."

Zelda spoke up. "Ruby, us girls need to talk!"

Randall felt some time pressures, so he urged the Queen Mary forward like he was the little tugboat that could. "Anybody else?"

Adele wanted in and rose to speak. "It ironic, you know. A long time I study subatomic physics. The deeper I go, I get feeling that I study what is infinite. It is eternal, not just finite science that we can understand it all. It start, to me, to feel spiritual. In physics literature, I now find many physicists who write books saying they find spiritual meaning in physics. I think these people who write such books crazy. Then, I think, I have much real physics to read. No time for nonsense. Now, I am older and I think, maybe, such ideas not so crazy. Maybe I see why they say these things. Now, I must read these books."

Adele sat back down. Randall stood silent, not quite knowing what to say as he rolled her comments around in his mind to digest them.

Joe was quite taken by what some would call a testimony of faith. He thanked Adele for her insight. "I find your candor quite refreshing, Adele. That's just the open-mindedness we are looking for. I'm afraid we need to cut things off here. Please, everybody, do what you need to. This time, come back in ten minutes. We will close with a one-hour session during which Randall and I will pose a special problem for you to help us solve."

CHAPTER 30

TRUTH BE TOLD

The more things change, the more things change.

—Not Telling

ROCK THE ROOM

With much shuffling about and chatter, the group, now down to ten members, returned to their seats. Randall was surprised there were no more defectors. He didn't get too overconfident, reasoning that the food and drink alone, not to mention entropy, could be a significant enough reason for some simply to stay. However, as he looked about the room, everyone looked quite expectant, a sign their collective curiosity had been aroused.

Joe clinked his attention glass and quiet was restored. "As promised, Dr. B and I will now pose a dilemma for you to discuss and, hopefully, help us resolve."

Before Joe could continue, Roland Walker rose somewhat noisily to speak. "Please excuse me, but during the break I was recalling some Shoshone folklore. If Dr. B still has the desert rock in his pocket, I wonder if he could pass it over to me?"

Randall patted his pants pocket. "Yeah, it's right here. Go ahead and take a closer look." He handed the rock to Adele to pass it down the line.

Adele took a moment to examine the stone more carefully. It was the size of an egg and mostly dark gray except for embedded white limestone layers, sort of like the white cream filling inside an Oreo cookie. The white layers spelled out 'IY.' "Wow! Rock is toasty!" she exclaimed. "You must have hot pocket in your pants." She got up quickly and handed the stone to Walker.

Randall shook his head. "Nah. I'm just really hot stuff." This evoked a collective groan.

Walker inspected the stone closely and suddenly dropped it. "*Koqtam keqsiw*! This thing is hot stuff, too! Nearly burn my hand. Someone else pick it up."

Dan Graham got up and went over to where the stone lay on the carpet. It had made no mark he could detect. He touched the stone gingerly with his forefinger. "Feels alright to me. Maybe a bit warm. Let's see your hand." Dan examined Walker's hand and found a barely visible red mark on the palm. "Red mark on the palm. Maybe a faint 'IY' imprint. What the heck? Dr. B, take a look at this."

Walker shook his hand and the room buzzed with excitement. Randall confirmed Dan's findings and took the stone from Dan. "Dang thing feels the same as before. Holy simoleons! Okay. This wasn't the dilemma I was planning on. Does anybody have a clue what just happened?"

There was a room full of head shaking, but no answers were offered except for a comment from Ruby Cosgrove. "It reminds me of the statue of Mary Magdalene that cried tears of blood. I never got over that one."

Walker raised his affected hand. "This is just like what I remember about Shoshone from reading about Rolling Thunder. Their clan lived for many years in the Nevada desert and mountain lands. They believe there are places of spiritual power, what they call *puha*, where one can pray for personal power or give thanks for answered prayers. Only the Shamans know where these votive places are, so they mark them with stones they etched with symbols. They also used stones, like this one, that the spirits of the mountain have formed for them."

The room was silent, taking this in. Zelda raised a hand. "Do we know how far back in time the Shoshone were doing this?"

Walker nodded. "Some archeologists believe it goes back big years, like 400,000. Way before white men take the land. Shoshone believe that *puha* is a living force that moves through our universe. It has no boundaries or fences. It is not divided between animals, plants or rocks. All have it and all these are considered 'people' talking one language."

Zelda let out a big breath. "Gee. That reminds me of the joke where Gandhi gets so thirsty that he walks into a bar for refreshment. The bartender asks him what he'd like to drink. Gandhi says 'Make me one with everything.' The bartender says 'I thought you already were.'"

Randall laughed. "Not quite the way I heard it, but apropos."

Elisa rose with a question for Walker. "When these Shoshone Shaman went to the *puha* points and prayed for something, what did they commonly ask for? And did they have to bring a sacrifice or something of value?"

Walker thought for a moment. "Wait. Let me think. I don't recall that animal sacrifices or valuables were offered. That's what the etched stones were for. The stones took many hours to make, but had no true value except as symbols. And the stones like yours, made by many years of geologic activity, were very hard to find, but, again, of no value for trading or buying things. These 'old stones' formed by natural forces were highly prized and used for the biggest asks like healing or bountiful hunting. The archeologists say the use of such stones as offerings have an 'asymmetrical' relationship with the request. Much gained for very little."

Roland Walker suddenly began to appear 'asymmetrical.' There was more there than initially met the eye. Randall and the members looked at the man with fresh eyes. Joe was next to enter the conversation. "So far we have no obvious explanation why others have easily handled the rock, and only Mr. Walker had been 'branded' by it. Mr. Walker, do you have any idea, based on Native American lore or anything else, why you were chosen for getting the hot potato treatment?"

Walker shrugged. "Umm, I've got some theories. Nothing that's fully worked out. Let me try some thinking out loud. It may be that Dr. B was led to a place of great *puha* in the desert. When did it start? Perhaps on the airplane or even before. His boss was going to go to Vegas, but plans changed to make Dr. B go instead. The power may have made him afraid and nervous. It led him to the desert with a Bible passage and alerted him with unusual sounds. He prayed for answers and the sacred stone answered in a loud voice. He chose to listen. Many would be afraid and push it away. He did not."

Simon Escaliente commented. "Many hear, but few listen."

Randall let that all sink in. "Okay. But why the difference in heat between the two of us? Does that mean you have a better connection than I do?"

Walker raised his hands palm up. "I have no answer for everything as yet. Maybe I just have more practice or was born with a better receiver, as you suggested in your talk of quantum entanglements. Perhaps we can put things to a test by passing the IY stone around the room, but very carefully this time."

Joe acted on Walker's suggestion. "So, let's take a vote. All in favor of continuing to pass the stone, raise your hand."

Everybody raised a hand except Walker. The group turned to look at him, somewhat surprised. He shrugged and commented. "What? Last time I passed a stone that hurt me this much it came from my kidney." He paused for effect. "Wisdom would say I've already handled the stone and I don't need extra proof that it burned me. Why should I get a vote?"

There was some forehead slapping and a few groans as the group saw the logic. Joe wished he had a gavel to garner attention, but resorted to dinging his juice glass again. "Alright, folks. The vote is unanimous for more stone passing. However, I'd like to present the dilemma to solve before we do that and then pass the stone around. As you each get the stone to hold, you'll discuss your idea for solving the dilemma. Does that sound alright with everyone? Randall?"

Randall and the members nodded their agreement. There were no objections to continuing, but some concerns about what holding the stone might do. After some discussion it was decided just to be cautious. Plus, each stone holder would get a stone buddy wearing gloves to remove the stone from the holder's hand if anything weird or dangerous happened.

Dilemma Time

Randall had possession of the stone again. It was back in his pants pocket. "Does anybody need a break before we venture forth with the moral/ethical dilemma? We are running a bit long. I don't want to cut off any discussion. Are we all alright with running over about 10 minutes, if needed?"

No one had bowel or bladder issues and they were too hooked on proceeding to have things cut short. The consensus was to proceed at flank speed.

Joe began the dilemma. "In our very finite wisdom, Randall and I have decided that the conundrum we'll work on will be regarding our new member, Elisa Angeles." Eyebrows went up but Elisa looked unaffected. "If that's copacetic with her," he added. Elisa nodded her approval.

Randall continued. "Elisa briefly mentioned her problems earlier this evening. Instead of me explaining the dilemma, I'll ask her to present the details. She can better express the full impact of how it affects her life. Elisa?"

Elisa did not hesitate and stood up immediately. The members applauded politely and some of the women looked a tad tearful. Zelda shouted. "You go, girl!"

Elisa took a deep breath and began. She started with her pride in landing the job at the VA. Then she described her initial excitement of engagement dulled by the unexpected pregnancy and the meritless departure of her erstwhile fiance. The tale segued into the diagnosis of Hodgkin's disease complicating the pregnancy and the difficult decision of whether to have immediate treatment and risk the viability of the fetus or to save herself with possible sacrifice of the child. As expected, her portrayal was accompanied by all the appropriate emotional responses from the group. There was sniffing, swearing, eye wiping, and some muffled sobbing in the room.

Elisa's story came to an end and she stood quietly making sure she hadn't left out anything important. "Well . . . that's pretty much the whole story. I suppose I should ask if there are questions."

Simon Escaliente was first to offer comment. "No questions, just a request. Give me the address of that *cabrón* boyfriend of yours. I'd like to have a mind-altering discussion with him."

The comment acted as a comic relief valve. There was some bitter laughter and offers from some of the members to alter non-brain portions of the boyfriend's anatomy.

Randall took the floor again and thanked Elisa for her willingness to share such an intimate story. He motioned for her to be seated again. "I suggest we each take the Talking Stone in turn and hold it for a few minutes with eyes closed. You know, like you're concentrating or meditating on it. Then, tell us what you're sensing. After that, give us your take on a solution to the dilemma. And make sure your Stone Buddy is ready to take a hand off, if needed. Is there anything else before we steam ahead?"

Joe surveyed the room for issues but found none. "Sounds like a plan to me. Like most battle plans, we'll be prepared to change strategies after the first skirmish. Randall, let's get this train rolling."

Escaliente suddenly raised a hand. "What if we don't have a solution worked out after we have all held the rock?"

Randall responded. "According to Hoyle or Mr. Murphy, you choose, no answer is an answer. All in favor, display your extended upper extremities." All hands rose.

Randall looked pleased. "Brilliant! Unanimity is good. So, who wants to hold the 'Talking Stone' first?"

Romancing the Stone

Randall had put on his winter gloves and served as perpetual stone buddy. Surprisingly, John Bingham volunteered to go first. He walked up to the front and bravely put out his hand to take the Talking Stone. After a few seconds, he began juggling it from hand to hand. "Damn thing is freezing. Take it away before I get frostbite."

Randall motored right over and took back the stone. He touched it with his ungloved hand and, again, there was no difference in temperature from when he'd first removed it from his pocket. "Dr. Bingham, can you tell us what you felt?"

Bingham looked dazed. "I think I've just been derailed by Mr. Murphy. That was one of the strangest things that's ever happened to me. Not only was that sucker cold as liquid nitrogen, I felt like the hand of death was on my shoulder. My spine still feels tingly. Am I going crazy? What does it mean?"

Joe and Randall shrugged their shoulders as everyone looked to them for an answer. Randall broke the questioning silence. "No idea, folks. Before now, my little rock was just that. A rock." He decided to invoke statistics. "I think we need more data. Let's move on to the next question. What are your thoughts about the dilemma and were they influenced by the stone?"

Bingham looked around the room as if the answer might be there somehow. "I guess . . . I mean, I believe . . . that I hadn't appreciated the gravity of Elisa's problems until I felt that death grip. Now, I think I understand how afraid she is for both herself and her unborn child. During the big chill, all I could think of was to grab life with both hands and hang on . . . for dear life . . . as it were."

There was a round of conversational chattering from the group. Joe took the floor and gestured for people to calm down. "Folks . . . Randall and I are just as baffled as you are. Thank you, Dr. Bingham, for being so candid. If I may be so bold, I think we have one vote to save both mother and child. Would that be a fair conclusion?"

Bingham nodded. "Indubitably!"

Randall tossed the stone in the air and caught it a few times. "Alrighty then. Who's my next involuntary volunteer?"

Dan Graham rose and joined Randall and Joe. "I've held Rocky Squirrel briefly, but not meditated upon it. I'll give that a try before I make my pronouncement. Give it to me."

Dan took the somewhat iconic rock in both hands, closed his eyes and meditated for a good two minutes, while the crowd got antsy. Dan opened his eyes and started sniffing the air. "Smells like your wife is brewing fresh coffee. All this meditating has made me sleepy. I could use a good wake up. What blend is it? I want some."

Joe looked puzzled. "Er, my wife has gone shopping. Nobody is brewing anything. I don't smell coffee. Does anybody else?"

There was lots of head shaking. As Dan realized he was the only one experiencing the aroma, his jaw dropped. "It's this damn rock! Or my smeller is performing hat tricks. Another stupefied customer!"

Randall had to laugh. "Brings new meaning to 'wake up and smell the coffee.' What were your other thoughts?"

Dan was a bit circumspect. "When I first smelled it, I felt like I was just waking up in the morning and was happy with the start of a new day. I don't wake up like that very often. I just felt glad to be alive. Do you suppose? Oh, yeah. That's got to be the message. And it was what I was thinking anyhow. Choose life!"

The group applauded and whistled. Dan smiled and pumped a fist. "Here, Randall, take this freaking rock back before I go coffee crazy. I want some French Roast!"

Randall relieved Dan of the rock and thanked him for his testimony. "Now, who's next? Don't all crowd to the front at once or there could be injuries."

Escaliente slow-stepped forward and put out his hand for the stone. He made a show of caressing it and then held it close to his chest with eyes closed. He waited for something to happen and sensed nothing different until he opened his eyes and looked down. He saw a yellow glow coming from the stone. His eyes went wide and he held it out on his palm as if on display. The group waited for some comment but he said nothing.

Escaliente finally shouted. "It took my speech away, too! Hardly anything shuts me up. See how lovely it is? The light is so soothing and refreshing."

"The light?" queried Joe.

"Yes, the light," said Escaliente. "See how the rock glows yellow and white? It makes me feel so peaceful."

Randall shook his head, then smiled. "Simon! You are the only one who can see that. The stone looks the same to us."

Escaliente's mouth went wide. " ¡Dios mío! Holy Mary, Mother of God! It is happening to me also! I get it. I get it! Light! Life! *Tienes que dar la luz.* The baby must see the light. It is so clear. How did I not see what I was seeing? Here, Dr. B. Take back this precious thing." He placed the stone into the nest of Randall's gloved hand and walked slowly back to his chair with his hand on his forehead.

Joe and Randall were temporarily at a loss. Joe finally carried on. "Well, we may not have seen everything yet. Next guinea pig?"

There was the same *ventrickled* voice from the back of the room again. "You go, Joe."

Joe shrugged and took the stone from Randall. Despite being one of the masters of ceremony, he looked a bit apprehensive as he did his closed eyes meditation. After a minute or so, he suddenly opened his eyes and turned his head towards the kitchen. Abruptly he yelled out. "Mom, I'm in here. I'm in the middle of a big meeting . . . holy shit!" He looked around in confusion.

"What's going on?" asked Randall.

"Oh, not much," squeaked Joe. "I just heard my mother saying hello from the kitchen."

"You did? Then you better go check on her," said Randall. "I must have missed it."

Joe's head sagged. "Not possible. My mother passed away two years ago."

"You sure it was her voice?" asked Randall.

"Oh, yeah," said Joe. "There's no mistaking it. From what I've seen so far tonight, I shouldn't be surprised. It must be part of my message. Let me think what it could be."

Zelda popped a question. "What was your mother like?"

Joe shook his head. "Like no one else. She was everybody's cheerleader and wouldn't hurt a fly . . . literally. Almost Buddhist. Frowned on killing spiders or stepping on ants. Oh, moldering mudslides. That's it. Respect all life. And she heard me when I whisper-yelled after falling out of the tree house."

Randall added on. "Your father did too. Maybe he's out in the kitchen."

Joe shook his head. "Not him. He was a hunter and fisherman. Despised insects. He'd never message me on this issue. I guess we have another notch for pro-life. I don't like to hallucinate. Take this thing back."

Randall took the stone. "I think we might be doing a disservice to my rock calling what it causes hallucinations, but that's just my opinion. Next candidate?"

There was a buzz of murmuring and muttering before Adele came forward. "I guess I'll go. No one has been harmed. Embarrassed maybe. That I am used to."

Adele's robust form drew some attention from the XY contingent. She took the rock gingerly in one hand and held it to her side while she meditated. It wasn't long before a small trickle of saliva rolled from mouth to chin and she grasped the rock so tightly her fingers turned white. Her face looked quite intense. She looked to be in a deep trance.

It had been well past three minutes when Randall decided to snap his fingers in an effort to rouse her. There was only a slight response to the snap, so he tapped her shoulder and she came awake. "Good morning, sunshine," said Randall. "You were down for the count. What was happening?"

Adele's face was shiny. "This was craziness. I was in Willy Wonka chocolate factory. I lay on my stomach sipping chocolate from the chocolate river when you poke me. Now, everybody here know the secret. I am chocoholic. If I don't eat many Milky Way bar, maybe I look more like Ruby than Oompa-Loompa."

Escaliente offered a different opinion. "You look nothing like an Oompa-Loompa. We Hispanic men like women with some meat on their bones. What are you doing after the meeting?" There was some hooting and catcalls.

Adele laughed. "Family must approve first. I have very big brothers. Oh, yes, and a rather largish husband."

Escaliente wasn't fazed. "Bring them on. You must meet my family also."

Randall tried to regain control. "Now, now, children. Let's behave. Adele, please contribute your recommendations for Elisa."

Adele turned to face Elisa and smiled broadly. "Oh, that's not a tough one. The question is not what life is without chocolate, but what chocolate is without life? Answer is we need both. Both mother and child must live. Signs telling us if mother wait to have baby until it ready to join world, then life will reward her for the risk to her own life to save baby. It say trust and have faith that both live and prosper. I hope this make sense."

Elisa could not help herself. "You are making perfect sense, Adele. You are so sweet in so many ways. Thank you."

Adele announced that her time was up and she pointed to Ruby. "You must go now. I very anxious what little stone does for you."

Randall agreed and soon Ruby was playing with the family stone. About halfway through her two-minute session, the hand holding the stone literally began to vibrate. Soon it was so intense she had to open her eyes and hand the stone back to Randall.

Randall took the stone and it became quite still once more. "You looked like you were having trouble holding on to the stone. Your hand was shaking like a paint mixer. What was happening?"

"It wasn't my hand, it was the stone," said Ruby. "It felt like I was trying to hold a buzzing pager. In my mind I kept repeating vibrate, vibrate.... Then it switched to vibrant...vibrant.... Then I couldn't help but think 'life is vibrant.' We feel the heartbeat of life inside. It tells us life is right there vibrating in our presence. Another bit of magic message. I think my vote is clear. I'm right there with Adele."

There was more applause and some whistles. Even Joe was smiling, not a common finding. Randall looked even more pleased. "Well, folks, we are running low on candidates. And, since we seem to be on a run of XX chromosomes, I'm going to select my wife Zelda for the next stone holder. Zelda, take it away!"

An energized Zelda sprang out of her chair and almost skipped to the front. She took the stone from Randall without hesitation, closed her eyes, and mimicked the prayer of the seven directions. She held the stone up high with both hands as she rotated briefly to each direction. When she finished the first four rotations, she held the stone to her heart for several minutes. Time seemed suspended and there were muffled whispers from the group. Suddenly her eyes popped open and she stared directly at Elisa like she was sending forth two laser beams. Elisa met her gaze and rose to her feet. The two stood staring at each other for a long moment. The whispering grew in intensity. Finally, Zelda let out a huge breath and both visibly relaxed.

Randall went to Zelda's side and relieved her of the stone. "So, wife of mine, can you enlighten us?"

Zelda shook her head and smiled weakly. "No. The conversation was just between us girls."

Randall knew that smile and calculated that Zelda was just taunting him and the group. He decided to fight the taunting with indifference. "So be it. You can just keep it confidential if you wish. What does the group say?"

The group hooted and booed its disapproval. Zelda felt herself going from hero to zero and bailed out. "Just kidding! What'll you give me for telling?"

The ventriloquist voice shouted from the back of the room. "We'll let you go home unbruised."

Zelda nodded. "That's excellent motivation. Alright. I'll do the reveal. Randy, you know that I've seen colored auras before, but the group doesn't know that. And it's okay if none of you believe me. But, when I held the stone, even before I opened my eyes, I 'saw' a green aura surrounding Elisa. There was a smaller red and orange aura right where the baby should be. Both auras were very intense. Could anybody else see it?"

Only one hand went up. It was Elena's. "I saw it, but not until you opened your eyes. I don't get how that worked, but it was what it was. I wasn't holding the stone, but I am her sister, so. . . . I guess that means I didn't have to hold the stone to see the result of your connection to Elisa.

I think the meaning of the aura is pretty clear to me. I'm not familiar with what aura colors mean, but I've got a feeling that green means life."

Zelda nodded. "I'm just a student of Yoga, but from what I know, I believe you are quite correct. Ruby's an expert. Let's ask her."

Ruby nodded. "This is right up my alley. You are both right on the money. Green represents the heart chakra and red the root chakra which connects us to the earth. Orange represents the sacral chakra, the source of new life and creativity. It tells me the baby already has its own spiritual energy. It would be abhorrent to nature to stifle that little bud."

Zelda and Elisa shared broad smiles. Elisa expanded on the phenomenon. "That whole time Zelda was staring at me, I could feel a warmth inside my belly. Kind of like I was part of everything around me. I can't explain it any better than that. All I can say is I feel like I could live forever."

The room became as silent as a stalking cat. It seemed like everyone was playing brain badminton with the new information and trying to figure out where it fit in their concept of life and the universe.

Randall was doing the same, then realized someone had to take the helm again. "Alright folks. That was a whole lot to take in. I'm still trying to process it. Let me just take a moment to ask if there are any further comments about the mother and child auras."

After a few seconds of head shaking from the group, Escaliente stood and blurted out a question. "I don't get why those two were the only ones to see the light. How do we know they weren't in cahoots to fake us out?"

Walker rose in response. "Are you daft, man? You weren't holding the rock and you are not her sister. Why would those two want to fake this? If you can't see the truth when it is right in front of you, you have no business in this group."

There was scattered applause from the group. Randall sensed it was time to move along the expository route again and not take the road to conflict. "Thanks for those opinions, but time dictates we must move along. Who's next to hold the stone? Raise a hand."

Zelda sat back down, but Elisa remained standing and raised her hand. "I haven't actually held the stone yet and neither have you, Dr. B."

Randall objected. "I have held it. It was in my pocket and I've been handing it around."

"Yes, but you haven't meditated with it," said Elisa. "So, I think it's your turn. Then I'll go."

Randall retracted the corner of his mouth. "Alright, have it your way. After all, you are the hour's person of honor."

Zelda rose and returned the stone to Randall. He held it firmly in both hands. First he raised it to the sky, then he rotated on his heel 360 degrees. It was sort of an abbreviated prayer of the seven directions. He finished by holding it to his temple with closed eyes. His body relaxed noticeably.

The back door of the house slammed shut and Joe's wife came back from shopping. She hollered "Honey, I'm home!"

Randall dropped the stone on the floor and shouted "What the hell was that noise?"

The entire group burst into uproarious laughter and Randall looked like he'd just been caught with his pants down. The laughter died down when Joe's wife came into the living room to see what the ruckus was all about. "Sorry, Joe. It's after 5:00. I thought your meeting was supposed to be over." Her transatlantic accent indicated she was used to a particular level of class and composure.

Joe was taken aback and stammered. "Ye . . . ess, honey, you're right. We've been running a tad late. We're just finishing up. Uh, Randall just told us a joke."

Joe's wife smiled. "Must have been a funny one. Can I hear it?"

Joe looked to Randall for help.

Randall thought quickly and improvised. "Sure, I can tell it again. In high school I got a bit part in the class play about the War of 1812. At the start of the play, I was to come out on stage alone in a soldier's uniform, then a recording of loud cannon fire was to go off backstage. After that, my line was 'Hark, hear the cannons roar.' It was my only line. I rehearsed it over and over at home so I wouldn't screw it up. For rehearsal, we didn't use the recording, but for the play we did. So for the first performance I went out on stage on cue, the cannons went off 'Kaboom!'and I yelled out 'What the hell was that noise?'"

The group burst out in laughter again, as if they'd not heard the joke before. Joe's wife joined in. When she finally stopped laughing, she wiped her eyes. "That really is funny."

Joe carried on the ruse. "Believe me, it's even funny the second time you hear it."

Joe's wife turned to leave the room. "Well, I'll leave you all to it."

Zelda shouted after her. "Thanks for all the great grub, Mrs. S."

"Don't thank me. Thank the caterer and Joe's now thinner wallet." Her voice trailed off as she walked down the hall.

Joe turned to Randall. "Nice save, partner. Let's get back to business. Please debrief us on what your rather strange session yielded."

Randall had to think momentarily to recall his vision. "Okay, sure . . . Believe it or else, I was not time traveling back to high school as my joke would suggest. My magic rock ride was a mental scene of a family singing 'Happy Birthday' and I was visualizing a kitchen table holding a birthday cake and one candle. I'm not really sure, but I think it was my mother's kitchen and her baking. It was all Good Housekeeping magazine until the dulcet tones of your wife interrupted my vision."

There was some chuckling and murmuring from the peanut gallery. Elisa spoke first. "Aha, I was right. I knew it would work on you. You never gave your rock the chance to speak to you by actually meditating on it. It may not have worked as easily for you removed from its special place of power in the desert. So what does your vision mean to you?"

Randall searched his thoughts. "I guess you can't have a birthday party for a baby who's never been born. In my vision the baby is one year old. And there's a mother there to bake the cake. To me the message is that your baby wants that one year old birthday cake and its mother to bake it."

Elisa smiled and nodded. "Seems pretty clear to me."

Escaliente played Devil's advocate again. "What you all are concluding from these vague imaginings sound like fortune cookie messages.

The messages are ambiguous enough to be interpreted any way that fits what you'd like to hear."

Walker had a riposte ready. "You're entitled to your own opinion, Escaliente. Mine is that the message received from the rock is unique to each person who holds it. It helps you find what you truly desire. It's the catalyst that releases the answer that is in your heart. It opens the path for you to seek and find."

Escaliente turned a bit red and muttered. *"No digas disparates!"*

Walker responded in kind. *"Ishaveka!"*

It was time for Randall to blow his referee's whistle. "Clearly we have some disagreement here. You two can take it outside, if needed, after the meeting. My beartrap-like memory tells me Elisa is last to play 'hold the stone.' Am I right?"

Elisa grinned, her face glowing with a soft light. "Yes, now it's my turn. I hope there are no more disputes. So far this rock holding has been quite revealing to me even if we don't all agree on what it reveals."

Elisa made her way past some chairs to the front. There were encouraging nods and glances from the group members. As Elisa stood up front and settled herself for the holding ceremony, the crowd went silent. She simply took the stone in both hands and held it to her belly. With closed eyes, she bowed her head.

Soon, she began to speak softly, but the words were crystal clear to everyone. *"Hola, hijo mío.* Hello to you too, my baby. *Sí, sí, estoy bien.* Yes, I am fine, baby of mine. *Sí, todo estará bien.* Yes, all will be well. *Conocemos pronto.* We will meet face to face soon enough. *No te preocupes.* Do not worry. *Tenemos amigos y familia.* We are not alone. Feel peaceful as I do."

Then, there was quiet.

The quiet settled as a blanket over the room. The conflicting beliefs and values that had ruffled feathers earlier descended as if it were a comforting quilt of compassion. Unconditional love became the hub that unified each of the participants. This eased the ending of the meeting into a sweetness that flowed out the door and into the homes of each participant as they repaired to their own orbits. Separate, yet still entangled.

CHAPTER 31

———

SYNCHRONICITY

Born, there will be, a baby boy. A font, he will be, of endless joy.

—Kyle Biedermeier

BUSHWHACKED

When Randall and Zelda returned home from the QEG meeting, it was almost an hour later than they had promised Mrs. Bush that they'd be home. They found her at the kitchen table playing Go Fish with Kyle and Addie.

Mrs. Bush rose from her chair and looked relieved. She was worse for wear after spending an afternoon with the kids. "Thank goodness you're home. These little upstarts are creaming me at Go Fish. I can't figure how they do it. I hope your meeting went well." Her thin lips clipped the words.

Zelda went over and hugged both kids. "Well enough. I hope you guys were good for Mrs. Bush."

Addie stood up straight, her hands to her heart. "We were angels."

Kyle stepped in front of Addie. "*She* was an angel. I was a gentleman."

Addie squealed. "You always try to correct me. You're so obstinate. Mrs. Bush said so."

Randall laughed. "So you learned a new word today? Sorry we're late. We got hung up with all kinds of questions after the meeting. It was

717

hard to break away. Mrs. Bush, thanks for the overtime and putting up with these two."

The praise made Mrs. Bush straighten up to her full six feet. Her height and her tight hair bun could make her seem rather intimidating. She reminded Randall of his old high school English teacher who controlled class deportment with a ruler. "Oh, I've managed worse. I raised five kids, you know. These two are no problem for me to handle. For kids their age, they're rather smart."

Zelda looked a bit surprised. "Oh, really? I hope you don't mean they smarted off to you. Anything we should know about?"

Mrs. Bush hesitated as if she had something to share, but then seemed to think better of it. "Nothing worth mentioning. I'd better run. Fred just called wondering if I'd ever feed him dinner. I swear, the poor man would starve without me pointing out the food."

Randall laughed and offered to pay Mrs. Bush for her trouble. She put up a hand. "Oh, posh! That's not necessary. I had more fun with Addie and Kyle than if I'd spent the day with Fred watching reruns on TV. I swear, that man...." She was out the door before the sentence was finished.

"Did you kids have fun?" asked Randall.

Kyle nodded. "Yeah, pretty much. Especially when we were whacking her fanny at Go Fish."

"But she says some weird stuff sometimes," observed Addie, her little eyebrows screwed into squiggles.

"Like what?" asked Zelda.

Addie scrunched up her face. "She said she was a daughter of the American *rebelution* or some word like that."

Zelda looked puzzled and then figured it out. "Oh, I think I know. The word is Revolution. She means she's related to people who fought in the American Revolution. It's a big thing with her." That did nothing to clear it up for either kid and they looked even more confused. "Don't worry about it. Your teachers will explain it in high school."

Kyle waved it off. "I don't care if I ever know."

"Me either," said Addie. "I'm glad you and Dad had a great meeting."

Randall cocked his head. "What makes you think it was great?"

"Because," said Addie. Sometimes one word from her held gravitas uncommon for such a small child.

Kyle stuck out his tongue and rolled his eyes. "Well, duh! Because Elisa decided to let the baby get older so it can be born."

"And you guys look happy," added Addie.

Randall felt his jaw drop. "Have you two been having a séance with Yoda and Uni or something? We haven't said anything about Elisa. Did she call here?" Both kids suddenly looked guilty and shook their heads.

Zelda looked at them wide eyed. "Then how do you know about the baby?"

Kyle backpedaled a bit and looked from side to side. "I guess we just know that's what she would do. Isn't that right, Sis?"

Addie felt put on the spot, so she just nodded assent.

Zelda thought briefly. "I guess that makes sense, but you two seem so sure about it. How's that?"

Now Addie was getting mad about being doubted. She stomped her foot for emphasis. "Don't you guys get it yet? When Kyle and me know stuff, we know stuff. And we're right, aren't we?"

After all of the family discussion of quantum connection, Addie's comment struck home. Randall nodded. "You guys are right. I guess Mom and I will just have to learn to listen to you two better."

Zelda began to tear up. "Mrs. Bush was right. You both are pretty bright for kids. What else do you know?"

Addie screwed up her face again. "Can't you tell? Kyle and I are so hungry we could eat two Big Boy burgers. Mrs. Bush didn't want to make dinner for us."

Randall laughed. "Got me again. At last, a problem we can solve. Get your coats on."

Burgers and Bed

Big Boy's was the hunger cure-all. Kyle and Addie scarfed their food like it might be outlawed the next day. After the kids pushed their plates away, they wanted a full review of the QEG meeting. They were mostly concerned about Elisa. It seemed like Kyle might have his first girl crush. Randall and Zelda went through the highlights. What really got Kyle and Addie's attention was the performance of the IY rock. They'd seen it on Randall's desk, but had never really handled it. Now, they wanted to. Randall and Zelda weren't certain they should let them do the meditation hold.

Kyle objected the loudest and got the attention of some people at tables nearby. "But why can't we?! We can see stuff, too."

Addie doubled down. "Yeah, better than you guys sometimes."

That comment set both Randall and Zelda back in their chairs. They couldn't immediately come up with a good reason to deny them a shot at the rock. Randall gave it a try. "The rock seems to be pretty powerful. It might hurt your young brains in some way I might not understand."

Zelda expressed concern as well. "Yeah, you two might get too freaked out and I don't want to be dealing with kid nightmares for the next month."

Kyle got up quickly and nearly knocked over his water glass. "Geez, Mom! This is not about YOU! I promise I won't have any bad dreams. And, if I do, I won't wake you up like a baby and cry for help."

"Me either," echoed Addie.

Zelda looked dubious. "You both say that now, but if the dream is bad enough, I'm betting you'll be waking me up anyhow."

"We promise we won't," pleaded Kyle. "Cross my heart and hope to . . . whatever. Besides, not even exploding lamps could wake you up!"

"I promise, too," said Addie, crossing her heart.

There was a long parents/kids staredown and the kids didn't waver. Then there was a husband and wife staredown followed by a simultaneous parental shrug. Randall knew when he was beaten. "Alright. We'll do it when we get home, but if you have dreams and wake us up, there will be no Big Boy burgers for two months."

"Three months," added Zelda.

"Goody goody flip flops," said Kyle. "Okay by me."

Me, too," echoed Addie. "Let's shake on it."

Parents shook hands with kids and the deal was done. Randall still looked uncertain. "I'm not sure who got the best deal on this."

Addie piped up like a lightbulb had just lit up above her head. "Speaking of shakes, I could go for a chocolate one. How about you, Kyle?"

"Great idea, Sis," answered Kyle. "Dad, How about you and Mom have one too? It'll make you feel better."

Randall rolled his eyes. "Oh, pish posh. Why not? In for a dollar . . . and all that."

Zelda harrumphed. "It'll cost more than a dollar. And add more than a pound! I'll have whipped cream on mine!"

It turned out the kids could drink the adults under the table when it came to chocolate shakes. Randall and Zelda were still feeling logy when they got home.

"Let's all sit around the kitchen table," directed Kyle. "Where's your special rock, Dad?"

"Right here in my pocket," said Randall.

Kyle's mouth opened wider than his head. "DAAAAD! You had it the whole time? What the heck!!"

Randall put up his hands. "Who died and made you director of affairs?"

"Randy, stop complaining and just do as he says," said Zelda. "Then we can get this over with and get them off to bed so we can have some 'quiet time.'"

That got Randall's attention and he fast-stepped to the table. When everyone was seated, Randall explained the rock meditation technique. "Do it just like that or bad things might happen. Got it?"

Both kids nodded solemnly. Randall carefully handed the rock to Kyle.

Kyle took the IY rock in both hands, closed his eyes and sat quietly for several minutes. His eyes popped open abruptly and his body shivered. His eyes had a hundred-mile stare.

Randall broke the silence. "What did you see, Buddy?"

Kyle shivered and then spoke. "I saw a lady with white hair lying in your bed upstairs. I'm pretty sure she was dead. There was a man standing next to the bed and crying. It was real clear but the lights were weird. The whole thing looked like it was inside a bubble. The bubble popped and I opened my eyes. Then I was back here in the kitchen."

Zelda turned her head to look at Randall. "Randy? Mr. Bush's story about . . . ?"

Randall waved her off. "Fred is just full of hot air. Let's not go there."

Kyle tried to decipher the exchange. "Oh, you mean Mr. Bush's story about the lady who died in your bedroom. I think that was it. I remember the man by the bed was the lady's husband. I think he was a doctor. They put him in jail for murder. Mr. Bush told me that story in the driveway last year. I thought he was just trying to scare me. I don't know. Maybe it was true."

Zelda shivered in response. "Whoa! Either that or he just planted that in your head and the rock went in and found it."

Addie had her own idea about it. "Or maybe it's true."

Kyle just shrugged. "Either way. I think it's no big deal. Old people die all the time. Why not in their own bed?"

Zelda was amazed by Kyle's blase reaction. "Kyle! That's no way to talk about people dying."

Kyle shrugged. "Sorry, Mom. What should I say instead?"

Zelda almost had to laugh. "It's nicer to just say something nice like 'passed away.'"

Kyle shook his head. "Mom, that's just lame. It sounds like she just drove by the house."

Zelda agreed but didn't say so and changed the subject. "So, you knew Mr. Bush's story already? Dad and I never told you because we didn't need you two to start worrying about ghosts in the house."

Kyle shook his head. "No worries, Mom. I already knew the passed away lady was ghosting us. But now I know her husband didn't kill her. She just suicided. Like Alexandra. She might scare us sometimes, but she won't hurt us."

Zelda shivered involuntarily. "Now I have the willies. How come Kyle is taking it better than me?"

Randall shivered in sympathy. "Don't ask me. My connections don't seem to be good enough."

Addie didn't look at all perturbed. "It's my turn now. Give me the rock."

Zelda was worried. "You sure you want to do this, Rosebud?"

"Do cats urp hairballs?" retorted Addie. She put out her hand and wiggled her fingers. "Gimme, gimme."

Addie took the rock from Kyle and repeated the procedure. Soon she started to giggle. Then, she shouted with her eyes still closed. "Stop! That tickles."

Randall snapped his fingers and Addie opened her eyes, still giggling a girlish giggle.

Zelda couldn't believe what she was seeing. "Sweetie, why were you giggling?"

Addie finally focused on her mother. "I was in my bedroom with all my stuffed friends around me. A nice lady in a purple dress came in and was playing with me. She was tickling me with my teddy bear right here on my side. At first I was scared, but then she told me she messed up my room one night because she was mad I wouldn't play with her. She said she was sorry and would never scare me again."

Randall's mouth dropped to full open. "Exhausted exhaust pipes! Could it be? Did she say anything else?"

Addie looked upwards trying to recall. "Oh, yeah. She said that we shouldn't call her the 'Witchy Woman' any more. She asked me to call her 'Wishy Woman.' Whenever I need something, I can ask her for help."

Zelda looked like she'd just put a finger in a 110 volt outlet. "Randy! I told you this was a bad idea. Now both kids are in touch with ghosts in the house. And we have no control over the dead spirits. We need to get them out of here."

"Now hold up a minute, Zel," countered Randall. "Even if they are 'real,' they don't seem malevolent. For some reason they are trapped here and maybe need our help to move on."

Zelda raised both arms in the air. "Then, why can't we sense them, but the kids can? Do they have some kind of connection to the kids?"

Randall reached into both back pockets for an explanation. "Maybe it's what I've been saying about QE and kids' brains. Kids have less stored trash in their brains and their receptors are more efficient. Maybe the ghosts can only reach clogged up adults through kids."

"Hmm . . . maybe," mused Zelda. "Well, enough of this nonsense. It's late. I'm tired and you kids need to get ready for beddy. Besides, your Dad and I need some time to relax and decompress. Got it?"

In unison the kids responded. "Yes, Mom."

Randall joined in. "Your mom is right. Hustle upstairs and get your PJs on, teeth brushed and we'll be up soon to do tucking in. Before you rush off, Addie, I want that IY rock back."

Addie backed away with the rock behind her back. "Aww, Dad!"

Randall reached out and tickled Addie's tickle spot. "You heard me, *gimme gimme*."

Addie laughed until she was weak and gave up the rock. With that, the two kids thundered up the stairs sounding like a cattle stampede. The kitchen was suddenly and eerily quiet.

Wind Up

"Whatcha thinking, Clyde?" asked Zelda.

Randall sighed. "Don't know about you, but my head is spinning. Lots of new input that needs sorting."

Zelda nodded. "I can't even begin to think about the ghost perception in our house. I gotta put that in my processor for a while. So, the QEG meeting was something else. I'm really glad you invited me. It was a real eye opener. I actually felt like I had something to contribute and the people there respected my opinion. And Elisa is one cool lady."

Randall nodded in agreement. "I really liked Roland Walker. When he was talking about ancient native cultures, I revised my opinion about the ancients. Perhaps they weren't as ignorant as we might imagine. Even thousands of years ago they intuited, without complex physics theories, that everything is connected and communicates. Not just human beings, but the land, plants, and animals. Now, here we are, millenia later, reaching the same conclusion with mind-numbingly complex mathematics and equipment of the highest order. Subatomic physics is 'discovering' what our distant forebears had already reasoned had to be the nature of things."

Zelda thought about that for a beat. "Dang! Randy, you're right. But you could have said that much more simply. Like 'what's old is new again.'"

Randall feigned grumpiness. "Must you always try to change me? You know I can't think or say anything the easy way. That's why I married you. You're my great simplifier."

Zelda wasn't sure if she'd been insulted or praised. "Hmm. How about something in the middle ground? 'We've just come full circle, from 2000 BC to 1979 AD.'"

Randall picked up on the new theme. "Yeah. And I feel like I'm split right down the middle. I'm the definition of a dichotomy. I have a foot in both camps—spiritual and scientific—trying to resolve how the two sides jibe."

Zelda was on a roll and became more expansive. "We are all spiritual beings having a human experience. When we try to distill the complexity of energy to just one electron plane, we deflate the sensory dimensionality of existence into a flat perspective that robs life of its spirit. I find hope and promise that we have this basic connectivity with everything through our basic make up."

Randall did a double take and laughed. "Excuse me, professor? Could you repeat that so I can write it down?"

Zelda laughed. "I don't think I can."

Randall laughed even harder. "Don't even try. I think I've got the gist. By 'same basic makeup' I assume you mean the subatomic quantal structure we share with everything."

Zelda nodded emphatically and touched her nose.

Randall wove his fingers together in illustration. "The entanglement is the multidimensionality of life experience. Probably the reason we are all struggling to get along in this world is that we haven't learned to employ our basic connections to their full potential."

Zelda reached out with her pointer finger. "Oh! And we, as individuals, worry that we don't matter and that we can't influence the world. That leads us to feelings of helplessness and depression, which we then broadcast to the world. It infects others like a virus and may become the world view. We all feel it and are doomed to replicate it unless we do something to change."

"Right!" said Randall, jumping onto the wavelength roller coaster. "Without realizing it, we constantly receive whatever communal feeling is being broadcast. Heisenberg and Einstein called the phenomenon of connective coincidences 'synchronicity.' We are all entangled. We don't need wars to change minds. We need minds to change minds. We need spirit to change reality. I bet we can make a difference in the world just by changing the way our electrons spin. Well, if enough of us do it together."

Zelda froze, stunned with mouth open for a beat. "Profound! You and I have just solved all the world's problems. We should be proud. I promise to start spinning in the positive direction if you do."

"We should all synchronize our minds," added Randall.

Zelda softened. "And our hearts."

EPILOGUE

Randall and Zelda high-fived. There was quiet for a time while both assimilated the concepts they'd been discussing. Then Zelda whispered. "Randy?"

Randall grimaced slightly. "Yes, my dear? What thought just popped up in your brain muscle?"

Zelda took Randall's hand. "I was just thinking about your special rock. Do you think the rock itself really has special *puha* or would any rock do? I mean, what would happen if we meditated on an ordinary rock from our backyard?"

Randall's eyes shifted left, then right. Then he crossed them. "Darn good question. My guess is that Roland Walker would probably say the only rocks with the juicy juju are the Shamanic etched stones or the spirit stones found in those mountain *puha* spots. Those sacred spots of power infuse the stones with a special force. Or, in physics speak, maybe their subatomic vibration fields have a unique alignment. Just saying."

Zelda looked askew at Randall. "If you keep talking like that, I might need to get an Allen wrench and tighten some of your screws."

Randall chuckled. "You can try that . . . or . . . I can go in the back yard and grab a stone. We can test your theory. We both got 'readings' from my IY rock. So, if any rock'll do ya, we should get a rise out of a backyard rock."

Zelda nodded. "It's no more crazy than what we did at Joe's. But, baby, it's cold outside. I might freeze my little tushy. Be my brave man and you go get one."

Randall overplayed a grumpy response, again. "If you insist!" He stomped outside and uncovered a rock from the snow covered rock garden. It was pretty nondescript but about the same size as the IY rock. He shivered when he came back in, then handed the rock to Zelda with overdone ceremony that included a formal bow. "Best I could do with the snow and no light. Do you think we should warm it up before we try?"

Zelda thought for a moment and then nuked a cup of water in the microwave. She dunked the rock in the hot water for several minutes until the rock was warm. She held it out to Randall. "You first."

Randall took the rock. "Makes a great hand warmer, if nothing else."

Zelda did not laugh. "Hold it in both hands and meditate, dummy!"

Randall did as commanded, but after three minutes he opened his eyes and shrugged. "Nothing. Your turn."

Zelda smiled and took the rock. She put both hands around it and sat back in the kitchen chair with her hands over her belly. As soon as she closed her eyes, she slid forward on the chair bottom until her head was atop the backrest and tilted upwards.

Randall's eyes grew wide as he sensed something was happening. Zelda started to make some odd sounds. "*Ooo, ah . . . mmmm . . .* that feels good. Lordy! Do me! *Ooo, ah . . . mmm!*" Writhing in the chair, she let out some squeaks and screams.

Randall rose from his chair and shook her shoulder. "Zel! Zel! Are you okay? What's going on? Sounded like you were having a seizure . . . or something."

Zelda opened her eyes and laughed an evil laugh. "Just as I suspected. You still can't detect a fake orgasm."

Randall turned red. "That's not fair! You're just too good at it. But, I have to admit. You got me. It was pretty convincing."

They both broke out laughing.

"Well, Randy, there's your scientific proof. The rock garden rock did nothing. Seems to take a special rock. Want to try your IY rock again?"

Randall shook his head with vigor. "The IY rock rule book says it can only be used by any one person once a day. No more readings tonight."

Zelda laughed. "That definitely sounds like a 'Calvin rule.'"

Randall made a squeezy face. He was stumped. "'Calvin rule?'"

Zelda nodded. "Yes. Come on. You know that one. It's from the comic strip Calvin and Hobbes, where Calvin plays a made up game with the cat, Hobbes, but keeps changing the rules to cheat and win."

Randall finally got the reference. "Well, fine then. I make the rules, so I win."

Zelda was about to protest when, as if on cue, Kyle and Addie appeared at the kitchen entrance. Zelda turned to face the two and the look on her face clearly said 'What are you two doing down here?' "I told you guys we'd be upstairs when we were done talking."

Kyle backed up a step but managed a cover story. "Yeah, Mom, we got that, but we heard you guys laughing. Did Dad tell a good joke? If he did, we want to hear it."

Randall looked over at the kids, but whispered to Zelda under his breath. "Careful what you say. The average age in the room just dropped."

Zelda had to giggle, but she got the message. "Yep. Your Dad told a really wild one, but it's not meant for children's little ears. If you two are ready to hit the hay, Dad can tell you a joke about unique rabbits that's not X-rated. Now, get your little behinds upstairs *lickety split*."

Addie's face lit up. "I love rabbit jokes!"

Kyle looked disgusted. "Rabbits are lame. I want an elephant poop joke."

Randall called a halt to the discussion. "That's enough backtalk. Get on upstairs. Now. You'll get what you get when I get there and you will laugh. Got it?"

Both kids nodded and hustled out of the kitchen. There was a cry from upstairs that the kids had put themselves in Kyle's bed and were ready for the joke. Addie yelled down that they also needed a bedtime story.

Randall rolled his eyes and sighed. "No rest for the wicked and tired."

Randall told the rabbit joke and even Kyle laughed. Then Randall and Zelda decided to construct a bedtime story together. They left the bedroom for a few minutes to spin up a story outline that they could improv from. They intentionally avoided a yarn that was at all spooky or nightmare inducing. At last, both young ones were tucked in their respective beds and snoring.

Randall and Zelda headed to their bedroom and asked for the Wishy Woman to take refuge in the attic while they studied anatomy. After their studies ended, both dropped off to "don't wake me until morning land."

Not long after the two were deep asleep, Addie came padding into their room clutching both her stuffed rabbit and Uni the unicorn. Addie knew there was little chance she'd be able to wake her mother, so she went to Randall's side of the bed and shook his shoulder.

"Daddy, Daddy, wake up," whispered Addie.

Randall raised his head off the pillow and rubbed his eyes. "Addie. What's wrong, sweetie?"

Addie was visibly shaking. "I had a bad dream and now I'm scared."

"What was the dream?" asked Randall.

Addie wiped a tear. "I think the 'Wishy Woman' was in it. She said in my dream that she wanted to play dolls with me."

Randall remembered Addie's solemn vow not to bother them if she had nightmares after using the IY rock. Yet, here she was awakened by a nightmare. He was so wasted and half awake that he didn't feel overly compelled to deal with Addie. "You promised not to bother me if you had a nightmare about a ghost. I need sleep. Go ask your brother to help. He's got dead reckoning." Randall laid back down and turned over.

Addie was too scared to move. She shook Randall again. "But Daddy, I'm too scared to go back to my room."

Randall's eyes opened wider. He sat up, fully awake. Now he felt guilty for ignoring Addie. "Alright, Rosebud. You can't control your dreams. I'll help you, but I'm not getting up. Crawl in next to me, Peapod."

Randall lifted up the covers and Addie crawled in between him and Zelda. He put his arm around Addie. Zelda subconsciously wove her arm around Addie, too, creating a nest of Beidermeiers.

Addie was much relieved and squeezed her parents' arms. "I love being entangled with you, Daddy. But just one thing. I'm not a Peapod. I'm a Rosebud."

"Got it," said Randall. "Now go to sleep, Rosebud."

THE END

Author's Note

If you, the reader, have made it this far by actually reading *Call of the Quantum*, I suspect you've noticed it is a bit long. Most authors would stop their story at about 150,000 words, or 350 pages, unless they are a Steven King or have 50 plus books under their belt. If you've skipped ahead to this note before reading this book, I urge you to have courage to proceed. I'm compelled to say that this book is long because it's a story worth telling. And, to give it the full flavor you have to include all the small bits. What's a banana split without the whipped cream, cherries, sauce and crushed nuts?

Also, of note, this book was written using AI, but not the artificial kind. It was written using actual intelligence. I am not claiming that my actual intelligence is anything spectacular. I wouldn't want your expectations to be over blown. Through analog application of my digits to a keyboard, my actual thoughts were converted to zeros and ones inside my laptop computer. Thus, it is a hybrid of analog and digital. I guess that makes it a new school book produced by an old school digitizer.

One of the most intriguing aspects of this book is the unusual patient and family stories within, all of which are based on real events (with details changed to protect the innocent). The exception to this is the character Elisa Angeles, who was not in the original first draft of this second book in the series. As the time approached to edit the first draft, my (much) younger sister, Diane, passed away after a brief but deadly encounter with ovarian cancer. Diane was a patient advocate in a large hospital. It's sadly ironic that she became so sick so quickly that she could not advocate for herself. That became the job of her friends and family, weighing especially heavy on her daughter.

Elisa's character was created to embody feminine power, compassion and vulnerability to honor Diane's memory and to illustrate the tragedy of a young person having to deal with cancer. While the circumstances in Elisa's case are not the same as Diane's, Elisa illustrates the struggles each cancer patient faces. The first book in this series talks about many patients with cancer, but in none of those cases did I include a more longitudinal look at the physical and mental hurdles they face. What is the same in most cancer cases is the surprising courage each patient finds to face those hurdles, especially the incurable cases.

In this world of billions, it's common to feel one's presence and activities have little impact. It's tempting to believe you can only affect those you interact with face to face and then only on a limited scale. I don't mean to understate the importance of even those direct encounters. If that's all we do in our lives, that's pretty darn good. But, as I hope the book suggests, each of us may have an unrealized effect on the world's inhabitants beyond those we can directly contact. We have the daily choice to add to the positive and healing energy in the world, rather than detract from it. When you get the call of the Quantum, will you listen?

If you've enjoyed this book and are jonesing to find out what happens to Elisa, Elisa's baby, and what the QEG finds out about quantum entanglement, stay tuned for Book Three of the series. What curveballs will the universe throw Randall's way next? How will he respond?

While the gum mystery has been solved, what other sticky issues will arise?

Will Kyle and Addie retain and refine their unique connections to the spirit realm?

Is life all that it's cracked up to be? Or will the Quantum unlock new mysteries that push the Beidermeiers to the edge?

Bonus. Only the divine is perfect. If you have found a blooper, perhaps it was part of the plan. Contact us about it to show how divinely in tune you are!

Picture Index and Attributions

742

福妮愛

ACKNOWLEDGEMENTS

Profound appreciation to Marilyn, my wife, for thoughtful copy editing, brainstorming and encouragement when my creative writing motivation waned. Kudos, as well, to my son Erik for his detailed and comprehensive copyediting. The check is in the mail. Thanks, too, to the readers of Book One who kept asking when Book Two would emerge. Finally, the book could not have been brought fully together without the help of Julie & Jess at Mayfly Design. —RB

Gratitude to my husband, Paul, for helping to provide a life where I can dedicate every Thursday afternoon to writing with my dad. And thanks to my dad for playing with me to create this series. These times of connection over thousands of miles have been beyond valuable. Thanks to my kids, Levi and Anya, for listening to their mom talk about the stories and characters in the book and adding perspective. Thanks to my cats, Sophie and Maeven, for inspiring kitty energy and love. —LBB

ABOUT THE AUTHORS

ROGER BYHARDT is a retired radiation oncologist who lives in Brookfield, Wisconsin, with his wife Marilyn and his cat Hobbes, a largish and always-hungry orange tabby. Breaks from writing include tennis, trumpet and trying to stay healthy. So far so good. Roger draws inspiration for writing from the "everyday" experiences he had when treating cancer patients and his "normal" family life. This comes seasoned with a fascination for the often-strange conjunction of reality and the unknown in our journey through life. As a student of Quantum and String Theory, he takes what we call reality with a grain of Nembutal and is often rewarded with the unexpected and unusual.

LYDIA BYHARDT BOLLINGER is a practicing clinical social worker, living in West Linn, Oregon. She's been doing that work long enough to have the hang of it and she no longer needs the practice. She is also the head of Remember the Joy Publishing (RtJP) which was inspired by her mental health practice and dedicated to remembering the joy of life.

Lydia's first publishing venture was a hair braiding book. Braiding has been a passion since second grade and she was "called" to publish *Her Dancing Fingers: The Art of Renaissance Hairbraiding* in 2014 as a celebration of beauty and connection.

Lydia wrote her next book to support her adopted children as they sought to figure out where they fit in the world. *Am I Family?: A Story for All Kinds of Families* is a warm and charming book for children in adoptive families, especially those who realize they do not physically resemble the other family members. Told from the perspective of the family cat, with excellent advice from the family dog. Published in 2016.

Fifty Catericks and Pix: A Poetic Photo Tale. What Your Cat is Trying to Tell You* is a collaboration by Roger Byhardt and his wife, Marilyn Corlew. This collection of paired poems and pictures provides critical insight into the inner thoughts and longings of a broad array of cats. These fabulous felines reveal a wide range of personalities and quirks that make them as diverse as snowflakes and almost as flaky. This little book is a fun ride for families of all ages. Published in 2023.

Last but not least, the first book in the Call You series, *I Was Just about to Call You!: And Other Mysteries*, was published in 2023. It was born of a father and daughter creating a book that had to be written to document the true and mysterious threads of life, down to the quantum level.